DIE BY THE GUN

DIE BY THE GUN

A CHUCKWAGON TRAIL WESTERN

WILLIAM W. JOHNSTONE
with J. A. Johnstone

PINNACLE BOOKS
Kensington Publishing Corp.
www.kensingtonbooks.com

PINNACLE BOOKS are published by

Kensington Publishing Corp.
119 West 40th Street
New York, NY 10018

PUBLISHER'S NOTE
Following the death of William W. Johnstone, the Johnstone family is working with a carefully selected writer to organize and complete Mr. Johnstone's outlines and many unfinished manuscripts to create additional novels in all of his series like The Last Gunfighter, Mountain Man, and Eagles, among others. This novel was inspired by Mr. Johnstone's superb storytelling.

All Kensington titles, imprints, and distributed lines are available at special quantity discounts for bulk purchases for sales promotions, premiums, fund-raising, educational, or institutional use. Special book excerpts or customized printings can also be created to fit specific needs. For details, write or phone the office of the Kensington sales manager: Kensington Publishing Corp., 119 West 40th Street, New York, NY 10018, attn: Sales Department; phone 1-800-221-2647.

PINNACLE BOOKS, the Pinnacle logo, and the WWJ steer head logo are Reg. U.S. Pat. & TM Off.

ISBN-13: 978-0-7860-4045-2
ISBN-10: 0-7860-4045-9

First Kensington hardcover printing: June 2018
First Pinnacle paperback printing: December 2018

10 9 8 7 6 5 4 3 2 1

Printed in the United States of America

Electronic edition: December 2018

ISBN-13: 978-0-7860-4078-0
ISBN-10: 0-7860-4078-5

CHAPTER 1

Dewey Mackenzie spun away from the bar, the finger of whiskey in his shot glass sloshing as he avoided a body flying through the air. He winced as a gun discharged not five feet away from his head. He hastily knocked back what remained of his drink, tossed the glass over his shoulder to land with a clatter on the bar, and reached for the Smith & Wesson Model 3 he carried thrust into his belt.

A heavy hand gripped his shoulder with painful intensity. The bartender rasped, "Don't go pullin' that smoke wagon, boy. You do and things will get rough."

Mac tried to shrug off the apron's grip and couldn't. Powerful fingers crushed into his shoulder so hard that his right arm began to go numb. He looked across the barroom and wondered why the hell he had ever come to Fort Worth, much less venturing into Hell's Half Acre, where anything, no matter how immoral or unhealthy, could be bought for two bits or a lying promise.

Two different fights were going on in this saloon, and they threatened to involve more than just the drunken cowboys swapping wild blows. The man with the six-gun in his hand continued to ventilate the ceiling with one bullet after another.

Blood spattered Mac's boots as one of the fist-fights came tumbling in his direction. He lifted his left foot to keep it from getting stomped on by the brawlers. A steer had already done that a month earlier when he had been chuckwagon cook on a cattle drive from Waco up to Abilene.

He had taken his revenge on the annoying mountain of meat, singling it out for a week of meals for the Rolling J crew. Not only had the steer been clumsy where it stepped, it had been tough, and more than one cowboy had complained. Try as he might to tenderize the steaks, by beating, by marinating, by cursing, Mac had failed.

That hadn't been the only steer he had come to curse. The entire drive had been fraught with danger, and more than one of the crew had died.

"That's why," he said out loud.

"What's that?" The barkeep eased his grip and let Mac turn from the fight.

"After the drive, after the cattle got sold off and sent on their way to Chicago from the Abilene railroad yards, I decided to come back to Texas to pay tribute to a friend who died."

The bartender's expression said it all. He was in no mood to hear maudlin stories any more than he was to break up the fights or prevent a disgruntled cowboy from plugging a gambler he thought was cheating him at stud poker.

"Then you need another drink, in his memory." When Mac didn't argue the point, the barkeep poured an inch of rye in a new glass and made the two-bit coin Mac put down vanish. A nickel in change rolled across the bar.

"This is for you, Flagg. I just hope it's not too hot wherever you are." Mac lifted the glass and looked past it to the dirty mirror behind the bar. A medium-sized hombre with longish dark hair and a deeply tanned face gazed back at him. The man he saw reflected wasn't the boy who had been hired as a cook by a crusty old trail boss. He had Patrick Flagg to thank for making him grow up.

A quick toss emptied the glass.

The fiery liquor burned a path to his belly and kindled a blaze there. He belched and knew he had reached his limit. Mac had no idea why he had come to this particular gin mill, other than he was foot-loose and drifting after being paid off for the trail drive. The money burned a hole in his pocket, but Dewey Mackenzie had never been much of a spend-thrift. Growing up on a farm in Missouri hadn't given him the chance to have two nickels to rub to-gether, much less important money to waste.

With deft instinct, he stepped to the side as two brawling men crashed into the bar beside him, lost their footing, and sprawled on the sawdust-littered floor. Mac looked down at them, then let out a growl. He reached out and grabbed the man on top by the back of his coat. A hard heave lifted the fighter into the air until the fabric began to tear. Mac swung the man around, deposited him on his feet, and looked him squarely in the eye.

"What mess have you gotten yourself into now, Rattler?"

"Hey, as I live and breathe!" the cowboy exclaimed. "Howdy, Mac. Never thought our paths would cross again after Abilene."

Rattler ducked as his opponent surged to his feet and launched a wild swing. Mac leaned to one side, the bony fist passing harmlessly past his head. He batted the arm down to the bar and pounced on it, pinning the man.

"Whatever quarrel you've got with my friend, consider it settled," Mac told the man sternly.

"Ain't got a quarrel. I got a bone to pick!" The drunk wrenched free, reared back, and lost his balance, sitting hard amid the sawdust and vomit on the barroom floor.

"Come on, Rattler. Let's find somewhere else to do some drinking." Mac grabbed the front of the wiry man's vest and pulled him along into the street.

Mayhem filled Hell's Half Acre tonight. In either direction along Calhoun Street, saloons belched customers out to continue the battles that had begun inside. Others, done with their recreation outside, crowded to get back in for more liquor.

Mac brushed dirt off his threadbare clothes. Spending some of his pay on a new coat made sense. He whipped off his black, broad-brimmed hat and smacked it a couple times against his leg. Dust clouds rose. His hair had been plastered back by sweat. The lack of any wind down the Fort Worth street kept it glued down as if he had used bear grease. He wiped tears from his cat-green eyes and knew he had to get away from the dust and filth of the city. It was dangerous on the trail, tending a herd of cattle, but it was cleaner and wide-open prairie. He might get stomped on by a steer but never had to worry about being shot in the back.

He knew better than to ask Rattler what the fight had been over. Likely, it had started for no reason other than to blow off steam.

"I thought you were going to find a gunsmith and get some work there," Mac said to his companion. "You're a better tinkerer than most of them in this town."

Mac touched the Model 3 in his belt. Rattler had worked on it from Waco to Abilene during the drive and had turned his pappy's old sidearm into a deadly weapon that shot straight and true every time the trigger was pulled. For that, Mac thanked Rattler.

For teaching him how to draw fast and aim straight, he gave another silent nod to Patrick Flagg. More than teaching him how to draw faster than just about anyone, Flagg had also taught him when not to draw at all.

Rattler said, "And I thought you was headin' back to New Orleans to woo that filly of yours. What was her name? Evie?"

"Evangeline," Mac said.

"Yeah, you went on and on, even callin' out her name in your sleep. With enough money, you shoulda been able to win her over."

Mac knew better. He loved Evangeline Holdstock, and she had loved him until Pierre Leclerc had set his cap for her. Leclerc's plans included taking over Evie's father's bank after marrying her—probably inheriting it when he murdered Micah Holdstock.

Being framed for Micah's murder had been enough to convince Mac to leave New Orleans. Worse, the frame had also convinced Evie to have nothing to do with him other than to scratch out his eyes if he got close enough to the only woman he had ever loved.

His only hope of ever winning her back was to prove Leclerc had murdered Holdstock. Somehow, his determination to do that had faded after Leclerc had sent killers after him to Waco.

Mac smiled ruefully. If he hadn't been dodging them, he never would have signed on with the Rolling J crew and found he had a knack for cooking and cattle herding. The smile melted away when he realized Evie was lost forever to him, and returning to New Orleans meant his death, either from Leclerc's killers or at the end of a hangman's rope.

"There's other fish in the sea. Thass what they say," Rattler went on, slurring his morsel of advice. He braced himself against a hitching post to point at a three-story hotel across the street. "The House of Love, they call it. They got gals fer ever' man's taste there. Or so I been told. Less go find ourselves fillies and spend the night, Mac. We owe it to ourselves after all we been through."

"That's a mighty attractive idea, Rattler, but I want to dip my beak in some more whiskey. You can go and dip your, uh, other beak. Don't let me hold you back."

"They got plenny of ladies there. Soiled doves." Rattler laughed. "They got plenny of them to last the livelong night, but I worry this town's gonna run outta popskull."

With an expansive sweep of his arm, he indicated the dozen saloons within sight along Calhoun Street. It was past midnight and the drinking was beginning in earnest now. Every cowboy in Texas seemed to have crowded in with a powerful thirst demanding to be slaked by gallons of bad liquor and bitter beer.

"Which watering hole appeals to you, Rattler?" Mac saw each had a different attraction. Some dance halls had half-naked women willing to share a dance, rubbing up close, for a dime or until the piano player keeled over, too drunk to keep going. Others featured exotic animals or claimed imported food and booze from the four corners of the world.

Mac had become cynical enough to believe the whiskey and brandy they served came from bottles filled like all the others, from kegs and tanks brought into Hell's Half Acre just after sunrise. That's when most customers were passed out or too blind drunk to know the fancy French cognac they paid ten dollars a glass for was no different from the ten-cent tumbler filled with the same liquor at the drinking emporium next door. It was referred to as poor man's whiskey.

"Don't much matter. That one's close enough so I don't stagger too much gettin' to it." The man put his arm around Mac's shoulders for support, turned on unsteady feet, and took a step. He stopped short and looked up to a tall, dark man dressed in black. "'Scuse us, mister. We got some mighty hard drinkin' to do, and you're blockin' the way."

"Dewey Mackenzie," the man said in a hoarse whisper, almost drowned out by raucous music pouring from inside the saloon.

"Yeah, he's my friend," Rattler said, pulling away from Mac and stumbling to the side.

When he did so, he got in the way of the dark man's shot. Mac had never seen a man move faster. The Peacemaker cleared leather so swiftly the move was a blur. Fanning the hammer sent three slugs ripping out in a deadly rain that tore into Rattler's body. He threw up his arms, a look of surprise on his face as he collapsed backward into Mac's arms.

He died without saying another word.

"Damn it," the gunman growled, stepping to the side to get a better shot at Mac.

Shock disappeared as Mac realized he had to move or die. With a heave he lifted his dead friend up and tossed him into the shooter. The corpse knocked the gunman's aim off so his fourth bullet tore past Mac and sailed down Calhoun Street. Almost as an afterthought, someone farther away let out a yelp when the bullet found an unexpected target.

Mac had practiced for hours during the long cattle drive. His hand grabbed the wooden handles on the S&W. The pistol pulled free of his belt. He wasn't even aware of all he did, drawing back the hammer as he aimed, the pressure of the trigger against his finger, the recoil as the revolver barked out its single deadly reply.

The gunman caught the bullet smack in the middle of his chest. It staggered him. Propped against a hitching post, he looked down at a tiny red spot spreading on his gray-striped vest. His eyes came up and locked with Mac's.

"You shot me," he gasped. He used both hands to raise his six-gun. The barrel wobbled back and forth.

"Why'd you kill Rattler?" Mac held his gun in a curiously steady hand. The sights were lined on the gunman's heart.

He never got an answer. The man's pistol blasted another round, but this one tore into the ground between them. He let out a tiny gurgling sound and toppled straight forward, like an Army private at attention all the way down. A single twitch once he hit the ground was the only evidence of life fleeing.

"That's him!" a man shouted. "That's Mackenzie. He gunned down Jimmy!"

Another man said, "Willy's not gonna take kindly to this."

Mac looked up to see a pair of men pushing hurriedly through the saloon's batwing doors. It didn't take a genius to recognize the dead gunman's family. They might have been chiseled out of the same stone—broad shoulders, square heads, height within an inch of each other. Their coats were of the same fabric and color, and the Peacemakers slung at their hips might have been bought on the same day from the same gunsmith.

Even as they took in how the dead man had found the quarry Leclerc had put a bounty on, their hands went for their guns. Neither man was too quick on the draw, taking time to push away the long tails of their coats. This gave Mac the chance to swing his own gun around and get off a couple of shots.

Flying lead whined past both men and into the saloon they had just exited. Glass broke inside and men shouted angrily. Then all hell broke loose as the patrons became justifiably angry at being targeted.

Several of them boiled out of the saloon with guns flashing and fists flying.

The two gunmen dodged Mac's slugs, but the rush of men from inside bowled them over, sending them stumbling out into the dusty street. Mac considered trying to dispatch them, then knew he had a tidal wave to hold back with only a couple of rounds.

"Sorry, Rattler," he said, taking a second to touch the brim of his hat in tribute to his trail companion. They had never been friends but had been friendly. That counted for something during a cattle drive.

He vaulted over Rattler's body, grabbed for the reins of a black stallion tethered to the side of the saloon, and jumped hard, landing in the saddle with a thud. The spirited animal tried to buck him off. Mac had learned how to handle even the proddiest cayuse in any remuda. He bent low, grabbed the horse around the neck, and hung on for dear life as the horse bolted into the street.

A new threat posed itself then—or one that had been delayed, anyway. Both of the dead gunman's partners—or brothers or whatever they were—opened fire on him. Mac stayed low, using the horse as a shield.

"Horse thief!" The strident cry came from one of the gunmen. This brought out cowboys from a half dozen more saloons. Getting beaten to a bloody pulp or even shot full of holes meant nothing to these men. But having a horse thief among them was a hanging offense.

"There he is!" Mac yelled as he sat up in the saddle and pointed down the street. "The thieving bastard just rounded the corner. After him!"

The misdirection worked long enough for him to

send the mob off on a wild goose chase, but that still left two men intent on avenging their partner. Mac put his head down again, jerked the horse's reins, and let the horse gallop into a barroom, scattering the customers inside.

He looked around as he tried to control the horse in the middle of the sudden chaos he had created. Going back the way he came wouldn't be too smart. A quick glance in the mirror behind the bar showed both of the black-clad men crowding through the batwings and waving their guns around.

A savage roar caught his attention. In a corner crouched a black panther, snarling to reveal fierce fangs capable of ripping a man apart. No wonder the black stallion was going loco. He had to be able to smell the big cat.

The huge creature strained at a chain designed to hold a riverboat anchor. The clamor rose as the bartender shouted at Mac to get his horse out of the saloon. The apron-clad man reached under the bar and pulled out a sawed-off shotgun.

"Out, damn your eyes!" the bartender bellowed as he leveled the weapon.

Mac whirled around and began firing, not at the panther but at the wall holding the chain. The chain itself was too strong for a couple of bullets to break.

The wood splintered as Mac's revolver came up empty. When the panther lunged again, it pulled the chain staple free and dragged it into the room. The customer nearest the cat screeched as heavy claws raked at him.

Then the bartender fired his shotgun and Mac yelped as rock salt burned his face and arm. Worse, the rock salt spooked the horse even more than the attacking panther.

The stallion exploded like a Fourth of July rocket. Mac did all he could do to hang on as the horse leaped through a plate glass window. Glittering shards flew in all directions, but he was out of the saloon and once more in the street.

The sense of triumph faded fast when both gunmen who'd been pursuing him boiled out through the window he had just destroyed.

"That's him, Willy. Him's the one what killed Jimmy!"

Mac looked back at death stalking him. A tall, broad man with a square head and the same dark coat pushed back the tails to reveal a double-gun rig. Peacemakers holstered at either hip quickly jumped into the man's grip. Using both hands, the man started firing. And he was a damned good shot.

CHAPTER 2

Dewey Mackenzie jerked to the side and almost fell from the horse as a bullet tore a chunk from the brim of his hat. He glanced up and got a quick look at the moon through the hole. The bullets sailing around him motivated him to put his heels to the horse's flanks.

Again the horse bolted through the open door of a saloon. This one's crowd stared at a half-naked woman on stage gyrating to bad piano music. They were too preoccupied to be aware of the havoc being unleashed outside. Even a man riding through the back of the crowd hardly pulled their attention away from the lurid display.

Mac slid from the saddle and tugged on the reins to get the horse out of the saloon. He had to shoulder men aside, which drew a few curses and surly looks, but people tended to get out of the way of a horse.

Finally he worked his way through the press of men who smelled of sweat and lust and beer. He emerged into the alley behind the gin mill. Walking slowly, forcing himself to regain his composure, he left the Tivoli Saloon behind and went south on Throckmorton Street.

The city's layout was something of a mystery to him, but he remembered the wagon yard was between Main and Rusk, only a few streets over. He resisted the urge to mount and ride out of town. If he did that, the gang of cutthroats would be after him before dawn. His best chance of getting away was to fade into the woodwork and let the furor die down. Shooting his way out of Fort Worth was as unlikely to be successful as was galloping off.

Where would he go? He had a few dollars left in his pocket from his trail drive pay, but he knew no one, had no friends, no place to go to ground for a week or two. Mac decided being footloose was a benefit. Wherever he went would be fine, with the gunmen unable to track him because he sought friends' help. He had no friends in Fort Worth.

"Not going to get anybody else killed," he said bitterly, sorry for Rattler catching the lead intended for him.

He tugged on the stallion's reins and worked his way farther south along Rusk until he reached the wagon yard. He patted the horse's neck. It was a strong animal, one he would have loved to ride. But it was distinctive enough to draw attention he didn't need.

"Come on, partner," Mac told the stallion quietly. The horse neighed, tried to nuzzle him, and then trotted along into the wagon yard. A distant corral filled with a dozen horses began to come awake. By the time he reached the office, the hostler was pulling up his suspenders and rubbing sleep from his eyes. He was a scarecrow of a man with a bald head and prominent Adam's apple.

"You're up early, mister," the man said. "Been on the trail? Need a place to stable your horse while you're whooping it up?"

"I'm real down on my luck, sir," Mac said sincerely. "What would you give me for the horse?"

"This one?" The liveryman came over and began examining the horse. He rested his hand on the saddle and looked hard at Mac. "The tack, too?"

"Why not? I need some money, but I also need another horse and gear. Swap this one for a less spirited horse, maybe? And a simple saddle?"

"This is mighty fine workmanship." The man ran his fingers over the curlicues cut into the saddle. "Looks to be fine Mexican leather work. That goes for top dollar in these parts."

"The horse, too. That's the best horse I ever did ride, but I got expenses. . . ." Mac let the sentence trail off. The liveryman would come to his own conclusions. Whatever they might be would throw the gunmen off Mac's trail, if they bothered to even come to the wagon yard.

He reckoned they would figure out which was his horse staked out back of the first saloon he had entered and wait for him to return for both the horse and his gear. Losing the few belongings he had rankled like a burr under his saddle, but he had tangled before with bounty hunters Pierre Leclerc had set on his trail. The man didn't hire stupid killers. Mac's best—his only—way to keep breathing was to leave

Fort Worth fast and cut all ties with both people and belongings.

A deep sigh escaped his lips. Rattler was likely the only one he knew in town. That hurt, seeing the man cut down the way he had been, but somehow, leaving behind his mare, saddle, and the rest of his tack tormented him even more.

"I know a gent who'd be willing to pay top dollar for such a fine horse, but you got to sell the saddle, too. It's mighty fine. The work that went into it shows a master leather smith at his peak, yes, sir." The liveryman cocked his head to one side and studied Mac as if he were a bug crawling up the wall.

"Give me a few bucks, another horse and saddle, and I'll be on my way."

"Can't rightly do that till I see if I can sell the stallion. I'm runnin' a bit shy on cash. You wait here, let me take the horse and see if the price is right. I might get you as much as a hundred dollars."

"That much?" Mac felt his hackles rise. "That and another horse and tack?"

"Don't see horses this spirited come along too often. And that saddle?" The man shook his head. "Once in a lifetime."

"Do tell. So what's to keep you from taking the horse and riding away?"

"I own the yard. I got a reputation to uphold for honesty. Ask around. You go find yourself some breakfast. Might be, I can get you as much as a hundred-fifty dollars."

"And that's after you take your cut?"

"Right after," the man assured him.

Mac knew he lied through his teeth.

"Is there a good restaurant around here? Not that it matters since I don't have money for even a fried egg and a cup of water." He waited to see what the man offered. The response assured him he was right.

"Here, take five dollars. An advance against what I'll make selling the horse. That means I'll take it out of your share."

"Thanks," Mac said, taking the five crumpled greenbacks. He stuffed them into his vest pocket. "How long do you think you'll be?"

"Not long. Not more 'n a half hour. That'll give you plenty of time to chow down and drink a second cup of coffee. Maggie over at the Bendix House boils up a right fine cup."

"Bendix House? That's it over there? Much obliged." Mac touched the brim of his hat, making sure not to show the hole shot through and through. He let the man lead the horse away, then started for the restaurant.

Only when the liveryman was out of sight did Mac spin around and run back to the yard. A quick vault over the fence took him to the barn. Rooting around, he found a serviceable saddle, threadbare blanket, bridle, and saddlebags. He pressed his hand against them. Empty. Right now, he didn't have time to search for food or anything more to put in them. He needed a slicker and a change of clothing.

Most of all he needed to leave. Now.

Picking a decent-looking mare from the corral took only a few seconds. The one who trotted over to him was the one he stole. Less than a minute later, saddle and bridle hastily put on, he rode out.

As he came out on Rusk Street, he caught sight of

a small posse galloping in his direction. He couldn't make out the riders' faces, but they all wore black coats that might as well have been a uniform. Putting his heels to his horse's flanks, he galloped away, cut behind the wagon yard's buildings, and then faced a dilemma. Going south took him past the railroad and onto the prairie.

The flat, barren prairie where he could be seen riding for miles.

Mac rode back past Houston Street and immediately dismounted, leading his horse to the side of the Comique Saloon. He had to vanish, and losing himself among the late night—or early morning now—imbibers was the best way to do it. The wagon yard owner would be hard-pressed to identify which horse was missing from a corral with a couple dozen animals in it. Mac cursed himself for not leaving the gate open so all the horses escaped.

"Confusion to my enemies," he muttered. Two quick turns of the bridle through an iron ring secured his mount. He circled the building and started to go into the saloon.

"Door's locked," came the warning from a man sitting in a chair on the far side of the door. He had his hat pulled down to shield his eyes from the rising sun and the chair tilted back on its hind legs.

"Do tell." Mac nervously looked around, expecting to see the posse on his trail closing in. He took the chair next to the man, duplicated his pose, and pulled his hat down, more to hide his face than to keep the sunlight from blinding him. "When do they open?"

"John Leer's got quite a place here. But he don't

keep real hours. It's open when it's needed most. Otherwise, he closes up."

"Catches some shut-eye?"

The man laughed.

"Hardly. He's got a half dozen floozies in as many bawdy houses, or so the rumor goes. Servicing all of them takes up his spare time."

"You figuring on waiting long for him to get back?"

The man pushed his hat back and looked over at Mac. He spat on the boardwalk, repositioned himself precariously in the chair, and crossed his arms over his chest before answering.

"Depends. I'm hunting for cowboys. The boss man sends me out to recruit for a drive. I come here to find who's drunkest. They're usually the most likely to agree to the lousy wages and a trip long enough to guarantee saddle sores on your butt."

"You might come here and make such an appealing pitch, but I suspect you offer top dollar." Mac tensed when a rider galloped past. The man wore a plaid shirt and jeans. He relaxed. Not a bounty hunter.

"You're the type I'm looking for. Real smart fellow, you are. My trail boss wouldn't want a drunk working for him, and the boss man was a teetotaler. His wife's one of them temperance women. More 'n that, she's one of them suffer-ay-jets, they call 'em. Can't say I cotton much to going without a snort now and then, and giving women the vote like up in Wyoming's just wrong but—"

"But out on the trail nobody drinks. The cook keeps the whiskey, for medicinal purposes only."

"You been on a drive?"

"Along the Shawnee Trail." Mac's mind raced. Losing himself among a new crew driving cattle would solve most of his problems.

"That's not the way the Circle Arrow herd's headed. We're pushing west along the Goodnight-Loving Trail."

"Don't know it," Mac admitted.

"Don't matter. Mister Flowers has been along it enough times that he can ride it blindfolded."

"Flowers?"

"Hiram Flowers, the best damned trail boss in Texas. Or so I'm told, since I've only worked for a half dozen in my day." The man rocked forward and thrust out his hand. "My name's Cletus Grant. I do the chores Mister Flowers don't like."

"Finding trail hands is one of them?" Mac asked as he clasped the man's hand.

"He doesn't stray far from the Circle Arrow."

"What's that mean?" Mac shifted so his hand rested on his gun when another rider came down the street. He went cold inside when he remembered he hadn't reloaded. Truth to tell, all his spare ammunition was in his saddlebags, on his horse left somewhere behind another saloon in Hell's Half Acre.

When the rider rode on after seeing the Comique was shuttered, Mac tried to mask his move by shifting in the chair. He almost toppled over.

He covered by asking, "You said the Circle Arrow owner was a teetotaler. He fall off the wagon?"

"His missus wouldn't ever allow that, no, sir. He upped and died six months back, in spite of his missus telling him not to catch that fever. Old Zeke Sullivan should have listened that time. About the only time he didn't do as she told him." Cletus spat again, wiped his mouth, and asked, "You looking for a job?"

"I'm a piss poor cowboy, but there's no better chuckwagon cook in all of Texas. Or so I'm told, since I've only worked for the Rolling J in my day."

Cletus Grant's expression turned blank for a moment, then he laughed.

"You got a sharp wit about you, son. I don't know that Mister Flowers is looking for a cook, but he does need trail hands. Why don't me and you mosey on out to the Circle Arrow and palaver a mite about the chance you'd ride with us to Santa Fe?"

"That where the herd's destined?"

"Might be all the way to Denver. It depends on what the market's like over in New Mexico Territory."

"That's fair enough. I might be willing to go all the way to Denver since I've never been there, but heard good things about the town."

Cletus spat and shook his head sadly.

"Too damn many miners there looking to get rich by pulling skull-sized gold nuggets out the hills. The real money comes in selling them picks, shovels . . . and beeves."

"Which is what the Circle Arrow intends," Mac said. "That suits me." He thrust out his hand for another shake to seal the deal, but Cletus held back this time.

"I can't hire you. Mister Flowers is the one what has to do that." The man looked up and down the street, then rocked forward so all four legs hit the boardwalk. One was an inch shy of keeping the chair level. When Cletus stood, his limp matched the uneven chair. He leaned heavily on his right leg. "Let's get on out to the ranch so's he can talk with you. I don't see much in the way of promising recruits."

Mac mounted and trotted alongside Cletus. The man's horse was a fine-looking gelding, well kept and eager to run. From the way the horse under him responded, Mac thought it would die within a mile, trying to keep pace.

"Yup," Cletus said, noticing Mac's interest. "The Circle Arrow has the best damned horses. Mister Flowers says it pays off in the long run having the best. We don't lose as many cattle—or drovers."

"That's good counsel. There're too many ways of dying on the trail without worrying about your horse dying under you." Mac thought a moment, then asked, "What's the trail like? The Goodnight-Loving?"

"The parts that don't kill you will make you wish you were dead. Drought and desert, Injuns and horse thieves, disease and despair."

"But the pay's good," Mac said, knowing the man tested him. "And if I'm cooking, the food will be even better."

"You got a wit about you, son. Let's hope it's not just half a one." Cletus picked up the gait, forcing Mac to bring his horse to a canter.

As he did so, he looked behind and saw two of the black-coated riders slowly making their way down the street. One pointed in Mac's direction but the other shook his head and sent them down a cross street. Being with Cletus Grant might just have saved him. The bounty hunters thought he was alone. That had

to be the answer to them not coming to question
them about one of their gang getting shot down.

The thought made Mac touch his S&W again.
Empty. He kept reminding himself of that. The saddle sheath lacked a rifle, too. If they caught up and a
fight ensued, and he couldn't bite them, he was out
of luck.

"You got a curious grin on your face," Cletus said.
"What's so funny?"

"Drought and desert, Indians and—"

"I get the drift. And I wasn't joking about them.
The trail's decent enough, but the dangers are real."

"Nothing like I'm leaving behind," Mac said. That
got a frown from Cletus, but he didn't press the matter. That suited Mac. He didn't want to lie to the
man.

Not yet. Not unless it became necessary to escape
the killers Pierre Leclerc had set on his trail.

Chapter 3

Hiram Flowers spun the tip of his knife a few more times, bored the hole in the pinewood, and finished carving himself a spinner to make a new horsehair lariat. His old lariat had worn out during the last trail drive. At the memory of that drive the prior year, he looked up and saw his boss's widow come out onto the ranch house porch and begin sweeping.

She had hired help for that. A maid. But Mercedes Sullivan preferred to keep her hand in running the house, the ranch, everything about the Circle Arrow. A tiny smile curled Flowers's chapped lips as the fiery redhead bent to flick away a bit of debris stuck between the porch boards. The sight of her made his heart race a little faster, and it wasn't just from how her perky rear end poked up into the air or the gentle sway under her blouse. He knew those emerald eyes of hers were bright and clear and hid none of her razor-sharp intelligence. She was a handsome woman, and a capable one when it came to business.

She was also his boss.

Flowers forced himself to pull his eyes away from her trim figure and mesmerizing ways. Her husband had been his best friend, no matter that Flowers had worked for Ezekiel Sullivan for more than fifteen years. He had struck up an immediate friendship with the man because of who he was, not just because of his wife.

Zeke had been his boss then. Mercedes was his boss now that the fever had taken Zeke six months back.

He muttered that over and over. Boss, boss, boss.

"You say somethin', Mister Flowers?"

He turned to Howard "Messy" Messerschmidt, a drover hired away from an adjoining ranch. Jake Church ran that spread in a slapdash way, hardly ever turned a profit but somehow kept stumbling along, and he treated his hired hands worse than he did his steers. That made it easy to hire away the best of the drovers, men like Messerschmidt and his partner, Klaus Kleingeld, who didn't speak much English. That didn't bother Flowers overly. He had found some good men, hard workers and dedicated cowboys among the men from down in New Braunfels. He wished he could hire one of those German women as a cook. He'd never found a single one who couldn't whip up a meal fit for a king.

"I was reflecting on how lazy you and Kleingeld are. You have chores to do out in the barn."

"Every bit of the chores are done, Mister Flowers. We rode through the cows corralled on the south forty, looking for any trace of splenic fever. Not a trace, not even a tick bite on the lot, and those are the last of the herd to be examined."

"You look in on Cassidy?" Flowers saw how the cowboy's face became a poker mask. That told him more than he wanted to know.

"He's still sleeping off his bender."

Both of them looked at the clear blue Texas sky and the sun hanging high in it. They had been up by sunrise, doing all the chores necessary to keep the ranch running and to prepare for the drive. Cassidy hadn't stirred, other than to roll over in his bunk and snore even louder.

"Mister Flowers!"

He looked up at the call and saw Cletus Grant waving at him. Cletus rode toward the house with another man on horseback beside him.

"He found a sucker," Messerschmidt said. "Be happy about that. We need all the trail hands we can find after so many of them went south to work on the railroad."

"What's a cowboy know about laying iron track?" Flowers stuck his knife in the bench beside him and stood. He ignored whatever Messy said in response. The man went on and on when he should have kept his yap shut. More important was the man riding alongside Grant.

He sized him up fast. Wherever did Grant find such losers?

The two men reined in, and Grant started to make the introductions. "Mister Flowers, this here's . . ."

Grant's words trailed off. It was apparent he hadn't bothered finding out the man's name, or if he had, he'd already forgotten it. Considering his age, either was possible.

"Dewey Mackenzie," the young man said. "Cletus here says you need cowboys, but my experience is more with cooking."

"You're a trail cook?" Flowers spat. The day was turning sourer the higher the sun got in the sky. "You don't look like one."

"I worked for Sidney Jefferson of the Rolling J, down around Waco. If you want to send him a telegram, he might not answer right away. He's mighty sickly and—"

"Not wasting time or money on a telegram. You don't have the look of a man willing to sit astraddle a horse all night long."

"I've ridden night herd and don't take much to it. Like I told Cletus, my skills are elsewhere."

Flowers took in the youngster. The revolver tucked into his belt had the look of being used hard and often, but he wasn't a gunfighter. Any gunslick worth his salt wore his iron on his hip. A gambler might use a shoulder rig, but having a pistol thrust into the belt like this spelled death if the hammer or cylinder caught on a vest or waistband during a quick draw. The only man he had ever heard of who carried his six-gun in a coat pocket and used it that way was a marshal out in El Paso. And he lined the pocket with leather to keep from getting the hammer tangled in cloth.

Dewey Mackenzie was no gunman, and he wasn't a cowboy.

"Can't use you. Sorry Cletus dragged you all this way for nothing."

"I can cook. I make the best darned biscuits any cowpoke ever ate. Keep the men happy and you get twice the work from them."

"He's right about that, Mister Flowers." Cletus shifted weight off his gimp leg and looked from one man to the other and back. "I'll work an extra hour just for a decent meal. Remember the last drive when—"

"Shut up, Cletus." Flowers tried to keep his shoulders from sagging. He faced Mac and said, "We got a cook. If you can't ride night herd as a wrangler, there's no place on the Circle Arrow drive for you."

He watched a curious ripple of emotion cross the young man's face. Mac took off his hat. The hole in the brim was fresh. There wasn't any fraying yet from wind or rain. His long dark hair was plastered down from sweat, although the day wasn't that hot. Something riled him, and whatever it was wouldn't surface. He had the look of a man with harsh secrets to keep. That meant a history Flowers had no desire to learn or have catch up with either the young man or anyone else on the drive. It was hard enough getting across West Texas and up into New Mexico Territory along the Goodnight-Loving Trail without keeping a close eye on your back trail.

"I can ride herd. I'm not too good, and I'd rather go as cook. I *am* good at that."

"Sorry." Flowers glared at Cletus Grant. The man had expected a finder's fee for another rider.

"But, sir, I—" Mac's words were drowned out by three quick gunshots, followed by a loud whoop like an Indian on the warpath coming after a scalp.

Flowers saw he was wrong about the boy not being

handy with his revolver. He had it out and cocked in the blink of an eye, the muzzle pointed up at the bunkhouse roof. Slower to turn, Flowers only touched the butt of his six-gun and didn't throw down when he saw Cassidy teetering on the edge of the roof, buck naked with a gun in one hand and a bottle in the other.

"I'm a ring-tailed, rootin' tootin' son of a bitch from Pecos, and I kin take any man on this godforsaken ranch." Cassidy raised his six-gun again. The motion unbalanced him and caused his feet to slip from under him. He sat hard, then slid down the shingled roof. He landed awkwardly, sprawled in the dirt, and didn't move.

He hadn't killed himself, though. His breath still wheezed and bubbled in his throat.

Cletus cringed at the inelegant sight of Cassidy's bare butt and muttered, "I ain't pulling the splinters from his cracker ass."

"Messerschmidt, get this drunken fool back into the bunkhouse and sober him up," Flowers ordered. "I don't care if you have to pour ten gallons of coffee down his throat. I want him sober before sundown."

"Can't see how that's possible, Mister Flowers. He's never sober. I declare, he's got whiskey instead of blood flowing through his veins."

Flowers glared. Messerschmidt kicked the pistol from Cassidy's unsteady hand, caught his wrist, and pulled the man to his feet. As the drunk toppled forward, he got a shoulder into Cassidy's belly and hoisted him like a sack of grain. A quick kick of his heel opened the door. He made no effort to keep from banging Cassidy's head against the frame as he carried him into the bunkhouse. In his drunken condition, the man never noticed.

"That's our cook," Cletus said. "Mister Flowers, you can't depend on Cassidy. No, wait, I'm wrong. That's exactly how you'll see him along the trail since he'll have the liquor supply under lock and key."

"Hush up. And you," Flowers said, spinning on Mac, "clear out."

He closed his eyes when a soft voice from the direction of the ranch house summoned him. Resolute, he left his problems with the men and went to see what Mercedes Sullivan had to say. Every step closer to the porch—where she stood with arms crossed over her breasts, foot tapping, and an expression just this side of a hellfire and brimstone sermon—convinced him climbing a gallows to be hanged was easier.

Disappointing Mercedes was worse for him than a noose around his neck.

"Yes, ma'am," Flowers said, stopping at the foot of the steps leading to the porch. From here he looked up at her.

"That's enough ruckus from Cassidy. He's drunk again, isn't he? I won't stand for that. No man who works for the Circle Arrow can be as soused as he is right now."

"I need him, Miz Sullivan. He's our cook."

"I heard about the trouble you had with him on the last drive. Zeke said he got into the cooking stores constantly and was seldom sober. If you hadn't stopped him, my husband would have sent Cassidy packing."

"It's not good to be on the trail and fire men, especially the cook. I can ride scout, and Messer-schmidt is as good with the herd as any man I've seen."

"Yes, yes," she said impatiently. "And Cletus Grant can soothe any horse in the remuda." She relaxed a little, her arms dropping. She sat down on the top step and pointed to a spot beside her. She pointed more emphatically when he hesitated to sit beside her. Flowers sighed and lowered himself stiffly to the plank step, being careful not to sit inappropriately close to her.

"It's a long drive," he said. "If we go all the way to Denver with this herd, I'll need seasoned men, and plenty of 'em."

"Hiram, you have to fire Cassidy."

"I—"

"I know he's your nephew, and it would break your sister's heart for her youngest to get fired. Do you want me to do your job for you? I will no longer permit a man to be that drunk and remain in my employ."

Flowers began, "Your work with the temperance league is—"

"That has nothing to do with firing Cassidy. He's a poor worker, plain and simple, and I have heard the men grumbling about his cooking. Whether he does a poor job because he's drunk—or not drunk enough—doesn't matter."

"Yes, ma'am." Flowers sighed heavily again. "I'll send him back to his ma."

"Hiram, trust me. She knows what a wastrel he is. Now. When do we hit the trail?"

"I'll be ready at dawn in two days."

"Good. That'll give me time to get my gear together. Have one of the men see that Majestic is ready then."

"Majestic? But that's your horse. I don't need to take your horse. We've got fifty head for the remuda, and what'd you ride here?"

She looked at him, redheaded, beautiful, and absolutely determined as she said, "You misunderstand me, Hiram. I want my horse ready because I'm riding along with you on this drive."

Flowers opened his mouth, then snapped it shut. No words came out. He stared at her, and all he could see were the high cheekbones, fair skin, and that flowing, long red hair. She might have been an Irish elf she was so pretty.

"Zeke always went with the herd. Since he's gone, it's my duty as owner."

"You can't!" He blurted out the denial. The shock on her face that he would speak to her that way turned to stubbornness he knew couldn't be changed. She was downright mulish when she set her mind to something. "Miz Sullivan, it's dangerous on the trail. Hard going every inch of the way. It's not like running the ranch and having a nice soft bed at night."

"You think so little of me, Hiram? I'm tough enough. I need to go along to get the best deal I can. You're not much of a haggler."

"Never had to be, not with Mister Sullivan along. I swear, I never saw a man better able to squeeze an extra dime out of a cattle buyer."

He realized as soon as he said it that he had played right into her hands.

"Since you lack the experience, it will be good for

you to see me use my feminine wiles to accomplish the same ends that Zeke achieved." She sounded smug, satisfied, as if she had practiced that line to recite for him. He refused to be convinced.

"Ma'am, all you have to do is bat those long eyelashes of yours and hearts melt."

"Like yours?" Her expression became unreadable. The words were light and joshing, but Flowers heard something else there he dared not believe.

"I won't be a party to you going. I'll quit. I'll take half the men with me, too."

"You'd leave me your nephew and no one else?" Anger rose now, turning her milky cheeks rosy. Her lips thinned to a line, and her green eyes flashed like warning beacons. Flowers had to tread carefully, or she might fire him and try to lead the drive by herself.

"I'll get rid of Cassidy. I promise you that. But I'll need a cook."

"And for me to stay at home, tallying accounts and minding the home fires?"

"Yes, ma'am, exactly." Flowers almost sagged in relief. He had convinced her to stay. The trail was no place for a lady like her. Then she drove another knife into his gut and twisted it around.

"I will remain behind on one condition. Desmond rides with you."

"Your son?" Flowers swallowed hard. It was almost better if he took Cassidy. He could deal with a drunk.

"His father's death hit him hard. It's time for him to snap out of the funk he's been in since the funeral and learn how to run a ranch. Watching you with the herd on the trail will stand him in good stead."

"Desmond?" The name came out in a croak. "He's not even here. He went back to town."

"I wondered where he had gotten off to. Fetch him. Get him outfitted and teach him what he needs to know. Otherwise, I must go along with you."

"I think I know where to find him," Flowers said, his voice hardening. "There's a special place in Fort Worth where he ends up after . . . after spending time there," he finished lamely. He didn't have the gumption to tell Mercedes Sullivan her son frequented whorehouses and raised such holy hell that many had banished him. Being banned from a brothel in Hell's Half Acre took a special amount of hell-raising.

"Then it's all settled. Thank you, Hiram." She bent over and lightly kissed his stubbled cheek.

"Ma'am, not where the men can see." He blushed under his weather-beaten hide.

"So I should kiss you when the men can't see?" Her joking tone had returned.

"I better go right away if I want to get back before midnight." He climbed to his feet and almost ran from the ranch house. Damn the woman! She got under his skin so quick.

He poked his head into the bunkhouse. Messer-schmidt had pinned Cassidy to the floor, his knees on the drunken man's shoulders. He tried to pour a cup of coffee into the gaping mouth. Only a few drops made it in.

"Cassidy, you're fired," Flowers said. "Get your gear out of here by the time I get back from Fort Worth. Tell your ma you're a drunken, no account, lazy weasel. If you can't remember, I'll tell her myself."

Cassidy choked and sputtered on the little bit of

coffee that had gone down his throat, then stared up at Flowers in drunken befuddlement and said, "But Uncle Hiram, you can't fire me. You pr-promised my ma."

"Out. Now." He motioned for Messerschmidt to get off the man. "Messy, I want you to tell your partner to get the horses ready. Dawn, day after tomorrow. We're hitting the trail."

"Yippee!" Messerschmidt took off his hat and waved it around his head. "We don't like it here on the ranch. We're cowboys meant to be on the trail."

Flowers left, grumbling. He saddled his horse and galloped after Cletus and that whippersnapper he'd found in town. When he overtook them, he drew to a halt and stared hard at Mackenzie.

"You weren't lying about being able to cook?"

"No, sir, I was not," Mackenzie said. He showed no sign of lying. He either believed his own lies or could serve as chuckwagon cook.

"You're hired, but I swear, if you poison my crew, I'll hog-tie you and drag you the entire way to Santa Fe behind the ugliest, meanest longhorn in the herd."

"I won't disappoint you, Mister Flowers." Mackenzie grinned from ear to ear.

"There's one chore you got to do before getting all the grub together for the drive."

"Mister Flowers, you can't ask him to—" Cletus Grant clamped his mouth shut when he saw how resolute Flowers was.

"Both of you will fetch back Desmond."

"Who's that?" asked Mackenzie, looking from Flowers to Cletus and not getting an answer from either.

"You're coming with us, aren't you, Mister Flowers?" Cletus was all choked up. Flowers smiled wickedly.

"You two will drag him out of that whorehouse by his heels, and I will be in a saloon drinking my fill of whiskey to shore up my resolve to face him."

Hiram Flowers liked the sound of that plan, but he knew he would go with Grant and the newly hired cook. It was his job as trail boss. More than that, Mercedes had asked him to bring her wastrel son back to the ranch, and whatever she wanted, he did. Anything.

CHAPTER 4

Mac shifted uneasily in the saddle. The signpost he'd just ridden past said Fort Worth was only three miles away. He had hightailed it from town and thought escape from the gang of bounty hunters was possible. Tempting fate by riding back so soon gave him the fantods.

"Look here, Mister Flowers, if I'm going to be your cook, why don't I get on back to the ranch and be sure the chuckwagon is all packed up proper-like? We both know how important it is for everything to be in its right place, secured when we hit rough terrain and—"

"We're going to pry Desmond loose from whatever hellhole he's crawled into. I need help with that."

"Hellhole?" Cletus Grant snickered. "Is that what you call them purty lil' things' private parts now?"

"I can cut that flapping tongue of yours out and stuff it in your ear," Flowers said. Mac tried to find even a hint of joking in what the trail boss said. He couldn't hear it. The man was deadly serious. From the look of the thick-bladed knife sheathed at his left side, it had seen hard use. Slicing out tongues might have been the least of what that steel had seen and done.

"Didn't mean anything by it, Mister Flowers. You know me. I'm always joshing, keeping a lighter way of seeing things."

Mac and Grant exchanged glances. Cletus shrugged and looked ahead down the road.

There was plenty of daylight left and that worried Mac. The owner of the wagon yard had undoubtedly taken the black stallion with the flashy tooled saddle straight to the bounty hunters. That told the gunmen their quarry was still around town. Mac had expected that and figured to use it as a diversion. He had been clever using Cletus as a shield to get out of the city before, but coming back to Fort Worth only stirred up the pot again.

"We had to come to town tomorrow anyway. Old man Mason at the mercantile's got the rest of the supplies I ordered for the drive," Flowers said. "We can lasso Desmond and take everything back. That'll save a trip in."

"I can go check the supplies. Making sure everything's ready is my job." Mac hoped he could lose himself in the commercial section of Fort Worth, away from the saloons and brothels in Hell's Half Acre where the bounty hunters were most likely to be prowling. Then again, they might have some of their gang watching the general stores to be sure he didn't buy supplies for the trail.

His head began to hurt. Too many ideas crowded

in, jumbled up, and tried to spill out in some sort of escape plan. Sticking with the Circle Arrow foreman gave him the best chance of avoiding trouble. At least he hoped so, but if necessary, he could take some of the supplies slated for the Circle Arrow trail drive and ride out of town. Stealing like that worried his conscience a mite, but getting caught by the bounty hunters and killed—or worse, taken back to New Orleans to hang for a murder Leclerc had committed—had to be a lot worse.

"Mason knows Cletus. You sign for the goods, then meet us just beyond the train station. It'll be dawn by then."

"Dawn?" Mac perked up. "You thinking it'll take us all night to find Miz Sullivan's son?"

Cletus laughed harshly, then tried to cover up with a fake cough.

By the time they crossed the railroad tracks, the sun had set and a brisk wind blew across the prairie, coming up from the south. Mac fancied he caught the salty scent of the Gulf of Mexico in the wind. If so, that meant a storm brewed somewhere out of sight. The way it rained here wiped out tracks within minutes. Travel became impossible in the driving rain, but having his trail washed away mattered more.

"Mason won't shut up shop for another half hour," Cletus said, fumbling open a pocket watch and holding it up to catch the light from a gas lamp. "I can get everything you bought and be waiting for you long before dawn."

"Git," Flowers said. Cletus wasted no time galloping away. When the man was out of earshot, Flowers spoke in a weary voice. "The last time I found Desmond he was in the Frisky Filly Sporting House. From the ruckus he put up as I dragged him out, he might have a favorite whore there."

"We can start there," Mac said. His head swiveled back and forth, jumping at every cowboy and rider dressed in a black coat. Either none was in the gang hunting him or they ignored a man with a partner. Mac doubted he had a big enough store of luck to use the same trick twice. Having Cletus riding with them would have given more, better, cover.

"You're as jumpy as a long-tailed cat on a porch full of rockin' chairs," Flowers commented. "What kind of trouble did *you* get into here in Fort Worth?"

"Some of Miz Sullivan's teetotaler ways must have rubbed off on me, maybe. All these drinking emporiums make me a tad uneasy." As they rode past every saloon, Mac glanced inside, worrying he would see the square-headed, broad-shouldered men hunting him down.

"Why do I doubt that?" Flowers asked dryly as he drew rein in front of a fancy three-story building.

Lights burned in every window on the top floor. Half-dressed women sat on a balcony circling the second story. They waved and hooted at anyone passing by. The ground floor had stained-glass windows, cut crystal fixtures visible through the open front door, and a parlor that was about the ritziest thing Mac had ever seen. He wouldn't have thought this was a frontier cathouse but rather one pulled up by the roots from Storyville in New Orleans and transplanted. It seemed out of place in a rough and tumble section of town like Hell's Half Acre, but Mac knew the rich folks liked to sneak down to the "wrong" part of town and revel in the danger.

Mac touched the revolver tucked into his belt to remind himself he had six empty chambers. The sight of a huge black man in a tailored, pearl-gray, swallowtail coat standing just outside the door, acting as gatekeeper, reminded him of his lack of firepower. There wasn't any way he could take a man that size and strength in a bare knuckles fight. From the way the mountain of a man stood, he had plenty of weapons of his own tucked away in a shoulder rig, in his coat pockets, and unless Mac guessed wrong, a couple of sheathed knives hidden under the broad lapels of his fancy jacket.

"We have to get past him?" Mac asked in awe.

"You man enough to bull past him?" Flowers laughed. This was as close to humor as Mac had heard from him, and it had to come at his expense.

"A full-grown bull's not bull enough to get past him."

Flowers nodded once.

"You might be a good hire, after all. You're the first one of the men I ever brought who's shown good sense."

"How loco are your cowboys? Who'd tangle with him?" Mac stepped down to stand beside his horse. He pressed close to hide his face from riders in the street. They shouted obscenities back at the ladies of the evening on the porch just above the street. In return, the Cyprians passed judgment on their manhood and anatomical endowments.

"We full up right now," the ebony giant said, stepping up and pressing a hand the size of a dinner plate against Flowers's chest.

"You mean we don't have the money to even get into the parlor. I know that. We're here to take Mister Sullivan home. He is here, isn't he?"

"That'd be tellin'. The boss don't like that none. Our customers deserve—and get—all the privacy we can give 'em."

Flowers lifted his shoulders and dropped them as he stepped forward. Mac almost laughed when he saw the servant's expression. Flowers might be the man's name, but he wasn't in the least bit fragrant like one. If he had taken a bath in the past week, it would have been a surprise.

"That'd be Harrison Judd?" Flowers said.

The broad, flat face betrayed no emotion.

"Who's inquirin' after me, Obediah?" On the heels of the question, a dapper man twirling a cane came from inside the whorehouse. The light caught the gold knob at one end of the cane and the steel tip at the other.

Mac had seen canes like this before. A sword inside the length came out with the twist of the knob and presented a formidable weapon. He began to get antsy at so much deadliness facing him and Flowers. His empty revolver taunted him now and made him wonder if a plot in the potter's field waited for him.

"Just the gent I want to see," Flowers said. "Come on out for a minute, Mister Judd. We wouldn't want to disturb any of the paying customers." Flowers pointedly looked at the well-dressed men in plush chairs with a drink in one hand and their other arm around trim waists of pretty waiter girls.

"This is becoming tedious," Judd said. "Let the boy sow his wild oats. You got no call dragging him out by his heels just when he's beginning to enjoy himself."

"Unless I miss my guess, Desmond is so drunk there's not a whale of a lot he can enjoy right now. Has he passed out?"

"Doesn't matter one bit to me. He pays for a lady's company. That's between the two of them."

"So you aren't the pimp running this whorehouse? You don't take the money from the gals and get them hooked on laudanum?"

Mac put his hand on Flowers's arm to quiet him. The man was building up a head of steam, and the safety valve wasn't going to hold much longer. Obediah moved his hand under his coat to get nearer the revolver in his shoulder holster. If lead started flying, Flowers would be the first to drop. Mac would be a close second.

Flowers jerked away from Mac angrily. He thrust out his chin and bumped his chest against Harrison Judd. The brothel owner, though considerably smaller, stood his ground.

"Might be we can come to an arrangement," Judd suggested. "I only learned recently that Desmond's last name is Sullivan. He wouldn't be the son of Mercedes Sullivan, would he? The widow owner of the Circle Arrow? That must mean he's actually as rich as he makes out with the girls."

"He doesn't have a penny to his name," Flowers said.

"But his ma does. What's it worth to her not to have him dragged through the streets naked as a jay-bird and humiliated? Or maybe the marshal comes by and arrests his ass for disturbing the peace."

"Peace? That's not what he's here for. He—"

"Arrested and his picture bannered on the front page of the *Fort Worth Daily Gazette* would cause his poor old ma considerable heartache. Why, she wouldn't be able to hold her head up if she ever came into town again. How'd such publicity help her with her temperance crusade? Makes her look like a hypocrite, doesn't it?"

"She'd disown him so it wouldn't reflect on her," Mac said. He squeezed harder on Flowers's arm to keep the man quiet. It didn't work.

"You go drag him out here this minute or we're going in and find him," Flowers declared.

"The Frisky Filly is a big place. You think you can find him before you get tossed out? Or worse?"

Hiram Flowers reared back to launch a haymaker. A dozen things flashed through Mac's head at the same instant. The black guard was pulling his revolver. Judd worked his hand over to a vest pocket where the butt of a derringer poked out. The argument had drawn the attention of the women on the balcony above them. Worse, Flowers shouting at the pimp drew a crowd of men who were flowing into town for a night's debauchery.

Mac looped his arm around the foreman's and twisted hard. This kept the punch from landing and unbalanced Flowers enough for Mac to steer him away. The foreman cursed and raged until they were across the street.

"What'd you stop me for, you young idiot? I could have taken him."

"It wouldn't have been a fair fight. Look upstairs."

Flowers sputtered and tried to deny that several of the scantily clad women had pistols of their own. Even if they aimed at Flowers and missed, hitting their pimp, the torrential downpour of lead would have been deadly.

"Get yourself killed and what good's that to Desmond?" Mac saw Obediah's attention fixed on them. He kept his hand hidden under his coat, resting on his revolver.

Then the guard had his hands full of cowboys trying to crowd into the Frisky Filly to sample the fleshy wares.

"He's in there. You heard what that snake said. He wants to blackmail Mercedes!"

"That makes it easier on us that Desmond is a man of habit." Mac studied the layout of the building. There had to be a back entrance. Judd didn't look to be the kind of man willing to pay for a guard on each door. Obediah was probably alone, his size and menacing look intended to keep out anyone who could be intimidated.

That included Mac, but he felt the pressure of time working on him. The bounty hunters wouldn't give up after he had plugged one of them. The way they had chased him through the saloons and up and down the streets the night before told him they were persistent, both from the need for revenge and the huge reward on his head. Either of those would be enough to keep them looking for him. Both insured they'd wear down the shoes on their horses chasing him to the ends of the earth.

"What's he look like? Desmond?"

"You're not going in there without me. I swear, I'll thrash him within an inch of his life for putting his poor ma in such a position. She'd die if he got his picture in the newspaper for doing half what he's likely doing in there." Flowers balled his hands into knobby fists as he ranted.

"Come around back. Let me do the talking," Mac said.

"I want that young reprobate out of there. If he doesn't ride with us on the drive, Mercedes said she'd come along."

"And you want her to stay safe and sound on the ranch," Mac said. He eyed Flowers closely, then shook his head. The grizzled old cowhand and the lovely ranch owner were as mismatched a pair as he could imagine. Still, he understood unrequited love and what it did to a man.

Evie had thrown him over for Pierre Leclerc and, so help him, Mac still loved her. Deep down, he still loved her although he knew fate had driven them apart for all time.

He didn't wait to see if Flowers was going to play along. Crossing the street, he went around the side of the building until he reached the far end of the balcony on the second floor. He waved to a young girl there.

"You can't—" Flowers started, then shut up when Mac shot him a cold look.

"Hello up there," Mac called. "You've got quite a view from that balcony."

"You want a better view? Here, mister, take a gander at this." The woman hiked her skirts and fluttered them about. She wasn't wearing anything under them.

"I'm a bit nearsighted. I'm not sure what I saw. Fact is, I do better fumbling around in the dark. My hands are a lot better at finding secret places than my eyes. Why not let me in?"

"Come on around to the front and tell Obediah it's all right."

"You didn't see the misunderstanding I had with him. He didn't think this was enough." Mac took out every bill he had left from his earnings. Folded triple and spread out in the dark, it looked like a wad of greenbacks big enough to choke a cow. "And that's just one pocket." He thrust his hand in and pulled out the same roll of bills, making it seem he was rolling in dough. "It'd all be yours 'cept he won't let me in."

"Come on, Mackenzie," Flowers said, tugging on his arm. "We can figure something else to get inside."

"My friend says there's a better house down the street. Too bad since you're real purty." Mac made no move to go after Flowers. He knew what the soiled dove's reaction would be. And he was right.

"Come on around. There's a door painted all red. I'll let you in there, but you got to give me all that money."

"Honey child, it's all yours."

Mac tried not to look too eager rounding the cathouse and standing in front of the red door the whore had mentioned. Flowers stood close.

"We rush in and—" the foreman began.

"And nothing," Mac broke in. "If she raises a ruckus,

finding Desmond will be impossible." He heard some-one fumbling with the doorknob. "There she is now. Keep quiet and follow me."

"You're mighty bossy for a hand I just hired this afternoon. I can fire you, you know."

"That's up to you, isn't it? I learned that a chuck-wagon cook's got to take charge or he'll get walked on. Nobody walks over me."

"You got quite a mouth on you." Flowers sounded ready to fight again.

"Stop being so riled you've got to pull Desmond's chestnuts out of the fire." Mac saw the slow realization dawn on Flowers that his anger was misdirected. He relaxed a little, but his fists were still ready for a fight.

The door swung open. "You all hot and ready or you just gonna talk?" The soiled dove stood with one hand on a cocked hip and tried to look alluring "Don't matter to me, as long as I get paid."

Mac went to her and pushed the door open more so he got a good look down the hallway. They were at the rear of the building and a staircase led upward just inside the door.

"Why don't you go to your room and get ready for me?" he suggested. "I like to make a grand entrance."

"Like an actor coming on stage?"

"Exactly like that," Mac said. He held out a few of his greenbacks. She snared them and made a big point of tucking them into her bodice.

"I'll expect the rest after you make that big entrance." She walked down the hall, putting as much of a hitch in her behind as possible to entice him.

She paused a moment at a door, shot him a sultry look and batted her eyelashes, then went in.

"Come on. We don't have much time to find Desmond," Mac said. He worried that Obediah might make a round through the halls to be sure everything was all right. Or Harrison Judd might check on his girls. Or any of a dozen other problems.

Flowers started up the stairs. Mac hung back and seriously considered hightailing it. He had gotten out of Fort Worth and away from the bounty hunters once. The more times he had to escape their six-guns the more likely his luck was to run out.

"Come on. I can't find the son of a bitch by myself." Flowers motioned urgently for him.

This decided Mac. He wanted the job with the Circle Arrow cattle drive, not only as a way to elude Leclerc's killers. He enjoyed being out on the trail, as dangerous as that could be.

He took the steps two at a time to reach the upper floor. Mac stared at the lavish decorations. Plaster statues of nude women lined the hallway. A soft carpet deadened the sound of Flowers's boots as he tromped along, opening each door as he went to take a quick look inside. Twice Flowers got furious cries to stop spying. At the third door he opened he simply stood and stared. Mac hurried to join him.

"That's Desmond?" Mac almost burst out laughing.

The rust-haired boy was only a year or two younger than Mac but had the look of being unfinished, soft . . . and drunker than a lord. He sprawled on his back across a big bed. His long johns had been put on backward so the drop flap was in the front and open.

"You boys want to join us? That'll be extra." A nude, blond strumpet perched on the edge of the bed, one foot up on the mattress and the other on the carpeted floor. She lounged back to expose herself.

"Come on, Desmond. Time to go." Flowers swung Mercedes Sullivan's son up and over his shoulder. He staggered a bit under the weight, then got his balance. "Get his clothes, Mackenzie."

Mac did as he was told, letting Flowers slip past into the hallway. He faced the harlot, who showed every sign of putting up a protest.

"What's he owe you?"

"A hundred dollars!"

"That's a lot of money."

With a sullen pout on her face, she said, "I'm worth it."

Mac pondered a moment, then said, "One of your friends down on the first floor's got the money."

"Angie? Bethany?"

"Yeah," Mac said, edging to the stairs. "She's the one."

Before the woman complained, he followed Flowers down the steps and out back.

"That's his horse. Bring it here," Flowers ordered Mac.

Running now, Mac grabbed the reins of the horse and tugged, getting it moving. Flowers met him halfway back to the whorehouse, heaved, and dumped Desmond belly down over the saddle.

"Let's get the blazes out of here," Flowers said. "I've had all of Fort Worth that I can stomach."

CHAPTER 5

Quick Willy Means sat in the corner of the dance hall, watching the ebb and flow of customers. Most came in to get drunk. Some came in to pay a dime and dance with the girl of their choice. Only a few did both.

This was one of the more expensive watering holes in Fort Worth, being right at the edge of Hell's Half Acre. It catered to a richer clientele but also saw some of the cowboys on their way to the dives and brothels south along Throckmorton Street. He liked the different types of men who came in. It gave him a chance to cover more territory in his hunt.

He slipped his revolver from his holster, snapped open the gate, and clicked the cylinder. Every chamber carried a fresh round. Another move closed the gate. He laid the pistol on the table next to the bottle of decent Kentucky whiskey.

Farther south, he couldn't get whiskey that didn't make him puke. In other parts of Fort Worth, he had to pay too much. This was just right. Plus he could reach any part of town in a flash, being centrally located. That suited him just fine after Jimmy Huffman was cut down. He had never liked Jimmy, or his brothers, but they were the best trackers he had ever hired and had no qualms about using their revolvers if the need arose.

And it did often. Means was the most efficient bounty hunter in the West. In eight years of hunting criminals, he had failed to find only two, and he thought one of them had died in a spring flood, his body washed all the way down the Mississippi to the Gulf of Mexico.

The other one he considered still to be found. Being hired by the shipping magnate in New Orleans added to the work, but the price Pierre Leclerc paid in advance made up for the detour from Kansas City and a man with a thousand-dollar reward on his head to this piss pot Texas town. Being derailed irritated him, but having Mackenzie cut down Jimmy Huffman caused a hatred to build. Quick Willy Means did not lose men working for him.

Ever.

He moved his gun a few inches on the table, poured himself another shot of the acceptable whiskey, and knocked it back before the rangy blond man crossed the dance floor to stand in front of him. Arizona Johnston might do to replace Jimmy Huffman. He had a quick hand, sharp eye, and didn't give much lip. Mostly Means appreciated that he was a thinker without being a jackass. But he really didn't know the man yet.

"I've got a line on him," Johnston said without preamble. "He and two others rode into town from the south. One went off on his own, but Mackenzie

and his partner made a beeline to a whorehouse."
He smiled crookedly. "A fine one by the look, too,
not just a crib like most of them in that part of town."

Means used the muzzle of his revolver to push a
shot glass in Johnston's direction and said, "Have a
drink."

"Later, when we've corralled him."

"You won't drink with me?" Means sat a little
straighter.

"I will when we catch Mackenzie and have the
bounty riding high in our pockets. Keeping my head
clear now lets me enjoy a celebration later."

Means gave the gunman another once-over. The
trail clothes he wore varied considerably from those
worn by the Huffman brothers. Arizona Johnston
wore a sand-colored duster, with canvas pants poking
out from under the frayed hem. A plain brown cloth
coat, paisley vest, and a boiled white shirt showed
some taste, but nothing out of the ordinary. His Stetson with a snake-skin hatband was pushed back on
his head.

The only thing that interested Means about the
man's attire were the two revolvers. One hung low on
his right hip just about the proper place for a quick
draw. The other rode high in a cross-draw holster on
his left side. Two guns but he wasn't rigged to fire
one in each hand.

"Let's go after our fugitive from justice," Means
said, pushing back from the table. He made a big
show of picking up the gun with his left hand, doing
a border shift to his right, spinning it around, and
slipping it expertly into his right holster.

He watched for Johnston's reaction. There wasn't

one. He either was unimpressed or he hid his admiration for a man so adroit with a shooting iron. Means needed to find out which it was before they hit the trail together.

As they walked out side by side, Johnston asked, "Is it true you have a pack mule so loaded down with wanted posters that it walks bowlegged?"

"I've got a couple hundred posters in a banker's folder. Any of those varmints might show up at any time, at any place. It's my duty to study them and to be sure new posters are added."

Means kept his voice level as he answered, but the flippant question peeved him. Hunting men was a business and one he took seriously. There was never room for joking.

"Where'd the Huffman boys get off to?" Johnston swung up into the saddle and waited for him to step up.

Means settled himself in the saddle, pushed back his coattails to expose the butts of both revolvers, then said, "They're mourning their brother. Lead the way. We can take Mackenzie ourselves."

"Do we split the reward with the Huffmans?"

"They're part of the crew."

"Not that good a part," Johnston said, eyes ahead as he rode. "One got himself cut down and the other two are drowning their sorrows."

"They're partners. My partners. Are you looking to take the entire reward for yourself?"

"Of course not. You've got the contact back in New Orleans. I just wanted to make sure where I stood. Equal share, right?"

"We're in this together," Means said. "You found him, so you've earned your share."

"And the Huffmans? How'd they earn theirs?"

"Being my partners," Means said, his ire rising now. "We've ridden together for quite a spell. Most bounty hunters concentrate on a lone outlaw at a time. We go after entire gangs."

"Loyal," Johnston said softly, almost to himself. "I can appreciate that."

Means tilted his head to one side when he heard the shouts ahead. A couple of shots made him reach for his left-hand gun, but he checked the move. All around him and Johnston flowed men like a bucking, churning ocean, running in the direction of the whorehouse.

"What's going on?" Means asked.

"I'll find out," Johnston said. He bent low and grabbed the collar of a man stumbling along. With an impressive show of strength he pulled the man off his feet. His boots kicked feebly in the air scant inches above the dirt. "Where are you going, partner?"

"Big fight. Riot. Men gonna get themselves kilt. I want to see."

"Where's this fight?"

"Somebody said it was at the Frisky Filly. Harry Judd's place." The man belched and turned slowly in Johnston's grip. "He don't like bein' called Harry. He's all stuck up and snotty. Harrison Judd, he says, 'cuz he runs the fanciest fancy house in the whole damn town."

Johnston dropped the man, who fell to his knees, then scrambled up and joined the flow of the crowd.

"Do you reckon it's Mackenzie causing the up-roar?"

"There's one way to find out," Means said. He kept

his horse walking through the crowd until the men were packed too close for any further progress.

Ahead rose the house of ill repute with a second-story balcony filled with whores all egging on the fighting down below. Means stood in his stirrups and tried to see who was responsible for the loud hoots and hollers, both from the women and from the crowd.

"See him?" Johnston asked.

Means didn't bother answering. He settled down and thought hard. Getting closer to the house wasn't possible. Hundreds of men barred his way. Worse, identifying Mackenzie in such a crowd would be like finding a particular straw stick in a haystack.

"There's nothing we can do with a crowd this big. If we tried to grab Mackenzie, the crowd would turn on us just for the hell of it."

"What are we going to do? Lose him?"

"Johnston, you haven't thought this through. He'll ride out of town. We follow. We'll grab him out on the prairie."

"What aren't you telling me?" Arizona Johnston craned his neck. "There's three men riding off. That might be them."

"I saw. One's Mackenzie, sure as rain. The old pelican riding with him is Hiram Flowers, about as tough a man as you'll ever run across."

"Does he have a reward on his head?"

Means shook his head slowly.

"Not that I ever saw, but that doesn't mean he hasn't done plenty that's against the law. With Mackenzie beside him, the two must be up to something."

With that, Means skirted the crowd and began riding

slowly in the direction Mackenzie and Flowers had taken. They had come to rescue the third man. Was Flowers getting a gang together? It had been five years since he'd run afoul of the man over in Abilene. There hadn't been any hint that Flowers broke the law, but Means always wondered. Seeing him with Dewey Mackenzie firmed up his opinion. They were up to no good.

"Willy, over there. A man with two pack mules."

He started to correct Johnston and order him to call him Mister Means, then saw what the man already had. One man didn't need so much in the way of supplies. This might be the target for Mackenzie and his gang.

"Go back and get the Huffman brothers. If Mackenzie is planning a robbery, I might need a passel of guns backing me up."

"You're not going to take them on by yourself? If Mackenzie is half as dangerous as you said that Leclerc made out, you'd have your hands full. With two others backing him in a robbery, there'd be no way any one man stood a beggar's chance of capturing them."

"I don't intend to ambush them since I'd have to know where the man with the pack mules is headed. Get Charles and Frank. If they try to rob him, they'll do it around dawn. I would."

Johnston started to make another comment about such craziness, then wheeled around and trotted away, finding a side street to avoid the crowd outside the Frisky Filly. It had grown even larger.

Quick Willy Means made sure his revolvers rode easy in their holsters, then gave his horse its head to walk along parallel to the drover with the pack mules. When the man disappeared over a rise, Means cut across the terrain and found the road leading to the southwest.

He kept his distance, wondering what the drover had in his packs that Mac and Flowers might want. Men like that would steal pennies off a dead man's eyes. It took all his willpower not to ride up to the man with the mules and offer to guard his shipment, hoping Mackenzie attacked anyway. Let the murderous outlaw come to him.

But he held back. Dawn began poking into the sky by the time Johnston and the Huffman brothers joined him.

"I let the drover get a mile ahead. Even if Mackenzie robs him, we can overtake him, especially if he tries to keep what all he's stolen."

"We want him dead, boss. He killed Jimmy."

Means ignored whichever of the Huffman brothers spoke. It made no difference to him if Mackenzie was taken back alive or dead, although Leclerc had promised a bonus if he was returned to New Orleans alive to stand trial. Leclerc had an ax to grind. For Means, it was a matter of expediency. Mackenzie might surrender right away. Cowards did that. If so, he'd be obligated to take him to Leclerc for justice. More likely, especially with Hiram Flowers at his side, Mackenzie would try to shoot it out.

That never came out good for the outlaws. Means had been returning escaped prisoners and road agents for eight years. Not one had survived a shoot-out with him. From all he could tell about Mackenzie, he was just starting his criminal career. That made him a greenhorn, a greenhorn outlaw and easy prey. His instincts would be wrong, and his skill with a gun would be lacking.

Means glanced over at Arizona Johnston. Even if Mackenzie went against Johnston, he had no chance. The Huffman boys were a different matter, but it wouldn't come to that. He wouldn't let it.

They topped a low rise and had a panoramic view of the dawn-lit Texas prairie. He caught his breath.

"They're riding together, the three from Fort Worth and the man with the supplies." Frank Huffman sounded confused. Means shared some of that puzzlement.

"It might be they're all in cahoots," he said, finally coming up with a new plan. "We won't try to grab Mackenzie now. We'll trail them for a while and see what they're up to."

"That might be dangerous, Willy," said Johnston. "With the supplies on those two mules, they can feed a small army. We could be up against a couple dozen outlaws."

Frank Huffman drew his pistol and aimed it in Mackenzie's direction. "You turning chicken, Arizona? We don't care. That son of a bitch murdered our brother. Even if he's backed up by a thousand men, we're gonna take him down."

Johnston said something under his breath about being stupid. But Means knew Frank wasn't going to fire. At this range the bullet would dig up prairie a hundred yards off. Alerting Mackenzie served no purpose. Frank only imagined what he would do when they got close enough.

Means didn't much care who plugged Dewey Mackenzie. If he had to track him down across half of Texas, he didn't want to take him back alive to New Orleans. That'd be too much trouble for too little reward.

"Let's see what supplies we've got between us, boys," he said to the other bounty hunters. "We're in for a longer hunt than I intended. We don't want to get too hungry before we bring in Mackenzie." Under his breath he added, "And Hiram Flowers."

CHAPTER 6

"It gets harder," Hiram Flowers told Mac. "A damned sight harder. You won't be enjoying the trip near as much when we get to the Pecos River."

"Is the river swollen this time of year?" As he asked the question, Mac went about his work fixing lunch for the Circle Arrow hands. They'd been on the trail four days and he still had plenty of the things they liked best. When he started running out of eggs and other perishables, the real grumbling would start.

He worked the dough for his biscuits until it oozed between his fingers with just the right texture. Of everything he fixed, biscuits were what kept the men happiest. That had been true when he had worked for the Rolling J, and it had been true with the Circle Arrow. So far.

"It's all swole up like a son of a bitch. Swole up worse 'n a rattlesnake-bit hound dog. Flowing over its banks, waiting to drown the lot of us." Flowers spat into the fire and caused a fragrant sizzling. He locked eyes with Mac, daring him to say anything.

Ever since leaving the ranch, Flowers had been in a foul mood. Mac thought much of that choler came from Desmond Sullivan being along. The trail boss had ignored the young rancher, but as he'd said, the going had been easy. Mac hoped the rest of the Goodnight-Loving Trail proved as smooth.

At this rate they'd be in Santa Fe before they knew it, though Flowers had been muttering about stopping at Fort Sumner to sell some beeves to the Army. If Mac was any judge, that would make the trip from the fort to Santa Fe all the easier. Fewer cattle meant fewer problems, and they had started with north of a thousand head.

Mac divided the dough and placed the lumps into the Dutch oven to get the first batch ready. The rest of the meal would go fast enough. The cowboys would eat their steaks raw. One had even complained that the steak he got for breakfast hadn't mooed loud enough to suit him when he cut a slice off. Mac had jabbed him with a fork, getting a cry of surprise from him that had kept the rest of the crew amused until they saddled up and went to get the ornery longhorns moving for the day.

"How much farther do you intend to get today?" Mac cleaned his utensils and sampled some of the peach cobbler left over from breakfast. The supply of fresh fruit was coming to an end, too.

"Another five miles," Flowers said. He took off his hat and ran a hand over his thinning hair. "I got a bad feeling about tonight."

Mac studied the sky. Clouds moved fast from the west like giant puffs of cotton. Not one of them showed an ugly gray underbelly that promised rain. He had never been trapped out on such flat land during one of the infamous Texas frog stranglers, but he had heard about them. The rain came down in buckets and had almost nowhere to go. Everything turned to mud, and deep ravines cut through the ground made travel by wagon hard. Getting a herd across those arroyos would be quite a job, too.

"It's not the weather that's worrying me," Flowers said. He looked back along their trail. A dust cloud rose where the herd moved toward them.

"Trouble with the men? Anything you want me to do?"

Flowers shot him a cold look and shook his head.

"Not the men that's worrying me. It's the men trailing the herd."

"Rustlers?" Mac sucked in his breath and looked at his revolver hanging in a holster he had won from one of the drovers in a poker game. He still didn't have any ammunition for the .44.

"Might be cowboys looking to join our company," Flowers said.

"You don't believe that. Why not? How long have they been trailing us?"

"I spotted them a couple days back. From the way they tried to stay out of sight, we might have had their unwanted company since leaving the ranch."

"My gun's mighty hungry," Mac said. "It'd feel better if it had a belly full of cartridges."

"Tell Messerschmidt to give you a box or two from our stores. You're one of the first they'd try to rob, being out front of the herd most of the time and all by your lonesome."

Mac always followed Flowers as the trail boss scouted

ahead for the entire herd. When he reached the spot the trail boss marked, he'd stop and prepare a meal, either midday or supper and breakfast where the herd bedded down for the night. As the cattle began their daily travels, he had to get after Flowers and repeat the routine, always leading and mostly on the trail alone unless he happened to find the trail boss.

"Much obliged."

Flowers fixed him with a steely, accusing look. "You can use that hog leg, can't you?"

Mac didn't answer. Anything he said would sound like bragging or worse. He might arouse Flowers's ire if he talked of the men he had shot down. Every last one of them had deserved it—and he was innocent of the one he was accused of killing in New Orleans. It hardly seemed fair. Whatever it was, Mac knew better than to talk about it.

"The men will get the herd here in another hour. I'm heading yonder." Flowers waved his hat toward a range of low hills in the distance. "Once everyone's chowed down, you skirt those hills to the south and then angle back toward me to the northwest."

"Is the going directly over the hills too rough for the chuckwagon?"

Flowers nodded, distracted. He swung into the saddle and headed out.

"You not eating?" Mac called after him.

"Not hungry." Flowers rubbed his belly. With that he trotted away, leaving Mac to wonder if the trail boss didn't like his food or if the man's stomach was hurting him. From the noises it made when he ate, his digestion was terrible.

Mac poked through the medicinal supplies he

had, hunting for something that might ease belly pain. He found a bottle of Sal Hepatica and wondered if this might help Flowers. He had other nostrums that might serve a man better who spent his day in the saddle. Flowers might enjoy life more by seeing a doctor in one of the towns they passed along the trail, though many frontier sawbones tended to be as dim as an old buffalo trail.

Humming to himself, Mac finished the cooking just as the first of the cowboys came in. He served them up the last of the fresh food, then talked with Messerschmidt about getting a box of ammunition.

"You thinking on starting a range war, Mac?" The man rummaged through the supply wagon until he found a box of .44s. He passed them over.

"Thanks, Messy. Flowers suggested I keep my revolver loaded since he thinks we're . . . getting away from the towns," he finished lamely. Telling Messerschmidt or any of the others that Flowers believed they were being followed by a gang of rustlers would spook them needlessly. While the cowboys ought to be on guard, worrying them over a few men who might just be heading in the same direction was pointless.

Besides, it was the trail boss's job to talk over such problems, not the cook's.

"How's he doing?" Mac didn't have to point out Desmond Sullivan. Messerschmidt knew right away who he meant.

"He does the work of five men."

"What?" This startled Mac. His eyebrows rose.

Messerschmidt laughed.

"What I mean, Mac, is that it takes five men to do

his work after he makes a complete botch of it. He knows nothing about being a drover. He should ride along and do nothing. That would keep all of us happy, but he meddles and makes things bad." Messerschmidt shook his head. "Flowers should never have let him come along. We must take care of the herd and ourselves *and* him."

Mac didn't want to share what he had overheard back at the ranch and in Fort Worth. Flowers had struck the bargain of wet-nursing Desmond to keep Mercedes Sullivan from accompanying them. He wondered if he was the only one who saw how Flowers wore his heart on his sleeve for their boss lady. Flowers would walk through hell barefoot for her.

This image caused a smile to curve his lips. If Flowers did just that, the Devil would throw him out of hell because of the stink. None of them on the drive had a chance to bathe, and some didn't want to. In Hiram Flowers's case, it was almost a matter of pride that he smelled worse than a stepped-on skunk.

"Time to drive on and set up for this evening. You got any requests, Messy?" Mac held up the ammo box. "I owe you for these."

"You do a good job, Mac. Better than Cassidy ever did."

"By better you mean I haven't poisoned anyone yet."

"Yeah, that." Messerschmidt slapped him on the shoulder and went around to climb into the driver's box of the supply wagon. He rode with the herd to get the cowboys anything they might need during the day.

Mac finished cleaning the last of the utensils, pots and pans, packed his chuckwagon, and settled in for the drive Flowers had outlined for him. This wasn't the first time he had taken a different route from the man riding scout. Being on horseback allowed the scout to travel faster and find better vantage points to study the lay of the land for the herd. When he had been with the Rolling J crew along the Shawnee Trail he had doubled as cook and scout, learning firsthand how difficult it was to find the right trail for a large herd.

He whistled tunelessly as he drove his team down the slight incline and found a trail to rattle along that took him around the taller hills and finally brought him out on the far side.

As his team struggled to pull along in sandy ground, the hair on the back of his neck rose the way it always did when he sensed someone watching him. Without being too obvious, he reached back and caught the holster swinging gently behind him. The loaded gun slid free of the leather, then was tucked securely into the waistband of his trousers. The gun had just settled in place when a solitary Indian rose from behind a tall mesquite bush and blocked his way.

Mac drew back slowly on the reins to bring his wagon to a halt. One brave posed little threat. A quick study of the man convinced Mac he had come upon a hunter and not a war party.

But he knew the Comanche wasn't out on the prairie alone. He didn't carry enough gear behind him on the pony. That meant a camp somewhere nearby. A lone Comanche had no reason to pitch

camp and ride around when he carried his entire
wealth with him. There would be others, perhaps a
dozen or more.

Not for the first time Mac wished he had eyes in
the back of his head. He heard the horses coming up
from behind where he couldn't see them. Turning
and making a show of counting them lowered his status in their eyes.

"Howdy," he called. "How's hunting? I haven't
seen anything the whole livelong day but a few
scrawny rabbits." As if trying to find a more comfortable spot on the hard wooden bench seat, he moved
his hand closer to the butt of his revolver.

From the soft thuds at least four rode up from behind. At least. He sucked in his breath when two
more joined the Indian blocking his way.

The brave who had stopped him pointed to the
rear of the chuckwagon. "You have food?"

"For the men riding herd. We are moving many
hundreds of longhorns. Many, many hundreds."

They exchanged silent looks. The other four drew
rein on either side and slightly behind him to make
it harder for him to open fire on them should they
attack. Seven braves, six rounds in his trusty .44? He
was a good shot but even assuming every round
found a target, that left one hunter unscathed.

He squinted a bit in the afternoon sun and again
tried to read their painted faces. A few streaks meant
decoration. And their horses lacked paint. Sometimes a war party put painted hand prints on their
horses' rumps. These needed currying and, judging
by their sunken flanks, decent fodder. But he saw no
indication he had run afoul of a war party.

He let out a small self-deprecating chuckle. How stupid could he be? If they'd been a war party, they wouldn't stop to talk. They'd ambush him and take whatever was left.

"Cows?" the spokesman said.

Mac nodded. "Many, many cows. Perhaps my chief would be willing to give your chief a few beeves as a show of friendship."

"Many, many cows?"

"A few. In exchange for your friendship."

The three ahead whispered. The one speaking shook his head. Mac turned so his hand rested on the pistol. He'd go down shooting, if it came to that.

"We hungry now."

"Then on the behalf of my chief, let me extend friendship now with a meal. I've got some food left over from my noon meal . . . for many, many cowboys." It didn't hurt to keep reminding them that he was alone right now but a veritable army of cowboys came along behind.

"You feed?"

"I will." Mac pushed hard on the brake and looped the reins around it. As he got down from the driver's box, he slipped his pistol from his waistband and left it on the floor. No gun, no mistakes.

They were hungry and jumpy. Shooting his way out of a jam wasn't possible if they got worked up. He'd had some contact with Comanches back in Waco and respected their fighting and riding skills. Talk—and a dollop of food—was the best way to avoid trouble now.

"Step right up," he said. "I'll get a fire going to boil some coffee. That'll help wash down the food."

Dried cow chips sent up a long, thin tendril of smoke when he got a pile of them lighted. Whether this warned Flowers or anybody with the herd of trouble, he didn't know, but he needed the fire anyway to make the coffee. As it boiled, he set out slabs of jerky, a pot of beans, and leftover biscuits for the Indians. They held back until he sampled each in turn, then he held out the various items for them. The way they gobbled down what the cowboys would have turned up their noses at told him how hard life was for them out here.

He stoked the fire with a few more dried cow chips. A gust of stinking gray smoke rose and got whipped around not fifty feet in the air. He only had two tin cups, but he filled those and passed them out to the Indians, who took turns gulping down his brew. The cowboys told him it tasted like varnish. The only response he got from the Comanches was a loud belch. They were so appreciative he was glad he didn't bother putting sugar in the coffee. This served the purpose of keeping them nice and peaceable. No reason to waste a valuable commodity out here on the range when anything he gave them was considered a banquet.

"Many, many cows?" The only one who spoke stabbed his finger in Mac's direction.

"Many, many cowboys herding them," he said.

The Comanches whispered again, then their spokesman said, "Many, many horses?"

"Not many," he answered slowly. For the Indians, horses were mobile wealth. They couldn't eat or ride gold. A brave with a dozen horses was a rich man. The Circle Arrow remuda had more than fifty horses in it. Without a mount, a cowboy was worthless. No-

body walked alongside a herd of longhorns and
kept up.

"Many. You lie!" The brave swung his rifle up and
pointed it at Mac.

He remembered how he had originally considered shooting it out with them. He would die, probably get scalped, and the entire chuckwagon filled
with supplies would be stolen, but a blazing six-gun
would let them know they'd been in a fight. Now he
stood unarmed and helpless.

Mac raised his hands and stood to face the Comanche. The Indian cocked the hammer on his rifle
and took aim.

CHAPTER 7

"Nice rifle. It'd be a damned shame if it got dropped in the dirt when I put a bullet through your head."

Hiram Flowers stepped from behind a greasewood, his Winchester trained on the Comanche with his rifle leveled at Mackenzie.

The cook took everything in with a single sweep of his eyes across the tableau. The Indians were frozen in place, but the bore of the rifle pointed at his face looked big enough to reach down with his fist and grab the bullet.

"You have many, many cows?" the Comanche asked.

"That's a crazy thing to say when you're an inch away from having your head blowed off." Flowers took another half step to get a better shot. He let out a curt "Stop!" when two of the Indians went to lift their rifles. None of them had six-guns that Mac saw, but all had wickedly sharp hunting knifes. Not for the first time, he regretted leaving his gun back on the chuckwagon driver's box.

"No ammo. Empty gun." The Indian lifted the muzzle and pointed it at the sky. He squeezed the trigger. Mac winced as it fell on an empty chamber.

"That's a good thing, since you ate our food. It's not neighborly to eat our food and then shoot the cook." Flowers shifted his aim a bit lower but kept the rifle pointed in the general direction of the Indians across from the cooking fire.

"This one promise cows," the Comanche insisted. "Many, many cows."

Flowers snorted disgustedly. "This one doesn't have the sense God gave a goose."

Mac started to protest, then held his tongue. He knew negotiating when he heard it, even if he was made out to be a fool. Better to look like a fool than to be a clever corpse.

"I sell cattle, I don't give them away to just anybody. But you're friends, aren't you? All seven of you are our friends?"

Seven heads bobbed up and down.

"For friends, I might be willing to give a steer. As a way to let you know how much I think of you and your hunters."

"Ten cows. We let you pass over Comanche land for ten."

"Two steers feed a passel of your tribe. How hungry are your squaws?"

Mac saw Flowers hit the nail right on the head. Hunting was poor this year, and from the look of the Indians' horses, they were next to be served up for dinner. The Comanche families wouldn't be in any better shape. Two cows would feed plenty of them for a week, maybe longer.

"Five. You go great way across Comanche land." The Indian made a sweeping motion using his rifle. This provoked Flowers to take aim again.

Mac fought back a laugh when he saw the Comanche jerk his rifle down, knowing he had made a mistake. To his credit, Flowers made no mention of this. It was going to be an act of charity to give even two steers to the Indians for their families because the Circle Arrow drovers had the edge with numbers and firepower. If a hunter couldn't even load his rifle, that meant they went out to set traps and club unwary rabbits with rocks. Fighting a crew of cowboys armed to the teeth meant sure death.

"We friends with three cows," the spokesman bargained.

Flowers lowered his rifle and stepped up. He held out his hand to shake. The Comanche stared at it for a moment, then grasped Flowers's forearm. Both exchanged quick nods of agreement.

"We're plenty good friends now," Flowers said. "It's my pleasure to give my *friends* three cows."

"I've already given them food," Mac pointed out.

"Good idea giving them coffee." Flowers sniffed as he stared at the smoking fire. The cow chips weren't very dry.

"Where we get cows?" the Indian wanted to know.

"Don't go getting so all fired anxious. The herd will come to us. Two miles. An hour's ride." Flowers pointed over his shoulder. "The land gets choppy, and I decided to make this a quick travel day." This he directed at Mac.

"I can lead them to the spot," Mac said. "I need to set up for supper. Our friends might want to stay for more food."

He saw this met with almost as much approval as Flowers giving them the cattle to avoid being harassed as they made their way to the Pecos River. It was extortion pure and simple, but he reckoned the Circle Arrow got off cheap. A few stragglers in exchange for safe passage was a good deal since those cattle were going to be the first eaten by the cowboys anyway.

"Go with him. I'll make sure the herd gets to the rendezvous." Flowers shook hands again with the Indian, spun and walked away as if he didn't have a care in the world.

Mac saw the tenseness across the trail boss's shoulders and knew he relied on his cook to keep from getting shot in the back. The one rifle might not have been loaded. That said nothing about the other six, though Mac guessed they were empty, too. The brave doing the talking carried some authority and the others deferred to him. The Comanches elected a leader of the hunt, just as they elected a war chief, so the man had his position only as long as they trusted him.

It paid to butter him up so they'd keep the deal he made.

"You want more coffee before I pack up?" Mac passed around the tin cups again. He considered using sugar this time, but common sense prevailed. Nothing different to show he had held back before.

Giving reason to go back on their deal was something only a greenhorn would do. He had been on another drive and had dealt with Shawnee Indians, who weren't that much different from the Comanche.

When his uninvited guests finished, he tossed the tin cups into the back of the chuckwagon and closed up. Washing the cups and utensils later seemed reasonable. Get the Indians on the trail with the promise of enough beef to feed their tribe for a week or two.

He clambered onto the driver's box, gathered the reins, and put his foot down on the revolver in the foot well to keep it from rattling around. It took him the better part of a half hour before he reached down and snared it, getting it back into the holster. He wished he had the holster belted on, but knowing the revolver was close enough for him to grab if the need arose made him happier. If it came to a shootout now, he knew those six rounds might go farther than expected because the Comanches had to rely only on their knives.

Finding a spot atop a low hill, he parked his wagon and began preparation for feeding the entire crew. The Indians stared at him with wide eyes. The amount of food he fixed would be enough to keep them and their families fed for the rest of the season.

He kept them occupied with more coffee until Messerschmidt came rattling up in the supply wagon. Mac saw the man wore his pistol strapped down. Beside him in the driver's box rode Klaus Kleingeld, fingering a double-barreled scattergun's triggers. Both men had been warned by the trail boss what they'd find.

Mac waved and considered going over to talk to them. Talking to Kleingeld did him no good since the Comanches understood him better—and he understood them better than he did the German. What Mac wanted to know was if Flowers had mentioned more than the Indians being in camp. Had he told anyone else about the men following the herd? The last thing they needed now with the Comanches here was a gang of rustlers stealing a sizable portion of the longhorns.

The confusion would open the door for the Indians to take plenty more than the three head that Flowers had promised them. So far, they hadn't lost but a few head to accidents. Two had stepped in prairie dog holes and broken their legs. They had furnished meals for almost a week. A few others turned sickly and had been shot and left for predators. All told, the Circle Arrow hadn't lost more than ten head.

Instead, he began cleaning up from the hasty midday meal he had provided. The Indians watched in silence as he did squaw's work and only showed life when Desmond Sullivan rode up. He galloped to within a half dozen feet of the Comanches, then pulled back so hard his horse dug in its hooves. A shower of dirt rose and covered the Indians.

"Watch what you're doing," Mac snapped. "You're getting dirt in the food."

"What're them redskins doing here? They got to clear out pronto. There's no way—"

"Mister Flowers said it was all right for them to wait. He's invited them to supper."

"Like hell! He can't do that. I own this damned herd, and I say who eats our food and who rides along."

"You don't own the herd," Mac said, his voice brittle. "Your ma does. Since she's not here, Mister Flowers is the one everyone takes orders from."

"I'm the owner." Desmond kicked free of the stirrups and dropped to the ground. The redhead was reaching for his revolver when Mac moved. Fast.

He dodged between Desmond and the Indians and got the young man's gun poked into his gut. The danger was high, but Mac didn't budge.

"Put down your gun," he told Desmond, tight-lipped with anger. "Unless you intend to plug me."

"I ought to. Who're you to meddle like this? I want them out of camp. I'm not eating food they eat."

"Then you'll get mighty hungry until breakfast." Mac reached down and pushed the pistol away. He breathed a sigh of relief when the muzzle pointed at the ground. "They'll get the three head of cattle Mister Flowers promised them, and they'll be on their way peaceably."

"What? He's giving away *my* beeves!"

Mac wasn't prepared for Desmond swinging the gun up and around in a wide arc. He felt the barrel collide with the side of his head. For an instant, he didn't think any damage had been done. Then his knees turned to butter, and he dropped to the ground, stunned. Not sure how he did it, as he fell he swung his nerveless arm around like a club. New pain lanced up into his shoulder, but he knocked the pistol out of Desmond's grasp.

This didn't stop the youth from barreling ahead, fists swinging. His clumsy blow caught one Indian in the middle of the face. Blood spurted from a broken nose. Desmond's second punch went wild and missed by a country mile. Mac fought to focus his eyes. He groaned and got to his feet, almost falling again until he got his balance back.

"Don't, no, don't!" he called out, and wasn't sure who he was ordering to stand down. Desmond was swinging like a windmill, but the Indians all drew their knives. The owner's son would be gutted and left for dead in a flash.

A distant roar filled Mac's ears. He thought it was thunder, then realized it was too close and the sky was clear of any storm clouds. A second blast solved the problem. Kleingeld had fired both barrels of his shotgun into the air.

The explosions startled Desmond, who half turned. The brave he had punched got in a good blow to his exposed belly. Desmond folded like a bad poker hand. But the other Indians all ran for their horses, getting astride and galloping away.

"They ride for the herd," Messerschmidt called. "They will steal our cows!"

Mac stepped over Desmond and grabbed the dangling reins to the young man's horse. It took most of his strength to pull himself up into the saddle. The horse was spooked by the shotgun and Mac used all of his skill as a rider to keep it from bucking him off.

He put his head down and clung to the horse's neck for dear life. The uneven gait jolted him and caused the world to spin. Slowly, his eyes focused and the ringing in his ears died down to a buzz. Ahead he saw the Indians fan out along a broad, wide ravine. The herd wasn't visible, but the lowing as they approached told the story. The Comanches readied for their theft of as many cattle as they could. Somewhere in the back of his head Mac thought they deserved whatever they could steal. Desmond had violated the uneasy truce with his impetuous attack.

Then Mac came to his senses. It was stealing Circle Arrow property. No matter what Desmond had done, the Indians were wrong taking more than the three Flowers had promised them. He saw the Indians swooping down. They cut at least thirty head from the main herd and tried to rush them through the gap. Only their scrawny horses kept them from succeeding.

"Stop! Those aren't yours," Mac shouted, but the sounds from the herd drowned out his orders. Mac slipped his revolver from its holster. Shooting the Indians would be akin to murder since he knew they were out of ammo. But if he didn't they would make off with three times as many cattle as they'd lost this far in the drive.

He fired at one Indian and instantly regretted it. The gunshot caused the lead steer to run. He had unintentionally started a stampede.

The Comanches tried to cut out a few of the cattle, but the tide of frightened gristle and immensely wide, long horns kept them from stealing any. Mac galloped alongside the herd as the steers scattered the Indians. In less than a minute the Comanches had vanished back onto the prairie—but Mac rode alongside tons of stampeding cattle.

His horse began to tire. He knew something had to be done fast, and he was the only one in position to do it. Before, on his previous trail drive, he had learned the dangers of a stampede, and how to stop it. Getting the beeves to mill was the only way to keep dozens or even hundreds of them from being run into the ground and killed. Turning the leaders was the answer. The cattle instinctively sought to gather rather than run out by themselves. Getting a few to turn and try to lose themselves in the middle of the herd would eventually rob them of leaders and get them spinning around and around rather than racing across the countryside.

Lather flecking its flanks, the horse's speed began to slacken. Mac fired his gun in the air and yelled until he was hoarse. Make the leaders run away from him, cross back in front of the rest of the herd, find a way to circle and begin to mill. It sounded easy. The longer his horse galloped, the more it faltered and the leaders of the stampede outdistanced him.

Then he caught a bit of luck. The herd shifted just a little in the right direction, forcing the leaders to run up a slope. This caused them to turn even more and definite milling began to occur. Mac fired until his revolver came up empty. The reports worked a miracle to force the cattle away from him.

The stampede was broken. And then his horse stepped into a prairie dog hole. The cannon bone snapping sounded louder than any of his gunshots. As the horse pitched forward on the broken leg, Mac sailed over the horse's head. He hit the ground hard enough to jolt him senseless, but in some distant part of his brain he knew the shaking ground beneath his back meant the herd was coming in his direction.

Moving was impossible. Staring up at the twilight sky, he saw a star. Irrationally, he began to make a wish on that first star of the night. He hoped for a quick death.

He didn't get it.

CHAPTER 8

Mac tried to call out when he heard a horse approaching rapidly. The air had been smashed from his lungs. Simply trying to suck in a breath sent knife stabs of pain throughout his chest. His legs kicked feebly. Trying to sit up caused more agony than he wanted. Ribs might be broken. Or worse. There had been a loud sound that might have been his spine snapping when he hit the ground.

His hand twitched. He tried to signal as the swift rataplan of hoofbeats came closer, but the rider didn't seem to notice him lying on the ground. Outlined against the stars, the man slowed his horse, turned in the saddle, and called out, "Frank? You see him?"

From a distance came the faint reply, "Son of a bitch ain't nowhere to be found."

Mac stopped his struggles and simply lay motionless, staring up at the sky. The voices weren't familiar.

"Quick Willy is scouting the far side of the herd. He's having a devil of a time avoiding those cowboys."

"We gotta meet up with him. We're not havin' any luck findin' the son of a bitch."

"It was the stampede that scattered everything. Horses, cattle, men."

"We done missed our best chance to nab him."

"Nab him, hell. I'll shoot the bastard down when I find him. I don't much care what Quick Willy says about a bonus reward for bringin' him back alive."

Mac's entire body quivered as his breathing began to return to normal. He fought down the loud gulping sound that tried to well up from his throat. His heart hammered so loudly in his ears the riders had to hear it. Frank. Quick Willy. Those names didn't belong to anyone on the drive. Bonus reward? These weren't Circle Arrow riders. They were bounty hunters after him.

After *him.*

The two men moved away, the thuds of their horses' hooves diminishing to nothing. Mac began rocking from side to side. Finally, he was able to roll over onto his belly. A huge effort brought him to his hands and knees. Only after a moment of dizziness did Mac get his feet under him to stumble to his horse.

The forward tumble had taken its toll on the animal. It had broken its neck right after its leg. Mac swallowed. This saved him a bullet—one he didn't have since he had emptied his gun turning the herd.

That thought made him turn in a full circle. Except for the dead horse, he stood alone on the range. The herd had vanished. Of the two riders hunting for him he saw not a trace. A deep breath hurt, but not as much as before, and settled his nerves.

At least three men were hunting for him. He knew two of their names. Quick Willy. Frank. Whoever Frank had been talking to earlier had been on the other side of a nearby rise. Taking a few more minutes to recover his strength, Mac got the tack off the horse, heaved it onto his shoulder, and hiked to the top of the hill where he believed the other bounty hunter had ridden.

Careful not to silhouette himself against the clear night sky, he looked around for the bounty hunters but didn't see them. In the distance he heard cattle lowing. That was where the herd had finished its stampede. Grunting with effort from the weight of the saddle, he began hiking.

Less than ten minutes later, a rider approached him. Mac touched the empty revolver in his holster, then jerked his head from side to side as he searched for a place to hide.

Too late. The rider homed in on him like an eagle swooping down on a rabbit.

He wished there had been a rifle in the saddle sheath, but Desmond hadn't carried one. Considering the boy's recklessness, Flowers had done well not letting him stick one in the scabbard before going on patrol. Mac dropped the saddle and widened his stance. A quick move pushed back his coat to get at the empty six-gun. Bluffing never worked for him as well as outright shooting, but he had no choice.

"That you, Mac?" called a voice with a familiar twang.

"Mister Flowers?" He relaxed his stance.

"Who'd you think it would be? Tarnation, Mac, you saved the herd from running itself into the ground. Three of the drovers said you turned it all by yourself. They were too far away to help, but they're singing your praises."

"Glad to hear they appreciate something other than my biscuits." Mac mulled over telling the trail boss about the men hunting him for the reward on his head back in New Orleans. There wasn't any reason to reveal that, he decided, since Hiram Flowers couldn't do anything about it.

"Desmond's not so fond of you right now. What happened to his horse?"

Mac explained about the horse's sad end. As he spoke, he rested his hand on the butt of his pistol. Flowers noticed.

"I didn't hear a gunshot, not after the herd came to rest."

"I was out of rounds," Mac said.

Flowers nodded grimly.

"Well, it's too damn bad. But I'll make it good with Desmond."

"The horse was his personal mount, not one from the remuda?"

"Climb on up behind me," Flowers said without answering Mac's question. "We'll get back to camp. You need to move the chuckwagon before breakfast."

"This is Desmond's tack."

"Leave it where it lays. I'll have him come out and get it himself." Flowers chuckled at this small punishment. He sobered quickly. "The way you lit out to turn the stampede—and he didn't—says a whole heap about the jobs you each do on the drive."

"I just wanted to choose which beeves I fed the

crew. Having to cut up meat that's been trampled doesn't suit anybody."

"Hamburger," Flowers said.

"I don't know what you mean." Mac perched behind the trail boss's saddle and settled down as Flowers walked his horse back to camp.

"That's something Messerschmidt told me about. Ground beef made into a patty and then cooked. It's something he heard about from back in Germany."

"Do tell." Mac shook his head. "That'll never be popular, not if you can get a nice, juicy steak."

"I'd have to lose all my teeth before I'd want one of them hamburgers."

"China clippers," Mac said, laughing. "False teeth work just fine for chewing up a tender slab of beef, especially if it's one I fixed up just for you."

"Get your chuckwagon moved." The change in Flowers's tone caused Mac to jump down. They were within earshot of many drovers, and Flowers had to keep his reputation as being a hardcase.

Mac stretched, which made every bone in his body hurt again. Landing flat on the ground had taken more than the wind out of him. He winced as he touched a spot in the middle of his back. He found a long spine from a Spanish bayonet plant stuck in him. He was lucky. If it hadn't broken, the spine could have run all the way through him as surely as a knife blade. The more he moved around, the more aches and pains he discovered.

He tried to climb up into the driver's box and couldn't. His legs refused to lift him.

"Give me a boost, will you?" he called out into the

dark as someone approached, not caring who knew how bad a shape he was in.

"Flowers just told me you killed my horse," Desmond said as he stalked up to the chuckwagon. "You stole my horse and gear and killed it. You killed my damned horse! I had that horse since he was a colt."

Mac sagged. He took a deep breath and regretted it as more pain stabbed through him. His ribs burned like liquid fire. A slow turn brought him face to face with Desmond Sullivan.

"I didn't want to hurt your horse," he said. "You trained him real good. Without his heart, I'd never have been able to turn the herd. He kept up and—"

Desmond launched a clumsy punch at Mac's face. Even in his debilitated condition, Mac had no trouble ducking the blow. As the knuckles slipped past his cheek, he stepped up and swung as hard as he could with his right fist. The punch landed smack in the middle of Desmond's belly. The young man gasped and backed off. He leaned forward and rubbed his belly, then spat. He doubled his fists.

"You sucker punched me."

"Better figure out what that really means." Mac ducked and weaved as Desmond came at him, flinging wild punches. "You weren't sucker punched. We were facing each other and you left your belly open. Like this!"

Mac let another punch slip past, then stepped up and drove his fist hard into Desmond's exposed midriff. His fist disappeared up to his wrist. The gush of air rushing from Desmond's lungs meant that the fight was over. Desmond folded up, fell to his knees, and then toppled onto his side.

Mac stepped over his opponent. Desmond struggled into a sitting position but couldn't maintain it. He fell onto his side and retched. When he finished losing his supper, Desmond tried to get back onto his feet. When he finally made it, he stumbled toward Mac.

"You can't . . ." he gasped out.

Mac pushed him away with just the tips of his fingers. Desmond lost his balance and sat down hard, back propped against the front wagon wheel. Tired, Mac sank down beside him and also leaned on the wheel.

"You've got quite a chip on your shoulder. More than that, you can't fight worth beans." He almost added that the young man's performance in the Fort Worth brothel probably rivaled his fighting skills, but he held that back. He had no reason to further inflame the boss's son.

"You'll pay," Desmond rasped. "I swear it. You're gonna pay." He turned to the side and leaned over to begin gagging again. However, this time he had nothing left in his stomach to lose.

"If you square off before launching a punch, you won't leave yourself open. Take your time, measure your opponent. And don't retreat. Stand your ground or advance." In a short, compact punch, Mac slammed his fist against a wheel spoke next to Desmond's head. "That's a lot more powerful than this." He duplicated the blow with his other hand, reaching a long way and keeping his elbow stiff when he hit.

"You're giving me boxing lessons?"

"Somebody has to. Didn't your pa ever show you anything about fighting?"

"Him?" Desmond snorted. "He was always doing

something out on the range, with the damned cattle. When he did come home, he spent all his time with my ma."

"Can't blame him for that," Mac said. Desmond's sudden reaction made him add hurriedly, "Whoa! I meant your ma's a mighty fine-looking woman. And you're one ugly little sprout."

"Why, you—" Desmond tried to swing a round-house punch, but his position seated next to Mac kept him from even coming close with the blow. Mac batted it away.

"You don't know when somebody's joshing you. Learn how to recognize that. Learn, or your life's going to be a living hell."

"It already is hell because of Flowers and you and all the others." Desmond levered himself to his feet and staggered off, clutching his belly. Within seconds the dark swallowed him entirely.

Mac closed his eyes and wanted nothing more than to go to sleep right then and there under his wagon. But Hiram Flowers had told him to move the chuckwagon and be ready for breakfast. A glance at the stars told him it was still three or four hours until sunrise, when a passel of hungry drovers would ride up demanding to be fed.

Using the wheel for support, he pulled himself to his feet. Still not up to climbing onto the box, he made a circuit and checked the harness on the team. He tried to soothe them and convince the horses he wasn't any happier than they were about traveling in the middle of the night. Returning to the box, feeling up to the chore—maybe—he stepped first onto the yoke and then pulled himself the rest of the way onto the driver's seat. A snap of the reins got the team pulling.

The stars blazed down with an intensity that turned the prairie into an eerie world unlike the daytime of heat and sharp shadows. He wished he could ride into it and leave all the bounty hunters and the troubles of the past behind.

The sound of hoofbeats behind him brought him back to the real world. He looped his reins around the brake and dived back into the wagon, fumbling in his gear for the box of cartridges Messerschmidt had given him. He should have already reloaded, he chided himself.

His fingers were numb and worked like giant sausages, but he slid fresh ammo into all six chambers. With a painful twist, he came to his knees and peered over the driver's seat, revolver cocked and ready.

The rider came up fast, slowed, and then halted just a few yards off. Mac tried to make out his face in the dark but couldn't.

"Where are you?"

The voice was familiar. Mac got his legs under him and climbed over the seat but kept the gun in his hand.

"What do you want, Desmond?"

"Not another whipping, that's for sure. Flowers sent me to help you, but he told me to pick up the gear you dropped after you killed my horse."

That wasn't the way Mac would have put it, but he lowered the hammer gently and tucked his pistol into his holster. Whatever threat dogged his steps, Desmond wasn't part of it. Not a deadly part, at least.

"About a quarter mile south of here. Follow the ground all cut up by the cattle. Where the ground's in good shape, look there."

"That's not much to go on." Desmond sounded skeptical. Mac didn't blame him since the directions were so vague. All he wanted was for the young man to leave him the hell alone.

"Go on. I've got to find where Mister Flowers wanted me to set up camp."

"I know that," Desmond said. He paused, as if thinking over something hard. "I'll help you if you show me where my saddle is."

"South," Mac said. Spending the rest of the night scouring the plains for the dropped gear wasn't in the cards. By the time he made it back to camp, the cowboys would be lining up for breakfast. An hour after they finished, he had to be back in the chuck-wagon making his way to wherever Flowers wanted him to serve the midday meal.

Nowhere in that next twelve hours was there any time to sleep. He didn't need much, but he had to get a few hours to keep him from falling asleep while he drove.

"Which way's that?" Desmond asked.

Muttering in impatience at the young man's ignorance, Mac leaned forward, found the Big Dipper and the Pole Star, then ran his finger from it across the dome of stars to due south. He stabbed out with his forefinger in the proper direction.

"Go to hell, you son of a bitch." Desmond yanked on his horse's reins and trotted off.

"A pleasant good night to you, too," Mac said tiredly, too worn out to raise his voice enough for Desmond to hear the sarcastic rejoinder. With the reins resting in his hands, he snapped them until the team began pulling.

Tangling with bounty hunters suddenly seemed like the lesser of two evils. He had to put up with that annoying little son of a bitch Desmond Sullivan for the rest of the trail drive.

CHAPTER 9

"Had better." The cowboy licked his fingers to get the last crumb of biscuit and dollop of thick gravy. When his fingers were clean—cleaner than the rest of his hand—he looked up expectantly. "Got any more, Mac?"

Mac forked over a couple more. The cowboy snatched them before anyone else claimed them.

"When did you ever have better?" Mac challenged. "Your mama? If you say your mama's done better, I won't argue. Otherwise, you have to prove it."

"Naw, don't ever remember my ma fixin' anything this good. Nope, it was a little place in Wichita Falls. Just a stone's throw from Seventh and Ohio Streets." The cowboy gobbled down the last of the biscuits, then wiped his hand on his jeans. "A tiny little café called the Green Frog. The woman doin' the cookin', she was danged near the size of one of them longhorns. Big woman. Sampled her own cooking too much."

"And it was that good? Her biscuits were better?" Mac enjoyed joshing the men as much as he enjoyed a good-natured argument. It was about all they had to pass the time between back-breaking, long, tedious, dangerous days in the saddle.

"You know, my memory ain't so good these days. Gimme another and let me see if I can remember. Got to give you a fair trial, I reckon."

"All gone," Mac told him. "You'll have to wait until this evening."

"Not this afternoon?" The man sounded genuinely sad at the prospect of waiting that long for another biscuit.

"Got a pot of stew ready to heat up, so that will be dinner. Flowers said we've got to make up all the time we lost because of the herd stampeding the way it did."

"Yup," the cowboy said, standing, hitching up his trousers, and settling his hat just so before he set off to work. "We're gettin' near the Pecos. Mister Flowers he says that's always a dangerous crossing. Don't know why we don't stay on this side of the river till we get up into New Mexico Territory and cross there."

"The closer to the headwaters you get, the bigger the river," Mac said.

"You talk just like Mister Flowers. You and him share a brain?"

"Something like that," Mac said.

He began cleaning up as the last of the cowboys left to ride herd. Getting the chuckwagon ready for the trail took a mite longer than starting the cattle moving again, but once he got rolling, he would outpace the beeves. It would take the better part of an hour to set up for dinner. Fixing several kettles of stew at a time more than fed even the always-famished drovers. Having leftovers for a second meal sped things up for at least that one meal.

As he fastened the tailgate, Flowers rode up.

"You're too late for breakfast, but I can find something for you," Mac offered. He started to unlatch the tailgate but Flowers stopped him.

"Not necessary. We got to move the herd farther in the next couple days and get across the Pecos."

"You're worried about that?" Mac wondered why. He waited for the trail boss to get to the point.

"The Comanches are still out there. I saw traces of them when I rode around the herd this morning. They left their tracks on purpose."

Mac nodded. "If they wanted to be sneaky, you'd never find any sign. That means they still want a few dozen cattle."

"The cattle they can have, as long as they leave us alone. They want our horses. I've doubled the night guard on the remuda."

"I wondered where Kleingeld got off to last night."

"Him and a lot of others are drawing double duty, guarding the horses and then riding herd. I want you to do some double duty, too, Mac."

"What more do you want? I can only drive the wagon so fast." The way his body ached and the cuts he had suffered in the stampede wouldn't heal for another week, and that was if he was lucky.

"I'm telling Desmond to drive the wagon."

"That'll keep him out of trouble, I suppose," Mac said, wondering if he was lying to himself by thinking that. "What do you want me to do?"

"Scout. I saw how you can do that. You've got a good

eye and a sense where the herd can travel easiest. The quicker we cross the river, the better I'll like it."

"Will the Comanches stay on this side of the Pecos?" Mac could tell something else was bothering the trail boss. If Flowers watched their back trail as closely as it seemed, he must know about the bounty hunters. But he wouldn't know *why* they were dogging the herd. Again Mac wrestled with telling the trail boss that the men were after him for the reward on his head back in New Orleans. But again he held his tongue.

"They go wherever they want, though they're not likely to follow us. The other side is Apache country. The Comanches and Apaches don't get on too well, stealing each other's squaws and using their children as slaves. I'm more worried about the weather. A good storm will send the Pecos over its banks and make fording it a chore, no matter where we cross."

Mac looked up at the blue sky. A few puffy white clouds meandered across it in a lazy way he wished he could copy. After everything he'd gone through the night before and the lack of sleep, he wanted to while away the day. Any chance of that was behind him before he ever signed on with the Circle Arrow crew.

"You don't see it up there. You don't even smell it, but I *feel* it in my bones. We've got a big storm coming at us."

"Should I leave the wagon here or drive it to wherever Desmond is?"

"He got back to camp just before sunrise." Flowers chuckled. "He spent the night hunting for his saddle. Not that I blame him. That's expensive tack. I wish he'd take better care of it."

Mac was glad he didn't have to lug it all the way back to camp, just to give it up to the boy.

"I tried to give him directions to where I left it. Might be I should have gone with him to speed up his hunt."

"Don't worry your head none over that, Mac. He's got to learn to do for himself. You get some of the spare gear and take a horse. Range out straight west, then curl on northward. I'm scouting straight to the northwest. If you come across a river, head straight on back and let me know. The Pecos winds all over the place. Even if I had a map, it wouldn't do me any good since the damned river is so cantankerous about keeping to its banks, year to year."

Mac nodded and started walking toward the remuda, wondering at how talkative the trail boss had become. Flowers kept to himself and seldom said much at the best of times. This sudden flood of words was a good indication of how worried he was about fording the Pecos.

Or was he worried about more than that? Mac shivered at what that might be.

He was out scouting within a half hour. As he left camp, he saw that Desmond had shown up and worked to hitch up the team. Mac considered helping him, then remembered what Flowers had said about the boss's son learning to do for himself. This chore wasn't anything Desmond hadn't done before. Driving the wagon could be difficult at times, especially over rough ground, but if Desmond got a move on, he'd be ahead of the herd and not have to drive through the prairie cut up by their hooves.

Settling into a rhythm as he rode, Mac tried to keep an eye out for the river and a route to it, but the swaying motion kept lulling him to sleep. Like most cowboys, he had learned to nap in the saddle, but this wasn't the right time.

Despite his best efforts, exhaustion caught up with him and he dozed off into a sound sleep. His horse shied and tried to bolt, causing him to snap awake. For a moment he panicked, unsure where he was or how long he had been asleep. The world around him looked different, as if he had ridden for months rather than—what?

A quick look at the sun's position in the sky showed he had been asleep for more than an hour. Shaking himself, he forced away some of the fuzzy feeling that stalked him.

To make sure he wasn't dreaming, he pulled out his pocket watch and studied it as if he had never seen its like before. The watch ran slow, but he had looked at it when he began preparing breakfast that morning. He had ridden more than two hours without realizing he had done so.

Grumbling, he tucked the watch back into his vest pocket. It was time to look around and do the job Flowers had given him. Finding a low rise, he gazed due west. No sign of the river. Nothing to the northwest, either. As his gaze slipped northward, he spotted several figures on horseback and caught his breath. Silhouetted on the hill like this, he made an easy target.

Backing his horse back over the crest, he got out of sight of the Comanches. Flowers had been right. The Indians hadn't moved on. The lure of so many beeves—and horses!—proved too powerful for them to let a stampede scatter them.

Mac took a better look around to fix the landmarks in his head. He had to let Flowers know right away that the Comanches lay in wait for the herd.

As he turned to go back eastward, a knot tightened in his belly. He drew rein and wished he had a spyglass to study the countryside spread out in front of him. For almost ten minutes he sat astride the increasingly restive horse, watching and waiting, before he decided that he hadn't seen anything suspicious after all. He patted the horse's neck and started to put his heels to the animal's flanks, his caution unnecessary.

He hadn't ridden a hundred yards when he stopped again. The sun burned hot on his back. And now it reflected from metal ahead of him. If he kept the sun behind him, he'd be harder to see. Not outlining himself against the sky almost assured he wouldn't be spotted by the men ahead of him. As he watched, this time with better knowledge of what to look for, he made out three men directly ahead blocking his route. A fourth rode to the north, probably scouting in that direction.

Indians behind him. Bounty hunters in front of him. The old saying about a rock and a hard place went through Mac's mind as he swallowed and tried to figure out his next move.

He was cut off from the herd by two gangs willing to kill him, though for different reasons. Humiliating the Comanches the way he had required them to lift his scalp to regain honor. The bounty hunters wanted only money for that scalp. More likely, they'd take his entire body to prove they had earned their reward. It didn't matter to him which of the two groups won. He was dead either way.

He turned toward the south, thinking to swing wide around the bounty hunters. The horse balked and began to snort and paw the ground. He struggled to control his mount. Something in this direction spooked the horse. He swung the animal around to quiet it.

Running away wasn't any answer. It he kept riding west, he could cross the Pecos and get to the Rio Grande. Cross that river and he could lose himself in Mexico within a week or two. All he had in the way of gear was stashed in the chuckwagon, but he had his gun and a coat pocket weighed down with a full box of ammunition. Taking the horse would make him a thief, and he didn't like the sound of that. Deep down, he was an honest man and had never stolen except in emergencies.

"Honest men don't run out on their jobs," he muttered to himself. Hiram Flowers had given him a job when he needed it. He had hired on to do that job. Sneaking away, stealing a horse, betraying Flowers's trust in him, none of that set well. In fact, it stuck in his craw, and he wouldn't do it.

Taking on the bounty hunters looked to be the worst trail to ride. They would open fire the instant they spotted him. The Indians, however, likely had no idea he was anywhere around. That gave him a small edge he had to use. How he was going to do that was something of a puzzle, but he turned due north and rode behind the ridge of sand hills in the direction where he had spotted the Comanches.

Staying in the shallow valley hid him from the bounty hunters, at least until he reached a point not a quarter mile from the Comanches. Careful observation told him that the bounty hunter riding to the north of his partners had spotted him and started for him. There wouldn't be any honor among men like that, who hunted others for money. If this one reached him first, they'd have to shoot it out. The bounty hunter intended to be the one to collect the entire reward on his head.

Mac picked up the gait and cantered more to the northwest now, directly toward the Comanches. When he topped a rise, he saw six of them below. They had dismounted from their ponies and now squatted down around a small fire cooking a rabbit. The odor wafted up to him and made his mouth water. He had missed a meal today, while he was asleep in the saddle.

At the moment, all he wanted was to be alive for supper. Twisting around, he dragged out his revolver and waved it high over his head as he let out a loud holler and galloped downhill toward the Indians.

Disturbing their meal had been a stroke of luck. They fumbled for their weapons and lifted their rifles. His heart seized up for a moment, fear striking him that they had found ammunition for their weapons since the previous encounter. Comancheros roved these plains. The Indians might have traded a few skins for cartridges. When they dropped their ri-

fles and picked up bows and arrows instead, he knew
his luck was holding.

"Thank you," he whispered to Lady Luck. Surely,
she rode on his shoulder. All he needed now was one
more turn in his favor.

He galloped straight through the camp. His horse
jumped the fire, dug in its hooves, and kicked up a
cloud of dust. Wheeling around, Mac kept up his
string of whoops and hoots to inflame the Comanches. When arrows began to fly in his direction,
he bent low and used the horse as a shield. They
wanted his horse alive as spoils of war as much as they
wanted him dead. The arrows flew well over his head
until he got out of range. He pulled himself upright
in the saddle and slowed his headlong pace.

The Indians, bless their hearts, jumped onto their
ponies and gave chase.

Judging distances and locations, Mac rode straight
for the bounty hunter who wanted to bring him in
and claim the whole reward. Mac burst over the crest
of a sandy hill, saw the man not fifty yards away, and
for the first time opened fire. At that range, on
horseback, hitting the bounty hunter would have
used up all his remaining luck. All he did was cause
the man's horse to rear.

That was good enough. He veered slightly and
forced the man to come after him . . . following him
so he ended up between Mac and the pursuing Indians.

The Comanches caught up fast, and when the
bounty hunter realized that, he twisted in his saddle
and threw a few shots from his Winchester in their di-

rection. Whether the Indians believed the bounty hunter to be Mac or simply didn't care, they shifted their attack from the fleeing cook to the man willing to use his rifle on them.

Mac's hastily formed plan was working so far, but he wasn't satisfied. He veered again, going to the southeast until he caught sight of the other three bounty hunters. A few more shots in their direction emptied his gun and brought them racing toward him.

Reloading on the gallop proved to be a challenge. He lost more than a few bullets as he fumbled in his pocket for cartridges to replace those spent already. When he got six more in the cylinder, he charged the bounty hunters, scattering them with a barrage of shots.

Now it was time to put the icing on the cake. He cut back again so the bounty hunters trailed him. Mac thundered up behind the Comanches and then veered sharply aside, behind one of the sand hills. The Indians never saw him, but they saw the three bounty hunters who seemed to be shooting at them, sure enough. Yipping frenziedly, they swung around and relaunched their attack in a different direction.

Arrows whistled through the air, met by the bounty hunters firing back. Mac halted and swung around, waiting for the three men to gallop past him. When they did, he opened fire in a flank attack, taking his time to aim and making every shot count. Whether he actually hit any of them wasn't the point. He stopped them in their tracks, confusing them and forcing them to deal with the Indians whooping toward them from the front.

Mac's gun came up empty again, but the bounty hunters weren't going to chase him any longer. They were too busy. They'd jumped down to take refuge behind the scanty cover of bushes and rocks poking out of the sandy soil.

Mac changed direction again, riding for the herd. He didn't know what had happened to the first bounty hunter. The Comanches might have killed him. But even if he had escaped, he was out of the way for now.

A large dust cloud rose on the horizon. That had to be where Mac would find a couple of dozen revolvers willing to back him up if necessary. The Circle Arrow cowboys would fight for him because he was one of them, part of their trail family.

That, and he made the best damned biscuits they'd ever tasted, Green Frog Café or not.

CHAPTER 10

"You go scout, Johnston. We need to find a place to set up an ambush." Quick Willy Means glared at the gunman. Johnston thought he was better than the rest of them. Maybe he was, but as long as he rode with this gang, he would take orders like everybody else.

Arizona Johnston shook his head, picked up a stick, and began scratching in the dirt.

"There's no reason for us to split up, Willy. See here? This is where the herd is. The last we saw, Mackenzie was driving the chuckwagon. There are only so many places he can go with that wagon. We don't need to split up. We all stay together and swoop in when he heads in this direction."

"Why's that gonna work?" Frank Huffman scratched himself. "How do we know what direction he'll head in?"

"Because," Johnston said, as if explaining to a simpleton, "he's their cook. He stays ahead of the herd.

They're following the Goodnight-Loving Trail, so we know the direction they're going already."

"Fort Sumner," Means said. "That's where they're most likely going to sell them beeves to the Army. I don't know about the rest of you, but chasing Mackenzie over into New Mexico Territory isn't what I want to do for the next couple weeks." He pitched his voice lower so it carried a menace that hadn't been there before. "Find us a place to ambush him *before* we get to New Mexico."

"All I'm saying is that we stand a better chance if we stay together." Johnston crossed his arms over his chest and looked at Means with cool, barely concealed defiance. Quick Willy saw that he stood so his right hand rested near the pistol in the cross-draw holster. As much as Johnston wanted them to think he stood easy, he was tighter than a drum and ready to throw down on the lot of them.

"You're nuthin' but a coward," Charles Huffman said abruptly. "You don't want to go traipsin' off by your lonesome 'cause Mackenzie might shoot you." Huffman was stupid enough not to see how close Johnston was to exploding.

"We'll be following," Quick Willy said in one final effort to defuse the tense situation. "You find the place and we'll—"

"No."

Arizona Johnston's flat-voiced refusal hardened something inside Quick Willy Means. Nobody challenged him for leadership of this gang. Being a bounty hunter was tough enough. Keeping these ya-hoos corralled and riding in the proper direction was almost as difficult as being trail boss for a big herd. Sometimes he thought it was harder. All Hiram Flowers had to deal with were cranky steers. They weren't too bright, either alone or in a herd, and had only a few things they did instinctively. The Huffman brothers were as stupid as a longhorn but always managed to find new and different ways to blunder on.

However, they always followed his orders. Arizona Johnston was another matter. He had plans he wasn't sharing, and Quick Willy figured those plans didn't include him. Not alive, anyway.

"You can ride out any time you want, Arizona," he said softly. By the different pitch to his voice, he added a quiet menace. The Huffmans wouldn't be threatened if he did it to them, because they were too dumb to notice. Shouting got better results with them.

Johnston caught on to the threat right away. Smart fellow, Johnston. Too smart.

"I'm not forfeiting my share of the reward for Mackenzie, not after I've come this far."

"Then ride. We can be done by the end of the day. Find where he's going to park that chuckwagon for dinner. It'll take the herd hours to reach that point. By then we'll have him in custody."

"Or dead," Johnston said. "In custody or dead."

"Leclerc wants him to stand trial and will give us a hefty bonus if we take him to New Orleans alive."

"Easier if he's dead." Johnston never twitched a muscle. He kept his hand near the gun on his left hip.

Quick Willy Means considered what he could do. Slowly nodding, he agreed with the gunman.

"Or dead. It *is* easier that way. If you get him, Arizona, you get an extra share from the pot."

The spark that lit in the gunman's eyes was everything Means could hope for. Greed won out over the need to be leader. Or maybe it was a lust for killing. Whatever moved Arizona Johnston kept him in line. For the moment. He wasn't a man to let sleeping dogs lie. There would be trouble eventually, even as soon as when they brought down Dewey Mackenzie. Quick Willy had to be ready for it and never turn his back.

"Don't get all caught up in a stampede," Charles Huffman called as Johnston stepped up into the saddle.

Means rested his hand on his revolver. If looks could kill, Huffman would be dead and buried. Johnston flicked his eyes from Charles to his brother, then fixed on him. Means made a mocking salute to send Johnston on his way.

When the rebellious bounty hunter was out of earshot, Frank Huffman said, "That's one dangerous galoot. Like a rattler all coiled and ready to strike. Only he don't know what direction to sink in his fangs."

Quick Willy Means eyed Frank. The man was smarter than his brother. He might be smarter than Means had given him credit for up to now.

Arizona Johnston never tried very hard to hide his contempt for the lot of them. Their paths had crossed just outside Fort Worth when Means had needed another gun hand after Jimmy Huffman had been cut down. He knew nothing about the man, other than the few sparse details Johnston had doled out. On the run from a Tombstone marshal meant nothing to Means. From what he'd heard about Tombstone, eventually everyone crossed the law there, be it sheriff, local, or federal marshal. The town was that rough and tumble.

For all he knew, Johnston had come from back east or up north or who the hell knew.

"Who the hell cares?" The sentiment was mumbled, but Frank overheard.

"If he uses those revolvers of his as good as he talks, you're right. Who the hell cares?"

"We didn't find Mackenzie last night. It's time we ended this," Means said. "Johnston will find him."

"Why can't we go 'n find him, Quick Willy? You'd give us an extra share if we done it, right? Like you promised Arizona?"

Charles drummed his fingers on the butt of his Colt dangling at his side as he spoke. Quick Willy had never decided if the man thought he was fast or hoped he was. Either way he was wrong. Clumsy, banging around like a bull in a china shop, Charles Huffman was better suited for lying in ambush and shooting his quarry in the back. Facing them in a gunfight, he would chicken out, turn tail and run, if he bothered to show up at all. His brother was the same way, too, but only because Frank was enough smarter to know he was going to die if he did anything else.

"Mount up. We're going to end this today. I'm tired of sneaking around all night, trying to find Mackenzie amongst those damn drovers."

"You don't want to tangle with their trail boss, do you, Quick Willy?"

Means considered how easy it would be to simply remove Charles Huffman. A shot between the eyes . . . No, that wasn't the way to do it. Blowing out his brains was too hard a shot. The brain was too small.

He said nothing, turned, and stepped up into the saddle. Johnston was a smart one. He'd find Mackenzie. Let him take the risk of a gunfight with a man reputed to have shot down a dozen hombres, including Jimmy Huffman. Even if that reputation was puffed up, he had to be dangerous or a rich, powerful man like Pierre Leclerc wouldn't put out such a lucrative reward.

The sound of a shot came through the hot air.

"You hear that, Quick Willy?" Charles exclaimed as he leaned sharply forward in his saddle. "A gunshot! It's gotta be Johnston. He's done found Mackenzie already!"

Charles whipped his horse into a gallop, his brother only a second behind.

"Wait up!" Means called after them. "Don't go rushing into something when you don't know who's firing."

They ignored him. Means shook his head, then galloped after his men.

For a minute, he thought Johnston was on to something. A rider galloped toward them, low in the saddle as if avoiding the gunfire. Quick Willy's heart sped up when he recognized Dewey Mackenzie. They must have Mackenzie caught in a vice, Means thought, with Johnston on one side and the rest of them on the other. He dragged out his rifle and levered a round into it. The time had come to end the manhunt.

But Mackenzie wasn't running. He was attacking, charging right into their midst as he threw lead. Quick Willy and the Huffman brothers had to scatter because of the bold, unexpected assault.

Then somehow, in the confusion, Mackenzie was headed back the other way. Quick Willy brought the rifle to his shoulder and squeezed the trigger, but the shot went wide.

Means slammed his boot heels against his horse's flanks. "Get that son of a bitch!" he shouted at the Huffman brothers as he galloped after Mackenzie.

Dust from all the flashing hooves roiled the air. Means could see his quarry up ahead, then suddenly Mackenzie was gone. Where in blazes had he gotten to? The sand hills in this region formed little tucks and folds in the landscape, and all Means could think of was that Mackenzie had ducked into one of them.

A bullet racketed through the air near Quick Willy's head. He had just realized it came from the side when Charles Huffman's horse suddenly screamed and bucked, its rump burned by another slug. Charles fought to get the animal under control while Means and Frank yanked their mounts to a halt and tried to figure out what was going on.

Out of the blue, an arrow almost skewered Quick Willy. He had ducked instinctively when he caught the blur of the arrow coming at him from off to one side, and that was the only thing that saved his life.

Quick Willy lived up to his name. Whipping around, he got off another shot, a killing shot. A Comanche fell from his horse and lay flat on his back. One threat gone. But a half dozen more thundered toward him.

Where the hell had *they* come from? And where was Johnston?

No time to worry about that now. "Get the hell out of here!" Means shouted to the brothers. "Mackenzie led us into a trap!"

He frantically hunted for their quarry, but Mackenzie was still nowhere to be seen. He was too smart to stick around to watch the massacre he had engineered.

Quick Willy winced as an arrow raked along his side, a shallow scratch that burned like hellfire. He pressed his hand into it. Wet heat oozed between his fingers, but he felt nothing more than the blood. He wasn't hurt bad, but he was madder than a wet hen. Fury rose. He lifted his rifle and got off a couple more shots. One took out a Comanche's horse and sent the brave tumbling to the ground. Means rode past without bothering to waste an extra bullet. The Indian was out of the fight and on foot. Better to find some cover.

Means dropped off his horse and clung to the reins with one hand while he rammed the rifle back in the saddle boot with the other. He knelt behind a rock and drew his revolver. A few yards away, the Huffman brothers were taking cover, too, Frank stretching out behind another rock while Charles knelt behind a scrubby bush. The growth wouldn't have stopped a bullet, but it might deflect an arrow.

Both of them had enough sense to hang on to their horses as they opened fire with their revolvers. Would wonders never cease? Quick Willy asked himself bitterly.

He fired three times and scared off a Comanche

intent on sticking a knife into Charles Huffman. Charles never noticed either the attacker or how he had been rescued. A lot of arrows were flying around and shots rolled like thunder over the plains, but not much actual damage was being done.

"Get outta here. Now!"

The shout came from Arizona Johnston as the gunman galloped in from the north. A trickle of blood ran down his forehead, a sign that he had tangled with the Comanches, too. He swiped it away.

Quick Willy locked eyes with Johnston and saw nothing but his own fury reflected there. He waved Johnston on past. Unlike the Huffman boys, Johnston didn't need to be told twice. If anything, he had figured it out for himself that they were outnumbered.

They outgunned the Indians, but numbers would wear them down if the fight went on much longer.

Quick Willy Means snapped another shot at the savage, then vaulted into the saddle, bent low, and urged his horse up to the crest of a sandy hill. From here he saw that retreat wasn't just their best course of action. It was their only one. A dozen more Comanches were coming on swift ponies from the south. Where their camp might be, Means couldn't tell, but the number told him there was an entire village not too far away and the warriors there had heard the gunfire.

Means took one more look around for Dewey Mackenzie. The murdering son of a bitch had caused this, but he was nowhere to be seen. He had poked the hornet's nest and then gotten out of the way of the real trouble. In a way, Quick Willy admired that. It was downright sneaky and showed Mackenzie had a sharp mind. Facing two different enemies, he had set them fighting each other rather than tangling with either—or both.

A Comanche struggling up the hill on foot provided Quick Willy a last chance to vent his anger. His first shot missed. He cocked the gun and tried again, only to have the hammer fall on an expended round. By the time he pouched the iron and yanked out his rifle again, the Indian was almost on him. Means fired three times.

At this range he couldn't miss. A trio of crimson flowers blossomed over the man's heart. Despite that, the man came on, his face twisted with hate and his knife raised. Means fired a fourth time and finally sent the Comanche falling facedown on the ground. The Indian was still twitching when Quick Willy's panicky horse reared and came down with its hooves on the Comanche's head, crushing the skull with a sound like a dropped melon busting open.

Quick Willy watched him die without so much as a flicker of emotion. He reserved that for Dewey Mackenzie.

He sawed at the reins, regained control of the bucking horse, turned, and galloped from the new spate of Indians thinking to join the battle. How many of their tribe had been killed wasn't something he wanted to consider. If enough had died, they might pursue. Or, seeing they lacked ammunition versus men who were not only armed but deadly accurate with it, the Comanches might break off the fight. The worst that could happen was them coming after his men, intending to slit their throats in the night.

That was all the more reason to finish off Mackenzie and clear out of West Texas.

Quick Willy's plans for the day hadn't included fighting to the death, so he hadn't made any provision for a rendezvous after a battle. He just kept riding north until he spotted Frank Huffman. The man joined him.

"Where's your brother?" Means asked.

"Comin'. He took an arrow in the shoulder. You got scratched, too, didn't you, Willy?" Huffman pointed to the oozing wound just above Means's gun belt.

"Doesn't amount to a hill of beans." He touched the cut again and shuddered in pain. Sewing up the wound struck him as a good idea. In order to do that, they had to camp for a spell.

Ten minutes later Charles joined them. They kept riding north and finally saw Johnston ahead of them. He slowed and let them catch up. The group was back together, without too much damage done. Johnston had a few cuts. A knife wound along his calf showed he'd let an Indian get too close to him.

"Blood's filled up my boot," he said, pressing his hand down on the leaking wound. "Walking's going to be a chore for a while."

Means saw how Johnston sized up the others' wounds. The look of expectation on the man's face didn't set well with him. He planned something, and it wasn't going to be acceptable.

"Let's pitch camp. The Comanches won't come

for us, not this soon, anyway," Quick Willy said. "We did enough damage they'll be licking their wounds for a while."

He rode down into an arroyo that provided some protection if he was wrong about the Indians' determination. Being lower than any attackers wasn't a smart move, but being able to shoot over the banks made for a better defense than being out in the open.

Within fifteen minutes, Frank had a small fire started. Means leaned back and pulled free his bloody shirt. As he had thought, the wound was hardly a scratch, but it bled furiously when he probed it. He used a burning twig from the fire to cauterize the wound. Sewing it up would have taken too long.

"You're gonna have one fine-lookin' scar there, Quick Willy. Somethin' to brag on to all the wimmen." Charles looked down with some admiration. He touched his own wound. "All I got for my trouble's a hole in my shoulder. That ain't gonna scar up good at all."

"Too bad the arrow didn't go through your damned skull," Means growled. He forced himself to sit up with his back against the dirt embankment.

Charles frowned, trying to figure out what his boss meant. Frank wore a disgusted look but said nothing. Arizona Johnston was another matter. The man limped over and towered above him.

"There's no point in keeping after Mackenzie," he said without preamble. "Admit it. We're on a hunt that's going to see us all killed."

"You let him go." Quick Willy worked his way to his feet. The pain subsided as he stood and stretched.

"He came for you, and you let him slip through your fingers."

"If you didn't notice, he was in front of a tornado of Comanches. I got off one shot at him, then I was fighting the Indians for my life."

"Which way did Mackenzie go? Back to join the others driving that herd? We can sneak in there tonight and find him. I want to grab him and be gone by sunrise."

"You're a fool. Let this one go, Means. Sometimes it's easy as pie. Other times, nothing will ever go right. This is one of those times. We fought off the Indians. Do we have to fight off a couple dozen drovers, too?"

"So you want to give up?"

Johnston looked away. When he spoke again, it was to the Huffman brothers.

"You see how it is. Come with me. There're plenty of wanted men out there that aren't half as hard to find and take in for a reward. We work together real good."

"You trying to take my men, Johnston?"

"No, Means. I don't care if they come with me or not. But if they've got a lick of sense, they'll ride out, too. I've had it with you getting us into jams where we have to shoot our way out and not have anything to show for it but our own spilled blood." Arizona Johnston took a step. There was a liquid squishing sound from his boot as he moved.

"Go on. Clear out," Quick Willy said.

Johnston turned to mount his horse. Means drew his gun, cocked, aimed, and fired in one smooth motion. The bullet hit Johnston in the back of the skull.

He fell forward into the sandy arroyo bottom. Means saw how the blood drained out of the man's boot and formed a puddle around it. If Means hadn't put him out of his misery, he would have died from blood loss.

"Bury him," he said. "No need to make the grave too deep."

"The coyotes will dig 'im up if we don't go down far enough," Charles said. He was a little wide-eyed with surprise from the sudden violence.

Means snorted.

"I hope they enjoy the meal." With that he sank back to the ground, hand pressed into the charred wound on his side. His brain spun in wild circles as he tried to figure out how to track down Dewey Mackenzie and bring him to the same justice he had just dished out to Arizona Johnston.

CHAPTER 11

"What do you think, Mac? Can we get across it?" Hiram Flowers asked as he stared across the wide expanse of the Pecos River.

This was the point along the Goodnight-Loving Trail Flowers worried about the most. Fording the river was dangerous at the best of times. Now it appeared swollen and several feet higher than the last time he and Zeke Sullivan had come this way with a herd.

When Mac didn't reply, he glanced over at the young man. For someone so young, Mac carried the weight of the world on his broad shoulders. Flowers wished Desmond Sullivan had the same dedication. Mac did the work of three men. He drove the chuck-wagon and fixed meals, he scouted, and from what Flowers had seen, he wasn't half bad at being a drover, though he denied it. The only thing he was piss poor at was singing to the herd at night. He couldn't carry a tune in a bucket, and if he knew more than two songs, he kept it hidden real good.

"Mac?"

"Sorry, I was thinking."

"Think how long it'll take to get across this stretch of water. You reckon scouting some more will help us?"

"We can find a shallower crossing," Mac said. "If not shallower, since this is a fast-moving river, maybe a spot that's not quite so far. I can't throw a rock hard enough to land on the other bank."

"It's too late in the day to begin fording," Flowers said, as much to himself as to Mackenzie. "We bed down for the night, then cross at first light."

"Sounds like a good idea. It'll give the men a chance to rest up, too. And get a good enough meal. I can take my time." Mac looked hard at him. "Are you going to eat?"

"Not hungry," Flowers said. His belly rumbled, as if putting that to the lie. He knew that food—even Mac's, which was tasty going down—caused a minor earthquake deep in his gut. He hadn't been puking lately, but the unsettled feeling kept him from aggravating it into full-blown rebellion by eating a full meal.

"I can see what's in the medicinal stores. Mostly, I brought along medicine for the trots and the reverse. Doesn't do a man good to have every meal he's ever eaten all packed up tight inside."

"Not my problem. Either of them."

"My ma used to whip up a medicine to soothe upset stomachs. Me and my brother Jacob used to eat anything that didn't run away from us fast enough. Once, I double-dirty-dog dared him to eat a bug. He did. He won the bet but was sick for a week." Mac chuckled. "That meant I got his dessert for a week, and that was in the autumn when Ma had a whole basket of peaches." He smacked his lips. "That peach cobbler was the best."

"I'd eat some peach cobbler." Just saying it brought back memories Flowers tried to keep tamped down. Mercedes Sullivan had a cook and a housekeeper, but she did most of her own cooking. The sensation of smelling a pie cooling on the windowsill had been the moment Flowers realized how much he loved her.

That memory caused his belly to rebel. He let out a belch, wiped his mouth, and said, "Fix the men whatever they want tonight. Get the chuckwagon ready to cross. Have Desmond help."

"I've been meaning to talk to you about him."

Flowers sighed. Being trail boss shouldn't require more than getting the herd to market. Dealing with a young snot carrying a chip on his shoulder wasn't high on his list of things to do when he faced a dangerous river crossing.

"What's the problem?" He knew what Mac was going to say. That didn't make it any easier to hear.

"He's been drinking the whiskey I keep for medicinal purposes. He takes a swig or two, then fills the bottle back up with water so it's still full to the same level. That cuts the whiskey left, making it almost useless to kill the pain for the men who need it."

"You sure it's him? There's more'n one riding for us with a taste for rotgut."

"I smell it on his breath. He has to know, but he doesn't give two hoots. There's not a whale of a lot I can do since I'm not his boss."

"He doesn't think I am, either." Flowers sighed as he looked across the river. Tree trunks the size of a large wagon raced past, carried all the way from New Mexico. This year the Pecos ran high and fast. He found himself wishing he was not only on the other bank but in Fort Sumner with a pocketful of cash from selling the herd to the Army. He was getting too old for the trail.

"I know the deal you made. It was either Desmond or Miz Sullivan coming with us. You made the right choice, but—"

"Don't give me no 'buts,' Mac. I'll talk to him. I'll send him home with his tail between his legs, if I have to."

"That'd mean your job."

Hiram Flowers shrugged. That might be for the best. The Circle Arrow was a fine ranch, and the Sullivan family the best he ever worked for. Zeke had been a decent man, and Mercedes, well, he tormented himself over her. She was too fine a woman to ever team up with a lowlife cowboy like him. Removing himself from all that frustration might be a good thing and give his belly a chance to settle down.

He drew in a deep breath and let it out fast so that his nostrils flared. He repeated it and felt even more responsibility crushing down on him.

"We might try crossing now. Most of the herd'd get across before it was too dark."

"You can't be serious," Mac said. "You want to split the herd like that? Having a bunch on this side and the rest across the river? Why would you divvy them up like that?"

"You don't smell it, do you? The storm?"

"The sky's clear. There are some clouds, but they're not rain clouds."

Flowers pointed to the south.

"The storm's movin' in on us from the Gulf of Mexico. Have you ever seen the gulf, Mac?"

"Not really. As close as I ever got was New Orleans."

The way the young man turned cautious warned Flowers not to press him on the subject. What he knew of Mac's background could be chiseled on the head of a pin. He'd just mentioned a brother and before he told of how his ma and pa died of typhus. The S&W hanging at his side had belonged to his pa. Other than that, all Mac had spoken of were his experiences on a cattle drive up the Shawnee Trail. Even then he had been tight-lipped about it. Flowers wondered what had happened and who had died.

It wasn't his place to pry. Not when he had problems of his own.

"The air tastes different, smells different. Everything changes, if you pay attention."

"Well, Mister Flowers, I'll try to pay more attention, but right now I need to see if Desmond has left any liquor at all and what I need to do to whip up a good meal for the crew."

"Are they really going to have a bullwhip contest?" Flowers had to ask. He'd never approve of such a thing since it always came down to one man trying to snap a rock off another's shoulder or head, missing, taking off an ear or eye, and then the fights started.

Still, the men were expert with their twelve-foot

whips. Using those to crack over horned heads moved the cattle easier than yelling at the beeves all day. He had seen the best of his cowboys crack straw from the lips of their friends, usually without taking off a nose in the process.

"If they are, I wouldn't be able to tell you. They know what you think of such foolishness."

"You ought to be a politician, Mac. You can give an answer without answering. Get on back to camp. I might just stop in and sample some of your vittles." He rubbed his belly. The pain wasn't too bad at all at the moment. Tempting fate with a decent steak would fortify him for the crossing in the morning.

"I'll fix a good meal especially for you. Don't disappoint me by letting it go to waste."

"What? Are we married? Are you nagging me? You're not that good at it. Get along, now." Flowers leaned over and smacked Mac's horse on the rump. It took off like a rocket, leaving him alone on the bank to stare across the river. If wishes were all it took, they'd already be across.

But he had to do more than wish. Another deep breath confirmed his suspicion that a big storm was on the way. They had to cross before it hit or be pinned down for several days. The sooner they got to Fort Sumner, the sooner he could push on up to Santa Fe and then return to the Circle Arrow.

Hiram Flowers snapped the reins and got his horse walking around the perimeter of the herd so he could estimate how long it'd take to cross the river.

* * *

The steak set well in his belly. When Flowers crawled out of his blankets before dawn the next morning and rubbed vigorously on his stomach, he expected the burning sensation inside to return. It didn't.

"Dang, Mac, you do serve a good meal," he said, even though the cook wasn't around at the moment. "Sorry I doubted you and ever tried to keep that drunkard Cassidy."

Keeping the wastrel around as long as he had had resulted in big trouble among the cowboys, but he had done it out of need. His sister's boy should have straightened up when he got a job. Instead, he used the money he earned to get drunker and drunker. That had never set well with Mercedes Sullivan and her temperance ways, but she had let him keep the boozehound on.

That made Flowers wonder why. She never meddled in how he ran the ranch, but everything about Cassidy went against her heartfelt beliefs. He had never been comfortable with her business associates, much less her social circle. He was a hired hand, not a ranch owner.

He snorted at that as he swung up into the saddle and rode out to check the river again. Without being too stuck on himself, he considered himself, Hiram Flowers, trail boss, to be a better man than Desmond Sullivan. He had a code of honor he followed as surely as Mercedes believed demon rum was evil.

A yawn almost cracked his jaw. He had set out only half the night riders on the herd that he usually posted, telling the rest to get a good night's sleep to prepare for the river crossing in the morning. He had told Mac to have breakfast ready an hour before sunrise so everyone would be tending the herd when the first light poked above the eastern horizon.

From the way the Pecos was swollen and flowing so fast, it might take most of the day getting across. He wanted every second of that to be in sunlight. And he wanted them across before the storm hit. Another sniff at the air convinced him he was right about the coming storm. The only question was when it would arrive.

His horse left sucking hoofprints in the muddy riverbank as Flowers tried to find the exact right spot to cross. Unless he took another couple of days scouting both directions along the Pecos, he wasn't going to find a better place than this. He shook his head sadly. This year that meant no single spot was better than any other due to the flooding.

Getting across fast mattered. If the river flooded any more than it already was, fording might become impossible for days or even a week. Urging his horse up a low rise, he had a decent vantage point to look out over the herd. He caught his breath when he saw thousands of horns dancing with blue fox fire in the darkness. Tiny, fuzzy patches formed along the ten-foot spans and crept to the very tips. There the fox fire shimmered and sometimes jumped from one horn tip to another, causing the steers to complain restively. He had seen this curious fairyland display before.

It always meant an electrical storm was on its way. In this part of Texas that might well mean a tornado. From the feelings he had in his gut and increasingly in his aching joints, his bet lay on a thunderstorm rushing up from the Gulf of Mexico. More than once while he worked a ranch down near Corpus Christi, this sensation had built in him. A storm always followed within a day or two. The fox fire glimmering along the cattle horns lent more credence to his belief that they were in for a gully washer.

He cocked his head to one side, heard the beeves beginning to stir, and knew dawn was on its way. Not wasting any time, he rode down into camp, saw Mac was already serving up breakfast, and smiled. That boy was always on top of his work and helped out when needed with everyone else's chores. He started to tell Mac to get a horse and help with the herd crossing the river, then realized that would leave Desmond to ferry the chuckwagon over the Pecos. Losing the chuckwagon would be a catastrophe for the drive. Better for Mac to use his expertise driving the wagon.

But then a different thought came to Flowers. He rode to where Mac was serving the last of the food.

"Take Desmond with you when you cross," the trail boss said. "He can help. You have the floats ready?"

"All ready, Mister Flowers." Mac seemed to want to say something else.

"Spit it out. What's eatin' you?"

"I'd be fine getting the chuckwagon across on my own. I don't need Desmond to help out."

"Take him." Flowers spoke with such force that it left no question of his intention. Mac might resent being a wet nurse, but the cowboys couldn't afford to be distracted once the cattle entered the water.

Flowers rode around, made sure the crew was ready.

Facing east, he waited for the first pink and gray fingers of a new day to claw at the sky.

"Get 'em movin'!" Flowers ordered when the time was right. "The sooner we get across the river, the sooner we can take another rest."

The promise of the opposite bank being as far as they had to go for the day spurred the cowboys to action. Some unlimbered their whips and sent them snaking out to crack above the lead steers' heads. This caused a ripple throughout the herd, a shrug, a stirring, then they began to move.

Flowers wheeled his mount around and led the way to the river. When the horse stopped, the water sloshing around its hooves, the morning light burned warm and inviting on Flowers's back. He took his time watching the river flow to be sure they weren't going to swim the cattle into submerged trees or other debris. As far as he could tell, submerged sandbars here and there provided the only impediment to crossing. With luck the cattle could rest on those sandbars before finishing their crossing, but he had to be sure they didn't get bogged down in mud. Suction on those sandbars could hold even a twelve-hundred-pound bull until it drowned.

So many problems to avoid, so many things to worry about.

No wonder his belly hurt so often.

Hiram Flowers lifted an arm high over his head, then lowered it like a cavalry general ordering a full charge of his horse soldiers. The cowboys began shouting, using their whips and crowding the cattle on the edges of the herd toward a single spot on the bank. The cattle protested, then started a slow walk into the water.

The first of the beeves got caught by the rush of the current. Flowers wanted to go out and make sure they didn't take the easy route and let the water carry them off to drown. But the Circle Arrow crew knew their jobs. They worked to do what he could never do as a solitary rider.

Flowers watched the steady stream of cattle enter the Pecos and swim their way across the raging river. Runoff had been extreme this year. He was glad to cross here and not farther north near the headwaters. If he had been that far north in New Mexico Territory he would have passed Fort Sumner and headed for Santa Fe instead. The decision to try to sell part of the herd at Fort Sumner had come to him in a dream of starving soldiers and Indians, now departed from Bosque Redondo, begging for beef. The more head he sold to the Army, the fewer he had to drive northward another couple hundred miles.

Back and forth he rode, keeping the cattle moving, having cowboys double up when necessary. As Mac drove the chuckwagon forward, Flowers waved it on. Desmond sat beside Mac, glowering. Flowers ignored the boy and studied the floats tied on both sides of the wagon. They were needed to keep the wagon from sinking. Mac had used tarpaulins to waterproof the interior the best he could. While the chuckwagon wasn't a real boat, it came close enough for the time it would take to make the crossing.

A sudden protest from a cow nearby forced him to help get the animal into the water. Some weren't happy but went with the rest of the herd. The ones that panicked made the ford the most dangerous, not only for themselves but for the riders. It took Flowers a few minutes to get the balky cow moving. He followed it until it had to swim, then started to return to the bank to urge the remainder of the herd across.

That's when he heard a loud shout. He jerked around to see the chuckwagon listing heavily to the side, shipping water as a huge wave broke over it. He started into the swollen stream to help, then saw a more immediate worry. Mac had been washed over the side of the chuckwagon and was being swept downstream in the middle of the river.

Mac held his arm up and waved it around, showing he was still alive. And then another wave rose over him and pushed him underwater.

CHAPTER 12

"You can't make me go." Desmond Sullivan had crossed his arms and thrust out his chin defiantly as he faced Mac a short time earlier.

"What'd I tell you about leading with your chin? Tuck it in or I'll plant a right jab on the point, knock you out, load you in the wagon, and go."

"Come on, then. Let's duke it out." Desmond shifted his weight and put up his fists, ready to fight.

Mac looked around. The cowboys cracked their whips and got the herd moving. Flowers had told him to get across the Pecos as quickly as he could. From their scouting yesterday, Mac knew the floats on the side of the chuckwagon might not be enough to keep it bobbing on top of the water. He had used a tarp to line the bottom of the wagon bed, turning it into a boat.

At least, he hoped it would be watertight enough to serve as a boat. The trick would be to get over to the far bank as fast as possible and not tempt fate.

"I don't have time to play around," he told Desmond, ignoring the young man's pugilistic stance. He cinched the last of the belly straps on the team and went to climb onto the driver's box.

"I ain't playing. This is for real. You gonna fight me or not?"

"Look at that, will you?" Mac pointed into the air just behind Desmond. As the young man turned to look, Mac stepped up, grabbed his right wrist, and twisted back hard. Then he leaned into the grip until Desmond cried out in pain.

"Here are your choices," Mac said coldly. "I can break your arm and leave you behind to get home any way you can. Don't expect Flowers to give you a horse."

"You killed my horse!"

Mac ignored him, applied a little more pressure, and shut Desmond's mouth with a new jab of pain.

"You can go on home with a broken arm. Tell your ma whatever story you like. Make yourself out to be the hero. I don't care. Or you can head south and vanish into Mexico. There's plenty of opportunity down there, I hear." Desmond squirmed. Mac did not loosen his hold. "The last choice is the one I'd take, if I were you. What might that be? Do you know?"

"G-get onto the driver's box."

"You're not as dumb as you act." Mac released him. Desmond clutched his tortured wrist while Mac pulled himself up onto the seat.

"You busted a bone," Desmond accused him.

"No, I didn't, since nothing snapped. Come on up." Mac reached out to help his unwilling assistant climb onto the box. Desmond ignored the out-

stretched hand. That suited Mac just fine. He had
work to do, and crossing the river required every bit
of concentration he had.

Once Desmond was on the seat beside him, he
snapped the reins and got the team moving. By the
time he reached the river a quarter of the herd had
dipped their noses in. He had to laugh at the sight of
so many longhorns in the water.

"What's so damn funny?" Desmond asked sullenly.

"They look like a hundred rocking chairs floating
across. I've never seen anything like that before." Mac
drove a bit downriver from where the herd waded in.

This close, the sight of what he was facing made
Mac swallow hard. The Pecos ran deep and swift. The
strongest cattle led the way. The rest followed, too
stupid to consider that they might never make it.

Mac, on the other hand, knew what the chances
were. They were good because of the preparations.
Bad because of the river's depth and the strength of
its flow. He refrained from checking the floats on either side of the chuckwagon. Having Desmond riding with him didn't make him any braver, but it caused
him to think about showing any concern. Besides,
what more could he do to prepare for the crossing
now?

He called out to the team and used the reins to
drive the horses forward. They balked when they got
chest deep in the river. Slapping the lines on their
backs and shouting at the top of his lungs got them
swimming.

The chuckwagon lurched as the current caught it
sideways. He kept the horses pulling. This kept the

wagon directly behind and held the force of the water at bay.

Everything went well until they were three-quarters of the way across. Then one of the wheels hit a sandbar. The chuckwagon canted to one side and let the water surge underneath, lifting it up.

"Pull! Keep going!" Mac jumped to his feet to better use the reins. As he stood the wagon tilted precariously.

He tried to take a step to keep his balance. His feet got tangled up together, forcing him to twist to the side. A wave hit the wagon and a giant watery hand lifted. Mac cried out as he flew through the air. The wet leather reins slid from his grip. He hit the edge of the driver's box, spun around because of the swirling water and then felt as if he had lost all weight. He was caught by the river and carried away from the chuckwagon.

"Get it on to shore!" he yelled at Desmond as he waved an arm. "The wagon. Get it—" He sputtered as he was pulled under.

The last thing he saw was the chuckwagon leaning precariously, Desmond shifting his weight in the other direction to counter it. Whether or not it capsized, he couldn't tell because muddy, filthy water filled his eyes and nose and mouth, blinding and choking him.

For a moment he fought the river's power, struggling so hard his arms went limp from the effort. But Mac refused to give up. To panic now meant certain death. He relaxed and let the current carry him along. He bobbed to the surface, sucked in a couple of quick breaths, and then was pulled back under.

He twisted and turned, prisoner to the river. Something banged against his arm. He grabbed it and hung on for dear life. The added buoyancy took him back to the surface where he saw he had seized a large tree limb. Using it as a float, he kicked hard and angled toward the shore. The tumult had scrambled his brains enough that he didn't know which side of the river was in front of him. Either promised safety.

He kicked and tried to swim but weakened fast. His wet clothes weighed him down. The revolver at his hip added another three pounds of iron he had to support. The wild notion of getting free of the gun belt flashed through his mind, but he rejected it immediately. His pa had given him that S&W. Lose it and he sacrificed the last thread connecting him to his family, to Missouri, to his life growing up. He kicked and dog paddled as hard as he could. The shore wasn't more than ten yards away. Close.

"I can make it. I can."

He couldn't. He surrendered more and more to the power of the river, and it wanted to sweep him downstream. Eventually he would wash up on the shore, but he would never know. He'd be dead.

"No, no, no," he spat out. His words bubbled as his head went underwater. He reached up.

A scream of pain ripped from his lips as it felt like his arm was being pulled out of joint. He fought, only to spin around and around, his arm the axle. The pain mounted in his shoulder until he quit fighting and let the new force drag him along. As he was pulled up facedown on the muddy bank, he saw the horsehair rope looped around his wrist. As he had reached up, someone had lassoed him and used this to pull him ashore.

"St-stop. You're d-draggin' me." He failed to get his feet under him and could hardly make a sound because of exhaustion and the mud coating his face. But his rescuer realized the danger from drowning was past and let the rope go slack.

The rope slid from his wrist. Forcing himself to sit up, he wiped mud from his eyes and saw about the prettiest sight he'd ever seen. Astride his horse sat Hiram Flowers.

"You make a lousy doggie, Mackenzie. Roping you was too easy. I don't even want to think about hogtying and branding you."

"I'm not going back out there to give you a fight." Mac tried to stand. His legs refused. He sat back down and wiped more mud from his face.

"I saw you get washed out of the chuckwagon. That wave was twice the height of the wagon."

"Desmond! He was in the wagon. Where is he?" Concern powered Mac to his feet. He took a few tentative steps back toward the river. "I don't see him. There's no sign of Desmond or the chuckwagon."

"Can't tell if they got swept downriver. I was concentrating on getting you out of the drink."

"Give me a hand up." Mac reached up for Flowers to hoist him behind. The trail boss hesitated, then pulled him up.

"Damn, boy, but you're filthy from the river. I thought bathing was supposed to get you all clean."

"How'd you know?" Mac shot back. "You haven't had a bath in a month of Sundays."

"That's because I spend all my time around cattle.

It's months past dipping time to get the ticks off them, so why bother sticking myself in water?"

"There!" Mac almost fell from the horse as he pointed. "That's a float from the wagon."

Flowers rode to where the crude pontoon was caught in some weeds. The rope holding it to the chuckwagon had been frayed, dragged repeatedly against the side of the wagon by the rise and fall of the river until it came free.

"There's no wreckage I can see." Flowers put his hand over his eyes as he peered into the rising sun.

"If the wagon went straight to the bottom, we might salvage it. If it got washed away, everything inside will be strewn along the river for miles and miles."

"We'll have to search," Flowers said.

"For Desmond's body," Mac finished. He felt beaten and battered by the river. Adding to that rose a sense of guilt. He should have taken better care of Desmond. The boy was a greenhorn on the trail, ornery and arrogant, but he never should have died the way he did. That was entirely Mac's fault. He should have looked after him better, and the chuckwagon with all their vittles, all their utensils—and maybe worst of all if there had been injuries—all their medical supplies.

"Kleingeld got across with the rest of the gear," Flowers said. "I see him waving."

"I should hunt for Desmond."

"You should stop blaming yourself. I told you to watch him. It's my fault he got into trouble out there. I knew he wasn't a trail hand. Hell, I should have made sure he had floats on him like the wagon. I don't even know if he could swim."

"Wouldn't matter much," Mac said. "The current's too powerful to fight for very long. If you hadn't roped me when you did, I'd be no better than one of those dead limbs sailing down the river."

"Shut your yap and save your strength. We've got the rest of the herd to get across the river. I knew it'd be tough goin'. I expected to lose upward of a quarter of the herd, but I hoped we wouldn't come up short because of men drowning." Flowers swallowed hard. Mac rode with his arms around the man's waist and felt him quaking. Losing Desmond hit him as hard as it did himself.

Flowers rode slowly up a rise to look down on the mud flats where the cattle filed past, wet and angry at being forced to endure such indignity. Kleingeld had parked his wagon a hundred yards inland from the river and worked to get what looked like half the river drained from the wagon bed. A couple of cowboys helped him.

Flowers suddenly reared back and almost knocked Mac from behind him.

"What is it?" Mac looked around the trail boss. His eyes went wide. He shook his head in disbelief and said, "That can't be. It just can't."

"Reckon you're wrong, Mac. It is." Flowers put his heels to his horse's flanks and galloped down to the riverbank, dodging cattle the entire way.

CHAPTER 13

"It's hardly dawn," Desmond had complained as the river crossing got underway. "There's no reason to ford the river this early."

Beside Desmond on the box, Mac had never twitched, never showed any sign he heard. Desmond started to poke him, then decided against it and settled down in a pile of dejection. Nothing ever went his way. The world kicked him in the teeth at every turn. Nothing he did was right or good enough. Flowers rode him constantly, and his ma ignored him, but at least she was better than his pa. Everybody worshiped the old man like he was some kind of saint. Desmond knew different. Zeke Sullivan had poked fun at him every chance he got.

Desmond yelped when the chuckwagon hit a rock and almost sent him sailing from the driver's box.

"You did that on purpose," Desmond protested, his accusation falling on deaf ears. Mac looked straight ahead. The roar of the river, its putrid, decaying smell, spray rising up to reach inland, occupied him more than answering the complaint. Nobody ever listened to Desmond. Nobody, and especially not a lowly cook, should boss him around like that.

"Hang on. We're going across."

"I don't want to go," Desmond said, staring at the choppy water of the Pecos. Logs the size of the chuckwagon tumbled in the dark, churning water. To ford here was crazy. It was sure death.

"Hop off if you want. This is your last chance. But I can use the help getting across."

"What? How?" Desmond looked at the cook, sure he was poking cruel fun at him.

"I'm going to be driving and won't be able to shift around to keep the chuckwagon from capsizing. You need to stand up, move your weight in the direction opposite that caused by the river. Keep us from turning over. Can you do that?"

"I . . . yes." Desmond doubted this was actually any kind of a job. It sounded stupid.

Then the team began pulling and got caught by the rush of the powerful current. Mac kept them moving with the wagon directly behind the horses. Desmond saw that the river wanted to spin the wagon around the tongue. If that happened the team would break free, and the wagon would be swept away, powerless against the flood.

He let out a yelp as the wagon tipped. The floats on the downriver side submerged and the upriver ones rose from the water. Desmond realized this was what Mac wanted from him. He jumped up and grabbed the brace immediately behind the driver's bench. Applying all his strength, he leaned into it. He thought he wasn't having any effect.

"That's the ticket. You're doing just fine," Mac shouted over the roar of the river.

Desmond thought he was taunting him. Mac never passed up a chance at sarcasm. Then Desmond felt the wagon tipping back. The floats on both sides dipped down into the water. He'd righted the wagon.

"We're halfway across. We're going to make it." Mac bent back, tugging hard on the reins to turn the horses toward a spot on the far bank off at an angle. They tired fast, fighting the current. He aimed them for a spot they could reach without exerting themselves as much.

Desmond had to jump up and lean into the wagon again. It righted fast, almost throwing him out into the river. He collapsed to the seat. His clothing clung to his body, as wet from the river spray as from sweat. Exerting every ounce of energy was taking it out of him. He saw that Mac's face was pale and drawn with strain. The cook fought the team every inch of the way, and it drained him.

A smirk came to Desmond's lips. So the great Dewey Mackenzie wasn't so great after all. He got tired and scared like everybody else.

"Help me. Take the reins. My hands are cramped up." Mac held out the leather straps. Desmond took them without realizing he did so.

The sudden jerk almost tore his arms from his shoulder joints. He shoved out his feet against sodden wood and pulled for all he was worth. The team began to move in the right direction, at an angle, through the river.

Mac took back the reins after flexing his hands for a minute or so. Desmond gave them back, glad to be freed of the responsibility but at the same time surly because Mac hadn't told him he'd done a good job.

Then a powerful invisible hand lifted the wagon straight into the air and dropped it down with a thud as if it hit solid ground.

"What do you think about that?" Desmond shouted over the roar of the water. It took him a moment to realize he was alone in the wagon. "Mackenzie? Mackenzie! Where'd you go?"

Frantic, he hunted for the cook. Mac was nowhere to be seen. He had been washed over the side of the wagon and carried away by the dark river. This startled Desmond so much, he almost didn't think to grab the wet reins that lay at his feet.

But those reins represented his only chance for survival, he realized. He knew he would die if he followed Mac into the river. His only chance to keep on living lay ahead. He had to get the team to pull him from the Pecos.

Desmond snatched up the reins and drove in a half crouch, controlling the team as he had never done before and using his shifting weight to counter the roll of the wagon. After an eternity, he realized the force of the river had diminished against the wagon because all four wheels were miring down in river bottom mud as he neared the shore.

"Pull, damn you! Keep going!" He whipped the tired horses. They saw dry land ahead and struggled to pull forward to reach it. Before he fully grasped what was happening, the horses were dragging the chuckwagon over dry ground and up an incline near the river.

Out of the river!

He stomped on the brake and set it, using the reins to hold it in place. Standing, he let out a wild whoop of glee. Then he collapsed to the bench seat, his legs the consistency of stewed okra. His insides were liquid and weak. Not a muscle worked right for him. He shook all over as if he had the ague.

Desmond sat up when he heard the rattle of another wagon.

"Mac!" a guttural voice called. "You made it, Mac! We celebrate, eh?"

He peered around the side of the wagon and saw Kleingeld driving up in the supply wagon. Their eyes locked. The German's faced melted into horror.

"Where is he? Where is Mac?"

"He got washed overboard," Desmond said. "Served him right. He was showing off. I had to drive the wagon the rest of the way."

"He is in the river? We must find him."

"You mean you're going to hunt for his body. As fast as the current is, he'll be halfway across Texas by now."

"Go. You go and hunt for him! I will tell the others!"

"What do they care? They have the cattle to tend. That's all that's important. The damned longhorns." Desmond let his bitterness gush forth. Kleingeld and the others would never have mounted a search if he had been the one dumped into the river. More than likely, they would have celebrated. He knew it because they all hated him so. Hiram Flowers would be the one doing the most cheering over his death.

Desmond jumped down and walked slowly around the wagon. He blinked in surprise when he saw one

of the floats had been ripped off. He had never noticed. Working with fingers that felt five times too
big, he untied the remaining floats and tossed them
into the back of the wagon.

As he stared inside, his mouth turned dry. He
poked around and found the crate with the whiskey
in it. Mac had been such a spoilsport about using it
for anything but medicine. He picked up the bottle
and held it.

His shaking went away at the touch of the smooth,
cool glass against his palm. He pulled out the cork
and let the fumes drift up to his nose. His nostrils
flared, and his mouth turned drier than the Chi-
huahuan Desert. A single sip. That's all. He had
sneaked a few drinks and Mac had never known.
Now that the cook was gone, he had the bottle all to
himself. Lifting it to his lips, he paused. Another
deep whiff. Then he put the cork back in and carefully packed the bottle in its crate again.

"Later," he muttered to himself. He'd sample the
whiskey later, to celebrate.

He finished bailing out the water inside the wagon,
mopping up what he could. By now the sun had risen
a good way and made it easier to hang out cloth and
get the tarps hung up to dry. The sound of the herd
kept him company. Nobody else came by, nobody
else cared.

"I'll show them. I'm as good as any of them."

Those words had barely left his lips when he heard
a loud hoot of glee. He turned and saw Hiram Flowers riding in his direction. For a moment, it didn't
penetrate to Desmond's fatigue-dulled brain that
someone came up alongside the trail boss, on foot.

Mackenzie. A broad grin stretched across the cook's muddy face.

"Desmond!" Mac shouted. "You saved the chuck-wagon!"

"Of course I did," he said. Had there ever been any doubt?

"I knew you could do it." Mac thrust out his hand. Desmond started to shake, then pulled back.

"Like hell you did. Why'd you leave me stranded in the middle of the river?"

Mac shot a look at Flowers, who shook his head.

"I've got a herd to bed down. There's a storm coming, mark my words." The trail boss put his heels to his horse's flanks and trotted off.

"Him and his weather sense," Mac said. "He's for certain sure we're in for a storm." He looked around. "I don't see it."

"You don't see much of anything," Desmond snapped.

Mac's lips thinned, but he held back any sharp words.

"Thanks for tending the wagon."

"It's still there."

Mac frowned slightly. "What's still there? I know we lost a float, but that doesn't matter. There aren't any more big rivers to cross like this."

"The whiskey, damn it. I didn't touch a drop of your precious whiskey." Desmond spun and stalked off. Mac said something, but he didn't try to understand. The cook had it in for him and would lie about the liquor. He'd probably drink it himself, then claim Desmond had drunk it.

He should have gone ahead and taken the whole damned bottle. Stomping to the top of a hill, he looked back over the river. If the Pecos wanted to really mock him, it would be all calm now.

The swollen river still sloshed against its banks, at flood level. He marveled at how he had driven the chuckwagon across such swollen, racing water and lived to tell about it. A thought crossed his mind that he ought to ask if everyone else had made it. Mac had, in spite of being washed out of the wagon.

Then Desmond decided it didn't matter one whit. If any of the cowboys had drowned, nothing would bring him back. And if they had all made it just fine, what did he care? They didn't like him. Why should he bother about them?

"Hey, Desmond!"

He saw Flowers waving to him. Reluctantly, he hiked down the hill to see what the trail boss wanted.

"Grab a horse and go out to the north side of the herd. Keep 'em all together. When the storm comes, it'll be a whopper. Get a slicker. Everybody's gonna get mighty wet before we hit the trail again."

"You putting everybody out riding herd or just me?"

"Doesn't concern you what anyone else is doing, but the answer's simple. I'm sending as many out as I can because the storm's going to break before sundown. Now get your ass on a horse and get to work."

Desmond watched him ride off, shouting orders to others. So much for gratitude, for saving the Circle Arrow's chow, utensils, everything that kept the drovers fed and happy. No matter what he did, they never appreciated it. No matter what.

He found a decent horse, saddled, and went out. At least being alone kept the others from mocking him all the time.

Desmond nodded off as he rode, then jerked awake. It wasn't right keeping him out here this long. Flowers had given him a break to eat supper and sent him back out without any sleep. Crossing the river had been enough for any given day, but riding herd the rest of the day while the cattle milled around irked him. They could have made another couple of miles, but Flowers insisted on bedding down not a quarter mile from the river.

He drifted off to sleep again, only to be awakened by a sharp crack. He thought someone was shooting at him. The cattle began making noises like they were afraid. Singing to them to soothe the stupid animals was beneath his dignity, but he worried that calming them wasn't possible any other way.

A new rumble caused him to look at the sky. The sunset had been spectacular, but what did he care about that? Clouds. Lots of them. But these coming up from the southeast now were dark, their leaden bottoms filled with flashes. The lightning in those storm clouds was still miles off, but the rain promised a long, wet night.

"Wet again." Desmond sighed. "Just when I dried out from getting across the river."

A single heavy, cold raindrop spattered against his hat brim. He turned his face up and caught another drop just under the right eye. He flinched. Flowers had doomed him for another terrible night. Licking his lips, he almost tasted the whiskey he had put back. The bottle would have gotten him through this miserable night.

The cattle moaned and began to stir as even louder thunder rolled over the land. The promise of more rain made Desmond twist around and fumble in his saddlebags for the slicker Flowers had told him to bring. That wouldn't make the night any better, but it kept him drier than he would have been without it.

As he kicked one foot from the stirrup to get a better reach, a lightning bolt tore through the sky directly overhead, well ahead of the storm as such things sometimes were. The violent electrical display startled him and terrified his horse. The animal bucked, hit hard, then reared. In his contorted position, Desmond couldn't keep his seat. He grabbed for the saddlebags to stay astride. The horse bucked again, sending him flying through the air. Desmond landed with a hard whack.

The fall stunned him for a moment. He climbed to his feet, every bone in his skeleton aching from being thrown. In his hand he clutched the yellow slicker.

"I may walk back to camp, but I won't get too wet," he grumbled as the horse tore off into the distance, thoroughly spooked. As he started to slip into the slicker, he felt the ground under his feet quiver and shake. He looked up and saw the dark mass of the herd shift. The cattle began to move.

"Oh, sweet Jesus, no!" Desmond turned and ran away from them, but the storm had spooked the biggest steers along the edge of the herd. They began to run. The others followed.

Stampede.

Heart pounding crazily, Desmond staggered along, his legs not working right. The herd snorted and let out a terrible sound that chilled him all the way to the soul. There was nowhere to run. Flowers had bedded the herd down in a shallow bowl away from the river. Desmond wished the cattle had stampeded toward the Pecos. Let them all drown. They came toward him instead, running away from the riverbank.

"Hang on, I'm coming!"

He looked over his shoulder, trying to see who called to him. The sun had set. Twilight should have let him see better than this, but already the onrushing storm had turned the evening pitch black. He tried to keep running. Whatever he heard might have been his imagination.

Then he saw the flashing hooves of a horse rush past him. The rider spun around and blocked his way, reaching down to help him up.

"Mackenzie!"

"We've got to get out of the way. Those cows aren't going to stop running for a month of Sundays. That's how scared they are."

Desmond started to reach up but held back. Mac would never let him hear the end of this, how he had pulled his fat from the fire, how he had saved the boss's son just like he had plucked him from a Fort Worth whorehouse.

"Damn it, get up here!" Mac looked behind Desmond. "Too late."

Desmond's heart threatened to explode. He saw the cook was right. The charging herd was too close to them. They couldn't get clear. In seconds they'd be goners.

Mac leaped off the horse. "What are you doing?" Desmond demanded. For a second he thought Mac had dismounted to give him the horse, but then the cook yanked the yellow slicker from his hand.

He began waving it around. The motion drew the herd's attention. The deadly cattle changed direction, but not much. Then Mac did something that confused Desmond. He yanked on his horse's reins, stuffed the slicker under the saddle and gave the horse a solid whack on the rump. Its eyes were rimmed in white with fear from the stampede. It galloped away, the slicker flapping behind.

"What are you doing?"

Mac didn't answer. He grabbed Desmond and threw both of them to the ground.

"Stay down. Keep your head down. These rocks might not be enough to protect us, even if the cattle chase after the horse."

Desmond looked up. The horse frantically tried to escape the cattle as it galloped away. It quickly became evident the race was not to the swift but to the frightened.

He heard the horse die. He couldn't see it because of the rippling mass of beef between him and the doomed animal.

Mac grabbed his collar and held him down. Desmond thrashed around, trying to get away, then stopped. The cook was right. They huddled behind rocks poking up from the ground. Not more than a couple of feet high, but enough. Maybe enough.

The stampede broke over their heads, deadly hooves whistling through the air only inches away.

CHAPTER 14

"Get up," Dewey Mackenzie said after what seemed like an eternity of being surrounded by roaring, pounding, certain death. "We've got to get away. There are still longhorns out there willing to trample us."

He grabbed Desmond by the coat collar and lifted. The young man's legs buckled. Mac supported him until he stood upright under his own power. If he hadn't realized the trouble they were still in, Mac would have felt the same. The closeness of death frightened anyone with an ounce of sense.

"You're bleeding." Desmond reached out and touched Mac's arm.

"A hoof caught me. Just missed my head." He took off his battered black hat and looked at it. Part of the crown had just vanished as the longhorn kicked past. "If it rains much more, I'll drown if I wear this."

Desmond snickered. Then he laughed harder. Hysteria hit him, and he doubled over guffawing at the bad joke. Mac didn't begrudge him this, either. They both knew how close they'd come to being killed. Finally as the paroxysms of laughter died down, Desmond straightened and stared at him.

"You saved my life. You didn't have to do that. You could have let me die."

"No way would I do such a thing," Mac said, shaking his head and regretting it as pain jabbed into him. That hoof hadn't just kicked away part of his hat. It must have grazed his skull. He pressed his fingers into the top of his head. They came away sticky with blood. "Flowers would never let me forget it. He might even dock my pay."

"We lost a horse," Desmond said.

"Two. And you lost your slicker."

That set Desmond off again, but the laughter died faster this time. Mac took him by the arm and guided him away from the herd and up a hillside. From here they had a better look at how the cattle had stampeded away from the river. In that, Flowers had had a touch of luck, but most of the longhorns were still running as the rain pelted down on them and lightning stabbed across the sky, jumping from cloud to cloud. If it ever flashed downward to blast apart a tree or even a cow, there'd be no stopping the stampede.

"How long can they run?" Desmond's voice sounded small, subdued.

"As long as they're scared. I heard tell of a stampede along the Chisholm Trail that lasted a week. They had to chase the beeves more than a hundred miles before they wore themselves out. What you have to do is get the leaders to turn back toward the center of the herd, get them to mill, to spiral around.

That breaks their forward run." Mac heaved a sigh. "Of course, that causes other problems."

"They trample each other."

Mac looked at Desmond. He hadn't expected an answer. His own fear was running out like sand through an hourglass, but he babbled rather than laughed.

"Not only that, they generate so damned much heat pressing together that it'll burn a cowboy riding close by."

"You're joshing me. That's not so."

"God's truth," Mac insisted. "They get all bunched together. Animals that big and frightened generate a lot of heat. Then there's the hooves pounding on the ground, hitting rocks. Never heard of a cowboy who got blisters from being too close by, but it's as bad as being out in the desert sun. Hotter than hell."

"You want me to put a tourniquet on your arm?"

Desmond stared at the steady flow of blood down Mac's left arm. It was a deep wound, but not as bad as it looked. Mac bunched up his coat and pressed it down hard. The blood turned sluggish and soon stopped flowing as it clotted over. It was his head hurting like a thousand wasps had built a nest in it that bothered him more.

"You two, are you all right?" The urgent shout came from down the slope.

"Up here, Mister Flowers," Mac called. "Me and Desmond. We dodged the worst of the stampede."

"Son of a bitch, Desmond, you got yourself caught in it," the trail boss said as he rode up the hill toward them. "I bet Mac here had to pull you out. Isn't that so?"

"I—"

"We lost two horses, Mister Flowers," Mac cut in. "It was a small price to pay for both of us getting away. I had to fasten his slicker to my horse and let it lead the cattle away from us."

"You're hurt. You two get back to the supply wagon." Flowers jerked a thumb over his shoulder. "Messy can patch you up. He's handy with needle and thread, if you have cuts needin' stitches. He said that he'd worked for a tailor when he was a young sprout."

"Thanks."

"Son of a bitch," Flowers grumbled under his breath as he turned his horse, but loud enough for both men to hear. "He's bound and determined to get himself killed. Mercedes would blame me for sure." He rode away to rally the cowboys and get the herd under control.

"He blames me," Desmond said bitterly. "He blames me for everything! Probably even for the storm!"

"Not that as much as he's blaming himself if anything were to happen to you."

"What's he care?" Desmond stormed away before Mac could explain. Maybe he didn't know how Hiram Flowers felt about his ma. Or maybe he did and that caused the bad blood between them, not that he saw Flowers as unnecessarily riding Desmond. The kid was pretty dumb when it came to most things, but he'd never had a chance to be on his own and learn.

Mac trailed him to the supply wagon, where Messerschmidt was already fixing up a couple of other cowboys. Mac sat on the tailgate. Messy had retrieved a bottle of whiskey from the chuckwagon and used it liberally on the men's open cuts. Mac picked it up, looked at it a moment, then called, "Desmond. Heads up!"

He tossed the half-full bottle. Desmond caught it. He stared at it, then looked up to Mackenzie.

"Go on, take a swig. It's for medicinal purposes."

Desmond pulled the cork, lifted it to his lips, then paused. He lowered the bottle and recorked it. He tossed it back.

"Not interested." He spun around and stalked off.

"What's that all about?" Messy took the bottle from Mac. "You're not seein' me pass up a chance to take a long pull." He expertly plucked out the cork with thumb and forefinger and, using the same hand to hold the bottle, upended it. A good inch of amber fluid disappeared down his gullet. He let out a sigh and recorked the bottle.

Messerschmidt held it out to Mac, who shook his head and said, "No thanks."

"You and the kid got a pact to see who can be more mule headed?"

"Something like that." Mac had to wonder at Desmond turning down the whiskey. Deciding if that was a good sign or bad gave him something to ponder.

"Better get everything packed up and ready for the trail," Mac went on. "Flowers never said, but since the herd stampeded in the direction he intended to go, there's a meal to be fixed before long, and I had better be ready."

"I wouldn't go more 'n three miles, not in this rain. There's still a passel of men to patch up, and I don't want to leave with them leakin' blood everywhere."

"See you at dinner, Messy." Mac waved as he walked off and added over his shoulder, "Obliged for the patching up!"

He trudged back to the chuckwagon, his head hurting worse than ever. He made a quick check and saw that Desmond had cleaned up the wagon enough to press on. The rain wasn't pelting down as hard as before and might stop soon. From the crash of thunder, the storm center had moved to the north and they were traveling northwest now. Let the rain swell the Pecos even more. They were across it.

"Desmond!" He climbed onto the driver's box and looked around. "Desmond, you riding with me?" No answer. "I'm pulling out. You'll have to catch up." As Mac sat, the world spun a little before settling down. He blinked hard. Having Desmond with him to be sure he wasn't seeing double would have been a boon, but the youngster had gone off somewhere to lick his wounds and be mad at the world.

The team moved, but they were difficult to control. The sporadic rain kept them shying one way and the other, but the distant sound of the running herd worried the horses the most. They were smarter than he was, Mac reflected. They knew better than to get in the way of a stampede.

After a few minutes, the team settled down and dutifully pulled the chuckwagon along the muddy track that passed for a road. Commerce came this way, wagons and mules and men driving stagecoaches. He hunted for traces that they actually followed the Goodnight-Loving Trail and found nothing. The rain had erased such obvious marks, leaving behind only the dual ruts baked into the ground by the sun most days of the year. Mac turned up his collar to keep the cold raindrops from running down his neck.

The rain was more of a fine mist now, but he had driven through worse. His mind drifted away from driving and went to fixing a meal for the hungry cowboys. They deserved something special for all the work they'd put in this day, from getting the herd across the river to stemming the raging tide of a fullout stampede.

At the thought of the mindlessly running cattle, he reached up and touched his tender scalp. He was lucky the hoof hadn't caught him a half inch lower or it would have split open his head.

If Mac was lucky, then Desmond Sullivan was even luckier that someone had come by just as he fell off his horse. There wouldn't have been more than a trampled, bloody corpse if Mac hadn't decoyed the steers away and forced Desmond to stay low behind the rocks. As it was, they had both come close to ending their days.

"Ingrate," Mac muttered. "I saved his life, and he seems to blame me."

As he ranted and raved on, he began gesturing with one hand and then the other. Switching the reins from one hand to the other proved easy for a man used to driving the wagon. But the horses balked when they came to a steep hill. The road was muddy, and getting up to the summit required a running start.

He applied the reins, snapping them and shouting to the horses to keep them pulling. The chuckwagon worked its way up the hill, sideslipping now and then in the slick mud. Mac let out one last hoarse shout to get the team to the top. From up there it would be easy to find a spot to set up camp and feed the men.

The chuckwagon began sliding. Mac tried to get the horses to pull faster. That was the only way he had of keeping the wagon from tilting precariously. The horses simply stopped. The wagon slid faster, sideways down the hill. A last effort to have the team pull him out of his predicament failed. He heard the wagon tongue snap as the wagon tilted far on its side. Freed of their burden, the team bolted. The wagon slammed back down on all four wheels, but it was completely out of control now.

Mac screamed as the wagon slid. He tried to stand and jump off, but the speed was too great. When the chuckwagon wheels hit a rock, the world went spinning. The wagon landed on its side and kept sliding down toward the bottom of the hill.

Mac had to hang on for dear life because he was on the wrong side of the runaway. If he jumped off, the chuckwagon would go over him and crush him. The mud lubricated the way until wagon and cook fetched up hard against a rocky patch. It felt like a giant fist had slammed down on them, stopping them.

Mac tried to move but couldn't. Looking down, he saw his legs were pinned under part of the wagon. The weight felt as if it increased with every passing second. Mac realized he was weakening from the fight to get free. He sagged, taking a moment to gather his strength. When he was again aware of the world, he realized he had passed out. The rain came down harder now. The gully between hills began to fill with runoff.

And Mac was held down as the water rose around him. It would take a lot more rain for him to drown, but gully washers out on the prairie dumped inches of rain at a time. That might be more than enough. He fought to pull his legs free, and again he failed.

Flopping back down, he tried to figure out how to escape. There had to be a way, but his head hurt worse than ever. Still, that was better than what he felt from the waist down—nothing. There wasn't any feeling at all in his hips and legs.

"Help!" he called out, but his voice was weak. He had turned hoarse shouting at the horses to keep them moving in the mud.

He wasn't sure how long he lay there, half aware of the world, but finally a new sound drifted to his ears over the constant pounding of the rain. A horse was approaching.

Mac used his arms to force his body up like a snake ready to strike. In this position he saw the rider coming through the sheets of rain.

"Here. Over here!"

His heart leaped when the rider turned and rode toward him.

"Desmond, get me out from under here. The chuckwagon flipped and . . ."

Mac lost all strength, all hope, as Desmond Sullivan turned his horse's face and rode off without saying a word.

CHAPTER 15

The rain washed dirt off Mac's face and out of his eyes, allowing him to see the full extent of his problems. Wiggling around, he began scooping at the soft earth in an attempt to free his legs from under the chuckwagon. His fingers quickly turned raw and his strength faded. He lay back, gasping, letting the rain hammer down on him.

The cold water renewed his determination, if not his strength. Muscles screaming in agony, he returned to burrowing under the wagon. He finally dug a tunnel to his right leg.

He ran his fingers along his leg. No sensation. Panic rose, then anger replaced it. He should have driven better. And Desmond Sullivan should have tried to help. Instead he had ridden away, leaving him to die. Fury filled him. Mac pinched his leg and yelped as pain lanced all the way down into his foot. For a second he let that build, then he realized what the pain meant. His legs were still good, only pressed down into the mud under the weight of the chuck-wagon.

Another five minutes of digging furiously exhausted him completely. He gasped for breath and tried to think of another way to get free. Nothing came to him.

"You need help?"

The voice came from far off. Mac knew it had to be a hallucination. But what did he have to lose? He answered.

"Whatever you can do would be mightily appreciated. I don't know what more I can do for myself."

"You done good, moving that much dirt with nothing but your hands."

"What choice did I have?"

"You're a mite hoarse from shouting, but you could have called for help. Hang on."

Mac closed his eyes and smiled. He had such good hallucinations. He even thought he heard wood creaking and the pressure on his legs vanishing. A yelp escaped his lips as strong hands gripped his arms and pulled him hard and fast.

"That's got him free. Let the wagon down real gentle. I don't want it more banged up than it already is."

"We ought to push it back onto its wheels, but it'll be easier if we turn it so the front end is pointing downhill."

Mac blinked. His eyes were filled with rainwater and tears. More blinking cleared them. Hiram Flowers stood over him. The trail boss had pulled him from under the wagon. Near the chuckwagon Messerschmidt and Kleingeld held a long pole they had used to lever it up.

Walking around from the rear came Desmond Sullivan.

"It's all set to move," Desmond said. He glanced at Mac.

"You went for help," Mac said in a choked voice.

"You thought I abandoned you. Figures."

"Thank you."

"Enough of this yammering," barked Flowers. "Messy, get him back to your wagon and fix him up the best you can. You get back to riding the herd, Desmond. You, too, Kleingeld. The stampede's over, but the rain is still spooking the beeves."

Mac looked up at the trail boss. Words didn't come. His throat felt as if someone were strangling him.

"Desmond came straight to me," Flowers said. "He saved you. Nobody would have missed you until they didn't get fed."

"Nice to be needed," Mac croaked. He closed his eyes and let them move him around. It felt good to be out from under the wagon. It felt even better knowing Desmond had had a hand in saving him.

"Some folks back east would kill to get steak every day," Desmond said. "I'd kill to have a fruit pie." He cut the steaks into strips, readying them for Mac to fry.

"Fruit pie?" Mac perked up. He hobbled as he went from one kettle to another, stirring the midday meal. His legs worked but were still stiff and sore, days after the mishap with the chuckwagon.

The savory smell from the kettles made his mouth water. It took all his willpower not to sample everything every time he stirred or checked. That was how cooks got to weigh twice what any cowboy did.

"That's one thing I remember," Desmond said. "My ma fixing peach pie. Or apple. Sometimes chokeberry. It'd depend on what she could find. She'd let the pie cool on the windowsill. I'd sneak over and sit underneath, just sniffing like I was a hound dog hunting down a rabbit." Desmond let out a sigh as the memory pushed away his darker moments.

"We don't have any fruit." Mac checked the larder to be sure. They were too long into the drive for any fresh fruit to remain uneaten. Even the dried fruit had run out before they crossed the Pecos. In the week since then, since he had been trapped under the wagon, they had worked northward but kept away from towns where he might trade a cow or two for more supplies. This stretch of New Mexico was sparsely populated desert.

"I know, but having a full belly isn't the same as pleasing your taste buds."

They finished preparations for the meal, Mac's mind racing. Desmond had settled down after rescuing him and had dutifully done whatever he was told. Some resentment still simmered in the young man. That was obvious by the narrowed eyes and the facial twitches, but he had been almost bearable.

"Are you riding herd this afternoon?"

"That's what Flowers said." Some antagonism sneaked into Desmond's answer.

"I won't need your help anymore," Mac said. "I'm getting around just fine now."

"You're still limping."

"Thanks for working as my cooking wrangler. It helped having someone to lean on rather than doing it all myself."

Desmond looked at him, expression unreadable. He shrugged and went back to his work.

He had come a ways from the way he acted before they crossed the river. A powerful lot of responsibility had been dropped on his shoulders, and he had stepped up to take it on. He had saved the chuck-wagon in the middle of the river after Mac had been washed over the side. The lapse riding herd where he had almost been trampled was something that could have happened to any of the cowboys. It had been an exhausting trip across the Pecos and the entire crew had been faced with a powerful thunderstorm immediately after. If Desmond hadn't been the one falling from his horse, another could have just as easily. Mac was glad he rode by when he had to save him.

Whether Desmond had saved him out of common decency or thought of it as evening the score worried Mac. On the trail they all depended on each other. This wasn't a poker game where the winner stacked the most chips in front of him on the table. He thought back on his own experience with the Rolling J crew and how that trail boss had fared. Patrick Flagg had saved more than one of the cowboys when they got into trouble, Mac included, only to lose all his chips at the end of the trail.

Some gave, some took, everyone worked together. Where Desmond fit into the Circle Arrow cattle drive remained to be seen. But that didn't mean Mac couldn't show some gratitude for what he had done.

Humming to himself, he packed up the last of the kettles and other utensils, checked to be sure the wagon tongue repair held, then got the wagon rolling toward the spot three miles north where Hiram Flowers decided to spend the night with the herd. As he drove along, Mac kept a sharp eye out for cactus. He saw a few barrel cactus and cholla everywhere, but they wouldn't suit his needs.

An hour along the trail, he halted, secured the reins, and jumped down. His leg threatened to give way under him, then strengthened.

With a smooth move he drew his knife. Spreading his bandana on the ground, he began cutting off the seedy fruit from a prickly pear cactus. Half a hillside was covered in the spiny plant and hundreds of purple-red bulbs poked out. A quick slash with his knife separated the fruit from the spiny, succulent pad. In less than five minutes he had a couple pounds of prickly pear fruit.

He tied the corners of his bandana together and put the precious package into the back of the wagon. The next two hours passed slowly as he thought about how to fix a special dessert for Desmond to thank him and maybe to win him over from his hostile ways.

Hiram Flowers stood near a clump of cottonwoods and waved to him. Mac veered over and came to a rattling halt.

"This where you want to set up camp for the night?" Mac secured the reins and climbed down, careful not to show any injury to the trail boss.

"Exactly right. You feeling up to fixing a full meal for those hungry drovers? I can get Desmond to help."

"He's been handy but use him how you want, especially if he's needed with the herd."

"He is," Flowers said. He chewed on his lower lip, then locked eyes with Mac. "You see anybody on our back trail?"

"The men who tangled with the Comanches? I haven't seen them since that dustup." Mac hesitated to say more. Flowers would fire him if he thought for an instant that bounty hunters were after him or if he ever learned that the wanted poster was legally issued, even if Mac had been framed for a murder he would never have committed under any circumstances.

"That's what I'm thinking." Flowers broke off, stared at his boots, and said in a voice almost too low to hear, "They're after me, I think. I tangled with one of them a year back. He didn't come out of the fight ever wanting to be partners, that's for sure."

Mac's eyebrows rose. It never occurred to him that the bounty hunters were after anyone but him.

"A guilty man flees when no one pursues," Mac muttered.

"Not sure how guilty I am, if I'm right about the man leading them. He's a snake in the grass. You keep your eye peeled for them, and let me know if you see anything out of the ordinary."

"I'll do that," Mac said.

"You're the most responsible man I've got here, Mac. Thanks."

Before Mac could reply, Flowers vaulted into the

saddle and trotted away. Mac watched the trail boss go, his head buzzing again. Being kicked in the head by a longhorn hadn't done him any good. It had led to him rolling the wagon down a hill and now it kept him from thinking this through. In a way he hoped Flowers was right about their pursuers being after him to settle an old score. But the night he had overheard two of them talking led him to believe they wanted to collect a reward—from New Orleans.

He looked around and found a decent spot to set up his wagon near a pond. Lugging water caused his already bruised body to complain. Painful or not, after getting what he needed for cooking, he refilled the water barrels. They were entering harder desert and water might be impossible to find unless they turned into Apaches. The chances of that were small.

"What Apache likes fruit pie?" Mac laughed as he began working on the pie for Desmond.

Taking out the prickly pear fruit, he began skinning them. He split each open. The juicy, sticky interior was mostly seeds. He worked to get them out, then tried one of the pieces. Biting down on it produced a curious taste. Slightly bitter, but he knew ways of making it taste better. He cleaned the rest of the prickly pear fruit of spines and skins, then worked to make a crust using his biscuit mix.

He popped the entire completed pie into a Dutch oven and turned his attention to preparing the meal for a herd of hungry cowboys. By the time he finished fixing the first batch of boiled greens and a few pounds of steak, the men began riding in.

He joked with them as he served their food. He was nearing the end of the meal when Desmond rode up and dismounted. The young man's nose wrinkled, and he looked around.

"What's wrong?" Mac asked.

"I thought I smelled a pie baking."

"Just for you." Mac popped it from the Dutch oven. "It'll take a spell to cool."

"What do you mean it's for me?"

"I appreciate you getting help to pull me from under the wagon. It was a damned stupid thing I did and you saved my life."

"Hey, I want a piece of that," one of the men spoke up.

"Me too!" called another.

The cry went up from the rest of the cowboys. They crowded around and reached out with their filthy hands, but Mac whacked their knuckles with his wooden cooking spoon.

"If Desmond wants to share, he can," Mac declared. "It's his reward."

"I'll save you. Go on, try to drown yourself in that pond," Messerschmidt said. "I will wade in and save you for a piece of this pie."

The jokes made the circuit, but Mac held firm. When the pie had cooled enough he gave it to Desmond. He dug into it, ate in silence, then spat some of the seeds out.

"Pie isn't supposed to be chewy. Here, you can divvy it up." He handed the plate to Messy, who began spooning out a tiny bit to every cowboy who wanted some.

"Desmond is right," the German said. "This is terrible, Mac. You got any more?"

This set off a new round of jokes. Mac took it

good-naturedly, but he watched Desmond. For all his complaint about the pie, he had eaten a fair amount. Passing it on, saying it tasted terrible, might have been his way of sharing. He had never learned to do that gracefully.

"Help me clean up, will you, Desmond?"

"I knew it was too good to be true. You bribed me to do extra duty."

Despite the griping, Desmond threw himself into the work, and Mac finished a half hour early. The others sat around a fire, swapping lies about their love lives and how much whiskey they could drink and still shoot the eye out of a flying eagle at a hundred yards.

Desmond moved as if he was on a spring, edging away and then hesitantly returning. He wanted company—and he didn't.

"You know how to use that revolver on your hip?" Mac asked.

"What?" Desmond perked up like a prairie dog on guard duty. "You calling me out?"

"I'm asking if you know how to use it, that's all. Before I went on my first trail drive, I had my pa's revolver and no idea how dangerous I was with it. The trail boss showed me how to draw. I can tell you what all he taught me."

"Why would you do that?" Desmond turned suspicious.

"You need to know things like that, or you'll end up in a world of trouble." Mac half turned and drew. He had the Smith & Wesson out, cocked and aimed, before Desmond blinked.

"You're as fast as anyone I ever saw."

"If the only ones you ever saw throw down were drunk cowboys in Hell's Half Acre, that's not much of a compliment. Wait. Watch this." Mac turned so he faced away from Desmond and drew the S&W again, this time slowly. "See all that I did?"

"No, I was watching how you stood."

"That's good, Desmond. It's important to keep your balance. Here's how to clear leather and not shoot your own foot off."

They worked for a half hour until Mac's shoulder began to hurt.

"You practice some, and you'll be good enough," Mac said.

"Good enough for what?" Desmond demanded.

"Good enough to stay alive. Take the cartridges out when you practice the draw."

"Why?" He got bristly. "Think I'll shoot myself?"

"You need to practice getting that smoke wagon out, cocked, and then fired. Do that a hundred times, and you've wasted a wagonload of ammo."

Desmond stared at him, a poker face betraying no emotion.

"Why?"

"I told you. You can practice the draw. When you get good, we can try some target practice, though too much shooting's likely to scare the cattle."

"No, not that. Why are you doing this?"

Mac hesitated, then said, "You remind me of somebody."

"Who's that?" Desmond pressed the matter.

Mac laughed harshly as he answered, "Me. You remind me of me. Now get your ass out on night herd. Flowers will chew us both out if you're late."

Desmond went off without another word, leaving Mac with a good feeling. He saw glimmerings of a real man inside the boy. All it took to bring it out was someone treating him as an equal. At least, he hoped that was true. It'd be hell teaching Desmond to use his gun, only to have him shoot down the first cowboy who crossed him.

CHAPTER 16

Quick Willy Means couldn't see ten feet in front of him. The rain came down in sheets that might as well have been shrouds. He kept his face turned down so most of the rain pelted hard against his hat and ran off the brim, but even so he got water in his eyes and had to wipe it away to see anything.

"We got to take cover, Quick Willy," Charles Huffman said. "Ain't possible to get wetter, but we might not get any more miserable."

"Shut up." Means spoke without malice. He worried over the potential for catching up with the herd and cutting out Dewey Mackenzie. Every passing minute made it less likely.

"He's right, Willy. There's no call to go blunderin' on in this rain. It's pure hell out here. I can't tell if it's day or night." Frank Huffman stood up for his brother, which was to be expected. But the edge in his voice surprised Means. After Quick Willy had cut down Arizona Johnston, the two men had been docile enough and willing to follow his every order.

Now the rain had washed that compliance out of them.

"Find a place where it's dry. I dare you," he said.

"We're close to the river. I hear it roarin' to beat the band." Frank cupped his hand behind his ear. "That's the bad boy. I know it. Them drovers have already crossed by now."

Means looked at his pocket watch, trying to determine what time it was. The heavy clouds and driving rain obscured any sunlight trying to filter through. It could be noon or midnight for all he knew. The watch face beaded right away with water. He wiped it against his vest, then tucked the watch away. Ten o'clock. He knew it had to be morning. By now Hiram Flowers had his herd across the river, but the rain would keep him from covering any real distance once he got bogged down in the mud.

Hiram damn Flowers, Means thought. He spat. He'd fix Flowers good and proper, but only after they snared Mackenzie. Business first, then pleasure.

"Trees over yonder. I can hear the leaves snappin' in the wind." Frank pointed.

Means turned and walked his horse in that direction. Huffman probably heard the sound of blood pumping in his own ears. How could anybody hear wind in tree limbs in this weather?

His horse veered suddenly, avoiding a tree. He looked up and saw a small grove of salt cedar holding back the worst of the wind and rain. It was hardly calm or dry in the middle of the grove, but it was better than being exposed on the flatlands.

"See, Quick Willy?" Charles said. "Frank was right. He's always right."

Means dismounted and scouted the area for an even drier section. The best he found was a tiny nest between four trees growing almost trunk to trunk. He tethered his horse in the lee of another large-boled tree, took his gear, and settled down with his back to the wind.

"What're we gonna do, Quick Willy? We can't get close enough to Mackenzie to nab him. I say we shoot the son of a bitch. They'll bury him, then we dig him up and take the body back." Charles sounded pleased with his gruesome plan.

"I'm not a grave robber," Means said glumly. "Doing it that way might get their whole crew on our trail."

"They'd never abandon a drive. I've heard about their trail boss. A mean one, he is. But determined. We kill Mackenzie and he'd keep right on herding his cattle toward Fort Sumner." Frank had it all worked out, too. Neither plan suited Means.

He wanted Mackenzie alive to collect the bonus from Leclerc. And he wanted Hiram Flowers dead. They had tangled in Abilene, and Flowers had pistol-whipped him until he passed out. The man's temper then meant his death now. No one did that to Quick Willy Means. No one, especially not a decrepit old drover who never took a bath.

"The rain's lettin' up," Charles called. "Lookee there. I see sunlight. The storm's danged near blowed itself out."

"We wait a spell," Means said. They had talked him into getting off the trail and out of the rain. He'd damned well enjoy a rest. Crossing the Pecos after a rain like this would be dangerous, and resting up before they tried it would increase their chances of reaching the other side. Their numbers were too diminished to lose any more.

He'd had to shoot Johnston. The man had challenged him for leadership. But Means missed Jimmy Huffman something fierce. He had been the smartest of the Huffman boys, even though that wasn't saying much.

How Jimmy had gotten himself gunned down in Fort Worth by Mackenzie was something he wished he had seen. Mackenzie would have died on the spot. Chances were good Frank and Charles had had something to do with their brother's death and lied about what had happened.

Hat pulled down to protect his face from the rain, Quick Willy drifted off to sleep. Sounds normally brought him awake. This time it was the rain stopping. It no longer pattered against his hat to drip off onto the ground. He sat up, stretched, then shook all over like a dog getting rid of water drops.

"We hit the trail. You men rested?"

"Ready to go, Willy." Frank kicked his brother to get him moving. For two cents, Means would have kicked them both just to vent some of his frustration. Tracking down Mackenzie had been a hell of a lot harder than he'd anticipated.

He would never give up, never stop hunting until he brought the murdering son of a bitch back. Preferably alive and hobbled in shackles, but if Mackenzie had to catch a few ounces of lead, Means wouldn't shed any tears over that, either.

They rode to the banks of the raging Pecos River. The turbulence looked worse than he expected. Means rode up and down the river for a quarter of a mile, hunting for an easier way across. In spite of the heavy rain, he saw tracks where Flowers had driven his herd across the river. From what he could tell, Flowers was a capable enough trail boss. He had been along this trail before and had to know the best spots to camp and to cross.

"This is it," Means said.

"I dunno, Quick Willy," Charles said, his voice slow and betraying a touch of fear. "That there river's runnin' mighty fast. We get caught in the current and we're goners. If the horse tires, we're goners, too."

"You don't start now, and you're a goner." Means rested his hand on the butt of his revolver. Even a dimwit like Charles Huffman got the message. Pulling his hat down until it mashed into his ears, Huffman let out a rebel yell and got his horse running as fast as he could into the water.

Means doubted this was a smart thing to do, then he saw how Huffman plunged a dozen yards into the swiftly flowing river. The horse tried to balk, but by then it was too late. All the horse could do was swim for the far bank. Huffman yelled and tried to put his spurs to the horse's flanks, but underwater that goad didn't amount to much.

"Can't let little brother have all the fun," Frank Huffman said. He duplicated Charles's plunge into the water and soon only his horse's head and everything above his own shoulders were visible.

Determined not to let his men show him up, Quick Willy Means rode to the edge of the water. He rushed in as they had worked, but he got his horse into the river gradually. Twice the horse denied him, then finally committed itself to the swift current. Means fought the river, in spite of it carrying him across at an angle. After what seemed an eternity, his horse found solid ground and pulled them onto the far bank. Both of the Huffman brothers already waited for him, shaking water off.

"Flowers got across without ending up this far downstream," Means said. He found deep, water-filled ruts left by a wagon. Whether this was the chuckwagon with its quarry or the supply wagon driven by one of the cowboys, he couldn't tell.

And it didn't matter. Both would follow the herd. Means only had to follow one set of tracks and Mackenzie would miraculously appear, the pot of gold at the end of the rainbow.

"They're makin' good time," Frank observed. "They crossed this morning, rode out the storm, and then pushed on. I don't see hide nor hair of them around."

"North," Means said. "If we ride hard we can over-take them before they set up camp for the evening. I want Mackenzie. That'll be the best time to grab him, before he's surrounded by all the cowboys as they chow down."

"Ground's kinda muddy, Willy. We ain't gonna make much speed in this slop. You got a plan to snatch him after the cowboys are fed?" Charles wrung out his bandana and mopped at his forehead. Water leaked out from under the hatband.

He turned away from the gunman and picked out the details of the trail they had to follow. Keeping tabs on his men wasted his time and annoyed them.

More than once he had given perfectly good advice, only to have the recipient consider it an insult and call him out for it.

Means's fight was with Mackenzie—and Hiram Flowers. Let Huffman drown himself by inches or all at once if he pulled off his hat.

It turned dark again as new storm clouds blew in. It was after sundown before he sighted the Circle Arrow camp. Anger welled up inside Means. Mackenzie had cleaned up and sat at a campfire with a half dozen cowboys. Even if he crawled into his bedroll under the chuckwagon, the number of drovers nearby would be difficult to avoid. The smallest disturbance—and they were all on edge, constantly listening for any threat to the herd—and they'd be up, revolvers ready. Anyway, creeping into camp would make him and the Huffmans look like sneak thieves, and Means wouldn't stand for that.

"We can wait for him to feed the sorry lot of 'em, then grab him when he heads off on his own in the morning." Frank picked at his teeth with the tip of a big knife.

Means knew that was the smart thing to do. But he was at the end of his tether. Chasing Mackenzie for so long had built up frustration that boiled over.

"We're not waiting," he said. "I want him as quick as possible."

"If Jimmy and Arizona was still with us, we could hurrah their camp, then you could sneak in and snatch Mackenzie." Frank Huffman finished cleaning his teeth and slipped the knife back into a sheath at his left side.

"We're shorthanded, that's for certain sure," Charles

said, agreeing with his brother. "What are we gonna do, Quick Willy?"

"That one, the kid with the red hair and strut in the way he walks. Him and Mackenzie spent a long time together at the campfire."

"So?"

"So they must be friends," Means said. "The red-haired kid is saddling up to ride night herd. We'll take him prisoner and use him as bait in a trap. A note will let Mackenzie know what he's up against, and if he tells any of the others, we'll kill his partner."

"That's a hell of a lot to put into a note. You reckon he can read?" Frank scratched himself.

"You're right about that, Frank," his brother said. "Can you write, Willy?"

Means glared at the two of them. Insulting his education was no more than he expected from them, but Charles had posed an actual problem. What if Mackenzie couldn't read?

"To hell with that. We'll take on an army, if we have to. We take the kid prisoner, find a spot to lay our ambush, and it won't matter if only Mackenzie or Mackenzie and the rest of the cowboys fall into the trap."

"Either way, we got Mackenzie," Frank said, nodding slowly.

Means found an old wanted poster and a pencil in his saddlebags. Chewing his tongue, he wrote the note that would lure Mackenzie away from the Circle Arrow and into shackles all the way back to New Orleans. He finished and studied his handiwork.

"This will do. Now all we need to do is nab the red-headed kid."

"I'm up for it." Charles grinned.

"Me, too," his brother added, but with less enthusiasm. Frank thought a moment, then asked, "Where're we gonna lay the ambush? Should we find a place and then kidnap him?"

"I know Flowers. He'll insist on keeping the herd moving. It doesn't matter if we have the perfect spot. Anywhere will do."

Frank Huffman looked skeptical, but Means didn't care. His patience was at an end. The time had come to grab Mackenzie, get the reward, and move on. As he rode to skirt the camp on his way to take the red-headed cowboy prisoner, he considered his alliance with the Huffman brothers. They weren't what he looked for in a partner anymore. Their brother had been the reason he teamed up with them. Once Jimmy took the bullet in his heart, Charles's and Frank's usefulness died with him.

"This is gonna be easy. He's doin' exactly what we want." Charles let out a whoop that drew the rider's attention.

Charles Huffman didn't have the sense God gave a goose. Now Means had to act too soon, too close to the camp.

The red-haired rider looked around but didn't reach for his revolver. That was a good sign. Means waved all friendly-like and trotted over to him.

"Howdy, mister. This the Circle Arrow herd?"

The cowboy got a sullen look and answered, "What's it to you?"

"I'm looking for a gent named Mackenzie. Dewey Mackenzie. You know him?" Mean rode closer so they were knee to knee.

"He's the cook. If you got any quarrel with him, you got to go through me first."

"Friends, are you? Good friends?" Before the cowboy answered, Quick Willy Means showed how he got the moniker. He drew his pistol left-handed and swung it in a wide arc that landed across the kid's nose.

The redhead threw up his hands to his broken, bleeding nose. Means drew with his right and jammed that pistol into the cowboy's exposed gut.

"You're coming with us. First, we got to leave a message for your good friend Dewey Mackenzie." He slipped his left pistol back into its holster so he could grab the cowboy's hat, put the note inside, and then yank the knife from the boy's belt. With a show of dexterity he rammed the knife through the hat crown and tossed, backhanded, hat and knife toward a tree. The blade dug deep, leaving the hat hanging as a signpost.

"He'll come for you. He's good with a gun." The cowboy used the end of his bandana stuffed up his nose to slow the bleeding.

"Yeah, he killed our brother. I want a piece of him." Charles Huffman rode over and tried to cuff the prisoner. The boy ducked so Charles missed and almost fell from his horse. "You little—"

"Enough of that," Means snapped. "We need to finish up. Our plan. We need to finish our plan." Means wondered if he had to repeat it a third time for Charles to get the idea that staying this close to the herd abusing one of the cowboys was a bad idea.

He motioned with his drawn gun for the boy to ride west. Seeing how his prisoner tensed and looked around furtively made him cock his revolver to emphasize the futility of trying to escape.

"You're holding me for ransom? Flowers won't give so much as a cow chip for me. He hates me."

"If you don't shut up, I'll take to hating you, too. You wouldn't like that. Faster." Means galloped hard when the captive lit out. If he thought to escape by outrunning his captors, he was wrong.

Means considered whether to make the young man dead wrong about that. A hostage added to complications he wanted to avoid. Most often he walked up to the fugitive he wanted to take in and shoved a gun in their gut. Using a hostage to get to Mackenzie was a hitch in an otherwise simple plan.

The three bounty hunters caught up to the redhead. The Huffman brothers flanked him while Means brought up the rear.

"Up there, Willy." Charles stood in his stirrups as he rode and gestured wildly. "That's a good spot."

Means took in what Huffman claimed about the terrain. For once, the idiot had it right.

"You and Frank get up on the hillside behind those rocks," Means ordered. "They don't give much cover, but you shouldn't need much. Take your rifles. If anything goes wrong, open fire and kill as many of them as you can."

This order caused Charles to grin from ear to ear. He and Frank galloped off to find decent spots to command the hollow where Means intended to stake out the cowboy to lure Mackenzie.

"Get off your horse," he ordered.

The redhead reluctantly obeyed. He had a truculent look that belied his position. Two men with rifles covered him, and Quick Willy Means could draw and fire twelve times before the youngster could even touch the butt of his revolver. Means staked out his horse and the cowboy's mount to one side and pointed to a rock exposed to anyone following the trail they had laid out.

"You didn't try to cover your tracks," the boy said. "You want to make it easy to find me. Well, nobody's gonna come. They don't like me. Flowers downright hates me because—"

"Shut up. Yammering the way you do bores me." Means drew and pointed his gun at the prisoner's head when he started to protest more. "Another word and I blow your brains out. I'll prop you up so from a distance nobody can tell you're dead."

The boy sucked in breath to protest, then let it out slowly when he realized Quick Willy Means didn't bluff. He meant what he said. The youngster sank to the rock and slumped forward, eyes on the ground as he muttered to himself.

Means walked around to find a better angle to shoot Mackenzie, if it came to that. He settled down behind another rock and considered what to do about the hostage. Letting him go free after they nabbed Mackenzie made no sense. Even if they tied him up and left him for the cowboys to find, he could identify them later. Means didn't care if he spilled his guts to a federal marshal and identified the Huffmans. Having the law breathing down *his* neck was another matter.

"You really don't think they'll come for you? That's a shame. If they don't, this is where you'll die." Means prodded his captive to see what response he got.

"He made me a fruit pie."

"What? What are you talking about?" Means perked up. The words showed how loco everyone working for the Circle Arrow ranch was.

"A pie. He didn't have to do that, but he did. Mac will come for me."

"That's what I'm counting on. I just don't want to wait forever. I get mighty impatient."

"Willy! Willy!"

Means looked up to where Charles stood, waving his arm frantically to get his attention. Before he shouted for the man to get back into hiding, he took a hard look along their back trail. A smile slowly curled his lips. The wait had been brief.

And it was over now. His hunt was over. Dewey Mackenzie made his way along the trail, eyes on the ground as he followed the hoofprints in the soft dirt. If he failed to look up in another minute, he would be in the middle of a firing squad of two rifles and both of Means's guns.

Quick Willy Means settled his mind and held his hands relaxed and ready over each holster. The moment of truth was at hand.

Chapter 17

Mac forced himself to keep his eyes on the ground. The tracks of at least four riders showed where Desmond had been taken. The difference in horseshoes made it obvious that Desmond rode flanked by the others. Mac's hand twitched, moving toward the gun holstered at his side, but he covered the action by scratching his belly.

He knew perfectly well where the gang that had kidnapped Desmond was. He had to pretend he didn't and that he was riding heedlessly into their ambush.

Mac slowed and finally stopped, as if confused about the trail. The earth, soft from the rains, took the prints well. He needed to play for time. He swung down from the saddle and continued pretending to study the tracks.

Then ignoring the outlaws was no longer possible. One of them stood up from behind a rock and called out to him.

Mac looked up. He tried to make it seem like he was taken by surprise.

"Come on over, or I'll put a bullet in his head." The man held a pistol to Desmond's temple. He thumbed back the hammer with an ominous sound.

For his part, Desmond showed great courage. He didn't flinch.

"There's no call for you to shoot him," Mac said. "What do you want in the way of ransom?"

"Ransom?" The man laughed harshly. "What'll you give me for him?"

"Five hundred head of cattle. That's half of what we have left."

Mac knew who he dealt with by the way the gunman jerked around and eyed his prisoner in surprise.

The reaction told Mac they had kidnapped Desmond to get him to surrender and had no idea who they held. He recognized the man from Fort Worth and later as the leader of the bounty hunters on his trail.

"Why so much for this kid? It's you we want, Mackenzie."

"I reckoned so," Mac said, slowly walking closer. He hunted for the others in the gang. At least two more lurked somewhere nearby, maybe three. He wished he had read sign better.

"Why's he worth so much?" The gunman moved around, standing half behind Desmond now, making a shot more difficult.

"You're bounty hunters. You want me. Let him go and take me."

"Who we got here?" the man insisted. "Is he wanted, too? If you wanted to buy me off with that many head, he must be somebody important. He's too young to be the rancher who owns that herd."

"I'm not that young," Desmond blurted. "My ma'd never give over that many beeves as ransom."

"Your ma?" the gunman laughed harshly. "This is my lucky day. I got me a fugitive from the law *and* a sprout who can get me half of that great, big herd."

Desmond should have kept his mouth shut when the bounty hunter revealed he had no idea who he had kidnapped. Mac couldn't blame the boy too much. He had planted that seed himself, trying to make sure these men were the bounty hunters who had been pursuing him.

His presence on the drive had been a fuse burning down to a keg of giant powder. When he learned that the bounty hunters were still on his trail, he should have left the Circle Arrow crew and hightailed it as far away from the drovers as possible. He respected Hiram Flowers and liked the others working for Mercedes Sullivan. Bringing down the wrath of these bounty killers on them was a great disservice.

"This is between us," Mac said loudly. "You don't want him."

Desmond struggled as the gunman circled his neck with a strong arm. The bounty hunter used him as a shield now.

"Drop your gun, murderer. Now!"

Mac looked around, trying to find the rest of the bounty hunters. No sign of them. His heart beat faster as he suddenly stepped behind the horse and used the animal as a shield just as Means used Desmond.

When he disappeared, he flushed out two more men. They popped up from the rocks higher on the hill, rifles in their hands. One had the stock snugged to his shoulder, ready to shoot. The other held his Winchester slanted across his chest.

Mac was done talking. His hand flashed to his gun. He felt like a machine, a smoothly oiled machine built to draw the Smith & Wesson, aim, cock, and fire. The first round sailed uphill to the bounty hunter with the rifle to his shoulder and knocked him back a half step.

Letting the momentum of his draw spin him around, Mac got off a shot at the second bounty hunter, the one lackadaisically holding his rifle. This shot went wide. He whirled in a complete circle and dropped to a knee, ignoring the men on the hill because the leader slugged Desmond with the revolver, then opened fire.

Mac had counted on the man's greed keeping him from putting a bullet through Desmond's head, and so far that hunch was right.

Mac got off a couple more shots as slugs whined over his head. To his surprise, the leader stood his ground. The man pulled his second gun and blazed away, right, left, right, left. His marksmanship was off, and that saved Mac. But at least one slug hit his horse and caused it to rear and paw at the air with its hooves.

Dodging the flying hooves as well as the bounty hunter's increasingly accurate fire sent Mac diving forward to skid along in the mud on his belly. Trying to aim as he slid proved impossible. All he could do was throw enough lead in the leader's direction to make him take cover behind a rock.

One round remained in the S&W's cylinder, but Mac reloaded as he wiggled his way to a shallow ditch. Rainwater stood a couple inches deep. Partly

submerged, he aimed in the leader's direction but
conserved his ammunition.

"Throw down that six-gun, Mackenzie. Give up
now or I'll plug your friend. What is he? Heir to the
ranch? What's his ma gonna think if you get away
alive and her son's caught a bullet in the head? Any
more menfolk left to inherit?"

Mac's bile rose. He held it down because he knew
the man intended to rile him, make him mad enough
to show himself. The best he could do was cover
Desmond, but the bounty hunter had a clear shot at
him from behind the rock.

"I got him, Willy. I got him in my sights!"

The shrill shout made Mac shift his attention back
uphill. The bounty hunter he had driven back readied his rifle, but he was aiming at Desmond. Resting
the butt of his pistol on the ground to steady it, Mac
drew back the trigger. Again he missed. The range
was too great for a handgun.

"I'm gonna kill that little son of a bitch!"

As the man stepped up to put his foot on a rock, a
shot echoed through the draw. Mac winced. He
thought the bounty hunter had fired. Then he saw
the man jerk around. A second shot took the man's
legs from under him. Flailing, he began sliding down
the hill. When he came to a halt at the bottom of the
slope, he lay unmoving.

"Charles!" the other man hidden in the rocks cried.
"You killed my brother, you bastard! You killed Jimmy
and now you killed my little brother!"

The man showed himself and charged down the
hill in blind rage. This time Mac began firing steady,
sending his lead dead on target, then aiming a little

left, a little right, and back to center. His hammer fell on an empty chamber with the last shot.

But he had hit his man at least twice and maybe three times. The bounty hunter sat down, out of sight, but no further cries of revenge came from him.

Reloading again, Mac wiggled forward in the shallow water. The sounds alerted the remaining bounty hunter, the leader of the bunch.

"Enough. You killed my men. You don't give up right now, I'll kill this one." The bounty hunter hauled Desmond half upright and shoved a gun into his spine. "Out where I can see you. Now. Do it now or I swear he dies."

"Don't give up, Mac," Desmond said as he thrashed about weakly. His captor shook him hard to make him stop trying to get away.

Mac called out, "Don't shoot him. I'm surrendering."

"No, no, Mac!"

"Let him go and—"

"Toss out your gun or I start shooting," the bounty hunter rasped. "Maybe only a bullet to his legs. He won't walk again. He won't ever ride one of his mama's horses or brand another of her calves. Throw down your gun!"

Mac slid his revolver into his holster and stepped out.

"You can hide behind him all you want, but if you shoot Desmond, I'll kill you."

"You want to face me down?"

"I think I heard you called Quick Willy. You really quick or are you just good at telling people you are?"

The man shoved Desmond out in front of him.

Mac looked for an opening, but the bounty hunter was too clever to expose much. Drawing and shooting at a patch of shoulder or an exposed leg wouldn't work. Rather than rush it, Mac waited. It was the hardest thing he had ever done, but he bided his time because he knew the man would make a mistake.

He had to if Desmond and a cook wanted for murder in New Orleans were going to escape alive.

"I'm faster than you," the bounty hunter said, "but I'm not stupid enough to try your hand. You're a killer, and I am entrusted to bring you in."

"So you're not that quick."

"I don't get mad, either. I'm too smart for that."

Desmond moved without warning. Instead of jerking away, he drove his elbow hard into his captor's belly. The bounty hunter's gun roared. Desmond groaned and Mac's hand flashed for his revolver.

The bounty hunter jerked as Mac's bullet sent his hat flying. He started firing the gun in his right hand as his left whipped out the other pistol. Mac found himself standing in a windstorm of lead. He crouched low and triggered again, but nothing happened. He knew he wasn't empty, so the cartridge must have misfired.

The bounty hunter yelled in triumph. Mac thumbed the hammer and got off another shot but missed. As he fired again, he knew there wouldn't be another chance.

The man grunted and took a step back.

"Damnation," he said. He clutched his right side.

Mac saw the hole in the bounty hunter's body begin to bleed. He shook off his shock and fanned the rest of his cylinder as he came to his feet. His wild fusillade joined another as a rifle high up behind him began firing.

The bounty hunter kept firing as he backed away and fell behind a rock. Rifle bullets spanged off it. In spite of the chance he would catch a ricochet, Mac ran forward and grabbed Desmond's arm. Digging in his heels, he pulled the young man out of the line of fire. They flopped back into the shallow muddy ditch.

"Are you hurt?" Mac hunted in his coat pocket for more cartridges. He found only three more rounds. With a snap, he broke open the S&W and ejected the spent brass. Working methodically, he inserted the three cartridges and snapped it shut.

"I don't think so. You risked your life to save me." Desmond stared at Mac as if he had grown another head.

"Not just me. That's Flowers with the rifle."

"He came to get me, too?"

Mac started to give a bad-tempered reply to that, but he held back. The threat remained. The bounty hunter was still dangerous. Until he saw the man's body, Mac couldn't let his guard down for an instant.

"Stay here."

"I can help," Desmond insisted.

"You'll get hurt. Stay put." Mac waved and from out of nowhere Hiram Flowers came huffing and puffing, his rifle pointed ahead of him.

"Did I get the varmint?"

"That's the man you were talking about? Quick Willy?"

"Quick Willy Means. We crossed paths before. He didn't come out so good." Flowers stared hard at

Mac. "He's after you, even if he knows me. He didn't want Desmond for ransom."

"Until Desmond told him, Means didn't even know who he was. And yeah, he's after me."

"The son of a bitch." Flowers checked his rifle to be sure the magazine was full. "Let's go get him."

"He's a bounty hunter and he and his gang have been after me."

"What? Can't hear you, Mac."

"I said—"

Abruptly, Mac shut his mouth. He realized that Flowers wanted to hear nothing of his past. It was enough that Flowers hunted Means for other reasons, for whatever had happened when they met before, for kidnapping Desmond. An attempt to take his cook back to New Orleans to stand trial wasn't necessary to add to the list of reasons Means had to die.

The bounty hunter was gone from behind the rocks, but he had left a trail of blood drops. With Flowers behind him, Mac began hunting for Means in earnest. Every step felt like his last. He knew Means intended to ambush him. "Dead or alive," read the wanted poster. A man willing to use Desmond as bait hardly cared about the condition of his quarry.

As he moved around the hillside, it occurred to Mac that the bounty hunter, although wounded, might check to see if either of his henchmen were alive. Revolver at the ready, Mac headed for the bodies while Flowers continued searching farther along the slope.

Both men were dead, and there was no sign of Means. Mac looked down at what appeared to be the older of the two brothers and shook his head. This one, Frank Huffman from the papers in his jacket pocket Mac pulled out, looked to be the twin of the man he had shot back in Fort Worth.

"Mac, over here," Flowers called. "I found the trail."

Mac hurried to join him. The trail boss knelt on the rocky ground and pointed out a blood smear. Means had bled enough to form a puddle and then carelessly stepped in it. Flowers pointed ahead to a sandy ravine.

"I'll go," Mac said. "Back me up."

"I'm not letting you have all the fun of killing that varmint."

Mac had no time to argue. The messy footprint had to be a trap. If it wasn't, Means had bled more freely than Mac expected from a wound through his side.

Flowers moved five yards away, and they advanced together. They reached the bank of the arroyo and poked their heads over the rim at the same time. Mac saw immediately that they were too late. Judging by the piles of dung, four horses had been staked out here. The one Desmond had taken from the remuda, a swayback mare long past its prime, stood beside a better quality horse.

"He got on his horse and took a spare. Catching him's going to be a full-time job." Flowers looked at Mackenzie. "That a job you intend on taking?"

Mac considered all the things he could do. Quick Willy Means was wounded, perhaps fatally. But if he wasn't, he might decide to stay on Mac's trail. That meant he should be tracked down and taken care of.

"We've got a herd to drive north."

"To Fort Sumner?"

"To Fort Sumner," Mac said. He looked down the sandy arroyo and hoped he was doing the right thing by letting Means get away. They would be at the Army post in another few days and the drive would be over. Disappearing would be easier with a pocketful of money he had earned.

CHAPTER 18

Dewey Mackenzie kept looking over his shoulder. Every bump in the trail made him sure he was going to slide down an embankment and be pinned under the wagon. Every strange noise caused him to reach for his revolver. He was driving himself loco.

"It'll be over soon. We're almost to Fort Sumner," he said over and over. It had been a week since he and Flowers had rescued Desmond from the bounty hunters. Two of the killers had become worm food. Burying the brothers seemed like a kindness they did not deserve, but Mac, Desmond, and Flowers had clawed out a shallow grave for one of them. The other's body was missing, likely dragged away by coyotes. Neither Mac nor Flowers had been willing to spend more time hunting for it. None of the bounty hunters deserved that kind of consideration.

He hadn't even wanted to say words over it, but Flowers had insisted. But the trail boss drew the line at putting a grave marker of any kind over the body. They deserved to be anonymous. Mac didn't even want a casual traveler to look over and wonder who was buried in the grave. He wanted them wiped from all human memory or thought.

A second grave would have been satisfying, but a third grave for Quick Willy Means would have satisfied him most. But with the bounty hunter escaped and on his own, that small pleasure had been denied him. As Mac drove, he made a gun out of thumb and forefinger and relived the fight that had freed Desmond. Moving to one side, he could have plugged Means. Or if Desmond had acted sooner. Or . . .

"Bang." He curled his thumb in mock firing. "He should have been a dead man."

There was no changing the fight. Desmond was safe. Two of the bounty hunters had gotten what they deserved. And the herd was within a day of Fort Sumner. The end of the drive, if they sold the beeves to the Army. Otherwise, it was on to Santa Fe or even Denver.

This journey had been entirely different from his drive to Abilene. The dangers changed, and the dread of a bounty hunter breathing down his neck caused him to be jumpy. But they hadn't lost near as many cattle as on his other drive, in spite of the dangerous Pecos crossing and the storm and stampede afterward. The Comanches hadn't made off with many cattle, and there had been few towns along the way to demand tribute in exchange for passage. Texas was wide open and lonely country, as was this part of New Mexico Territory.

Mac liked that.

He jerked around, his revolver out and ready as he heard a galloping horse closing on the chuckwagon from behind. When he saw Hiram Flowers, he slipped the pistol back into the holster.

"No call to be that jumpy, Mac. If Means didn't bleed to death a hundred miles behind us, he gave up."

"Means didn't have the look of a man who would give up. And we never found the other brother's body."

"Is that why every night you take a horse and ride back along the trail? Looking for any trace of him?"

Mac changed the subject by asking, "What's ahead? I've never been to Fort Sumner before."

He felt uneasy talking about the bounty hunters they had cut down. He realized he was turning into a belt-and-suspenders man, never feeling quite secure enough. Seeing the bullet-riddled bodies of his enemies would have smoothed his ruffled feathers.

"The only time I was there was with Desmond's pa," Flowers said in answer to Mac's question about their destination. "The post is an important one for the Army, and they like to keep it well supplied, but that's not saying too much. Their paymaster up at Fort Union, north of Santa Fe, sorta forgets about frontier outposts now and again. They might be flush with money to buy beef or they might not have two nickels to rub together. Since they closed Bosque Redondo and let the Navajos and Mescaleros go back to their reservations, there's not much going on at the post. We're going to put the herd to pasture to fatten them up for a week or so while me and you go on into the post to palaver with the quartermaster."

"Why not bring Desmond along?" Mac suggested. "This is his herd, more or less."

Flowers rubbed his stubbled chin and nodded.

"Good idea, Mac. You've got a head on your shoulders. I hope you'll consider stayin' with the Circle Arrow after the drive. Most of them cowboys will head for other jobs. I'd appreciate it if you considered staying on permanent-like."

Mac had been afraid Flowers would ask him to do this very thing. Only willpower kept him from glancing back again, just to be sure Means wasn't catching up. Or some other bounty hunter Pierre Leclerc had set on his trail. Returning to the Circle Arrow outside Fort Worth would give him a permanent address and make it easier for anyone hunting for him to find him. But he liked Flowers. Hell, he even liked Desmond, just a little.

And his curiosity was eating him alive about Flowers and Mercedes Sullivan. How would that romance turn out, even if Flowers was down in the mouth about even saying more than "Good morning, ma'am" to the lovely ranch owner?

"Is this all open range? We just find a patch of grass and let the cattle graze?"

"That's about it. Most of the countryside is Spanish land grant. The king of Spain deeded it to his loyal soldiers and financial backers more'n a hundred years ago. Parts are open. New ranchers have moved in, but they don't have much claim to the land, unless they buy it from the Spanish. Then the Mexicans have come up with their herds and ways in the past ten or fifteen years. In spite of so many folks crowding in, there's plenty of land for us to use."

Mac looked into the hazy distance to the west where purple mountains rose. The Sacramento Mountains, he had been told. It was quite a ways over there. And the land between was prime grassland, perfect for fattening cattle. The Circle Arrow beeves would appreciate it.

"You going right on into town?" Mac tried to settle down. Losing himself in the middle of a crowd, even if the town was as small as Fort Sumner, pleased him. A drink or two would go down the gullet smooth and warm after being on the trail so long.

"Park the chuckwagon and let's go. And it's a good idea to take Desmond with us." Flowers added dryly, "You can look after him."

Mac bristled, then saw Flowers was joking. He smiled ruefully.

It took the better part of an hour to get the wagon set up and the team tended to before he joined Flowers and Desmond. Both were antsy about getting into town.

"Sure are a lot of cattle around here," Desmond said. "Can we get a fair price?"

"Doesn't matter that much," Flowers said. "If they won't buy our beeves, we'll push on to Santa Fe or even Denver and sell them there. The railroad can ship them west, and we'll see a handsome profit."

"That's another six hundred miles," Mac said. Staying with the Circle Arrow outfit that much longer worried him. Then he decided Denver was as good a place to part company as Fort Sumner. It added another month of pay to his poke, and the company wasn't all that bad.

"There's the Army purchasing office. Let's get business out of the way," Flowers said.

The town looked like any other sleepy southwest-

ern settlement. Mac guessed the Army post lay somewhere to the north. Places like this were peaceable
enough, especially after the Navajos had been sent
packing from Bosque Redondo. The Apaches who
had been on the reservation with them trickled back
to their homes in the Sacramento Mountains and beyond. Yes, sir, this was a quiet enough place now.

"Do I have to go? Business bores me."

Both Mac and Flowers glared at Desmond. He reluctantly dismounted and followed the trail boss into
the cramped office.

Inside was cool because of the thick adobe walls
and small windows. A few maps provided the only
wall decorations. A lieutenant sat behind the battered desk poring over a ledger. His uniform was
crisp and he looked hardly old enough to have grad-
uated from West Point, although the heavy ring on
his finger told a different story. His rumpled blond
hair showed he had worn his hat recently and had
not bothered to comb the mop. That told Mac the
officer had arrived just ahead of them. From his expression when he saw who walked into his office,
Mac doubted they'd be in Fort Sumner longer than
it took to let the cattle rest and graze.

He was both right and wrong.

"What's the Army's need for cattle? We got a herd
of prime longhorns waiting to be bought and et by
hungry soldiers," Flowers said.

"The Army's got quite a need for fresh meat, sir."
The lieutenant pointed to a single chair. Flowers
took it while Mac stood to one side and Desmond
prowled about the sparse office, bored.

"Then we can do business. I—"

"Wait. Before you go on, let me inform you about our . . . situation."

"There's no situation we can't handle," Flowers said with some confidence.

"Our operating funds have been held up for another few weeks. In truth, I am not sure when the funds will arrive. They are being sent down from Fort Union."

"Fort Union's up north," Mac said. "On the trail to Denver. Maybe we can drive the herd up that direction and sell there."

"I am sure they would appreciate such a gesture, though Union is the central supply depot for all of New Mexico Territory. They, of all the posts, will have adequate supplies." The lieutenant got a sour look. "Unlike here. We struggle in the midst of plenty."

"Plenty of cattle, you mean?"

The lieutenant nodded.

"Our problem is keeping a cork tamped into a bottle full of animosity here. The ranchers engage in what amounts to war between one another, and—" He stopped suddenly, took a breath, and let it out slowly. "That is none of your concern. If you wait a week, we will dicker for your cattle, or at least some of them, depending on how many you offer."

"Got close to nine hundred head," Flowers said.

"More than we need, but we can use two hundred head immediately."

"Fork over some money and you've got a deal."

"You weren't listening, Mister Flowers," Mac said, eyeing the officer carefully. "They don't have one red cent."

"Not right now. I can issue an IOU guaranteed by the U.S. Army, to be paid when our disbursement funds arrive."

"But you don't know when that'll be?"

The answer was written on the lieutenant's face. Not only did he not know, there was a chance the money would never arrive.

"I have to pay my hands. Giving them a piece of paper with a mark on it promising pay at some future time isn't going to set well with any of them. It don't with me, either."

"Then, sir, I suggest you find other markets for your beef. As much as the military's need for it is great, you must either sell elsewhere or wait."

"Reckon that settles the matter. We'll wait." Flowers cleared his throat. "We'll wait and find some other market."

Mac wondered how often the lieutenant had heard those very words. The young man closed the ledger and leaned forward, elbows on the desk. It wobbled a little because one leg was shorter than the others. The lieutenant adjusted unconsciously, used to it.

"Selling around here might be more difficult than you realize. I do, however, wish you luck. Good day."

Dismissed, they left and stepped out into the bright New Mexico sun. Mac pulled his hat brim down to shield his eyes. The hat almost fell to pieces. The crown had been kicked out by a cow, and a couple of bullet holes in the brim had grown until they were the size of a two-bit piece. If he'd received his trail pay, he would have gone hunting for a new hat.

"I need to ask around about selling some of the

cattle. If I get enough, we'll have money to buy supplies to get us to Denver." Flowers shook his head. "I'd prefer to sell here to the Army. What do you think the chances are of them seeing any money soon?"

Mac had no idea. Desmond said, "Hanging around for a while isn't going to hurt us. I'm not looking forward to another drive, this time all the way up to Denver."

"You can always go back to Fort Worth," Mac said. He had a sour taste in his mouth from hearing the lieutenant's tale of woe and why the Army wasn't in the market for cattle right now. Getting what was owed him wasn't possible. He knew how low on cash Flowers was. Without the cattle being sold, nobody on the drive would get paid.

"Trying to get rid of me? Because you're embarrassed at baking such a terrible fruit pie? You ought to be. I've still got seeds stuck between my teeth."

Mac started to snap back, then realized this was the first time Desmond had made any kind of a joke. Desmond was funning him when all he had done until now was gripe his fool head off. That was real progress.

"Go on, find a window and sit under it so you can smell a cooling pie and tell me mine wasn't better."

"The only way it'd be better is that I can't afford to buy even a slice, no matter what it's made from," Desmond said.

"Here, you two. I've got almost fifty cents. Go get yourselves some pie." Flowers looked disgusted. "Real men would buy a drink, but no, I got a cook and a drover who want *pie*. Get on along now. I have to do some business so we can all get a shot of real rotgut."

The trail boss stalked off, leaving Mac and Desmond on their own.

"There's a restaurant that looks like it sells pie." Mac pointed to a hole-in-the-wall adobe building down the street. A buggy parked to the side gave the only hint that the place was open for business.

They went in and looked around the cool, dim dining room. Both men froze when they saw the lone customer.

Mac forced himself to let out the breath he unconsciously held. He had seen prettier women in his day, but right now he couldn't remember where or when.

The young woman at the back table eating with precise bites wore a Mexican-style dress, bright and cheerful and matching her looks perfectly. She glanced up and smiled almost shyly. Mac thought the sun had come out. Her dark eyes and delicate face, high cheekbones, and carefully plucked eyebrows showed both intelligence and genteel upbringing.

"I want what she's having," Desmond said.

"Sit down and let's order. We've got no call to bother her while she's eating." Mac's mind raced trying to find such a reason to introduce himself. If he had known the women in Fort Sumner looked this lovely, he wouldn't have complained at all about the trail drive. The destination was worthy of shooting his way through murderous bounty hunters and crossing swollen rivers.

"What'll you gents like?" The waiter gave them a

quick once-over and said, "You're likely sick of steak. Got good fried chicken."

"Pie," Desmond said. "What kind of pie do you have?"

"I knew it. You're straight off the trail and haven't seen any fruit in a spell. Well, you're in luck. We got peach and we got apple."

"All right," Mac said.

"Which will it be?" The waiter grinned. "Both? A slice of each for both of you?"

"That'll be so close to heaven that I am speechless," Desmond said.

"If you knew him, you'd know how unusual that is." Mac enjoyed being able to joke with Desmond. All it took to break through his arrogance was saving him from a stampede, rescuing him from being kidnapped, and serving up a prickly pear pie that was hardly fit for consumption by man or beast.

The pie came. Both men tucked into it. Mac started with the peach, Desmond the apple. It looked like a race to the last crumb when they each finished. They leaned back and eyed the spotless plates in front of them.

"I could eat the whole damned pie," Desmond said. He hastily looked at the woman, worried he might have been overheard and his language offended her.

Mac hoped it had so he could apologize to her. He swung around in the chair and hesitated. The waiter was speaking in low tones to the woman. She looked distraught and he wasn't pleased.

With a surge, Mac was out of the chair. Desmond was right behind as they went to see what the trouble was. The woman looked up, stricken.

"Please, Señor Weatherby. I did not do this on purpose."

"Miss Abragon, I know that, but I can't just *give* you the meal."

"Is there a problem?" Mac planted his feet and gave the impression of a solid, dependable rock.

"No, *por favor*, please." She fidgeted, her hands turning over and over on her small clutch purse.

"She can't pay. I'm not the mercantile or the dress shop. I don't run a tab."

"I forgot my money. I promise to pay."

Mac saw the waiter—also the owner from the way he spoke—wasn't going along with that. He wondered why. In a town the size of Fort Sumner, everyone ought to know and trust everyone else. Unless something was going on he hadn't heard about.

Before he could say anything, Desmond spoke up. "I'll be happy to cover the lady's meal. How much is it?"

"Forty cents," Weatherby said.

"Give him the money, Mac." Desmond prodded him to fish out the four bits Flowers had given them. Desmond snatched the coins from his grip and handed both of them to the restaurant owner. "No need for change. The dime's a tip."

"Much obliged. You gents want anything more? Another piece of pie? Coffee?"

"I'll escort Miss Abragon out, then we'll see," Desmond said, offering her his arm.

Mac tried to get in on the action but Weatherby took his arm, and it wasn't to escort him out. The man's fingers cut into his biceps.

"You owe me forty cents, ten cents for each slice of pie. No need to give me a tip."

Mac felt a sinking feeling. Flowers had given him the fifty cents because he didn't have a penny to his name and wouldn't until he got his trail wages. Desmond wasn't any better heeled. But Mac had been in similar straits before, back in Waco, and knew what to do.

"I can work it off. I'm the best damned cook you're going to find, and I don't mind cleaning and doing fix-up jobs around here."

"My big business starts in an hour. You sure you can cook and not poison anyone?"

"You'll have them coming back wanting more," Mac promised.

"Ten cents an hour, four hours and we're even." Weatherby thrust out his hand.

Mac wasted no time shaking. Four hours doing what he enjoyed wasn't any punishment . . . but what he would do to Desmond for leaving with the lovely Miss Abragon would be.

CHAPTER 19

Luther Wardell sat astride his black stallion, taking in the herd grazing on the section of land below him.

"Are those damned beeves on our land, Joe?" Wardell asked.

His foreman, Joe Ransom, pursed his lips and finally said, "Can't tell, Mister Wardell. I'd say they are on open range, maybe a couple miles from your property."

"Doesn't make no never mind to me. Those longhorns came all the way up from Texas. Whoever headed the drive did a good job."

"Why do you say that, sir?"

Wardell brushed dust from his fancy frock coat, then tended the accumulation of brown grit on his expensive Stetson with the hammered silver and turquoise hat band. He made sure every last speck was gone. He disliked the constant dust in the air in this part of New Mexico Territory, but the potential for wealth was greater here than up north where the Spanish controlled every inch of land.

Down here in the southeast section, the desert was more open and the land deeds always in contention. The Spanish king's surveyor had been drunk most of the time—that was Wardell's guess for such sloppy work. In places, the property lines were off by as much as five miles.

A clever man took advantage of such discrepancies. Luther Wardell was a very clever man and one itching to become another rancher of the stature of Richard King and Gideon Lewis. Their ranch in South Texas stretched over six counties and thirteen hundred sections. Lincoln County was going to be his. Lincoln and the surrounding land. De Baca and more.

He settled his hat back squarely on his head and poked his glossy black hair up under the band. Moving the coattails away, he rested his hand on the ivory butt of his Colt .44. That ivory had come all the way from Africa and some monster elephant. His one regret in paying so much for the ivory was not being able to shoot the beast himself so he personally harvested the ivory. He'd have to be content to take on anything—or anyone—charging straight at him right here in Fort Sumner.

After he owned all the land fair and square, he considered how traveling to Africa and bagging some big game himself would be the perfect reward. Maybe he'd bring a few of them back and let them roam the desert—his desert, his land, his empire. After all, Jeff Davis had put African camels down at the Texas fort bearing his name. Why shouldn't

Luther Wardell do the same with elephants and lions?

"You hear any more about the Army's budgetary allotment arriving?"

"You mean their grubstake from Fort Union? The gossip says it won't be sent for another couple weeks. Maybe later."

"Maybe later," Wardell mused. He rubbed his clean-shaven chin, then the billowy muttonchops. The bushy facial hair belied his whipcord thin body. A man had once told him it made him look like a mushroom, with a scrawny stem and puffy head.

The authorities never looked much for that loud-mouth, but even if they had the marshal would never have found the body. Ever.

"You want me to run them drovers off? Me and some of the boys can do it and never break a sweat."

"No, Joe. I have other plans for that herd. What's the ranch?"

"Circle Arrow by the brand. I can send José down to be sure."

"Knowing the Circle Arrow brand is fine." Wardell turned toward town. He had a lieutenant in the quartermaster corps to speak to—after he located the trail boss for the herd.

He trotted along, thinking how best to proceed. Joe Ransom kept pace a few yards to his right.

"Joe?" His foreman rode closer. "Did Don Jaime come to town this morning?"

"That's what I heard. I didn't see him with my own eyes, but a couple of the outriders saw him riding up from his rancho like his ass was on fire."

"He heard that the Circle Arrow drovers arrived. That's what's got him so riled."

"He thinks the Circle Arrow boys will sell to the Army and cut him out of the military market?"

"That's part of it. I spoke with the banker a few days ago. Don Jaime is falling behind on his payments."

"A place like that," Ransom said, a touch of glee in his tone, "can cost a man dearly. An arm and a leg."

"It won't come to that." Wardell glanced at his bloodthirsty foreman. Ransom enjoyed killing a little too much. "His claim that he controls a Spanish land grant is on shaky legal grounds."

"You saw to that, Mister Wardell."

"I did, Joe, I did."

Wardell rode the rest of the way into Fort Sumner, going over his plan in his head. Try as he might, he saw no downside to any part of it. Before the end of the month, he would own twice the land that his Big W now covered. Another year and the King ranch would be small potatoes in comparison.

"He's there, Mister Wardell," Ransom said as they rode along the street and approached the lieutenant's office. "Don Jaime. That's his horse tied outside, the one with the fancy Mexican saddle."

"So it is. Let's not bother him and his palaver with the lieutenant. I don't think it will last long when the lieutenant makes it clear he has no money for Mexican cattle. If you were the Circle Arrow trail boss, where would you be?"

"In a saloon. There's plenty around. Bob Hargrove's saloon is right over there and Beaver Smith's is—"

"No, that's not where you would go if you brought

so many longhorns all the way along the Goodnight-Loving Trail."

"It ain't? There're some more saloons over a few streets, out by the fort."

"You find that the Army isn't buying your cattle because they don't have the funds. You look for someone else to buy your longhorns." Wardell suppressed the irritation he felt at having to explain such a simple matter to his foreman. Ransom had his uses, many of them in fact, but deep thinking was not one of them.

Wardell kept moving down the street and halted in front of the grain and feed store. He dismounted, smoothed wrinkles from his frock coat, and rubbed the toes of his boots on the backs of his pants legs to get them all nice and shiny.

Only then did he march into the store and look around. A slow smile came to his thin lips. Three men sat at the table near the back of the store. He knew Garton, the store owner, and Maxwell, a newcomer to the county and potential rival. A quick snort dismissed them as he focused on the third man, the stranger. His time on the trail was cut into every line in his forehead. Hands tanned tougher than leather by sun and holding reins rested on the table, palms down as he leaned forward earnestly.

This was the man Wardell wanted to see.

"Good afternoon, gentlemen."

"What do you want, Wardell?" Maxwell asked curtly. He recognized Wardell as a rival for control of the area and instinctively got his back up.

Wardell ignored him. He thrust out his hand in the drover's direction.

"I'm Luther Wardell, and you must be the trail boss for the Circle Arrow herd grazing outside town."

"Pleased to make your acquaintance," the man said. "At least I think I am. That's not your land my longhorns are chewing up grass on, is it?"

"No, sir, it's not."

"Then I'm the trail boss, Hiram Flowers."

"Pleased to make your acquaintance as well, Mister Flowers." Wardell gestured. Joe Ransom fetched a chair and had it under him as he sat between the drover and Maxwell, effectively blocking any chance the rancher had to continue his talk.

"I was dickering with these gentlemen. I'll be happy to talk to you when I'm done."

"Well, Mister Flowers, Maxwell wants a bull and a few heifers to improve his chance of raising a good herd in a few years. And Mister Garton is thinking on selling you grain to fatten up your prime animals, possibly the ones Maxwell is most interested in." Wardell took a cigar from his vest pocket. "Is that correct?"

"What's your game, Mister Wardell?"

Maxwell said something obscene under his breath. Wardell moved his chair around a little more to cut off any chance of Maxwell speaking with the Circle Arrow trail boss.

Leaving the cigar unlit, he gestured with it to emphasize his words as he said, "I want to buy some of your herd, sir."

"Some?"

"Three hundred head."

"Well, now, that's something we can discuss. Since

you're not making an offer for the entire herd, I'd have to say . . ." Hiram Flowers considered how much to ask. Wardell knew it would be high. "A hundred dollars a head."

"Very well, sir, that is a fair price. Let's get the bill of sale drawn up. I think Mister Garton has a blank or two we can use."

Flowers stared, his mouth hanging open. He closed it, then held out his hand. "We got a deal."

Maxwell stood, kicked over his chair, and stormed out of the grain store. Wardell moved his chair around the table, reached into his pocket, and pulled out a thick, tooled leather wallet. He put the cigar in the corner of his mouth, then laid the wallet open on the table and began counting out the bills.

Wardell enjoyed the look of surprise on the drover's face. Hiram Flowers might never have seen so much cash in one pile in all his born days. The act of dumbfounding the ignorant cowboy made him feel just a little bigger.

"There you are. Do you have the bill of sale, Mister Garton?"

"Right here." The store owner dropped the paper on the table, then placed pen and ink beside it. "You want me to fill it out?"

"If you would be so kind. I hate getting ink on my fingers." Wardell wiggled them in front of his eyes, staring between them at Flowers.

"You want them for what you claimed Maxwell did? Breeding stock?" Flowers asked.

"Not at all, sir. I want them for their meat."

"Here? In Fort Sumner?"

Wardell enjoyed seeing how confused the drover was. That added to his overall enjoyment of the transaction.

"I intend to make a tidy profit, sir." Wardell got Flowers to sign, then added his name, blew on the wet ink until it dried, and tucked the paper into his pocket. "I need to conclude my business now. Thank you, sir."

"Any more you want, let me know," Flowers said, his eyes on the stack of greenbacks and not on the man who had bought his cattle.

"Three will be sufficient for my purposes."

He left, Joe Ransom trailing. His foreman knew better than to ask what he intended. Wardell paused outside to light the cigar and puff on it in great satisfaction with both the fine tobacco . . . and himself.

They rode back to the quartermaster's office. Don Jaime was still there. This made Wardell's triumph all the more joyful—for him. He went in, removed his Stetson, and held it in front of him, waiting for the officer to notice him.

It took only a second. Don Jaime had bent the lieutenant's ear long enough about his troubles and he undoubtedly sought relief. He found it in Luther Wardell.

"Today's the day for cattlemen to come calling," the officer said. "I'd've thought you heard there's no money yet to buy cattle, Mister Wardell. I don't know when there will be."

"I have heard, Lieutenant." He nodded in Don Jaime's direction. The Mexican rancher turned a little pale, or so it seemed. That added to Wardell's enjoyment.

"I offered the Army my cattle at fifty dollars a head," Don Jaime said.

"But, as I told you repeatedly, as much as we need the beeves, I don't have enough money to buy even ten head from you at that price. And you won't let us have the cattle on a promissory note."

"I must be paid immediately, Lieutenant. Being paid at some time in the future that none of us know will not do."

"Three hundred head of prime Texas longhorns," Wardell said. He took the bill of sale from his pocket and laid it on the officer's desk. "You can send your soldiers out to pick which of the cattle you want."

"Mister Wardell, I—"

"I consider it my civic duty to let you have the cattle on consignment." Wardell waved the cigar he held between the first two fingers of his left hand. "You can pay when you receive your funds."

"That's all well and good, but even then I won't have enough to cover three hundred head. Not at a price where you'd make a profit." The lieutenant pressed his finger down on the bill of sale next to the total amount. "You'd do well to keep the cattle for breeding and—"

"I said I wanted to do my civic duty. Don Jaime's price was fifty a head?"

"That is so," the Mexican said. "It is a rock bottom offer, but I need the money now. Cash on the barrelhead, as you say." The rancher crossed his arms over his chest. He wore a colorful vaquero jacket with intricate embroidered patterns. At his hip, a revolver rode high in a holster. Tight dark pants with the legs tucked into his tooled boots and silver spurs with large Spanish rowels completed the image of a successful Mexican rancher.

"Civic duty," Wardell said again. "The Army protects us from the Mescaleros and the Lipans."

"What's your point, Mister Wardell?" The lieutenant began to look uneasy.

"Ten dollars. When you get the money from Fort Union."

"What's that?" The lieutenant sat bolt upright. His eyes narrowed. "What exactly are you offering?"

"Three hundred head at ten dollars each, payable whenever you have adequate funds."

"What if I don't get as much as three thousand dollars to pay you? You know how appropriations go." The lieutenant's face flushed, and his breathing became strained.

Wardell hoped the man would not die of a heart attack when he finally realized this was not a joke. He was being given a deal no one else in the territory would ever hear.

"You cannot give away those cattle!" Don Jaime began to fume. "This is not right! You cannot make a profit. This bill of sale says you will lose ninety dollars a head. Why are you doing this?"

"As I said, my civic duty commands me to help the Army in whatever way I can. They need meat. This is an excellent chance for me to show my gratitude for all they do."

"You do this to prevent me from selling my cattle to them!" Don Jaime accused.

"Not at all. You already turned down their offer." Wardell looked over at the lieutenant, who had started quickly scribbling the terms onto a contract. "Be sure to leave the final payment date open."

"Whenever we get adequate money, yes, thank you, Mister Wardell." The officer wrote even faster, as if afraid that Wardell would change his mind.

That was the last thing in the world Wardell wanted. When the contract was signed, he would have cut off any chance for Don Jaime to sell enough cattle to pay the mortgage on his ranch. The land would be foreclosed soon and put up for auction by the bank. Wardell would see his ranch more than double in size, all for little more than the price of the Circle Arrow cattle. Who wouldn't pay less than a dollar an acre for prime ranch land? Don Jaime would never sell under any circumstances.

It was a sweet deal for Hiram Flowers—and the new king of the ranchers in New Mexico Territory, Luther Wardell.

CHAPTER 20

Don Jaime Abragon stood, his horse nervously pawing the ground beside him, and looked out over his rancho. He had inherited it from his uncle, a Spanish don, a man of great importance to the king. To lose a land grant would be the ultimate shame. All he needed was a little more time to pay the loan he had taken out the year before from the bank to double the size of his herd.

How was he to know the Army would stop buying beeves because they had no money? That hardly seemed possible, the government with so much money from far-off Washington. He had so many cattle, and no place to sell them. Because of Luther Wardell he could never sell to the Army this year.

"How did he sell for so little?" He chewed on his lower lip as he considered what the upstart rancher had done. Bit by bit he pieced together the scheme. Without realizing it, he drew his pistol and cocked it. If Wardell had been in front of him just then, the man would have died with six bullets in his worthless, black heart. The loss he sustained buying the Texan longhorns and virtually giving them to the Army mattered little since it allowed him to bid for the rancho, the hacienda, everything that Don Jaime saw stretching to the very horizon.

"The land is worth hundreds of thousands of dollars, and he will buy it for pennies, because I cannot sell my cattle to pay the bank." The unfairness struck him hard. More than this, he saw no way around what was being done to him because of his heritage, his legacy, his beloved rancho.

He let out a heartfelt bellow of rage and fired into the air. The report caused his horse to rear. Strong hands jerked its reins to hold it down. His fury mounted. Killing Wardell would solve some of his problems, but how would he pay off the bank? The debt was real, the debt was owed. No Abragon defaulted on such an obligation. He had asked for the money of his own free will, and now he must find a way to repay it.

Lowering the pistol, Don Jaime watched the last curls of white smoke wreath from the barrel.

"I am no highwayman. I cannot rob those in stagecoaches or banks or trains. I am descended from nobility. The king of Spain honored my family with this land for their bravery and loyalty to the throne. How can I disgrace such a legacy?" He hung his head in shame that such an idea had ever occurred to him. "I cannot. I, Don Jaime Abragon y Suarez, will not descend to acts of the common criminal, an outlaw who should be hanged for his misdeeds. But then what am I to do?"

No one was there to answer. He was alone as he gazed out over his imperiled domain.

He slipped his revolver back into the high, soft leather holster, mounted, and rode the still skittish stallion across the pastures where his cattle grazed. No finer cattle were to be had in all of New Mexico Territory, but he could not sell them because of Luther Wardell. Because of the Army turning him away when he needed their patronage the most.

Because of the Texas longhorns.

He turned toward the hacienda but drew rein when a cloud of dust popped up along the road leading from town. A tiny smile crept to his lips. He put his heels to his horse, tapping the rowels to get the most speed possible. The stallion rocketed away to intercept Don Jaime's daughter as she drove her buggy.

The closer he got, the more he frowned. Something was wrong. A horse had been tied to the back of the buggy. Someone rode with her. A man. Don Jaime bent over and let his horse race at full speed. He had told her to have nothing to do with the men in Fort Sumner. They were all beneath her station. When the time came for her to marry, he would find a ranchero of property and breeding.

She slowed and pulled the buggy to a halt as he skidded past. The horse had been trained to follow darting cattle during branding and closed back in as if she were nothing more than a calf. His hand went to the pistol at his side.

"Whoa," the man seated beside his daughter said. He handed her the reins and put his hands up to show he had no weapon.

Don Jaime came close to squeezing off a round

anyway. This was not the kind of man his daughter should consort with. This was not only a cowboy; he was one of the Texas drovers. They were worse than those of the nearby ranches.

"Don't get an itchy trigger finger," the young, red-headed man said. "I'm Desmond Sullivan, with the Circle Arrow. You might say that's my brand since my ma owns the spread outside Fort Worth. That's in Texas."

"I know where it is," Don Jaime said as he trained his revolver on the young man. His lips curled with hostility under the thin mustache.

"Wait, don't shoot!" Desmond whipped off his hat and let it dangle behind him, his bright red hair shining like spun gold in the sun. "I was only escorting your lovely daughter home. She got into some trouble back in town, and I helped her out."

"Papa, please," Estella said. "Put down your gun. Mister Sullivan has been nothing but a gentleman, and what he says is true."

"You were in trouble? What happened? If Wardell did anything—"

"No, not *him.*" Estella spat the word out. Her opinion and Don Jaime's were the same of the upstart rancher and his ways. He had tried to court her, but Don Jaime had run him off. Estella would have sent him on his way with his horse's tail ablaze to make certain he did not slow down as he left the rancho.

"Who's this Wardell hombre?" Desmond asked. "If he's giving you any grief, Miss Abragon, I'll take care of him."

"This is not your concern, Tejano," Don Jaime snapped.

"Sir, we got off on the wrong foot. I worried that your daughter had to drive all the way from Fort Sumner by herself. Escorting her has been my honor and privilege."

"I invited him for dinner, Papa."

"No!"

"That's all right, Miss Abragon. I have to be getting on back to the outfit. The trail boss will have the entire crew out hunting for me."

"Go. Go now," Don Jaime said. He slowly holstered his revolver when he saw the brightly haired man climb down from the buggy. Desmond settled his hat on his head, politely touched the brim in Estella's direction. Then he said something to her that made her smile, look down, and blush.

Don Jaime started to pull his gun again.

Estella shot a hot, dark stare in his direction. How she looked like her *madre* in that moment, rest her soul. She was easily as beautiful—and headstrong.

He shoved his pistol back firmly into the holster as the cowboy mounted.

"Have a good day, sir." He cast one last look at Estella, turned and trotted away.

"What did he do?" Don Jaime demanded. "What is this little trouble that he rescued you from?"

"Oh, Papa, I feel like such a fool. I forgot to take any money in my purse. I ate a small meal and could not pay for it. Desmond—Mister Sullivan—paid for it since I could not. Mister Weatherby refused to give me credit. I don't know what I would have done if Mister Sullivan had not been there." She heaved a deep sigh. "Perhaps I would have been forced to sweep and wash dishes until the debt was paid."

"If only it were that easy," Don Jaime muttered, thinking of the bank loan.

"What, Papa? I did not hear you."

"He did not try to take advantage of you? Not even a little?" He studied her for any hint that she lied. Estella was a fine girl of good morals, but she was increasingly feisty since her mother died. How he wished she were here to speak to their daughter and convince her not to run off with the first wild cowboy who smiled at her and told her tempting lies.

"Not at all. He was a gentleman, unlike so many in this town." She looked a little bitter. "Unlike some who work for you."

"The vaqueros are not cultured. I shall send you to Spain for a proper education. You might find a husband there of your station."

"Or I might find one of those dashing Italians I hear about. The handsome ones, the suave ones who cheat on their wives. I could be his mistress with a villa on the Costa del Sol."

"Do not say such things. Do not even joke of that!"

"But why not? I enjoy seeing you squirm about like a flea on a hot griddle. You are so cute when you sputter and turn red in the face."

"Estella!"

"Oh, very well, Papa. I will be the sour old woman you want me to be, never having any fun." She looked straight ahead, snapped the reins, and got the buggy horse moving.

Don Jaime trotted alongside, wondering what he should do with her. Sending her to Spain for finishing school was a possibility, but she needed a chaperone. Her sainted *madre* had died more than a year ago of a fall from her horse.

He involuntarily looked toward a stand of oak trees where the solitary grave with its elaborate marble marker lay. Burying her in the town cemetery had been possible. The priest had been reluctant to bury anyone outside the church graveyard. Either would have been sanctified ground, but he had wanted her nearby. Fray Esteban had argued with him about his choice but finally acceded to his wishes for the burial site.

Not a day passed that Don Jaime didn't go to his beloved's grave, kneel, say a quiet prayer for her soul, then begin the work demanded of him by the rancho, the work that would give Estella the life they both had wanted for her.

It was certainly not a life that included a cowboy. A Tejano cowboy, at that.

"Who is that riding so hard?" Estella looked over her shoulder as a swift rataplan of hoofbeats sounded behind them. "Do you think Mister Sullivan returns so soon?"

"Estella!"

"Papa, *un chiste. Nada más. Canto un chiste.*"

"You tell a joke." He felt like shouting, not laughing. He rested his hand on his pistol as the dust cloud hiding the galloping rider came closer. Don Jaime relaxed when he saw that his foreman caused the small storm.

"I have it, I have the telegram!" Fernando waved a flimsy yellow sheet about, as if displaying a flag in a parade.

"What telegram is this?" Estella looked hard at her father. "Your expression is . . . strange. You fear what is in the telegram?"

"I fear nothing. Nothing that concerns you." He swung his horse around so he could take the telegram from his foreman. The dust kicked up by Fernando's horse swirled around both riders and the buggy.

"What do we do, Don Jaime?"

"You've read this?" He saw that Fernando had. Hastily unfolding the paper, he scanned it. Estella had been right. He feared what he read, but he also felt immense relief. That relief turned to anger, but he muted that. Too many conflicting emotions threatened to swamp him.

"Do we go?" The foreman looked expectant.

Don Jaime's mind raced.

"We have no choice. Prepare for the journey."

"All?"

"All the cattle, Fernando, and as many of the men as will volunteer. I know some cannot return and respect that." He smiled grimly. "Some must stay on the rancho to defend it while we are gone."

"Where are you going?" Estella asked. "A trail drive, Papa?"

He took a deep breath and nodded.

Estella's beautiful dark eyes widened. "No, Papa. Say you are not selling the cattle to Don Pedro. He is a hateful man."

"He is my bitterest enemy, but no one other than Don Pedro Escobar will buy my cattle."

"All of them? You sell them all? What will we do for next year and the year after?"

"The price he agreed to will barely pay off the bank debt. I will find ways to replenish the herd—after I have saved the rancho."

"You're driving the cattle into Mexico?"

"Some of the men are wanted for crimes there." Don Jaime shrugged. "We will have enough for the drive without them."

"Only ten vaqueros, Don Jaime," Fernando said. "That is not so many for such a large herd. It will be difficult."

"So be it. We begin the drive at dawn."

"So soon?" Estella said. She took a deep breath and let it out in a gust. "Then I have little time to pack."

"Pack? What are you saying?"

"I'm going with you." Estella Abragon spoke in a way that brooked no argument. For a heart-stopping moment, he almost told his foreman to forget the trail drive to keep his daughter safe.

"Very well," he said, giving in to the inevitable. "Dawn."

"Of course, Papa. I will be ready." Estella snapped the reins and drove to the hacienda to begin preparations for the long trip across New Mexico Territory and far into Chihuahua.

CHAPTER 21

"This is more money than I expected to see any time soon," Dewey Mackenzie said, riffling through the wad of greenbacks. "And most of the herd's still to be sold."

"Do you think the gent who bought the three hundred head will buy the rest?" Desmond rubbed his fingers over the bills he had received as his due for the work done on the drive to Fort Sumner. Some of the ink smeared and left colored marks on his thumb. The greenbacks he spent so freely at Fort Worth saloons and brothels didn't smear like this, but these were genuine U.S. Government bills. The banker vouched for these poorly printed bills and so did the Army quartermaster when Flowers had asked him to verify they were legit. Watching the lieutenant count out each and every bill, examining each in turn as if they were his and he spent them personally, had been amusing. With both men authenticating the money, Flowers had agreed to let Wardell cut out whichever cattle he wanted from the Circle Arrow herd.

Desmond wondered what the rancher's real interest was. He sent his men into the herd, not to find the fattest, healthiest cattle but to cut out the nearest three hundred. Even then his count was off by a few in the Circle Arrow ranch's favor. Mac had wanted to speak up about it, but Flowers shushed him. The more that remained, the more money they made. If a man didn't claim what was rightfully his, that wasn't anyone else's business.

"He wanted the cattle for some reason that had nothing to do with quality, that's for sure," Mac said. "From what Flowers said, he just about gave them to the Army to keep another rancher from selling his stock."

Desmond shifted his weight from foot to foot and looked around nervously.

"You got a bug up your ass? Settle down. Whenever Flowers decides what to do will be plenty soon enough to get antsy. My guess is that he'll push on to Denver. He sent a couple of telegrams and found out that the market there will take seven hundred cattle, maybe more, but at nowhere near as good a price as we got from Wardell. And that the Santa Fe market's as soft as the one here in Fort Sumner."

"How much can he get in Denver?"

"Might be as low as fifty a head, but we got the time to drive them a thousand more miles and let them graze along the way. Up near Las Vegas is supposed to be wide open grassland, about the best place to spend a week or so before pushing over Raton Pass and on up to Denver."

"But prime beef would sell for more than fifty dollars a head in Denver?"

"Could be as much as eighty. You know the business. If we get there during a lull, we might get paid well. If a half dozen other outfits show up when we do, it'll be a bidding war." Mac lounged back in the shade of the chuckwagon. "What's the difference? You suddenly taking an interest in your ma's profits?"

Desmond held back a sharp reply. He tucked his wages into his vest pocket, spun, and stalked off without a word. Mac had no call to say things like that. The horse Desmond had been riding came to him at the side of the corral and nickered. A quick pat, then he climbed over the makeshift fence and saddled up. Business in town called his name, and he wasn't going to keep her waiting.

The buggy he had driven for Estella was parked outside the restaurant where he had rescued her the day before. Its springs were depressed from the heavy boxes piled into it, leaving only a small space for her to drive. He hitched his horse to the back of the buggy and went into the cool, dim interior.

It took a few seconds for his eyes to adjust from the bright sun. As far as he was concerned, the smile that spread across her face when she saw him was brighter than the sun and more welcome. He went to the table, touched the brim of his hat politely, and said, "Miss Abragon. I'd hoped to see you again. May I sit down?"

Desmond didn't wait for her answer. Nothing she said would drive him off, manners or not. Besides, she had told him she would be here today before her pa had galloped up, waving his revolver as if he intended to fight off bandidos. She wouldn't have said a word if she hadn't wanted to see him again.

"You are very forward, sir."

"I will leave if you ask." He saw her pixie smile and knew she preferred that he stay. He moved the chair closer to the table to better look at her.

"You ordering a meal?" a voice asked. "One that you can pay for?"

Desmond looked up. The restaurant owner towered over him.

"I have plenty of money." He put his entire pay on the table. "All I want is a cup of coffee." He fixed his eyes on Estella Abragon. "Anything the lady wants, she can have."

"Why, thank you, Señor Sullivan, but I am content with what I have."

"You eat like a bird," he said, "and sound like a nightingale."

"You want anything but coffee?" Weatherby cleared his throat. "Truth to tell, I was hoping you'd order and not be able to pay again."

Desmond stared at him.

"What do you mean?"

"For the price of a couple pieces of pie, I got about the best danged cook I ever did see workin' his butt off for four hours. Anytime that friend of yours wants a full-time job, and not shoveling food to a bunch of smelly cowboys, he's got a job here. A fine cook. Danged fine."

"Coffee," Desmond repeated.

Weatherby went off, mumbling to himself about how good a worker Dewey Mackenzie had proven to be.

"You paid for my food yesterday but couldn't pay for your own? I own you a debt of gratitude," Estella said. "Here. Forty cents, I believe."

Desmond pushed it back in her direction.

"My friend wanted to work here. You heard the waiter. Mac breaks into people's houses and cooks a meal, then sneaks out."

"No!"

"It's true. He's a prince of a fellow and my best friend."

"He is quite handsome." Estella smiled.

"Nowhere near as good-looking as me," Desmond said. "And certainly not in your class. You stand out like the brightest star at night, the shiningest rainbow during the day, you're—"

"Here's your coffee," Weatherby interrupted. "Sure you don't want anything else? Pie? Got some huckleberry pie."

"Nothing more," Desmond said, "from you." He leaned on the table, eyes only on Estella. She blushed just a little under his appreciative stare.

"You come on strong, sir," she told him.

"In this life, a man has to if he's going to get what he wants."

"Oh? What is it you want? Me?" She slid back in her chair and crossed her arms over her breasts.

"To buy you another meal," he said, slipping a dollar bill from his stack. "To please you."

"Nothing more?"

"Everything more, but in time," he said. This confounded her. She blushed more vividly and sipped at her coffee to cover her reaction. "What plans do you have for the rest of the day? I'm thinking there must be somewhere we could go with a picnic basket and watch the world go by."

"Sit by a stock pond?" She laughed at this. "I do so

enjoy sitting on a lake shore, but water is difficult to come by."

"Except in the Pecos." Desmond launched into a description of fording the river and how he had saved the chuckwagon from certain destruction. He embellished his role in saving Mac because he saw how wide-eyed she got at his tale of braving the dangerous water and coming through with the herd intact.

"You are very brave. But your friend Mac seems to be, also. To ride beside you requires great courage."

Desmond almost told her of how he'd been kidnapped and held for ransom because the bounty hunters wanted Mac, but he realized no one came out sounding brave in that story.

"A picnic doesn't have to be near water, though that can be very . . . romantic. Where else can we go?"

"Why, nowhere, Mister Sullivan. I came to town to get supplies and must return immediately."

"I can ride with you again, but what's the hurry?" Desmond worried she was trying to brush him off. Mention of getting back to her hacienda turned her distant, as if her thoughts were there rather than on him.

"We leave in the morning. At dawn. We were supposed to leave this morning but supplies were necessary that we did not have. We have them now."

Desmond sat speechless. He wasn't going to lose her so soon after he had found her.

"Where are you going?" he asked when he found his voice again.

"Back to Mexico. Oh, don't look so forlorn. I will

return after Papa sells our cattle there. That horrible Luther Wardell made certain we couldn't sell any cattle to the Army, so we must find other markets."

"There's Denver," he said. "The Circle Arrow is moving out what's left of our herd in a few days. We could combine our herds. That'd be safer for all of us and make it easier to handle the cattle."

"You have longhorns. They do not mix well with our breed. And no, it is too far, too long on the trail, for us to sell in Denver. Mexico is closer. Besides, Papa has received a telegram assuring him of a sale." She made a face.

"To someone you don't like? Maybe I can convince Mister Flowers to buy your cattle."

"Does he have more money than that which Wardell gave him for the three hundred head? We need more than that to . . . We need more than that." She covered her lack of forthrightness by taking one long, last sip of coffee. "Now I must go."

"You're riding along with the herd? You can stay here in Fort Sumner."

"I bullied Papa into letting me go. He would never permit me to stay now. I cannot go back on my word to help, either. We have too few vaqueros for the size of our herd. I will help however I can."

"You can ride night herd? I bet you've got a great singing voice."

"Oh, you. Thank you, Mister Sullivan, for your kindness. I must go. Really." Estella Abragon stood.

Desmond shot to his feet.

"How many more hands do you need on the drive?"

"We have ten. My Papa, me. That makes twelve. I can do many things. I am not what you call a hot-house flower."

"But you are as beautiful as one." Desmond took her hand, tugged a little until she yielded, then kissed it in what he hoped was a gallant, courtly fashion. Estella should be in high society and not riding along a dusty trail with hundreds of beeves threatening to stampede at every turn.

"Please, sir, return my hand to me." She tugged it free, then graced him with one of her sunshiny smiles. With that she left.

But he had to grin when she paused at the door and glanced back at him before leaving. If she had rushed out without a backward look, it would have left him disconsolate. That look meant she cared as much for him as he did for her.

So why did they have to go their separate ways? By the time she returned from Mexico, he would be on the trail and almost in Denver, a thousand miles to the north. He'd sparked many women and had even more he paid for, but none of them held a candle to Estella Abragon. Not a single one.

"I'm not letting you go, not alone," he said.

"You sure you don't want some pie?" came the ringing question. The restaurant owner leaned against the door leading to the kitchen, arms crossed and looking smugly satisfied. How much he had seen, Desmond didn't know. It wouldn't take much to guess what was going on, him making dewy cow eyes at such a beautiful woman and she playing coy.

"When we get back. Both of us will have a piece." Desmond rushed from the restaurant. Estella's heavily laden buggy was gone. She had moved his mount's reins from the back wheel to an iron ring set up high on the restaurant wall for the purpose of tethering horses. He should have looked at what she carried, though he had no reason to doubt she had purchased supplies for the trail drive, as she claimed.

She couldn't get far or drive very fast with so much cargo. He started after her, then drew rein. All he could do was ride alongside, then watch her leave him behind. A dozen excuses rattled around in his head, but he realized none would hold water with Hiram Flowers. The best way for him to proceed was both sneaky and straightforward.

Asking Flowers for permission to leave the drive would be futile. He might as well hammer nails into his own skull. Flowers hadn't wanted to let him come in the first place but agreed to wet-nurse him to keep his ma from riding along.

He smiled crookedly. Estella Abragon and his ma had a lot in common. Fear didn't make up any part of their personality.

Galloping hard got him back to the Circle Arrow camp just as Mac had supper ready. Desmond picked at his food and thought he might tell the cook what he planned. Then he figured that was the same as telling Hiram Flowers. Mac and the trail boss were thicker than thieves. Expecting Mac to keep a secret wasn't too smart.

"What's eating you?"

Desmond jumped a foot and spilled some of his beans on the ground. He hastily kicked dirt over them. They had enough trouble with bugs without advertising for more.

"Nothing special. Just thinking about the drive up to Denver. You ever been there before?"

"Nope," Mac said. "This is all new country for me. Can't say I like it as much as East Texas, but it has its appeal, I suppose. From what Mister Flowers says, once we get to Colorado, the land's a whole lot different. Tall trees, cooler, greener."

"That's good."

"Are you feeling all right, Desmond? You act like you're a million miles away."

"I'm just a tad tired. I rode night herd last night."

Mac looked at him strangely, then shook his head slowly and said, "No, you didn't. At least somebody who snored like a ripsaw cutting through tall timber curled up under your blanket all night long."

"Must have been the night before."

"No, that was—"

"I don't want to talk about it." Desmond shot to his feet, tossed his plate into the slop bucket, and marched away. He knew Mac stared at him, unconvinced. It didn't matter one little bit. He had made up his mind, and nothing would change it. Nothing.

Around midnight, just as the first of the night herders came in and the next wave of wranglers went to keep the herd bedded down safely, Desmond saddled his horse and packed what supplies he could in a pack. He rummaged through the chuckwagon for food. His fingers touched cool glass. The whiskey bottle taunted him.

"Medicinal," he said. "That's for medicinal use only." He held it in his hand, considered popping the cork and taking one long pull to get him on the way, and made his decision. He replaced the cork without so much as taking a sniff of the potent rotgut.

With the bag of food, he silently walked from camp and stowed the supplies on his horse. A pang of guilt hit him. He was stealing from the drive. A deep breath settled his thoughts. His ma owned the ranch and cattle. In a way, they were all his, so how could he steal from himself?

He stepped up into the saddle, wheeled around, and cut across country for the Abragon ranchero. Don Jaime wouldn't turn down an experienced cowboy, not when he had only ten men to handle his entire herd.

Desmond looked forward to the trip into Mexico with Estella riding alongside. He might even learn some Spanish.

CHAPTER 22

"You all packed up until the noon meal?" Hiram Flowers chewed on his lower lip and kicked at a rock as he spoke. He hated the uncertainty. He wanted Mac to get ready for the drive to Denver, but giving that order meant he had to commit himself—and the herd. A mistake now meant Mercedes Sullivan wouldn't get as much as possible for the beeves.

"What do you need from me, Mister Flowers?" Mac jumped up and sat on the chuckwagon tailgate, swinging his feet back and forth. To be as confident, as at ease, as the young man eluded Flowers. He wanted nothing more than to turn around, go back to Fort Worth and the Circle Arrow ranch, and—

And what?

"Near her," Mac said.

Flowers jumped as if he had been stuck with a pin. He had been thinking about getting home to be near Mercedes, to just *see* her again.

"What?"

Mac frowned, licked his chapped lips, and combed

his fingers through his hair. "Mister Flowers? Mister Flowers!"

"Sorry," Flowers said as he gave a little shake of his head. "Got my mind on other things. The herd, getting on up to Denver."

And Mercedes . . . but Flowers wasn't going to say that.

"You've decided the Army won't take any more cattle?" Mac asked.

"You heard what Luther Wardell did with the three hundred he bought from us, eh?" Flowers nodded slowly. Mac kept his ear to the ground, especially since he kept on talking about that rancher's daughter he had met in town.

"He's trying to run the Abragons off their rancho," Mac said. "Now that the Army has all the cattle they can use, Don Jaime can't sell any of his cattle to the quartermaster. And neither can we."

"I about came to that decision on my own," Flowers said. "With the grasslands around here being so lush, the ranchers are raising big herds. Wardell, Don Jaime, several others. I think that fellow, the newcomer, Maxwell, has a decent herd, too."

"He's just started breeding. It'll be a year or two before he's ready to start selling," Mac said. "But you're right about too many head looking for a market." He paused. "Denver? When are we heading out?"

"You don't sound too happy about it. You will stay with the drive for another thousand miles? We can sell the rest of the herd for good money. The pay'll be worth it."

"It's a long way back to Texas."

"Don't sound so down in the mouth. We can take the train across to Abilene, then ride on down to the Circle Arrow from there in a week or two. There's no reason we have to backtrack the trail from here to Denver."

"Crossing the Pecos again, even without a herd, is not much to my liking, so I'm glad of that."

"What's Desmond think?" Flowers looked around. "Where is he, anyway? I saw him on night herd."

"He ate breakfast, or at least he grabbed a couple biscuits. I thought you had him watching the herd this morning."

Flowers suddenly had a bad feeling. "Show me where he spread his bedroll."

"You think something's wrong, Mister Flowers?" Mac asked as he slid down from the tailgate.

The trail boss took a deep breath and let it out slowly. His heart sped up, and he heard blood hammering in his ears.

"I don't look for things to go wrong, but that doesn't mean they don't find me now and then. Desmond was sweet on the same girl you are. I heard the two of you arguing about her. Estella? That was her name?"

"Estella," Mac confirmed. "We weren't arguing, exactly. He owed me some money from when we met her in town." Mac spat. "He owed me more than the money. I put in four hours working for the restaurant because Desmond walked out on me."

"With the girl."

Mac's sour expression answered his suspicions.

"Show me where he flops," Flowers said.

Mac walked around the chuckwagon hunting for a spot nestled between three mesquite trees and a large creosote bush. The ground showed where Desmond had scooped out for his hips and shoulders, but the blanket and the rest of his tack were missing.

Flowers stared at the empty, sandy patch, his mind racing. Mac completed a circuit of the area and came back, shaking his head.

"He's nowhere to be found. Did you send him out to ride herd?"

"I gave him the day off. He said he was feeling poorly, but it might just be that he was feeling frisky. Do you think he's off to pay court to Estella?"

Mac said nothing, which answered the question better than a lie. Flowers wrestled with the problem. He had hired on to get the herd to market. Watching after Mercedes's boy had become an additional chore, one he wasn't paid for, but if he let anything happen to Desmond she would never forgive him. Being in Mercedes's bad graces was worse than ignoring his duty as trail boss. He wanted nothing to happen to the boy, but choosing what to do tossed him on the horns of a dilemma broader than the span of a longhorn.

"Tell Messy he's in charge while I'm gone."

"You thinking on being gone long?"

"Can't say, but I intend to be back to get some of those biscuits you fix up so good." Flowers sighed. "The fact is, I might be longer. You go tell Messerschmidt for me."

He felt Mac's eyes boring into his back as he walked away. The cook knew what was going on and that his trail boss had just abandoned the herd in favor of finding the boss's kid. What trouble Desmond might be in mattered less to Flowers than get-

ting him out of it. As always. Whether it was a whorehouse in Hell's Half Acre or stepping between him
and an irate gambler, or now keeping him from getting mixed up in what might turn into a range war, it
was always the same. Desmond Sullivan blundered
into a mess, and Hiram Flowers got him out of it.

He got the boy out of it because of what he felt for
the boy's ma.

"Damn me." He saddled a mount from the remuda, stepped up, and said, "Damn me," again for
good measure. Tapping his heels, he got the horse
galloping in the direction of Don Jaime's rancho.

He knew vaguely where the place was, and his instincts steered him right, as usual. When he reached
the front gate, he slowed his breakneck pace and
looked around. Something was wrong. His stomach
knotted tight and his heart hammering away, he
rode to the hacienda. Before he dismounted he took
another look around. The place felt like a ghost
town. The usual bustle around a place where people
lived was gone.

Dropping to the ground, he walked to a wrought-
iron gate in a thick adobe wall. As with most houses
of Spanish design, this opened into a courtyard surrounded by the house itself. He stopped to admire
the garden, then jerked around when he heard soft
footsteps coming from the house.

Flowers was quick on the draw. He might be an old
man, but he cleared leather and fired accurately with
the best of them. Quick Willy Means had found that
out the hard way, and all that had happened to him
was being whomped on the head with a pistol—before he kidnapped Desmond. Flowers wished they

had found the body. He was certain he had put at least one hunk of lead into the bounty hunter's worthless carcass, but he wanted to bury the son of a bitch.

"Who are you?"

Flowers took off his hat respectfully as he faced the servant, dressed Mexican style in a flowing skirt, snow-white blouse, and with a red sash tied around her ample waist. They were of an age and, if Flowers judged matters rightly, of similar positions. He worked for Mercedes Sullivan in an important job. This woman had the same air of command he did when he rode with the herd.

"I'm looking for a young man, Desmond Sullivan. Red hair, about so tall—" He started to indicate Desmond's height but the woman put up both hands, palms toward him, and waved them to stop him.

"I know of him. He is no good."

"We can agree on some things, then," Flowers said. "I want to get him back to his job working the Circle Arrow herd. Where is he?"

"Gone. He is gone with the rest of them."

"What do you mean?" He looked around again and the sense of abandonment hit him even harder. The only two people in the house were standing in the garden. Everyone else was . . . gone.

"Don Jaime has taken the herd to Mexico to sell. To Don Pedro." She spat the name out as if it burned her tongue like a red-hot chili pepper.

"What about Desmond?" The sinking feeling became more akin to drowning now. He hardly dared breathe.

"He rides with Don Jaime." She shook her head

angrily. "No, he rides with *her*. I thought she had better sense. She likes him."

"She? Estella Abragon?"

"Who else?" She looked at him as if he had been out in the sun too long. Maybe he had.

"Don Jaime and his vaqueros are driving the herd into Mexico and Estella rode along? With Desmond, too?"

She glared at him, tapped her toe, and crossed her arms. Never had he seen a more emphatic dismissal.

"Did they leave at dawn?"

"They did. And I do not know where Don Pedro's rancho is. Mexico. That is what I do know." She pointed to the gate leading out to where he'd left his horse.

He put his hat on, touched the brim politely, muttered a "thank you," and hightailed it. Astride his horse again, he spun in a circle, trying to figure out what to do. As if by its own accord, the horse walked southward. Here, Flowers saw where Don Jaime's men had rounded up their horses for the drive and headed south. If the herd was of any real size, tracking it would be simple. *If* he went after Desmond. For two cents and a plugged nickel he'd let the boy go off on his own. What did he owe him, anyway? Desmond had been nothing but trouble.

He had been hired to get the Circle Arrow herd to market and wrangle the best price that he could. Selling about a third of the beeves for a hundred a head made him glow with pride. The reason Luther Wardell paid so much hardly mattered. The money covered all the Circle Arrow hands' salaries and then some. The sale of what remained, in Denver or elsewhere, was pure gravy.

Flowers rode steadily back to the Circle Arrow herd. The closer he got, the less sure he was what to do. By the time he reached the chuckwagon, he was too confused to know which end was up. Mac was working to clean the harness for the chuckwagon team and looked up when Flowers came closer.

"You find him?" Mac tossed aside the harness and saddle soap.

"He's on his way to Mexico. With Don Jaime and his herd."

Mac pursed his lips. Flowers saw the wheels spinning in the man's head as he ground everything into a fine dust before spitting it out.

"You're going after him, aren't you?" Mac said.

"No! He's old enough to make his own decisions."

"What's Miz Sullivan going to say? She wanted you to look out for him."

"I never agreed to that."

"But you didn't have to say it out loud," Mac said. "You and her, you've got a verbal contract. She stayed at the Circle Arrow, and Desmond was supposed to stay with the herd until it was sold. He was supposed to learn the business of running a ranch."

"You think I should go after him?"

Mac wiped his lips. His brain still churned. Watching the process would have been funny if Flowers hadn't had so much riding on Desmond and the herd.

"I do, Mister Flowers. How hard is it letting the herd stay here and graze?"

"There's no market here. Wardell sold our cattle

to the Army. There aren't other markets big enough for seven hundred head. Almost that many." He did a quick inventory in his head. "Too many of them are steers for the local ranchers for breeding into their own herds."

"We could drive the herd down into Mexico. If Don Jaime has a market there, we might do all right, too," Mac said.

"I don't know anybody there. I don't know the markets, and I sure don't speak Spanish."

Mac laughed and said, "You don't hardly speak English."

Flowers glared at him for a second, then laughed, too.

"Got me on that." He relaxed a mite and thought as hard as Mac had been on the subject. Everything clicked into place, like dice falling in a chuck-a-luck cage.

"Messy can be the trail boss and get the herd started for Denver. I'll corral Desmond, bring him back, and catch up before a week's out."

"You trust the German with that much responsibility?"

"I've ridden with him and his buddy, Kleingeld, for a couple years. Nothing rattles him. And I don't intend being gone all that long. He's somewhere out riding herd. You can tell Messy what I decided. He gets my pay and his own while I'm gone. That'll please the hardheaded German."

Mac said nothing.

"You behave yourself, Mac. It's hard enough dealing with Desmond. I don't want you acting up, too."

Flowers led his horse to the corral, chose another

that wasn't all tuckered out, mounted, and rode back. He nodded in Mac's direction.

Then he galloped off, knowing he had to put distance between himself and the herd or his resolve would weaken. Getting Desmond back mattered. That might not get him into Mercedes's good graces since he let her son light out for Mexico in the first place, but it helped. Let her fire him. In his heart he knew he was doing the right thing.

After a mile, he slowed to keep the horse from collapsing under him. If he kept up a decent pace, Don Jaime's herd would be within reach by nightfall, maybe sooner. From everything he'd heard, the rancher had only a few vaqueros. That would slow down the drive. Feeling good, Flowers began singing one of the songs the nighthawks crooned to keep the cattle settled down.

He jumped a foot when another voice joined in on the chorus. Hand on his revolver, he twisted around in the saddle.

"Mac!" he exclaimed when he saw the cook trotting toward him on horseback. "What are you doing here? Something wrong?"

"Nothing's wrong." Mac pulled even with him and made no move to stop or head back toward Fort Sumner.

"Messy refused to be trail boss?"

"He liked the idea. You might have to fight him to get your job back."

"So why are you here?"

"I decided to help you fetch back Desmond. I owe him."

"You're that good a friend?" Flowers laughed

harshly. The two young men had a wary truce and nothing more.

"More like a grudging respect. Desmond is fighting to climb out of a bad hole and is doing a good enough job."

"What you're saying in polite words is that he's not as big of an asshole as he once was."

"That," Mac said. "And we worked good as partners before."

"We won't have Quick Willy Means to deal with anymore. Not like in Fort Worth." Flowers hesitated, then asked, "What're the men going to do for a cook if you're coming with me to Mexico?"

"Kleingeld claims he can do better. Let him try with his stuffed skunk cabbage and sausage. If I get back and the men like him better, I'll move on and everyone will be happy."

Flowers heard something more in what Dewey Mackenzie said. If he liked Mexico, he'd never go back to the Circle Arrow herd. Desmond might be traveling with the herd again, but the drive was going to lose a cook, a damned good one, to boot, sooner or later.

He'd deal with that problem when it happened. First, he had to hog-tie Desmond and drag him back. Then he'd worry about Mac.

CHAPTER 23

The day was as perfect as it could get. Luther Wardell shifted his feet, hiked them up on the porch railing, leaned back a bit farther, and sipped at the Kentucky bourbon he had special ordered six months ago for celebrations. Snookering Don Jaime counted as reason to sip at the whiskey and enjoy the fine late summer day, with the wispy clouds high in the bright blue sky, the gentle breeze, and land that he owned as far as he could see. Even if he climbed to the roof of his two-story house, he wouldn't be able to see the boundaries of his ranch.

After he bought Don Jaime's ranch for the price of a few mortgage payments, he wouldn't be able to ride around the perimeter of his land in a day. Two, maybe, but even galloping on a fast horse wouldn't take him off his own property. He was on his way to being a power in De Baca County. Some of Don Jaime's land stretched out to Lincoln County. That would be the next direction to expand.

He laughed.

"What's so funny, boss?" Joe Ransom asked as he came up to the porch.

He motioned for his foreman to join him.

"Ransom, my good man, I am going to expand my spread. Don't you like the play on words? I'm going to own all of southeastern New Mexico Territory within a couple years."

Joe Ransom dragged a chair over and put it at polite distance from his employer. He looked at the chair as if not understanding what good it was, then settled down into it.

"Something's eating you, Ransom. What is it? Don't ruin my good mood."

"I'd better go check the herd on the south forty." He started to stand, but Wardell motioned him to stay put.

"You *are* going to ruin my day. I can tell. What's wrong?"

"Don Jaime and the bank," Ransom said. "I just heard that the banker's giving him another month to make his back payments before putting the ranch up for sale."

"So? Another month? I'm a patient man. I can wait that long." Wardell fixed a cold stare on Ransom. The man was more gunman than foreman and had ice water in his veins. That he looked downright fidgety now caused Wardell to knock back his whiskey. It burned down to his belly. He didn't taste it, and that put him in a foul mood. He had spent a hundred dollars getting a couple of bottles from the distillery.

"Don Jaime rounded up all his cattle and is driving them to Mexico."

"He's abandoning his ranch? Good. That'll make . . ." Wardell's words trailed off. The reason for Don Jaime's trail drive wasn't cowardice or welshing on the bank loan. "He has a buyer for the entire herd? Willing to pay enough to cover his debts?"

"All of them, if my ciphering's right, boss. He sent a telegram to Don Pedro Escobar. I asked around. The two of them don't get along, but Don Jaime's got the cattle and Don Pedro's got the markets farther down in Mexico. He sells to the Federales and a half dozen Indian tribes, including the Yaquis." Ransom grinned wolfishly. "Rumor has it he also sells guns to the Indians. That might be where his real money comes from."

"Real money," Wardell said. He spat. "He's got plenty to buy cattle. Do you think Don Jaime might be smuggling guns into Mexico?"

"He wouldn't have the crust for that."

"That's the way I see him, too," Wardell said.

"I can catch up with his herd and gun him down."

"That won't get me his ranch anytime soon. If it gets tied up in court, I have to buy off judges and lawyers. You know what crooks they are."

"So he doesn't end up with a couple ounces of lead in his belly?" Ransom sounded disgruntled at this. His fingers twitched, as if they circled the butt of his six-gun and pulled back on the trigger.

"There're all sorts of dangers to face on a trail drive. Stampedes can destroy most of your cattle. What if his horses were stolen and his vaqueros had to walk?"

"He has to pay off the loan in a month. The banker won't give him more time."

"Why'd Amos Dunphy give him one second longer to pay up? Dunphy would foreclose on his own grandmother if there was an extra nickel in it for him." Wardell thought hard. Then he shook his head in disbelief. "I can't believe he gave Don Jaime the extra time because he's sweet on Estella."

"The fat banker man and a *chica bonita* like that?" Ransom laughed. It was an ugly sound that made Wardell wonder if the gunman wasn't sweet on her, too

"It makes sense. He thinks giving Don Jaime a break might ingratiate him to his daughter. He either doesn't see too clearly how she'd react to an arranged marriage with a fat, pasty-white banker or there's something more at stake."

"What does it matter? He gave Don Jaime the time."

"Will he give him one second longer if he doesn't get his money? Maybe with a bonus tacked onto it."

"I can see that. Dunphy gets a bribe, paid under the table so his shareholders never find out. That's what I'd do, then find a way to foreclose on his ranch." Ransom sounded proud of such a scheme. Wardell knew that much was true, but Estella's hand, with the ranch as dowry, still intrigued Ransom.

"How many men can you get into the saddle?"

"To overtake Don Jaime? A half dozen. If I take any more, tending the cattle out on the range will suffer. We've got Mescaleros raiding almost nightly. Without enough guards, they'd run off the entire herd within a week."

"Damned Indians," Wardell groused. "Get the

men ready to leave as fast as possible. I'll stay here to deal with the Apaches."

"And the banker?" suggested Ransom.

"Dunphy must have a weak spot. I'll find it and dig my thumbs in to see how deep the bruise goes." Wardell recovered some of the good nature he had experienced before Ransom delivered such bad news. There wasn't any call to get upset. Things would work out for him soon enough. All he needed was patience.

Patience and a way of applying pressure to Don Jaime and Amos Dunphy and anyone else who got in his way.

CHAPTER 24

Mac pulled his battered hat down until the brim was just over his eyebrows. This shielded his eyes enough to slowly survey the land ahead even as it let the hot sun bake down on the top of his head through the hole in the hat's crown.

Small ranges of low mountains perked up all around, but the main path any cattle would take lay wide and green with juicy grass. Try as he might, he couldn't find Don Jaime's herd. This worried him. The rancher might have taken some other route from Fort Sumner. Going straight into the Sacramento Mountains had to be the worst choice. They were high and passes would need to be found. Mac had never driven a herd through mountains, but it didn't look easy.

He turned more to the south. The Circle Arrow herd had come from the southeast. Don Jaime had no reason to cross the Pecos. Texas was filled with longhorns, and the price of any given steer was too low to get him the money he needed.

"There," Hiram Flowers said, pointing due south. "He's made good time to get that far."

"Are you sure?" Mac finally spotted the dust on the far horizon. "It's only a dust devil."

"Don Jaime's herd," Flowers insisted. "He's in a hurry."

"He'll run those beeves until they're nothing but skeletons." Mac pushed his hat back up in a more comfortable position. He eyed the dust as it died down. The brown haze lay in the right direction.

"Let's ride. We can overtake them by sundown."

"We should have brought a second horse for each of us. Swapping out when one got tired would have let us double the distance we can ride."

"We'll get there, Mac. What worries me most is if something's happened to Desmond. Sometimes, he doesn't have the sense God gave a goose."

"You mean you worry that Don Jaime catches him fooling around with Estella?" In a perverse way, Mac hoped Don Jaime did catch them and booted Desmond off the drive. He smiled, just a little, at the notion of Estella turning from Desmond to someone else. *He* was that someone else. Ever since he had seen her in the restaurant, she had dominated his thoughts and dreams.

Desmond had been able to corner her when he hadn't. Desmond gave her a way off the ranch that her pa was driving into the ground. Mac wasn't sure what he offered her, but it had to be better than the ne'er-do-well. Desmond had hardly worked a day in his life before the trail drive.

Mac had worked every day since he was eight or nine. His pa had made sure of that. When he moved on after his parents died and his brother Jacob upped and left without so much as a good-bye, life had turned difficult. All the time he'd spent in New Orleans had shown he coped well and met any challenge, even the snake eyes he rolled with Pierre Leclerc.

A momentary pang caused him to catch his breath as he thought of Evie. She had been so lovely. For all he knew, she enjoyed her life with Leclerc, though he doubted it if she got wind that the shipping tycoon had murdered her pa. He shuddered, remembering how he had found Micah Holdstock's body tied up on the oak tree, his body slashed and his throat slit with Mac's knife.

He still used that knife for cooking on the drive.

"What's wrong? You forget something? Your knife's sheathed at the small of your back, if that's what you're feeling around for." Flowers looked curiously at him.

"I worry about forgetting things. I'm ready to ride."

"Gallop a mile, walk half, trot for a half, then gallop until the horses tire. If we change their gait they won't get as worn out." Hiram Flowers patted his horse's neck. The animal turned a big brown eye around to glare at its rider, as if it understood what the trail boss said and disagreed.

"You've done this before," Mac said. "Was it chasing after Desmond then, too?"

"You've got a mouth on you, boy. You just shut it and ride. Otherwise, you'll end up with a mouth full of bugs and dust." Flowers lowered his head and brought his horse to a gallop.

Mac followed him. His horse wasn't anywhere near as strong as the trail boss's but kept up well enough, lagging only a few dozen yards by the time Flowers drew back to a walk.

Mac closed the distance and said, "You see what I do?"

Flowers jerked around, eyes narrowed.

"What are you talking about?"

Mac felt a momentary pride that he had paid attention to his surroundings and Flowers hadn't. The satisfaction died when he realized how second nature that had become to him with bounty hunters on his trail and a murder trial waiting for him in New Orleans.

"Not a mile to the west. At least five riders. They're making tracks for Don Jaime's herd, too. They might be rustlers."

"That's mighty quick of them, if they are. From what I can tell, Don Jaime got the bug up his ass to drive his cattle to Mexico in the last day or two. Maybe only hours before he set out."

"This isn't the usual trail that a cattle drive takes, is it?"

"The Goodnight-Loving Trail is miles and miles to the east and doesn't go anywhere near Mexico. Men don't ride this section of the territory for fun, not with the Indians always riled up about something."

Mac hazarded a guess. "Apache scouts?"

"Apache war party is more like it. You didn't get any better look at them, did you?"

Mac started to snap back an answer. He had seen the riders; Flowers hadn't. How much more was he supposed to do? Count the number of gold teeth in their heads? Find out their horses' names?

He held back his sass.

"From the way they're headed, we can cross in front and find out what they're up to. Or we can dog their back trail and sneak up when they camp."

"And spy on them?" Flowers spat out the words. "That's downright uncivil."

"If they're honest men traveling for honest reasons, that's not overly polite. You're the one who said there's no such critter as an honest man out in this part of the territory. Other than us. And Don Jaime and his vaqueros."

"We take it on faith they're up to no good. Asking their business is likely to get us filled full of holes, no matter what their intentions."

Mac put what he knew into his head and let it all tumble around to see what finally came out. The determination of the gang, the way they rode fast and hard, heading straight for Don Jaime's herd, decided him. They were up to no good.

"Don Jaime got all the men he could from his ranch. These gents aren't intending to join up and help him get his cattle south of the border. If I was a betting man, I'd lay odds on them being sent by Luther Wardell."

"Why's that, Mac?" Flowers worked on his own ideas, but this one distracted him.

"If Don Jaime gets the money to save his ranch, Wardell wasted the money he spent buying our beeves and almost giving them to the Army. The Circle Arrow and the Army will be the only winners.

And Don Jaime, if he collects enough for his cattle. Wardell loses all around."

"That makes sense," Flowers said. "The question comes to mind, what do we do? If we mix it up with them for no good reason, that's not going to get Desmond back."

"If the gang tries to rustle the herd or just stampede it, Desmond is in serious danger. He's barely got the experience to wipe his own nose."

"He can do more than that. He saved your damned chuckwagon crossing the Pecos. Don't you forget that."

Mac recognized a desperate defense when he heard one. The trail boss knew that Desmond had been caught in the stampede during the thunderstorm and would have died if he hadn't saved him. After that, Mac had taught him close to everything he knew about being a cowboy. Mac remembered how Desmond had come close to shooting off his own foot until taught how to draw and fire. He needed more practice with his revolver, but the lessons Mac had given him were enough to keep him alive. Unless the hothead did something he thought was heroic to impress Estella.

"It won't hurt to watch them," Mac said, choosing his words carefully. "If it looks like they're going to try their hand at some rustling, we can always let Don Jaime know. After all, it's his herd to protect."

"That's sensible enough," Flowers said. He spat, turned his horse, and slowed to a walk.

Mac kept pace beside him, letting his horse rest up. They might have to hightail it. He wanted as fresh a horse under him as possible if it came down to shooting.

They made their way through the desert, finding ways to stay out of sight until Flowers couldn't stand it any longer. He dropped to the ground, tossed his reins to Mac, and started up a steep hillside for a look.

"Don't let them see you," Mac called. He got a dirty look in return. Flowers was savvy enough not to silhouette himself against the sky, even if the sun had moved around and would be in his eyes.

He reached the crest, hunkered down, and inched forward. He flopped on his belly so fast that Mac jumped. In less than a minute Flowers worked his way back downhill, stood, and ran the rest of the way. Panting harshly, he grabbed the reins from Mac's hands and pointed to the rifle in the saddle sheath.

He gasped out, "Rifle. Get your damned rifle. They're on the other side of the hill fixing to start a stampede."

"You heard them?"

Flowers's head bobbed up and down. He mounted, drew his own rifle, and levered a round into the chamber. Not waiting to see if Mac followed, he lit out around the base of the hill.

"Wait for me," Mac cried. He felt a little queasy going into a fight and not knowing what he faced. How many rustlers were there? Or had he been right that these men worked for Wardell and intended nothing but mischief to keep Don Jaime from selling the cattle to save his ranch?

He found out quick. Trailing Flowers by a dozen yards, he pounded around the hill. Nestled between two smaller hillocks, eight men worked to fasten bandanas over their faces and checked their revolvers. They looked up when Flowers and Mac raced toward them, but they didn't react. Mac saw them call out to one man, their leader.

"That's Ransom, Wardell's foreman," he shouted to Flowers. He had seen the man in Fort Sumner and learned his name.

The trail boss never heard. His horse's hooves pounded too hard against the dry ground. Then he opened fire. His rifle spat foot-long tongues of orange flame and filled the air with white gun smoke.

Mac raced right behind him. The notion of shooting down the men churned at his gut. This wasn't self-defense, not strictly. To ease his conscience, he saw that all his rounds missed their intended targets, but the volley they fired spooked the mounts under Wardell's henchmen. Confusion, rearing horses, animals bolting threw several of the riders to the ground. As Mac charged past one, he heard a sick crunch as his horse's front hoof collided with the man's arm. The bone not only broke but poked out through his duster. He fell away, screaming in pain and adding to the commotion.

"It's just two of them. Don't let them scare you!" Ransom fought for control of his horse. He waved his gun around, but every time he leveled it, the horse sunfished and threatened to throw him off. "Kill them! Shoot the bastards!"

Mac tried to do just that to Ransom, but he had raced clean through where they'd gathered. He leaned to the side, avoided a couple bullets sent his way, turned his horse, and came back for a second attack. He changed his tactics when he saw Flowers on the ground, his horse next to him. The horse was dead. Hiram Flowers had drawn his revolver and fired as accurately as he could as he knelt behind the meager shelter of the horse's body.

To protect the trail boss, Mac rode between him and three men closing in on him. Two rounds cracked from his rifle, but then it was empty. He whipped out his S&W. The trusty gun fired four rounds with accuracy unlike anything he had experienced before. Or it might have been Lady Luck smiling on him. He winged one of Wardell's gunmen, shot another's horse from under him, and caused the third to veer away.

"Get up behind me," Mac called. He had to use both hands on the reins to stop the horse close enough to Flowers. Otherwise, it would have kept running until it died under him.

"Two of us will tire it out."

"*Get on!*" Mac was in no mood to argue. His tone lit a fire under the trail boss. Flowers jumped up, caught at the saddle, and awkwardly pulled himself forward.

Mac saved his last two rounds for when he might need them. He bent low and rode straight into a tight knot of would-be stampeders. Two scattered. Another was thrown when his horse reared.

"What are you doing?" He looked behind. Flowers had jumped away. He saw the reason. The riderless horse had stepped on a rein and jerked its head around. As it tried to figure out how to get away, Flowers snatched the rein, pulled it free, and vaulted into the saddle.

They were both mounted again.

Mac used his final two rounds to send Wardell's men running. It took all his willpower not to keep firing on empty chambers. The click-click-click might have drawn them back to fight some more if they knew he had run out of rounds.

Flowers hooted and hollered and dropped the man who had been tossed from his horse as he tried to scramble over a hill. Flowers grabbed and caught the bridle of the now stray horse.

"We showed them," Mac said. Reaching into his coat pocket, he pulled out six cartridges and re-loaded his revolver. It took longer to find a box of shells and get his rifle reloaded. "Let them come back. I'm ready for bear."

"How many are dead?" Flowers swayed as if a high wind buffeted him. He turned in a full circle, then threw up his hands. "How many?"

"They're running, Mister Flowers. They won't stop until they get back to Fort Sumner." Mac had to grin. "Chances are good they won't go back and tell Wardell what happened. They'd prefer him to think they're dead, rather than cowards who couldn't tangle with two cowboys and win."

"Their leader. Ransom. He's a mean one. He won't go back. He'll get mad."

"He'll be alone. I saw the expressions on those owlhoots' faces. They won't come back."

"I hope you're right, Mac. I hope you're right." Flowers tipped his head to one side, listened hard, then pointed. "Don Jaime's herd is over that way. I hear them stirring."

"They stayed put and didn't stampede. His vaqueros can settle them down."

"That's none of our business. Getting Desmond back to the Circle Arrow is."

Mac heaved a sigh. The trail boss had a one-track mind. This time that proved to be a good idea. Ransom and the rest of Wardell's gunmen had run away, but if they took long enough, they'd forget why they ran, build up some courage—maybe with the help of a bottle of whiskey—and decide they feared Ransom and Wardell more than two cowboys.

He settled in the saddle, hunted for any dropped weapons, and found two revolvers. It took him a few seconds to dismount and grab them. The more firepower he carried, the better their chance of fulfilling Flowers's pipe dream of prying Desmond loose from the Mexican's trail drive.

Desmond had plenty to prove. He'd take every chance he could to show off for Estella Abragon. Mac caught up and cantered beside the trail boss until they sighted the trailing edge of the herd. Two vaqueros turned in their direction. Both uncurled ten-foot-long whips and cracked them behind the steers. This moved the reluctant beeves—and it gave ample warning to the pair of intruders not to cross them.

Mac politely waved. Flowers rode, eyes straight ahead as if he pierced the cloud of dust and saw Desmond. A few minutes' ride brought them around the side of the herd where Don Jaime rode. His fancy embroidered sombrero had turned dust brown. The gold threads poked through in places but both the quality and craftsmanship were veiled by trail dust already.

"What do you want?"

"A good day to you, too, Don Jaime," Flowers said. "We're here to take Desmond back where he belongs."

Mac rode between the two men. Flowers lacked even a hint of diplomacy in his makeup. He focused on one thing only, and nothing moved him until he finished it. In a trail boss that kept the herd together and the crew safe. For retrieving the boss's son as he worked another herd, it lacked a great deal of diplomacy.

"Desmond Sullivan's needed back in Fort Sumner," Mac said. "We'd like your permission to talk it over with him."

Mac saw the ranch owner thaw a little at that. "He has hired on to work for me until we reach market in Mexico."

"We understand that, Don Jaime. We only want to talk."

A cloud of dust rose when Don Jaime took off his sombrero and waved it above his head. He loosed a whistle that hurt Mac's ears before the dust from that broad-brimmed hat choked him. Riding through a New Mexico dust devil had nothing on the tiny storm stirred up by simply whacking the hat a few times.

"There he is." Flowers started to ride to Desmond until Mac reached out to hold him back. Flowers angrily jerked free. "Don't you ever try to stop me, boy. Never."

"He's coming to us, Mister Flowers. Rock the boat now, and we return empty handed."

Mac was aware that Don Jaime took in every word they said. What his role was in letting Desmond ride with the herd remained to be seen. Having the young man on the same drive as his daughter had to be a burr under his fancy saddle.

"What are you two doing here?" Desmond drew rein and glared at them. "I'm not being kidnapped."

"Not again," Flowers said, his tone surly. "You've already done that so you keep making new mistakes. Go fetch your gear. We're going back to the Circle Arrow herd right away."

"I gave Don Jaime my word. I promised I'd work as a cowboy—a vaquero—until he reaches a market below the border."

"Your ma won't like you running off like this." Flowers turned even more belligerent. Mac saw this was the wrong thing to say, the wrong tack to take.

"Why don't we get a cup of coffee and talk this over?" Mac suggested.

"The chuckwagon's a mile that way," Desmond said, pointing due south, the direction of the herd. "You mind, Don Jaime?"

The rancher dismissed them with a wave, shouted in Spanish, and rode to chew out one of his vaqueros for some minor offense. Mac felt sorry for the man because he hadn't done anything but provide Don Jaime a convenient reason to leave his unwanted visitors to work out their problems alone.

Mac, Flowers, and Desmond rode in silence. The herd moved like a sluggish river beside them. The cattle were well fed from the lush grasslands around Fort Sumner, but Mac saw how fragile they looked in comparison to the sturdy longhorns. Without cutting into one of the cows, he figured their meat lacked the tenderness and flavor of the Texas cattle.

Life in New Mexico Territory was hard enough that it toughened the animals.

"Here," Desmond said. "Here's the chuckwagon. Dinner will be ready in another hour."

"We won't be around that long." Flowers dismounted and lashed his reins to the wagon's rear wheel. He took a deep breath. The odor of cooking food obviously pleased him.

It certainly did Mac. He had learned to cook as much by smell as by taste. If food smelled bad, no amount of salt and pepper turned it palatable. The man with an apron wrapped fully around his waist and then half again worked on a mess of pinto beans. He stirred them, then worked to fry tortillas.

"That's Felipe. He's been with Don Jaime going on twenty years." Desmond reached out to pluck a morsel from a Dutch oven. He jerked back when Felipe rapped his knuckles with a wooden spoon and loosed a string of Spanish that none of the three men understood. But the meaning was clear.

"You eat with the rest of the vaqueros."

Felipe went about his work with quick moves and efficiently produced enough food for a small army. Mac approved of the man's skill and, if the taste matched the smell, his cooking was even better.

"We should hit the trail right now," Flowers said. "Trouble's brewing that isn't your concern."

"What do you mean?" Desmond perked up. His hand pushed back his duster so his revolver rested where a quick draw was possible.

Mac wondered if Flowers intended to force Desmond to stay with Don Jaime. Everything he said backed Desmond into a corner where he either fought or ran. No matter which he chose, he wasn't heading back to Fort Sumner and the Circle Arrow herd.

"We shot it out with some owlhoots. They had the look of working for Luther Wardell."

"That snake," blurted Desmond. "He's out to get Don Jaime's ranch. If this herd's not sold for a decent price, the bank forecloses and Wardell buys it for a song and dance."

"That's his worry, not yours."

"Mister Flowers, let me talk to him." Mac had to repeat his request before it soaked into Flowers's thick skull. He waved him off to one side.

Mac took Desmond by the arm and kept him from jerking free. When they were out of earshot of both Flowers and Felipe, Mac spun on him and shoved his face within inches.

"You want to get yourself killed? There's a range war brewing. You're going to be smack in the middle of it."

"I'll side with Don Jaime. Estella says—"

"There's the problem," Mac said. "Estella. She's got your brain all scrambled up. This isn't your fight. It's hers. Hers and Don Jaime's. They'd as soon shoot you as any of Wardell's men. And Ransom—Wardell's foreman—has the look of a gunslick. He's a hired killer. He won't think of you twice except to decide how few rounds it'll take to kill you so he can save the bullets for Don Jaime."

"For Don Jaime and Estella. I'm not leaving her to a man like that."

Mac backed off. Desmond hadn't budged. In his way he was as mule-headed as Hiram Flowers.

"We're not friends, not exactly, but we've saved each other's life. We've come to a truce, if you can call it that. I'm telling you, not so much as a friend but as an outsider with no stake in this game, go with Flowers. Get back to your ma's herd and drive them up to Denver. Sell them, go back to Fort Worth, and put in the hard work raising next year's longhorns."

"You just want me to go so you can cut in on Estella," Desmond accused. "I know how you look at her. If she's going to end up with anyone, it'll be me."

Desmond looked past Mac, who turned and saw the woman helping Felipe prepare the food.

"She's almost as good a cook as Felipe." Desmond sounded proud of that.

"As good as your ma? Is that what you see in her?" Mac ducked as Desmond swung. Even so, the fist grazed his cheek and caused him to reel back, off balance. His heel caught on something and he sat down hard.

Desmond stood over him, hand on his revolver, fire in his eyes.

"I taught you how to use that," Mac said. "I hope I also taught you when not to use it."

"Go to hell." Desmond stepped back and took his hand off his pistol. He stormed off to go talk with Estella. She looked at Mac wide-eyed and with some fear, as if she knew about Desmond's unchecked anger. They walked away from camp, arguing.

Flowers came over and crouched down beside Mac.

"I'm glad I let you handle him. I'd've made him so mad he couldn't be pried from this herd using a crowbar."

"What are we going to do?" Mac let Flowers help him to his feet. He brushed off the dirt from his jeans.

"You can go on back to Fort Sumner and save the men from Kleingeld's cooking. Me, I've got no choice. I go along into Mexico to be sure he stays out of trouble. If anything happened to him, his ma would skin me alive."

Mac watched Desmond and Estella standing inches apart. He wasn't sure but the tension between them turned the distance into miles.

"I'll go along to keep you company. Might be I can help Felipe whip up chow for the crew."

"I'll lend a hand herding the cattle. We won't get paid, but I'll see that Mercedes puts a little extra into your pay when we get back."

Mac considered the bonus, then thought about staying in Mexico. The bounty hunters had gotten too close, and Ransom was the sort to carry a grudge all the way to the grave. Money was good. Freedom from being hunted like an animal was better. He'd have to see.

South of the border.

CHAPTER 25

Quick Willy Means stared down at the man who
had been his partner for the better part of a
year. Charles Huffman moaned and thrashed, his
arms pulled in tight to his belly to stop the bleeding.
It didn't work. Red leaked out around his hands and
dripped to the thirsty ground to make a gory mix of
mud and sticky sand.

Means hadn't helped his partner's wounds any by
dragging him away from the gunfight, rolling him
down a hillside, and then draping him over his saddle to lead them out. There had been nothing he
could do for Frank Huffman—he was deader than a
doornail from Hiram Flowers's deadly aim.

"Do somethin', Willy. I'm hurtin' something fierce.
My guts are on fire and there's a ringin' in my ears so
loud I can hardly hear."

Means stared at him. There wasn't anything he
could do. There wasn't anything a doctor could do.
Three hunks of lead had lodged in the man's stomach. Another had caught him high in the shoulder.

Even if the other three hadn't spelled certain death, the one in the shoulder would have eventually killed the man since it was still lodged deep against the bone.

"Frank's dead. He died in the gunfight. It's a wonderment to me that you're still kicking."

"Kickin'? Hurts to move anything. Can't hardly feel my feet. Are my boots on? I don't want to die with them on. I promised my ma that I wouldn't die with them on."

"You lied." Means came to a decision after listening to the caterwauling and whines of pain. He slid his gun from its holster, aimed and fired. The bullet struck Huffman in the middle of the forehead. He died before he knew what happened.

Means slowly replaced his revolver. It had been a waste of ammunition to put Huffman out of his misery since Huffman was dying anyway, but he would have done the same thing for a horse that had broken its leg.

"Getting shot was a mistake." Means flexed his own arm and knew he had come close to sharing the Huffmans' fate. Four bullets had torn through his coat and shirt sleeve. Only one had drawn blood. This left his arm achy and stiff, but not enough to affect his draw or his aim.

He closed his eyes and took in the world around him. The drone of flies coming for Charles drowned out other, more subtle sounds. But he noted the sun against his face, the puff of wind through his hair, the feel of the earth beneath his boots. He experienced it all.

Then he mentally pictured the men who had

done this to him. Dewey Mackenzie had a bounty on his head. Bringing him in—bringing him down—would be a pleasure. Whatever money Leclerc offered for Mackenzie's scalp would put a decent bonus in his pocket. But Hiram Flowers wasn't a wanted man, not so far as Means knew.

That took away any profit from cutting him down, but not the sheer animal pleasure of seeing him die. Means imagined facing the grizzled old cowboy, seeing his face wrinkled and tanned by the hot Texas sun begin to furrow even more as he realized he was going to die. A quick draw, an accurate shot, Hiram Flowers gasping as death ripped through his chest. That was how it would be, and Means would watch him crumple to the ground, kick feebly, and then die in the hot sun. The old man had pistol-whipped him. That had left a deep scar on Means's soul.

Flowers and Mackenzie gunning down all three of the Huffman brothers called for punishment beyond a quick death. A dozen tortures came to mind, many of them stolen from the Apaches. But when all was said and done, Quick Willy was a businessman. Taking the time to properly torture Flowers would keep him from tracking down outlaws wanted by the law.

"You'll die fast, old man." He opened his eyes and stared at Charles Huffman. The man's face was black with flies and crawling insects.

He considered burying him to keep the coyotes from feasting on his dead flesh. Means decided not to waste the time. Charles Huffman hadn't been that bright, and he had never liked taking orders from anybody but Frank.

Means spun around and walked to his horse. Both

Huffmans had lost their horses in the gunfight. A spare horse would have meant quicker, easier riding. So, of course they had let their mounts run off to make life that much more disagreeable for him. When he killed Mackenzie and Flowers, taking their horses wouldn't be that much of an advantage. He had seen the scrawny nags the Circle Arrow crew rode.

His horse pawed nervously at the ground. The gunshot had scared it, but not as much as the smell of blood. Means stepped up, wheeled the horse, and started for Fort Sumner. When Flowers and Mackenzie had saved the young punk, the only place they'd ride would be back to the Circle Arrow herd grazing outside the town.

Ignoring the aches and pains in his body proved difficult. He needed a shot of whiskey. Hell, he needed a bottle to ease the anguish wracking him from head to toe. As he rode past the fort, he garnered a few curious looks from sentries patrolling the perimeter. Like most frontier forts, there wasn't a palisade, just a low adobe wall to keep the livestock from running away. He wondered what kept the soldiers from deserting. This was a lonely, terrible place.

He almost fell from the saddle in front of the first saloon he rode up to. Means straightened, worked the kinks from his shoulder, and rubbed his arm before entering. The cantina was in a small adobe house with a bar hardly eight feet long. On a wooden shelf behind the barkeep proudly stood four bottles. They were the only things in the cantina not covered with a thin coating of dust.

"You don't have much selection," Means said.

"Nope. We got rye, we got bourbon, we got brandy, and there's a bottle of—" The barkeep peered at the fourth bottle, then leaned closer to it as he tried to read the label. "We got whatever that is."

"You don't sell a lot of it, do you? Give me a shot."

"From this one? Mister, that's living high, wide, and dangerous." The bartender sloshed the muddy fluid around in the bottle. "It might have been tequila."

"It's almost black," Means said.

"The worm fell apart?" The barkeep hesitated and asked, "You still want it?"

"Gimme a shot and information." Means let a silver dollar spin on the bar, then come to rest, its ringing pure music to the bartender's ears.

"Anybody who'd drink this can hear whatever I got to say." He poured a shot into a glass. With some distaste he pushed it across the bar to Means.

"The cowboys from the herd grazing outside town. What do you know about them?" He toyed with his glass as the barkeep spewed forth everything he already knew. He lifted the glass, sniffed, and then knocked back the vile liquor. It tasted like nothing he had ever sampled before. There wasn't much kick. Then there was. He felt as if he went bare knuckles with the liquor, ducked a feint, and then got hit by a sucker punch.

"What's it taste like?" The bartender leaned closer to hear, in case it had robbed Means of his voice.

"You want to know, you try it."

"No, sir, not me. You're a better man than I am."

"That's as plain as that big nose on your face," Means said. "Do the trail boss and cook come in here?"

"Naw, they ain't much in the way of drinkers, or so the Circle Arrow cowboys say. But there's a new trail boss, and I seen a German fellow who don't speak much English over at the mercantile. Now that I think on it, the new trail boss is German, too, but he speaks good English, unlike the cook."

"What happened to the old ones?"

Means listened to a highly improbable tale unfold, then the barkeep mentioned Desmond Sullivan and how he had gone south with Don Jaime's herd because of Estella. This explained both Mackenzie and Flowers leaving their jobs and close to seven hundred head of cattle to be sold. Desmond Sullivan. He didn't know what draw the arrogant little pup had over the other two, but it explained them leaving. They were off to rescue him. Again.

"Keep that bottle ready for me. I'll be back to celebrate."

"Ain't been nobody daring enough to even smell it in a year. It'll be here for you. First one's on the house."

"I'll hold you to that," Means said, hitching up his gun belt. He had some riding to do to overtake the herd driving south toward Mexico. He hoped Don Jaime wouldn't miss that extra gringo helping with his herd. And he wondered how long his daughter would bawl her eyes out when her gringo lover was shot down along with Mackenzie and Flowers.

Means tried to make sense of the tracks in the sandy ground. The wind had scrambled much of the evidence, but picking out the bloody patches reminded him of his own fight with Flowers and Mackenzie. Someone had died here, judging by the amount of blood soaked into the ground. Rocks had been painted a dull red and more than a few bright scratches showed where bullets had ricocheted off into the distance.

"So a couple riders came galloping in from that direction." He imagined seeing the riders. A sneer crossed his lips. "Flowers. Mackenzie." He walked around the spot. "They rode down on men waiting here and shot them up. Why were the men here?"

He scratched his stubbled chin trying to work through what happened. All he could tell was that two or three men were ambushed and escaped. Two or three others had been killed or severely wounded to spill that much blood. He ran his finger over a rock. The blood had died fast in the hot sun, making it difficult to determine when the fight had happened.

"Within a couple of days," he mused. "And they're after Don Jaime's herd. Rustlers?" That didn't ring true. Or maybe it did. The rumors he had heard in Fort Sumner alerted him to a fight between Don Jaime and Luther Wardell. "These were Wardell's men," he decided.

He mounted and circled the area, finding the direction taken by the two riders who had charged into camp. Letting his horse have its head, he meandered southward. The tracks disappeared over sunbaked ground, but he pressed on. Just before sundown Means felt a little prickly. The hair rose on the back of his neck, a sure sign he was being watched.

Spied on or riding into trouble. Not slowing, not

looking around, he slid first one gun from its holster and then the other, checking to be sure he carried full wheels in each. The rifle under his right knee begged to be checked, too. The rifle was an old Henry, but it served its purpose in a fight. He was a crack shot with it, and that mattered more than having a Yellow Boy or some other fancy long gun.

In the distance he heard cattle lowing. He kept riding, but at an angle to his original path. The setting sun caught metal and gave off glints that allowed him to locate the source of his uneasiness. Not a half mile off he made out the dim shadows of three riders intent on working their way toward the herd. If they'd been vaqueros or otherwise working for Don Jaime, there'd be no reason for skulking. He caught his breath. It hardly seemed possible that his luck had dealt him a hand with three aces—Mackenzie, Flowers, and the snot-nosed kid.

He shook off that notion. From what he'd been told in Fort Sumner, Desmond Sullivan rode with Don Jaime as one of the cowboys. If Mac and Flowers had gone to fetch him back to the Circle Arrow herd, the three of them would be at odds. These riders huddled together, taking turns leading the single-file advance that took them toward the beeves.

Standing off and watching what Wardell's men did next made sense. Tackling Hiram Flowers, Mackenzie, and Sullivan on his own did not. Help might be at hand. Help or pawns to be sacrificed as he took his revenge on the Circle Arrow trio for what they'd done to his partners. His mind raced until everything came together.

He rode slowly toward the men, making sure they

heard him coming, then saw that he wasn't a threat. Keeping his hands outstretched to show he wasn't aiming a gun at them, he stopped a few yards off.

"Evening," he said. "I'm looking for the trail down into Mexico. You gents heading that way, too?"

"Who're you?" One of the men stepped out, hand resting on his pistol. Means sized him up fast. Not only was he the leader, he thought he was a fast hand and smarter than anyone else.

"My name's . . . Shiloh. Antietam Shiloh."

"You're a damned liar!"

"Why? You come across somebody else claiming that name?" Means almost laughed. He had given the first names that had come to mind. His uncle and his pa had died at Shiloh and Antietam, fighting for the wrong side. If the need arose in the future, he'd have to come up with a name that wasn't so outrageously fake. But the deed had been done, and he had to live with it. For the moment.

"Those are battles, not names."

"My pa had a fondness for those places long before they were battle sites. What kind of man makes fun of another's name?" Means waited to see the reaction.

"My name's Ransom."

Means laughed. "That a name or is that what you pay a kidnapper?" He saw he had taken the right path. The two men with Ransom laughed, causing their boss to turn and shush them.

"It's your worst nightmare," Ransom said.

"You mean it's my worst nightmare, Mister Shiloh." Means paused a few seconds, then said, "I was looking for trail companions. I'll keep looking." Before he turned his horse, Ransom snapped at him. "You hold on, mister." He swallowed his pride. "Mister Shiloh."

"Yes, Mister Ransom?" This reply put oil on troubled water.

"You got the look of being able to use those revolvers." Ransom moved closer to get a good look. "Fact is, you got the look of a man on the run from the law."

"Yes, no."

Ransom sputtered.

"Yes, I know how to use my sidearms. No, I'm not on the run from the law, local or federal. I just want to go to Mexico and see if I can't find a job. I've heard tell men with my skills are in demand to protect the towns and ranches from the Indians."

"The cavalry does that north of the border," Ransom said. "That's why New Mexico Territory is filthy with Army posts, all a day's ride apart."

"I've found that out. I get antsy if life's too quiet." Means considered adding more. Better to let Ransom lead the way.

"Do you have any problem taking a job right now? To get back cattle that've been rustled from my boss?"

Means had wondered what lie Ransom would tell. As fibs went, this wasn't too bad. He wouldn't have to press Ransom for more details.

"You ride out of Fort Sumner? There are plenty of ranches up there with fat cattle just itching to be rustled. That's the way I saw it, at any rate."

"You want to hire on for Luther Wardell's spread,

five dollars a day until we get the stolen cattle back to their pastures?"

"That's a mighty rich payoff. All the cattle in the herd along the trail yours? Mister Wardell's?"

"How'd you know—?" Ransom laughed harshly. "You were on the same trail as the herd."

"Hard to miss that many cow chips. Fresh ones, to boot."

"Not all the cows are Mister Wardell's. We'll have to cut out the ones that are and to hell with the rest. They might be from other ranches around Fort Sumner. That's not our concern. For all I care, what's not our property can be sold in Mexico."

Means nodded slowly. "Sensible way to approach it. You don't want to shoot it out with the rustlers? Just sneak in, get your beeves back, then go home?"

"Something like that," Ransom said.

Quick Willy Means grinned, dismounted, and went to Ransom, his hand outstretched.

"We got a deal. Let's go get some strays all rounded up, and damn the rustlers."

Ransom shook. From the small tremor, Means knew he'd have no trouble throwing down on Ransom and leaving the man dead in the dirt, if the need arose. Up close, he studied the man's face and knew he had a hundred wanted posters that might carry the man's visage.

A bounty hunter's job never ended.

CHAPTER 26

"Go. I do not want you." Don Jaime Abragon crossed his arms and rocked back as if distancing himself from Dewey Mackenzie and Hiram Flowers would get rid of them.

Mac almost laughed. If anything, this made him even more intent on staying. The man would do anything to protect Desmond, even take on the rancher as he made his way into Mexico.

Mac cut off the trail boss's response, knowing whatever Flowers said it would only make Don Jaime madder. He wanted to smooth ruffled feathers, not pluck them out.

"Don Jaime, please. Our interest is Desmond and nothing more. We have the same goal, I suspect." He glanced to where Desmond sat close to Estella Abragon. She made no effort to push him away. "His ma would have a fit knowing he ducked across the border when he was supposed to be going in the opposite direction."

"He is young." The rancher's lip curled. "So is she."

"Too young to understand what they're doing," Mac hurried on, realizing he was hardly older than Desmond. His own travails with women had almost gotten him hanged. "We agree on so much more. You want to get your herd to market. That's none of our business. Desmond's well-being is."

"You think to hog-tie him and take him with you?" Don Jaime laughed harshly.

"It'd work," Flowers said.

"It would work. And then my daughter would go after him. That distracts me. I would have to go after her, and then who drives my cattle to Don Pedro?"

Mac realized Don Jaime was right.

"You'd lose your ranch to Luther Wardell," Mac said. He took a deep breath and looked at Desmond and Estella making cow eyes at each other. "You'd lose your daughter, too. She'd never forgive you."

"You see a great deal," Don Jaime said. He uncrossed his arms and gestured with his hands, waving them in the air. "I do not know what to do. Do you know?"

"We can drag him off so she'd never know where he went," Flowers said. "We can hide our trail."

"She's not stupid, Mister Flowers," Mac cut in. "There's only one place he would go—back to Fort Sumner and the herd."

"It's his herd!"

"Whether she believes that or not doesn't matter. She'll go there and Don Jaime has the very problem he wants to avoid. The problem *we* want to avoid," Mac emphasized. "There is a way around this."

Both Don Jaime and Flowers stared at him as if he had grown a hand out of the top of his head.

"What is this magic? You know a *brujo* to cast a spell on her?"

"She'll stay with the herd as long as he's riding with you as a vaquero. So Mister Flowers and I go along until you sell your cattle in Mexico. We'll work. You don't have to pay us."

"So?" Don Jaime frowned, trying to figure Mac's angle.

"At that age, passions run high and burn out fast. By the time we get to Mexico, they'll be tired of each other. There'll be an argument. They will see someone else who excites them more. I understand there are many pretty señoritas where we're going." He had no idea where that was, but assuming there were women there helped his argument.

"He is not so stupid. He would never turn from my Estella." Don Jaime smiled broadly after a moment. "But she will see many of the young bucks from wealthy families. They are in favor in the Spanish court, with the king. They appreciate my land grant."

Flowers started to say something about forcing Estella to marry the son of a wealthy landowner. Mac elbowed him and got a dark look. Flowers subsided.

"We look after Desmond, and you do the same for your daughter." Mac saw Don Jaime come around to his way of thinking. He wondered if Don Jaime cottoned to the idea of Desmond fading away, only to be replaced by another gringo. Mac had never seen a lovelier woman than Estella and knew he offered her more than Desmond ever could, in spite of the youngster being heir to the Circle Arrow.

"Do not get in my way." Don Jaime pointed. "And keep him away from her. As much as possible." With that he stalked off, barking orders to his foreman. Men hurried around as he gave orders to bed down the herd for the night.

"I don't know if we came out on top or not, Mac." Flowers scratched his head. "We got to work for him all the way to market? For nothing?"

"Not for nothing. Miz Sullivan's still paying us, only not to be trail boss or cook. She'll be paying us to watch over her son."

"You're playing some other game, aren't you, Mac? I can tell. You and Desmond weren't such good friends that you'd do all this for his sake."

"You accused me of wanting to disappear into Mexico before. Let's take it one day at a time."

"We already helped Don Jaime more than he knows, scaring off Wardell's men the way we did."

"There'll be other problems. Rustlers. Indians. Once we get into Mexico, I have no idea what we'll face. Have you been in Mexico?"

"Not for years. There's nobody left who remembers me, not that this is where I was in Mexico. I crossed the Rio Grande down south of Eagle Pass."

"And?" Mac nudged him to tell more. There had to be a good story, one that'd keep the cowboys laughing around the campfire.

"And nothing. You're too young to hear. It'd burn your delicate ears."

"Show me when we get to Mexico," Mac said, laughing.

"We better get mounted and see if Don Jaime wants

us to take a turn at night herd." Flowers stretched. "Been a while since I rode like that."

"You're always up, checking on the cowboys who are on night herd," Mac said. "I've done it a few times, but mostly preparing food is the one thing that keeps me busier than a cat in a mouse factory."

Mac stepped up and brought his horse alongside Flowers. They rode slowly until they were away from the main camp and not likely to have anyone overhear what they said.

"Keep an eye out for rustlers," Flowers said. "We've seen more than enough evidence that this herd is a prime target." He sniffed. "Prime. Not the beef. The Circle Arrow longhorns are better. Prime Texas beef."

Mac slowly drifted away from his trail boss, letting Flowers carry on because the sound of the man's voice soothed the cattle. On the far side of the herd a vaquero sang in a deep, melodic voice some song Mac did not recognize. He didn't know if it gentled the cattle, but it made him begin to nod off. Now and then he jerked awake. He had been through too much that day not to be exhausted. His horse walked without stumbling; he wasn't sure he could do the same.

As he circled the herd and shooed a few cattle back to the main herd, a clicking sound brought him fully awake. A smooth move pulled his revolver from its holster. Turning from the cattle, he rode due south in the direction the herd would travel the next morning. A sliver of moon poked up in the sky, but the brilliant stars provided most of the light. Eerie shadows danced as he rode, only to stop dead a quarter mile from the herd. The clicking sound was louder here.

Mac lifted his pistol in that direction. A small shadow became a larger one as a rider appeared. The rider stopped. Mac kept his pistol aimed in the rider's direction. The rider lit a quirley and puffed on it. The sudden flare of the lucifer gave Mac an instant to see the man's face. He had a serape slung over his shoulder and wore a broad-brimmed sombrero. He took his time with the smoke, then tossed the stub away. It trailed embers all the way to the ground where it vanished. With a shrug, the rider pulled the serape around, turned his horse, and walked off. Again came the clicking sound of steel horseshoes against rock. He listened until only the soft wind disturbed the desert silence.

Going after the rider gained him nothing. Mac returned to the herd, completed his circuit and two hours on duty. In camp, he found himself a place to spread his bedroll, forcing himself to stay away from the chuckwagon. He felt out of place having the stars overhead as he stretched out, rather than looking up at the chuckwagon's bottom. In a short time he had developed habits that proved hard to break.

He slept fitfully, waking before dawn. To be sure he was ready to ride, he gathered his gear, tended his horse, and called out when he saw Don Jaime.

"I wanted to tell you what I saw last night."

"Do I care?" The ranch owner's foul mood almost made Mac hold his tongue.

"You should." He described the rider and how the man had watched the herd, as if judging the number of vaqueros in preparation for an attempt to rustle as many head as possible.

"We are close to the border. He rode from the south?"

"Yes, sir, he did. I didn't see anyone with him, but his confidence tells me he's not alone."

"You did well to tell me. The Rurales are in cahoots with many bandidos. We must avoid them as well as any lone rider thinking to lure us into an ambush."

"You're the boss."

Don Jaime's eyes narrowed as he studied Mac, hunting for any trace of sarcasm. There wasn't any, but he still thought less of what Mac told him than if one of his own vaqueros had.

"Get breakfast. We hit the trail in an hour." Don Jaime went about his business, rousting his men and bellowing for chores to be done.

Mac made his way to the chuckwagon and watched Felipe work. The cook prepared food differently, in an order that made Mac want to help. Somehow, in spite of what had to be a poor use of time and food, the cook had everything ready for the men. Mac missed his own biscuits, but the freshly fried tortillas made up for the lack of them. He used bits of the last tortilla, as he would a biscuit, to sop up whatever remained on his plate.

Felipe took his tin plate without a word. His reluctance to acknowledge Mac carried over to the rest of the vaqueros. As he mounted, Mac saw one exception. Estella Abragon had no trouble chatting brightly with Desmond. The two of them rode side by side until Don Jaime trotted up and sent Desmond out to the front of the herd. Mac had to smile. Assigning Desmond the responsibility of keeping to the trail showed Don Jaime had grown some respect for the cowboy.

Or was there something else going on?

He caught up with Flowers to share his concern.

"He sent Desmond ahead, and there might be trouble brewing."

"I know," Flowers said. "Last night I went scouting after I finished night herd and saw a campfire a few miles ahead of us. From the size of the fire, there were a dozen men there."

"Rustlers," Mac said. "That's what I think."

"And Desmond will be the one who springs the trap. Don Jaime is using him as bait."

"There," Mac said, "is a path leading off the main trail. We take it and come up from the side at about the place where Desmond calls a halt for Felipe to set up the chuckwagon."

"The chuckwagon," Flowers said. "I knew I'd missed something. The chuckwagon is behind the herd, not in front of it." He looked around hastily. He saw the path Mac had mentioned. He pulled out his rifle and checked it.

"Let's ride," Mac said. He had already made certain his weapons were ready for a fight.

They set off at a gallop. Slowing to a canter let their horses regain their wind, then they galloped for another two miles before reaching a small canyon opening out into a wider plain. Desert plants dotted the sandy ground. Waiting behind half a dozen mesquite trees were bandidos, bandanas pulled up over their faces and their pistols drawn.

"That's half of them. The rest are over yonder." Flowers pointed.

Mac couldn't see them but believed the older man. Flowers had been on enough trail drives to have an instinct for such things. Mac felt a tension that showed he was developing a similar nature.

"There's Desmond," Mac said quietly as he spotted the young man ambling along a couple of hundred yards to the right. "They'll let him ride in and then what? Reckon the herd will come on because he didn't warn the vaqueros?" Mac stood in the stirrups and shaded his eyes. "There's a second rider, one joining Desmond." His stomach tightened into a knot.

Both he and Flowers exclaimed at the same time, "Estella!"

Their outcry ruined any hope they had of a surprise ambush on the rustlers. The one closest spun, shouted a warning in Spanish, and opened fire. He used a six-gun and was out of range, but others had rifles and turned them on Mac and Flowers.

"Desmond, run! Get Estella out of here!" Mac shouted, then had to duck as the air around him filled with lead. He swung his rifle up and fired, but his horse started crow hopping and ruined his aim.

Flowers had better luck. His first shot winged the bandido nearest them. Then he, too, was forced to break off and try to reach safety.

Desmond and Estella had wheeled their horses and were galloping away from the canyon. Mac saw Estella's horse go down suddenly. It had stepped in a prairie dog hole or somehow else failed her. She hit the ground and rolled. Desmond didn't seem to have noticed what had happened.

"Keep down!" His shouted warning was drowned out by a rising thunder of gunfire. He bent forward, head pressed low by his horse's neck as he raced toward Estella. The hail of bullets diminished thanks to Flowers and his accurate return fire. He had pulled up and was spraying lead among the bandidos.

By the time Mac got to Estella, she was sitting up, dazed. He reached down to help her up behind him. His horse balked, then screamed, reared, and keeled over. One of the rustlers had finally found the range and shot the horse out from under him. Mac had to kick his feet free of the stirrups and dive from the saddle to keep the horse from falling on him. He crashed to the ground, shook off the fall, and rolled onto his belly. Somehow he had held on to his rifle.

A flash of sunlight off a rifle's front sight presented a decent target. Mac got his first killing shot in, saw the bandido throw up his arms and topple from his horse. This did nothing to slow the rate of firing.

"Desmond!" the young woman cried out, and reached up.

Mac saw Desmond galloping toward them. He hit the ground running and dropped beside Estella, holding her. She clung to him and buried her face in his shoulder.

For a brief second, the shooting stopped. In that pause, Mac saw he had no chance with Estella, not with Desmond around.

"Get down, both of you." Mac broke the lull in the

fight in an attempt to get both Desmond and Estella to safety.

He jerked as two bullets hit him at the same instant. One ripped away part of his duster and left a crease in his left side. The other slug jerked him around as it tore at his scalp. His left temple felt as if it would explode. He fell facedown and lay stunned. Through the ground he felt vibration.

At first he thought it was Flowers's galloping horse. He pushed himself up and saw Flowers a dozen yards away astride his mount. Not moving. Flowers kept his horse steady with his knees as he fired methodically. The vibration didn't come from his horse's hooves. Twisting his head around despite the thunderous pain inside his skull, he saw the real cause of the earthquake.

Don Jaime's herd was stampeding directly toward him. He forced himself to his feet, wobbled, and found it impossible to keep upright. Mac crashed back to the ground in the path of the frightened cattle.

CHAPTER 27

How many times could one man get trapped in the path of a stampede and survive? Mac didn't know, but he had a hunch the odds had just caught up to him.

He hoped he would die quick. Being maimed and hanging on to a thread of life for days or weeks wasn't for him. Mac worried even more about being so crippled for life he couldn't get around. Fumbling, he tried to lift his rifle and shoot himself rather than be stomped on by the cattle. His fingers had turned into sausages, big and greasy and not working.

Then he felt light and floating.

"Walk, damn you," a voice said urgently in his ear. "Help me."

"What?" He turned his head and almost lost his balance again. "Desmond?"

"Walk. Run, if you can. Get over there with Estella. It's not far."

"Not far." The words echoed in Mac's head. His dizziness passed, just a little, and he saw Estella Abragon hunkered down behind a mesquite perched on the edge of a deep arroyo. Everything clicked in his head. If he could get there, the steep bank would protect him. The cattle would blunder into the thorny bush and veer away, no matter how frightened they were.

His feet worked a little better as Desmond's arm around his shoulders supported him. Then he ran—stumbled. He fell forward and hit the bottom of the arroyo with enough force to send pain jabbing into his head. And side. And everywhere in his body. Hands pulled him upright, so he pressed his back against the tall, crumbling, sunbaked arroyo wall. In the distance he heard gunfire and pounding hooves and shouts.

Closing his eyes helped him regain his senses. Then he forced himself to look around. Desmond held Estella, cradling her, and turned so any steer coming over the edge of the arroyo would hit him first.

"The herd's not stampeding anymore," Mac croaked out. He pressed his fingers into the side of his head. They came away sticky with blood. He straightened and examined his side. His duster was shredded and stained with blood seeping from the shallow wound in his side. Moving around, he gingerly examined the wound. He wasn't so bad off, after all.

"They turned the herd," Desmond said.

Mac looked at him. Estella hung on him, her arms circling him as if she were drowning and he was her lifeline.

"Thanks," Mac said. "You pulled my fat from the fire."

"You saved me," Desmond said. Then he wasn't talking. Estella kissed him.

Mac turned away. This wasn't any of his business. Then he saw Flowers riding down the arroyo. He waved, but Flowers had already spotted him—them.

"Well, isn't this a fine reunion," the trail boss said. "Everybody still have all their parts attached to their bodies?"

"Mostly," Mac said. He grabbed an exposed root and pulled himself to his feet. "What's happened to the bandidos?"

"The ones that weren't stomped to death mounted up and galloped away. Don Jaime says we're already over the border and in Mexico, so there's no reason for the cavalry to go after them."

"What about the Rurales?" Mac took a few hesitant steps. The dizziness passed, and he was sure he was going to be all right. But he needed a horse if he intended to get very far. Hoofing it in this desert, he wouldn't get half a mile before he keeled over.

"They don't risk their necks unless they're paid," Flowers said. "Might be some of the rustlers were Rurales. I thought I saw a couple of them wearing uniforms. Might be they took them, might be they threw in with the rustlers."

"How far do we have to go?"

"Not more than three days," Estella said. "I went to Don Pedro's rancho a few times when I was younger. He owns land stretching for many miles along the border and then down into Mexico."

"He sounds like a prosperous rancher," Flowers said.

"He is. He is also a terrible man. But *muy rico.*"

"Let's get back to work," Flowers said. "You need a ride?" He reached down to help Mac up behind him. The trail boss chuckled. "I'd rather have her riding behind me, but Desmond beat me to it."

"He'd fight you off," Mac said. Estella had already settled behind Desmond on his horse as they made their way up the brittle slope. He kept it to himself how Desmond had saved his life. In spite of the way he had started out, Desmond was turning into a decent man. There hadn't been any call for him to come to Mac's aid. He could have stayed with Estella and protected her. He'd saved her, and he'd saved Mac.

Seeing the two on horseback made Mac wonder what Flowers would do when Desmond refused to return to the Circle Arrow. He fell into the rhythm of Flowers's horse, almost going to sleep by the time they caught up with Don Jaime and the herd.

"He won't let me use any of his horses," Mac said to Felipe. The cook shrugged. "I can't ride herd, so I'm stuck here with you."

Felipe glared at him as he peeled potatoes. He glared even more when Mac sat next to the sack of potatoes, hefted a spud, and pulled out his cooking knife. The blade flashed four times and the potato skin surrendered. The naked potato went into the pot and another joined it a few seconds later.

"I do not need help."

"Then teach me." Mac's simple statement made Don Jaime's cook jerk around and stare at him.

"What do you mean?"

"I'm a cook, a danged good one, but what I fix for the Circle Arrow crew isn't anything like you do. Those pinto beans are about the best tasting beans I ever had."

"Green chile," Felipe said. "That is how I do it. And some other spices."

"Show me, and I'll do whatever work you don't want to."

"You are a strange gringo."

"I'm a cook. I like it, I want to do it better."

"Then you will learn from a master." Felipe grinned broadly.

Mac settled down and watched, with Felipe speaking only a little. When Felipe asked questions about why Mac prepared parts of the meal the way he did, Mac knew he was accepted. Working as a wrangler, a cook's assistant, didn't bother him too much. He earned a few dollars, or more likely his choice of horse from Don Jaime's remuda when they arrived. Estella had said it would be a couple more days.

That suited him just fine. He wanted to ask what life was like in Mexico so he could make a better decision whether to drift on further into the center of the country or return with Flowers. Estella would follow her father back to Fort Sumner once the money was securely in hand, but Mac began to doubt if Desmond would budge an inch without the woman. Flowers had lost himself any chance of winning Mercedes Sullivan's approval by taking her son on the drive and teaching him ranching.

Whether Don Jaime allowed the Texan to stay and work on his ranch was another matter. Mac foresaw gunplay if the land grant holder tried to separate Desmond from his daughter.

Thinking on it as he prepared food for Don Jaime's vaqueros, Mac decided he would back Desmond's play, whatever it was. If he even returned to Fort Sumner.

"You're looking mighty thoughty," Flowers said, settling down and holding out his tin plate for Mac to slop a little of this and more of that on it.

"What are you going to do about Desmond?" There was no call to explain what he meant. Flowers had to have the same ideas.

"I've been talking to Don Jaime. He's not too keen on having a gringo as a son-in-law. He's planning on arranging a marriage between Estella and some Mexican rancher's boy."

"Does he have anyone in mind?"

"He's going to shop around and see what the best match is." Flowers began shoveling the food into his mouth, chewing once and swallowing almost whole. The way he wolfed it down made it seem he was in a hurry.

Mac asked about that.

"Estella said we were a couple days away from Don Pedro's ranch. Truth is, we're not only south of the border, we're on the ranch and the two of them, Don Pedro and Don Jaime, are fixing to meet around sundown to discuss the sale."

"So soon?" Mac held back a moment's panic. Being rushed into a decision put him on edge after he had anticipated another couple of days to mull over his choices.

"Don Jaime refused to go to Don Pedro's hacienda. There's plenty of bad blood between them. From what I overheard of the vaqueros gossiping, and my Spanish is not too good, Don Pedro didn't want Don Jaime inside his house, either. There was talk he'd only meet him out by the pigsty. Whatever's gone wrong between the two of them, it's bad wrong."

"Will Don Pedro try to cheat Don Jaime on payment?" Mac's hand drifted to the S&W at his side. He hadn't signed on to be a hired gunman, but protecting Desmond and seeing him returned to his own herd might require some exchange of lead.

"Don't know. I do know Desmond is riding out with Don Jaime because Estella is going along, too." Flowers scraped the rest of his food straight from the plate into his mouth. A gulp got it down, followed by the full cup of coffee made from boiled mesquite beans. "You up for a twilight ride?"

"Thought you'd never ask." Mac finished his chores to Felipe's satisfaction and went with Flowers to the rope corral.

"Go on, take a horse. You can always say you're riding night herd."

"In a way, I reckon I am," Mac said. He wasn't going to work long enough to justify being given a horse. The few pesos Don Jaime might pay him for helping Felipe would hardly buy a shot of tequila.

They rode through the gathering gloom, the desert coming alive with hunters and hunted. Mac knew the feeling. In spite of riding with Flowers to make sure that Desmond didn't get into too much trouble, he watched over his shoulder constantly in case somebody was creeping up on him. It was ridiculous to react like this, he knew. He had rid himself of bounty hunters and others wanting to ventilate him.

"There they are," Flowers said.

Peering through the shadowy desert, Mac saw what Flowers already had. Two groups stood a few feet apart, looking for all the world like they were going to throw down on each other. Behind Don Jaime stood Desmond, two vaqueros, and at the rear, Estella.

Despite everything that had happened, despite knowing better, Mac felt a pang of desire for her. So lovely. But so devoted to Desmond. Mac forced himself not to linger on her grim form silhouetted in the night against the starlit sky.

Facing Don Jaime was a shorter man, stockier and even more voluble as he waved his arms around. Compared to the Fort Sumner rancher, he had an army with him. Mac lost count at eight vaqueros.

The voices carried in the still night, but Mac didn't understand enough Spanish to know what insults were being swapped. Whatever Don Pedro said, it wasn't complimentary. Don Jaime's answer was no less biting.

"What's happening?" Flowers came up in the stirrups, hand going to his gun. "They're moving toward each other."

"Papers," Mac said. "Don Jaime has papers. That must be the bill of sale for his herd. Don Pedro is handing over money."

The business transaction continued with more insults bouncing back and forth. Mac held his breath when Don Pedro thrust out his hand. And waited. Don Jaime finally shook, completing the deal. Don Jaime handed the money to Estella, who clutched it to her breast. She spoke quietly with Desmond. Then they backed away a few paces, turned, mounted, and rode off.

"What do we do?" Mac felt at loose ends. He had a horse that would take him into central Mexico. Leaving behind the suspicion he felt every time he saw a stranger coming toward him meant a simpler life. If he stayed in the U.S., every man might turn out to be a bounty hunter after him. In Mexico, no one knew him or cared about his past.

"Follow Desmond back. The sooner we're out of this country, the better I'll feel. We tangled with rustlers. Some got away. Sure as hell and damnation, they'll recruit some of the Rurales to come for us. Then we're fighting the whole damned Mexican Army."

"Don Pedro sounds like the kind of man who'd set them on Don Jaime to steal back his money. If he split it with the soldiers he'd come out way ahead."

"More than that, Mac. He hates Don Jaime enough to let the soldiers have all the money. He's got a big herd of prime cattle at a bargain. Killing Don Jaime is a bonus for him since his hands would be clean of the deed."

This decided Mac about where to ride and what to do. At least for a while. Don Pedro controlled the entire stretch of border. Killing everyone who rode with Don Jaime seemed to be something that the Mexican cattle baron would revel in.

Without a word, Mac swung his horse around and

trotted after Don Jaime and the others. He quickly
discovered how fast they rode, wanting to get away
from Don Pedro. Within a half hour they had returned to the herd. Don Jaime was already bellowing
orders about packing up and heading north.

The vaqueros complained about riding in the
dark, but Don Jaime cursed them and used a short
whip on one to roust him from his bedroll and get
him on the trail. Mac dropped to the ground to help
Felipe pack up the chuckwagon. The cook had left
out the fixings for breakfast.

"We return home," Felipe said. "It is good Don
Jaime has the money."

"I've got experience driving at night," Mac said.
"You want me to take the reins?"

"My chuckwagon, my duty," Felipe said. He slapped
Mac on the shoulder. "You are a good cook." With
that compliment, he climbed onto the driver's box
and got the six-mule team pulling hard. Seeing how
balky a pair of them were, Mac silently thanked Felipe for insisting on driving.

He mounted and rode to where Flowers spoke in
low tones with Desmond. Mac left them alone and
went to Estella. He remembered her pa had given
her the sale money. She had stuffed it down the front
of her riding blouse. A dozen unworthy thoughts
raced across Mac's mind.

"Did your pa get the price he asked?"

She nodded. With a quick toss of her head, she
moved the broad-brimmed dark hat back and let it
drop behind, held around her neck by a stampede
string. She was just about the loveliest woman Mac
had seen.

"He worries there will be treachery from Don Pedro."

"So much so that he's not going to stay and find you a husband?"

Mac almost laughed at her reaction. She whirled around, her dark eyes flashing anger.

"I have told him I will have no part in such a thing. I . . . I have other plans." She looked toward Desmond.

"You and your pa are going to lock horns over him." Mac thought a moment, then said, "He's a better man since he met you."

"You are his friend?"

Mac shook his head. Exactly what Desmond was to him remained a mystery. They had saved each other's lives more than once, but he felt no bond with the young ranch heir. Desmond rode his own trail. Mac had to, also, and it wasn't in the same direction.

The tight knot of vaqueros rode past them, joking and laughing. After the night's sale, they were getting paid. Don Jaime's ranch was safe from being sold at auction by the bank. All was well.

But the longer Mac rode alongside Estella, the uneasier he felt. Desmond cantered over, and he and the woman rode together a few yards from Mac. The night had turned even darker, making it difficult to see, even in the bright starlight. The moon rose in a few hours, but it was a sliver and gave no real brightening to ride by.

He jumped when Flowers said in a low voice, "You feel it, too, don't you, Mac?"

He didn't know what he felt, but a vague dread clutched at him. Then all hell broke loose.

Again.

CHAPTER 28

Bullets tore past Mac, forcing him to fight to keep his horse from bolting. Flowers wasn't as lucky. His horse lit out like its tail was on fire. Mac knew the trail boss rode like his butt was glued to the saddle and would soon bring the frightened horse under control, so he whirled around to see what happened with Desmond and Estella.

Estella's horse stood stolidly, unaffected by the deadly lead filling the air around her. From the way Desmond's horse bucked and reared, it might have been grazed by a stray bullet meant for its rider.

"This way, this way!" Mac waved to the others. He spotted an arroyo leading away into a cluster of rocky hills that would provide good cover—if they reached it.

He foolishly sat upright in the saddle to get a better look at who was attacking them. The flash of gunfire off brass and medals told the story. As Flowers had worried, the Rurales had come for them with guns blazing. Whether dispatched by Don Pedro or they recognized easy pickings when they saw it, the

Rurales put everyone riding with Don Jaime in danger.

Estella galloped toward Mac. Desmond had more difficulty because his horse wanted to run away from the gunfire. If it did, both rider and horse would be out in the open, good targets even in the dark. From what Mac saw, they were only a few minutes from being caught in the jaws of a cross fire set up by the Mexican soldiers. Don Jaime and his men had ridden through, but the Rurales waited for the stragglers. Maybe they knew Estella carried the money from the cattle sale.

Or maybe they simply saw an easy way to split Don Jaime's forces in half. Whatever the reason, they fought like wildcats, with Don Jaime on the far side of the group. If there had been a way to communicate with the ranch owner and his vaqueros, Mac saw that the Rurales would be the ones in a trap, fighting on two fronts. As it was, he and the others were forced to take refuge or die.

Desmond had finally gotten his horse under control. He rode around so he positioned himself between the soldiers and Estella. "Where's Flowers? Wasn't he with you?"

"His horse took off in the other direction," Mac said. "If we're lucky, he can get through the Rurales and tell Don Jaime to counterattack."

"Shoot the no-account bastards in the back," Desmond said. He glanced at Estella, as if he worried that such language offended her. She paid no heed. Her expression said that she had come to that conclusion without Desmond's profane urging.

Mac dragged his rifle from the saddle sheath. He

spat. Checking his gear before riding from camp would have served him better now. This rifle needed patches of rust wire-brushed off the barrel. As he cocked it, he heard grinding. It hadn't been oiled in too long. If luck rode with him, the gun wouldn't blow up when he fired it.

The answer came faster than he liked. A soldier galloped toward them. Not even thinking, Mac lifted the rifle to his shoulder, aimed, and fired. The recoil almost knocked him from horseback. He recovered in time to see the Rurale throw up his hands and topple backward from his horse. The shot had been more luck than skill. His luck had run out after he pulled the trigger. Part of the bore had been peeled back as the bullet left the barrel. He tossed the useless rifle away and pulled his trusty revolver. He fired several times, driving back another soldier.

Desmond, Estella, and Mac drew into a crude circle at the mouth of the arroyo, their horses' hindquarters rubbing together. This let them fire outward and, temporarily, drive back their attackers. Mac saw immediately there wasn't any way to survive if they stayed here.

"Ride for the hills. I'll slow them down."

"Go," Desmond urged Estella. "We'll keep them from hurting you."

Mac was in no position to argue. He had fallen into the job of protecting Desmond ever since he and Flowers had pulled the young man from the Fort Worth brothel. Things had changed since then. They had to rely on each other, and Desmond willingly pulled his weight now.

Estella leaned over and gave Desmond a quick kiss.

She missed his lips and pressed briefly against his cheek. Then she drew her right arm across her belly to cradle the money from selling the herd and lit out at full speed. Her horse tried to slow, showing good sense in the darkness. Heels raking, she dug her Spanish rowels into horseflesh. This convinced the reluctant nag to ignore the chance of stepping into a hole and to race like the wind.

Desmond looked at Mac, who grinned and said, "Let's see who gets to her first."

Desmond started to protest. He spoke to empty air. Mac charged out of the arroyo and cut off at an angle to give Estella more time to reach the foothills. Desmond quickly overtook him, his horse stronger and not ridden into the ground by a careless vaquero during the drive. They began to zigzag, drawing fire and forcing the Rurales to waste their ammo. Mac barely had time to tense as his horse gathered its hind legs and made a mighty jump over a huge patch of prickly pear cactus. He landed hard but held on. Desmond skirted the spiny clump.

A few more shots emptied his six-gun. Mac crammed it back into his holster and concentrated on outpacing the squad of soldiers now giving chase. He slid down an embankment, then crossed to a steeper climb into the rocky foothills. From here all he could do was follow a game trail meandering through increasingly large boulders. Even if he had a loaded gun, firing over his shoulder would have been futile. The rocks gave him cover. He popped out from between two towering rocks that formed a channel so tight he thought the horse might get stuck.

"Up here. Hurry!" Estella waved to him from a

hundred feet farther along the trail. The elevation changed quickly, affording her a view of the desert behind them.

Mac was panting with exhaustion by the time he drew alongside the young woman.

"Where's Desmond?"

"He comes along a different trail." She pointed, but Mac failed to see. He closed his eyes and listened. A rider approached, making good time.

"Are you sure it's Desmond?" He broke open the S&W and kicked free the spent cartridges. Wanting to hurry but knowing that rushing made him clumsy, he reloaded with mechanical precision. The gun snapped back shut, ready for action, when a dark shape came from between two rocks to his left. He started to fire, then checked himself.

"Desmond!" Estella rode to him and they awkwardly hugged.

"We've got bandidos on our trail," Mac said. "You want to deal with them first?"

"There is no need," Estella said. "I saw Papa and a few vaqueros riding to fight them."

Mac strained to hear gunfire and was greeted with only the silence of the desert.

"They are chasing them away," Estella went on. "We are safe."

Mac wanted to see for himself. He dismounted, climbed to the top of a boulder, and studied the ground they had just ridden across. It was as desolate and devoid of life as any desert he had ever seen. Don Jaime might be chasing off the Rurales. It didn't matter. The soldiers were gone and no longer a threat. He turned in a slow circle, hunting for Hiram Flowers. If things had gone right, Flowers had eluded the Rurales and fetched Don Jaime and his men.

"I don't see him," he said. "Mister Flowers."

"He can take care of himself," Desmond said. Swinging his leg over the saddle horn, he slid to the ground and took a couple stumbling steps.

"*Mi novio*, you are hurt!"

Estella rushed to Desmond's aid. When he dismounted, his legs caved under him. He fell to his knees, still hanging on to the reins. He used his stirrup to pull back to his feet. The places he had been shot earlier pained him anew. His side ached like a son of a bitch and dizziness sent the world spinning around him. Carefully walking, letting his horse support him, he found a comfortable-looking rock and sank to it. His knees hurt from scraping along the rocks leading to this refuge.

He slowly regained his strength. Protecting Desmond looked less likely in his condition than Desmond protecting him—if Desmond ever noticed. He and Estella were too busy kissing and carrying on.

Mac sucked in a deep breath and let it out slowly. His heart raced faster as he did so. He sucked in another breath, taking it in so he caught every hint of scent on the faint breeze blowing from higher elevations. Trying not to look too obvious, he slid his revolver from its holster and laid it across his lap. Gritting his teeth at the noise, he broke it open and checked to be sure he carried a full load. When he was sure, when his strength was enough, he drew back the hammer, half stood, and looked into the rocks above them. His finger curled on the trigger the instant he spotted a hat rising up from behind the crest of a boulder.

The report startled both Desmond and Estella, but it took his target by even more surprise. The man rose, pushed his hat back from his head, touched the hole in his forehead where oozing blood turned inky black in the starlight, and slumped forward. Mac had drilled him through the brain with one shot.

"Who's that?" Desmond asked.

"Don't know, don't care," Mac said. He tugged at his horse's reins to get it back down the trail he had just ridden. Pushing between the tall rocks gave protection on either side. It also funneled a volley of shots coming from the rocks near the man he had killed.

"Those are not Rurales," Estella cried. "They are gringos. They do not wear uniforms."

"Chances are good they're Wardell's men," Mac told her. He silently cursed. They should have killed them, all of them, rather than believing they would hightail it for Fort Sumner. "Keep moving. Your pa has run off the Mexican soldiers. We have to go back that way." He ducked involuntarily as another round spanged off a rock beside his head. Hot chips of splintered rock stung his cheek.

"How'd you know they were up there?" Desmond pushed forward to stand between the gunmen and Estella.

"I caught the smell of tobacco. I don't partake, and I've never seen you build a smoke."

"You saved us," Estella said.

"We're not out of this yet. Check farther downhill and see if they're circling us."

"Wait, no!" Desmond tried to stop her but Mac grabbed his arm and spun him around.

"It gets her out of the line of fire. They're not down there. They're above us. All of them."

"How can you tell?" Desmond looked worried. He scowled when Estella vanished around a bend in the trail.

"Instinct," Mac said. Actually, he had no idea, but his show of confidence settled Desmond's nerves and focused him on the narrow gap between the rocks and the sandy pit just beyond where they had first taken refuge.

Mac looked around. Their attackers had chosen a poor spot for an ambush, unless they had intended to gun the trio down. Mac wished about now he was with Felipe riding along on the chuckwagon, heading for Fort Sumner. Might as well wish he was on the moon, he reflected wryly. Escaping wasn't going to be easy, especially with Desmond and Estella to look after.

"We can't make a stand here," Desmond said. "There's no way to move around. We either attack them straight ahead or get on down the trail."

Mac reached into his coat pocket and fingered the spare ammo there. Desmond was right. He had a dozen rounds plus the six chambered in the S&W. Then he remembered his shot that reduced the attackers' number by one. Five rounds in his six-gun. Even if Desmond had more, the men coming after their scalps could wait them out.

"I can't see what's happening," Desmond said. "It's too dark."

Mac avoided staring at the deep shadows and looked instead at the spots where the stars shone the brightest. On a cloudless night the illumination was enough to see clearly. In this tumble of rocks, he caught glimpses of movement but listening hard gave him more information on what the gunmen were doing. When he took another deep whiff, he raised his pistol and fired three times. He heard a grunt, then a curse. He hadn't killed the man trying to sneak up on them but he'd certainly winged him.

"Who are you?" Mac called. "We don't have any feud with you." He held up his hand to keep Desmond quiet. Whatever answer he got was likely to be a lie. All he wanted was a hint as to how many men they faced and where they had positioned themselves in the rocks.

"We're only bandidos," the answer came back. "We want the money you got from the cattle sale!"

Mac pressed Desmond back. They quietly retreated. He had located the one who answered. That had to be the leader.

They inched away and finally came to the base of the small hill. Estella waited anxiously a hundred yards away.

"Go to her, get away," Mac said softly. "I'll keep them back until you find Flowers or her pa."

"I'm not leaving you to face them alone," Desmond insisted.

"They want her, or the money she's got. The only way they'd know about it is if Wardell sent them to steal it."

"They might be Mexicans," Desmond said. Then, "Oh. They aren't. They don't have accents."

"I think I recognize the leader. His name's Ransom."

"Wardell's foreman!"

"You go on now," Mac said. "Make a lot of noise as you go so they'll think I'm with you. I'm going to lay an ambush for the ambushers."

He handed the reins of his horse to Desmond.

"I won't need it, and you have to decoy them. If they see or hear only one horse leaving, they'll know what I'm up to. Now *go*."

Mac knew Desmond obeyed when he heard the thudding of hooves going toward Estella. He bent double and ran to a spindly greasewood bush and crouched behind it. Hands sweaty, heart hammering, he waited. It took only a minute for a trio of men on foot to come from the narrow trail and spread out.

Ransom would be in the middle. His henchmen would flank him. Mac steadied his revolver, squeezed off a shot, and cried out in triumph when the middle man collapsed as if his knees had turned to water. Mac swung to the left and triggered a second shot, then hurriedly flung lead to the right. He winged one man and scared the other. Not letting himself think too much about what he was doing, he got his feet under him, ignored the pain twisting him around from his prior wounds, and ran forward shouting.

The man he had winged switched hands and tried to fire. Mac dispatched him with two more shots. He stumbled and went to a knee. This saved him from catching a wild shot from the third man. Using both hands to steady his aim, he fired.

The third man straightened, then toppled like a tall tree sawed off at the roots.

"Mackenzie!"

His head snapped up at the sound of his name. His heart jumped into his throat.

"You know me, Dewey Mackenzie. I could take you in to the law. I could drag your worthless carcass all the way back to New Orleans. But I won't. You know why? You killed three of my men. The Huffman brothers. All dead."

Quick Willy Means came from the rocks, widened his stance, and pushed his coattails back on both sides. He wore two revolvers and looked able to draw and fire both of them.

"The only thing missing is Hiram Flowers," Means went on. "I got a beef with him, but you were the one I was sent after. I can deal with him later since that's personal, not business."

Mac raised his gun and fired. The hammer fell on a spent chamber.

"I was counting, Mackenzie. Six rounds fired. How'd you survive this long being so careless?" Means started walking toward him. "Go on. Try to reload. I can plug you from here, but I want to see you squirm for all you've done."

Mac had nothing to say. Anything that came from his lips would be futile. Means intended to cut him down. Why goad him? Why give him even an instant's satisfaction? Mac wasn't the type to grovel or beg for mercy. Getting compassion or leniency from the bounty hunter was a waste of the last few seconds he had on earth.

He cracked open his S&W and ejected the spent brass. Means came down the slope even faster.

"Time to die, Mackenzie. Time to die!"

The bounty hunter went for his guns, both of them. Mac cringed when a shot rang out, but when he opened his eyes, he was startled that the bullets hadn't ripped through him. He hadn't thought Means was that bad a shot, either left- or right-handed.

More shots rang out. The thunder of a galloping horse from behind caused him to look over his shoulder. Desmond Sullivan fired his rifle repeatedly.

Means was distracted by the new attacker, giving Mac time to fumble in his coat pocket and find a cartridge. He stuffed it into an empty cylinder and reached for another when he heard a heavy thud. Desmond's horse ran past him. His eyes following the horse, he saw it pass where the bounty hunter stood, his guns smoking after shooting Desmond from the saddle.

Mac snapped the gun closed.

"He died for you, Mackenzie. Now you'll die!" Quick Willy Means turned his revolvers on his victim. Lead whined past Mac's head. He grunted as a bullet hit him in the side, about where he had been shot before.

Seeing double from the impact, he raised his pistol and fired. One shot. That was all he had. One shot. He fell facedown on the ground, waiting for

Means to finish the job he had started. Through the hard ground where his cheek pressed down, he felt vibration. Another horse. He tried to warn Estella away. No words came. All that came for him was darkness.

CHAPTER 29

Mac was lifted straight up and dropped on a hard surface. He cried out from the shock and pain. His eyes refused to focus for a few seconds, then he saw Hiram Flowers.

"You aren't dead. I wondered . . ." Mac said. His words sounded strange. Flowers poured water over Mac's chapped lips. He swallowed enough to repeat what he'd said. By now he saw beyond Flowers. He lay in the back of a wagon bouncing along. Every bump the wagon hit jolted him and increased his misery.

Moaning, he rolled onto his side and forced himself to sit up. His shirt had been cut away and a fresh bandage circled his waist. It not only covered his fresh bullet wounds but held his bruised ribs in place.

"I fetched Don Jaime and his men," Flowers said. "We ran off the Rurales, then heard more gunfire."

"What about Desmond?" Mac looked around. "He

saved my life. He distracted Means long enough for me to reload."

A chill passed through him. Reloaded? He had slipped *one* cartridge into his pistol. One. His life— and Desmond's—had rested on one single shot. Closing his eyes, he called up the image of Ransom and his men, then Quick Willy Means, as if they were players on a stage and he was in the audience. He watched it all as if it had been dipped in molasses.

"Desmond took a bullet in the thigh, but the fall from his horse shook him up even more." Flowers sounded disgusted. "He's in good enough shape to ride, even though *she* protested."

Mac didn't have to ask who Flowers meant. Estella would be nursing her beau every inch of the way.

"We're back in the U.S.?"

"Yup, we are."

"Good," Mac said. He wondered why he had ever considered riding farther into Mexico. He had been greeted with more lead and death than he wanted to consider, even if most of it had followed him. The bounty hunters, Wardell's men, they had trailed him down from New Mexico Territory. Only the Rurales, and maybe Don Pedro inciting the bandidos, had been new dangers. Now all that lay behind him, across the border.

"Are you considering drifting on, Mac? I'm not funning you when I say you've got a permanent job with the Circle Arrow. We can reach Denver, take a train to Kansas City, and then ride on back to Fort Worth."

"Denver," Mac said softly. A thought poked into

his head but stayed just beyond the reach of his brain.

"You got any ideas about making sure Desmond gets home?" Flowers asked.

Mac looked hard at the trail boss. This was the first time Flowers had ever admitted he had no answer for a thorny question. Even more surprising, he was asking a chuckwagon cook for advice.

"That's not my problem," Mac said. "Truth is, it shouldn't be yours, either. Desmond's proved himself capable of taking care of any trouble that comes his way. And if what you say's true about Estella, she sees that in him."

"Don Jaime will never let them get hitched."

"They'll light out, and he'll never see his daughter again. You willing to let her go back to the Circle Arrow with Desmond and explain it all to Mercedes Sullivan?"

Flowers groaned.

"I don't have any idea how I'd explain that her son's found a girlfriend and intends to get married. Mercedes is a Methodist, and I reckon Estella is Catholic. How *that'll* play out is anyone's guess." Flowers shook his head. "What are we gonna do, Mac? I can't think of a single thing that makes a lick of sense."

Again a thought rose and—almost—came spilling from Mac's lips. His head hurt so bad it threatened to split open. His bullet wounds and ribs were bound up so tightly they didn't give him much pain. That was something to be thankful for, anyway.

"Where are we?" He turned his head to look

through the opening at the front of the wagon. "We're almost back to Fort Sumner!"

"You were out of your mind for a day or two, then settled down for the last few." Flowers peered at him, squinting as if this gave him better insight. "You're looking mighty good, considering what you were like before."

Mac started to respond, then stopped. He grinned broadly.

"I need to talk to Desmond and Estella. And Don Jaime."

"That can be a chore, at least as far as getting Desmond's attention. We're almost back to our herd. When we get there, that'd be the best time before he and Estella hightail it to parts unknown." Flowers cleared his throat. "That's what I expect to happen. Not saying it will, but finding anybody to bet against me isn't possible."

Mac settled back, working over his scheme. The fog had finally cleared and let him see things better now. Try as he might, he couldn't find any drawbacks with the idea. When the wagon rattled to a halt at the Circle Arrow camp, he climbed down and went hunting for Desmond and Estella. Finding them proved easy enough.

Estella had her beau stretched out on a blanket as she held a cool compress on his forehead. His leg was bandaged where the bullet had ripped off a hunk of flesh. Every move the man made showed a touch of pain. Mac didn't doubt Desmond ached all over from falling off his horse, but he also believed much of the apparent pain was feigned to keep Estella fussing over him.

Somehow, Mac couldn't find it in his heart to fault Desmond for doing that. Estella was a lovely woman.

"I wanted to thank you for distracting Means," Mac said. He sank to the ground and sat cross-legged near Desmond. "I was a goner until then."

"You took on a powerful lot." Desmond looked at Estella. "You risked your life to save us. I had to return the favor."

"We're even," Mac said.

This caused Desmond to sit upright. His demeanor changed.

"We're not going to Denver with the herd." He looked at Estella, then back at Mac. "Her pa and my ma don't have any say-so. We love each other."

"Yeah, about that. I've got a proposal that might work out for all of us."

"What is it?" Desmond's suspicious nature showed how much he had learned on the trail drive. Before he would have opposed anything Mac had to say, just on general principles. Now he would listen and if he liked what he heard, agree. That was all any man could do.

Dewey Mackenzie launched into his plan. Desmond remained unconvinced, until Estella warmed to the notion and started talking to him in low, confidential tones. Mac got to his feet and left them discussing what he'd suggested. He had others to corral.

"I don't see what good I'll be," Hiram Flowers said. "That so-and-so isn't gonna listen to anything I have to say. All I want to do is get on the trail to Denver. You coming with us, Mac? I hope so."

Flowers tugged on the reins and brought his horse to a halt. Don Jaime's hacienda loomed in the twilight, spacious and sprawling, more a fortress than a house. The high adobe walls encircled the entire hacienda. Inside were garden views for the rooms facing inward. Whether Don Jaime allowed them inside didn't matter as long as he listened to what Mac had conjured up, more in a fever dream than through rational thought.

"Looks like we've been noticed."

A man carrying a rifle came from the gates protecting the hacienda's interior. The gates stood partly open, letting out a heady aroma of growing plants and flowers. After breathing trail dust, this buoyed Mac and made him even more sure he was on the right track.

"Don Jaime, good evening," he called as the rancher planted himself in their path.

"What do you want?"

"You've paid off the banker? Your ranch is still yours?"

Don Jaime nodded. "Dunphy took the money. Reluctantly. He wanted to sell my land for a big fee."

"To Luther Wardell," Mac said. He saw how the rancher tensed and brought the rifle muzzle around, as if his adversary had appeared in front of him.

"What do you want? You did not work enough for me to pay. You lost a horse. You owe me money, but I will forgive the debt for all you did to protect my daughter."

"Glad the debt's canceled," Flowers said dryly. "I'd hate to tally up all you owe us for protecting you from bandidos, Rurales—and Wardell's killers."

"Mister Flowers here has a proposal for you." Mac walked his horse closer but did not dismount. Don Jaime gave no indication of relaxing.

"I do?" Flowers scowled. "What proposal?"

Mac spoke louder to drown out the trail boss.

"It's a mighty long trail for the Circle Arrow crew to drive the rest of the cattle all the way to Denver."

"It is." Don Jaime lowered his rifle. Mac hoped the man had an inkling of what he was going to be offered.

"You've sold all your cattle. What good is it having a ranch if you don't have any cattle left?"

"It will take two or three years to rebuild."

"There are some heifers and more than a few bulls in the Circle Arrow herd."

"Wait a second, Mac," Flowers said. "You can't offer breeding rights to him. I can't without Miz Sullivan's permission."

Mac ignored the trail boss and plowed on.

"You have the land, the Circle Arrow has the cattle."

"Many steers in your herd," Don Jaime said.

"What you need to sell next season while the rest of the herd grows."

"To graze on my land, what will you pay?"

"Nothing," Mac said. "Nothing because there's going to be a merger of your ranch and the Circle Arrow, whether you like it or not."

"A merger? No! I will never permit my daughter to marry him!" Don Jaime jerked the rifle back up.

"You don't have a choice. Estella will sneak away to be with Desmond, no matter what you do. Even if you try to put her in a convent."

328 *William W. Johnstone*

"There is one in Mexico City. She—"

"She'll escape. He'll find her. Give in to the inevitable."

"The cattle would be mine? In exchange for the grazing?"

"The money you get is shared. After all, your land will be the western extension of the Circle Arrow back in Fort Worth. Desmond and Estella will be the owners some day—she of your rancho, him of the Circle Arrow—they'll own both."

Don Jaime mumbled. Mac pushed his final argument.

"You want to make it as comfortable as possible for them to stay here, on the old land grant, rather than living over in Texas."

"She would never do that," Don Jaime insisted. "Give up this hacienda for some Texas ranch house."

"I don't know why not," Flowers cut in. "I've never seen a purtier house than the one Miz Sullivan has, a bigger one, or one with more servants."

Mac almost laughed. Mercedes Sullivan did most of the chores herself. The ranch house was nice, but he thought Don Jaime's hacienda might be more lavishly appointed. The trail boss had hit the right chord, though. Don Jaime's complaints melted like ice in the bright New Mexico sun.

"They will marry?" Don Jaime said, glaring. "When?"

"That's up to them," Mac said. "I do know Desmond wants to take Estella back to Texas, at least for a spell, to show off a new bride to his ma."

In a whisper only Mac heard, Flowers said, "I need to get the money from the cattle to her, too. I don't know what the hell I'll tell her about most of the herd being left here to graze for another year."

"Desmond can explain it," Mac told him.

"My daughter, married." Don Jaime shook his head. He didn't have to add, "to a gringo like Desmond Sullivan." He didn't have to. That went unsaid. But he was giving in to Mac's argument, that was obvious.

"The way I see it, the Army will need more beef later in the year. You'll have a herd waiting to be butchered."

"Wardell will sell more to them to undercut my market," Don Jaime protested.

"He can't do that forever," Flowers said. "He has to make a profit somewhere or he'll risk losing his own ranch." He coughed, spat, and said, "You've got the Circle Arrow money behind you now, too. Or Estella does. Estella and Desmond."

"So, where are they? My daughter and her . . . man."

"He's recuperating at our camp, but having a bed would go a ways toward speeding his recovery," Flowers said.

"I will order a room prepared for him. On the far side of the house, away from my daughter's room." Don Jaime went back through the gate and closed it. The sound of the locking bar falling into place echoed through the still night.

Flowers and Mac sat for a moment, then the trail boss said, "I don't know if this is any kind of a deal. Miz Sullivan's not going to take it kindly, losing out on selling so many of the herd."

"She's probably doubling the size of the Circle Arrow. Don Jaime's land grant is huge."

"But there's five hundred miles between the east and west pastures," Flowers said.

"It's going to be up to Desmond to make some decisions. His ma can run the Circle Arrow. Running this spread is going to be hard if Don Jaime won't let loose of the reins. My thought is that he'll come around and let his son-in-law run things while he takes it easy."

"There might be a grandbaby someday to keep him busy."

Mac and Flowers both laughed at that.

They walked their horses away. Mac rubbed his eyes when he saw shadows moving not too far away, as if a man eavesdropped and now ran off. Or it could have been a coyote skulking about.

"I hope Desmond is up to it."

"I think he is," Mac said. "After all he's been through, I *know* he is."

Mac was confident enough in his opinion, but the nearby shadow that had vanished worried him more than a little.

CHAPTER 30

Luther Wardell paced behind his desk, fists beating at the air. Nothing had worked right. Not a damned thing, and he had planned so carefully. Everyone worked against him in a huge conspiracy, but how did he get even with men like Amos Dunphy? The banker had cooked up some deal with Jaime Abragon to let the man keep his land grant. That had to be the answer. Wardell's men had tried to stop the herd from being sold, and they had failed. Then Ransom had gone to steal the money Don Jaime had received for the herd, and he had failed. Somebody warned the damned Mexican rancher of every move against him. That was the only answer.

Wardell spun and slammed both fists down hard on his desk as his new foreman came into the room, timidly holding his hat and looking like he was going to piss himself at any instant.

"Well? What'd you find out?"

Guy Brooks ran his fingers around the hat brim, then found his voice. Wardell wished Ransom was still here, but the man had been murdered in an ambush by the Circle Arrow cowboys.

"Well, sir, like you said, I followed Don Jaime around town. He didn't do much. He paid off his bill at the general store, then spent a while at the feed store. I couldn't get close enough to hear, but he must be wanting a line of credit to buy feed for—"

"The bank. He went to the bank. What happened there, dammit?"

"Well, now, Mister Wardell, he wasn't in the bank too long, but the banker, Dunphy, came out with him and shook hands. It looked for all the world like they parted on good terms. He must have paid off his loan."

Wardell sank into his chair and put his forehead in his hands, elbows on the desk. How was he cursed with such idiots? Ransom had been trigger happy, but the man had a brain and used it.

"Of course he paid off his loan. He had money from selling his herd."

"About that, Mister Wardell, it happened just like I said. Those Texans hid and shot at us and killed everyone. I was lucky to get away."

"Without a scratch. You shot your way out of an ambush that killed Joe Ransom and a half dozen gunmen and didn't get so much as a scratch." He rocked back in his chair and cursed being saddled with such cowards and incompetents. For two cents he'd put a bullet through Brooks's fat gut and keep shooting him until he spewed forth the truth.

Then he decided that would be a waste of good ammunition.

"I ain't lucky in cards or with the ladies. I musta

used up all my luck getting away, Mister Wardell. Really."

"Where'd Abragon go after he left town? Straight back to his ranch house?"

"Straight as an arrow. He went into his compound and locked the gates. I smelled food cooking." Brooks rubbed his bulging gut. "I got powerful hungry 'cause it smelled so good. Them Meskins fix mighty good food. He—"

"You stood outside sniffing at that dog's supper. How lucky I am to have such a devoted employee."

"I am as devoted as they come, sir. Really, I am. But he didn't stay inside. Don Jaime came out wavin' a rifle around when they rode up."

Wardell gritted his teeth. Getting information out of this fool was worse than pulling his own teeth with pliers. He gripped the edge of his desk and forced himself to stay quiet. That lingering silence wormed the facts from Brooks.

"Them Texans. The trail boss and his cook. They rode up, and Don Jaime came out to talk with them. I was close enough to hear them make a deal."

"A deal?" The question burst from Wardell like a bull from the chutes at a rodeo.

"One of the Texas cowboys and Don Jaime's daughter are getting hitched. The herd they didn't sell—"

"That I didn't buy," Wardell said, his belly tightening into a cold knot.

"Yeah, that. They're goin' to leave them to graze on Don Jaime's pasture, then split the money when he sells them."

"He sold every last cow to Don Pedro to save his

ranch. I could have bought his land next year because there wouldn't be another herd. But there will be now. The Circle Arrow herd."

"Our cows are prime, Mister Wardell."

"They're not as good as the longhorns. Abragon is going to sell them to the Army over the next year and then still have a big enough herd to drive to market, down in Mexico or up in Denver. He's going to be a rich man because of the damned longhorns."

He closed his eyes. Estella and one of the Texas cowboys. It had to be the red-haired one. Their union was more than of the flesh. Somehow this merged the Circle Arrow and Don Jaime's land grant. After paying so much for those three hundred head he had almost given to the Army, his funds ran low. Dunphy would loan him whatever he wanted, but Abragon held the winning hand with the Texas longhorns pasturing on his vast range.

"Why didn't you shoot the son of a bitch? You were within earshot. A single bullet would have ended this farce." Wardell pushed to his feet and began pacing again.

Killing Abragon accomplished nothing, he realized. The deal between the Texans and Abragon revolved around the marriage of his daughter with the redheaded cowboy. Remove Estella Abragon and her sweetheart and the deal fell apart. Killing Estella Abragon might be all it took for the two sides to break their pact. He hated that idea since she was such a beautiful woman, but sacrifices had to be made if he wanted to keep his ranch and prosper.

If he wanted to expand onto Abragon's land.

"How many men does Abragon have at his hacienda?"

"What? Not so many. He paid them and they all went into town to get drunk."

"Is his daughter at the hacienda?"

"And Desmond Sullivan. That's her boyfriend, sir. Her betrothed, from what the Texans said."

"How many men can you get together?"

"In town? If there's a payoff involved, I can get a couple dozen."

"No, no, not that," Wardell said, his mind racing to other ways of getting what he wanted. "How many of our Big W wranglers can you find right now?"

"Not so many, sir. Three?" Brooks sounded unsure.

He was that kind of foreman, unimaginative . . . and a coward.

"Never mind. Come with me. Make sure your revolver's loaded." Wardell opened his desk drawer and pulled out a holster. He checked the Colt Navy to be sure it carried six rounds in the cylinder, then stood, strapped on the gun belt, and practiced a quick draw. He wasn't anywhere near as fast as Joe Ransom had been, but tonight he wouldn't have to be.

"What're you gonna do, sir?" Brooks shifted nervously from foot to foot.

"We're going back to Abragon's spread and shoot us a couple varmints. Are you up to it?" He squared off and considered throwing down on his new foreman. It would be good practice, shooting worthless—

Brooks spun around suddenly, facing out into the main house.

"What is it?" Wardell came around the desk, pushed Brooks out of the way, and stepped out into the main room. A hiss like a striking rattler escaped his lips, and his hand moved to his six-gun.

"You got us all tangled up in promises nobody wants to keep, Mac." Hiram Flowers slumped as he rode. "I don't know how Mercedes is going to take this."

"Go back to the Circle Arrow with the money from the cattle Wardell bought. Desmond will go, too. Him and Estella. You might be surprised at how she takes the news. Then let things take their course."

"Like spring runoff? Water gushing down a mountain and into a river?"

"New tributaries can be cut if the runoff is strong enough," Mac told the trail boss. "Why don't you go on ahead? I've got a few things to deal with."

"What're those?"

Mac ignored the question. He left Flowers grumbling but not inclined to follow his cook. The trail boss rode on through the darkness, heading for the Circle Arrow herd now slated to be pastured on Don Jaime's spread.

Mac kept his horse's gait at a slow walk to hold down the sound of hooves hitting the dried ground. His head hurt and he worried his vision had doubled from all the falls and wallops he had taken in the past week. Imagining haints in the night wasn't out of the question. A smile curled his lips when he spotted the man on foot, running toward a stand of cottonwoods. His eyes hadn't betrayed him back at Don

Jaime's. There had been a man spying on them as they negotiated the merger between the New Mexico and Texas cattle empires.

The only one that mattered to was Luther Wardell. The man riding away at a dead gallop had to report to Wardell. Mac felt as sure of that as he ever had anything in his life. The speed the rider showed leaving in the direction of the Big W ranch told Mac more than he needed to know. This wasn't Wardell himself but one of his errand boys. At the U.S. border where the gunfight had left so many dead, Don Jaime had identified not only Wardell's foreman, Ransom, but also the others as being his henchmen. Wardell sent others to do his dirty work.

Tonight, Mac was going to end the skulking around once and for all.

A half hour later, he dismounted outside Wardell's ranch house and stepped up to the front porch. From inside he heard voices—two. From the snatches of argument he caught, he had trailed Wardell's new foreman from Don Jaime's. He made sure his S&W rode easy, then slowly opened the front door and went inside.

The only sounds in the house came from the direction of the parlor and the office beyond it. He took a deep breath, settled his nerves, and went into the parlor. His spurs jingled and the click of his boot heels echoed in the stillness. Two kerosene lamps in the office provided most of the light, but another small one on a table in the middle of the parlor cast dimmer light. He made certain to keep from being silhouetted by it and turning himself into an easy target.

"What is it?" Luther Wardell came around his desk and pushed his foreman out of the way. He stepped into the parlor. "Who's out there?"

"You sent Ransom to kill me," Mac said.

"How'd you get here?" Wardell jerked around and glared at Brooks. "You let him follow you?"

"He's not much of a trailsman," Mac said. "And you're not much of a rancher. You spend all your time and money trying to steal Don Jaime's land instead of running your own herd."

Wardell laughed harshly.

"Listen to you. A cook? That's all you are, and you're lecturing me how to run my ranch?"

"A cook," Mac said softly. "That's all I want to be." Louder, he said, "You're going to keep meddling where you're not wanted. I promised Flowers I'd help him look after Desmond."

"The red-haired kid? What's he to you?"

"A duty. A job I never wanted. You might even say he's a curse, but he saved me from Ransom and the bounty hunter that rode with your men."

"Bounty hunter?" Wardell moved farther into the parlor. He pushed back his frock coattails to better get to the gun at his side.

"Quick Willy Means, he called himself." Mac's heart beat faster. Then he settled down. The showdown was going to happen at any instant. He felt it.

"I don't know anybody named that, but you have bounty hunters on your tail? You're running from the law? That means I can claim a reward when I—"

Luther Wardell went for his gun. Mac was faster. And more accurate. The rancher's shot blasted into the floor. The cook's tore through Wardell's chest.

Mac swung around, aiming for Wardell's foreman. Brooks threw his hands up and stepped back. His heel caught on the rug, and he sat down hard. Somehow he kept his hands high above his head. Mac cocked his pistol again and leveled it at the man's face. Sweat poured down Brooks's forehead and his lips quivered in fear.

"Don't come after me," Mac said. "Try and you'll end up like your boss." He lowered the hammer and backed away, then turned. Brooks was too cowed to try shooting him in the back. Mac got out of the house at a fast walk.

He vaulted into the saddle and galloped away. A light came on in the bunkhouse. He wanted to put some distance between him and any pursuit by Wardell's cowboys. Brooks had to tell them something, but his cowardice might keep him from identifying Mac.

He couldn't take that chance. He swerved from the road leading back to where the Circle Arrow crew bedded down. He wouldn't have minded wishing Desmond and Estella well, and not saying goodbye to Hiram Flowers bothered him, too. The trail boss had a passel of problems ahead of him with Mercedes Sullivan, and dealing with Don Jaime had to be a mountain of trouble, if he failed to say the right words.

Flowers had complications enough to deal with. Having his cook chased by Wardell's men or the local law or even the cavalry would just make things worse. And there was no telling how many more bounty hunters Pierre Leclerc had set snapping at Mac's heels.

He rode northward, following the Pole Star until

after midnight, then turned so it stayed on his right side. West? If he went far enough, he might end up looking out over the Pacific Ocean. He'd seen the Mississippi River, and it was a huge stretch of water, but he could see across it. An ocean was something else, too vast to understand. That would be a sight.

Or maybe somewhere else would beckon more after a week or two in the saddle. Dewey Mackenzie had plenty of time to figure that out.

And somewhere along the way, he mused, he needed to buy himself a new hat.

Turn the page for an exciting preview!

Johnstone Country.
The Good Die Young. The Bad Die Younger.

When Smoke Jensen is summoned to a small Texas town under siege by a scourge of kill-crazy bandits, volunteers line up to take out the Mountain Man. Being Smoke Jensen, he wouldn't have it any other way.

A gunshot wound has robbed Audubon, Texas, of its top lawman at the worst possible time. Clete Lanagan and his band of outlaws have hatched a scheme to plunder the town bank of a small fortune in railroad money. When the acting sheriff, Dalton Conyers—half-brother of Smoke's niece Rebecca—is unable to raise a posse to hunt down Lanagan's gang, he calls on Smoke for help.

But with so much cash at stake, Lanagan won't go down without a fight. With a bounty on his head, Smoke finds himself marked for death by a legendary gunslinger, a wrathful ranch hand bent on revenge for his brother's death, and an army of trigger-happy recruits with nothing to lose but their lives.

NATIONAL BESTSELLING AUTHORS
William W. Johnstone
and J. A. Johnstone

TORTURE OF THE MOUNTAIN MAN

Live Free. Read Hard.

PROLOGUE

From the *Fort Worth Democrat:*

TERRIBLE CRIME !

When the sexton of St. Luke's Episcopal Church arrived to carry out his assigned duties on Monday most recent, he made a most appalling discovery. Seeing that the rector was not in his office, and knowing that to be unusual, Bill Donohue went to the parsonage to inquire as to why the priest had not arrived at his usual time and place.

He had no idea of the gruesome scene he would behold when he looked through the window. There, he saw a sight that would make the blood run cold on even the most insentient person.

Hurrying inside he discovered the bodies of Fr. Damon Grayson, his wife Millicent, and their two small children, Jerome and Marie. It is believed that the motive for the murder was the theft of the previous Sunday's collection of $117.37.

So heinous is the crime that a five thousand dollar reward has been offered for any information leading to the capture of the unknown perpetrator.

Tyrone Greene was the blacksmith, machinist, and all-round handyman for Live Oaks Ranch, a 120,000-acre spread that lay just north of Ft. Worth. His position was second only to that of Clay Ramsey, the ranch foreman. He had been very disturbed by the murder of Father Grayson, particularly since Tyrone was not only a parishioner, but a vestryman.

It was three weeks after the murder when Tyrone was moving the saddles of the cowboys so he could do some repairs to the wall. When he moved the saddle belonging to Cutter MacMurtry, one of the cowboys, a silver cup fell from the saddlebag. Tyrone picked it up and gasped. He examined the inscription.

In honor of the
First Communion
Of my daughter
———————
TAMARA GREENE

Tyrone had given this very cup to St. Luke's Church ten years earlier for the christening of his daughter, Tamara. He knew there was only one way Cutter Mac-Murtry could have it, and that was to have stolen it. Going into his quarters, Tyrone got his pistol belt down from the hook where it hung and belted it around his waist.

One month later, after Cutter MacMurtry was tried and convicted for the murder of Father Grayson and his family, Tyrone Greene was presented with a check for five thousand dollars. He had not taken Cutter MacMurtry in to the sheriff for the money. He had done it because he wanted justice for Father Grayson.

But the money promised a bright future for him and his family.

When Mel Saddler, jailer for the Tarrant County jail, looked up, he saw a man with rough, blunt features and eyes as gray as a dreary winter day. This was Hatchett MacMurtry.

"I'm here to see my brother."

"You've been here before, MacMurtry, so you know the routine," Saddler said. "Take off your gun belt."

Hatchett MacMurtry did so.

"Now, hold your arms out while I search you for any weapons."

Hatchett MacMurtry complied, and Saddler made

a thorough check for any hidden guns or knives. Finding none, he stepped back.

"All right, you can go back there to tell your brother good-bye," Saddler said with a little chuckle.

"What do you mean, good-bye? I just got here."

"We'll be hangin' 'im tomorrow, 'n there will be a crowd gathered around for the show," Saddler said. "When I said you could tell 'im good-bye, that's 'cause I figured you'd want to do it alone, when there was just the two of you."

"Yeah," Hatchett said.

Saddler led Hatchett back to Cutter MacMurtry's cell.

"Hello, brother," Hatchett said.

"I wasn't sure you'd come to see me," Cutter replied.

Hatchett turned toward Saddler. "I thought you said this would be a private meeting."

"I'm supposed to stay here to keep an eye on all the visitors," Saddler replied.

"Why? You done searched me pretty good, you know I ain't got no gun to give 'im."

Saddler sighed, then looked around. "All right, seein' as your brother's goin' to get hung tomorrow anyhow, I can't see as it be any way wrong to let you talk amongst yourselves. I'm goin' to close 'n lock this outer door, call me when you're ready to leave."

"All right," Hatchett agreed.

"You goin' to watch me hang tomorrow?" Cutter asked, after the deputy closed and locked the outer door.

"No."

"Why not? It might be good to have a friendly face in the crowd."

"I ain't goin' to watch you, 'cause you ain't goin' to hang.'

"You got some way to get me out of it?"

Hatchett smiled. "Go back there 'n look at the bars on your window."

"What for?"

"Just do it, Cutter," Hatchett said, the tone of his voice reflecting his irritation.

Cutter walked to the back of his cell to examine the bars that were on the back window.

"Do you see a piece of rawhide tied around one of the bars?"

"Yeah."

"Pull it up, but be careful, you don't want to lose what's on the other side."

Cutter did as he was instructed, and when the other end of the string drew even with the window, he saw a Colt .44 suspended by the rawhide string tied around the trigger guard.

"Damn!" Cutter said with a broad smile. He pulled the gun in, then untied the cord.

"Now, pass it through to me," Hatchett ordered.

Cutter did so, and as soon as he had the gun back in hand, he called out for the jailer.

"Damn," Saddler said as he returned and unlocked the outer door. "That wasn't a long visit.'

"It don't take long to say good-bye," Hatchett said.

As soon as Slater stepped inside, Hatchett put the barrel of the pistol against Saddler's head.

"Where did you . . ."

That was as far as he got with the question before Hatchett pulled the trigger and blew the jailer's brains out.

Moving quickly, Hatchett got the jailer's keys and unlocked the cell door.

"What do we do now?" Cutter asked.

"We get out of here. I borrowed some money and a couple of horses from Live Oaks," Hatchett said.

"Colonel Conyers loaned us some money and horses?" Cutter asked, surprised by the news.

Hatchett chuckled. "Yeah, only he don't know it. 'N this here ain't the kind of loan that's ever goin' to be paid back."

CHAPTER ONE

Four years later, Sugarloaf Ranch

Smoke Jensen, the owner of Sugarloaf Ranch, stood out on the front porch, one hand leaning against one of the porch rails, and the other hand holding a cup of coffee. Smoke was a big man, over six feet tall, and with a spread of shoulders that could just about cover an axe handle. He had hair the color of ripened wheat, though not much of it could seen at the moment since it was covered with a low-crowned, brown hat.

To the east, the sun had not yet crested Casteel Ridge, but it had pushed the early morning darkness away. Pearlie, Smoke's ranch foreman, came toward him.

"Good mornin', Pearlie."

"Mornin', Smoke. We picked up six cows overnight."

"What?"

"Herefords, they were easy enough to pick out. According to the brand, they belong to Mr. Greene. I'll get one of the hands to take the cows back."

"I thought you had a full day planned for all the hands," Smoke said.

"Yeah I do, we're re-fencing some of the south quarter. There's gaps all along the fence. More 'n likely that's how these cows got through."

"You keep the men working," Smoke said. "I'll take the cows back."

"You sure you want to do that? It'll take up half your mornin', over there and back," Pearlie said.

"I don't mind. Sally has some books she wants to take over to Tyrone's daughter, so this will give me a chance to do it."

"I'll get the cows gathered up for you," Pearlie offered.

Diamond T Ranch

"Tamara, go out to the barn and tell your father to come to breakfast," Edna said.

"Yes, Mama," Tamara replied. Tamara was a very pretty fourteen-year-old girl, a good student who had it in mind to be a schoolteacher.

"What on earth would make you want to be a schoolteacher?" one of her classmates had asked. "Why, schoolteachers can never get married."

"Yes, they can," Tamara had answered. "Miz Sally used to be a schoolteacher, and now she is married to Mr. Smoke Jensen. I want to be just like her . . . she's the smartest person I've ever met."

That conversation had taken place on the last day of school. Now, even though school was out for the summer, Tamara continued to study, reading books that their neighbor Sally Jensen had provided.

"Papa? Papa, are you out here?" Tamara called, carrying out her mother's bidding.

"I'm in the barn, darlin'," a man's voice answered. Tamara's father, Tyrone Greene, appeared in the barn door.

"Mama says to wash up, and come to breakfast."

"Your mother told me to wash up?" Tyrone asked, a grin spreading across his face.

"No, Papa, I'm saying that. You've been working in the barn where there are all kinds of dirty things. Wouldn't you want to clean up?"

Tyrone laughed. "For you, I'll clean up."

As father and daughter walked back to the house, they saw a strange horse out front.

"Who's here?" Tyrone asked. "Whose horse is that?

"I don't know," Tamara replied. "It wasn't there when I came to get you."

"It looks like we may have company for breakfast. I hope your mama made enough."

"She always makes enough biscuits and bacon, you know that. All she'll have to do is fry a couple more eggs," Tamara said.

"Well, let's go see who it is, shall we?"

Tyrone and Tamara stepped up onto the porch, then Tyrone opened the door.

"Tell me, Mrs. Greene, what vagabond have you agreed to feed this morning? I hope you have enough . . ."

The smile left Tyrone's face to be replaced by an expression of fear and horror. There was a man

stand- ing next to his wife, with an evil grin on his
face and a pistol in his hand. He was holding the pistol to Edna's temple. The uninvited visitor was a big
man with a bald head, a protruding brow, and practically no neck. It was someone that Tyrone knew well.

"Hello, Greene," the man said.

"Cutter MacMurtry, what are doing here? I thought
you . . ."

"You thought I'd been hung? Well, they was plan-
nin' on doin' that, but me 'n my brother thought it
might be a good idea to leave Texas, before it was
that they could ever actual get around to a-doin' it,"
MacMurtry said.

Tyrone looked around. "Is Hatchett here with
you?"

"I don't rightly know where he is now. We sort of
separated oncet we come to Colorado." MacMurtry
grinned again. "I see that you have yourself a nice little ranch. How'd you get it?"

"I bought it."

"You was one of Colonel Conyers' top hands, 'n
I've heard he paid some of you a lot better 'n he paid
me 'n a lot of the other workin' hands. But I don't
figure that even the Colonel paid enough for you to
buy a ranch like this. Where'd you get the money?"

Tyrone didn't answer.

"How much of a reward did you collect for turning me in? Five thousand dollars, is what I heard. Yes,
sir, five thousand dollars would be enough money to
buy yourself a real nice little ranch. So, you come up
here from Texas 'n used that five thousand dollars of
blood money to do just that, didn't you?"

Tyrone still didn't answer.

"Fact is, I wouldn't be surprised if you didn't still have some o' that money here, in the house."

"I don't keep money in the house," Tyrone said. "I have very little money anyway, as I have everything invested in this ranch."

"Well then, in that case I'll have to find some other way of gettin' back at you, won't I?"

MacMurtry turned his pistol toward the rancher and pulled the trigger. Tyrone grunted once, put his hand over the bullet hole, then collapsed

"Tyrone!" Edna yelled in horror. "You have killed him!"

"Don't worry, I'll send you to join him," MacMurtry said, and putting the pistol back up to her temple again, he pulled the trigger a second time. Blood, brain tissue, and skull fragments blew out of the exit wound in Edna's head as she went down.

Tamara had watched the whole thing in a state of shock. She had wanted to beg him not to shoot her mother or father, but she was totally unable to make a sound.

"Well, now, you warn't much more 'n a little girl the last time I seen you. You've growed up some, 'n ain't you a purty thing, though?" MacMurtry said. He put his pistol back in his holster and started toward her. "You been made a woman yet?" he asked.

Tamara's eyes got wider in terror.

"You know what I think? I think you ain't never had no man before. This is your lucky day, girlie. I'm goin' to show you what it's all about."

MacMurtry reached up to put his hand on the collar of her dress, then jerked it down. The dress parted, exposing more of her.

"Yes, ma'am, you're goin' to enjoy this," MacMurtry said. "Though prob'ly not as much as I am."

Just over an hour later Smoke Jensen was driving six Hereford cows in the direction of Tyrone Greene's ranch. Smoke was a rancher and it wasn't unusual to see him driving cattle, but it was unusual to see him driving Herefords, since he was now running only Angus cattle on Sugarloaf Ranch.

The cows he was pushing all had the Diamond T brand, indicating that they had, somehow, strayed over onto Smoke's ranch from his neighbor, Tyrone Greene. Greene had only lived in the area for a little over a year, having come up from Texas to buy the ranch when it came available. Greene had worked for Big Ben Conyers, one of the largest and most successful ranchers in Texas. And it was through Colonel Conyers' connection with Smoke that Greene was able to locate a ranch that he could afford. Tyrone and his wife Edna had become very good friends of Smoke and Sally, and Sally had all but adopted their precocious fourteen-year-old daughter.

When Smoke reached the Diamond T, he saw a gathering of cattle, and he shouted at the cows he was herding.

"Here now, go join your friends!" he called out to them, and with shouts, whistles, and vigorous waving of his hat, he pushed the wayward cows back toward the others.

Having come this far, Smoke decided to drop in and visit with Tyrone for a few minutes. He didn't want to stay too long, because if he did, Edna would insist that he remain for lunch, and he didn't want to impose, because he knew they were still on a tight budget until he got his ranch fully operational.

He also didn't want to take too much of Tyone's time, since he had no hands, and had to run the ranch all by himself. He was a good rancher, though. He knew cattle and horses, and because he had been a blacksmith, mechanic, and all around handyman for the Colonel, so he knew what it took to be successful. He also knew the value of hard work, and Smoke knew that if success depended upon hard work, Tyrone would succeed.

As he approached the house, though, he heard a cow bawling from the barn, and it was a bawl he recognized. The cow needed to be milked. That was odd. It wasn't like Edna or even Tamara to go this late into the day without milking the cow.

Now, what had been the pleasant anticipation of a visit with good friends changed to apprehension. Smoke had a very powerful feeling that something was amiss, and, dismounting, he pulled his pistol, stepped quietly up onto the porch, then, deciding against knocking, he pushed the door open and stepped into the house.

Had he gone a step farther, he would have tripped over Tyrone's body. Across the room, near the table, still set for breakfast, he saw Edna; she, too, was lying on the floor with her head in a pool of blood.

Then he saw Tamara. Tamara was sitting on the floor, leaning back against the wall. She was staring at Smoke through eyes that were open wide, but she made no sound. There were bruises on her face and her shoulders. Smoke could see the bruises on her shoulders, because they were bare. And the shoulders were bare, because Tamara was naked, preserving what modesty she had by holding what was left of her torn dress over her.

"Tamara, who did this?" Smoke asked.

Tamara didn't respond.

Smoke, realizing that he was still holding his gun, slipped it back in its holster.

"It's all right, sweetheart, nobody is going to hurt you again."

Tamara gave no sign that she had even heard him speak.

"I'm going to take you home," Smoke said.

Just over half an hour later, Sally was standing out on the porch when she saw Smoke riding up the long approach from Eagle Road to the compound of houses and ancillary buildings that made up Sugarloaf Ranch headquarters. Her smile changed to confusion, then to concern as she saw that he was cradling someone in front of him.

"Smoke! Who is that? What has happened?"

"It's Tamara, Sally. Tyrone and Edna have been murdered. Tamara has been raped. I . . . uh . . . didn't think it would be right for me to dress her, so I just wrapped her in a bedsheet."

"Oh, bless her heart!" Sally said. "Bring that child into the house!"

"I'm going in town to see Sheriff Carson, and I'll get Tyrone and Edna . . ." Smoke started to say "bodies" but thinking of Tamara, he changed his comment to "taken care of."

"I'm going to get this child cleaned up," Sally said.

"Don't worry, Smoke, I'll send some people out there to pick up Mr. and Mrs. Greene," the undertaker said. "And I'll take care of them. The little girl need not worry about that."

"Oh, and Gene, there's quite a bit of blood out there, could you . . ."

"I'll get that taken care of as well," Gene promised.

"Does the girl know who did it?" Sheriff Carson asked, as the undertaker left the sheriff's office to take care of the situation. "Has she given you any hints?"

Smoke shook his head. "So far she hasn't said a word."

"Was she . . . uh . . . what I mean is, do you think she was?" Sheriff Carson paused in mid-question, unable to go any further.

"If you are asking if she was raped, I'm sure she was," Smoke replied.

Sheriff Carson shook his head, sadly. "We've got to find out who did this, Smoke. Any son of a bitch who would do something like kill her mama and papa right in front of her eyes, then rape a young girl like that, doesn't deserve to live. I'm going to take an intense, personal pleasure in seeing that rope put around his neck. In fact, I'll do it myself."

Another person came into the sheriff's office then, and looking up, Smoke saw his foreman, Pearlie.

"Pearlie?"

"Sally wants you to come home, Smoke," Pearlie said. "Tamara is talking now."

* * *

"How is she?" Smoke asked half an hour later when he stepped into the foyer of his house. He looked through the door into the living room. There, he saw Tamara sitting on the sofa wearing one of Sally's dresses. The expression on her face had changed from a blank stare to great sadness.

"She has come out of her shock," Sally said, having met him in the foyer.

"Has she said anything?"

"We've talked a little, nothing substantive, but she is coherent. And of course, she is aware of what happened, not only to her parents, but the ordeal she went through as well."

"Does she know who did it?"

"She says that she does, but she didn't tell me. She wants to talk to you."

Because the conversation between Smoke and Sally had taken place in the entry foyer, and was quiet, Tamara couldn't overhear it. Smoke nodded at Sally, then stepped into the living room. When Tamara looked up at him, he could see that her eyes were brimming with tears, and there were tear tracks down her cheeks.

"Hello, Tamara," Smoke said quietly. "Cutter Mac-Murtry," Tamara said.

"Cutter MacMurtry is the name of the man who did this?"

"Yes."

"How do you know that was his name?"

"Because I remember Mr. MacMurtry. He used to work for Colonel Conyers, same as Papa. But he killed some people and Papa found out about it, and

Papa took him to the sheriff. Papa got a reward for it, and that's how he had enough money to buy the ranch."

"So, you knew him in Texas. Have you seen him up here? Before this morning, I mean."

"No sir. This morning is the first time I've seen him since we moved."

Smoke reached out to put his hand on Tamara's cheek.

"Thank you, sweetheart. You have been a big help."

Excel Data Analysis For Dummies®

Cheat Sheet

Quick Statistical Measures

To perform some other statistical calculation of the selected range list, right-click the Sum of the selected range shown in the status bar. When you do, Excel displays a pop-up menu of statistical measures that you can make on the selected range.

Statistical Measures Option	What It Does
None	Tells Excel that you don't want it to calculate and then show a statistic on the status bar.
Average	Finds the meaning of values in selected range.
Count	Tallies the cells that hold labels, values, or formulas. Use this when you want to count the number of cells that aren't empty.
Count Nums	Tallies the number of cells in a selected range that hold values or formulas.
Max	Finds the largest value in the selected range.
Min	Finds the smallest value in the selected range.
Sum	Adds the values in the selected range.

Using Boolean Expressions

To construct a Boolean expression, such as when you filter criteria, use a comparison operator and then a value used in the comparison: >5, for example.

Comparison Operator	What It Means
=	Equals
>	Greater than
>=	Greater than or equal to
<	Less than
<=	Less than or equal to
<>	Not equal to

Excel Database Functions

Excel provides a set of handy-to-use database functions for making statistical calculations using information from lists, as described in Chapter 8:

Function	Description
DAVERAGE	Calculates arithmetic mean
DCOUNT	Counts the number of cells with values
DCOUNTA	Counts the number of cells that aren't empty
DGET	Returns a value from a database list
DMAX	Finds the largest value in a list
DMIN	Finds the smallest value in a list
DPRODUCT	Calculates the product of values matching criteria
DSTDEV	Calculates the standard deviation of a sample
DSTDEVP	Calculates the standard deviation of a population
DSUM	Calculates the sum of values matching criteria
DVAR	Calculates the variance of a sample
DVARP	Calculates the variance of a population

All of these database functions function use a standard three-argument syntax. For example, the DAVERAGE function looks like this:

```
=DAVERAGE(database,field,criteria)
```

where database is a range reference to the Excel list that holds the value you want to examine, field tells Excel which column in the database to examine, and criteria is a range reference that identifies the fields and values used to define your selection criteria. The field argument can be a cell reference holding the field name, the field name enclosed in quotation marks, or a number that identifies the column (1 for the first column, 2 for the second column, and so on).

Excel Data Analysis For Dummies®

Cheat Sheet

Key Statistics Terms

Average: Typically, an average is the arithmetic mean for a set of values. Excel supplies several average functions.

Chi Square: Use chi-squares to compare observed values with expected values, returning the level of significance, or probability (also called a *p value*). A p value helps you to assess whether differences between the observed and expected values represent chance.

Cross-tabulation: This is an analysis technique that summarizes data in two or more ways. Summarizing sales information both by customer and product is a cross-tabulation.

Descriptive statistics: Descriptive statistics just describe the values in a set. For example, if you sum a set of values, that sum is a descriptive statistic. Finding the biggest value or the smallest value in a set of numbers is also a descriptive statistic.

Exponential smoothing: Exponential smoothing calculates the moving average but weights the values included in the moving average calculations so that more recent values have a bigger effect.

Inferential statistics: Inferential statistics are based on the very useful, intuitively obvious idea that if you look at a sample of values from a population and if the sample is representative and large enough, you can draw conclusions about the population based on characteristics of the sample.

Kurtosis: This is a measure of the tails in a distribution of values.

Median: The median is the middle value in a set of values. Half of the values fall below the median, and half of the values fall above the median.

Mode: Mode is the most common value in a set.

Moving average: A moving average is one that's calculated using only a specified set of values, such as an average based on just the last three values.

Normal distribution: Also known as a Gaussian distribution, normal distribution is the infamous bell curve.

P value: A p value is the level of significance, or probability.

Regression analysis: Regression analysis involves plotting pairs of independent and dependent variables in an XY chart and then finding a linear or exponential equation that best describes the plotted data.

Skewness: This is a measure of the symmetry of a distribution of values.

Standard deviation: A standard deviation describes dispersion about the data set's mean. You can kind of think of a standard deviation as an *average* deviation from the mean.

Variance: A variance describes dispersion about the data set's mean. The variance is the square of the standard deviation; the standard deviation is the square root of the variance.

Z value: This is the distance between a value and the mean in terms of standard deviations.

For Dummies: Bestselling Book Series for Beginners

Excel Data Analysis

FOR

DUMMIES®

Excel Data Analysis

FOR

DUMMIES®

by Stephen L. Nelson

Wiley Publishing, Inc.

Best-Selling Books • Digital Downloads • e-Books • Answer Networks • e-Newsletters • Branded Web Sites • e-Learning

Excel Data Analysis For Dummies®

Published by
Wiley Publishing, Inc.
909 Third Avenue
New York, NY 10022

www.wiley.com

About the Author

Stephen L. Nelson is the author of more than two dozen best-selling books, including *Quicken For Dummies* and *QuickBooks For Dummies* (Hungry Minds, Inc.). In fact, Nelson's books have sold more than 4,000,000 copies in English and have been translated into more than ten other languages.

Nelson is a certified public accountant and a member of both the Washington Society of CPAs and the American Institute of CPAs. He holds a Bachelor of Science in Accounting, magna cum laude, from Central Washington University, and a Masters in Business Administration in Finance from the University of Washington (where, curiously, he was the youngest person ever to graduate from the program).

Nelson's work experience includes stints as a book publisher and packager, as the chief financial officer, treasurer, and controller of a high-technology manufacturer, and as a senior consultant with one of the Big Five public accounting firms.

Nelson lives in the foothills east of Redmond, Washington with his wife, two daughters, and a guinea pig.

Author's Acknowledgments

The curious thing about writing a book is this: Although an author's name appears on the cover, it's always really a team project. Take the case of this book, for example. Truth be told, the book was really the idea of Andy Cummings, the publisher of *For Dummies* technology books, and Bob Woerner, my long-suffering acquisitions editor. I wrote the manuscript, and then a lot of folks at Wiley expended a lot of effort into turning my rough manuscript into a polished book. Linda Morris, project editor, Teresa Artman, copy editor, Kerwin McKenzie, technical editor, and a host of page layout technicians, proofreaders, and graphic artists are just some of the people who helped this book come to life.

Publisher's Acknowledgments

We're proud of this book; please send us your comments through our online registration form located at www.dummies.com/register/.

Some of the people who helped bring this book to market include the following:

Acquisitions, Editorial, and Media Development

Project Editor: Linda Morris

Acquisitions Editor: Bob Woerner

Copy Editor: Teresa Artman

Technical Editor: Kerwin McKenzie

Editorial Manager: Constance Carlisle

Media Development Manager: Laura VanWinkle

Media Development Supervisor: Richard Graves

Editorial Assistant: Amanda M. Foxworth

Production

Project Coordinator: Maridee Ennis

Layout and Graphics: Scott Bristol, Jackie Nicholas, Brent Savage, Betty Schulte, Mary J. Virgin

Proofreaders: Laura Albert, John Greenough, Andy Hollandbeck, TECHBOOKS Publishing Services

Indexer: TECHBOOKS Publishing Services

Publishing and Editorial for Technology Dummies

Richard Swadley, Vice President and Executive Group Publisher
Mary C. Corder, Editorial Director
Andy Cummings, Vice President and Publisher

Publishing for Consumer Dummies

Diane Graves Steele, Vice President and Publisher
Joyce Pepple, Acquisitions Director

Composition Services

Gerry Fahey, Vice President of Production Services
Debbie Stailey, Director of Composition Services

Contents at a Glance

Cartoons at a Glance

By Rich Tennant

page 323

page 293

page 165

page 77

page 7

Cartoon Information:
Fax: 978-546-7747
E-Mail: richtennant@the5thwave.com
World Wide Web: www.the5thwave.com

Table of Contents

Introduction

· ·

So here's a funny deal: You know how to use Excel. You know how to create simple workbooks. And how to print stuff. And you can even, with just a little bit of fiddling, create cool-looking charts.

But I bet that you sometimes wish that you could do more with Excel. You sometimes wish, I wager, that you could use Excel to really gain insights into the information, the data, that you work with in your job.

Using Excel for this kind of stuff is what this book is all about. This is a book that assumes that you want to use Excel to learn new stuff, discover new secrets, and gain new insights into the information that you're already working with in Excel — or the information stored electronically in some other format, such as in your accounting system.

About This Book

This book isn't meant to be read cover to cover like a Lemony Snicket novel. Rather, it's organized into tiny, no-sweat descriptions of how to do the things that must be done. Hop around and read the chapters that interest you.

If you're the sort of person who, perhaps because of a compulsive bent, needs to read a book cover to cover, that's fine. I recommend that you only delve in to the chapters on inferential statistics, however, if you've taken at least a couple of college-level statistics classes. But that caveat aside, feel free. After all, maybe *CSI* is a rerun tonight.

What You Can Safely Ignore

This book provides a lot of information. That's the nature of a how-to reference. So I want to tell you that there are some chunks of the book that it's pretty darn safe for you to blow off.

For example, in many places throughout the book, I provide step-by-step descriptions of the task. When I do so, I always start each step with a bold-faced description of what the step entails. Underneath that bold-faced step description, I provide detailed information about what happens after you perform that action. Sometimes I also offer help with the mechanics of the step, like this:

1. Press Enter.

Find the key that's labeled *Enter*. Extend your index finger so that it rests ever so gently on the Enter key. Then, in one sure, fluid motion, press the key by using your index finger. Then release the key.

Okay, that's kind of an extreme example. I never actually go into that much detail. My editor won't let me. But you get the idea. If you know how to press Enter, you can just do that and not read farther. If you need help — say with the finger-depression part or the finding-the-right-key part — then you can read the nitty-gritty details.

You can also skip the paragraphs flagged with the Technical Stuff icon. These icons flag information that's sort of tangential, sort of esoteric, or sort of questionable in value . . . at least for the average reader. If you're really interested in digging into the meat of the subject being discussed, go ahead and read 'em. If you're really just trying to get through your work so that you can get home and watch TV with your kids, skip 'em.

I may as well also say that you don't have to read the information provided in the paragraphs marked with a Tip icon, either. I assume that you want to know an easier way to do something. But if you're someone who likes to do things the hard way because that improves character and makes you tougher, go ahead and skip the Tip icons.

What You Shouldn't Ignore (Unless You're a Masochist)

By the way, don't skip the Warning icons. They're the text flagged with a picture of a 19th century bomb. They describe some things that you really shouldn't do.

Out of respect for you, I don't put stuff in these paragraphs such as, "Don't smoke." I figure that you're an adult. You get to make your own lifestyle decisions.

I reserve these warnings for more urgent and immediate dangers — things that you can but shouldn't do. For example: "Don't smoke while filling your car with gasoline."

Three Foolish Assumptions

I assume just three things about you:

1. **You have a PC with Microsoft Excel installed.**
2. **You know the basics of working with your PC and Microsoft Windows.**
3. **You know the basics of working with Excel, including how to start and stop Excel, how to save and open Excel workbooks, and how to enter text and values and formulas into worksheet cells.**

How This Book is Organized

This book is organized into five parts:

Part 1: Where's the Beef?

In Part I, I discuss how you get data into Excel workbooks so that you can begin to analyze it. This is important stuff, but fortunately, most of it is pretty straightforward. If you're new to data analysis and not all that fluent yet in working with Excel, you definitely want to begin in Part I.

Part II: PivotTables and PivotCharts

In the second part of this book, I cover what are perhaps the most powerful data analysis tools that Excel provides: its cross-tabulation capabilities using the PivotTable and PivotChart commands.

No kidding, I don't think there is any more useful Excel data analysis skill then knowing how to create pivot tables and pivot charts. If I could, I would give you some sort of guarantee that the time you spent reading how to use these tools is always worth the investment you make. Unfortunately, after consultation with my attorney, I find that this is impossible to do.

Part III: Advanced Tools

In Part III, I discuss some of the more sophisticated tools that Excel supplies for doing data analysis. Some of these tools are always available in Excel, such as the statistical functions. (I use a couple of chapters to cover these.) Some of the tools come in the form of Excel add-ins, such as the Data Analysis and the Solver add-ins.

I don't think that these tools are going to be of interest to most readers of this book. But if you already know how to do all the basic stuff and you've got some good statistical and quantitative methods, training or experience, you ought to peruse these chapters. There are some really useful whistles and bells available to advanced users of Excel. And it would be a shame if you didn't at least know what they are and the basic steps that you need to take to use them.

Part IV: The Part of Tens

In my mind, perhaps the most clever element that Dan Gookin, the author of the original and first Dummies book *DOS For Dummies*, came up with are the chapters that just list information in David Letterman-ish fashion. These chapters let us authors list useful tidbits, tips, and factoids for you.

Excel Data Analysis For Dummies includes three such chapters. In the first, I provide some basic facts most everybody should know about statistics and statistical analysis. In the second, I suggest ten tips for successfully and effectively analyzing data in Excel. Finally, in the third chapter, I try to make some useful suggestions about how you can visually analyze information and visually present data analysis results.

The Part of Tens chapters aren't technical. They aren't complicated. They're very basic. Anybody should be able to skim the information provided in these chapters and come away with at least a few nuggets of useful information.

Part V: Appendix

The appendix contains a handy glossary of terms you should understand when working with data in general and Excel specifically. From *kurtosis* to *histograms*, these sometimes baffling terms are defined here.

Special Icons

Like other *For Dummies* books, this book uses icons, or little margin pictures, to flag things that don't quite fit into the flow of the chapter discussion. Here are the icons that I use:

✔ **Technical Stuff:** This icon points out some dirty technical details that you might want to skip.

✔ **Tip:** This icon points out a shortcut to make your life easier or more fulfilling.

✔ **Remember:** This icon points out things that you should, well, remember.

✔ **Warning:** This icon is a friendly but forceful reminder not to do something . . . or else.

Where to Next?

If you're just getting started with Excel data analysis, flip the page and start reading the first chapter.

If you have a bit of skill with Excel or you have a special problem or question, use the Table of Contents or the Index to find out where I cover a topic and then turn to that page.

Good luck! Have fun!

Part I
Where's the Beef?

The 5th Wave — By Rich Tennant

©RICHTENNANT

"Get ready, Mona — here come the stats."

In this part . . .

In Part I, I talk about how you get data into Excel workbooks so that you can begin to analyze it. This is important stuff, but fortunately, most of it is pretty straightforward. Read here to discover what makes an Excel list, how to get data from external sources, and how to clean your data.

Chapter 1

Introducing Excel Lists

*F*irst things first. I need to start my discussion of using Excel for data analysis by introducing Excel lists. Why? Because except in the simplest of situations, when you want to analyze data with Excel, you want that data stored in a list. In this chapter, I discuss: what defines an Excel list; how to build, analyze, and sort a list; and why using filters to create a sublist is useful.

What Is a List and Why Do I Care?

A list is, well, a list. This definition sounds circular, I guess. But take a look at the simple list shown in Figure 1-1. This list shows the items that you may shop for at a grocery store on the way home from work.

As I mention in the introduction of this book, many of the Excel workbooks that you see in the figures of this book are available in a compressed Zip file available at the Dummies Web site. You can download this Zip file from the Internet address www.dummies.com/extras. To unzip the Zip file, you either need to use a decompression utility like WinZip or have Windows XP.

Commonly, lists include more information than Figure 1-1 shows. For example, take a look at the list shown in Figure 1-2. In column A, for example, the list names the store where you might purchase the item. In column C, this expanded list gives the quantity of some item that you need. In column D, this list provides a rough estimate of the price.

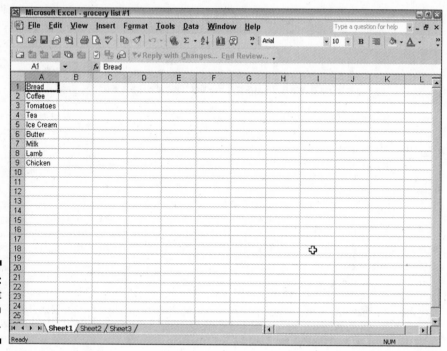

Figure 1-1:
A list: Start out with the basics.

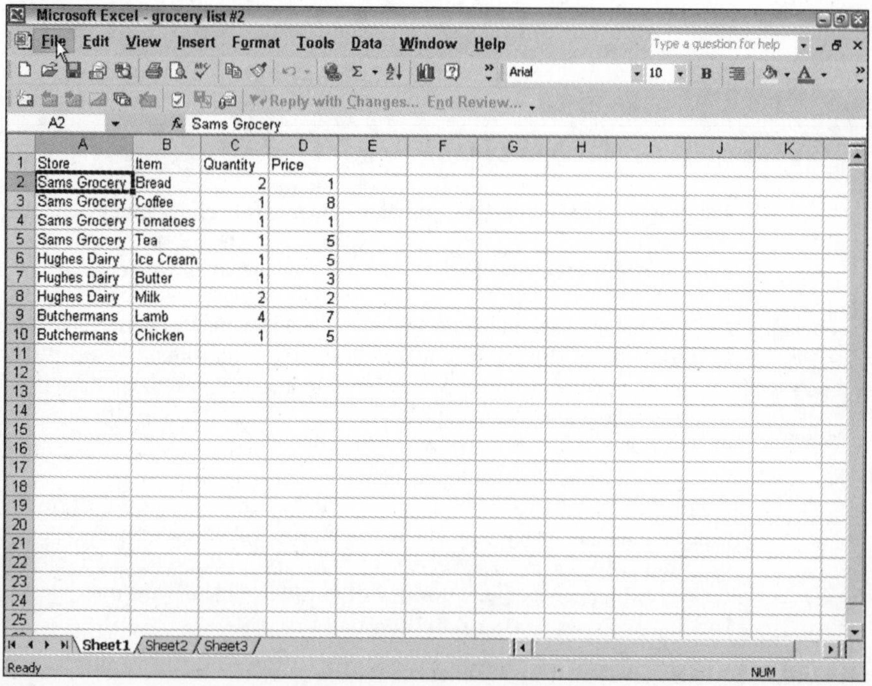

Figure 1-2:
A grocery list for the more serious shopper . . . like me.

An Excel list usually looks more like the list shown in Figure 1-2. Typically, the list enumerates rather detailed descriptions of numerous items. But a list in Excel, after you strip away all the details, essentially resembles the expanded grocery-shopping list shown in Figure 1-2.

Let me make a handful of observations about the list shown in Figure 1-2. First, each column shows a particular sort of information. In the parlance of database design, each *column* represents a field. Each *field* stores the same sort of information. Column A, for example, shows the store where some item can be purchased. (You might also say that this is the Store field.) Each piece of information shown in column A — the Store field — names a store: Sams Grocery, Hughes Dairy, and Butchermans.

The first row in the Excel worksheet provides field names. For example, in Figure 1-2, row 1 names the four fields that make up the list: Store, Item, Quantity, and Price. You always use the first row of an Excel list to name, or identify, the fields in the list.

Starting in row 2, each row represents a record, or item, in the list. A *record* is a collection of related fields. For example, the record in row 2 in Figure 1-2 shows that at Sams Grocery, you plan to buy two loaves of bread for a price of $1 each. (Bear with me if these sample prices are wildly off; I usually don't do the shopping in my household.)

Row 3 shows or describes another item, coffee, also at Sams Grocery, for $8. In the same way, the other rows of the super-sized grocery list show items that you will buy. For each item, the list identifies the store, the item, the quantity, and the price.

TECHNICAL STUFF

Something to understand about Excel lists

An Excel list is a *flat-file database*. The flat-file-ish-ness means that there's only one list, also called a *table*, in the database. And the flat-file-ish-ness also means that each record stores every bit of information about an item.

In comparison, popular desktop database applications such as Microsoft Access are *relational databases*. A relational database stores information more efficiently. And the most striking way in which this efficiency appears is that you don't see lots of duplicated or redundant information in a relational database. In a relational database, for example, you might not see

Sams Grocery appearing in cells A2, A3, A4, and A5. A relational database may eliminate this redundancy by having a separate list of grocery stores.

This point may seem a bit esoteric; however, you may find it handy when you want to grab data from a relational database (where the information will be efficiently stored in separate lists, or tables) and then combine all this data into a super-sized flat-file database in the form of an Excel list. In Chapter 2, I discuss how to grab data from external databases.

Building Lists

You build a list that you want to later analyze by using Excel in one of two ways:

- ✔ Export the list from a database.
- ✔ Manually enter items into an Excel workbook.

Exporting from a database

The usual way to create a list to use in Excel is to export information from a database. Exporting information from a database isn't tricky. However, you need to reflect a bit on the fact that the information stored in your database is probably organized into many separate lists or tables that need to be combined into a large flat-file database or list.

In Chapter 2, I describe the process of exporting data from the database and then importing this data into Excel so it can be analyzed. Hop over to that chapter for more on creating a list by exporting and then importing.

Even if you plan to create your lists by exporting data from a database, however, read on through the next paragraphs of this chapter. Understanding the nuts and bolts of building a list makes exporting database information to a list and later using that information easier.

Building a list the hard way

The other common way to create an Excel list (besides exporting from a relational database) is to do it manually. For example, you can create a list in the same way that I create the list shown in Figure 1-2. You first enter field names into the first row of the worksheet and then enter individual records, or items, into the subsequent rows of the worksheet. When a list isn't too long, this method is very workable. This is the way, obviously, that I create the list shown in Figure 1-2.

Building a list the semi-hard way

Another related way to create a list manually is to enter the field name into row 1, select those field names and the empty cells of row 2, and then choose the Data➪Form command. From a form dialog box that Excel displays, use its text boxes to describe the records that belong in your database.

The form dialog box is often — or at least sometimes — overkill. In some circumstances, however, you may want to use this method for building a database.

Manually adding records

To manually create a list by using the Form command, follow these steps:

1. **Identify the fields in your list.**

   To identify the fields in your list, enter the field names into row 1 in a blank Excel workbook. For example, Figure 1-3 shows a workbook fragment. Cells A1, B1, C1 and D1 hold field names for a simple grocery list.

2. **Select the Excel list.**

   The Excel list must include the row of the field names and at least one other row. This row may be blank or it may contain data. In Figure 1-3, for example, you can select an Excel list by dragging the mouse from cell A1 to cell D2.

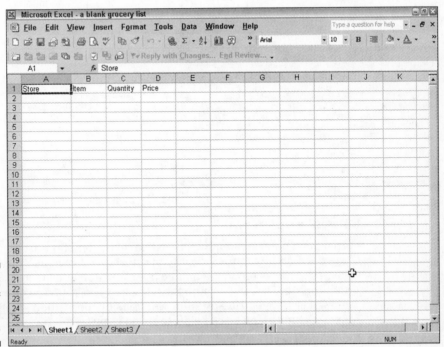

Figure 1-3:
The start of something important.

3. Choose Data⇨Form to tell Excel that you want to use a data form to enter items into a list.

If Excel can't figure out which row holds your field names, Excel displays the dialog box as shown in Figure 1-4. Essentially, this dialog box just enables you to confirm that the first row in your range selection holds the field names. To accept Excel's guess about your list, click OK. Excel displays the data form dialog box, as shown in Figure 1-5.

Figure 1-4: Excel tries to figure out what you're doing.

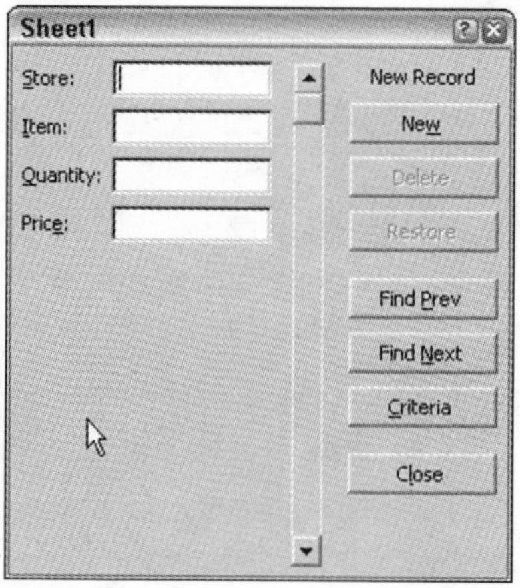

Figure 1-5: Describe a data form here.

4. Describe each record.

To enter a new record into your list, fill in the text boxes. For example, use the Store text box to identify the store where you purchase each item. Use the — oh, wait a minute here. You don't need me to tell you that the store name goes into the Store field, do you? You can figure that out. Likewise, you already know what bits of information go into the Item, Quantity, and Price fields, too, don't you? Okay. Sorry.

5. Store your record in the list.

Click the New button when you finish describing some record, or item, that goes onto the shopping list. Excel adds the item to the list and clears the text boxes so that you can add another item. In this manner, you can use the data form dialog box to describe and add each record to the list.

Excel uses the worksheet name to label the data form dialog box, as shown in Figure 1-5. To re-label the data form dialog box, rename the worksheet. To name or rename a worksheet, double-click the Sheet1 tab. When Excel selects the sheet name, type the new sheet name you want.

Editing records

You can also edit a list by using the data form dialog box. To edit the list, follow these steps:

1. Identify your list.

To select your database, click a cell in the list.

2. Choose the Data⇨Form command.

Excel displays the data form dialog box, as shown in Figure 1-6.

The box tells you how many records are in the list.

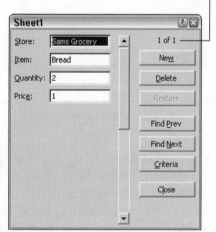

Figure 1-6:
Edit records
here.

3. Find the record that you want to change.

Use the Find Prev and Find Next buttons to move through the Excel list one record at a time. You can also scroll through the list by clicking the scroll bar's arrow buttons, or dragging the scroll bar marker, or by clicking on the scroll bar itself. Pretty standard stuff, really.

Note that the data form dialog box lists the number of records in the list: That's kind of cool.

Click the Criteria button to display the Criteria version of the data form dialog box, as shown in Figure 1-7. When the Criteria version of the data form dialog box displays, you enter information about the record that you're looking for into the dialog box's text boxes. For example, you could enter **Sams Grocery** into the Store text box. Then when you click either the Find Prev or Find Next buttons, Excel displays the previous or next record that shows *Sams Grocery* in the Store field.

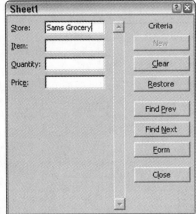

Figure 1-7:
Search for a record with Criteria.

To flip-flop between the Form and Criteria versions of the data form dialog boxes, click the Form or Criteria command buttons.

4. **Edit the record.**

When you find the record that you want to edit, change the contents of the text boxes to change the record. Click the New button, and Excel updates the record in the list with your changes.

If you change a field in a record but want to return to the original value after making your edits, click the Restore button. Note that you must click Restore before moving to a new record.

To delete a record, click the Delete command button.

When you delete a record in an Excel list, the record is permanently deleted. You can't undo your deletion by clicking Restore. Or by using the Edit⇨Undo command. Or by waving your arms in the air and screaming, "Oh, what have I done . . . what have I done?!"

5. Close the data form dialog box.

In what I'm sure is a big surprise to you, you click the Close button to close the data form dialog box.

Some cruel editorializing about the data form command

Although the data form dialog box looks good — those folks at Microsoft know how to design attractive windows and dialog boxes — you need to not let a pretty face override your better judgment.

In many cases, you'll find it easier to manually build a list by entering information directly into rows. For one thing, you can easily copy redundant data from cell to cell or from a cell to a range of cells. For example, if you need to enter the information **Sams Grocery** into 20 or 50 cells, you could easily just copy the label.

Excel also includes an AutoFill feature, which is particularly relevant for list building. Here's how AutoFill works: Enter a label into a cell in a column where it's already been entered before, and Excel guesses that you're entering the same thing again. For example, if you enter the label **Sams Grocery** in cell A2 and then begin to type **Sams Grocery** in cell A3, Excel guesses that you're entering **Sams Grocery** again and finishes typing the label for you. All you need to do to accept Excel's guess of the label is press Enter. Check it out in Figure 1-8.

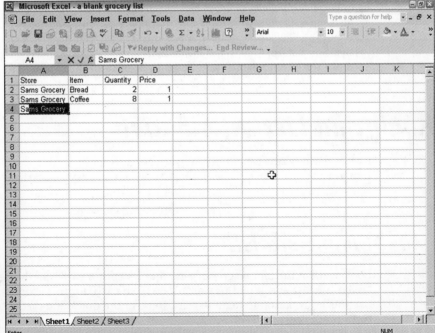

Figure 1-8: A little workbook fragment compliments of AutoFill.

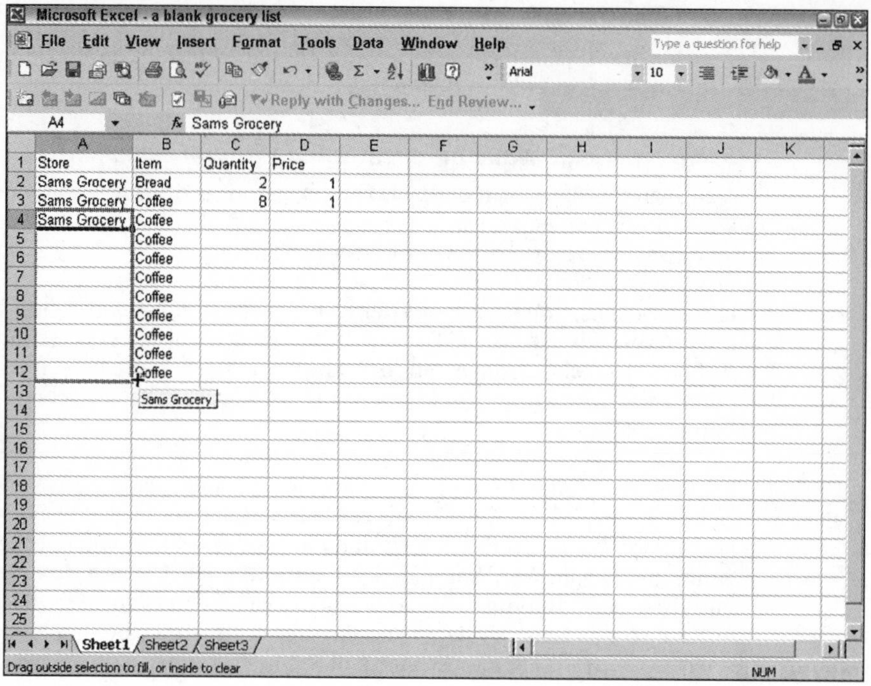

Figure 1-9:
Another
little
workbook
fragment
compli-
ments of
the Fill
Handle.

Excel also provides a Fill command that you can use to fill a range of cells —
including the contents of some column in an Excel list — with a label or value.
To fill a range of cells with the value that you've already entered in another cell,
you drag the Fill Handle down the column. The Fill Handle is the small plus sign
(+) symbol that appears in the lower-right corner of the active cell. In Figure
1-9, I use the Fill Handle to enter **Sams Grocery** into the range A5:A12.

Analyzing List Information

Excel provides several handy, easy-to-use tools for analyzing the information
that you store in a list. Some of these tools are so easy and straightforward
that they provide a good starting point.

Simple statistics

Look again at the simple grocery list that I mention earlier in the section
"What Is a List and Why Do I Care?" See Figure 1-10 for this grocery list as I
use this information to demonstrate some of the quick-and-dirty statistical
tools that Excel provides.

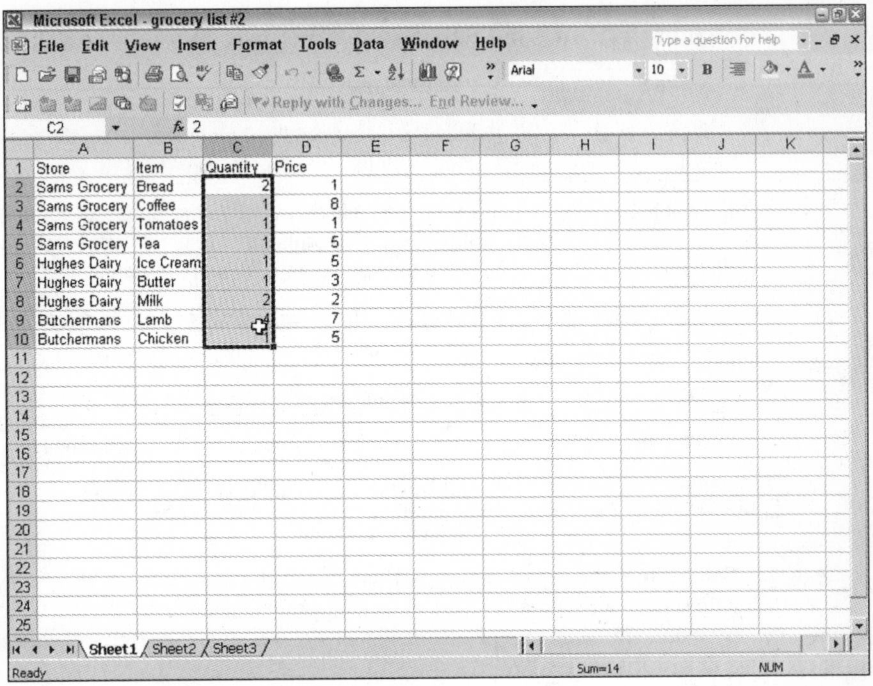

Figure 1-10:
Start at the
beginning.

One of the slickest and quickest tools that Excel provides is the ability to effortlessly calculate the sum, average, count, minimum, or maximum of values in a selected range. For example, if you select the range C2 to C10 in Figure 1-10, Excel sums the quantity counts and displays this information in the status bar. In Figure 1-10, note the phrase *Sum=14* on the status bar (lower-right of the workbook). This indicates that the grocery list includes 14 items: Two loaves of bread, one can of coffee, one tomato, one box of tea, and so on.

You aren't limited, however, to simply summing fields in your list. You can also calculate other statistical measures.

To perform some other statistical calculation of the selected range list, right-click the Sum shown in the status bar. When you do, Excel displays a pop-up menu of statistical measures that you can make on the selected range: None, Average, Count, Count Nums, Max, Min, and Sum. In Table 1-1, I describe each of these statistical measures briefly, but you can probably guess what they do. If you choose the average, Excel calculates the arithmetic mean, or average, of the values in the selected range. If you choose a count measure, Excel counts the cells with labels, values, or formulas in a selected range, and so on.

Table 1-1	Quick Statistical Measures Available on the Status Bar
Option	*What It Does*
None	Tells Excel that you don't want it to calculate and then show a statistic on the status bar.
Count	Tallies the cells that hold labels, values, or formulas. In other words, use this statistical measure when you want to count the number of cells that are *not* empty.
Count Nums	Tallies the number of cells in a selected range that hold values or formulas.
Max	Finds the largest value in the selected range.
Min	Finds the smallest value in the selected range.
Sum	Adds up the values in the selected range.

No kidding, these simple statistical measures are often all that you need to gain wonderful insights into data that you collect and store in an Excel list. By using the example of a simple, artificial grocery list, the power of these quick statistical measures doesn't seem all that earthshaking. But with real data, these measures often produce wonderful insights.

In my own work as a writer, for example, I first noticed the slowdown in the computer book publishing industry that followed the dot.com meltdown when the total number of books that one of the larger distributors sold — information that appeared in an Excel list — began dropping. Sometimes, simply adding, counting, or averaging the values in a list gives extremely useful insights.

Sorting lists

After you place information in an Excel list, you'll find it very easy to sort the records. To do so, follow these steps:

1. **Select the database.**

   To select the database, drag the mouse from the top-left corner of the list to its lower-right corner. You can also select an Excel list by: clicking the cell or selecting the cell in the top-left corner, holding down the Shift key, pressing the End key, pressing the right arrow, pressing the End key, and pressing the down arrow. This technique selects the Excel list range by using the arrow keys.

2. Choose the Data⇨Sort command.

Excel displays the Sort dialog box, as shown in Figure 1-11.

Figure 1-11:
Set sort
parameters
here.

3. Select the first sort key.

Use the Sort By drop-down list box to select the field that you want to use for sorting. Then indicate whether you want records arranged in ascending or descending order by selecting either the Ascending or Descending radio button. Ascending order, predictably, alphabetizes labels and arranges values in smallest value to biggest value order. Descending order arranges labels in reverse alphabetical order and values in largest-value-to-smallest-value order.

4. Specify any secondary keys (optional).

If you want to sort records that have the same primary key with a secondary key, use choices from the Then By drop-down list boxes and their Ascending and Descending radio buttons to specify which secondary keys that you want to use.

Note: The Sort dialog box provides a set of My List Has radio buttons — Header Row and No Header Row — that enable you to indicate whether the range selection includes the row and field names. If you include the Header Row — a top row of field names in your range selection — select the Header Row radio button. If you don't include the row of field names, select the No Header Row radio button.

5. Fiddle-faddle with the sorting rules (really optional).

If you click the Options button in the Sort dialog box, Excel displays the Sort Options dialog box, as shown in Figure 1-12. Make choices here to further specify how the first key sort order works.

Typically, you want the key to work in an alphabetic or reverse-alphabetic or ascending or descending fashion. However, you may want to sort records using a chronological sequence such as Sunday, Monday, Tuesday, and so on. Or January, February, March, and so forth. Select one of these other ordering methods from the Sort Options dialog box.

The Sort Options dialog box also enables you to indicate whether case sensitivity (uppercase versus lowercase) should be considered.

Finally, use the Sort Options dialog box to tell Excel that it should sort rows instead of columns or columns instead of rows. You make this specification by using either Orientation radio button: Sort Top to Bottom or Sort Left to Right.

6. **Click OK.**

   Excel then sorts your list.

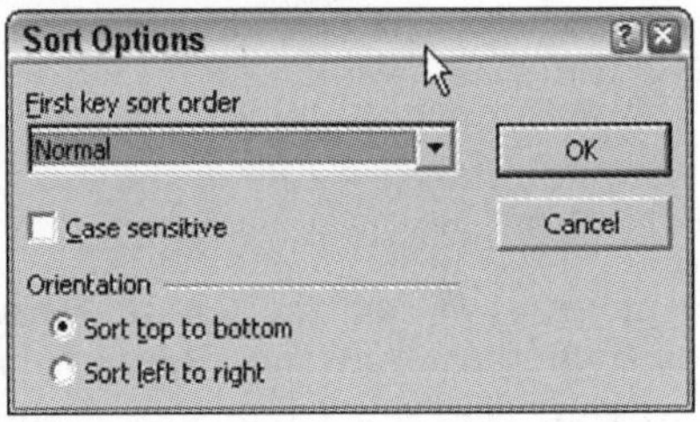

Figure 1-12:
Sorting out
your sorting
options.

Using AutoFilter on a list

Excel provides an AutoFilter command that's pretty cool. When you use AutoFilter, you produce a new list that's a subset of your original list. For example, in the case of a grocery list, you could use AutoFilter to create a subset list that shows only those items that you'll purchase at Butchermans. Or, a subset list that shows only those items that cost more than, say, $2.

To use AutoFilter on a list, take these steps:

1. **Select your list.**

   Select your list in the usual way. You can click the cell in the upper-left corner of the list and then drag the mouse to the cell in the lower-right corner of the list. Or you can click the cell in the upper-left corner of the list, hold down the shift key, press End, press right arrow, press End, and press the down arrow.

2. **Choose the AutoFilter command.**

   Choose Data⇨Filter⇨AutoFilter. Excel turns the header row, or row of field names, into drop-down list boxes. See Figure 1-13 for how this looks.

Drop-down list boxes appear when you turn on AutoFiltering.

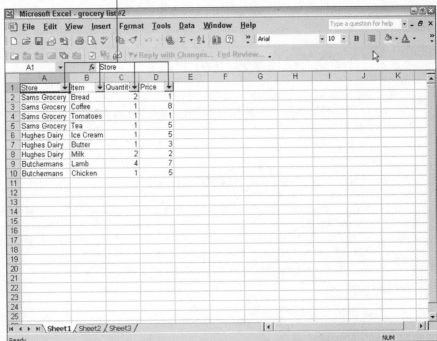

Figure 1-13:
How an
Excel list
looks after
using
AutoFilter.

3. **Use the drop-down list box to filter the list.**

Each of the drop-down list boxes that now make up the header row can be used to filter the list.

To filter the list using the contents of some field, select (or open) the drop-down list box for that field. For example, in the case of the little workbook shown in Figure 1-13, you might choose to filter the grocery list so that it shows only those items that you'll purchase at Sams Grocery. To do this, click the Store drop-down list down-arrow button. When you do, Excel displays a list of AutoFilter options: All, Top Ten, Custom, Butchermans, Hughes Dairy, and Sams Grocery. To see just those records that describe items you've purchased at Sams Grocery, select Sams Grocery. In Figure 1-14 is the filtered list with just the Sams Grocery items visible.

To unfilter the list, open the Store drop-down list box and choose All.

If you're filtering a list using a value field, you can also choose to see the records with the ten largest values by choosing the Top 10 AutoFilter option. When you choose the Top 10 AutoFilter option, Excel displays its dialog box, as shown in Figure 1-15. You use this dialog box to indicate whether you want the biggest values or top values or the smallest values or the bottom values. You can also choose whether you want the top one, two, three, and so on. Or the bottom one, two, three, and so on values. You can also choose to sort items or include items based on either their value or a percentage value.

Undoing an AutoFilter

To remove a custom AutoFilter, use the blank filter from the AutoFilter drop-down list box. The blank, or empty, filtering operation is the first operation listed in the drop-down list box.

Turning off AutoFilter

The AutoFilter command is actually a toggle switch. When AutoFilter is turned on, Excel places a checkmark in front of the AutoFilter command. When you turn off AutoFilter, Excel removes the checkmark. To turn off AutoFilter and remove the AutoFilter drop-down list boxes, select the list and then choose the Data⇨Filter⇨AutoFilter command.

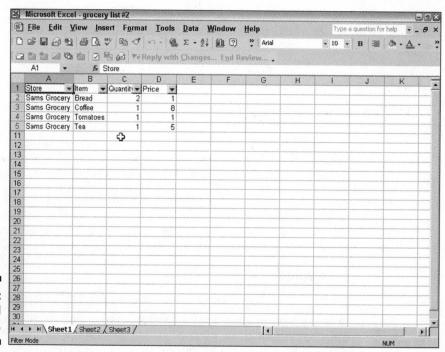

Figure 1-14:
Sams and
Sams alone.

Figure 1-15:
Quick filter:
The Top 10.

Using the custom AutoFilter

You can also construct a custom AutoFilter. To do this, select the Custom AutoFilter option from the AutoFilter drop-down list box. Excel displays the Custom AutoFilter dialog box, as shown in Figure 1-16. This dialog box enables you to specify with great precision what records you want to appear on your filtered list.

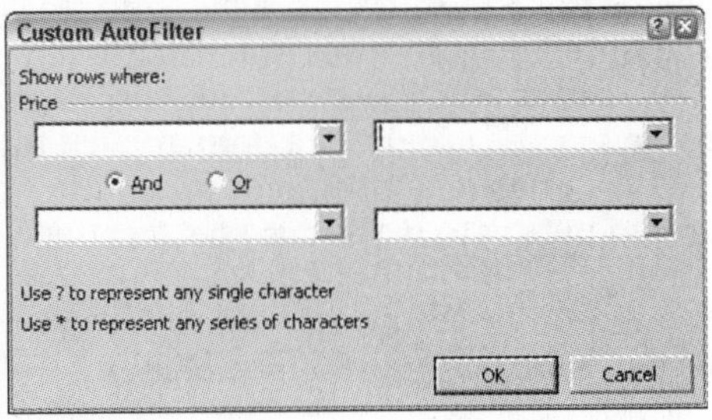

Figure 1-16:
Customize
an
AutoFilter.

To create a custom AutoFilter, take the following steps:

1. **Turn on the Excel AutoFilter.**

   As I mention earlier in this section, just select the list and then choose Data⇨Filter⇨AutoFilter.

2. **Select the field that you want to use for your custom AutoFilter.**

   To indicate which field list you want to use, open the AutoFilter drop-down list box for that field and choose the Custom AutoFilter option. When you do this, Excel displays the Custom AutoFilter dialog box. (Refer to Figure 1-16.)

3. **Describe the AutoFilter operation.**

   To describe your AutoFilter, you need to identify the filtering operation and the filter criteria. Use the left side set of drop-down list boxes to select a filtering option. For example, in Figure 1-17, the filtering option selected in the first Custom AutoFilter set of dialog boxes is *begins with*.

If you open this drop-down list box, you'll see that Excel provides a series of filtering options including equals, does not equal, is greater than or equal to, is less than, is less than or equal to, begins with, does not begin with, ends with, does not end with, contains, and does not contain. The key thing to be aware of is that you want to pick a filtering operation that, in conjunction with your filtering criteria, enables you to identify the records that you want to appear in your filtered list.

In practice, you won't want to use precise filtering criteria. Why? Well, because your list data will probably be pretty dirty. For example, the names of stores may not match perfectly because of misspellings. For this reason, you'll find filtering operations based on *begins with* or *contains* and filtering criteria that use fragments of field names or ranges of values most valuable.

4. Describe the AutoFilter filtering criteria.

After you pick the filtering option, you describe the filtering criteria using the right-hand side drop-down list box. For example, if you want to filter records that equal *Sams Grocery* or, more practically, that begin with the word *Sams*, you enter **Sams** into the right-hand side box. Figure 1-17 shows this custom AutoFilter criterion. You can use more than one AutoFilter criterion. If you want to use two custom AutoFilter criteria, you need to indicate whether the criteria are both applied together or the customer AutoFilter criteria are applied independently. You select either the And or Or radio button to make this specification.

5. Click OK.

Excel then filters your list using your custom AutoFilter.

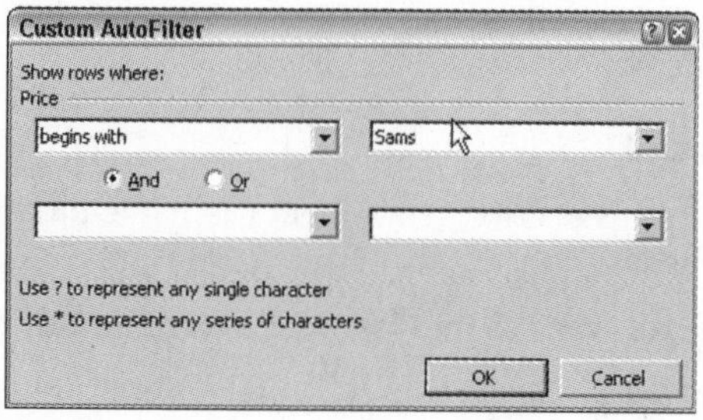

Figure 1-17: Setting up a custom AutoFilter.

Custom AutoFilter	
Show rows where:	
Price	
begins with	Sams
● And ○ Or	
Use ? to represent any single character	
Use * to represent any series of characters	
	OK Cancel

Filtering a filtered list

You can filter a filtered list.

What this often means is that if you want to build a highly filtered list, you will find your work easiest if you just apply several sets of filters.

If you want to filter the grocery list to show only the most expensive items that you purchase at Sams Grocery, for example, you might first filter the list to show items from Sams Grocery only. Then, working with this filtered list, you would further filter the list to show the most expensive items or only those items with the price exceeding some specified amount.

The idea of filtering a filtered list seems, perhaps, esoteric. But applying several sets of filters often reduces a very large and comprehensible list to a smaller subset of data that provides just the information that you need.

Building on the earlier section "Using the custom AutoFilter," I want to make this important point: Although the Custom AutoFilter dialog box does enable you to filter a list based on two criteria, sometimes filtering operations apply to the same field. And if you need to apply more than two filtering operations to the same field, the only way to easily do this is to filter a filtered list.

Using advanced filtering

Most of the time, you'll be able to filter lists in the ways that you need using an AutoFilter or a combination thereof. However, in some cases you may want to exert more control over the way filtering works. When this is the case, you can use the Excel advanced filters.

Writing Boolean expressions

Before you can begin to use the Excel advanced filters, you need to know how to construct Boolean logic expressions. For example, if you want to filter the grocery list so that it shows only those items that cost more than $1 or those items with an extended price of more than $5, you need to know how to write a Boolean logic, or algebraic, expression that describes the condition in which the price exceeds $1 or the extended price exceeds or equals $5.

See Figure 1-18 for an example of how you specify these Boolean logic expressions in Excel. In Figure 1-18, the range A13:B14 describes two criteria: one in which price exceeds $1, and one in which the extended price equals or exceeds $5. The way this works, as you may guess, is that you need to use the first row of the range to name the fields that you use in your expression. After you do this, you use the rows beneath the field names to specify what logical comparison needs to be made using the field.

To construct a Boolean expression, you use a comparison operator from Table 1-2 and then a value used in the comparison.

Table 1-2	Boolean Logic
Operator	*What It Does*
=	Equals
<	Is less than
<=	Is less than or equal to
>	Is greater than
>=	Is greater than or equal to
<>	Is not equal to

In Figure 1-18, for example, the Boolean expression in cell A14 (>1), checks to see whether a value is greater than 1. And the Boolean expression in cell B14 (>=5) checks to see whether the value is greater than or equal to 5.

Here's an important point: Any record in the list that meets the criteria in *either* one of the rows gets included in the filtered list. For example, the criterion in row 14 can be used to identify some list record that belongs on the filtered list. Or, the criterion in row 14 can be used to identify some list record that belongs on the filtered list.

If you want to include records for items that *both* cost more than $1 apiece and that totaled at least $5 in shopping expense (after multiplying the quantity times the unit price), you use one row that includes both criteria. (I put this new column into the workbook shown in Figure 1-18 just to make this discussion a little richer.)

Running an advanced filter operation

After you set up a list for an advanced filter and the criteria range — what I did in Figure 1-18 — you're ready to run the advanced filter operation. To do so, take these steps:

1. **Select the list.**

   To select the list, drag the mouse from the top-left corner of the list to the lower-right corner. You can also select an Excel list by clicking the cell or selecting the cell in the top-left corner, holding down the Shift key, pressing the End key, pressing the right arrow, pressing the End key, and pressing the down arrow. This technique selects the Excel list range using the arrow keys.

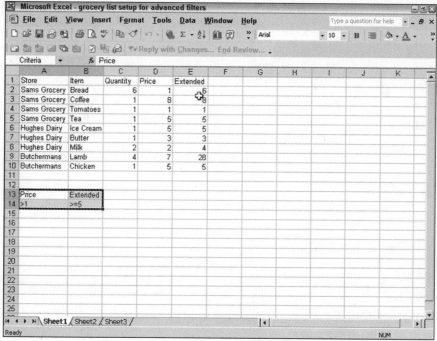

Figure 1-18:
A list set
up for
advanced
filters.

2. Choose Data⇨Filter⇨Advanced Filter.

Excel displays the Advanced Filter dialog box, as shown in Figure 1-19.

Figure 1-19:
Set up an
advanced
filter here.

3. Tell Excel where to place the filtered list.

Use either Action radio button to specify whether you want the list filtered in place or copied to some new location.

4. Verify the list range.

The worksheet range shown in the List Range textbox — $A$1:$E$10 in Figure 1-19 — should correctly identify the list if you perform Step 1. If your text box doesn't show the correct worksheet range, however, enter it.

5. Provide the criteria range.

Make an entry in the Criteria Range text box to identify the worksheet range holding the advanced filter criteria. In Figure 1-19, the criteria range is $A$13:$B$14.

6. If you're copying the filtering results, provide the destination (optional).

If you tell Excel to copy the filter results to some new location, use the Copy To text box to identify this location.

7 Click OK.

Excel filters your list.

And that's that. Not too bad, eh? Advanced filtering works in a pretty straight-forward manner. All you really do is write some Boolean logic expressions and then tell Excel to filter your list using those expressions.

Chapter 2

Grabbing Data from External Sources

• •

• •

*I*n many cases, the data that you want to analyze with Excel resides in an external database or in a database application such as a corporate accounting system. Thus, often your very first step and very first true challenge are to get that data into an Excel workbook and in the form of an Excel list.

You have two basic approaches that you can use to grab the external data that you want to analyze. You can export data from another program and then import that the data into Excel, or you can query a database directly from Excel. I describe both approaches in this chapter.

Getting Data the Export-Import Way

You can usually easily export data from popular database programs and accounting systems. Excel is the dominant data analysis tool available to business. Because of this, most database programs and most management information systems export data in a format that makes it simple to easily import the data into Excel later.

Exporting: The first step

Your first step when grabbing data from one of these external sources, assuming that you want to later import the data, is to first use the other application program — such as an accounting program — to export the to-be-analyzed data to a file.

You have two basic approaches available for exporting data from another application program: direct exporting and exporting to a text file.

Direct exporting

Direct exporting is available in many accounting programs because accountants love to use Excel to analyze data. For example, the most popular small business accounting program in the world is QuickBooks from Intuit. When you produce an accounting report in QuickBooks, the report document window includes a button labeled *Excel*. Click this button, and QuickBooks displays the Export Report To Excel dialog box, as shown in Figure 2-1.

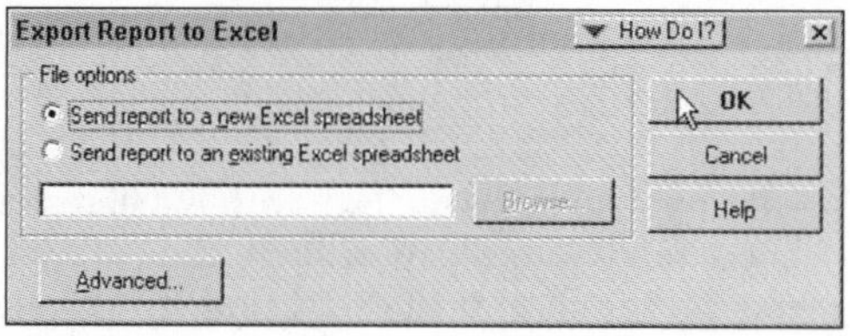

Figure 2-1:
Begin
exporting
here.

The Export Report To Excel dialog box provides two radio buttons with which you indicate whether you want to send the report to a new Excel spreadsheet or to an existing Excel spreadsheet. To send (*export*) the report to an existing Excel spreadsheet, you need to identify that workbook by entering the workbook path name and filename into the text box provided. Or, click the Browse button and use the Open Microsoft Excel File dialog box that appears (as shown in Figure 2-2) to identify the folder and workbook file.

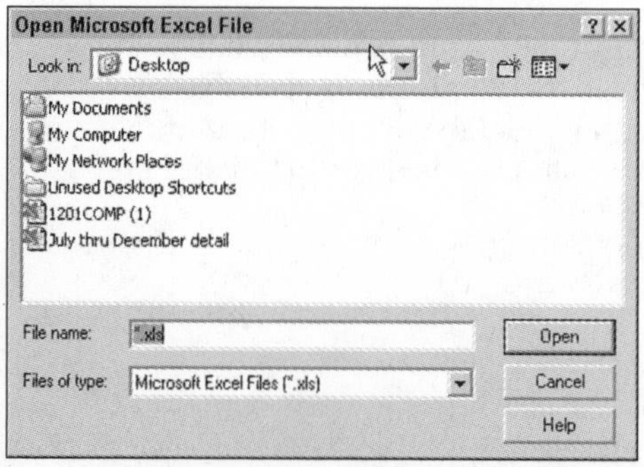

Figure 2-2:
Find the
file to be
exported
here.

In Figure 2-3, you can see how the QuickBooks report looks after it's been directly exported to Excel.

In this example using QuickBooks, the Export Report to Excel dialog box also includes an Advanced command button. Click this button, and QuickBooks displays a dialog box in which you control how the exported report looks. For example, you get to pick which fonts, colors, spacing, and row height that you want. You also get to turn on and turn off Excel features in the newly created workbook, including AutoFit, Gridline, and so on.

Okay, obviously, you may not want to export from QuickBooks. You may have other application programs that you want to export data from. You can export data directly from a database program like Microsoft Access, for example. But the key thing that you need to know — and the reason that I discuss in detail how QuickBooks works — is that application programs that store and collect data often provide a convenient way for you to export information to Excel. Predictably, some application programs work differently. But usually, the process is little more than clicking a button labeled _Excel_ (as is the case in QuickBooks) or choosing a command labeled something like _Export_ or _Export to Excel._

	B	C Item Description	D	E On Hand	F	G Avg Cost	H	I Asset Value	J	K % of Tot Asset	L	M Sales Price	N	Ret
1														
2	0-9672981-3-X	Executive FrontPage Web Sites		2,996.00		1.77		5,302.92		2.86%		24.95		
3	0-9672981-4-8	Executive's PowerPoint 2000		412.00		2.27		935.24		0.5%		24.95		
4	0-9672981-6-4	MBA's Internet		3,531.00		4.11		14,512.41		7.83%		39.95		14
5	0-9672981-8-0	Executive's Windows 2000		3,909.00		1.96		7,661.64		4.13%		24.95		5
6	09672981-0-5	MBA's Excel 2000		672.00		3.41		2,291.52		1.24%		39.95		
7	09672981-1-3	Executive Project 2000		397.00		1.90		754.30		0.41%		24.95		
8	09672981-2-1	Ask the Expert GT Money		3,879.00		1.55		6,012.45		3.24%		19.95		
9	09672981-7-2	Executive's Internet		3,863.00		1.89		7,301.07		3.94%		24.95		5
10	09672981-9-9	Executive's Dreamweaver Web Sites		3,043.00		2.06		6,268.58		3.38%		24.95		5
11	1-931150-00-1	Executive's PowerPoint 2002		3,855.00		1.71		6,592.05		3.56%		24.95		5
12	1-931150-01-X	MBA Excel 2002		1,981.00		3.97		7,864.57		4.24%		39.95		7
13	1-931150-02-8	New Webmaster's FrontPage 2002		4,327.00		1.97		8,524.19		4.6%		24.95		10
14	1-931150-03-6	Executive's Word 2002		3,928.00		1.81		7,109.68		3.84%		24.95		5
15	1-931150-04-4	Exec Outlook 2002		4,064.00		2.16		8,778.24		4.74%		24.95		10
16	1-931150-05-2	New Webmaster's Dreamweaver 4		2,407.00		1.95		4,693.65		2.53%		24.95		6
17	1-931150-06-0	Executive's GT Access 2002		3,745.00		1.87		7,003.15		3.78%		24.95		
18	1-931150-07-9	Executive's Office XP		3,046.00		1.83		5,574.18		3.01%		24.95		
19	1-931150-08-7	Executive's Excel 2002		4,204.00		1.72		7,230.88		3.9%		24.95		10
20	1-931150-18-4	Effective Executive's GT Windows XP		2,253.00		3.08		6,939.24		3.74%		24.95		
21	1-931150-19-2	MBA's GT Windows XP		1,805.00		4.63		8,357.15		4.51%		39.95		2
22	1-931150-20-6	MBA Office XP		4,429.00		3.90		17,273.10		9.32%		39.95		12
23	1-931150-21-4	Word 2002 A to Z		3,753.00		1.15		4,315.95		2.33%		11.95		
24	1-931150-22-2	Excel A to Z		3,734.00		1.07		3,995.38		2.16%		11.95		
25	1-931150-23-0			3,823.00		1.10		3,985.30		2.15%		11.95		

Figure 2-3:
A Quick-Books report that's been directly exported to Excel.

Therefore, when exporting data from some other application program, your first step is to do a little bit of digging and research to see whether there's a way to easily and automatically export data to Excel. This fact-finding shouldn't take much time if you use the online Help.

Microsoft Access includes an Export command on its File menu. Choose the File➪Export command to export an Access table, report, or query to Excel. Just choose the appropriate command and then use the dialog box that Access displays to specify where the exported information should be placed.

Exporting to a text file

When you need to export data first to a text file because the other application won't automatically export your data to an Excel workbook, you need to go to a little more effort. Fortunately, the process is still pretty darn straightforward.

When you work with application programs that won't automatically create an Excel workbook, you just create a text version of a report that shows the data that you want to analyze. For example, to analyze sales of items that your firm makes, you first create a report that shows this.

The trick is that you send the report to a text file rather than sending this report to a printer. This way, the report gets stored on disk as text rather than printed. Text files are then later easily imported by Excel.

See how this works in more concrete terms by following how the process works in QuickBooks. Suppose, for sake of illustration, that you really did want to print a list of items that you sell. The first step is to produce a report that shows this list. In QuickBooks, you produce this report by choosing the appropriate command from the Reports menu. Figure 2-4 shows such a report.

The next step is to print this report to a text file. In QuickBooks, you click the Print button or choose File➪Print Report. Using either approach, QuickBooks displays the Print Reports dialog box, as shown in Figure 2-5.

Pay attention to the Print To radio buttons shown near the top of the Settings tab. QuickBooks, like many other programs, gives you the option of either printing your report to a printer or to a file.

To later import the information on the report, you print the report to a file. In the case of QuickBooks, this means that you select the File radio button. (Refer to Figure 2-5.)

The other thing that you need to do — if you're given a choice — is to use a delimiter. In Figure 2-5, the File drop-down list box shows ASCII text file as the type of file that QuickBooks will print. Often, though, application programs — including QuickBooks — will let you print delimited text files.

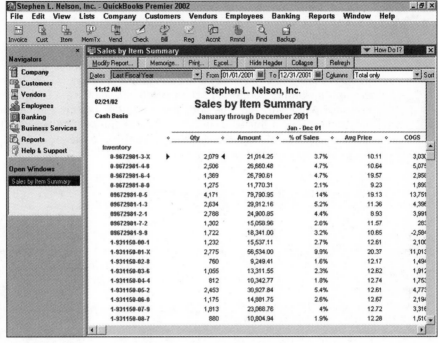

Figure 2-4:
Begin to
export a text
file from a
QuickBooks
report.

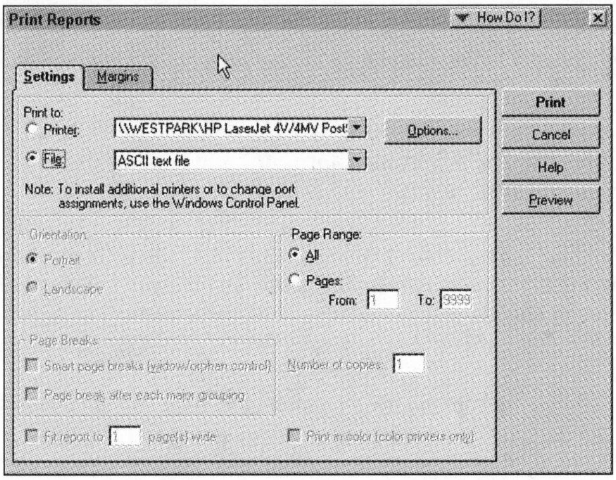

Figure 2-5:
Print a
QuickBooks
reports
here.

Delimited text files use standard characters, called *delimiters*, to separate fields of information in the report. You can still later import a straight ASCII text file, but importing a delimited text file is easier. Therefore, if your other application program gives you the option of creating delimited text files, do so. In QuickBooks, you can create both comma-delimited files and tab-delimited files.

In QuickBooks, you indicate that you want a delimited text file by choosing Comma Delimited File or Tab Delimited File from the File drop-down list box of the Print Reports dialog box.

To print the report as a file, you simply click the Print button of the Print Reports dialog box. Typically, the application program (QuickBooks, in this example) prompts you for a path name, like in the Create Disk File dialog box shown in Figure 2-6. The *path name* includes both the drive and folder location of the text file as well as the name of the file. You provide this information, and then the application produces the text file . . . or hopefully, the delimited text file. And that's that.

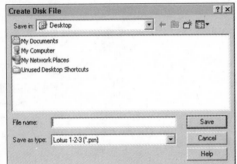

Figure 2-6:
The Create
Disk File
dialog box.

Importing: The second step (if necessary)

When you don't or can't export directly to Excel, you need to take the second step of importing the ASCII text file that you create using the other program. (To read more about this, see the previous section.)

To import the ASCII text file, first open the text file itself from within Excel. When you open the text file, Excel starts the Text Import Wizard. This wizard walks you through the steps to describe how information in a text file should be formatted and rearranged as it's placed in an Excel workbook.

One minor wrinkle in this importing business is that the process works differently depending on whether you're importing straight (ASCII) text or importing delimited text.

Importing straight text

Here are the steps that you take to import a straight text file.

1. **Open the text file by choosing File⇨Open.**

   Excel displays the Open dialog box, shown in Figure 2-7.

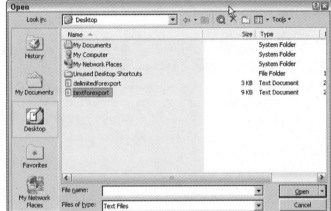

Figure 2-7:
Open the
text file that
you want to
import.

2. **Choose Text Files from the Files of Type drop-down list box.**

3. **Use the Look In drop-down list box to identify the folder in which you placed the exported text file.**

   You should see the text file listed in Open dialog box.

4. **To open the text file, double-click its icon.**

   Excel starts the Text Import Wizard, as shown in Figure 2-8.

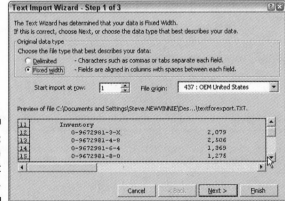

Figure 2-8:
Step 1 of the
Text Import
Wizard.

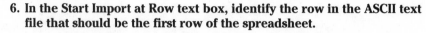

5. Select the Fixed Width radio button.

This tells Excel that the fields in the text file are arranged in evenly spaced columns.

6. In the Start Import at Row text box, identify the row in the ASCII text file that should be the first row of the spreadsheet.

In general, ASCII text files use the first several rows of the file to show report header information. For this reason, you typically won't want to start importing at row 1; you'll want to start importing at row 10 or 20 or 5.

Don't get too tense about this business of telling the Text Import Wizard which row is the first one that should be imported. If you import too many rows, you can easily delete the extraneous rows later in Excel.

Preview the to-be-imported report shown on the bottom section of the Text Import Wizard dialog box.

7. Click Next.

Excel displays the second step dialog box of the Text Import Wizard, as shown in Figure 2-9. You use this second Text Import Wizard dialog box to break the rows of the text files into columns.

You may not need to do much work identifying where rows should be broken into columns. Excel, after looking carefully at the data in the to-be-imported text file, suggests where rows should be broken and draws vertical lines at the breaks.

8. In the Data Preview section of the second wizard dialog box, review the text breaks and amend them as needed.

- If they're incorrect, drag the break lines to a new location.
- To remove a break, double-click the break line.
- To create or add a new break, click at the point where you want the break to occur.

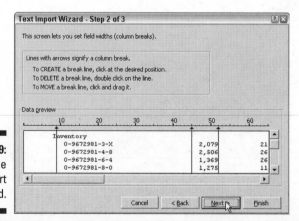

Figure 2-9:
Step 2 of the
Text Import
Wizard.

9. **Click Next.**

   Excel displays the third step dialog box of the Text Import Wizard, as shown in Figure 2-10.

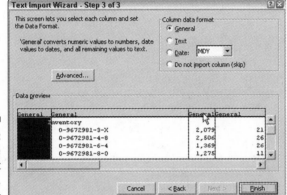

Figure 2-10:
Step 3 of the
Text Import
Wizard.

10. **Choose the data format for the columns in your new workbook (optional).**

    You can pick default formatting from the third Text Import Wizard dialog box for the columns of the new workbook.

    • To choose the default format for a column, click that column in the Data Preview box and then select one of the four Column Data Format radio buttons.

    • If you choose the Date format radio button as the default for a column, use the Date drop-down list box to choose a Date format.

11. **Identify any columns that Excel should skip importing (optional).**

    If you don't want to import a column, select a column in the Data Preview box and then select the Do Not Import Column (Skip) radio button.

12. **Nit-pick how the data appears in the text file (optional).**

    You can click the Advanced button (on the third Text Import Wizard dialog box) to display the Advanced Text Import Settings dialog box, as shown in Figure 2-11. The Advanced Text Import Settings dialog box provides text boxes that you can use to specify in more detail or with more precision how the data in the text file is arranged.

    • Choose what symbol is used to separate whole numbers from decimal values by using the Decimal Separator drop-down list box.

    • Choose what symbol is used to separate thousands by using the Thousands Separator drop-down list box.

Click OK after you make choices here; you return to the third wizard dialog box.

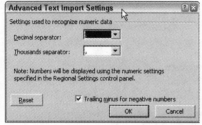

Figure 2-11:
The
Advanced
Text Import
Settings
dialog box.

13. Click Finish.

Excel imports the text file according to your specifications and places it into a new Excel workbook, as shown in Figure 2-12. The data probably won't be perfectly laid out. Still, when you have very large data sets, you'll find importing a tremendous timesaver. In general, you won't find it terribly difficult to clean up the new workbook. You only need to delete a few rows or perhaps columns, or maybe do a bit of additional formatting or row and column resizing.

	A	B	C	D	E	F	G	H	I	J	K	L
1	I											
2		Inventory										
2		0-9672981	2,079	21,014.25	3.70%	10.11	3,030.22	1.46	17,984.03	85.60%		
3		0-9672981	2,506	26,660.48	4.70%	10.64	5,075.75	2.03	21,584.73	81.00%		
4		0-9672981	1,369	26,790.61	4.70%	19.57	2,958.00	2.16	23,832.61	89.00%		
5		0-9672981	1,275	11,774.31	2.10%	9.23	1,899.13	1.49	9,871.18	83.90%		
6		09672981-4	4,171	79,790.95	14.00%	19.13	13,751.39	3.3	66,039.56	82.80%		
7		09672981-	2,634	29,912.16	5.20%	11.36	4,396.50	1.67	25,515.66	85.30%		
8		09672981-	2,788	24,900.85	4.40%	8.93	3,991.49	1.43	20,909.36	84.00%		
9		09672981-	1,302	15,058.96	2.60%	11.57	283.85	0.22	14,775.11	98.10%		
10		09672981-	1,722	18,341.00	3.20%	10.65	-2,584.74	-1.5	20,925.74	114.10%		
11		1-931150-0	1,232	15,537.11	2.70%	12.61	2,100.79	1.71	13,436.32	86.50%		
12		1-931150-0	2,775	56,534.00	9.90%	20.37	11,013.67	3.97	45,520.33	80.50%		
13		1-931150-0	760	9,249.41	1.60%	12.17	1,494.03	1.97	7,755.38	83.80%		
14		1-931150-0	1,055	13,311.55	2.30%	12.62	1,912.28	1.81	11,399.27	85.60%		
15		1-931150-0	812	10,342.77	1.80%	12.74	1,753.60	2.16	8,589.17	83.00%		
16		1-931150-0	2,453	30,927.84	5.40%	12.61	4,773.30	1.95	26,154.54	84.60%		
17		1-931150-0	1,175	14,881.75	2.60%	12.67	2,194.76	1.87	12,686.99	85.30%		
18		1-931150-0	1,813	23,068.76	4.00%	12.72	3,316.67	1.83	19,752.09	85.60%		
19		1-931150-0	880	10,804.94	1.90%	12.28	1,510.93	1.72	9,294.01	86.00%		
20		1-931150-1	4	4	0.00%	1	49.34	12.34	-45.34	########		
21		1-931150-1	4	8	0.00%	2	1,917.07	479.27	-1,909.07	########		
22		1-931150-2	402	8,139.97	1.40%	20.25	1,565.81	3.9	6,574.16	80.80%		
23		1-931150-2	1,151	6,859.75	1.20%	5.96	1,318.65	1.15	5,541.10	80.80%		
24		1-931150-2	1,099	6,572.81	1.10%	5.98	1,179.65	1.07	5,393.16	82.10%		
25		1-931150-2	1,098	6,498.65	1.10%	5.92	1,206.60	1.1	5,292.05	81.40%		

Figure 2-12:
The
imported
text file in
an Excel
workbook.

Importing delimited text files

Here are the steps that you take to import a delimited text file.

1. **Choose the File➪Open command to open the text file.**

   Excel displays the Open dialog box; refer to Figure 2-7.

2. **Choose Text Files from the Files of Type drop-down list box.**

3. **Use the Look In drop-down list box to identify the folder in which you placed the exported text file.**

   You should see the text file listed in Open dialog Box.

4. **To open the text file, double-click its icon.**

   Excel starts the Text Import Wizard, as shown in Figure 2-13.

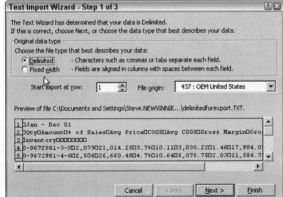

Figure 2-13:
The first
Text Import
Wizard
dialog box.

5. **Select the Delimited radio button.**

   This tells Excel that the fields in the text file are separated with delimiters.

6. **In the Start Import at Row text box, identify the point in the ASCII text file that should be the first row of the spreadsheet.**

   In general, ASCII text files use the first several rows of the file to show report header information. For this reason, you typically want to start importing at row 10 or 20 or 5.

   Don't get too tense about this business of telling the Text Import Wizard which row is the first one that should be imported. You can easily delete the extraneous rows later in Excel.

   Preview the to-be-imported report shown on the bottom section of the Text Import Wizard dialog box.

7. Click Next.

Excel displays the second dialog box of the Text Import Wizard, as shown in Figure 2-14. You use this second Text Import Wizard dialog box to identify the character or characters used as the delimiter to break the text into columns. For example, if the file that's being imported is a tab-delimited file, select the Tab check box in the Delimiters area.

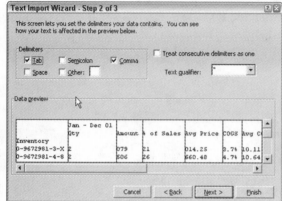

Figure 2-14: The second Text Import Wizard dialog box.

8. Click Next.

The third Text Import Wizard dialog box appears, as shown in Figure 2-15. Here you choose the data format for the columns in your new workbook (optional).

- To choose the default format for a column, click that column in the Data Preview box and then select one of the Column Data Format radio buttons.

- To use the Date format as the default for a column, select the Date radio button and use the Date drop-down list box to choose a Date format.

The Data Preview box on the second Text Import Wizard dialog box shows how the file looks after it's imported based on the delimiters that you identify. For this reason, do experiment a bit to make sure that you import the data in a clean format.

9. Identify any columns that Excel shouldn't skip importing (optional).

If you don't want to import a column, select a column and then select the Do Not Import Column (Skip) radio button.

10. Nit-pick how the data appears in the text file (optional).

Click the Advanced command button of the third Text Import Wizard dialog box to display the Advanced Text Import Settings dialog box. (Refer to Figure 2-11.) Here you can specify in more detail how the data in the text file is arranged.

Click OK to return to the third Text Import Wizard dialog box.

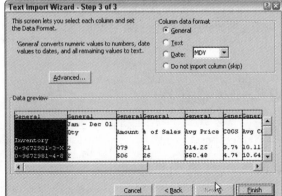

Figure 2-15:
The third
Text Import
Wizard
dialog box.

11. **Click Finish.**

   Excel imports the delimited text file according to your specifications. As
   for a straight text file, the data probably won't be perfectly laid out. But
   you won't find it difficult to clean up the new workbook. A few deletions,
   a little resizing, and pretty soon the workbook will look the way you want.

Querying External Databases and Web Pages Tables

Another approach to collecting data that you want to analyze is to extract
data from a Web page or from an external database.

Excel 2002 provides three very neat ways to grab this sort of external data:

- ✔ You can perform a Web query, which means that you can grab data from
  a table stored in a Web page.

- ✔ You can import tables stored in common databases such as Microsoft
  Access.

- ✔ You can use Microsoft Query to first query a database and then place
  the query results into an Excel workbook.

All three approaches for grabbing external data are described in the paragraphs that follow.

The difference between importing information that you want to analyze using the File⇨Open command (read the preceding paragraphs of the chapter) and importing information by using one of the Data⇨Import Data commands (read the following paragraphs of the chapter) is somewhat subtle. In general, using the Data⇨Import Data command enables you to grab data directly from some external source without first massaging the data so that it's more recognizable.

Running a Web query

One of the neatest ways to grab external data is through a Web query. As you know if you've wasted any time surfing the Web, Internet Web sites provide huge volumes of interesting data. Often you'd like to grab this data and analyze it in some way. Unfortunately, in the past, you haven't had an easy way to get the data from a Web page into Excel.

With the Excel Query tool, as long as the data that you want to grab or analyze is stored in something that looks like a table — that is, in something that uses rows and columns to organize the information — you can grab the information and place it into an Excel workbook.

To perform a Web query, follow these steps:

1. **Click the New toolbar button to open a blank workbook.**

   You need to place query results into a blank worksheet. Therefore, your first step may need to be to open a workbook with a blank worksheet.

   If you need to insert a blank worksheet into an existing workbook, choose Insert⇨Worksheet.

2. **Tell Excel that you want to run a Web query by choosing Data⇨Import External Data⇨New Web Query.**

   Excel displays the New Web Query dialog box, as shown in Figure 2-16.

3. **Open the Web page containing the table that you want to extract data from by entering its URL into the Address text field.**

4. **Identify the table by clicking the small yellow arrow button next to the table.**

   Excel places this small yellow right arrow button next to any tables that it sees in the open Web page. All you need to do is to click one of the buttons to grab the data that the arrow points to.

   Excel replaces the yellow arrow button with a green check button.

5. **Verify the green check button marks for the table that you want to import and then import the table data by clicking the Import button that appears near the bottom of the New Web Query window.**

   Excel displays the Import Data dialog box, as shown in Figure 2-17.

Click these arrow buttons next to data you want to import.

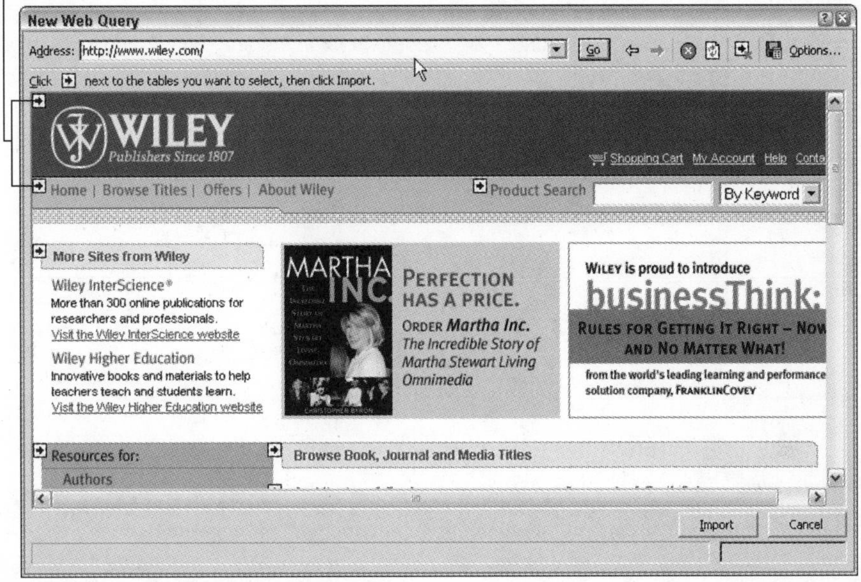

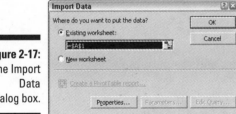

Figure 2-16:
The New
Web Query
dialog box.

Figure 2-17:
The Import
Data
dialog box.

6. In the Import Data dialog box, tell Excel where to place the imported Web data.

Select the Existing Worksheet radio button to place the table data into the existing open empty worksheet. Alternatively, select the New Worksheet radio button to have Excel place the table data into a newly inserted blank sheet.

7. Click OK.

Excel places the table data into the specified location. But I should tell you that sometimes grabbing the table data may take a few moments. Excel goes to some work to grab and arrange the table information. Figure 2-18 shows worksheet data retrieved from a Web page table.

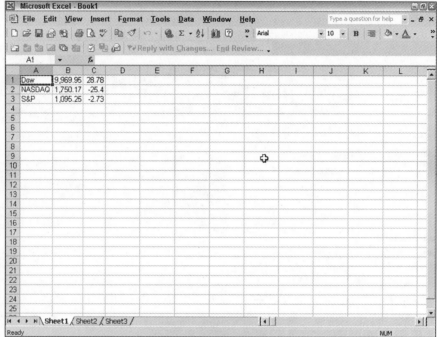

Figure 2-18:
Import
worksheet
data from a
Web page
table.

Web query operations don't always work smoothly. In this case, you may want to revisit the Web page that displays the table and verify that you clicked the correct select button. The select button, again, is the small yellow button with the arrow that points to the table data.

Importing a database table

Another powerful method for retrieving data from an external data source, such as a database, is to retrieve the information directly from one of a database's tables. In relational databases, information gets stored in tables. *Tables* are essentially lists that store information. In fact, an Excel list is a table.

To import data from a database table, follow these steps:

1. **Choose the Data⇨Import External Data⇨Import Data command.**

   Excel displays the Select Data Source dialog box, as shown in Figure 2-19.

2. **Identify the database that you want to query by using the Look In drop-down list box to identify the folder that stores the database from which you will grab information.**

3. **After you see the database listed in the Select Data Source dialog box, select it by clicking and then click the Open button.**

   Excel displays the Select Table dialog box, as shown in Figure 2-20.

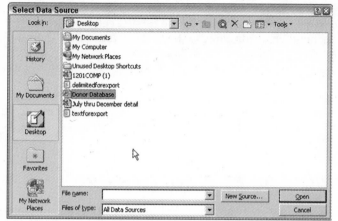

Figure 2-19:
The Select
Data Source
dialog box.

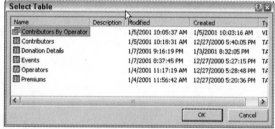

Figure 2-20:
The Select
Table
dialog box.

4. **Select the table that you want to retrieve information from by clicking it; then click OK.**

   Excel displays the Import Data dialog box, as shown in Figure 2-21.

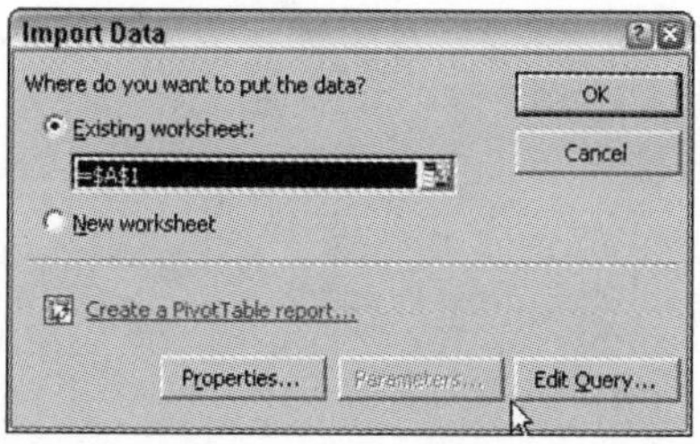

Figure 2-21:
The Import
Data
dialog box.

5. **Specify where Excel should place the information retrieved from the table.**

   Select either the Existing Worksheet radio button or the New Worksheet radio button to place the table data into an existing worksheet or into a new worksheet, respectively.

If you want to place the data in an existing worksheet, use the Existing Worksheet text box to specify the top-left cell that should be filled with data. In other words, specify the first cell into which data should be placed.

6. **Click OK.**

Excel retrieves information from the table and places it at the specified worksheet location. Figure 2-22 shows an Excel worksheet with data retrieved from a database table in the manner just described.

Querying an external database

Excel provides one other powerful method for retrieving information from external databases. You aren't limited to simply grabbing all the information from a specified table. You can, alternatively, query a database. By querying a database, you retrieve only information from a table that matches your criteria. You can also use a query to combine information from two or more tables. Therefore, use a query to massage and filter the data before it's actually placed in your Excel workbook.

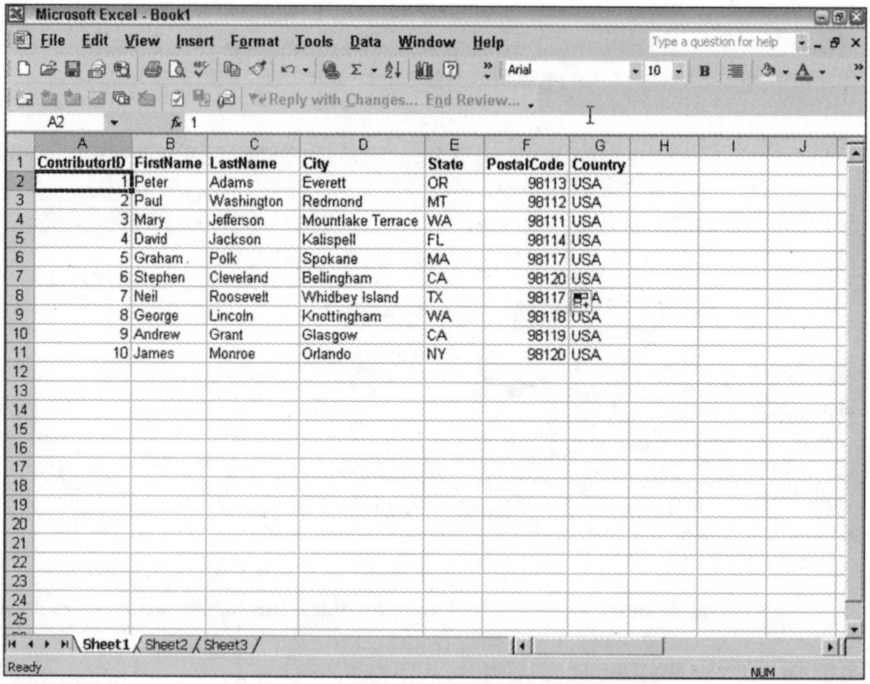

Figure 2-22:
An Excel worksheet with imported data.

ContributorID	FirstName	LastName	City	State	PostalCode	Country
1	Peter	Adams	Everett	OR	98113	USA
2	Paul	Washington	Redmond	MT	98112	USA
3	Mary	Jefferson	Mountlake Terrace	WA	98111	USA
4	David	Jackson	Kalispell	FL	98114	USA
5	Graham	Polk	Spokane	MA	98117	USA
6	Stephen	Cleveland	Bellingham	CA	98120	USA
7	Neil	Roosevelt	Whidbey Island	TX	98117	USA
8	George	Lincoln	Knottingham	WA	98118	USA
9	Andrew	Grant	Glasgow	CA	98119	USA
10	James	Monroe	Orlando	NY	98120	USA

Querying is often the best approach when you need combined data before importing it and when you need to filter the data before importing it. For example, if you were querying a very large database or very large table — one with hundreds of thousands of records — you would need to run a query in order to reduce the amount of information actually imported into Excel.

To run a database query and import query results, follow these steps:

1. **Choose the Data➪Import External Data➪New Database Query command.**

   Excel displays the Choose Data Source dialog box, as shown in Figure 2-23.

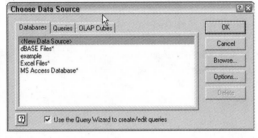

2. **Using the Databases tab, identify the type of database that you want to query.**

   For example, to query a Microsoft Access database, click the MS Access Database entry.

   You can query the results of a query by clicking the Queries tab and then selecting one of the items listed there.

   You can also query an OLAP cube and grab information from that. If you want to query a query or an OLAP cube, consult with the database administrator. The database administrator can tell you what query or OLAP cube that you want to grab data from.

3. **Select the database by clicking OK.**

   Excel displays the Select Database dialog box, as shown in Figure 2-24. Use this dialog box to identify both the location and the name of the database that you want to query.

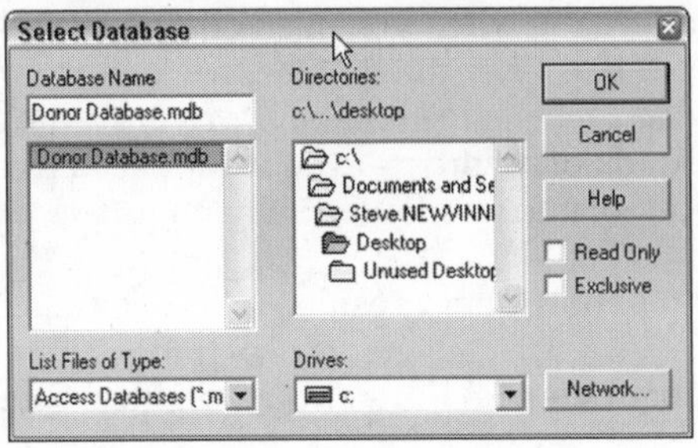

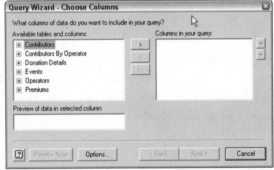

Figure 2-24:
The Select
Database
dialog box.

4. **Identify the correct database that you want from the directories list and then click OK.**

Excel displays the Query Wizard - Choose Columns dialog box, as shown in Figure 2-25.

Figure 2-25:
The Query
Wizard -
Choose
Columns
dialog box.

You use the Query Wizard - Choose Columns dialog box to pick which tables and which table fields that you want to appear in your query results. In the Available Tables and Columns box, Excel lists tables and fields. Initially, this list shows only tables. But you can see the fields within a table by clicking the + symbol next to the table.

5. **When you see a field that you want as a column in your Excel list, click its field and then click the right-facing arrow button that points to the Columns in Your Query list box.**

To add all the fields in a table to your list, click the table name and then click the right-facing arrow button that points to the Columns in Your Query list box.

To remove a field, select the field in the Columns in Your Query list box and then click the left-facing arrow button that points to the Available Tables and Columns list box.

This all sounds very complicated. But it really isn't. Essentially, all you do is to identify the columns of information that you want in your Excel list. Figure 2-26 shows how the Query Wizard - Choose Columns dialog box looks if you want to build a data list that includes the contributor's first and last name, the contributor's ID, and the donation amount.

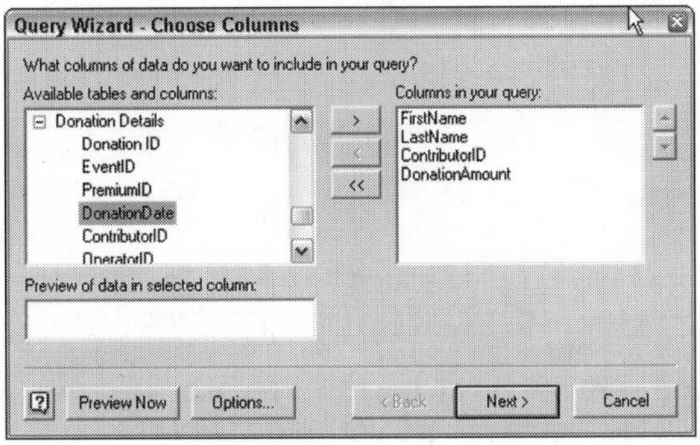

Figure 2-26: The Query Wizard - Choose Columns dialog box query information is defined.

6. **After you identify which columns you want in your query, click the Next button to filter the query data as needed.**

   Excel displays the Query Wizard - Filter Data dialog box, as shown in Figure 2-27.

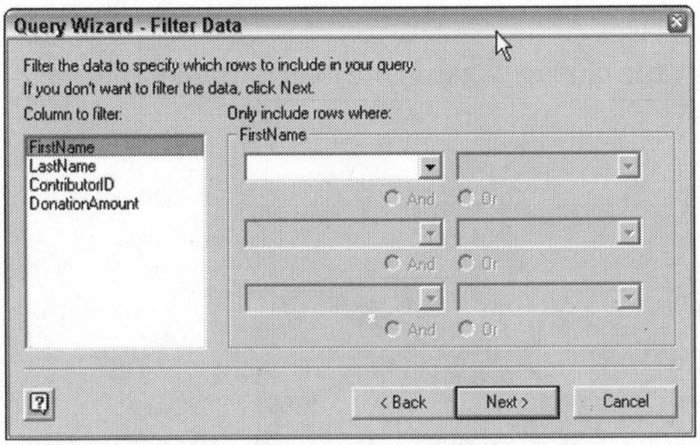

Figure 2-27: The Query Wizard - Filter Data dialog box.

You can filter the data returned as part of your query using the Only Include Rows Where text boxes. For example, to only include rows where the donation amount is greater than $50, click the DonationAmount field in the Column to Filter list box. Then select the Is Greater Than filtering operation from the first drop-down list box and enter the value **50** into the second drop-down list box; see how this looks in Figure 2-28.

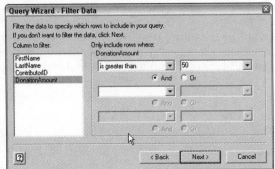

Figure 2-28:
Add filter
descriptions
here.

The Query Wizard - Filter Data dialog box performs the same sorts of filtering that you can perform using the AutoFilter command and the Advanced Filter command. Because I discuss these tools in Chapter 1, I won't repeat that discussion here. However, note that you can perform quite sophisticated filtering as part of your query.

7. **Filter your data based on multiple filters by selecting the And or Or radio buttons (optional).**

   - **And:** Using *And* filters means that for a row to be included, it must meet each of the filter requirements.

   - **Or:** Using *Or* filters means that if a row meets any filtered condition, the row is included.

8. **Click Next.**

   Excel displays the Query Wizard - Sort Order dialog box, as shown in Figure 2-29.

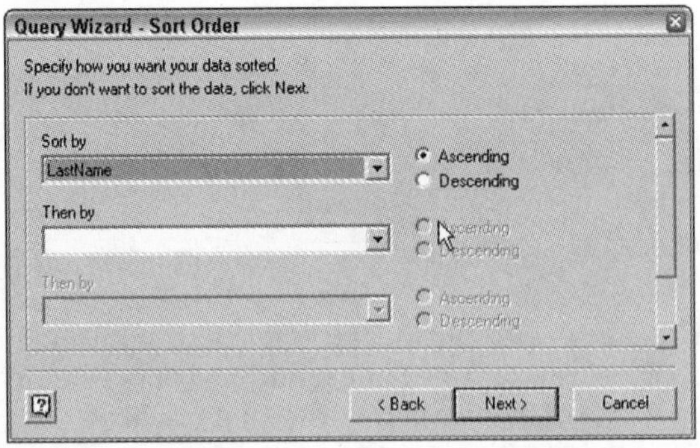

Figure 2-29:
The Query
Wizard -
Sort Order
dialog box.

9. Choose a sort order from the Query Wizard - Sort Order dialog box for the query result data.

Select the field or column that you want to use for sorting from the Sort By drop-down list box.

By selecting either the Ascending or Descending radio button, choose whether the field should be arranged in an ascending or descending order, respectively.

You can also use additional sort keys by selecting fields in the first and second Then By drop-down list boxes.

You sort query results the same way that you sort rows in an Excel list. If you have more questions about how to sort rows, refer to Chapter 1. Sorting works the same whether you're talking about query results or rows in a list.

10. Click Next.

Excel displays the Query Wizard - Finish dialog box, as shown in Figure 2-30.

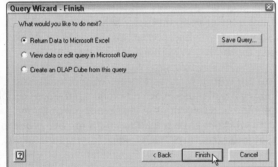

Figure 2-30:
The Query
Wizard -
Finish
dialog box.

11. In the Query Wizard - Finish dialog box, specify where Excel should place the query results.

This dialog box provides three radio buttons from which you choose where you want to place your query result data: in Excel, in a Microsoft Query window that you can then review, or in an OLAP cube. Typically (and this is what I assume here in this book), you simply want to return the data to Microsoft Excel and place the data in a workbook. To make this choice, select the Return Data to Microsoft Excel radio button.

12. Click the Finish button.

After you click the Finish button to complete the Query Wizard, Excel displays the Import Data dialog box; refer to Figure 2-21.

13. **In the Import Data dialog box, choose the worksheet location for the query result data.**

    Use this dialog box to specify where query result data should be placed.

    - To place the query result data in an existing worksheet, select the Existing Worksheet radio button. Then identify the cell in the top-left corner of the worksheet range and enter this in the Existing Worksheet text box.

    - Alternatively, to place the data into a new worksheet, select the New Worksheet button.

14. **Click OK.**

    Excel places the data at the location that you chose.

It's Sometimes a Raw Deal

By using the instructions that I describe in this chapter to retrieve data from some external source, you can probably get the data rather quickly into an Excel workbook. But it's possible that what you've also found is that the data is pretty raw. And so you are saying to yourself, (or at least if I were in your shoes, I would be saying this), "Wow, this stuff is pretty raw."

But don't worry: You are where you need to be. Your information may be raw at this point. In Chapter 3, I discuss how you clean up the workbook by eliminating rows and columns and information that's not part of your data. I also cover how you scrub and rearrange the actual data in your workbook so that it appears in a format and structure that's useful to you in your upcoming analysis.

The bottom line is this: Don't worry that your data seems pretty raw right now. Getting your data into a workbook is accomplishing an important step. All you need to do now is spend a little time on your housekeeping. Read through the next chapter for the lowdown on how to do that.

By the way, if the process of importing data from some external source has resulted in very clean and pristine data — and this may be the case if you've grabbed data from a well-designed database or with help from the corporate database administrator — that's great. You can jump right into the data analysis techniques that I describe starting in Chapter 4.

Chapter 3

Scrub-a-Dub-Dub: Cleaning Data

In This Chapter

▶ Editing an imported workbook

▶ Cleaning data with text functions

▶ Keeping data clean with validation

*Y*ou will greatly benefit from exploring the techniques often necessary for cleaning up and rearranging workbook data. You know why? Because almost always the data that you start with — especially data that you import from other programs — will be pretty disorganized and dirty. Getting your data into a clean form makes it easier to work with and analyze the data.

Editing Your Imported Workbook

I start this discussion with some basic workbook editing techniques. If you take a look at the workbook shown in Figure 3-1, you see that the data, although neatly formatted, doesn't appear as an Excel list. The workbook shown in Figure 3-1, for example, includes blank columns and rows. The workbook also uses some columns that are inadequately sized. The column width for column I, for example, is too small to display the values stored there. (That's why those #s appear.)

You will often encounter situations like this. The workbook shown in Figure 3-1, for example, has actually been imported from QuickBooks. You can use several workbook-editing techniques to clean up a workbook. In the following sections, I give you a rundown of the most useful ones.

Delete unnecessary columns

To delete unnecessary columns (these might be blank columns or columns that store data that you don't need), click the column letter to select the column. Then choose Edit➪Delete.

Figure 3-1:
This
worksheet
needs to
clean up
its act.

	A	B	C	D	E	F	G	H	I	J	K	L
1												
2												
3												
4	8:46 AM	Stephen L.Nelson, Inc.										
5	Feb-00	7/02	Sales by Item Summary									
6	Cash	Basis	January through December 2002									
7												
8						Jan - Dec 01						
9		Qty		Amount	% of Sales	Avg Price	COGS		Avg COGS	Gross Ma	Gross Margin %	
10												
11		ProdID										
12		0-9672981	2,079	21,014.25	3.70%	10.11	3,030.22	1.46	#######	85.60%		
13		0-9672981	2,506	26,660.48	4.70%	10.64	5,075.75	2.03	#######	81.00%		
14		0-9672981	1,369	26,790.61	4.70%	19.57	2,958.00	2.16	#######	89.00%		
15		0-9672981	1,275	11,770.31	2.10%	9.23	1,899.13	1.49	9,871.18	83.90%		
16		09672981-	4,171	79,790.95	14.00%	19.13	13,751.39	3.3	#######	82.80%		
17		09672981-	2,634	29,912.16	5.20%	11.36	4,396.50	1.67	#######	85.30%		
18		09672981-	2,788	24,900.85	4.40%	8.93	3,991.49	1.43	#######	84.00%		
19		09672981-	1,302	15,058.96	2.60%	11.57	283.85	0.22	#######	98.10%		
20		09672981-	1,722	18,341.00	3.20%	10.65	-2,584.74	-1.5	#######	114.10%		
21		1-931150-0	1,232	15,537.11	2.70%	12.61	2,100.79	1.71	#######	86.50%		
22		1-931150-0	2,775	56,534.00	9.90%	20.37	11,013.67	3.97	#######	80.50%		
23		1-931150-0	760	9,249.41	1.60%	12.17	1,494.03	1.97	7,755.38	83.80%		
24		1-931150-0	1,055	13,311.55	2.30%	12.62	1,912.28	1.81	#######	85.60%		
25		1-931150-0	812	10,342.77	1.80%	12.74	1,753.60	2.16	8,589.17	83.00%		

You can select multiple columns for multiple deletions by holding down the
Ctrl key and then individually clicking column letters.

Delete unnecessary rows

To delete unnecessary rows, you follow the same steps that you do to delete
unnecessary columns. Just click the row number and then choose
Edit⇨Delete. To delete multiple rows, hold down the Ctrl key and then select
the row numbers for each of the rows that you want to delete. After making
your selections, choose the Edit⇨Delete command.

Resize columns

To resize (enlarge the width of) a column so that its contents clearly show,
double-click the column letter box's right corner. For example, in Figure 3-2,
column H is too narrow to displays its values. Excel displays several pound
signs (########) in the cells in Column H to indicate the column is too
narrow to adequately display its values.

	A	B	C	D	E	F	G	H	I	J	K	L
1												
2												
3												
4	AMStephen L. Nelson, Inc.											
5	7/02Sales by Item Summary											
6	BasisJanuary through December 2002											
7												
8					Jan - Dec 01							
9	Qty		Amount	% of Sales	Avg Price	COGS	Avg COGS	Gross Ma	Gross Margin %			
10												
11	ProdID											
12	0-9672981-	2,079	21,014.25	3.70%	10.11	3,030.22	1.46	########	85.60%			
13	0-9672981-	2,506	26,660.48	4.70%	10.64	5,075.75	2.03	########	81.00%			
14	0-9672981-	1,369	26,790.61	4.70%	19.57	2,958.00	2.16	########	89.00%			
15	0-9672981-	1,275	11,770.31	2.10%	9.23	1,899.13	1.49	9,871.18	83.90%			
16	09672981-	4,171	79,790.95	14.00%	19.13	13,751.39	3.3	########	82.80%			
17	09672981-	2,634	29,912.16	5.20%	11.36	4,396.50	1.67	########	85.30%			
18	09672981-	2,788	24,900.85	4.40%	8.93	3,991.49	1.43	########	84.00%			
19	09672981-	1,302	15,058.96	2.60%	11.57	283.85	0.22	########	98.10%			
20	09672981-	1,722	18,341.00	3.20%	10.65	-2,584.74	-1.5	########	114.10%			
21	1-931150-0	1,232	15,537.11	2.70%	12.61	2,100.79	1.71	########	86.50%			
22	1-931150-0	2,775	56,534.00	9.90%	20.37	11,013.67	3.97	########	80.50%			
23	1-931150-0	760	9,249.41	1.60%	12.17	1,494.03	1.97	7,755.38	83.80%			
24	1-931150-0	1,055	13,311.55	2.30%	12.62	1,912.28	1.81	########	85.60%			
25	1-931150-0	812	10,342.77	1.80%	12.74	1,753.60	2.16	8,589.17	83.00%			

Figure 3-2:
Column H needs to gain a little weight.

Just double-click the column letter label, and Excel resizes the column so that it's wide enough to display the values or labels stored in that column. Check out Figure 3-3 to see the column after Excel has resized the width of column H to display its values.

You can also resize a column by selecting the column and then choosing Format⇨Column⇨Width. When Excel displays the Column Width dialog box, as shown in Figure 3-4, you can enter a larger value into the Column Width text box and then click OK. The value that you enter is the number of characters that can fit in a column.

For you manually inclined fiddlers, you can also resize a column by clicking and dragging the left corner of the column letter label box. You can resize the column to any width by dragging this border.

Resize rows

You can resize rows like you resize columns. Just select the row number label and then choose Format⇨Row⇨Height. When Excel displays the Row Height dialog box, as shown in Figure 3-5, you can enter a larger value into the Row Height text box.

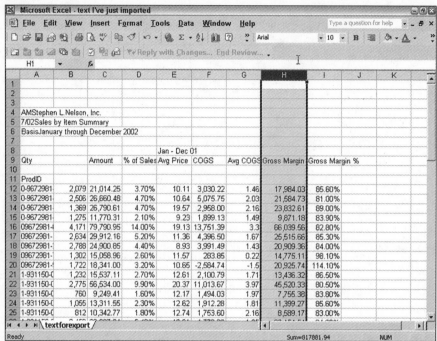

Figure 3-3:
Ah . . . now
you can see
the data.

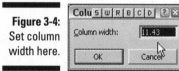

Figure 3-4:
Set column
width here.

Figure 3-5:
Set row
height here.

Row height is measured in points. (A point equals one-seventy-second of an inch.)

Erase unneeded cell contents

To erase the contents of a range that contains unneeded data, select the worksheet range and then choose the Edit⇨Clear⇨All command. Excel erases both the contents of the cells in the selected range and any formatting assigned to those cells.

Format numeric values

To change the formatting of values in a workbook that you want to analyze, first select the range of what you want to reformat. Then choose Format⇨Cells. When Excel displays the Format Cells dialog box, as shown in Figure 3-6, choose from its tabs to change the formatting of the selected range. For example, use choices from the Number tab to assign numeric formatting to values in the selected range. You use options from the Alignment tab to change the way the text and values are positioned in the cell, from the Font tab to choose the font used for values and labels in the selected range, and from the Border tab to assign cell border borders to the selected range.

Copying worksheet data

To copy worksheet data, first select the data that you want to duplicate. You can copy a single cell or range of cells. Choose the Edit⇨Copy command and then select the range into which you want to place the copied data. Remember: You can select a single cell or a range of cells. Then choose Edit⇨Paste.

You can also copy worksheet ranges by dragging the mouse. To do this, select the worksheet range that you want to copy. Then, hold down the Ctrl key and drag the range border.

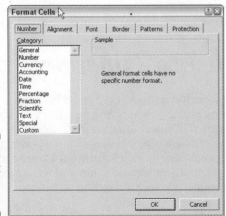

Figure 3-6:
Format
numeric
values here.

Moving worksheet data

To move worksheet data to some new location, select the range that stores the data. Choose Edit⇨Cut and click the cell in the upper-left corner of the range into which you want to move the worksheet data. Then choose the Edit⇨Paste command.

You can also move worksheet ranges by dragging the mouse. To do this, select the worksheet range that you want to copy and then drag the range border.

Replacing data in fields

One of the most common commands that I find myself using to clean up a list is Edit⇨Replace. To use this command, first select the column with the data that you want to clean by clicking that column's letter. Next choose Edit⇨Replace so that Excel displays the Find and Replace dialog box, as shown in Figure 3-7.

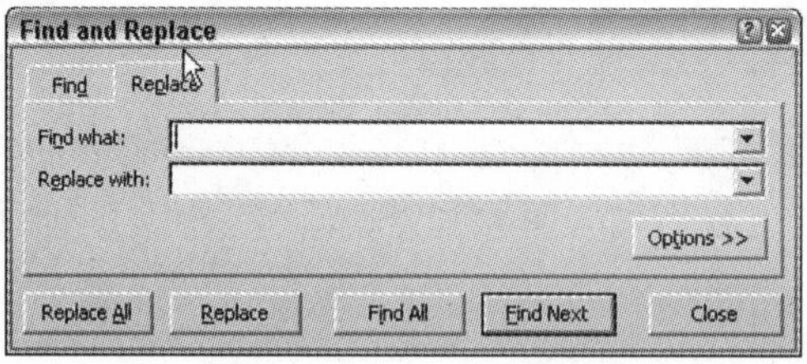

Figure 3-7:
Keep data in its place with the Find and Replace dialog box.

Enter the incorrect text that you want to find in the Find What text box and then enter the correct text in the Replace With text box. Then click the Replace All button to fix the incorrect text.

Cleaning Data with Text Functions

One of the common problems with data that you import is that your text labels aren't quite right. For example, you may find yourself with the city, state, and Zip code information that's part of an address stored in a single cell rather than in three separate cells. Or, you may find that same information stored in three separate cells when you want the data stored in a single cell. You may also find that pieces of information that you want stored as labels instead are stored as values and vice versa.

What's the big deal, Steve?

Just to give you a quick idea of what I mean here, take a look at Figures 3-8 and 3-9. Okay, this is fake data, sure. But the examples show a common situation. The list information shown in Figure 3-8 uses unnecessarily lengthy product names, goofs up some customer names by appending store numbers to customer names, and then puts all of the city and state information into one field. Yuk.

In Figure 3-9, see how I rearrange this information so that it's much more easily sorted and filtered. For example, the PRODUCT2 field abbreviates the product name by changing *Big Bob's Guide to* to just *BBgt*. The store names are essentially edited down to just the first word in the store name — an easy change that enables you to see sales for Bean's Tackle, Mac's Shack, and Steve's Charters. The ADDRESS information is split into two fields: CITY and STATE.

Here's one other important point about Figure 3-9. The rearrangement shown in Figure 3-9 makes it possible to cross-tabulate the data using a pivot table (something I talk more about in Chapter 4).

Figure 3-8:
Good worksheet data; tough to analyze.

	A	B	C	D
1	PRODUCT	CUSTOMER	ADDRESS	SALE
2	Big Bob's Guide to Flyfishing	Bean's Tackle (Store #1)	Redmond WA	379.4013
3	Big Bob's Guide to Flyfishing	Mac's Shack	Bellingham WA	882.3254
4	Big Bob's Guide to Flyfishing	Bean's Tackle (Store #1)	Redmond WA	529.4157
5	Big Bob's Guide to Flyfishing	Bean's Tackle (Store #3)	Oak Harbor WA	602.958
6	Big Bob's Guide to Tying Flies	Bean's Tackle (Store #1)	Redmond WA	861.9961
7	Big Bob's Guide to Tying Flies	Bean's Tackle (Store #2)	Westport WA	875.4814
8	Big Bob's Guide to Tying Flies	Bean's Tackle (Store #3)	Oak Harbor WA	313.9593
9	Big Bob's Guide to Tying Flies	Bean's Tackle (Store #1)	Redmond WA	605.3213
10	Big Bob's Guide to Tying Flies	Bean's Tackle (Store #1)	Redmond WA	71.48089
11	Big Bob's Guide to Tying Flies	Bean's Tackle (Store #3)	Oak Harbor WA	225.1029
12	Big Bob's Guide to Tying Flies	Bean's Tackle (Store #1)	Redmond WA	947.1249
13	Big Bob's Guide to Steelhead Fishing	Bean's Tackle (Store #1)	Redmond WA	924.9809
14	Big Bob's Guide to Steelhead Fishing	Bean's Tackle (Store #2)	Westport WA	448.7892
15	Big Bob's Guide to Steelhead Fishing	Bean's Tackle (Store #3)	Oak Harbor WA	769.8975
16	Big Bob's Guide to Steelhead Fishing	Mac's Shack	Bellingham WA	375.0785
17	Big Bob's Guide to Salmon Fishing	Mac's Shack	Bellingham WA	857.5768
18	Big Bob's Guide to Salmon Fishing	Bean's Tackle (Store #2)	Westport WA	472.9414
19	Big Bob's Guide to Salmon Fishing	Bean's Tackle (Store #1)	Redmond WA	968.4072
20	Big Bob's Guide to Salmon Fishing	Bean's Tackle (Store #1)	Redmond WA	938.2165
21	Big Bob's Guide to Salmon Fishing	Steve's Charters	Westport WA	436.0216

Figure 3-9: Much better: Rearranged worksheet data that's easy to analyze.

	E	F	G	H	I
1	PRODUCT2	CUSTOMER2	CITY	STATE	SALES
2	BBgt Flyfishing	Bean's	Redmond	WA	379.4013
3	BBgt Flyfishing	Mac's	Bellingham	WA	882.3254
4	BBgt Flyfishing	Bean's	Redmond	WA	529.4157
5	BBgt Flyfishing	Bean's	Oak Harbor	WA	602.958
6	BBgt Tying Flies	Bean's	Redmond	WA	861.9961
7	BBgt Tying Flies	Bean's	Westport	WA	875.4814
8	BBgt Tying Flies	Bean's	Oak Harbor	WA	313.9593
9	BBgt Tying Flies	Bean's	Redmond	WA	605.3213
10	BBgt Tying Flies	Bean's	Redmond	WA	71.48089
11	BBgt Tying Flies	Bean's	Oak Harbor	WA	225.1029
12	BBgt Tying Flies	Bean's	Redmond	WA	947.1249
13	BBgt Steelhead Fishing	Bean's	Redmond	WA	924.9809
14	BBgt Steelhead Fishing	Bean's	Westport	WA	448.7892
15	BBgt Steelhead Fishing	Bean's	Oak Harbor	WA	769.8975
16	BBgt Steelhead Fishing	Mac's	Bellingham	WA	375.0785
17	BBgt Salmon Fishing	Mac's	Bellingham	WA	857.5768
18	BBgt Salmon Fishing	Bean's	Westport	WA	472.9414
19	BBgt Salmon Fishing	Bean's	Redmond	WA	968.4072
20	BBgt Salmon Fishing	Bean's	Redmond	WA	938.2165
21	BBgt Salmon Fishing	Steve's	Westport	WA	436.0216

Cell E2: =REPLACE(A2,1,19,"BBgt ")

The answer to some of your problems

All the editing performed in Figure 3-9 is performed using text functions, so here, I discuss these babies.

You can grab a Zip file from the Dummies Web site that includes most of the Excel workbooks shown in the pages of this book. I mention this because if you're really curious about how text functions are used in Figure 3-9, you can grab the actual workbook and check out the formulas. The Zip file is available at www.dummies.com/extras.

Excel provides two dozen text functions that enable you to manipulate text strings in ways to easily rearrange and manipulate the data that you import into an Excel workbook. In the following paragraphs, I explain how to use the primary text functions.

If you've just read the word *function* and you're scratching your head, you might want to review the contents of the Appendix.

By the way, I skip discussions of three text functions that I don't think you'll have occasion to use for scrubbing data: BAHTEXT (rewrites values using Thai characters); CHAR (returns the character represented by an American National

Standards Institute [ANSI] code number); and CODE (returns the ANSI code represented by character). To get descriptions of these other text functions, choose Insert⇨Function, select the Text entry from the Or Select A Category box, and then scroll through the list of text functions that Excel displays in the Select a Function box until you see the function that you have a question for — most likely, the function that I incorrectly assume you don't need information about.

The CLEAN function

Using the CLEAN function removes nonprintable characters text. For example, if the text labels shown in a column are using crazy nonprintable characters that end up showing as solid blocks or goofy symbols, you can use the CLEAN function to clean up this text. The cleaned-up text can be stored in another column. You can then work with the cleaned text column.

The CLEAN function uses the following syntax:

```
CLEAN(text)
```

The *text argument* is the text string or a reference to the cell holding the text string that you want to clean. For example, to clean the text stored in Cell A1, you use the following syntax:

```
clean(A1)
```

The CONCATENATE function

The CONCATENATE function combines, or joins, chunks of text into a single text string. The CONCATENATE function uses the following syntax:

```
CONCATENATE(text1,text2,text3,...)
```

The text1, text2, text3, and so on arguments are the chunks of text that you want to combine into a single string. For example, if the city, state, and Zip code were stored in fields named city, state, and zip, you could create a single text string that stores this information by using the following syntax:

```
CONCATENATE(city,state,zip)
```

If city were Redmond, state were WA, and zip were 98052, this function returns this text string:

```
RedmondWA98052
```

The smashed together nature of the concatenated city, state, and Zip code information isn't a typographical mistake, by the way. To concatenate this information but include spaces, you need to include spaces as function arguments. For example, the following syntax:

```
CONCATENATE("Redmond", " ","WA"," ","98052")
```

returns the text string

```
Redmond WA 98052
```

The EXACT function

The EXACT function compares two text strings. If the two text strings are exactly the same, the EXACT function returns the logical value for true, which is 1. If the two text strings differ in any way, the EXACT function returns the logical value for false, which is 0. The EXACT function is case-sensitive. For example, *Redmond* spelled with a capital *R* differs from *redmond* spelled with a lowercase *r*.

The EXACT function uses the following syntax:

```
EXACT(text1,text2)
```

The text1 and text2 arguments are the text strings that you want to compare. For example, to check whether the two strings "Redmond" and "redmond" are the same, you use the following formula:

```
EXACT("Redmond","redmond")
```

This function returns the logical value for false, 0, because these two text strings don't match exactly. One begins with an uppercase *R* and the other begins with a lowercase *r*.

The FIND function

The FIND function finds the starting character position of one text string within another text string. For example, if you want to know at what position within a text string the two-letter state abbreviation WA starts, you could use the FIND function.

The FIND function uses the following syntax:

```
FIND(find_text,within_text,start_num)
```

The find_text argument is the text that you're looking for. The within_text argument identifies where or what you're searching. The start_num argument tells Excel at what point within the string it should begin its search. For example, to find at what point the two-letter state abbreviation WA begins in the string Redmond WA 98052, you use the following formula:

FIND("WA","Redmond WA 98052",1)

The function returns the value 9 because WA begins at the ninth position.

The start_num function argument is optional. If you omit this argument, Excel begins searching at the very beginning of the string.

The FIXED function

The FIXED function rounds a value to specified precision and then converts the rounded value to text. The function uses the following syntax:

FIXED(number,decimals,no_commas)

The number argument supplies the value that you want to round and convert to text. The optional decimals argument tells Excel how many places to the right of the decimal point that you want to round. The optional no_commas argument needs to be either 1 (if you want commas) or 0 (if you don't want commas) in the returned text.

For example, to round to a whole number and convert to text the value 1234.56789, you use the following formula:

FIXED(1234.56789,0,1)

The function returns the text 1,235.

The LEFT function

The LEFT function returns a specified number of characters from the left end of a text string. The function uses the following syntax:

LEFT(text,num_chars)

The text argument either supplies the text string or references the cell holding the text string. The optional num_chars argument tells Excel how many characters to grab.

For example, to grab the leftmost seven characters from the text string Redmond WA, you use the following formula:

LEFT("Redmond WA",7)

The function returns the text Redmond.

The LEN function

The LEN function counts the number of characters in a text string. The function uses the following syntax:

LEN(text)

The text argument either supplies the text string that you want to measure or it references the cell holding the text string. For example, to measure the length of the text string in cell I81, you use the following formula:

LEN(I81)

If cell I81 holds the text string Semper fidelis, the function returns the value 14. Spaces are counted as characters, too.

The LOWER function

The LOWER function returns an all-lowercase version of a text string. The function uses the following syntax:

LOWER(text)

The text argument either supplies the text string that you want to convert or references the cell holding the text string. For example, to convert the text string PROFESSIONAL to professional, you use the following formula:

LOWER("PROFESSIONAL")

The function returns professional.

The MID function

The MID function returns a chunk of text in the middle of text string. The function uses the following syntax:

MID(text,start_num,num_char)

The text argument either supplies the text string from which you grab some text fragment or it references the cell holding the text string. The start_num argument tells Excel where the text fragment starts that you want to grab. The num_char argument tells Excel how long the text fragment is. For example, to grab the text fragment tac from the text string tic tac toe, you use the following formula:

```
=MID("tic tac toe",5,3)
```

The function returns tac.

The PROPER function

The PROPER function capitalizes the first letter in every word in a text string. The function uses the following syntax:

```
PROPER(text)
```

The text argument either supplies the text string or references the cell holding the text string. For example, to capitalize the initial letters in the text string ambassador kennedy, you use the following formula:

```
PROPER("ambassador kennedy")
```

The function returns the text string Ambassador Kennedy.

The REPLACE function

The REPLACE function replaces a portion of a text string. The function uses the following syntax:

```
REPLACE(old_text,start_num,num_chars,new_text)
```

The old_text argument, which is case-sensitive, either supplies the text string from which you grab some text fragment or it references the cell holding the text string. The start_num argument, which is the starting position, tells Excel where the text starts that you want to replace. The num_chars argument tells Excel the length of the text fragment (how many characters) that you want to replace. The new_text argument, also case-sensitive, tells Excel what new text you want to use to replace the old text. For example, to replace the name Chamberlain with the name Churchill in the text string Mr. Chamberlain, you use the following formula:

```
REPLACE("Mr. Chamberlain",5,11,"Churchill")
```

The function returns the text string Mr. Churchill.

The REPT function

The REPT function repeats a text string. The function uses the following syntax:

```
REPT(text,number_times)
```

The text argument either supplies the text string or references the cell holding the text string. The number_times argument tells Excel how many times you want to repeat the text. For example, the following formula:

```
REPT("Walla",2")
```

returns the text string WallaWalla.

The RIGHT function

The RIGHT function returns a specified number of characters from the right end of a text string. The function uses the following syntax:

```
RIGHT(text,num_chars)
```

The text argument either supplies the text string that you want to manipulate or it references the cell holding the text string. The num_chars argument tells Excel how many characters to grab.

For example, to grab the rightmost two characters from the text string Redmond WA, you use the following formula:

```
RIGHT("Redmond WA",2)
```

The function returns the text WA.

The SEARCH function

The SEARCH function calculates the starting position of a text fragment within a text string. The function uses the following syntax:

```
SEARCH(find_text,within_text,start_num)
```

The find_text argument tells Excel what text fragment you're looking for. The within_text argument tells Excel what text string that you want to search. The start_num argument tells Excel where to start its search. The start_num argument is optional. If you leave it blank, Excel starts the search at beginning of the within_text string.

For example, to identify the position at which the text fragment `Churchill` starts in the text string `Mr. Churchill`, you use the following formula:

```
SEARCH("Churchill","Mr. Churchill",1)
```

The function returns the value `5`.

The SUBSTITUTE function

The `SUBSTITUTE` function replaces occurrences of text in a text string. The function uses the following syntax:

```
SUBSTITUTE(text,old_text,new_text,instances)
```

The `text` argument tells Excel what text string you want to edit by replacing some text fragment. The `old_text` argument identifies the to-be-replaced text fragment. The `new_text` supplies the new replacement text.

As an example of how the `SUBSTITUTE` function works, suppose that you need to replace the word `Governor` with the word `President` in the text string `Governor Bush`.

```
SUBSTITUTE("Governor Bush","Governor","President")
```

The function returns the text string `President Bush`.

The `instances` argument is optional, but you can use it to tell Excel for which instance of `old_text` you want to make the substitution. For example, the function

```
SUBSTITUTE("Governor Governor Bush","Governor","President",1)
```

returns the text string `President Governor Bush`.

The function

```
SUBSTITUTE("Governor Governor Bush","Governor","President",2)
```

returns the text string `Governor President Bush`.

If you leave the instances argument blank, Excel replaces each occurrence of the `old_text` with the `new_text`. For example, the function

```
SUBSTITUTE("Governor Governor Bush","Governor","President")
```

returns the text string `President President Bush`.

The T function

The T function returns its argument if the argument is text. If the argument isn't text, the function returns nothing. The function uses the following syntax:

```
T(value)
```

For example, the formula T(123) returns nothing because 123 is a value. The formula T("Seattle") returns Seattle because Seattle is a text string.

The TEXT function

The TEXT function formats a value and then returns the value as text. The function uses the following syntax:

```
TEXT(value,format_text))
```

The value argument is the value that you want formatted and returned as text. The format_text argument is a text string that shows the currency symbol and placement, commas, and decimal places that you want. For example, the formula

```
=TEXT(1234.5678,"$#,###.00")
```

returns the text $1,234.57.

Note that the function rounds the value.

The TRIM function

The TRIM function removes extra spaces from the right end of a text string. The function uses the following syntax:

```
TRIM(text)
```

The text argument is the text string or, more likely, a reference to the cell holding the text string.

The UPPER function

The UPPER function returns an all-uppercase version of a text string. The function uses the following syntax:

UPPER(text)

The text argument either supplies the text string that you want to convert or it references the cell holding the text string. For example, to convert the text string professional to PROFESSIONAL, you can use the following formula:

UPPER("professional")

The function returns the text string PROFESSIONAL.

The VALUE function

The VALUE function converts a text string that looks like a value to a value. The function uses the following syntax:

VALUE(text)

The text argument either supplies the text string that you want to convert or it references the cell holding the text string. For example, to convert the text string $123,456.78 — assume that this isn't a value but a text string — you can use the following formula:

VALUE("$123,456.78")

The function returns the value 123456.78.

Converting text function formulas to text

You may need to know how to convert a formula — such as a formula that uses a text function — to the label or value that it returns. For example, suppose you find yourself with a worksheet full of text-function-based formulas because you used the text functions to clean up the list data. And now you want to just work with labels and values.

You can convert formulas to the labels and values that they return by select-ing the worksheet range that holds the formulas, choosing Edit⇔Copy, and then immediately choosing Edit⇔Paste Special without deselecting the cur-rently selected range. When Excel displays the Paste Special dialog box, as shown in Figure 3-10, select the Values radio button and click OK.

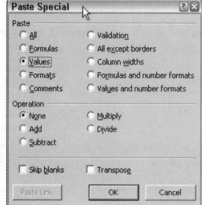

Figure 3-10:
Convert
formulas to
text here.

Using Validation to Keep Data Clean

One useful command related to this business of keeping your data clean is the Data Validation command. Use this command to describe what informa-tion can be entered into a cell. The command also enables you to supply mes-sages that give data input information and error messages that attempt to help someone correct data entry errors.

To use Data Validation, follow these steps:

1. **Select the worksheet range where the to-be-validated data will go.**

   You can do this by dragging your mouse or by using the navigation keys.

2. **Choose Data⇔Validation to tell Excel that you want to set up data vali-dation for the selected range.**

   Excel displays the Data Validation dialog box, as shown in Figure 3-11.

3. **On the Settings tab of the Data Validation dialog box, use the Validation Criteria text boxes to describe what is valid data.**

   Use choices from the Allow drop-down list box, for example, to supply what types of information can go into the range: whole numbers, deci-mal numbers, values from the list, valid dates, valid times, text of a par-ticular length, and so on.

Use choices from the Data drop-down list box to further define your validation criteria. The Data drop-down list box provides several comparisons that can be made as part of the validation: between, not between, equal to, not equal to, greater than, and so on.

Refine the validation criteria, if necessary, using any of the other drop-down list boxes available. *Note:* The other validation criteria options depend on what you enter into the Allow and Data drop-down list boxes

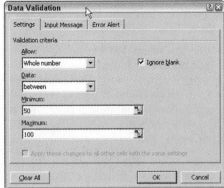

Figure 3-11:
Keep data
clean with
the Data
Validation
dialog box.

For example, as shown in Figure 3-11, if you indicate that you want to allow only whole numbers between a particular range of minimum and maximum values, Excel provides Minimum and Maximum text boxes for you to enter or define the range. However, if you select other entries from the Allow or Data drop-down list boxes, you see other text boxes appearing on the Settings tab. In other words, Excel customizes the Settings tab depending on the kind of validation criteria that you define.

4. **Fine-tune the validation.**

   After you describe the validation criteria, either select or deselect (clear) the Ignore Blank check box to indicate whether blank cells are allowed.

5. **Consider expanding the scope of the data validation (optional).**

   Select the Apply These Changes to All Other Cells with the Same Settings check box to indicate whether the validation criteria should be expanded to other similar cells.

   Click the Clear All command button, and Excel clears (removes) the validation criteria.

6. **Provide an input message from the Input Message tab of the Data Validation dialog box.**

   The Input Message tab, as shown in Figure 3-12, enables you to tell Excel to display a small message when a cell with specified data validation is selected. To create the input message, you enter a title for the message into the Title text box and message text into the Input Message text box. Make sure that the Show Input Message When Cell Is Selected check box is selected. Look at Figure 3-13 to see how the Input Message entered in Figure 3-12 looks on the workbook.

7. **Provide an error message from the Error Alert tab of the Data Validation dialog box. (See Figure 3-14.)**

   You can also supply an error message that Excel displays when someone attempts to enter invalid data. To create an error message, first verify that the Show Error Alert After Invalid Data is Entered check box is selected. Then, use the Style drop-down list box to select what Excel should do when it encounters invalid data: Stop the data entry on the user without the incorrect data entry, or simply display an informational message after the data has been entered.

   Just like creating an input message, enter the error message title into the Title text box. Then enter the full text of the error message into the Error Message text box. In Figure 3-14, you can see a completed Error Alert tab. Check out Figure 3-15 for how the error message appears after a user enters invalid data.

   Curious about the options on the Style drop-down list box (as shown in Figure 3-14)? The style of the error alert determines what command buttons that the error message presents when someone attempts to enter bad data. If the error style is Stop, the error message box displays Retry and Cancel command buttons. If the error style is Warning, the error message box displays Yes, No, and Cancel command buttons. If the error style is informational, the error message box displays OK and Cancel command buttons.

Figure 3-12:
Create a
data entry
instruction
message.

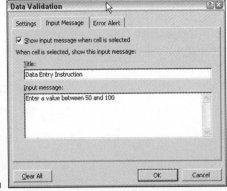

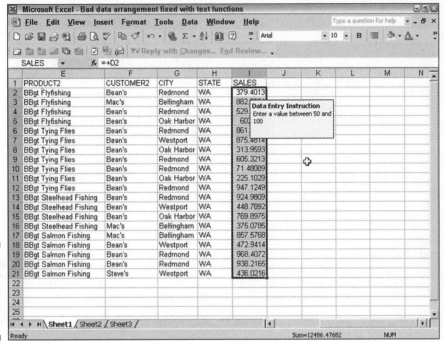

Figure 3-13:
A data entry
instruction
message is
helpful.

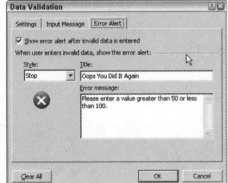

Figure 3-14:
Create
an annoying
data
entry error
message.

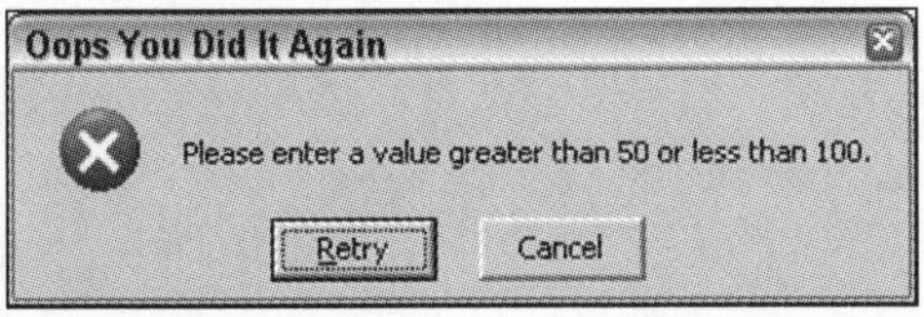

Figure 3-15:
Britney
would be
proud, you
dunderhead.

Part II
PivotTables and PivotCharts

The 5th Wave   By Rich Tennant

"WELL, SHOOT! THIS EGGPLANT CHART IS JUST AS CONFUSING AS THE BUTTERNUT SQUASH CHART AND THE GOURD CHART. CAN'T YOU JUST MAKE A PIE CHART LIKE EVERYONE ELSE?"

In this part . . .

*1*n this part of the book, I discuss the most powerful data analysis tool that Excel provides — its cross-tablation capability, which is available through the PivotTable and PivotChart command. Discover here how to unlock the power of this tool as I cover how to create pivot tables and charts, customize pivot charts, and build pivot table formulas.

Chapter 4

Working with PivotTables

*P*erhaps the most powerful analytical tool that Excel provides is the Pivot Table command, with which you can cross-tabulate data stored in Excel lists. A cross-tabulation summarizes information in two (or more) ways: for example, sales by product and state, or sales by product and month.

Cross-tabulations, performed by pivot tables in Excel, are a basic and very interesting analytical technique that can be tremendously helpful when you're looking at data that your business or life depends on. Excel's cross-tabulations are neater than you might at first expect. For one thing, they aren't static: You can cross-tabulate data and then re-cross-tabulate and re-cross-tabulate it again simply by dragging buttons. What's more, as your underlying data changes, you can update your cross-tabulations simply by clicking a button.

Looking at Data from Many Angles

Cross-tabulations are important, powerful tools. Here's a quick example: Assume that in some future century that you're the plenipotentiary of the Freedonian Confederation and in charge of security for a distant galaxy. (Rough directions? Head toward Alpha Centauri for about 50 million light years and then hang a left. It'll be the second galaxy on your right.)

Unfortunately, in recent weeks, you're increasingly concerned about military conflicts with the other major political-military organizations in your corner of the universe. Accordingly, assume for a moment that a list maintained by the

Confederation tracks space trooper movements in your galaxy. Assume that the list stores the following information: troop movement data, enemy name, and type of troop spaceships involved. Also assume that it's your job to maintain this list and use it for analysis that you then report to appropriate parties.

With this sort of information, you could create cross-tabulations that show the following information:

- **Enemy activity over time:** One interesting cross-tabulation is to look at the troop movements by specific enemy by month over a two- or five-year period of time. You may see that some enemies were gearing up their activity or that other enemies were dampening down their activity. All this information would presumably be useful to you while you assess security threats and brief Freedonian Confederation intelligence officers and diplomats on which enemies are doing what.

- **Troop movements by spaceship type:** Another interesting cross-tabulation would be to look at which spaceships your (potential) enemies are using to move troops. This insight may be useful to you to understand both the intent and seriousness of threats. As your long experience with the Uglinites (one of your antagonists) might tell you, for example, if you know that Jabbergloop troop carriers are largely defensive, you might not need to worry about troop movements that use these ships. On the other hand, if you notice a large increase in troop movements via the new photon-turbine fighter-bomber, well, that's significant.

Pretty powerful stuff, right? With a rich data set stored in an Excel list, cross-tabulations can give you remarkable insights that you would probably otherwise miss. And these cross-tabulations are what pivot tables do.

Getting Ready to Pivot

In order to create a pivot table, your first step is to create the Excel list that you want to cross-tabulate. Figure 4-1 shows an example Excel list that you might want a pivot table based on. In this list, I show sales of herbal teas by month and state. Pretend that this is an imaginary business that you own and operate. Further pretend that you set it up in a list because you want to gain insights into your business's sales activities.

Note: This Herbal Teas Excel Data List Workbook, available in the Zip file of sample Excel workbooks related to this book, can be found at the Dummies Web site (www.dummies.com/extras). You may want to download this list in order to follow along with the discussion here.

	A	B	C	D	E	F	G	H	I	J	
1	Month	Product	State	Sales $							
2	January	Shining Seas	California	$370							
3	January	Purple Mountains	California	$39							
4	January	Purple Mountains	Oregon	$302							
5	January	Huckleberry Heat	Oregon	$465							
6	January	Blackbear Berry	California	$877							
7	January	Raspberry Rocket	California	$211							
8	January	Blackbear Berry	Oregon	$891							
9	January	Amber Waves	Oregon	$678							
10	February	Amber Waves	Washington	$105							
11	February	Huckleberry Heat	Washington	$735							
12	February	Purple Mountains	California	$828							
13	February	Raspberry Rocket	California	$712							
14	February	Blackbear Berry	California	$988							
15	February	Shining Seas	California	$669							
16	February	Amber Waves	Oregon	$71							
17	February	Huckleberry Heat	Oregon	$9							
18	February	Purple Mountains	Oregon	$283							
19	February	Raspberry Rocket	Oregon	$704							
20	February	Blackbear Berry	Oregon	$743							
21	February	Shining Seas	Oregon	$184							
22	February	Amber Waves	Washington	$637							
23	February	Huckleberry Heat	Washington	$353							
24	February	Purple Mountains	Washington	$105							
25	February	Raspberry Rocket	Washington	$825							

Figure 4-1:
This Excel data list can be the basis for a pivot table.

Running the PivotTable Wizard

You create a pivot table — Excel calls a cross-tabulation a *pivot table* — by using the PivotTable Wizard. To run the PivotTable Wizard, take the following steps:

1. **Choose Data⇨PivotTable and PivotChart Report.**

   Excel displays the first step of the PivotTable and PivotChart Wizard, as shown in Figure 4-2.

Figure 4-2:
Use the wizard to set up a pivot table.

2. Answer the question about where the data you want to analyze is stored.

If the to-be-analyzed data is in an Excel list, for example, select the Microsoft Excel List or Database radio button. I demonstrate this approach here. And if you're just starting out, you ought to use this approach because it's the easiest.

If the data is in an external data source, select the External Data Source radio button. I don't demonstrate this approach here because I'm assuming in order to keep things simple and straightforward that you've already grabbed any external data and placed that data into a worksheet list. (If you haven't done that and need help doing so, skip back to Chapter 3.)

If the data is actually stored in a bunch of different worksheet ranges, select the Multiple Consolidation Ranges radio button. (This approach is more complicated, so you probably don't want to use it until you're comfortable working with pivot tables.)

If you have data that's scattered around in a bunch of different locations in a worksheet or even in different workbooks, pivot tables are a great way to consolidate that data.

3. Select the PivotTable radio button.

I describe how to create pivot chart reports in Chapter 6.

4. Click the Next button to move to the second screen of the PivotTable and PivotChart Wizard, as shown in Figure 4-3.

Figure 4-3: Identify pivot chart data from the wizard.

5. Use the second screen of the PivotTable and PivotChart Wizard to tell Excel where the to-be-analyzed data is stored.

If you're grabbing data from a single Excel list, enter the list range into the Range text box. You can do so in two ways.

- You can type the range coordinates: For example, if the range is cell A1 to cell D225, you can type **$A$1:$D$225**.

- Alternatively, you can click the button at the right end of the Range text box. Excel collapses the PivotTable and PivotChart Wizard, as shown in Figure 4-4.

Now use the mouse or the navigation keys to select the worksheet range that holds the list that you want to pivot. After you select the worksheet range, click the button at the end of the Range text box again. Excel redisplays the second dialog box of the PivotTable and PivotChart Wizard. (Refer to Figure 4-3.)

If you're grabbing data from multiple worksheet ranges, Excel first asks whether you want a single page field or multiple page fields. Indicate that you want a single page field and click Next. Then use the PivotTable and PivotChart Wizard dialog box that Excel displays (but which I haven't shown) to identify each of the worksheet ranges that you want to include in your pivot table by entering a range address into the text box provided and clicking the Add button.

6. **After you identify the data that you want to analyze in a pivot table, click Next.**

   Excel displays the third and final page of the PivotTable and PivotChart wizard, as shown in Figure 4-5.

7. **On the third page of the wizard, select either the New Worksheet or Existing Worksheet radio button to select a location for the new pivot table.**

   Most often, you want to place the new pivot table report into a new worksheet in the existing workbook: namely, the workbook that holds the Excel list that you're analyzing with a pivot table. (Select the New Worksheet radio button to accomplish this.)

However, if you want, you can place the new pivot table report into an existing worksheet. To do this, select the Existing Worksheet option button and also identify the worksheet range in the text box beneath the Existing Worksheet radio button. To identify the worksheet range, enter the cell in the top-left corner of the worksheet range.

Two final quick points about the third wizard screen. Don't pay any attention to the Layout button. That button displays a redundant dialog box that you don't need and shouldn't use. (I take care of all the layout stuff in Steps 9, 10 and 11, in case you're interested.) Also, ignore the Options button for the time being. Clicking that button opens the PivotTable Options dialog box, which I discuss later in the section "Setting pivot table options."

8. Click the Finish button.

Excel displays the new workbook with the partially constructed pivot table in it, as shown in Figure 4-6.

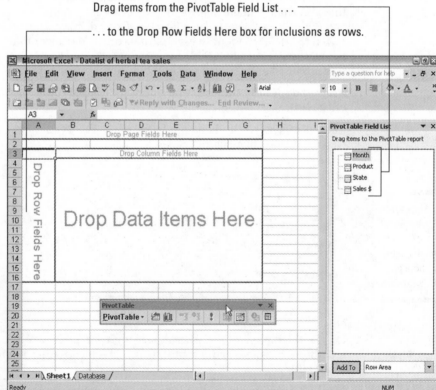

Drag items from the PivotTable Field List . . .

. . . to the Drop Row Fields Here box for inclusions as rows.

Figure 4-6:
Create an empty pivot table; then tell Excel what to cross-tabulate.

9. Select the Row field.

You need to decide first which field from the list that you want to summarize by using rows in the pivot table. After you decide this, you drag the field from the PivotTable Field List box (on the right side of Figure 4-6) to the large empty rectangle field marked Drop Row Fields Here (on the left side of Figure 4-6). For example, if you want to use rows that show product, you drag the Product field to the Drop Row Fields Here box.

Using the example data from Figure 4-1, after you do this, the partially constructed Excel pivot table looks like the one shown in Figure 4-7.

10. Select the Column field.

Just like you did for the Row field, indicate what list information you want stored in the columns of your cross-tabulation. After you make this choice, drag the field item from the PivotTable Field List to the box marked Drop Column Fields Here. Figure 4-8 shows the way the partially constructed pivot table looks now, using columns to show states.

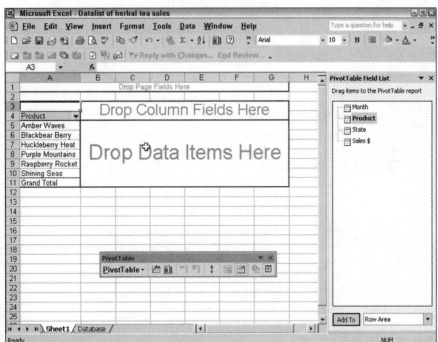

Figure 4-7:
Your cross-tabulation after you select the rows.

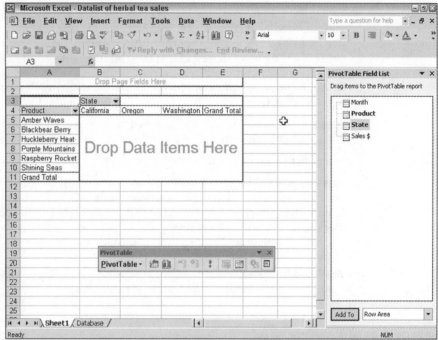

Figure 4-8:
Your cross-
tabulation
after you
select rows
and
columns.

11. **Select the data item that you want.**

   After you choose the rows and columns for your cross-tabulation, you indicate what piece of data you want cross-tabulated in the pivot table. For example, to cross-tabulate sales revenue, drag the sales item from the PivotTable Field List to the open rectangle labeled Drop Data Items Here. Figure 4-9 shows the completed pivot table after I select the row fields, column fields, and data items.

   Note that the pivot table cross-tabulates information from the Excel list shown in Figure 4-1. Each row in the pivot table shows sales by product. Each column in the pivot table shows sales by state. You can use column E to see grand totals of product sales by product item. You can use row 11 to see grand totals of sales by state.

   Another quick note about the data item that you cross-tabulate: If you select a numeric data item — like sales revenue — Excel cross-tabulates by summing the data item values. That's what you see in Figure 4-9. If you select a textual data item, Excel cross-tabulates by counting the number of data items.

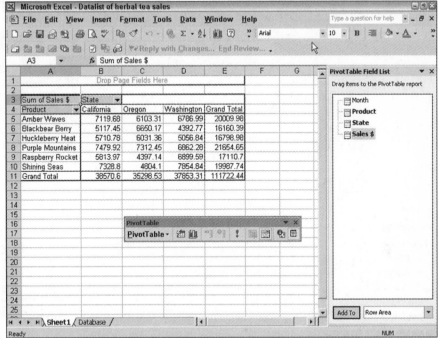

Figure 4-9:
Tah dah! A
completed
cross-
tabulation.

TIP

Although you can use pivot tables for more than what this simple example illustrates, this basic configuration is very valuable. With a list that reports the items you sell, to whom you sell, and the geographic locations where you sell, a cross-tabulation enables you to see exactly how much of each product you sell, exactly how much each customer buys, and exactly where you sell the most. Valuable information, indeed.

Fooling Around with Your Pivot Table

After you construct your pivot table, you can further analyze your data with some cool tools that Excel provides for manipulating information in a pivot table.

Pivoting and re-pivoting

The thing that gives the pivot table its name is that you can continue cross-tabulating the data in the pivot table. For example, take the data shown in Figure 4-9: By swapping the row items and column items (you do this merely by swapping the State and Product buttons), you can flip-flop the organization of the pivot table. Figure 4-10 shows the same information as Figure 4-9; the difference is that now the state sales appear in rows and the product sales appear in columns.

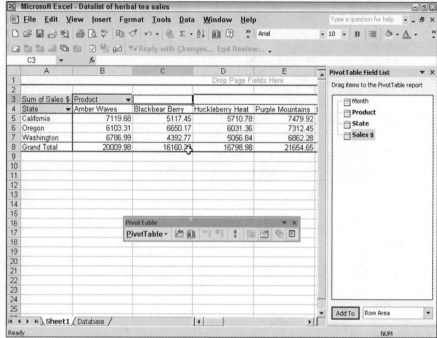

Figure 4-10:
Change
your focus
with a
repivoted
pivot table.

Note: The observant ones in the audience will notice that some of the work-sheet now appears to the right of the portion viewable in the Excel workbook window in Figure 4-10. You'd need to scroll to see the rest of this information.

Another nifty thing about pivot tables is that they don't restrict you to using just two items to cross-tabulate data. For example, in both the pivot tables shown in Figures 4-9 and 4-10, I use only a single row item and only a single column item. You're not limited to this, however: You can also segregate data by putting information on different pages. For example, if you drag the month data item to the Drop Page Fields Here open rectangle, Excel creates the pivot table shown in Figure 4-11. This pivot table enables you to view sales informa-tion for all the months, as shown in Figure 4-11, or just one of the months.

To show sales for only a single month, click the arrow button to the right of the Month drop-down list box (cell B1 in Figure 4-11). When Excel displays the drop-down list box (as shown in Figure 4-12), select the month that you want to see sales for and then click OK. Figure 4-13 shows sales for just the month of January (check out cell B1 again).

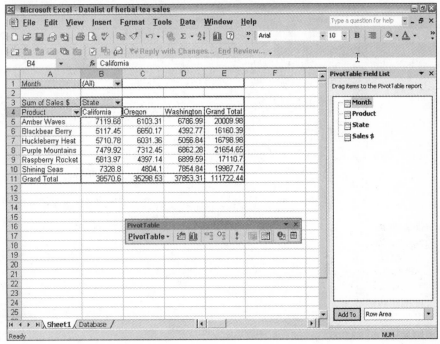

Figure 4-11:
Use page
fields to
cross-
tabulate.

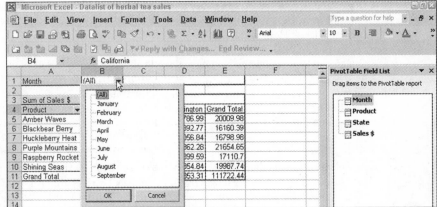

Figure 4-12:
You can
filter page
fields.

Here are some other handy pivoting tricks:

✔ **See ya:** To remove an item from the pivot table, you simply drag the item's button back to the PivotTable Field List.

✔ **Gettin' fancy:** To use more than one row item, drag the first item that you want to use to the Drop Row Items Here box and then also drag the second item that you also want to use to Drop Row Items Here.

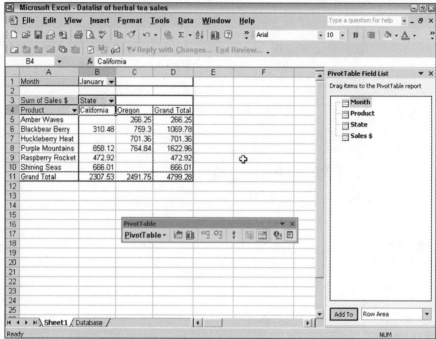

Drag them from the PivotTable Field List. Do the same for columns: Drag each column item that you want from the PivotTable Field List Here to the Drop Column Items Here box.

Check out Figure 4-14 to see how the pivot table looks when I also use Month as a column item. Based on the data in Figure 4-1, this pivot table is very wide when I use both state and month items for columns. For this reason, only a portion of the pivot table that uses both month and state column items shows in Figure 4-14.

Sometimes having multiple row items and multiple column items makes sense. Sometimes it doesn't. But the beauty of a pivot table is that you can easily cross-tabulate and re-cross-tabulate your data simply by dragging those little item buttons. Accordingly, try viewing your data from different frames of reference. Try viewing your data at different levels of granularity. Spend some time looking at the different cross-tabulations that the PivotTable command enables you to create. Through careful, thoughtful viewing of these cross-tabulations, you can most likely gain insights into your data.

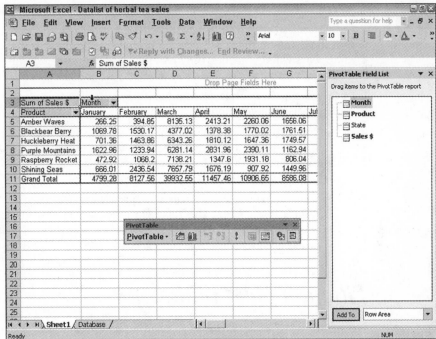

Figure 4-14:
Slice data
however
you want in
a cross-
tabulation.

Refreshing pivot table data

In many circumstances, the data in your Excel list changes and grows over
time. This doesn't mean, fortunately, that you need to go to the work of recre-
ating your pivot table. If you update the data in your underlying Excel list,
you can tell Excel to update the pivot table information.

You have five methods for telling Excel to refresh the pivot table:

    ✔ Click the Refresh data tool — it shows an exclamation point — on the
      PivotTable toolbar button, as shown in Figure 4-15.

Figure 4-15:
Refresh
data from
the
PivotTable
toolbar.

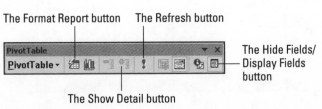

The Format Report button   The Refresh button

The Hide Fields/
Display Fields
button

The Show Detail button

- ✔ You can always learn which tool is which by pointing to the tool. Excel displays the name of the tool you're pointing to in a tool tip pop-up box.

- ✔ Choose the Refresh Data command from the PivotTable menu, which appears when you click the PivotTable tool on the PivotTable toolbar. Cleverly, the PivotTable tool is labeled with the word *PivotTable*.

- ✔ Choose the Refresh Data command from the shortcut menu that Excel displays when you right-click a pivot table.

- ✔ Tell Excel to automatically refresh the pivot table whenever the pivot table is opened. To do this, click the PivotTable tool, choose the Table Options command, and then after Excel displays the PivotTable Options dialog box, select the Refresh on Open check box.

- ✔ Tell Excel to periodically refresh the pivot table. To do this, click the PivotTable tool, choose the Table Options command, and then after Excel displays the PivotTable Options dialog box, select the Refresh Every [X] Minutes check box and enter a value into the text box.

Filtering pivot table data

As I mention in the earlier section "Pivoting and re-pivoting," you can filter pivot table data. Don't use the Data➪Filter menu's commands, but rather click the arrow button next to the item button. For example, to see only sales to the state of California in my example pivot table, click the arrow button next to the State item. When you do this, Excel displays a drop-down list box like the one shown in Figure 4-16.

Click to filter data

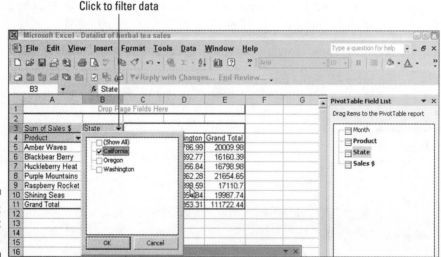

Figure 4-16: Filter pivot table data.

To see only sales from California, select the check box next to California and make sure that the other check boxes are unselected (blank). Click OK, and Excel re-cross-tabulates the data showing sales to California. See the results in Figure 4-17.

Sorting pivot table data

You can sort pivot table data in the same basic way that you sort an Excel list. Say that you want to sort the pivot table information shown in Figure 4-18 by product in descending order of sales to see a list that highlights the best products. In order to sort pivot table data in this way, take the following steps:

1. **Identify the sort key.**

    Click a cell in the column that holds the sort key. For example, in the case of the pivot table shown in Figure 4-18, and assuming that you want to sort by sales, you click a cell in the worksheet range C5:C10.

2. **Choose Data⇨Sort.**

    Excel displays the Sort dialog box, as shown in Figure 4-19.

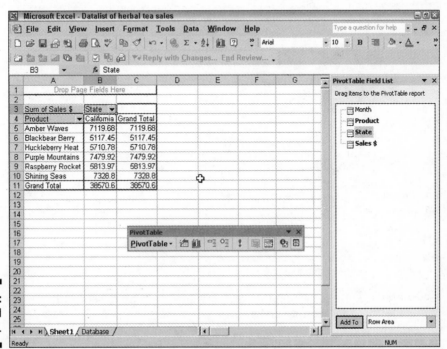

Figure 4-17:
A filtered
pivot table.

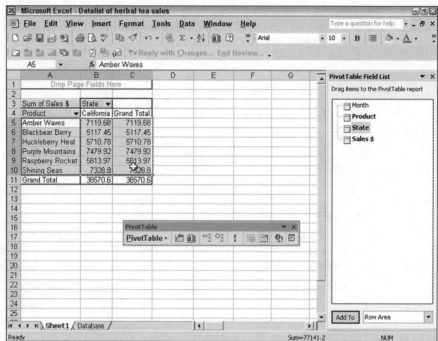

Figure 4-18:
First select the sort range of a pivot table.

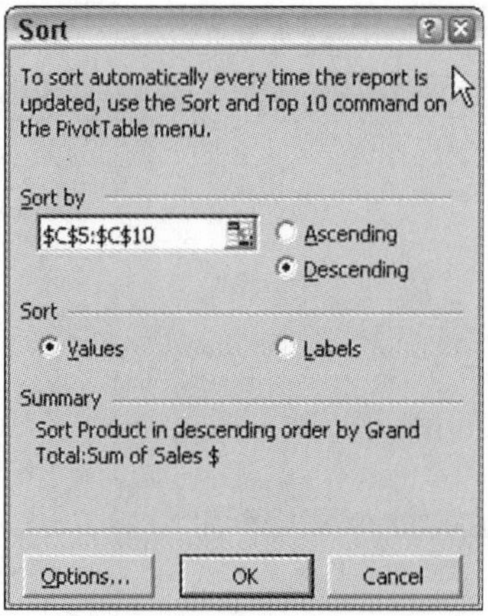

Figure 4-19:
Tell Excel what to sort.

3. **Describe whether the sorting should be in ascending or descending order.**

To describe how sorting should work, select either the Ascending or Descending radio button. To sort product sales in descending order, for example, select the Descending radio button.

You can ignore the Values and Labels radio buttons. Excel marks the appropriate button for you depending on what you're sorting. Just in case you're curious, however, if you select a cell in the column that you want to use for sorting (which is what I suggest in Step 2), Excel marks the Values button. If you select one of the pivot table's buttons, Excel marks the Labels button. In other cases, Excel sorts in the predictable order.

4. Click OK to sort the data.

Excel re-sorts the pivot table's rows according to the sort order that you specify. See the result in Figure 4-20 from the choices in the previous step: Product sales are arranged in descending order. Purple Mountain produces the most sales, and thus appears in the first row in the pivot table. Shining Seas, the next highest grossing herbal tea, appears as the second row in the pivot table, and so on.

You also tell Excel to automatically sort, or AutoSort, pivot tables. To use AutoSort, you use the PivotTable Sort and Top 10 command, which you can find in the PivotTable menu of commands. (To activate this menu, click the PivotTable tool available on the PivotTable toolbar; refer to Figure 4-15.) When you choose this command, Excel displays the PivotTable Sort and Top 10 dialog box, as shown in Figure 4-21. If you mark either the Ascending or Descending buttons, Excel automatically sorts the pivot table. Use the Using Field list box to select the sort key.

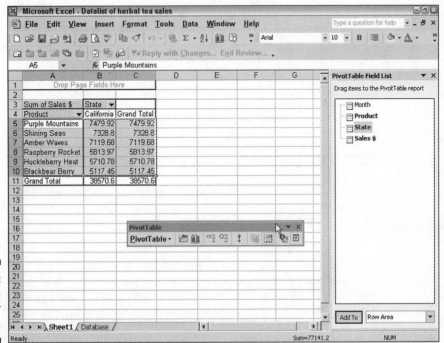

Figure 4-20:
Sort data
by your
parameters.

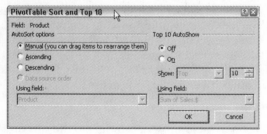

Figure 4-21:
Déjà vu à la
Letterman:
Excel's Sort
and Top 10.

A tangential point: The PivotTable Sort and Top 10 dialog box also lets you tell Excel to filter your pivot table so that only the top data items (top ten, top three, whatever) should display in the pivot table. To perform this top-data-items filtering, select the On radio button and use the Show boxes to indicate which data items you want to see (such as the Top 3, or whatever). Next, use the Using Field list box to pick the field that Excel should use to filter your pivot table.

Pseudo-sorting

You can manually organize the items in your pivot table, too. You might want to do this so the order of rows or columns matches the way that you want to present information or the order in which you want to review information.

To change the order of items in your pivot table, right-click the pivot table row or column that you want to move. From the shortcut menu that Excel displays, choose the Order command. You should see a list of submenu commands: Move to Beginning, Move Up, Move Down, and so forth. Use these commands to rearrange the order of items in the pivot table. For example, you can move a product down in this list. Or you can move a state up in this list.

Grouping and ungrouping data items

You can group rows, columns, and even pages in your pivot table. You may want to group columns or rows when you need to segregate data in a way that isn't explicitly supported by your Excel list.

In this chapter's running example, suppose that I combine Oregon and Washington together. I want to see sales data for California, Oregon, and Washington by salesperson. I have one salesperson who handles California and another who handles Oregon and Washington. I want to combine (group) Oregon and Washington sales in my pivot table so that I can compare the two salespersons. The California sales (remember that California is covered by one salesperson) appear in one column, and Oregon and Washington sales appear either individually or together in another column.

To create a grouping, select the items that you want to group, right-click the pivot table, and then choose Group and Show Detail⇨Group from the shortcut menu that appears.

Excel creates a new grouping, which it names in numerical order starting with Group1. As shown in Figure 4-22, Excel still displays detailed individual information about Oregon and Washington in the pivot table. However, the pivot table also groups the Oregon and Washington information into a new category: Group1.

You can rename the group by clicking the cell with the Group1 label and then typing the replacement label.

Important point: You don't automatically get group subtotals. You get them when you filter the pivot table to show just that group. (I describe filtering earlier in the section "Filtering pivot table data.") You also get group subtotals when you hide the details within a group. To hide the detail within a group, right-click a column or row in the group and choose Group and Show Detail⇨Hide from the shortcut menu that appears.

To ungroup previously grouped data, right-click the pivot table to again display the shortcut menu and then choose Group and Show Detail⇨Ungroup. Excel removes the grouping from your pivot table.

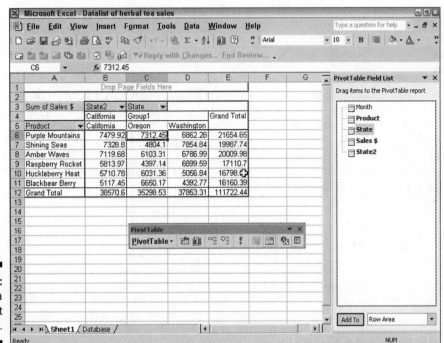

Figure 4-22:
Group data in a pivot table.

Selecting this, selecting that

At your disposal is the Excel Select submenu of commands: Label, Data, Label and Data, Entire Table, and Entire Selection. The Select submenu appears when you right-click a pivot table to display the shortcut menu and then choose the Select command.

Essentially, when you choose one of these submenu commands, Excel selects the referenced item in the table. For example, if you choose Select⇨Label, Excel selects all the labels in the pivot table. Similarly, choose Select⇨Data command, and Excel selects all the data cells in the pivot table.

The only Select menu command that's a little tricky is the Enable Selection command. That command tells Excel to expand your selection to include all the other similar items in the pivot table. For example, suppose that you create a pivot table that shows sales of herbal tea products for California, Oregon, and Washington over the months of the year. If you select the item that shows California sales of Amber Waves and then you choose the Enable Selection command, Excel selects the California sales of all the herbal teas: Amber Waves, Blackbear Berry, Purple Mountains, Shining Seas, and so on.

Where did that cell's number come from?

Here's a neat trick. Click a cell and then click the Show Detail button on the PivotTable toolbar. (Refer to Figure 4-15.) Excel adds a worksheet to the open workbook and creates an Excel list that summarizes individual records that together explain that cell's value.

For example, I click cell B8 in the workbook shown in Figure 4-22 and then click the Show Detail button on the PivotTable toolbar. Excel creates a new list, as shown in Figure 4-23. This list shows all the information that gets totaled and then presented in Cell B8 in Figure 4-22.

You can also show the detail that explains some value in a pivot table by double-clicking the cell holding the value.

Setting field settings

The field settings for a pivot table determine what Excel does with a field when it's cross-tabulated in the pivot table. This sounds complicated, but this quick example shows you exactly how it works. If you right-click one of the sales revenue amounts shown in the pivot table and choose Field Settings from the shortcut menu that appears, Excel displays the PivotTable Field dialog box, as shown in Figure 4-24.

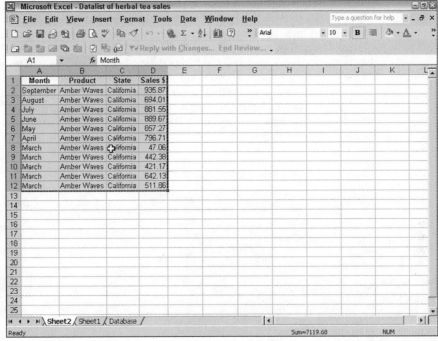

From the PivotTable Field dialog box, you can indicate whether the data item
should be summed, counted, averaged, and so on, in the pivot table. By
default, data items are summed. But you can also arithmetically manipulate
data items in other ways. For example, you can calculate average sales by
selecting Average from the Summarize By list box. You can also find the
largest value using the Max function, the smallest value using the Min function, the number of sales transactions using the Count function, and so on.
Essentially, what you do with the PivotTable Field dialog box is to pick the
arithmetic operation that you want Excel to perform on data items stored in
the pivot table.

If you click the Number button in the PivotTable Field dialog box, Excel displays a scaled-down version of the Format Cells dialog box. From the Format Cells dialog box, you can pick a numeric format for the data item. Click the Options button in the PivotTable Field dialog box, and Excel adds several boxes to the expanded Field Settings dialog box, as shown in Figure 4-25. These additional boxes enable you to specify how the data item should be manipulated for fancy-schmancy summaries. I postpone a discussion of these calculation options until Chapter 5. There's some background stuff that I should cover before moving on to the subject of custom calculations, which is what these boxes are for.

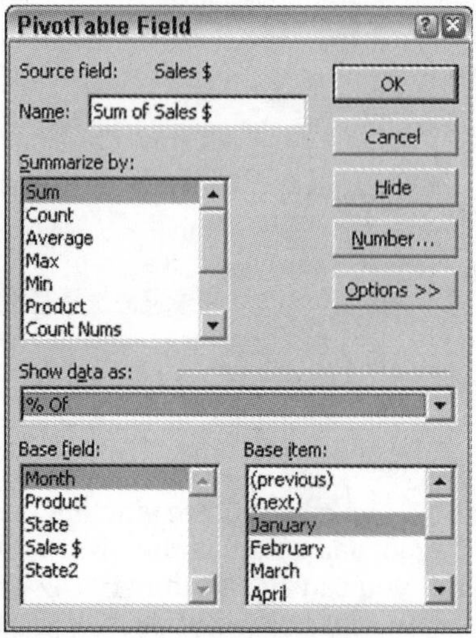

Figure 4-25:
Make more choices from the expanded PivotTable Field dialog box.

Customizing How Pivot Tables Work and Look

Excel gives you a bit of flexibility over how pivot tables work and how they look. You have options to change their names, formatting, and data manipulation.

Setting pivot table options

Right-click a pivot table and choose the Table Options command from the shortcut menu to display the PivotTable Options dialog box, as shown in Figure 4-26.

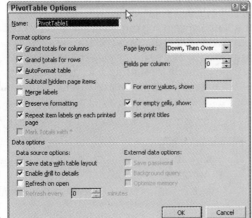

Figure 4-26:
Change a
pivot table's
look
from the
PivotTable
Options
dialog box.

The PivotTable Options dialog box provides a series of check and text boxes with which you tell Excel how it should create a pivot table. Use choices from the Format Options check boxes (top half of the dialog box) to specify whether you want grand totals for columns or rows, whether the table should be automatically formatted, and so forth.

Your best bet with these options is to just experiment. If you're curious about what a check box does, simply mark (select) the check box. You can also click the Help button (the question mark button, top-left corner of the dialog box) and then click the feature that you have a question about.

The Data Options check boxes (bottom of the PivotTable Options dialog box) enable you to specify whether Excel stores data with the pivot table and how easy it is to access the data upon which the pivot table is based. For example, select the Save Data with Table Layout box check box, and the data is saved with the pivot table. Select the Enable Drill to Details check box, and you can get the detailed information that supports the value in a pivot table cell by right-clicking the cell to display the shortcut menu and then choosing Group and Show Detail⇨Show Detail.

Predictably, selecting the Refresh on Open check box tells Excel to refresh the pivot table's information whenever you open the workbook that holds the pivot table.

Formatting pivot table information

You can and will want to format the information contained in a pivot table. Essentially, you have two ways of doing this: using standard cell formatting and using an auto format for the table.

Using standard cell formatting

To format a single cell or a range of cells in your pivot table, select the range and then choose Format⇨Cells. When Excel displays the Format Cells dialog box, as shown in Figure 4-27, use its tabs to assign formatting to the selected range. For example, if you want to assign numeric formatting, click the Number tab, choose a formatting category, and then provide any other additional formatting specifications appropriate — such as the number of decimal places to be used.

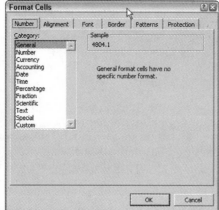

Figure 4-27:
Format one cell or a range of cells here.

Using AutoFormat

You can also format an entire pivot table. Just select a cell in the pivot table and then click the Format Report tool on the PivotTable toolbar. (Refer to Figure 4-15.) Excel displays the AutoFormat dialog box, as shown in Figure 4-28. You can pick one of the formats shown in this dialog box by clicking it. After you identify the format that you want, click OK. Excel uses this format to reformat your pivot table information. Look at Figure 4-29 to see how my running example pivot table of this chapter looks after I apply an AutoFormat choice.

Note: Selecting an AutoFormat choice may rearrange the information shown in your pivot table. For example, in the case of the pivot table shown in Figure 4-29, choosing AutoFormat puts the product item into a column. Previously, the product item was shown in rows. This table still provides the same information, as does the original unformatted pivot table; AutoFormat just rearranges information.

Customizing the pivot table tools

Excel also provides you with ways that you can change and customize its pivot table tools.

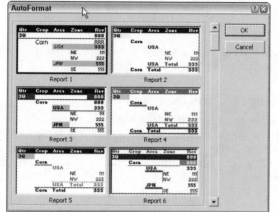

Display hidden ~~Field~~ Column

Select column
adjacent
Format → Column
→ unhide

Figure 4-28:
Choose a
format for
an entire
pivot table.

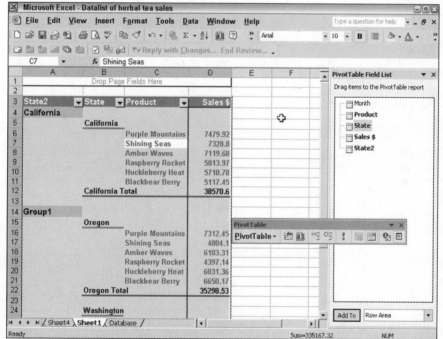

Figure 4-29:
My pivot
table
formatted
from
AutoFormat.

Removing and redisplaying the field list

You can remove and redisplay the PivotTable Field List. To hide — perhaps to show a large portion of the pivot table — click the Hide Field List tool on the PivotTable toolbar. (Refer to Figure 4-15.) To show a previously hidden field list, click the Show Field List tool on the PivotTable toolbar. (Refer to Figure 4-15.)

Predictably, whether the PivotTable toolbar displays the Show Field List tool or the Hide Field List tool depends on whether the field list shows or not.

You can point to any toolbar button and see its name in a pop-up tool tip. Use this technique when you don't know which tool is which.

Hiding and unhiding the PivotTable toolbar

To hide and later show the PivotTable toolbar itself, right-click a pivot table to display its shortcut menu. From there, hide the PivotTable toolbar by choosing the Hide PivotTable Toolbar command. To show the PivotTable toolbar again, right-click the pivot table and choose the Show PivotTable Toolbar command.

Chapter 5

Building PivotTable Formulas

*M*ost of the techniques that I discuss in this chapter aren't things that you need to do very often. Most frequently, the cross-tabulated data that appears in a pivot table after you run the PivotTable wizard are almost exactly what you need. And if not, a little bit of fiddling around with the item buttons gets the information into the perfect arrangement for your needs. (For more on the PivotTable Wizard, read through Chapter 4.)

On occasion, however, you'll find that you do need to either grab information from a pivot table so that it can be used some place else or that you need to hard code calculations and add them to a pivot table. In these special cases, the techniques that I describe in this chapter may save you much wailing and gnashing of teeth.

Adding Another Standard Calculation

Take a look at the pivot table shown in Figure 5-1. This pivot table shows coffee sales by state for an imaginary business that you can pretend that you own and operate. The data item calculated in this pivot table is sales. Sometimes, sales may be the only calculation that you want made. But what if you also want to calculate average sales by product and state in this pivot table?

To do this, right-click the Sum of Sales $ button and choose Field Settings from the shortcut menu that appears. Then, when Excel displays the PivotTable Field dialog box, as shown in Figure 5-2, select Average from the Summarize By list box.

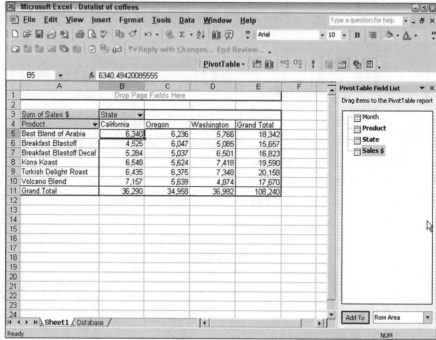

Figure 5-1:
Add
standard
calculations
to basic
pivot tables
for more
complex
data
analysis.

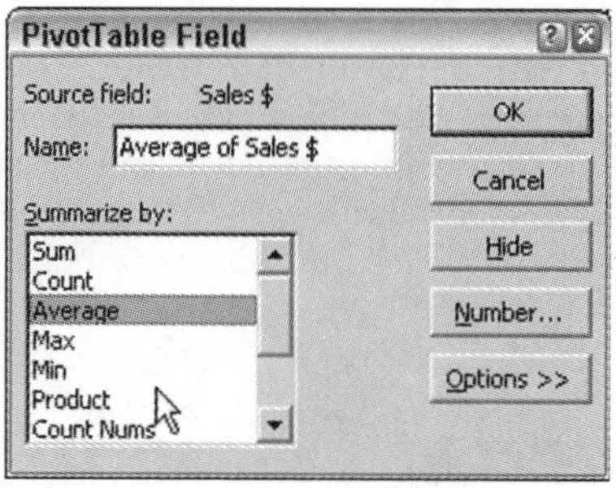

Figure 5-2:
Replace
calculations
here.

Now assume, however, that you don't want to replace the data item that
sums sales. Assume instead that you want to add average sales data to the
worksheet. In other words, you want your pivot table to show both total sales
and average sales.

To add a second summary calculation, or standard calculation, to your pivot
table, drag the data item from the PivotTable Field dialog box Summarize By
list to the data item area. Figure 5-3 shows how the roast coffee product sales
by state pivot table looks after you drag the sales data item to the pivot table
a second time.

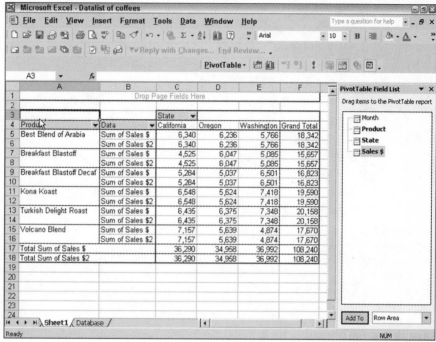

	A	B	C	D	E	F
1			Drop Page Fields Here			
2						
3			State			
4	Product	Data	California	Oregon	Washington	Grand Total
5	Best Blend of Arabia	Sum of Sales $	6,340	6,236	5,766	18,342
6		Sum of Sales $2	6,340	6,236	5,766	18,342
7	Breakfast Blastoff	Sum of Sales $	4,525	6,047	5,085	15,657
8		Sum of Sales $2	4,525	6,047	5,085	15,657
9	Breakfast Blastoff Decaf	Sum of Sales $	5,284	5,037	6,501	16,823
10		Sum of Sales $2	5,284	5,037	6,501	16,823
11	Kona Koast	Sum of Sales $	6,548	5,624	7,418	19,590
12		Sum of Sales $2	6,548	5,624	7,418	19,590
13	Turkish Delight Roast	Sum of Sales $	6,435	6,375	7,348	20,158
14		Sum of Sales $2	6,435	6,375	7,348	20,158
15	Volcano Blend	Sum of Sales $	7,157	5,639	4,874	17,670
16		Sum of Sales $2	7,157	5,639	4,874	17,670
17	Total Sum of Sales $		36,290	34,958	36,992	108,240
18	Total Sum of Sales $2		36,290	34,958	36,992	108,240

Figure 5-3:
Add a
second
standard
summary
calculation
to a pivot
table.

After you add a second summary calculation — in Figure 5-3, this shows as the Sum of Sales $2 data item — right-click that data item, choose Field Settings from the shortcut menu that appears, and use the PivotTable Field dialog box to name the new average calculation and specify that the average calculation should be made. In Figure 5-4, you can see how the PivotTable Field dialog box looks when you make these changes for the pivot table shown in Figure 5-3.

See Figure 5-5 for the new pivot table. This pivot table now shows two calculations: the sum of sales for a coffee product in a particular state and the average sale. For example, in cell C5, you can see that sales for the Best Blend of the Arabia coffee are $6,340 in California. And in cell C6, the pivot table shows that the average sale of the Best Blend of Arabia coffee in California is $488.

Figure 5-4:
Add a
second
standard
calculation
to a pivot
table.

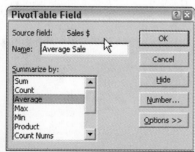

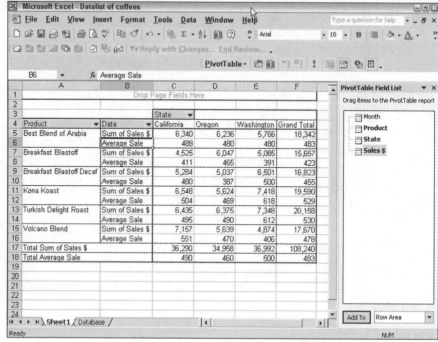

Figure 5-5:
A pivot table
with two
standard
calcu-
lations.

If you can add information to your pivot table by using a standard calculation, that's the approach you want to take. Standard calculations are the easiest way to calculate information, or add formulas, to your pivot tables.

Creating Custom Calculations

Excel pivot tables provide a feature called *Custom Calculations*. Custom Calculations enable you to add many semi-standard calculations to a pivot table. By using Custom Calculations, for example, you can calculate the difference between two pivot table cells, percentages, and percentage differences.

To illustrate how custom calculations work in a pivot table, take a look at Figure 5-6. This pivot table shows coffee product sales by month for the imaginary business that you own and operate. Suppose, however, that you want to add a calculated value to this pivot table that shows the difference between two months' sales. You may do this so that you easily see large changes between two months' sales. Perhaps this data may help you identify new problems or important opportunities.

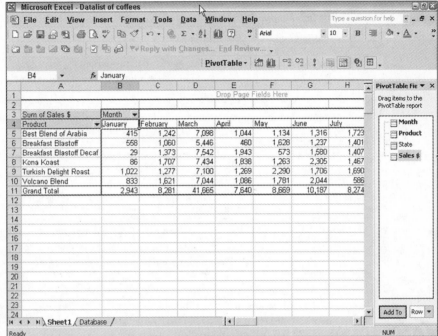

Figure 5-6:
Use custom calculations to compare pivot table data.

To add a custom calculation to a pivot table, you need to complete two tasks: You need to add another standard calculation to the pivot table, and you need to then customize that standard calculation to show one of the custom calculations listed in Table 5-1.

Table 5-1	Custom Calculation Options for Pivot Tables
Calculation	*Description*
Normal	You don't want a custom calculation.
Difference From	This is the difference between two pivot table cell values: for example, the difference between this month's and last month's value.
% of	This is the percentage that a pivot table cell value represents compared with a base value.
% Difference From	This is the percentage difference between two pivot table cell values: for example, the percentage difference between this month's and last month's value.

(continued)

Table 5-1 *(continued)*

Calculation	Description
Running Total In	This shows cumulative or running totals of pivot table cell values: for example, cumulative year-to-date sales or expenses.
% of Row	This is the percent that a pivot table cell value represents compared with the total of the row values.
% of Column	This is the percent that a pivot table cell value represents compared with the total of the column values.
% of Total	This is the pivot table cell value as a percent of the grand total value.
Index	Kind of complicated, dude. The index custom calculation uses this formula: ((cell value) x (grand total of grand totals)) / ((grand total row) x (grand total column)).

To add a second standard calculation to the pivot table, add a second data item. For example, in the case of the pivot table shown in Figure 5-6, if you do want to calculate the difference in sales from one month to another, you need to drag a second sales data item from the field list to the pivot table. Figure 5-7 shows how your pivot table looks after you make this change.

After you add a second standard calculation to the pivot table, you must customize it by telling Excel that you want to turn the standard calculation into a custom calculation. To do so, follow these steps:

1. **Click the new standard calculation field, right-click, and then choose Field Settings from the shortcut menu that appears.**

2. **When Excel displays the PivotTable Field dialog box, as shown in Figure 5-8, click the Options button.**

   Excel displays three additional list boxes at the bottom of the PivotTable Field dialog box: Show Data As, Base Field, and Base Item.

   The list boxes or boxes that Excel adds after you click the Options button on the PivotTable Field dialog box depends on which type of custom calculation you're making.

3. **Select a custom calculation by clicking the down-arrow at the right side of the Show Data As list box and then selecting one of the custom calculations available in that drop-down list.**

   For example, to calculate the difference between two pivot table cells, select the Difference From entry. Refer to Table 5-1 for explanation of the possible choices.

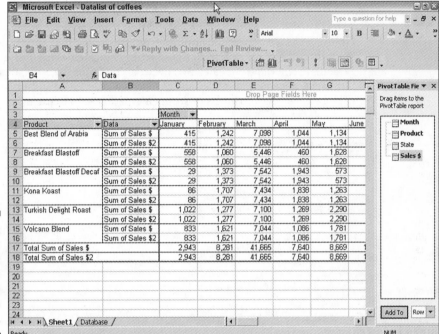

Figure 5-7:
Add a
second
standard
calculation
and then
customize it.

Click to select a custom calculation.

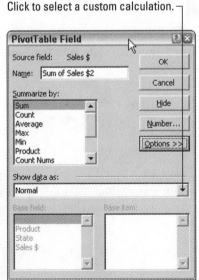

Figure 5-8:
Customize a
standard
calculation
here.

4. Instruct Excel how to make the custom calculation.

After you choose the custom calculation that you want Excel to make in the pivot table, you make choices from the Base Field and Base Item list boxes to specify how Excel should make the calculation. For example, to calculate the difference in sales between two months, you select Month from the Base Field list box and Previous from the Base Item list box. Figure 5-9 shows how this custom calculation gets defined.

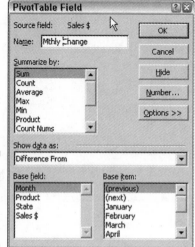

Figure 5-9:
Define a custom calculation here.

5. Appropriately name the new custom calculation in the Name text box of the PivotTable Field dialog box.

For example, to calculate the change between two pivot table cells and the cells supply monthly sales, you may name the custom calculation *Change in Sales from Previous Month*. Or, more likely, you may name the custom calculation *Mthly Change*.

6. Click OK.

After you choose a custom calculation, identify the inputs to the custom calculation, and name the custom calculation, click OK. Excel adds the new custom calculation to your pivot table, as shown in Figure 5-10.

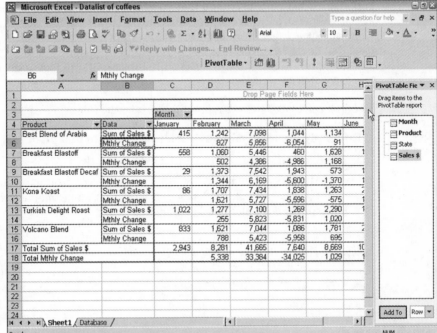

Figure 5-10:
Your pivot table now shows a custom calculation.

Using Calculated Fields and Items

Excel supplies one other opportunity for calculating values inside a pivot table. You can also add calculated fields and items to a table. With these calculated fields and items, you can put just about any type of formula into a pivot table. But, alas, you need to go to slightly more work to create calculated fields and items.

Adding a calculated field

Adding a calculated field enables you to insert a new row or column into a pivot table and then fill the new row or column with a formula. For example, if you refer to the pivot table shown in Figure 5-10, you see that it reports on sales both by product and month. What if you want to add the commissions expense that you incurred on these sales?

Suppose for sake of illustration that your network of independent sales representatives earns a 25 percent commission on coffee sales. This commission expense doesn't appear in the data list, so you can't retrieve the information from that source. However, because you know how to calculate the commissions expense, you can easily add the commissions expense to the pivot table by using a calculated field.

To add a calculated field to a pivot table, take the following steps:

1. **Identify the pivot table by clicking any cell in that pivot table.**

2. **Tell Excel that you want to add a calculated field.**

   Click the PivotTable button on the PivotTable toolbar, click Formulas, and then choose Calculated Field from the Formulas menu. Excel displays the Insert Calculated Field dialog box, as shown in Figure 5-11.

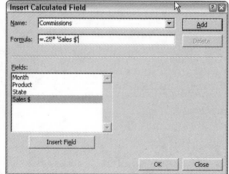

Figure 5-11:
Add a
calculated
field here.

3. **In the Name text box, name the new row or column that you want to show the calculated field.**

   For example, if you want to add a row that shows commissions expense, you might name the new field *Commissions*.

4. **Write the formula in the Formula text box.**

   Calculated field formulas work the same way as formulas for regular cells:

   1. Begin the formula by typing the equal (=) sign.

   2. Enter the operator and operands that make up the formula.

      If you want to calculate commissions and commissions equal 25 percent of sales, you enter **=.25***.

   3. The Fields box lists all the possible fields that can be included in your formula. To include a choice from the Fields list, click the Sales $ item in the Fields list box and then click the Insert Field button.

See in Figure 5-11 how the Insert Calculated Field dialog box looks after you create a calculated field to show a 25 percent commissions expense.

5. Click OK.

Excel adds the calculated field to your pivot table. Figure 5-12 shows the pivot table with coffee product sales by state with the Commissions calculated field now appearing. For example, on California sales of the coffee Best Blend of Arabia, commissions equal $1,585. This amount is calculated in cell C6 by using a calculated field formula.

After you insert a calculated field, Excel adds the calculated field to the PivotTable field list. You can then pretty much work with the calculated item in the same way that you work with traditional items.

Adding a calculated item

You can also add calculated items to a pivot table. Now, frankly, adding a calculated item usually doesn't make any sense. If, for your pivot table, you have retrieved data from a complete rich Excel list or from some database, creating data by calculating item amounts is more than a little goofy. However, in the spirit of fair play and good fun, here I create a scenario where you may need to do this using the sales of roast coffee products by months.

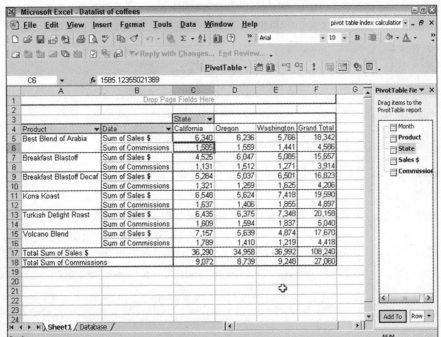

Figure 5-12:
A pivot table with a calculated field.

Assume that your Excel list omits an important product item. Suppose that you have another roast coffee product called *Volcano Blend Decaf*. And even though this product item information doesn't appear in the source Excel list, you can calculate this product item's information by using a simple formula.

Also assume that sales of the Volcano Blend Decaf product equal exactly and always 25 percent of the Volcano Blend product. In other words, even if you don't know or don't have Volcano Blend Decaf product item information available in the underlying Excel data list, it doesn't really matter. If you have information about the Volcano Blend product, you can calculate the Volcano Blend Decaf product item information.

Here are the steps that you take to add a calculated item for Volcano Blend Decaf to the Roast Coffee Products pivot table shown in earlier figures in this chapter:

1. **Select the Product button by simply clicking the button in cell A4 of the pivot table.**

2. **Tell Excel that you want to add a calculated item to the pivot table.**

   Click the PivotTable button on the PivotTable toolbar. When Excel displays the PivotTable menu, click Formulas and then choose Calculated Items from the Formulas submenu that appears. Excel displays the Insert Calculated Item in "Product" dialog box, as shown in Figure 5-13.

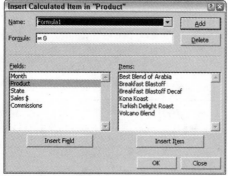

Figure 5-13: Insert a calculated item here.

3. **Name the new calculated item in the Name text box.**

   In the example that I set up here, the new calculated item name is *Volcano Blend Decaf*, so that's what you enter in the Name text box.

4. **Enter the formula for the calculated item in the Formula text box.**

   Use the Formula text box to give the formula that calculates the item. In the example here, you can calculate Volcano Blend Decaf sales by multiplying Volcano Blend sales by 25 percent. This formula then is =.25*'Volcano Blend'.

• To enter this formula into the Formula text box, first type =.25*.

• Then select Volcano Blend from the Items list box and click the Insert Item button.

See Figure 5-14 for how the Insert Calculated Item in "Product" dialog box looks after you name and supply the calculated item formula.

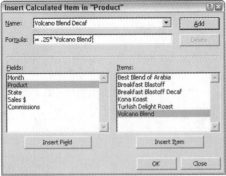

Figure 5-14: The Insert Calculated Item dialog box after you do your dirty work.

5. **Add the calculated item.**

After you name and supply the formula for the calculated item, click OK. Excel adds the calculated item to the pivot table. Figure 5-15 shows the pivot table of roast coffee product sales by month with the new calculated item, Volcano Blend Decaf. This isn't an item that comes directly from the Excel data list, as you can glean from the preceding discussion. This data item is calculated based on other data items: in this case, based on the Volcano Blend data item.

Removing calculated fields and items

You can easily remove calculated fields and items from the pivot table.

To remove a calculated field, click a cell in the pivot table. Then click the PivotTable button on the PivotTable toolbar, click Formulas, and then choose Calculated Field on the Formulas submenu that appears. When Excel displays the Insert Calculated Field dialog box, as shown in Figure 5-16, select the calculated field that you want to remove from the Name list box. Then click the Delete button. Excel removes the calculated field.

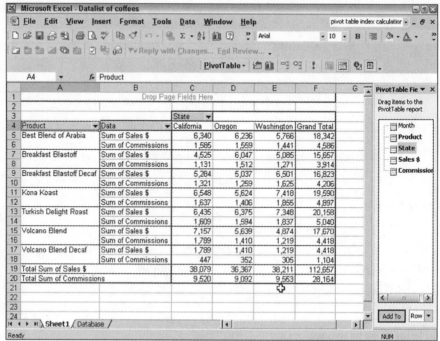

Figure 5-15:
The new
pivot table
with the
inserted
calculated
item.

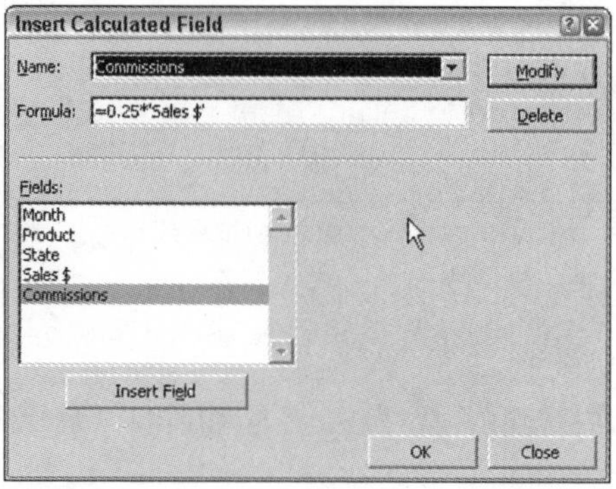

Figure 5-16:
Use the
Insert
Calculated
Field dialog
box to
remove
calculated
fields from
the pivot
table.

To remove a calculated item from a pivot table, perform the following steps:

1. **Click the button of the calculated item that you want to remove.**

   For example, if you want to remove the Volcano Blend Decaf item from
   the pivot table shown in Figure 5-15, click the Product button.

2. **Click the PivotTable button on the PivotTable toolbar, click Formulas, and then click Calculated Item from the menu that appears.**

   The Insert Calculated Item dialog box appears.

3. **In the Insert Calculated Item dialog box, select the calculated item from the Name list box that you want to delete.**

4. **Click the Delete button.**

5. **Click OK.**

Figure 5-17 shows the Insert Calculated Item in "Product" dialog box as it looks after you select the Volcano Blend Decaf item to delete it.

Figure 5-17: Delete unwanted items from the Insert Calculated Item dialog box.

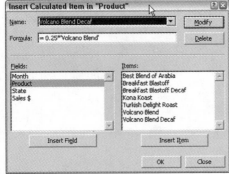

Reviewing Calculated Field and Calculated Item formulas

If you click the PivotTable button on the PivotTable toolbar, click Formulas, and choose List Formulas from the Formulas submenu that appears, Excel adds a new sheet to your workbook. This new sheet, as shown in Figure 5-18, identifies any of the calculated fields and calculated item formulas that you add to the pivot table.

For each calculated field or item, Excel reports on the solve order, the field or item name, and the actual formula. If you have only a small number of fields or items, the solve order doesn't really matter. However, if you have many fields and items that need to be computed in a specific order, the Solve Order field becomes relevant. You can pick the order in which fields and items are calculated. The field and item columns of the worksheet give a field or item name. The formula column shows the actual formula.

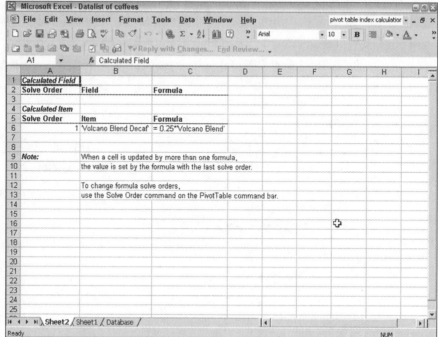

Figure 5-18:
The
Calculated
Field and
Calculated
Item list of
formulas
worksheet.

Reviewing and changing solve order

If you click the PivotTable button on the PivotTable toolbar, click Formulas, and choose Solve Order from the Formulas submenu that appears, Excel displays the Calculated Item Solve Order dialog box, as shown in Figure 5-19. In this dialog box, you tell Excel in what order the calculated item formulas should be solved.

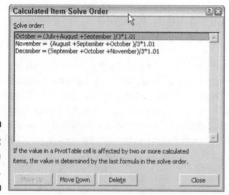

Figure 5-19:
Set solve
order here.

In many cases, the solve order doesn't matter. But if, for example, you add calculated items for October, November, and December to the Kona Koast coffee product sales pivot table shown earlier in the chapter (refer to Figure 5-6), the solve order might just matter. For example, if the October calculated item formula depends on the previous three months and the same thing is true for November and December, you need to calculate those item values in chronological order. Use the Calculated Items Solve Order dialog box to do this. To use the dialog box, simply click a formula in the Solve Order list box. Click the Move Up and Move Down buttons to put the formula at the correct place in line.

Retrieving Data from a Pivot Table

You can build formulas that retrieve data from a pivot table. Like, I don't know, say that you want to chart some of the data shown in a pivot table. You can also retrieve an entire pivot table.

Getting all the values in a pivot table

To retrieve all the information in a pivot table, follow these steps:

1. **Select the pivot table by clicking a cell in the pivot table.**

2. **Click the PivotTable button from the PivotTable toolbar, click Select, and choose Entire Table from the Select submenu that appears.**

   Excel selects the entire pivot table range.

3. **Copy the pivot table.**

   You can copy the pivot table the same way that you would copy any other text in Excel. For example, you can click the Copy toolbar button or you can choose Edit⇨Copy. After you copy the pivot table range, Excel places a copy of your selection onto the Clipboard.

4. **Select a location for the copied data by placing the cursor there.**

5. **Paste the pivot table into the new range.**

   You can paste your pivot table data into the new range in the usual ways: by clicking the Paste button on the toolbar or by choosing Edit⇨Paste. Note, however, that when you paste a pivot table, you get another pivot table. You don't actually get data from the pivot table.

   If you want to get just the data and not the pivot table — in other words, you want a range that includes labels and values, not a pivot table with pivot table buttons — you need to use Edit⇨Paste Special. When you choose the Edit Paste Special command, Excel displays the Edit⇨Paste Special dialog box, as shown in Figure 5-20. In the Paste section of this dialog box, select the Values radio button to indicate that you want to paste just a range of simple labels and values and not a pivot table itself. When you click OK, Excel pastes only the labels and values from the pivot table and not the actual pivot table.

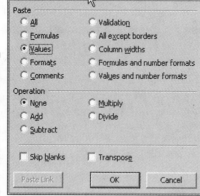

Figure 5-20: Paste information from a pivot table rather than the entire pivot table.

Getting a value from a pivot table

To get a single value from a paragraph using a formula, create a cell reference. For example, suppose that you want to retrieve the value shown in cell C8 in the worksheet shown in Figure 5-21. Further suppose that you want to place this value into cell C15. To do this, click cell C15, type the = sign, click cell C8, and then press Enter. Figure 5-21 shows how your worksheet looks before you press Enter. The formula shows.

As you can see in Figure 5-21, when you retrieve information from an Excel pivot table, the cell reference isn't a simple cell reference as you may expect. Excel uses a special function to retrieve data from a pivot table because Excel knows that you may change the pivot table. Therefore, upon changing the pivot table, Excel needs more information about the cell value or data value that you want than simply its previous cell address.

Look a little more closely at the get pivot table formula shown in Figure 5-21. The actual formula is

```
=GETPIVOTDATA("Sales$",$A$3,"Product","KonaKoast","State",
"Oregon")
```

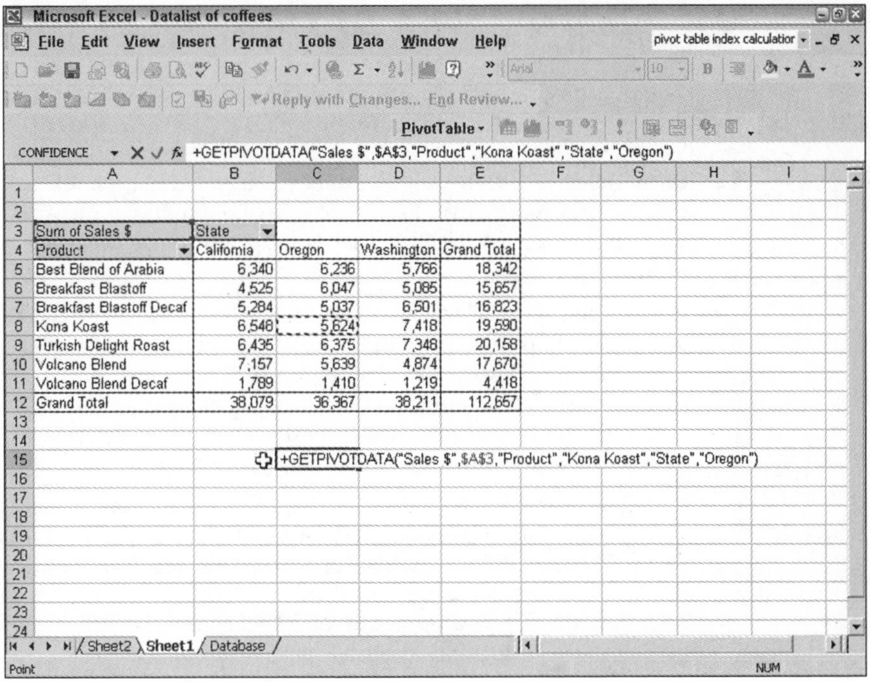

Figure 5-21: How the worksheet looks after you tell Excel you want to place the Kona Koast sales for Oregon value into cell C15.

The easiest way to understand the GETPIVOTDATA function arguments is by using the Insert Function command. To show you how this works, assume that you do enter a Get Pivot Data function formula into cell C15. This is the formula that Figure 5-21 shows. If you then click cell C15 and choose the Insert⇨Function command, Excel displays the Function Arguments dialog box, as shown in Figure 5-22. The Function Arguments dialog box, as you may already know if you're familiar with Excel functions, enables you to add or change arguments for a function. In essence, the Function Arguments dialog box names and describes each of the arguments used in a function.

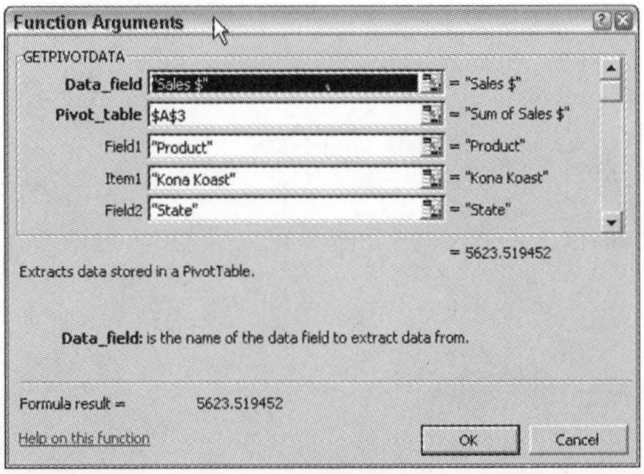

Figure 5-22: The Function Arguments dialog box for the GETPIVOT-DATA function.

Arguments of the GETPIVOTDATA function

Here I quickly go through and describe each of the GETPIVOTDATA function arguments. The bulleted list that follows names and describes each argument:

- **Data_field:** The data_field argument names the data field that you want to grab information from. The data_field name in Figure 5-22 is Sales $. This simply names the item that you drop into the Drop Items Here area of the pivot table.

- **Pivot_table:** The pivot_table argument identifies the pivot table. All you need to do here is to provide a cell reference that's part of the pivot table. In the GETPIVOTDATA function that I use in Figure 5-21, for example, the pivot_table argument is $A$3. Because cell A3 is at the top-left corner of the pivot table, this is all the identification that the function needs in order to identify the correct pivot table.

- **Field1** and **Item1:** The field1 and item1 arguments work together to identify which product information that you want the GETPIVOTDATA function to retrieve. Cell C8 holds Kona Koast sales information. Therefore, the field1 argument is product, and the item1 argument is Kona Koast. Together, these two arguments tell Excel to retrieve the Kona Koast product sales information from the pivot table.

- **Field2** and **Item2:** The field2 and item2 arguments tell Excel to retrieve just Oregon state sales of the Kona Koast product from the pivot table. Field2 shows the argument state. Item2, which isn't visible in Figure 5-22, shows as Oregon.

Chapter 6

Working with PivotCharts

*I*n Chapter 4, I discuss how cool it is that Excel easily cross-tabulates data in pivot tables. In this chapter, I cover a closely related topic: how to cross-tabulate data in pivot charts.

You may notice some suspiciously similar material in this chapter compared with Chapter 4. But that's all right. The steps for creating a pivot chart closely resemble those that you take to create a pivot table.

If you've just read the preceding paragraphs and find yourself thinking, "Hmmm. *Cross-tabulate* is a familiar-sounding word, but I can't quite put my finger on what it means," you may want to first peruse Chapter 4. Let me also say that, as is the case when constructing pivot tables, you build pivot charts by using data stored in an Excel list. Therefore, you should also know what Excel lists are and how they work and should look. I discuss this information a little bit in Chapter 4 and a bunch in Chapter 1.

Why Use a PivotChart?

Before I get into the nitty-gritty details of creating a pivot chart, stop and ask a reasonable question: *When would you or should you use a pivot chart?* Well, the correct answer to this question is, "Heck, most of the time you won't use a pivot chart. You'll use a pivot table instead."

Pivot charts, in fact, only work in certain situations: Specifically, pivot charts work when you have only a limited number of rows in your cross-tabulation. Say, less than half a dozen rows. And pivot charts work when it makes sense to show information visually, such as in a bar chart.

These two factors mean that for many cross-tabulations, you won't use pivot charts. In some cases, for example, a pivot chart won't be legible because the underlying cross-tabulation will have too many rows. In other cases, a pivot chart won't make sense because its information doesn't become more understandable when presented visually.

Getting Ready to Pivot

As with a pivot table, in order to create a pivot chart, your first step is to create the Excel list that you want to cross-tabulate. You don't have to put the information into a list, but working with information that's already stored in a list is easiest, so that's the approach that I assume you'll use.

Figure 6-1 shows an example data list — this time, a list of specialty coffee roasts that you can pretend sell to upscale, independent coffeehouses along the West Coast.

The roast coffee list workbook is available in the Zip file of example Excel workbooks related to this book and stored at the Dummies Web site. You may want to download this list in order to follow along with the discussion here. The URL is www.dummies.com/extras.

Figure 6-1:
A simple
Excel data
list that
shows sales
for your
imaginary
coffee
business.

	A	B	C	D
1	Month	Product	State	Sales $
2	January	Volcano Blend	California	$912
3	January	Turkish Delight Roast	California	$876
4	January	Turkish Delight Roast	Oregon	$548
5	January	Breakfast Blastoff	Oregon	$248
6	January	Best Blend of Arabia	California	$35
7	January	Kona Koast	California	$462
8	January	Best Blend of Arabia	Oregon	$511
9	January	Breakfast Blastoff Decaf	Oregon	$476
10	February	Breakfast Blastoff Decaf	Washington	$930
11	February	Breakfast Blastoff	Washington	$60
12	February	Turkish Delight Roast	California	$383
13	February	Kona Koast	California	$846
14	February	Best Blend of Arabia	California	$909
15	February	Volcano Blend	California	$986
16	February	Breakfast Blastoff Decaf	Oregon	$901
17	February	Breakfast Blastoff	Oregon	$394
18	February	Turkish Delight Roast	Oregon	$250
19	February	Kona Koast	Oregon	$198
20	February	Best Blend of Arabia	Oregon	$156
21	February	Volcano Blend	Oregon	$800
22	February	Breakfast Blastoff Decaf	Washington	$748
23	February	Breakfast Blastoff	Washington	$910
24	February	Turkish Delight Roast	Washington	$122
25	February	Kona Koast	Washington	$483

Running the PivotTable Wizard

Because you typically create a pivot chart by starting with the PivotTable Wizard, I describe that approach first. (Actually, the wizard is technically called the PivotTable and PivotChart Wizard, but that gets a little long-winded.) At the very end of the chapter, however, I describe briefly another method for creating a pivot table: using the PivotChart Wizard on an existing pivot table.

To run the PivotTable Wizard to create a pivot chart, take the following steps:

1. Select the Excel list.

For example, click the upper-left corner of the list's worksheet range and then drag the mouse to the bottom-right corner of the list's worksheet range. Alternatively, you can click the upper-left corner, hold down the Shift key, press the End key, press the right-arrow key, press the End key, and then press the down-arrow key.

2. Tell Excel that you want to create a pivot chart by choosing Data⇨PivotTable and PivotChart Report.

Excel displays the PivotTable and PivotChart Wizard dialog box, as shown in Figure 6-2.

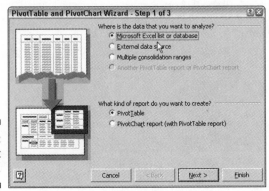

Figure 6-2:
Create pivot tables here.

3. Answer the question about where the data that you want to analyze is stored.

I recommend you store the to-be-analyzed data in an Excel list. If you do so, select the Microsoft Excel List Or Database radio button. (You can, if you want, analyze data stored in some external data source, in multiple worksheet ranges, and in another pivot table or pivot chart report. Just select one of the other radio buttons here to make this choice.)

4. Indicate that you want to create a pivot chart.

To answer the wizard's question `What kind of report do you want to create?`, select the PivotChart Report (with PivotTable Report) radio button.

5. Click the Next button.

Excel displays the second PivotTable and PivotChart Wizard dialog box page, as shown in Figure 6-3.

6. Use the second page of the PivotTable and PivotChart Wizard dialog box to tell Excel in what worksheet range the to-be-analyzed data is stored.

If you followed Step 1, Excel should already have filled in the Range text box with the worksheet range that holds the to-be-analyzed data, but you should verify that the worksheet range shown in the Range text box is correct.

If you skipped Step 1, enter the list range into the Range textbox. You can do so in two ways. You can type the range coordinates. For example, if the range is cell A1 to cell D225, you can type $A$1:$D$225. Alternatively, you can click the button at the right end of the Range textbox. Excel collapses the PivotTable And PivotChart Wizard dialog box, as shown in Figure 6-4. Now use the mouse or the navigation keys to select the worksheet range that holds the list you want to pivot.

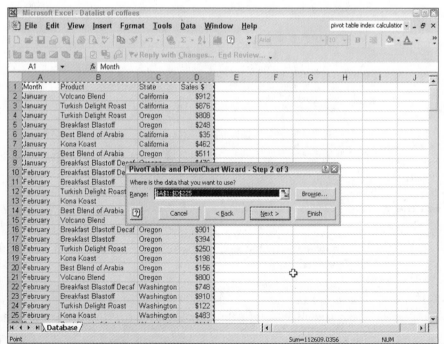

Figure 6-3:
Tell the
wizard
where your
data is.

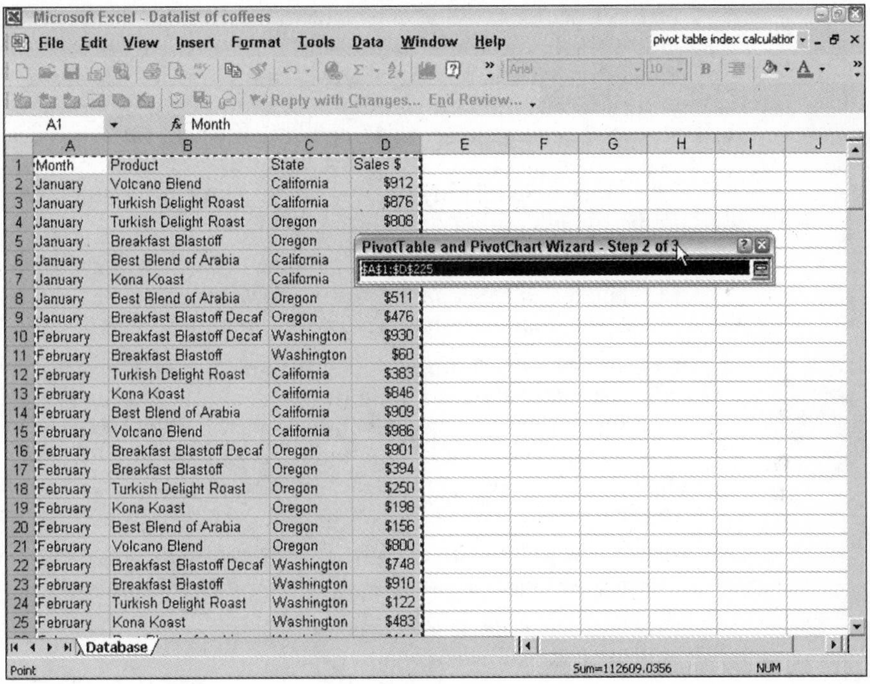

Figure 6-4:
Enter a pivot table range here.

After you select the worksheet range, click the range button again. Excel redisplays the second step page of the PivotTable and PivotChart Wizard dialog box. (Refer to Figure 6-3.)

7. Click Next.

Excel displays the third and final step of the PivotTable and PivotChart dialog box, as shown in Figure 6-5.

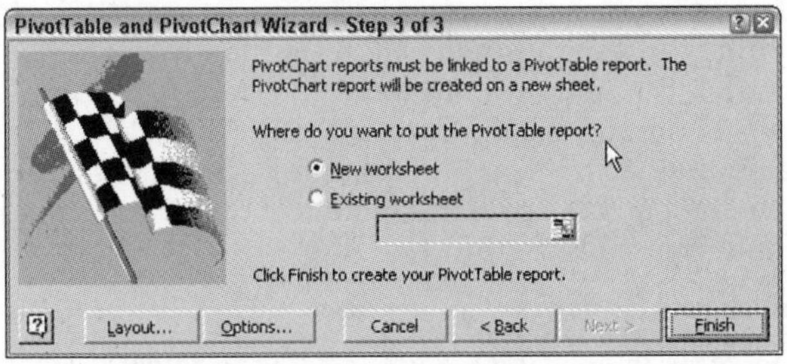

Figure 6-5:
Decide where to put your pivot table report.

8. Tell Excel where to place the new pivot table report that goes along with your pivot chart.

Select either the New Worksheet or Existing Worksheet radio button to select a location for the new pivot table that supplies the data to your pivot chart. Most often, you want to place the new pivot table onto a new worksheet in the existing workbook — the workbook that holds the Excel list that you're analyzing with a pivot chart. However, if you want, you can place the new pivot table into an existing worksheet. If you do this, you need to select the Existing Worksheet radio button and also make an entry in the Existing Worksheet text box to identify the worksheet range. To identify the worksheet range here, enter the cell name in the top-left corner of the worksheet range.

You don't tell Excel where to place the new pivot chart, by the way. Excel inserts a new chart sheet in the workbook that you use for the pivot table and uses that new chart sheet for the pivot table.

Ignore the Layout button. It just displays a dialog box that gives you another, inferior way to build the pivot chart. You can also ignore the Options button. Clicking it just displays the PivotTable Options dialog box, which I describe in Chapter 4. (Essentially, the PivotTable Options dialog box enables you to describe what formatting Excel should apply to the pivot table.)

9. **When you finish with the third and final page of the PivotTable and PivotChart Wizard dialog box, click the Finish button.**

   Excel displays the new workbook with the partially constructed pivot chart in it, as shown in Figure 6-6.

10. **Select the data series.**

    You need to decide first what you want to plot in the chart — or what data series should show in a chart.

If you haven't worked with Excel charting tools before, determining what the right data series are seems confusing at first. But this is another one of those situations where somebody's taken a ten-cent idea and labeled it with a five-dollar word. *Charts* show data series. And a *chart legend* names the *data series* that a chart shows. For example, if you want to plot sales of coffee products, those coffee products are your data series.

After you identify your data series — suppose that you decide to plot coffee products — you drag the field from the PivotTable Field list box to the rectangle marked Drop Series Fields Here. To use coffee products as your data series, for example, drag the Product field to the Drop Series Fields Here box. Using the example data from Figure 6-1, after you do this, the partially constructed Excel pivot chart looks like the one shown in Figure 6-7.

11. **Select the data category.**

    Your second step in creating a pivot chart is to select the data category. The data category organizes the values in a data series. That sounds complicated, but in many charts, identifying the data category is easy. In any chart (including a pivot chart) that shows how some value changes over time, the data category is *time*. In the case of this example pivot chart, to show how coffee product sales change over time, the data category is *time*. Or, more precisely, the data category uses the Months field.

Drag one of these Data Series to the Drop Series Fields Here box.

Drop Series Fields Here

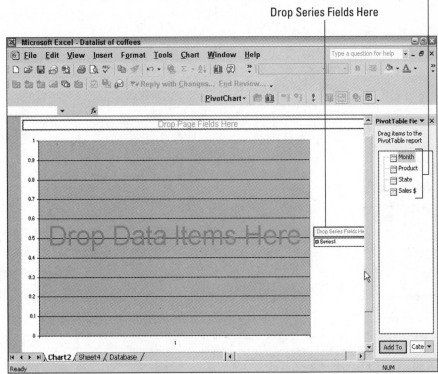

Figure 6-6:
A cross-tabulation before you tell Excel what to cross-tabulate.

After you make this choice, you drag the data category field item from the PivotTable Field list to the box marked Drop Category Fields Here, which isn't visible in Figure 6-7 but appears beneath the horizontal axis. Figure 6-8 shows the way that the partially constructed pivot chart looks after you specify the data category as Months.

12. Select the data item that you want to chart.

After you choose the data series and data category for your pivot chart, you indicate what piece of data that you want plotted in your pivot chart. For example, to plot sales revenue, drag the Sales $ item from the PivotTable Field list to the rectangle labeled Drop Data Items Here.

Figure 6-9 shows the pivot table after the Data Series (Step 10), Data Category (Step 11), and Data Items (Step 12) have been selected. This is a completed pivot chart. Note that it cross-tabulates information from the Excel list shown in Figure 6-1. Each bar in the pivot chart shows sales for a month. Each bar is made up of colored segments that represent the sales contribution made by each coffee product. Obviously, you can't see the colors in a black-and-white image like the one shown in Figure 6-9. But on your computer monitor, you can see the colored segments and the bars that they make.

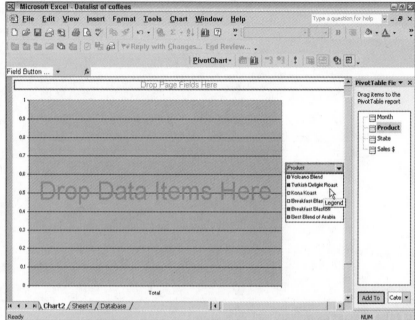

Figure 6-7:
The cross-tabulation after you select a data series.

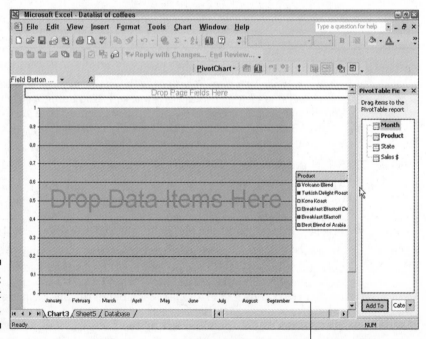

Figure 6-8:
And it just gets better.

The Months category is now visible on the horizontal axis.

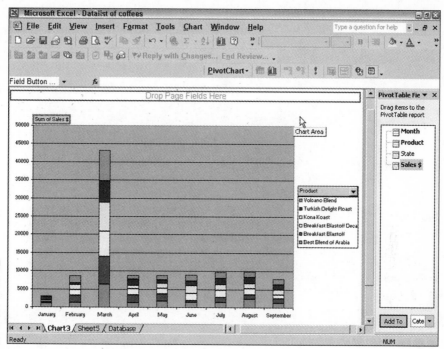

Figure 6-9:
The
completed
pivot chart.

Fooling Around with Your Pivot Chart

After you construct your pivot chart, you can further analyze your data. Here I briefly describe some of the cool tools that Excel provides for manipulating information in a pivot chart.

Pivoting and re-pivoting

The thing that gives the pivot tables and pivot charts their names is that you can continue cross-tabulating, or pivoting, the data. For example, you could take the data shown in Figure 6-9 and by swapping the data series and data categories — you do this merely by dragging the State and Product buttons — you can flip-flop the organization of the pivot chart. The chart in Figure 6-10 shows the same information as Figure 6-9. The difference is that the new pivot chart uses the State field rather than the Month field as the data category. The new pivot chart continues to use the Product field as the data series.

Another thing to note is that pivot tables don't restrict you to using just two items to cross-tabulate data. For example, in both the pivot charts shown in Figures 6-9 and 6-10, I use only a single chart to show cross-tabulated data.

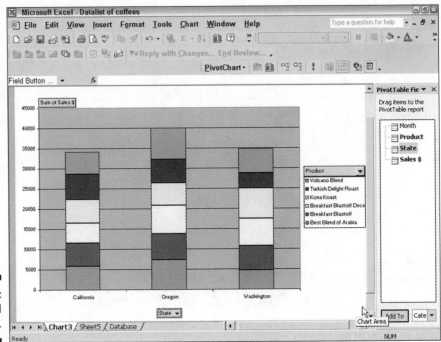

Figure 6-10:
A re-pivoted
pivot chart.

You can also segregate data by putting information on different charts. For example, if you drag the month data item to the Drop Page Fields Here rectangle, which appears at the top of the chart sheet, Excel creates the pivot table shown in Figure 6-11. This pivot table lets you view sales information for all the months, as shown in Figure 6-11, or just one of the months. In Figure 6-11, note the Month drop-down box in the upper-left corner. This box is by default set to display all the months (All), so the chart in Figure 6-11 looks just like Figure 6-10. Things really start to happen, however, when you want to look at just one month's data.

To show sales for only a single month, click the down-arrow button to the right of the Month drop-down list box. Then, when Excel displays the drop-down list box shown in Figure 6-12, select the month that you want to see sales for and then click OK. Figure 6-13 shows sales for just the month of January.

To remove an item from the pivot chart, you simply drag the item's button back to the PivotTable Field list.

You can also filter data based on the data series or the data category. In the case of the pivot chart shown in Figure 6-13, you can indicate that you want to see only a particular data series information by clicking the arrow button to the right of the Product drop-down list box. When Excel displays the drop-down list box of coffee products, you select the coffee that you want to see sales for. You can use the State drop-down list box in a similar fashion to see sales for only a particular state.

Let me mention one other tidbit about pivoting and re-pivoting. If you've worked with pivot tables, you may remember that you can cross-tabulate by more than one row or column items. You can do something very similar with pivot charts. You can become more granular in your data series or data categories by dragging another field item to the Drop Series Items Here or Drop Category Items Here box.

Figure 6-14 shows how the pivot table looks if State is used to add granularity to the Product data series.

Sometimes lots of granularity in a cross-tabulation makes sense. But having multiple row items and multiple column items in a pivot table makes more sense than adding lots of granularity to pivot charts by creating superfine data series or data categories. Too much granularity in a pivot chart turns your chart into an impossible-to-understand visual mess, a bit like the disaster that I show in Figure 6-14.

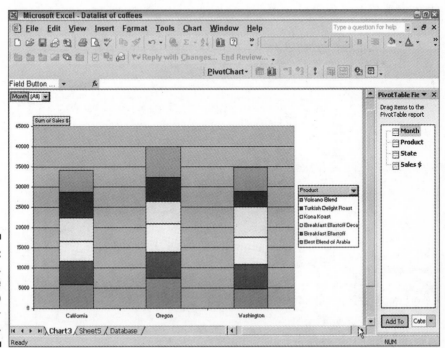

Figure 6-11: Whoa. Now I use months to cross-tabulate.

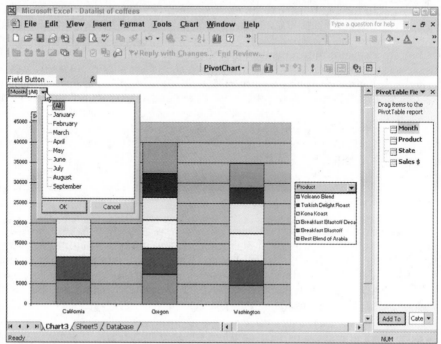

Figure 6-12:
The filter
drop-down
list box.

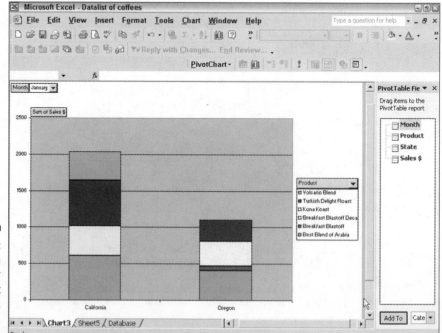

Figure 6-13:
You
can filter
pivot chart
information,
too.

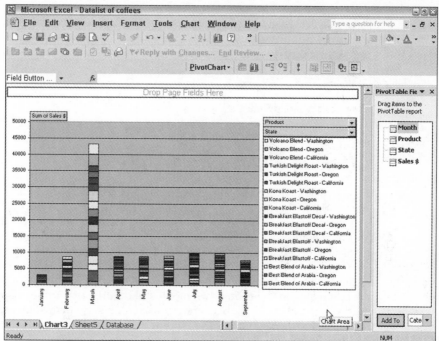

Figure 6-14:
Yet another
cross-
tabulation
of the data.

Refreshing pivot chart data

As the data in an Excel list changes, you need to update the pivot chart. You have three methods for telling Excel to refresh your chart:

- ✔ **You can click the Refresh data tool** — it bears an exclamation mark — on the PivotTable toolbar. (See Figure 6-15.)

- ✔ **You can choose the Refresh Data command from the PivotTable menu.** The PivotTable menu appears when you click the PivotTable tool on the PivotTable toolbar. (See Figure 6-15.)

- ✔ **You can choose the Refresh Data command** from the shortcut menu that Excel displays when you right-click a pivot chart.

Figure 6-15 shows the PivotTable toolbar.

Point to an Excel toolbar button, and Excel displays pop-up tooltips that give the button name.

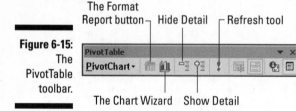

The Format
Report button— Hide Detail — Refresh tool

Figure 6-15:
The
PivotTable
toolbar.

The Chart Wizard Show Detail

Filtering Pivot Chart Data

You can filter pivot chart data. However, you don't use the Data⇔Filter menu commands. Rather, you click the down-arrow button next to the item button. For example, if you want to see only sales for the state of California in the pivot table, you could click the down-arrow button next to the State item. When you do this, Excel displays a drop-down list box like the one shown in Figure 6-16.

To see only sales from California, you would verify that the California check box is selected in the drop-down menu and that the other check boxes are clear. When you click OK, Excel re-cross-tabulates the data showing sales to California. Figure 6-17 shows the pivot table after this change is made.

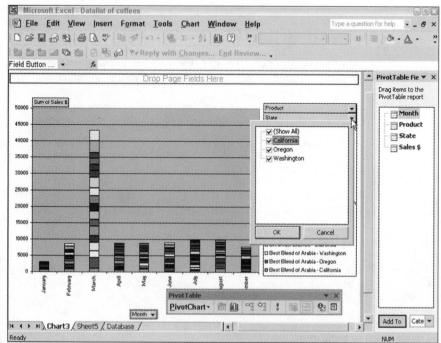

Figure 6-16:
The filter
drop-down
list box.

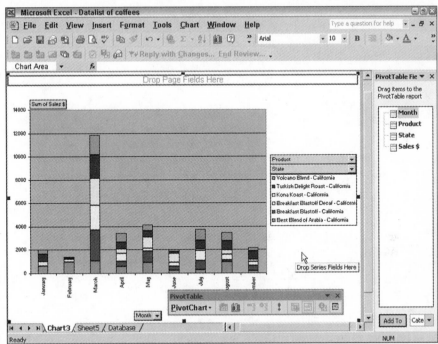

Figure 6-17:
A filtered
pivot chart.

Grouping and ungrouping data items

You can group together and ungroup values plotted in a pivot chart. For example, suppose that you want to take the pivot chart shown in Figure 6-18 — which is very granular — and hide some of the detail. You might want to combine the detailed information shown for Volcano Blend and show just the total sales of Volcano Blend.

To do this, select a Volcano Blend data marker. In the case of the pivot chart shown in Figure 6-18, this means that you click one of the bars that show information about sales of Volcano Blend.

Different types of charts use different types of data markers. A bar chart, for example, uses bars as data markers. A line chart uses lines, and so on.

After you hide the detail — this is what happens when you group data, of course — Excel groups the detailed information and reports just the group total. As shown in Figure 6-19, Excel still displays information about Volcano Blend sales in the pivot chart, but not detailed information by month, which is what shows in Figure 6-18.

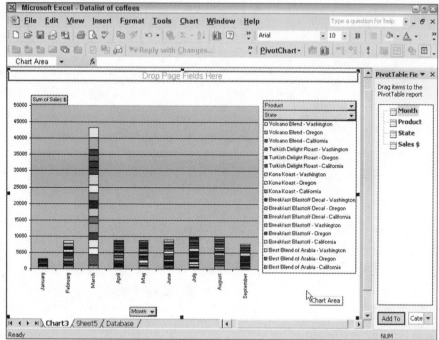

Figure 6-18:
A pivot
chart with
too much
detail.

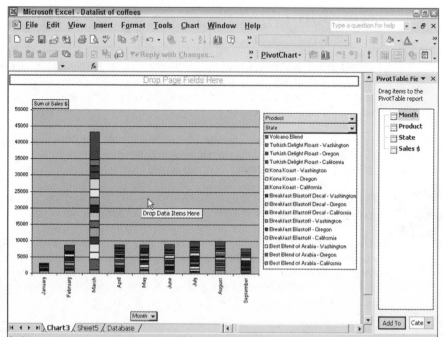

Figure 6-19:
A pivot
chart that
looks a little
bit better.

To show previously hidden detail, right-click the data marker that shows the grouped detail. Then choose the Show Detail command from the menu that appears. Excel removes the grouping from your pivot table.

You can also drill down and see more detail about a data marker's value by using the Show Detail command. Right-click a data marker that shows the lowest level of detail and choose the Show Detail command; then Excel displays the Show Detail dialog box, as shown in Figure 6-20. You select the field that you want to use to further breakdown the data and then click OK.

Figure 6-20:
The Show Detail dialog box.

What are field settings?

The field settings for a pivot chart work the same way as field settings for a pivot table. The settings determine what Excel does with a field when it's cross-tabulated in the pivot chart. For example, if you right-click one of the sales revenue amounts shown in the pivot chart and then choose Format PivotChart Field from the shortcut menu that appears, Excel displays the PivotTable Field dialog box, as shown in Figure 6-21.

Figure 6-21:
The PivotTable Field dialog box.

From the PivotTable Field dialog box, you indicate whether the data item should be summed, counted, averaged, and so on. By default, data items are summed. But you can also arithmetically manipulate data items in other ways by choices that you can select from the Summarize By list box. You can calculate average sales (Average), find the largest value (Max) or the smallest value (Min), the number of sales transactions (Count), and so on. Essentially, the PivotTable Field dialog box identifies the arithmetic operation that you want Excel to perform on data items stored in the pivot table.

I describe the options that appear when you click the Options button in Chapter 5. So if you have questions, you might want to refer there.

Using Chart Wizard to Create PivotCharts

You can use Excel's standard charting tool, called *Chart Wizard*, to create pivot charts. You might choose to use the Chart Wizard tool when you've already created a pivot table and now want to use that data in a chart.

To create a pivot chart using Chart Wizard, follow these steps:

1. **Create a pivot table.**

   For help on how to do this, refer to Chapter 4 for the blow-by-blow account.

2. **Click a cell in the pivot table.**

3. **Tell Chart Wizard to create a pivot chart by choosing the Insert➪Chart command.**

   Alternatively, you can click the Chart Wizard toolbar button. This button shows a picture of a chart, but remember that you can point to any toolbar in Excel and see the toolbar name in a pop-up screen tip.

   The Chart Wizard creates a pivot chart that matches your pivot table.

How Chart Wizard normally works, by the way, is that you set up a worksheet with the data that you want to plot in a chart. Then you select the data and tell Chart Wizard to plot the data. You can tell Chart Wizard to chart either by choosing the Insert➪Chart command or by clicking the Chart Wizard button on the toolbar. Excel then runs the Chart Wizard. It just walks you through the steps for charting your data using three dialog boxes. To do this, you essentially verify your data selection, pick a chart type (line chart, bar chart, pie chart, or whatever) and then make some formatting choices. When you use Chart Wizard to create a pivot chart, as the preceding steps indicate, the Chart Wizard doesn't ask you any additional questions or walk you through screens. It just charts.

By the way, in this chapter, I don't describe how to customize the actual pivot chart . . . but I didn't forget that topic. Pivot chart customization as a subject is so big that it gets its own chapter: Chapter 7.

How about just charting pivot table data?

You can chart a pivot table, too. I mean, if you just want to use pivot table data in a regular old chart, you can do so. Here's how. First, copy the pivot table data to a separate range. Start the Chart Wizard by selecting Insert⇨Chart. Then use the Chart Wizard in the usual way to create a chart based on the copied data.

Chapter 7

Customizing PivotCharts

· ·

· ·

Although you usually get pretty good-looking pivot charts by using the wizard, you'll sometimes want to customize the charts that Excel creates. Sometimes you'll decide that you want a different type of chart . . . perhaps to better communicate the chart's message. And sometimes you want to change the colors so that they match the personality of the presentation or the presenter. In this chapter, I describe how to make these and other changes to your pivot charts.

Selecting a Chart Type

The first step in customizing a pivot chart is to choose the chart type that you want. When the active sheet in an Excel workbook shows a chart, Excel adds the Chart menu to the Excel menu bar. The first command on the Chart menu is Chart Type. If you choose the Chart⇨Chart Type command, Excel displays the Chart Type dialog box, as shown in Figure 7-1.

The Chart Type dialog box, as shown in Figure 7-1, has two tabs (Standard Types and Custom Types) from which you pick the type of chart that you want. Most often you make choices from the Standard Types tab; here the Chart Type list box identifies each of the 14 chart types that Excel plots. You can choose chart types such as Column, Bar, Line, Pie, and so on. For each chart type, Excel also displays several subtypes; pictographs of these display on the right side of the Standard Types tab. You can think of a chart subtype as a flavor or model or mutation. You choose a chart type and chart subtype by selecting a chart from the Chart Type list box and then clicking a Chart Sub-Type button.

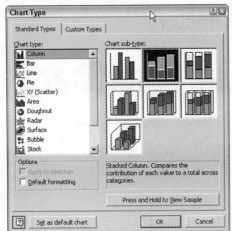

Figure 7-1:
Select your
chart type
here.

At the bottom-right of the Standard tab, Excel provides a Press and Hold to View Sample button. Clicking this button previews what the selected chart type and sub-type look like based on your data. For example, look at Figure 7-2 to see how a sample chart appears based on the line chart type and one of the line chart sub-types.

The Custom Types tab of the Chart Type dialog box, as shown in Figure 7-3, displays the special chart types. You use custom chart types that create area block charts, black and white area charts, black and white (B&W) column charts, and so on. But you typically don't use these chart types. That's why they're not on the standard tab.

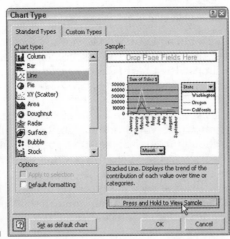

Figure 7-2:
Preview
your
chart type
choices
here.

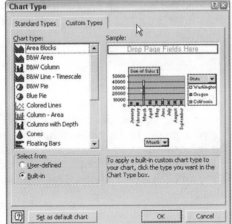

Figure 7-3:
Choose
custom
chart types
here.

Setting Chart Options

Choosing Chart⇨Chart Options displays the Chart Options dialog box. The Chart Options dialog box provides six different tabs that let you customize just about any element of your pivot chart, including titles, axes, gridlines, legends, data labels, and data tables.

Chart titles

The Titles tab of the Chart Options dialog box, as shown in Figure 7-4, provides text boxes that you can use to provide labels for the chart title, the category axis, and the value axis. When you have a secondary category or value axis, the Titles tab also provides text boxes that you can use to supply these bits of descriptive information.

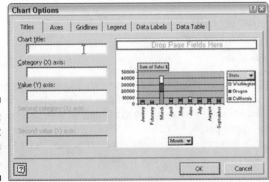

Figure 7-4:
Set chart
and axis
titles here.

Like the other Chart Options tabs, the Titles tab provides a small picture of your pivot chart. This picture shows the effect of your chart option selections and changes.

Chart axes

The Axes tab of the Chart Options dialog box, as shown in Figure 7-5, is where you tell Excel whether your pivot chart should include a category (X) axis and a value (Y) axis. You indicate that you want an axis by selecting the appropriate axis check box. For example, if you want a category axis on your pivot chart, you select the Category (X) Axis text box. The same steps work for adding or removing a value axis.

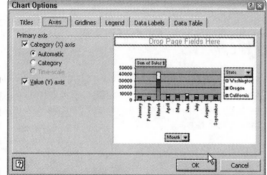

Figure 7-5:
Set category and value axes here.

If you do include or add a category axis to your pivot chart, Excel provides radio buttons (Automatic, Category, and Time-scale) that you can select to fine tune the appearance of the category axis. The best way to find out what these radio buttons do is to just experiment with them. In some cases, selecting the different category axis radio button has no effect. You can't use the Time-scale option unless your chart shows time series data — and Excel realizes it.

Chart gridlines

Options on the Gridlines tab of the Chart Options dialog box, as shown in Figure 7-6, enable you to add and remove gridlines to the category (X) axis and to the value (Y) axis. To add or remove gridlines to either axis, simply select or deselect the appropriate check box. When you make these choices, Excel updates the small picture of the chart shown on the Chart Options dialog box, and you see the effects of your changes.

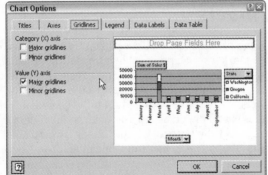

Figure 7-6:
The
Gridlines
Tab of the
Chart
Options
dialog box.

Chart legend

Use the Legend tab of the Chart Options dialog box, as shown in Figure 7-7, to add or remove a legend to a pivot chart. Here you can also choose where a chart legend should be placed. A *chart legend* simply identifies the data series plotted in your chart.

You can guess how the Legend tab works. To add a legend to your pivot chart, select the Show Legend check box; to remove it, clear the Show Legend text box. Duh.

Use the Placement radio buttons to choose a location for your pivot chart legend. If you want the legend to appear to the right of the pivot chart, for example, select the Right radio button. To direct Excel to locate the legend in some other position, select one of the other placement radio buttons: Bottom, Corner, Top, or Left.

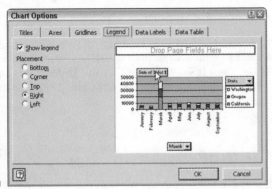

Figure 7-7:
Add a
legend and
set its
placement
here.

Chart data labels

From the Data Labels tab of the Chart Options dialog box, as shown in Figure 7-8, you can label data markers with pivot table information or list information. To add data labels, just select the check box that corresponds to the bit of pivot table or Excel list information that you want to use as the label. For example, if you want to label data markers with a pivot table chart using data series names, select the Series Name check box. If you want to label data markers with a category name, select the Category Name check box. To label the data markers with the underlying value, select the Value check box.

Different chart types supply different data label options. Your best bet, therefore, is to experiment with data labels by selecting and deselecting the check boxes in the Label Contains area of the Data Labels tab.

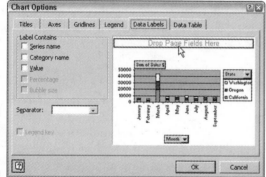

Figure 7-8:
Set data labels here.

Note: The Data Labels tab also provides a Separator drop-down list box, from which you can select the character or symbol (a space, comma, colon, and so on) that you want Excel to use to separate data labeling information.

Selecting the Legend Key check box tells Excel to display a small legend key next to data markers to visually connect the data marker to the legend. This sounds complicated, but it's not. Just select the Legend Key check box to see what it does. (You have to select one of the Label Contains check boxes before this check box is active.)

Chart data tables

A data label may make sense for non-pivot charts, but not for pivot charts. (What a data table does is duplicate the pivot table data that Excel creates as an intermediate step in creating the pivot chart.) Nevertheless, just because I have an obsessive-compulsive personality, I'll explain what the Data Table tab does.

From the Data Table tab of the Chart Options dialog box, as shown in Figure 7-9, you can add a data table to the chart sheet. A *data table* just shows the plotted values in a table and adds the table to the chart. To tell Excel that you want a data table that's part of a chart, select the Show Data Table check box. Figure 7-10 shows a pivot chart with the data table.

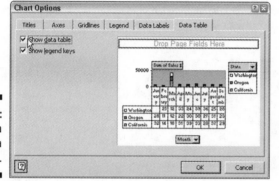

Figure 7-9:
Add a data table to a chart here.

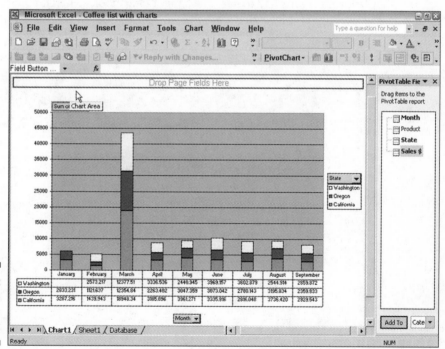

Figure 7-10:
Add a data table to a pivot chart.

Changing a Chart's Location

When you choose the Chart⊃Location command, Excel displays the Chart
Location dialog box, as shown in Figure 7-11. From here, you tell Excel where
it should move a chart. In the case of a pivot chart, this means that you're telling
Excel to move the pivot chart to some new chart sheet or to move the pivot
chart to a worksheet. When you move a pivot chart to a worksheet, the pivot
chart becomes a chart object in the worksheet.

Figure 7-11:
Move a
pivot chart
from here.

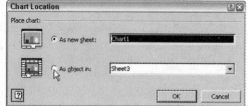

Check out Figure 7-12 to see how a pivot chart looks when it appears as
an object on top of a sheet.

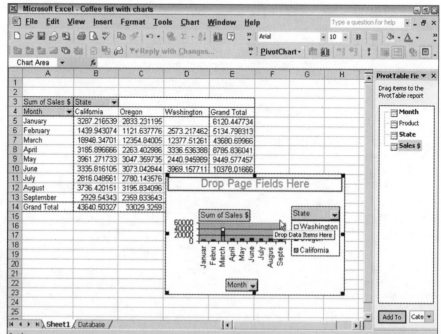

Figure 7-12:
Add a chart
object to a
worksheet.

To tell Excel to place the pivot table on to a new sheet, select the As New Sheet radio button in the Chart Location Dialog Box (refer to Figure 7-11). Then name the new sheet that Excel should create by entering some clever sheet name in the As New Sheet text box.

To tell Excel to add the pivot chart to some existing chart sheet or worksheet as an object, select the As Object In radio button. Then select the name of the chart sheet or worksheet from the As Object In drop-down list box.

Formatting the Plot Area

If you right-click a pivot chart's plot area — the area that shows the plotted data — Excel displays a shortcut menu. Choose the first command on this menu, Format Plot Area, and Excel displays the Format Plot Area dialog box, as shown in Figure 7-13. This dialog box provides a single tab — Patterns — from which you can choose a border for the plot area as well as a background color and pattern.

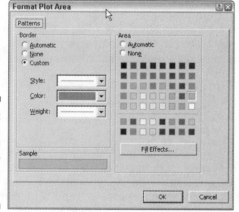

Figure 7-13:
Add a border and fill colors for a plot area here.

To choose a border or change the border for a plot area, select the Custom radio button. Make choices from the Style, Color, and Weight list boxes to choose the line style, color, and thickness that you want to use for your pivot chart's border.

To specify what color and pattern should be used for the pivot chart's plot area, click one of the colored square buttons in the Area section of the Patterns tab. Or, take a walk on the wild side and click the Fill Effects button (bottom-right) to display the Fill Effects dialog box, as shown in Figure 7-14.

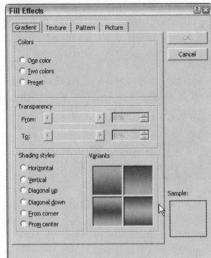

Figure 7-14:
Add plot
area fill
effects here.

The Fill Effects dialog box displays four tabs — Gradient, Texture, Pattern, and Picture — that enable you to pick fill effects for the chart's plot area. I could spend pages describing in painful and tedious detail the buttons and boxes that these four tabs provide, but I have a better idea. If you're really interested in fiddling with the pivot chart plot area fill effects, just noodle around. You'll easily be able to see what effect your changes and customizations have.

Formatting the Chart Area

If you right-click a chart sheet or object outside of the plot area and then choose the Format Chart Area command, Excel displays the Format Chart Area dialog box. From here you can set chart area patterns and also choose fonts and any special character formatting for your charts.

Chart area patterns

The Patterns tab of the Format Chart Area dialog box looks and works like the Patterns tab of the Format Plot area dialog box. (Refer to Figure 7-13.) To choose a border, select the Custom radio button. Use the Style, Color, and Weight list boxes to choose the line style, color, and thickness that you want. To specify what color and pattern should be used for the pivot chart, click one of the colored square buttons. Or, click the Fill Effects button to display the Fill Effects dialog box and use its radio buttons and boxes to make your formatting choices. (Refer to Figure 7-14.)

Chart area fonts

From the Font tab of the Format Chart Area dialog box, as shown in Figure 7-15, you can pick default fonts for the text that appears in the chart area. You can guess or figure out how this works, right? Choose a font from the Font box, and then make that font regular, italic, bold, or bold italic from the Font Style box. Use the Size box to pick a point size. (One point — *pt* — equals ½ inch; the text in this book is 10 pt.)

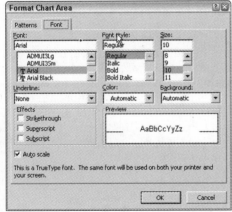

Figure 7-15: Set font formatting here.

The Underline, Color, and Background boxes do what you expect. Use the Underline box to pick a style of underlining for the text; pick a text color from the Color box. Use the Background box to make text background either transparent or opaque.

If you have questions, don't worry. The Preview box shows what your changes look like.

Select the Effects check boxes to add special effects such as strikethrough, superscripts, and subscripts. You wouldn't use these effects, typically, as the default for chart area text. But note that you can also use the Fonts tab to format just a selection of text. In this case, you might use these settings for just that selected blurb. You select text, by the way, by dragging the mouse.

Formatting 3-D Charts

If you choose to create a three-dimensional (3-D) pivot chart, you should know about a couple of commands that apply specifically to this case: the Format Walls command and the 3-D View command.

Formatting the walls of a 3-D chart

After you create a 3-D pivot chart, you can format its walls if you want. Just right-click the wall of the chart and choose the Format Walls command from the shortcut menu that appears. Excel then displays the Format Walls dialog box. The Format Walls dialog box provides a single Patterns tab.

The walls of the 3-D chart are its sides and backs — the sides of the 3-D cube, in other words.

From this tab, select the Custom radio button and then use the Style, Color, and Weight list boxes to choose the line style, color, and thickness for the wall. To specify what color and pattern should be used for the wall, click one of the colored square buttons in the Area portion of the Patterns tab.

If you just can't go on without seeing what the Patterns tab looks like, refer to Figure 7-13 to see the Patterns tab for the Format Plot Area dialog box. The Patterns tab of the Format Walls dialog box is identical.

Using the 3-D View command

After you create a 3-D pivot chart, you can also change the appearance of its 3-D view. Just right-click the chart and choose the 3-D View command from the shortcut menu that appears. Excel then displays the 3-D View dialog box, as shown in Figure 7-16.

The easiest way to work with the 3-D View dialog box is just to click those big buttons labeled with directional arrows. They tell Excel to redraw the pivot chart by using a different elevation, rotation, or perspective. As you click these arrow buttons, you can see what effect you create by looking at the picture shown in the middle of the 3-D View dialog box. When you finish, you can click Apply (to make your changes but leave the dialog box open) or OK (to make your changes and close the dialog box).

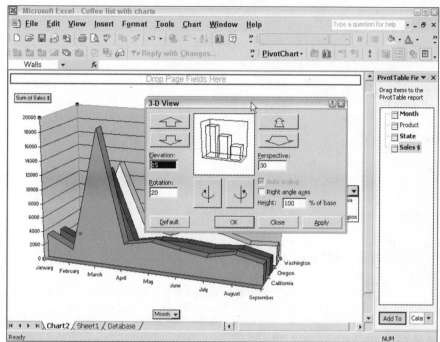

Figure 7-16:
Change the
3-D view of
your chart
here.

Formatting Gridlines

To change the format of a chart gridline, right-click that gridline and choose
the Format Gridlines command from the menu that appears. Excel displays
the Format Gridlines dialog box, which contains two tabs that you can use
to change the appearance of gridlines and to scale gridlines.

Gridline patterns

The Patterns tab of the Format Gridlines dialog box appears in Figure 7-17.
What you use it for is probably pretty obvious. Select from the Line radio buttons to indicate whether you want Excel to automatically choose gridlines or
whether you want to choose a custom gridline. When you select the Custom
radio button, you then use the Style, Color, and Weight list boxes to pick a
gridline style, color, and thickness.

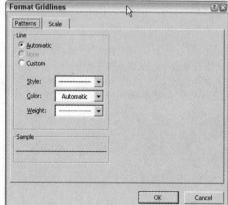

Gridline scale

Use choices from the Scale tab of the Format Gridlines dialog box, as shown in Figure 7-18, to tell Excel how to scale a chart's axes and, as a result, where to draw gridlines. Select the Auto check boxes, for example, to tell Excel to automatically scale the gridline minimum, maximum, major unit, minor unit, and for 3-D charts, the floor. To manually control scaling, deselect (clear) the appropriate check box and then enter a value into its corresponding text box. To manually set the minimum, for example, clear the Minimum check box and then enter the minimum value that you want into the Minimum text box.

Figure 7-18:
Set gridline
scale here.

The Display Units drop-down list box enables you to choose a display scaling unit for the chart, such as Hundreds, Thousands, Millions, and so on. If you don't want to use some display scaling unit, select None from the Display Units drop-down list box.

Don't ignore the three check boxes at the bottom of the Scale tab. They can be pretty darn useful at times:

- ✔ **Logarithmic Scale:** Select the Logarithmic Scale check box to tell Excel to logarithmically scale a chart's gridlines. A *logarithmic scale*, by the way, lets you view rates of change in your plotted data rather than absolute changes. In Chapter 13, I discuss how cool logarithmic scaling is.

- ✔ **Values in Reverse Order:** Select the Values in Reverse Order check box to tell Excel to flip the chart upside down and plot the minimum value at the top of the scale and the maximum value at the bottom of the scale. If this description sounds confusing — and I guess it is — just try this reverse order business with a real chart. You'll instantly see what I mean.

- ✔ **Floor (XY Plane) Crosses at Minimum Value:** Select the Floor (XY Plane) Crosses at Minimum Value check box to tell Excel to place the floor of a 3-D chart at value shown in the Minimum text box.

Formatting Legends

To format a legend, right-click it and choose the Format Legends command from the menu that appears. Excel displays the Format Legends dialog box, which provides three tabs: Patterns, Font, and Placement. (To add a legend to your chart, read the earlier section "Chart legend.")

Legend patterns

The Patterns tab of the Format Legend dialog box looks like the Patterns tab of other formatting dialog boxes. Use the Style, Color, and Weight list boxes to choose the line style, color, and thickness for the box that Excel draws around the legend. To specify what color and pattern should be used for the legend box, click one of the colored square buttons in the Area portion of the Patterns tab. You can preview your choices in the Sample box.

Legend font

The Font tab of the Format Legend dialog box provides text and check boxes that you use to tell Excel what the legend text should look like. Refer to Figure 7-15; the Font tab that you see there is pretty much the same thing. Use choices from the Font tab to specify what font should be used, whether boldface or italics should be used, what point size should be used, and so forth.

Legend placement

The Legend Placement tab of the Format Legend dialog box, as shown in Figure 7-19, provides radio buttons that you use to tell Excel where to locate a legend. I don't need to tell you that you select the radio button that corresponds to the location that you want. You would, of course, guess that immediately. On the subject of legend placement, here's something you might not immediately guess: You can also reposition a legend by dragging it to a new location.

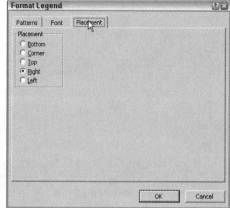

Figure 7-19:
Set legend
placement
here.

Formatting Axes

Ah, Grasshopper, I save the best for last: how to format axes. If you right-click a chart axis and choose the Format Axis command, Excel displays the Format Axis dialog box. This dialog box provides five tabs: Patterns, Scale, Font, Number, and Alignment. Each deserves at least a few words of discussion.

Axis patterns

The Patterns tab of the Format Axis dialog box, as shown in Figure 7-20, sort of resembles the Patterns tab of other chart formatting dialog boxes. The tab provides Style, Color, and Weight list boxes to choose the line style, color, and thickness for the axis, for example. However, the Axis Patterns tab provides some other radio button choices, too. From these you can indicate where Excel should show draw tick marks on the axis and whether Excel should label the tick marks. Tick marks, as the radio button descriptions suggest, can appear on the side of the axis that's outside the plot area, on the side of the axis that is inside the plot area, and so on.

Axis scale

Use choices from the Scale tab of the Format Axis dialog box, as shown in Figure 7-21, to tell Excel how to scale an axis and draw gridlines. You can select the Auto check boxes, for example, to have Excel automatically scale the axis minimum, maximum, major unit, minor unit, and for 3-D charts, the floor. If you want to manually control scaling, you can clear the appropriate check box and then enter a value into its corresponding text box. To manually set the minimum, for example, deselect the Minimum box and then enter the minimum value that you want into the Minimum text box.

Note: The Scale tab of the Format Axis dialog box displays the same options as the Scale tab of the Format Gridlines dialog box. (Refer to Figure 7-18.) For example, if you use the Scale tab of the Format Axis dialog box to fiddle-faddle with the axis scaling, those changes affect gridline scaling — and they show up on the Scale tab of the Format Gridlines dialog box.

The Scale tab of the Format Axis dialog box provides several other scaling options, too:

- ✔ Select from the drop-down list box of Display Units to choose a display scaling unit for the chart, such as Hundreds, Thousands, Millions, and so on.

- ✔ Select the Logarithmic Scale check box to tell Excel to logarithmically scale the chart's gridlines.

- ✔ Select the Values in Reverse Order check box to tell Excel to flip the chart upside down and plot the minimum value at the top of the scale and the maximum value at the bottom of the scale.

- ✔ If you're working with a three-dimensional chart, select the Floor (XY Plane) Crosses at Minimum Value check box to tell Excel to place the floor of a 3-D chart at value shown in the Minimum text box.

Axis font

Hey, this will be a big surprise. The Font tab of the Format Axis dialog box provides text and check boxes that you use to tell Excel what axis text should look like. From choices on the Font tab, you can specify what font should be used, whether boldface or italics should be used, what point size should be used, and so forth. (Refer to Figure 7-15 for a similar Font tab.)

Axis number style

The Number tab of the Format Axis dialog box, as shown in Figure 7-22, provides text and check boxes that you use to tell Excel what numeric formatting that it should use for the numbers that describe an axis's scale. This is the same Number tab that you use (and may be already familiar with) for formatting values in a worksheet range. You first pick a numeric format from the Category list box. Then, if available, you use any additional text or check boxes to fine-tune the formatting. In Figure 7-22, for example, you can specify how many decimal places Excel should use, pick a thousands separator symbol, and specify how negative values should be handled.

The Linked to Source check box, if marked, tells Excel to use the same formatting for the numbers as the values being displayed.

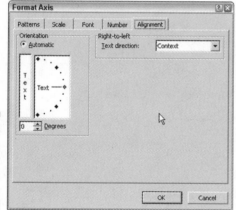

Figure 7-22:
Format axis
numerals
here.

Axis alignment

The Alignment tab of the Format Axis dialog box, as shown in Figure 7-23, provides options and controls that you use to tell Excel how axis text should be oriented and in what direction text should be read.

Figure 7-23:
Orient axis
text
alignment
here.

If you just want Excel to automatically orient text, select the Automatic radio button. If instead you want to manually orient text, drag the text rotation tool (drag on the red diamond) or adjust the value in the Degrees text box. To specify that text should read in some direction other than from left to right, select an option from the Text Direction drop-down list box.

Part III
Advanced Tools

The 5th Wave · By Rich Tennant

"NIFTY CHART, FRANK, BUT NOT ENTIRELY NECESSARY."

In this part . . .

Read here to find out about some mighty useful whistles and bells available to advanced Excel users. It'd be a shame if you didn't at least know what they are and the basic steps that you need to use them. In Part III, I cover using database and statistical functions, descriptive and inferential statistics, and how to use the Excel Solver.

Chapter 8

Using the Database Functions

*E*xcel provides a special set of functions, called *database functions*, especially for simple statistical analysis of information that you store in Excel lists. In this chapter, I describe and illustrate these functions.

Interested in statistical analysis of information that's *not* stored in an Excel list? Then you can use Chapter 8 as a resource for descriptions of functions that you use for analysis when your information isn't in an Excel list.

Note: Excel also provides a rich set of statistical functions, which are also wonderful tools for analyzing information in an Excel list. Skip to Chapter 9 for details on these statistical functions.

Quickly Reviewing Functions

The Excel database functions work like other Excel functions. In a nutshell, when you want to use a function, you create a formula that includes the function. Because I don't discuss functions in detail anywhere else in this book — and because you need to be relatively proficient with the basics of using functions in order to employ them in any data analysis — I review some basics here, including function syntax and entering functions.

Understanding function syntax rules

Most functions need arguments, or *inputs*. And all database functions need arguments. You include these arguments inside parenthesis marks. If a function needs more than one argument, you separate arguments by using commas.

For illustration purposes, here are a couple of example formulas that use simple functions. These aren't database functions, by the way. I get to those in later sections of this chapter. Read through these examples to become proficient with the everyday functions. (Or just breeze through these as a refresher.)

You use the SUM function to sum, or add up, the values that you include as the function arguments. In the following example, these arguments are 2, 2, the value in cell A1, and the values stored in the worksheet range B3:G5.

```
=SUM(2,2,A1,B3:G5)
```

Here's another example. The following AVERAGE function calculates the average, or arithmetic mean, of the values stored in the worksheet range B2:B100.

```
=AVERAGE(B2:B100)
```

Simply, that's what functions do. They take your inputs and perform some calculation, such as a simple sum or a slightly more complicated average.

Entering a function manually

How you enter a function-based formula into a cell depends on whether you're familiar with how the function works — at least roughly.

If you're familiar with how a function works — or at the very least, you know its name — you can simply type the function name into the cell. SUM and AVERAGE are good examples of easy-to-remember function names. When you type that first parenthesis mark [(] after entering the full function name, Excel displays a pop-up screen tip that names the function arguments and shows their correct order. (Refer to the previous section "Understanding function syntax rules" if you need to brush up on some mechanics.) In Figure 8-1, for example, you can see how this looks in the case of the loan payment function, which is named PMT.

 If you point to the function name in the screen tip, Excel turns the function name into a hyperlink. Click the hyperlink to open the Excel Help file and see its description and discussion of the function.

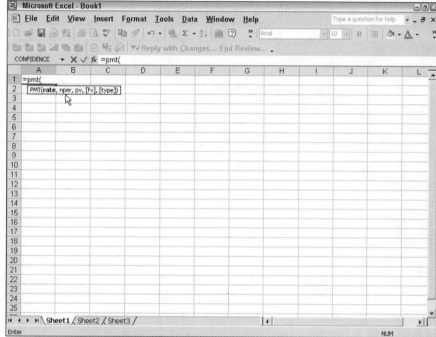

Figure 8-1:
The screen
tip for
the PMT
function
identifies
function
arguments
and shows
their correct
order.

Entering a function with the Function command

If you're not familiar with how a function works — maybe you're not even sure what function that you want to use — you need to use the Insert➪Function command to find the function and then correctly identify the arguments.

To use the Insert➪Function command in this manner, follow these steps:

1. **Position the cell selector at the cell into which you want to place the function formula.**

   You do this in the usual way. For example, you can click the cell. Or, you can use the navigation keys, such as the arrow keys, to move the cell selector to the cell.

2. **Choose Insert➪Function.**

   You may also be able to simply click the Function tool. Depending on how you've configured Excel, the standard Excel toolbar may provide a Function toolbar button.

   Either way, after you choose the Function command or click the

Function tool button, Excel displays the Insert Function dialog box, as shown in Figure 8-2.

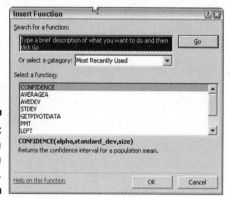

Figure 8-2:
Select a
function
here.

3. **In the Search for a Function text box, type a brief description of what you want to calculate by using a function.**

For example, if you want to calculate a standard deviation for a sample, type something like **standard deviation**.

4. **Click the Go button.**

In the Select a Function list box, Excel displays a list of the functions that may just work for you, as shown in Figure 8-3.

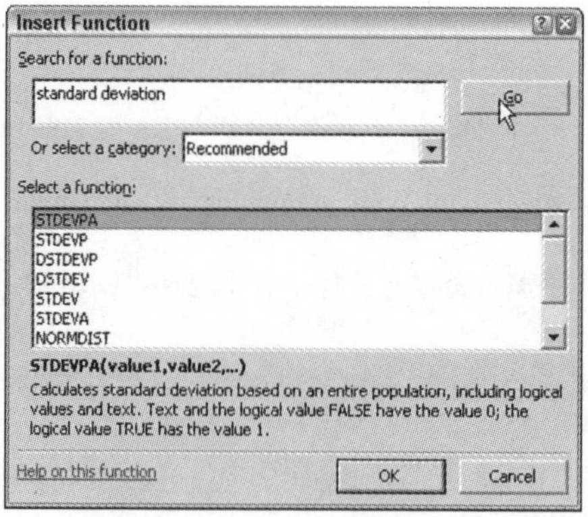

Figure 8-3:
Let Excel
help you
narrow
down the
function
choices.

Note: The STDEV function in Figure 8-3 isn't a database function, so I don't describe it here in this chapter. Read through Chapter 9 for more on this function.

5. **Find the right function.**

To find the right function for your purposes, first select a function in the Select a Function list. Then read the full description of the function, which appears beneath the function list. If the function you select isn't the one you want, select another function and read its description. Repeat this process until you find the right function.

If you get to the end of the list of functions and still haven't found what you want, consider repeating Step 3. Only this time use a different (and hopefully better) description of the calculation you want to make.

6. **After you find the function you want, select it and then click OK.**

Excel displays the Function Arguments dialog box, as shown in Figure 8-4.

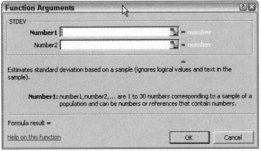

Figure 8-4: Supply function arguments here.

7. **Supply the arguments.**

To supply the arguments that a function needs, click an argument text box (Number1 and Number2 in Figure 8-4). Next, read the argument description, which appears at the bottom of the dialog box. Then supply the argument either by entering a value, a formula, or a cell or range reference into the argument text box.

If a function needs more than one argument, repeat this step for each argument.

Excel calculates the function result based on the arguments that you enter and displays this value at the bottom of the dialog box next to Formula Result =, as shown in Figure 8-5.

8. **If you need help with a particular function, browse the Excel Help information (optional).**

If you need help using some function, your first resource — yes, even before you check this chapter — should be to click the <u>Help on This Function</u> hyperlink, which appears in the bottom-left corner of the Function Arguments dialog box. In Figure 8-6, you can see the help information that Excel displays for the STDEV function.

9. **When you're satisfied with the arguments that you enter in the Function Arguments dialog box, click OK.**

   And now it's party time. In the next section, I describe each of the database statistical functions that Excel provides.

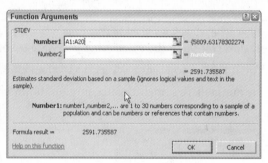

Using the DAVERAGE Function

The DAVERAGE function calculates an average for values in an Excel list. The unique and truly useful feature of DAVERAGE is that you can specify that you only want list records that meet specified criteria included in your average.

The Or Select a Category drop-down box

After you learn your way around Excel and develop some familiarity with its functions, you can also narrow down the list of functions by selecting a function category from the Or Select a Category drop-down list in the Insert Function dialog box. For example, if you select Database from this drop-down list, Excel displays a list of its database functions. In some cases, this category-based approach works pretty darn well. It all depends, really, on how many functions that Excel puts into a category. Excel provides 12 database functions, so that's a pretty small set. Other sets, however, are much larger. For example, Excel supplies more than 70 statistical functions. For large categories, such as the statistical functions category, the approach that I suggest in the section "Entering a function with the Function command " (see Step 3 there) usually works best.

If you want to calculate a simple average, use the AVERAGE function. In Chapter 9, I describe and illustrate the AVERAGE function.

The DAVERAGE function uses the following syntax:

```
=DAVERAGE(database,field,criteria)
```

where *database* is a range reference to the Excel list that holds the value you want to average, *field* tells Excel which column in the database to average, and *criteria* is a range reference that identifies the fields and values used to define your selection. The *field* argument can be a cell reference holding the field name, the field name enclosed in quotation marks, or a number that identifies the column (1 for the first column, 2 for the second column, and so on).

As an example of how the DAVERAGE function works, suppose that you've constructed the worksheet shown in Figure 8-7. Notice that the worksheet range holds a small list. Row 1, predictably stores field names: Name, State, and Donation. Rows 2–11 store individual records.

If you're a little vague on what an Excel list is, you should take a peek at Chapter 1. Excel database functions analyze information from Excel lists, so you need to know how lists work in order to easily use database functions.

Rows 14 and 15 store the criteria range. The *criteria range* typically duplicates the row of field names. The criteria range also includes at least one other row of labels or values or Boolean logic expressions that the DAVERAGE function uses to select records from the list. In Figure 8-7, for example, note the Boolean expression in cell C15, <500, which tells the function to include only records where the Donation field shows a value less than 500.

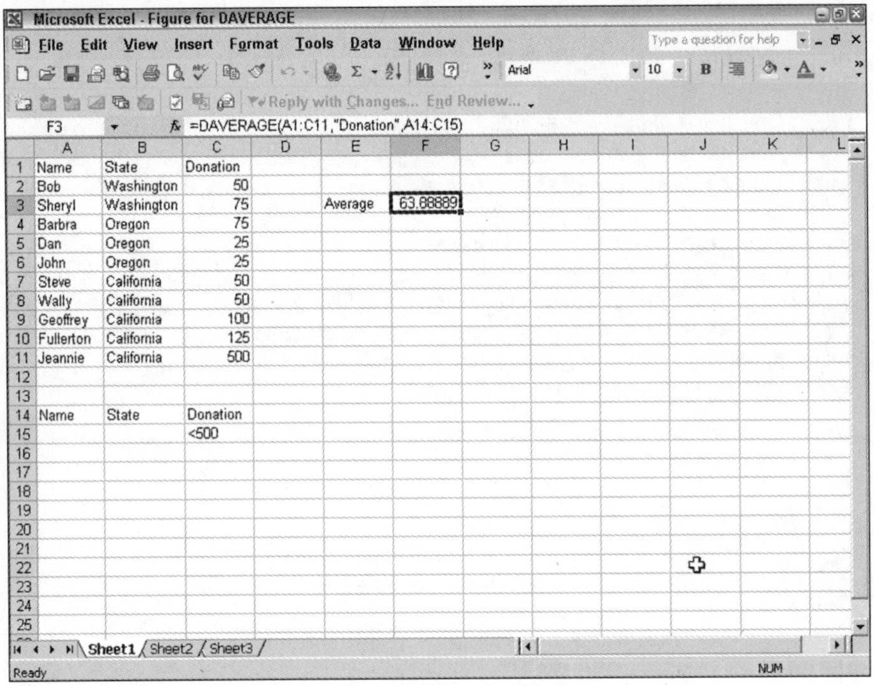

Figure 8-7:
Use the
DAVERAGE
database
statistical
functions to
calculate an
average for
values in an
Excel list.

The DAVERAGE function, which appears in cell F3, is

```
=DAVERAGE(A1:C11,"Donation",A14:C15)
```

and it returns the average donation amount shown in the database list excluding the donation from Jeannie in California because that amount isn't less than 500. The actual function result is 63.88889.

Although I mention this in a couple of other places in this book, I want to be a little redundant about something important: Each row in your criteria range is used to select records for the function. For example, if you use the criteria range shown in Figure 8-8, you select records using two criteria. The criterion in row 15 tells the DAVERAGE function to select records where the donation is less than 250. The criterion in row 16 tells the DAVERAGE function to select records where the state is California. The DAVERAGE function, then, uses every record in the list because every record meets at least one of the criteria. The records in the list don't have to meet both criteria; just one of them.

To combine criteria — suppose that you want to calculate the DAVERAGE for donations from California that are less than 250 — you put both the criteria into the same row, as shown in row 15 of Figure 8-9.

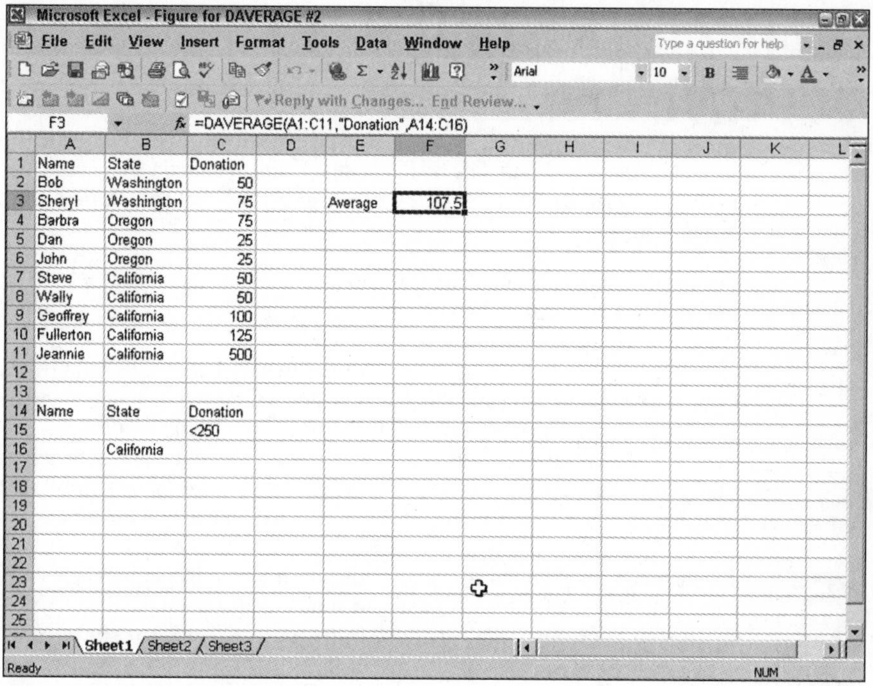

Figure 8-8:
Using a criteria range that's a little more complicated.

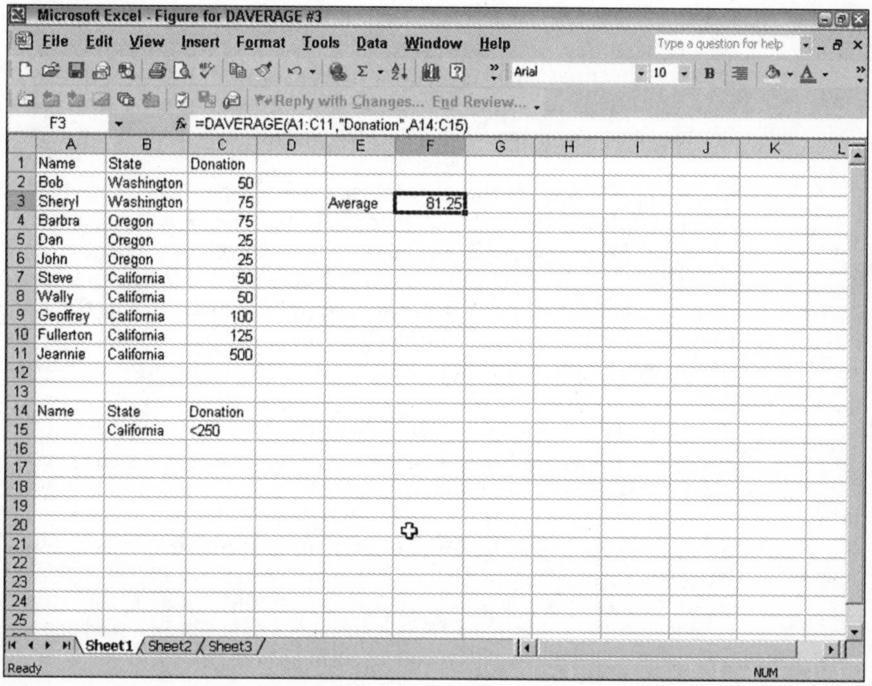

Figure 8-9:
You can combine the criteria in a range.

Using the DCOUNT and DCOUNTA Functions

The DCOUNT and DCOUNTA functions count records in a database list that match criteria that you specify. Both functions use the same syntax, as shown here:

```
=DCOUNT(database,field,criteria)
=DCOUNTA(database,field,criteria)
```

where *database* is a range reference to the Excel list that holds the value that you want to count, *field* tells Excel which column in the database to count, and *criteria* is a range reference that identifies the fields and values used to define your selection criteria. The *field* argument can be a cell reference holding the field name, the field name enclosed in quotation marks, or a number that identifies the column (1 for the first column, 2 for the second column, and so on).

Excel provides several other functions for counting cells with values or labels: COUNT, COUNTA, COUNTIF, and COUNTBLANK. Refer to Chapter 9 or the Excel online help for more information about these tools.

The functions differ subtly, however. DCOUNT counts fields with values; DCOUNTA counts fields that aren't empty.

As an example of how the DCOUNT and DCOUNTA functions work, suppose that you've constructed the worksheet shown in Figure 8-10, which contains a list of players on a softball team. Row 1 stores field names: Player, Age, and Batting Average. Rows 2–11 store individual records.

Rows 14 and 15 store the criteria range. Field names go into the first row. Subsequent rows provide labels or values or Boolean logic expressions that the DCOUNT and DCOUNTA functions use to select records from the list for counting. In Figure 8-10, for example, there's a Boolean expression in cell B15, >8, which tells the function to include only records where the Age shows a value greater than eight. In this case, then, the functions count players on the team who are older than 8.

The DCOUNT function, which appears in cell F3, is

```
=DCOUNT(A1:C11,C1,A14:C15)
```

The function counts the players on the team who are older than 8. But because the DCOUNT function looks only at players with a batting average in the Batting Average field, it returns 8. Another way to say this same thing is that in this example, DCOUNT counts the number of players on the team who are older than 8 and have a batting average.

Microsoft Excel - Figure for DCOUNT and DCOUNTA

File   Edit   View   Insert   Format   Tools   Data   Window   Help   Type a question for help

Arial   10   B

Reply with Changes... End Review...

F3   fx   =DCOUNT(A1:C11,C1,A14:C15)

	A	B	C	D	E	F	G	H	I	J	K
1	Player	Age	Batting Average								
2	Julie	9	0.135								
3	Beth	10	0.598		DCOUNT	8					
4	Melanie	10	0.266								
5	Stephanie	11	0.233		DCOUNTA	9					
6	Christina	11	NA								
7	Maddie	8	0.444								
8	Kelsey	9	0.093								
9	Susie	11	0.256								
10	Cathy	10	0.325								
11	Kathy	10	0.236								
12											
13											
14	Player	Age	Batting Average								
15		>8									
16											
17											
18											
19											
20											
21											
22											
23											
24											
25											

Sheet1 / Sheet2 / Sheet3 /

Ready   NUM

Figure 8-10:
Use the
DCOUNT
and
DCOUNTA
database
statistical
functions to
count
records in a
database
list.

If you want to get fancy about using Boolean expression to create your selection criteria, take a peek at the earlier discussion of the DAVERAGE function. In that section, "Using the DAVERAGE function," I describe how to create compound selection criteria.

The DCOUNTA function, which appears in cell F5, is

```
=DCOUNTA(A1:C11,3,A14:C15)
```

The function counts the players on the team who are older than 8 and have some piece of information entered into the Batting Average field. The function returns the value 9 because each of the players older than 8 have something stored in the `Batting Average` field. Eight of them, in fact, have batting average values. The fifth player (Christina) has the text label `NA`.

If you just want to count records in a list, you can omit the field argument from the DCOUNT and DCOUNTA functions. When you do this, the function just counts the records in the list that match your criteria without regard to whether some field stores a value or is nonblank. For example, both of the following functions return the value 9:

```
=DCOUNT(A1:C11,,A14:C15)
=DCOUNTA(A1:C11,,A14:C15)
```

Note: To omit an argument, you just leave the space between the two commas empty.

Using the DGET Function

The DGET function retrieves a value from a database list according to selection criteria. The function uses the following syntax:

```
=DGET(database,field,criteria)
```

where *database* is a range reference to the Excel list that holds the value you want to extract, *field* tells Excel which column in the database to extract, and *criteria* is a range reference that identifies the fields and values used to define your selection criteria. The field argument can be a cell reference holding the field name, the field name enclosed in quotation marks, or a number that identifies the column (1 for the first column, 2 for the second column, and so on).

Go back to the softball players list example in the previous section. Suppose that you want to find batting average of the single eight-year-old player. To retrieve this information from the list shown in Figure 8-11, enter the following formula into cell F3:

```
=DGET(A1:C11,3,A14:C15)
```

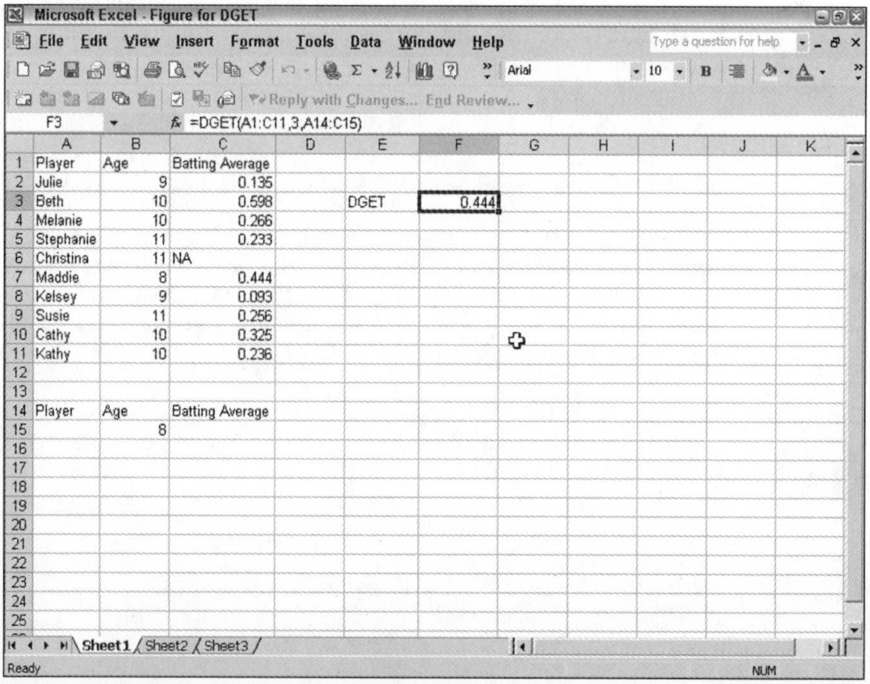

Figure 8-11:
Use DGET to retrieve a value from a database list based on selection criteria.

This function returns the value 0.444 because that's the eight-year-old's batting average.

By the way, if no record in your list matches your selection criteria, DGET returns the #VALUE error message. For example, if you construct selection criteria that look for a twelve-year-old on the team, DGET returns #VALUE because there aren't any twelve-year-old players. Also, if multiple records in your list match your selection criteria, DGET returns the #NUM error message. For example, if you construct selection criteria that look for a ten-year-old, DGET returns the #NUM error message because there are four ten-year-olds on the team.

Using the DMAX and DMIN Functions

The DMAX and DMIN functions find the largest and smallest values, respectively, in a database list field that match the criteria that you specify. Both functions use the same syntax, as shown here:

```
=DMAX(database,field,criteria)
=DMIN(database,field,criteria)
```

where *database* is a range reference to the Excel list, *field* tells Excel which column in the database to look in for the largest or smallest value, and *criteria* is a range reference that identifies the fields and values used to define your selection criteria. The field argument can be a cell reference holding the field name, the field name enclosed in quotation marks, or a number that identifies the column (1 for the first column, 2 for the second column, and so on).

Excel provides several other functions for finding the minimum or maximum value, including MAX, MAXA, MIN, and MINA. Refer to Chapter 9 for more information about using these related functions.

As an example of how the DMAX and DMIN functions work, suppose you construct a list of your friends and some important statistical information, including their typical golf scores and their favorite local courses, as shown in Figure 8-12. Row 1 stores field names: Friend, Golf Score, and Course. Rows 2 through 11 store individual records.

Rows 14 and 15 store the criteria range. Field names go into the first row. Subsequent rows provide labels or values or Boolean logic expressions that the DMAX and DMIN functions use to select records from the list for counting. In Figure 8-12, for example, note the text label in cell C15, Snohomish, which tells the function to include only records where the Course field shows the label Snohomish.

Microsoft Excel - Figure for DMAX and DMIN

File   Edit   View   Insert   Format   Tools   Data   Window   Help   Type a question for help

F3   fx   =DMAX(A1:C11,"Golf Score",A14:C15)

	A	B	C	D	E	F	G	H	I	J	K
1	Friend	Golf Score	Course								
2	Harold	105	Carnation								
3	Mike	95	Carnation		DMAX	98					
4	Rick	75	Snoqualmie								
5	Don	75	Snoqualmie		DMIN	96					
6	Les	110	Snoqualmie								
7	Steve	130	Everett								
8	Peter	95	Everett								
9	Tom	96	Snohomish								
10	Dean	97	Snohomish								
11	Jim	98	Snohomish								
12											
13											
14	Friend	Score	Course								
15			Snohomish								
16											
17											
18											
19											
20											
21											
22											
23											
24											
25											

Sheet1 / Sheet2 / Sheet3 /

Ready   NUM

Figure 8-12:
Use the
DMAX and
DMIN
database
statistical
functions
to find the
largest and
smallest
values.

The DMAX function, which appears in cell F3, is

```
=DMAX(A1:C11,"Golf Score",A14:C15)
```

The function finds the highest golf score of the friends who favor the Snohomish course, which happens to be 98.

If you want to get fancy about using Boolean expression to create your selection criteria, take a peek at the earlier discussion of the DAVERAGE function. In that section, "Using the DAVERAGE Function," I describe how to create compound selection criteria.

The DMIN function, which appears in cell F5, is

```
=DMIN(A1:C11,"Golf Score",A14:C15)
```

The function counts the lowest score of the friends who favor the Snohomish course, which happens to be 96.

Using the DPRODUCT Function

The DPRODUCT function is weird. And I'm not sure why you would ever use it. Oh sure, I understand what it does. The DPRODUCT function multiplies the values in fields from a database list based on selection criteria. I just can't think of a general example about why you would want to do this.

The function uses the syntax:

```
=DPRODUCT(database,field,criteria)
```

where *database* is a range reference to the Excel list that holds the value you want to multiply, *field* tells Excel which column in the database to extract, and *criteria* is a range reference that identifies the fields and values used to define your selection criteria. If you're been reading this chapter from the very start, join the sing-along: The field argument can be a cell reference holding the field name, the field name enclosed in quotation marks, or a number that identifies the column (1 for the first column, 2 for the second column, and so on).

I can't construct a meaningful example of why you would use this function, so no worksheet example this time. Sorry.

Note: Just so you don't waste time looking, the Excel Help file doesn't provide a good example of the DPRODUCT function either.

Using the DSTDEV and DSTDEVP Functions

The DSTDEV and DSTDEVP functions calculate a standard deviation. DSTDEV calculates the standard deviation for a sample. DSTDEVP calculates the standard deviation for a population. As with other database statistical functions, the unique and truly useful feature of DSTDEV and DSTDEVP is that you can specify that you only want list records that meet the specified criteria you include in your calculations.

If you want to calculate standard deviations without first applying selection criteria, use one of the Excel non-database statistical functions such as STDEV, STDEVA, STDEVP, or STDEVPA. In Chapter 9, I describe and illustrate these other standard deviation functions.

The DSTDEV and DSTDEVP functions use the same syntax:

```
=DSTDEV(database,field,criteria)
=DSTDEVP(database,field,criteria)
```

where *database* is a range reference to the Excel list that holds the values for which you want to calculate a standard deviation, *field* tells Excel which column in the database to use in the calculations, and *criteria* is a range reference that identifies the fields and values used to define your selection criteria. The *field* argument can be a cell reference holding the field name, the field name enclosed in quotation marks, or a number that identifies the column (1 for the first column, 2 for the second column, and so on).

As an example of how the DSTDEV function works, suppose you construct the worksheet shown in Figure 8-13. (This is the same basic worksheet as shown in Figure 8-7, in case you're wondering.)

The worksheet range holds a small list with row 1 storing field names (Name, State, and Donation) and rows 2 through 11 storing individual records.

Rows 14 and 15 store the criteria range. The criteria range typically duplicates the row of field names. The criteria range also includes at least one other row of labels or values or Boolean logic expressions that the DSTDEV and DST-DEVP functions use to select records from the list. In Figure 8-13, for example, note the Boolean expression in cell C15, <250, which tells the function to include only records where the Donation field shows a value less than 250.

The DSTDEV function, which appears in cell F3, is

```
=DSTDEV(A1:C11,"Donation",A14:C15)
```

and it returns the sample standard deviation of the donation amounts shown in the database list excluding the donation from Jeannie in California because that amount is not less than 250. The actual function result is 33.33333.

The DSTDEVP function, which appears in cell F5, is

```
=DSTDEVP(A1:C11,"Donation",A14:C15)
```

and returns the population standard deviation of the donation amounts shown in the database list excluding the donation from Jeannie in California because that amount isn't less than 250. The actual function result is 31.42697.

You would not, by the way, simply pick one of the two database standard deviation functions willy-nilly. If you're calculating a standard deviation using a sample, or subset of items, from the entire data set, or population, you use the DSTDEV function. If you're calculating a standard deviation using all the items in the population, you use the DSTDEVP function.

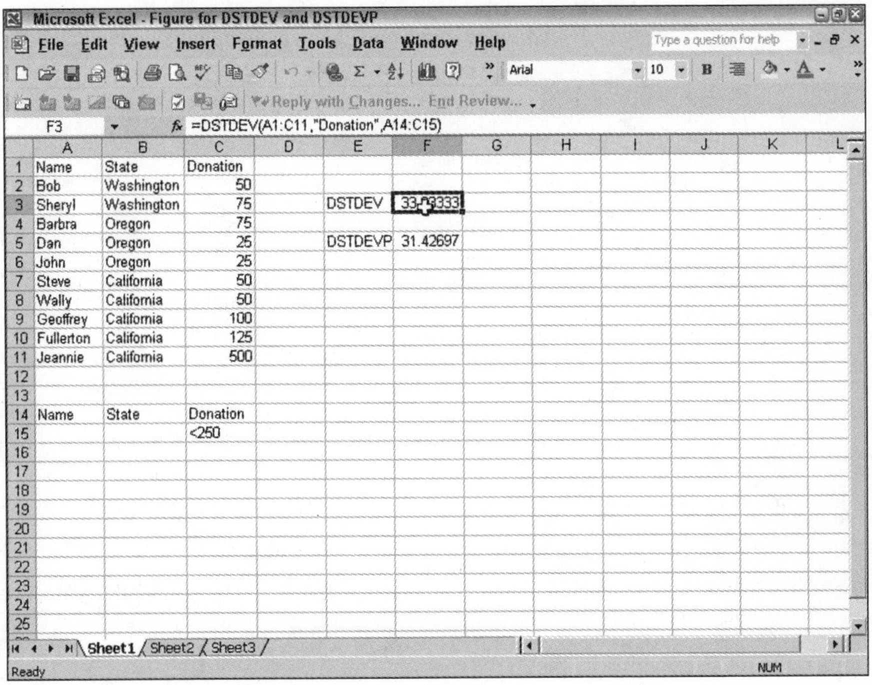

Figure 8-13:
Calculate a
standard
deviation
with the
DSTDEV
and
DSTDEVP
functions.

Using the DSUM Function

The DSUM function adds values from a database list based on selection criteria. The function uses the syntax:

```
=DSUM(database,field,criteria)
```

where *database* is a range reference to the Excel list, *field* tells Excel which column in the database to sum, and *criteria* is a range reference that identifies the fields and values used to define your selection criteria. The field argument can be a cell reference holding the field name, the field name enclosed in quotation marks, or a number that identifies the column (1 for the first column, 2 for the second column, and so on).

In Figure 8-14, you can see shows a simple bank account balances worksheet that illustrates how the DSUM function works. Suppose that you want to find the total of the balances that you have in open accounts paying more than .02, or 2 percent, interest. The criteria range in A14:D15 provides this information to the function. Note that both criteria appear in the same row. This means that a bank account must meet both criteria in order for its balance to be included in the DSUM calculation.

Microsoft Excel - Figure for DSUM										

F3   =DSUM(A1:D11,3,A14:D15)

	A	B	C	D	E	F	G	H	I	J
1	Bank	Rate	Balance	Status						
2	Big National	0.04	10000	Open						
3	Big National	0.05	10000	Open	DSUM	39000				
4	Little National	0.03	2000	Open						
5	Little National	0.03	10000	Open						
6	Seattle Savings	0.06	2000	Open						
7	Seattle Savings	0.08	10000	Close						
8	Big National	0.02	5000	Open						
9	Little National	0.03	5000	Open						
10	Seattle Savings	0.04	10000	Close						
11	Seattle Savings	0.04	8000	Close						
12										
13										
14	Bank	Rate	Balance	Status						
15		>.02		Open						
16										
17										
18										
19										
20										
21										
22										
23										
24										
25										

Sheet1 / Sheet2 / Sheet3 /

Ready   NUM

Figure 8-14:
Add values from a database list with DSUM.

The DSUM formula appears in cell F3, as shown below:

```
=DSUM(A1:C11,3,A14:D15)
```

This function returns the value 39000 because that's the sum of the balances in open accounts that pay more than 2 percent interest.

Using the DVAR and DVARP Functions

The DVAR and DVARP functions calculate a variance, which is another measure of dispersion — and actually, the square of the standard deviation. DVAR calculates the variance for a sample. DVARP calculates the variance for a population. As with other database statistical functions, using DVAR and DVARP enable you to specify that you only want list records that meet selection criteria included in your calculations.

If you want to calculate variances without first applying selection criteria, use one of the Excel non-database statistical functions such as VAR, VARA, VARP, or VARPA. In Chapter 9, I describe and illustrate these other variance functions.

The DVAR and DVARP functions use the same syntax:

```
=DVAR(database,field,criteria)
=DVARP(database,field,criteria)
```

where *database* is a range reference to the Excel list that holds the values for which you want to calculate a variance, *field* tells Excel which column in the database to use in the calculations, and *criteria* is a range reference that identifies the fields and values used to define your selection criteria. The *field* argument can be a cell reference holding the field name, the field name enclosed in quotation marks, or a number that identifies the column (1 for the first column, 2 for the second column, and so on).

As an example of how the DVAR function works, suppose you've constructed the worksheet shown in Figure 8-15. (Yup, this is the same worksheet as shown in Figure 8-12.)

The worksheet range holds a small list with row 1 storing field names and rows 2–11 storing individual records.

Rows 14–17 store the criteria, which stipulate that you want to include golfing buddies in the variance calculation if their favorite courses are Snohomish, Snoqualmie, or Carnation. The first row, row 14, duplicates the row of field names. The other rows provide the labels or values or Boolean logic expressions — in this case, just labels — that the DVAR and DVARP functions use to select records from the list.

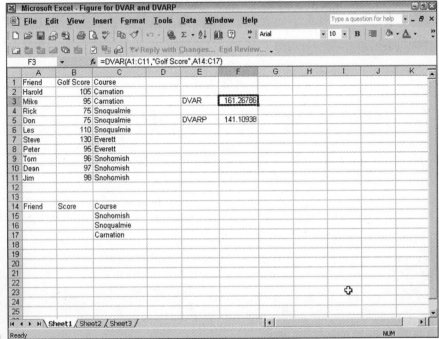

Figure 8-15:
Calculate a variance with the DVAR and DVARP functions.

The DVAR function, which appears in cell F3, is

```
=DVAR(A1:C11,"Golf Score",A14:C17)
```

and it returns the sample variance of the golf scores shown in the database list for golfers who golf at Snohomish, Snoqualmie, or Carnation. The actual function result is 161.26786.

The DVARP function, which appears in cell F5, is

```
=DVARP(A1:C11,"Golf Score",A14:C17)
```

and it returns the population variance of the golf scores shown in the database list for golfers who golf at Snohomish, Snoqualmie, and Carnation. The actual function result is 141.10938.

As when making standard deviation calculations, you don't simply pick one of the two database variances based on a whim, the weather outside, or how you're feeling. If you're calculating a variance using a sample, or subset of items, from the entire data set, or population, you use the DVAR function. To calculate a variance using all the items in the population, you use the DVARP function.

Chapter 9

Using the Statistics Functions

*E*xcel supplies a bunch of statistical functions . . . more than 70, in fact. These functions help you dig more deeply into the characteristics of data that you've stored in an Excel worksheet, list, or pivot table. In this chapter, I discuss and illustrate each of the statistical functions that you're likely to use. I also briefly describe some of the very esoteric statistical functions.

Counting Items in a Data Set

Excel provides four useful statistical functions for counting cells within a worksheet or list: COUNT, COUNTA, COUNTBLANK, and COUNTIF. Excel also provides two useful functions for counting permutations and combinations: PERMUT and COMBIN.

COUNT: Counting cells with values

The COUNT function counts the number of cells within a specified range that hold values. The function, however, doesn't count cells containing the logical values TRUE or FALSE nor cells that are empty. The function uses the syntax

```
=COUNT(range)
```

If you want to use the COUNT function to count the number of values in the range B1:B10 in the worksheet shown in Figure 9-1, you might enter the formula

```
=COUNT(B1:B10)
```

into cell G2, as shown in the Figure. The function returns the value 9.

Note: You can include several arguments as part of the range argument in the COUNT function. For example, in Figure 9-1, you might also use the syntax =COUNT(B1,B2:B5,B6:B7,B8,B9), which would return the same result as the formula shown in the figure.

COUNTA: Alternate counting cells with values

The COUNTA function counts the number of cells within a specified range that aren't empty. The function uses the syntax

```
=COUNTA(range)
```

If you want to use the COUNTA function to count the number of nonempty cells in the range A1:B2 in the worksheet shown in Figure 9-1, for example, enter the formula

```
=COUNTA(A1:B2)
```

into cell G4. The function returns the value 3.

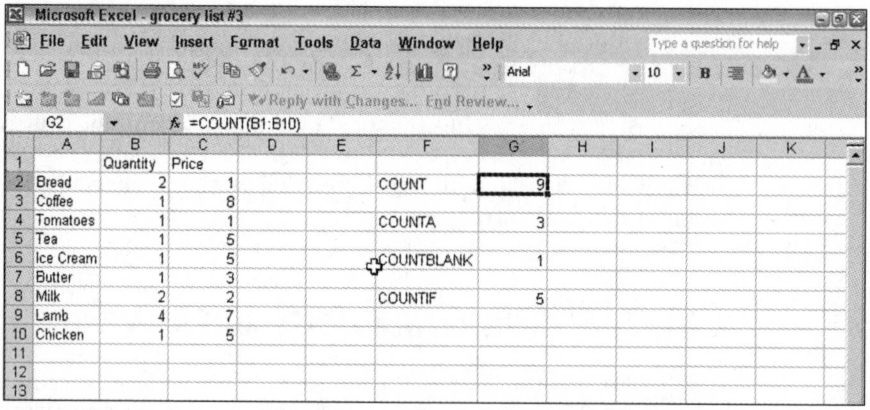

Figure 9-1: A worksheet fragment for illustrating the counting functions.

COUNTBLANK: Counting empty cells

The COUNTBLANK function counts the number of cells within a specified range that are empty. The function uses the syntax

```
=COUNTBLANK(range)
```

To use the COUNTBLANK function to count the number of empty cells in the range A1:B2 in the worksheet shown in Figure 9-1, for example, you could enter the formula

```
=COUNTBLANK(A1:B2)
```

into cell G6. The function returns the value 1.

COUNTIF: Counting cells that match criteria

The COUNTIF function counts the number of cells within a specified range that match criteria that you specify. The function uses the syntax

```
=COUNTIF(range,criteria)
```

where range is the worksheet range in which you count cells and criteria is a Boolean expression, enclosed in quotation marks, that describes your criteria.

As an example of how this works, suppose you want to use the COUNTIF function to count the number of cells within the worksheet range C1:C10 that hold values greater than 4. To make this count, you use the following formula:

```
=COUNTIF(C1:C10,">4")
```

This formula is what appears in cell G8 of the worksheet shown in Figure 9-1.

Other Boolean operators can be used to construct other match criteria: Use the < operator for a less-than comparison, the <= operator for a less-than-or-equal-to comparison, the >= operator for a greater-than-or-equal-to comparison, the = operator for the equal-to comparison, and the <> operator for a not-equal-to comparison.

PERMUT: Counting permutations

The PERMUT function counts the number of permutations possible when selecting a sample from a population. Note that for a permutation, the order does matter in which items are selected. The function uses the syntax

```
=PERMUT(number,number_chosen)
```

where number is the number of items in the population and number_chosen is the number of items selected. Given a population of six items and three selections, for example, you calculate the number of permutations by using the formula

```
=PERMUT(6,3)
```

The function returns the value 120, indicating that 120 different ways exist in which three items can be selected from a set of six.

COMBIN: Counting combinations

If the order in which items are selected doesn't matter, you use the COMBIN, or combination, function, which uses the syntax

```
=COMBIN(number,number_chosen)
```

The number of combinations possible when three items are selected from a set of six can be calculated using the formula

```
=COMBIN(6,3)
```

This function returns the value 20. The COMBIN isn't technically an Excel statistical function, by the way. But it seems so closely related to the PERMUT function that I want to include a description here.

Means, Modes, and Medians

Excel provides a handful of functions for calculating means, modes, and medians.

AVEDEV: An average absolute deviation

The AVEDEV function provides a measure of dispersion for a set of values. To do this, the function looks at a set of values and calculates the average absolute deviation from the mean of the values. The function uses the syntax

```
=AVEDEV(range)
```

where `range` is a worksheet reference to the range that stores the values.

Note: As is the case with many other simple statistical functions, you can include several arguments as part of the range argument in the AVEDEV function. For example, the formulas =AVEDEV(B1,B2:B5,B6:B7,B8,B9) and =AVEDEV(B1:B9) are equivalent.

Suppose you have three values — 100, 200, and 300 — in the worksheet range that you supply to the AVEDEV function. The average of these three values is 200, calculated as (100+200+300)/3. The average of the deviations from the mean is 66.6667, calculated as:

```
(|100-200|+|200-200|+|300-200|)/3
```

Note: The AVEDEV function calculates the average of the absolute value of the deviation. For this reason, the function calculates absolute differences, or deviations, from the mean.

The AVEDEV function isn't used in practice. Mostly a teaching tool, educators and trainers sometimes use the average deviation measure of dispersion to introduce the more useful but also more complicated measures of dispersion: the standard deviation and variance.

AVERAGE: Average

The AVERAGE function calculates the arithmetic mean for a set of values. The function uses the syntax

```
=AVERAGE(range)
```

where `range` is a worksheet reference to the range that stores the values.

If your `range` argument includes the three values — 100, 200, and 300 — the function returns the value 200 because (100+200+300)/3 equals 200.

Note: You can supply up to 30 arguments to the AVERAGE function either as values, cell addresses, or range references.

AVERAGEA: An alternate average

The AVERAGEA function, like the AVERAGE function, calculates the arithmetic mean for a set of values. The difference with the AVERAGEA function, however, is that AVERAGEA includes cells with text and the logical value for

FALSE in its calculations as 0. The AVERAGEA function includes the logical value for TRUE in its calculations as 1. The function uses the syntax

```
=AVERAGEA(range)
```

where `range` is a worksheet reference to the range that stores the values — and possibly text as well as logical values.

If your `range` argument includes three values — 100, 200, and 300 — and three text labels in the worksheet range that you supply to the AVERAGEA function, the function returns the value 100 because (100+200+300+0+0+0)/6 equals 100.

Note: As is the case with the AVERAGE function, you can supply up to 30 arguments to the AVERAGEA function.

TRIMMEAN: Trimming to a mean

The TRIMMEAN function calculates the arithmetic average of a set of values but only after discarding a specified percentage of the lowest and highest values from the set. The function uses the syntax

```
=TRIMMEAN(array,percent)
```

where `array` is the range holding the values and `percent` is the decimal value that gives the percentage of values that you want to discard. For example, to calculate the arithmetic mean of the values stored in the worksheet range C2:C10 in Figure 9-2 but after discarding 10 percent of the data — the top 5 percent and the bottom 5 percent — you use the following formula:

```
=TRIMMEAN(C2:C10),0.1)
```

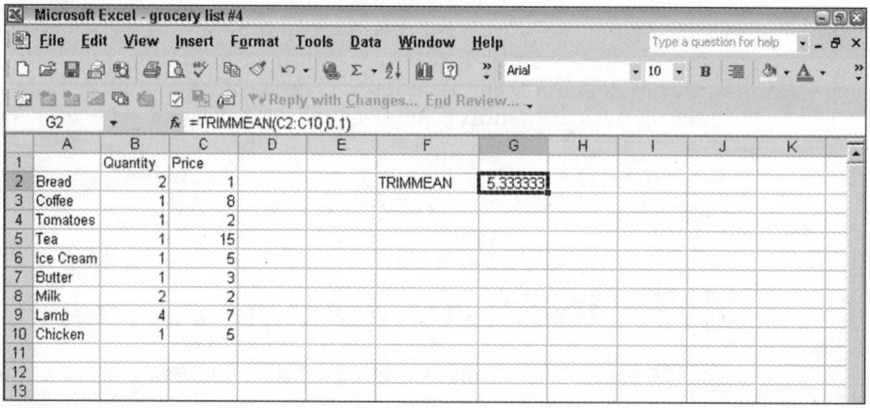

Figure 9-2:
A worksheet fragment that shows how TRIMMEAN works.

MEDIAN: Median value

The MEDIAN function finds the middle value in a set of values: Half the values fall below and half the values fall above the median. The function uses the syntax

```
=MEDIAN(range)
```

If you use the MEDIAN function to find the median of a range holding the values 1, 2, 3, 4, and 5, for example, the function returns the value 3.

Note: You can supply up to 30 arguments to the MEDIAN function.

If you use the MEDIAN function find the median of a range holding the values 1, 2, 3, and 4, the function returns the value 2.5. Why? Because if your data numbers an even number, Excel calculates a median by averaging the two middle values.

MODE: Mode value

The MODE function finds the most common value in your data set, but the function ignores empty cells and cells that store text or return logical values. The function uses the syntax

```
=MODE(range)
```

If you use the MODE function to find the most common value in a range holding the values 1, 2, 3, 4, 4, and 4, the function returns the value 4.

Note: You can supply up to 30 arguments to the MODE function.

GEOMEAN: Geometric mean

The GEOMEAN function calculates the geometric mean of a set of values. The *geometric mean* equals the *n*th root of the product of the numbers. The function uses the syntax

```
=GEOMEAN(number1,[number2]...)
```

where number1 and, optionally, other similar arguments supply the values that you want to geometrically average.

HARMEAN: Harmonic mean

The HARMEAN function calculates the reciprocal of the arithmetic mean of the reciprocals of a data set. The function uses the syntax

```
=HARMEAN(number1,[number2]...)
```

where `number1` and, optionally, other similar arguments supply the values that you want to harmonically average.

Finding Values, Ranks, and Percentiles

Excel provides functions for finding the largest or smallest values in a data set and also for finding values with a particular rank and for ranking values within the data set. Excel also provides a couple of tangentially related functions for calculating frequency distributions and simple probabilities for data sets. I describe all these function tools in the next paragraphs.

MAX: Maximum value

The MAX function finds the largest value in your data. The function ignores blank cells and cells containing text or logical values such as TRUE and FALSE and uses the syntax

```
=MAX(range)
```

If the largest value in the range A1:G500 is 50, the function =MAX(A1:G500) returns the value 50.

Note: You can supply up to 30 arguments to the MAX function.

MAXA: Alternate maximum value

In a fashion similar to the MAX function, the MAXA function also finds the largest value in your data. However, unlike the MAX function, the MAXA function includes logical values and text. The logical value TRUE equals 1, the logical value FALSE equals 0, and text also equals 0. The MAXA function uses the syntax

```
=MAXA(range)
```

MIN: Minimum value

The MIN function finds the smallest value in your data. The function ignores blank cells and cells containing text or logical values such as TRUE and FALSE and uses the syntax

```
=MIN(range)
```

If the smallest value in the range A1:G500 is 1, the function =MIN(A1:G500) returns the value 1.

MINA: Alternate minimum value

The MINA function also finds the smallest value in your data, but the MINA function includes logical values and text. The logical value TRUE equals 1, the logical value FALSE equals 0, and text also equals 0. The MINA function uses the syntax

```
=MINA(range)
```

If the smallest value in the range A1:G500 is 1 but this range also includes text values, the function =MINA(A1:G500) returns the value 0.

LARGE: Finding the kth largest value

You can use the LARGE function to find the kth largest value in an array. The function uses the syntax

```
=LARGE(array,k)
```

where `array` is the array of values and k identifies which value you want the function to return. For example, if you store the values 1, 3, 5, 8, and 9 in the worksheet range A1:A5 and you want the function to return the second largest value, you use the following formula:

```
=LARGE(A1:A5,2)
```

The function returns the value 8 because that's the second largest value in the array.

SMALL: Finding the kth smallest value

The SMALL function finds the kth smallest value in an array. The function uses the syntax

```
=SMALL(array,k)
```

where `array` is the array of values and `k` identifies which value you want to find and have the function return. For example, if you store the values 1, 3, 5, 8, and 9 in the worksheet range A1:A5 and you want the function to return the second smallest value, you use the following formula:

```
=SMALL(A1:A5,2)
```

The function returns the value 3 because that's the second smallest value in the array.

RANK: Ranking an array value

The rank function determines the rank, or position, of a value in an array. The formula uses the syntax

```
=RANK(number,ref,order)
```

where `number` is the value you want to rank, `ref` is the array of values, and optionally `order` indicates whether array values should be arranged in descending order (indicated with a 0 or logical FALSE value) or in ascending order (indicated with a 1 or logical TRUE value). By the way, Excel ranks duplicate values the same, but these duplicates do affect the rank of subsequent numbers. If you leave out the order argument, Excel ranks values in descending order.

To demonstrate how the RANK function works, suppose you want to rank the values shown in the worksheet range A1:A9 in Figure 9-3.

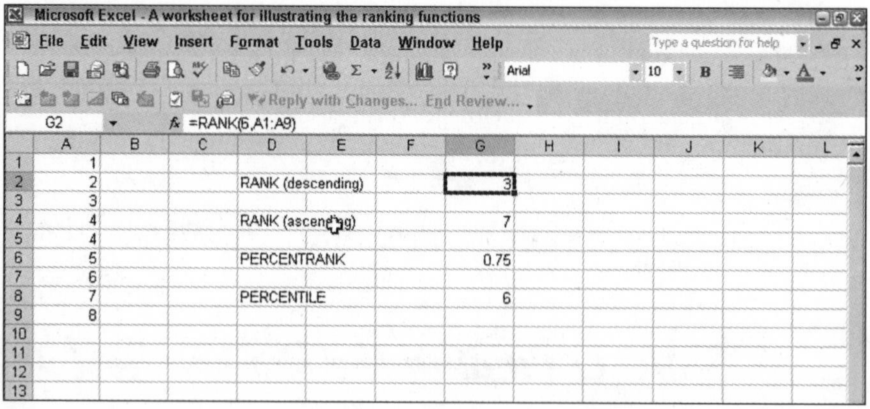

Figure 9-3:
A worksheet fragment with the array 1, 2, 3, 4, 4, 5, 6, 7, 8.

The formula in cell G2

```
=RANK(6,A1:A9)
```

returns the value 3, indicating that when a descending order is used, the value 6 is the third value in the array.

The formula in cell G4

```
=RANK(6,A1:A9,1)
```

returns the value 7, indicating that when an ascending order is used, the value 6 is the seventh value in the array.

PERCENTRANK: Finding a percentile ranking

The PERCENTRANK function determines the percentage rank, or percentile, of a value in an array. The formula uses the syntax

```
=PERCENTRANK(array,x,significance)
```

where `array` gives the array of values, `x` identifies the value you want to rank, and `significance` identifies the number of decimal places that you want in the percentage. The `significance` argument is optional. If you omit the argument, Excel assumes that you want three significant digits.

To demonstrate how the PERCENTRANK function works, again suppose you want to rank the values shown in the worksheet range A1:A9 in Figure 9-3 — only this time, you rank the values using percentages.

The formula in cell G6

```
=PERCENTRANK(A1:A9,6,2)
```

returns the value 0.75, which is the same thing as 75 percent.

Excel calculates the percentage rank by looking at the number of array values greater than the X value and the number of array values smaller than the X value. For array shown in Figure 9-3, the array includes the values 1, 2, 3, 4, 4, 5, 6, 7, 8. The percent rank of 6 in the array equals 0.75 because six array values are smaller than 6 and two array values are larger than 6. The actual formula that the function calculates is 6/(2+6), which equals 0.75.

PERCENTILE: Finding a percentile ranking

The PERCENTILE function determines the array value at a specified percentile in an array. The formula uses the syntax

```
=PERCENTILE(array,k)
```

where `array` gives the array of values and `k` gives the percentile of the value that you want to find.

To find the value at the 75-percent percentile in the array of values shown in the worksheet range A1:A9 in Figure 9-3, you use the formula

```
=PERCENTILE(A1:A9,.75)
```

The function returns the value 6 because the value 6 is at the 75th percentile in this array. This formula appears in cell G8 in the worksheet shown in Figure 9-3.

To repeat something in the earlier discussion of the PERCENTRANK function, note that Excel calculates the percentage rank by looking at the number of array values greater than the X value and the number of array values smaller than the X value. For the array shown in Figure 9-3, the array includes the values 1, 2, 3, 4, 4, 5, 6, 7, 8. The percent rank of 6 in the array equals 0.75 because six array values are smaller than 6 and two array values are larger than 6.

FREQUENCY: Frequency of values in a range

The FREQUENCY function counts the values in an array that fall within a range, or bin. The function uses the syntax

```
=FREQUENCY(data_array,bins_array)
```

where `data_array` is the worksheet range that holds the values that you want to count and `bins_array` is a worksheet range that identifies the ranges of values, or bins, that you want to use to create a frequency distribution. Take a look at Figure 9-4, for example.

To categorize the values in the worksheet range A2:A20 using the bins shown in B2:B6, you select the worksheet range C2:C6 and enter the formula

```
=FREQUENCY(A2:A20,B2:B6)
```

Then press Ctrl+Shift+Enter to tell Excel that the function formula should be entered as an array. Excel enters your formula into each of the cells in the worksheet range C2:C6, with the result shown in Figure 9-4.

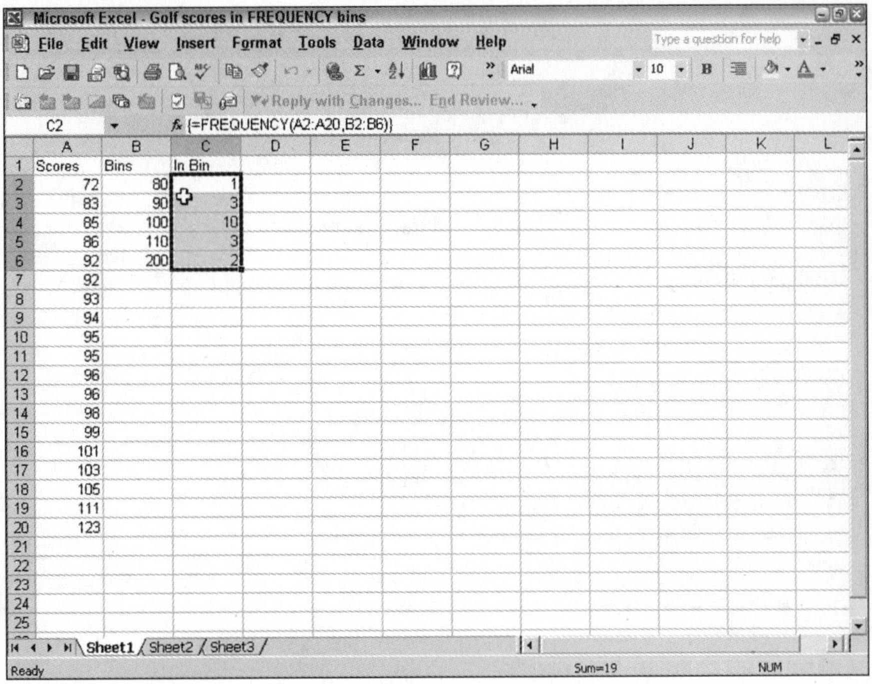

Figure 9-4:
A work-
sheet that
illustrates
how the
FREQUENCY
function
works.

In cell C2, the function uses the bin value in cell B2 to count up all the data values greater than 0 and less than or equal to 80. In cell C3, the function counts up all the data values greater than 80 but less than 90, and so on. Note that you need to arrange your bin range values in ascending order.

PROB: Probability of values

The PROB function uses a set of values and associated probabilities to calculate the probability that a variable equals some specified value or that a variable falls with a range of specified values. The function uses the syntax

```
=PROB(x_range,prob_range,lower_limit,upper_limit)
```

where x_range equals the worksheet range that holds your values and prob_range holds the worksheet range that specifies the probabilities for the values from x_range. To calculate the probability that a variable equals a specified value, enter that value using the lower_limit argument. To calculate the probability that a variable falls within a range, enter the bounds of that range using the lower_limit and upper_limit arguments.

Although the PROB function seems complicated at first blush, take a peek at the worksheet shown in Figure 9-5. The worksheet range A1:A10 holds the values, and the worksheet range B1:B10 holds the probability of those values.

Working with array formulas

You can use array formulas to return arrays. For example, you can create an array formula that adds the array 1, 2, 3 to the array 4, 5, 6. This formula produces an array result: 5, 7, 9. The worksheet fragment below shows this. The array in range A1:C1 is added to the array in range A2:C2, and the resulting array is placed into the range A3:C3.

If you want to try entering this formula yourself, create a worksheet that holds the values shown in A1:C2. Then, select the range A3:C3, type the formula **=A1:C1+A2:C2**, and press Ctrl+Shift+Enter. Excel enters the same formula, {=A1:C1+A2:C2}, into each of the cells in the

worksheet range A3:C3. You don't enter the braces, by the way. Excel enters those for you when you press Ctrl+Shift+Enter. The array formula tells Excel to calculate different values for different cells. Excel calculates the value for cell A3 by adding the values in A1 and A2. Excel calculates the value in cell B3 by adding the values in B1 and B2, and so on.

A3	▼		_fx_ {=A1:C1+A2:C2}		
	A	B	C	D	E
1	1	2	3		
2	4	5	6		
3	5	7	9		
4					

To calculate the probability that a value equals 4, use the formula

```
=PROB(A1:A10,B1:B10,4)
```

In what should not be a surprise to you, given the value shown in cell B4, this function returns the value 15.00%, as shown in cell G3 in Figure 9-5. To calculate the probability that a value falls from 4 to 7, use the formula

```
=PROB(A1:A10,B1:B10,4,7)
```

The function returns the value 68.00%, which is the sum of the values in the range B4:B7. Figure 9-5 also shows this formula result in cell G5.

Figure 9-5:
A work-
sheet
fragment
for demon-
strating
the PROB
function.

	Microsoft Excel - Illustrating the PROB function											
	File Edit View Insert Format Tools Data Window Help											
	G3		_fx_ =PROB(A1:A10,B1:B10,4)									
	A	B	C	D	E	F	G	H	I	J	K	L
1	1	1.00%										
2	2	5.00%										
3	3	10.00%		Probability value equals 4			15.00%					
4	4	15.00%										
5	5	19.00%		Probabiliy value between 4 and 7			68.00%					
6	6	19.00%										
7	7	15.00%										
8	8	10.00%										
9	9	5.00%										
10	10	1.00%										
11												
12												

Standard Deviations and Variances

I'm sure that this will be a big surprise to you. Excel provides almost a dozen functions for calculating standard deviations and variances. A *standard deviation*, by the way, describes dispersion (spread of data) about (around) the data set's mean. You can kind of think of a standard deviation as an *average* deviation from the mean. A *variance* is just the squared standard deviation. You often use variances and standard deviations in other statistical calculations and as arguments to other statistical functions.

STDEV: Standard deviation of a sample

The STDEV function calculates the standard deviation of a sample, a measure of how widely values in a data set vary around the mean — and a common input to other statistical calculations. The function uses the syntax

```
=STDEV(number)
```

To calculate the standard deviation of the worksheet range A1:A5 using the STDEV function, for example, use the formula

```
=STDEV(A1:A5)
```

If the worksheet range holds the values 1, 4, 8, 9, and 11, the function returns the standard deviation value 4.037326.

The STDEV function lets you include up to 30 arguments as inputs; those arguments can be values, cell references, formulas, and range references. The STDEV function ignores logical values, text, and empty cells.

STDEVA: Alternate standard deviation of a sample

The STDEVA function calculates the standard deviation of a sample but unlike the STDEV function, STDEVA doesn't ignore the logical values TRUE (which is 1) and FALSE (which is 0). The function uses the syntax

```
=STDEVA(number)
```

STDEVA arguments, which can number up to 30, can be values, cell references, formulas, and range references.

STDEVP: Standard deviation of a population

The STDEVP function calculates the standard deviation of a population to measure how widely values vary around the mean. The function uses the syntax

```
=STDEVP(number)
```

To calculate the standard deviation of the worksheet range A1:A5 using the STDEVP function, for example, use the formula

```
=STDEVP(A1:A5)
```

If the worksheet range holds the values 1, 4, 8, 9, and 11, the function returns the standard deviation value 3.611094.

The STDEVP function lets you include up to 30 arguments as inputs; the arguments can be values, cell references, formulas, and range references. The STDEV function ignores logical values, text, and empty cells.

STDEVPA: Alternate standard deviation of a population

The STDEVPA function calculates the standard deviation of a population but unlike the STDEVP function, STDEVPA doesn't ignore the logical values TRUE (which is 1) and FALSE (which is 0). The function uses the syntax

```
=STDEVPA(number)
```

STDEVPA arguments, which can number up to 30, can be values, cell references, formulas, and range references.

VAR: Variance of a sample

The VAR function calculates the variance of a sample, another measure of how widely values in a data set vary around the mean. The VAR function uses the syntax

```
=VAR(number)
```

A standard deviation is calculated by finding the square root of the variance.

To calculate the variance of the worksheet range A1:A5 using the VAR function, for example, use the formula

Population statistics compared with sample statistics

How do you know whether you're supposed to be using sample-versions of statistical functions (such as STDEV and STDEVA) or population-versions of statistical functions (such as STDEVP and STDEVPA)? If you're looking at all the values — the key word is *all* — then you're working with the entire population. In this case, you use one of the population standard deviation functions. If you're working with samples — which are just portions of the population — you use one of the sample standard deviation functions.

```
=VAR(A1:A5)
```

If the worksheet range holds the values 1, 4, 8, 9, and 11, the function returns the standard deviation value 16.3.

The VAR function lets you include up to 30 arguments as inputs; the arguments can be values, cell references, formulas, and range references. The VAR function ignores logical values, text, and empty cells.

VARA: Alternate variance of a sample

The VARA function calculates the variance of a sample but unlike the VAR function, VARA doesn't ignore the logical values TRUE (which is 1) and FALSE (which is 0). The function uses the syntax

```
=VARA(number)
```

VARA arguments, which can number up to 30, can be values, cell references, formulas, and range references.

VARP: Variance of a population

The VARP function calculates the variance of a population. The function uses the syntax

```
=VARP(number)
```

To calculate the variance of the worksheet range A1:A5 using the VARP function, for example, use the formula

```
=VARP(A1:A5)
```

If the worksheet range holds the values 1, 4, 8, 9, and 11, the function returns the standard deviation value 13.04.

The VARP function lets you include up to 30 arguments as inputs; the arguments can be values, cell references, formulas, and range references. The VARP function ignores logical values, text, and empty cells.

VARPA: Alternate variance of a population

The VARPA function calculates the variance of a population but unlike the VARP function, VARPA doesn't ignore the logical values TRUE (which is 1) and FALSE (which is 0). The function uses the syntax

```
=VARPA(number)
```

VARPA arguments, which can number up to 30, can be values, cell references, formulas, and range references.

COVAR: Covariance

The COVAR function calculates a covariance, which is the average of the products of the deviations between pairs of values. The function uses the syntax

```
=COVAR(array1,array2)
```

where `array1` is the worksheet range holding the first values in the pair and `array2` is the worksheet range holding the second values in the pair.

DEVSQ: Sum of the squared deviations

The DEVSQ function calculates the deviations of values from a mean, squares those deviations, and then adds them up. The function uses the syntax

```
=DEVSQ(number1,[number2]...)
```

where `number1` and, optionally, `number2` are worksheet ranges or arrays that hold your values.

Normal Distributions

Excel provides five useful functions for working with normal distributions. Normal distributions are also known as *bell curves* or *Gaussian distributions*.

Pssst. Hey buddy, wanna to see how a normal distribution changes when you noodle with its mean and standard deviation? Visit the Stanford University Web page at

```
http://www-stat.stanford.edu/~naras/jsm/NormalDensity/
            NormalDensity.html
```

NORMDIST: Probability X falls at or below a given value

The NORMDIST function calculates the probability that variable X falls below or at a specified value. The NORMDIST function uses the syntax

```
=NORMDIST(x,mean,standard_dev,cumulative)
```

where `x` is the variable that you want to compare, `mean` is the population mean, `standard_dev` is the population standard deviation, and `cumulative` is a logical value that tells Excel whether you want a cumulative probability or a discrete probability.

Here's an example of how you might use the NORMDIST function: Suppose you want to calculate the probability that some goofball with whom you work actually does have an IQ above 135 like he's always bragging. Further suppose that the population mean IQ equals 100 and that the population standard deviation for IQs is 15. (I don't know whether these numbers are true or not. I do vaguely remember reading something about this in *Zen and the Art of Motorcycle Maintenance* when I was in high school.)

In this case, you use the following formula:

```
=NORMDIST(135,100,15,1)
```

The function returns the value .990185 indicating that if the inputs are correct, roughly 99 percent of the population has an IQ at or below 135. Or, slightly restated, this means the chance that your co-worker has an IQ above 135 is less than 1 percent.

If you want to calculate the probability that your co-worker has an IQ equal to exactly 135, use the following formula:

```
=NORMDIST(135,100,15,0)
```

This function returns the value .001493 indicating that .1493 percent, or roughly one-sixth of a percent, of the population has an IQ equal to 135.

To be very picky, statisticians might very well tell us we can't actually calculate the probability of a single value, such as the probability that somebody's IQ equals 135. When you set the cumulative argument to 0, therefore, what actually happens is that Excel roughly estimates the probability by using a small range about the single value.

NORMINV: X that gives specified probability

The NORMINV function makes the inverse calculation of the NORMDIST function. NORMINV calculates the variable X that gives a specified probability. The NORMINV function uses the syntax

```
=NORMINV(probability,mean,standard_dev)
```

where `probability` is percentage that you want the variable X value to fall at or below, `mean` is the population mean, and `standard_dev` is the population standard deviation.

Okay, here's something that I do remember from *Zen and the Art of Motorcycle Maintenance*. In that book, the protagonist says that he has an IQ that occurs only once in every 50,000 people. You can turn this into a percentile using this formula 1-1/50000, which returns the value .99998.

To calculate the IQ level (which is the variable X) that occurs only every 50,000 people and again assuming that the IQ mean is 100 and that the standard deviation is 15 IQ points, you use the following formula:

```
=NORMINV(.99998,100,15)
```

The formula returns the value 162, when rounded to the nearest whole number.

NORMSDIST: Probability variable within z-standard deviations

For normal distributions, the NORMSDIST function calculates the probability that a random variable is within z-standard deviations of the mean. The function uses the syntax

```
=NORMSDIST(z-value)
```

To find the probability that a randomly selected variable from a data set is within 2 standard deviations from the mean, you use the following formula:

```
=NORMSDIST(2)
```

which returns the value 0.97725, indicating that there is a 97.725-percent chance that the variable falls within 2 standard deviations of the mean.

NORMSINV: z-value equivalent to a probability

The NORMSINV function is the inverse of the NORMSDIST function. If you know the probability that a randomly selected variable is within a certain distance of the mean, you can calculate the z-value by using the NORMSINV function to describe the distance in standard deviations. The function uses the syntax

```
=NORMSINV(probability)
```

where `probability` is a decimal value between 0 and 1.To find the z-value for 99 percent, for example, you use the following formula:

```
=NORMSINV(0.99)
```

The function returns the z-value 2.326347, indicating that there is a 99-percent chance that a randomly selected variable is within the 2.326347 standard deviations of the mean.

STANDARDIZE: z-value for a specified value

The STANDARDIZE function returns the z-value for a specified variable. The z-value describes the distance between a value and the mean in terms of standard deviations. The function uses the syntax

```
=STANDARDIZE(x,mean,standard_dev)
```

where `x` is the variable for which you want to calculate a z-value, `mean` is the arithmetic mean, and `standard_dev` is the standard deviation.

For example, to calculate the z-value for the variable 6600 given a mean equal to 6000 and a standard deviation equal to 800, you use the following formula:

```
=STANDARDIZE(6600,6000,800)
```

The function returns the z-value .75.

With a z-value, you can use the NORMSDIST function to calculate the probability that a randomly selected variable falls within the area calculated as the mean plus or minus the z-value. The probability that a randomly selected variable falls within the area that equals the mean plus or minus the z-value .75 is calculated using the formula =NORMSDIST(0.75). This function returns the probability value 0.773373, indicating that there's a 77.3373 chance that a variable will fall within .75 standard deviations of the mean.

CONFIDENCE: Confidence interval for a population mean

The CONFIDENCE function calculates a value that you can use to create a confidence interval for the population mean based on the sample mean. This definition amounts to a mouthful, but in practice what the CONFIDENCE function does is straightforward.

Suppose that, based on a sample, you calculate that the mean salary for a chief financial officer for a particular industry equals $100,000. You may wonder how close this sample mean is to the actual population mean. Specifically, you may want to know what range of salaries, working at a 95-percent confidence level, includes the population mean.

The CONFIDENCE function calculates the number that you use to create this interval using the syntax

```
=CONFIDENCE(alpha,stdev,size)
```

where alpha equals 1 minus the confidence level, stdev equals the standard deviation of the population, and size equals the number of values in your sample.

If the standard deviation for the population equals $20,000 and the sample size equals 100, you use the formula

```
=CONFIDENCE (1-.95,20000,100)
```

The function returns the value $3920 (rounded to the nearest dollar). This interval suggests that if the average chief financial officer's salary in your sample equals $100,000, there's a 95-percent chance that the population mean of the chief financial officers' salaries falls within the range $96,080 to $103,920.

KURT: Kurtosis

The KURT function measures the tails in a distribution. The function uses the syntax

```
=KURT(number1,[number2]...)
```

where `number1` is a value, cell reference, or range reference. Optionally, you can include additional arguments that provide values, cell references, and ranges.

The kurtosis of a normal distribution equals 0. A kurtosis greater than 0 means the distribution's tails are larger than for a normal distribution. A kurtosis less than 0 means the distribution's tails are smaller than for a normal distribution.

SKEW: Skewness of a distribution

The SKEW function measures the symmetry of a distribution of values. The function uses the syntax

```
=SKEW(numbers)
```

The skewness of a symmetrical distribution, such as a normal distribution, equals 0. For example, the formula

```
=SKEW(1,2,3,4,5,6,7,8)
```

returns the value 0.

If a distribution's values *tail* (that is, stretch out) to the right, it means the distribution includes greater numbers of large values (or larger values) than a symmetrical distribution would. Thus the skewness is positive. For example, the formula

```
=SKEW(1,2,3,4,5,6,8,8)
```

returns the value .09884.

If the distribution's values tail (stretch out) to the left, meaning that the distribution includes greater numbers of small values or smaller values than a symmetrical observation would, the skewness is negative. For example, the formula

```
=SKEW(1,1,3,4,5,6,7,8)
```

returns the value -.09884.

t-distributions

When you're working with small samples — less than 30 or 40 items — you can use what's called a *student t-value* to calculate probabilities rather than the usual z-value, which is what you work with in the case of normal distributions. Excel provides three t-distribution functions, as I discuss in the following paragraphs.

TDIST: Probability of given t-value

The TDIST function returns the probability of a given t-value. The function uses the syntax

```
=TDIST(x,deg_freedom,tails)
```

where x equals the t-value, `deg_freedom` equals the degrees of freedom, and `tails` indicates whether you want to calculate the probability assuming one tail or two tails: This value can be either 1 or 2. For example, to calculate the two-tailed probability of the t value 2.093025 given 19 degrees of freedom, you use the following formula:

```
=TDIST(2.093025,19,2)
```

which returns the value 0.05, including that there's a 5-percent chance that a value will fall within the range calculated as the mean plus or minus 2.093025 t-values.

Student t-distribution measures let you estimate probabilities for normally distributed data when the sample size is small (say, 30 items or fewer). You can calculate the degrees of freedom argument by subtracting 1 from the sample size. For example, if the sample size is 20, the degrees of freedom equal 19.

TINV: t-value of a given probability

The TINV function calculates the t-value for a given probability. The function uses the syntax

```
=TINV(probability,deg_freedom)
```

where `probability` is the probability percentage and `deg_freedom` equals the degrees of freedom. To calculate the t-value given a 5-percent probability and 19 degrees of freedom, for example, you use the following formula:

```
=TINV(0.05,19)
```

which returns the t-value 2.093025.

TTEST: Probability two samples from same population

The TTEST function returns the probability that two samples come from the same populations with the same mean. The function uses the syntax

```
=TTEST(array1,array2,tails,type)
```

where `array1` is a range reference holding the first sample, `array2` is a range reference holding the second sample, `tails` is either the value 1 (representing a one-tailed probability) or 2 (representing a two-tailed probability), and `type` tells Excel which type of t-test calculation to make. You set `type` to 1 to perform a paired t-test, to 2 to perform a *homoscedastic* test (a test with two samples with equal variance), or to 3 to perform a *heteroscedastic* test (a test with two samples with unequal variance).

f-distributions

f-distributions are probability distributions that compare the ratio in variances of samples drawn from different populations. That comparison produces a conclusion regarding whether the variances in the underlying populations resemble each other.

FDIST: f-distribution probability

The FDIST function returns the probability of observing a ratio of two samples' variances as large as a specified f-value. The function uses the syntax

```
=FDIST(x,degrees_freedom1,degrees_freedom2)
```

where x is specified f-value that you want to test; `degrees_freedom1` is the degrees of freedom in the first, or numerator, sample; and `degrees_freedom2` is the degrees of freedom in the second, or denominator, sample.

As an example of how the FDIST function works, suppose you compare two sample's variances: one equal to 2 and one equal to 4. This means the f-value equals 0.5. Further assume that both samples number 10 items, which means both samples have degrees of freedom equal to 9. The formula

```
=FDIST(2/4,9,9)
```

returns the value 0.841761297, suggesting that there's roughly an 84-percent probability that you might observe an f-value as large as .5 if the samples' variances were equivalent.

FINV: f-value given f-distribution probability

The FINV function returns the f-value equivalent to a given f-distribution probability. The function uses the syntax

```
=FINV(probability,degrees_freedom1,degrees_freedom2)
```

where `probability` is probability of the f-value that you want to find; `degrees_freedom1` is the degrees of freedom in the first, or numerator, sample; and `degrees_freedom2` is the degrees of freedom in the second, or denominator, sample.

FTEST: Probability data set variances not different

The FTEST function compares the variances of two samples and returns the probability that variances are not significantly different. The function uses the syntax

```
=FTEST(array1,array2)
```

where `array1` is a worksheet range holding the first sample and `array2` is a worksheet range holding the second sample.

Binomial Distributions

Binomial distributions let you calculate probabilities in situations: in which you have a limited number of independent trials, or tests, which can either succeed or fail; and success or failure of any one trial is independent of other trials.

I also discuss Excel's sole hypergeometric distribution function here with the binomial functions because, as you'll see if you slog through this discussion, hypergeometric distributions are related to binomial distributions.

BINOMDIST: Binomial probability distribution

The BINOMDIST function finds the binomial distribution probability. The function uses the syntax

```
=BINOMDIST(number_s,trials,probability_s,cumulative)
```

where `number_s` is the specified number of successes that you want, `trials` equals the number of trials you'll look at, `probability_s` equals the probability of success in a trial, and `cumulative` is a switch that's set to either the logical value TRUE (if you want to calculate the cumulative probability) or the logical value FALSE (if you want to calculate the exact probability).

For example, if a publisher wants to know the probability of publishing three best-selling books out of a set of ten books when the probability of publishing a best-selling book is ten percent, the formula is:

```
=BINOMDIST(3,10,.1,FALSE)
```

which returns the value 0.0574. This indicates that there's roughly a six-percent chance that in a set of ten books, a publisher will publisher exactly three best-selling books.

To calculate the probability that a publisher will publish either one, two, or three bestsellers in a set of ten books, the formula is

```
=BINOMDIST(3,10,.1,TRUE)
```

which returns the value 0.9872, which indicates that there is roughly a 99-percent chance that a publisher will publish between one and three best-sellers in a set of ten books.

NEGBINOMDIST: Negative binominal distribution

The NEGBINOMDIST function finds the probability that a specified number of failures will occur before a specified number of successes based on a probability-of-success constant. The function uses the syntax

```
=NEGBINOMDIST(number_f,number_s,probability_s)
```

where `number_f` is the specified number of failures, `number_s` is the specified number of successes, and `probability_s` is the probability of success.

For example, suppose you're a wildcat oil operator and you want to know the chance of failing to find oil in exactly ten wells before you find oil in exactly 1 well. If the chance for success is 5 percent, you can find the chance that you'll fail ten times before drilling and finding oil by using the formula

```
=NEGBINOMDIST(10,2,.05)
```

which returns the value 0.016465266, indicating that there's less than a 2-percent chance that you'll fail ten times before hitting a gusher.

CRITBINOM: Cumulative binomial distribution

The CRITBINOM function finds the smallest value for which the cumulative binomial distribution equals or exceeds a criterion value. The function uses the syntax

```
=CRITBINOM(trials,probability_s,alpha)
```

where `trials` is the number of Bernoulli trials, `probability_s` is the probability of success for each trial, and `alpha` equals your criterion value. Both the `probability_s` and `alpha` arguments must fall between 0 and 1.

HYPGEOMDIST: Hypergeometric distribution

The HYPGEOMDIST function returns the probability of a specified number of sample successes. A hypergeometric distribution resembles a binomial distribution except with a subtle difference. In a hypergeometric distribution, the success in one trial affects the success in another trial. Typically, you use a the HYPGEOMDIST function when you take samples from a finite population and don't replace the samples for subsequent trials. The function uses the syntax

```
=HYPGEOMDIST(sample_s,number_sample,population_s,number_population)
```

where `sample_s` equals the specified number of sample successes, `number_sample` gives the size of the sample, `population_s` gives the number of successes in the population, and `number_population` gives the size of the population.

As an example of a hypergeometric distribution, suppose you want to calculate the probability that in a sample of 30 items, 5 will be successful. Further suppose you know that within a 4,000-item population, 1,000 are successful. You use the following formula to make this calculation:

```
=HYPGEOMDIST(5,30,1000,4000)
```

which returns the value 0.01046, indicating that the chances that exactly 5 items will be successful in a set of 30 items given the characteristics of the population equals roughly 10 percent.

Chi-Square Distributions

I get very confused, personally, when I start working with statistical measures that are more complicated than those simple calculations that you learn in junior high. Yet the chi-square functions, which I discuss next, really are practical. I take this one slow and use an easy-to-understand example.

Even if you're only going to use one of the chi-square functions, read through all three function descriptions. Viewed as a set of statistical tools, the functions make quite a bit more sense.

CHIDIST: Chi-square distribution

The CHIDIST function calculates a level of significance using the chi-square value and the degrees of freedom. The chi-square value equals the sum of the squared standardized scores. The function uses the syntax

```
=CHIDIST(x,degrees_freedom)
```

where x equals the chi-square value and `degrees_freedom` equals the degrees of freedom.

As an example of how all this works, suppose you're more than a little suspicious of some slot machine that shows one of six pictures: diamonds, stars, cowboy boots, cherries, oranges, or pots of gold. With six possibilities, you might expect that in a large sample, each of the six possibilities would appear roughly one-sixth of the time. Say the sample size is 180, for example. In this case, you might expect that each slot machine possibility appears 30 times because 180/6 equals 30. If you built worksheet fragment like the one shown in Figure 9-6, you could analyze the one-armed bandit.

To calculate the level of significance using the data shown in Figure 9-6 and the chi-square distribution function, you could enter the following formula into D10:

```
=CHIDIST(D8,5)
```

The function returns the value 0.010362338, which is the level of significance that a chi-square value of 15 is due to sampling error.

Cell D8 holds the chi-square value, which is simply the sum of the squared differences between the observed and expected values. For example, the value in cell D2 is calculated using the formula =+(B2-C2)^2/C2 to return the value 3.333333333. Predictably, similar formulas in the range D3:D7 calculate the squared differences for the other slot machine symbols. And, oh, by the way, the formula in cell D8 is =SUM(D2:D7).

The bottom line: It doesn't look good, does it? I mean, that there's only a 1-percent chance that the slot machine that you're worried about could actually produce the observed values due to chance. Very suspicious. . . .

CHIINV: Chi-square value for a given level of significance

The CHIINV function returns the chi-square value equivalent to a specified level of confidence. The function uses the syntax

```
=CHIINV(probability,deg_freedom)
```

where `probability` equals the level of significance and `deg_freedom` equals the degrees of freedom.

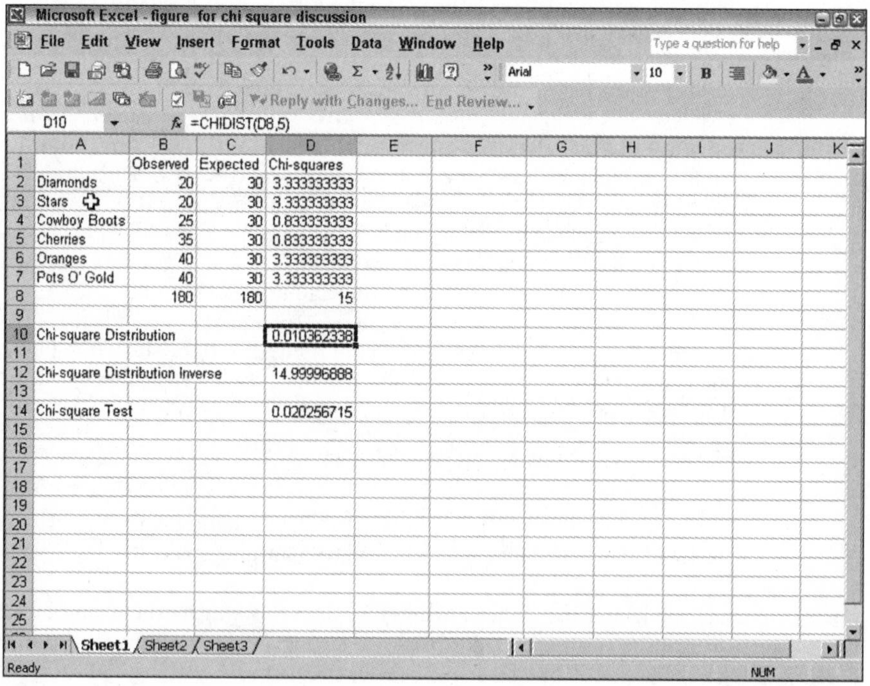

	Observed	Expected	Chi-squares								
Diamonds	20	30	3.333333333								
Stars	20	30	3.333333333								
Cowboy Boots	25	30	0.833333333								
Cherries	35	30	0.833333333								
Oranges	40	30	3.333333333								
Pots O' Gold	40	30	3.333333333								
	180	180	15								

D10 fx =CHIDIST(D8,5)

Chi-square Distribution — 0.010362338

Chi-square Distribution Inverse — 14.99996888

Chi-square Test — 0.020256715

Figure 9-6: A worksheet fragment to look at chi-square measures.

To show you an example of the CHIINV function, refer to the worksheet fragment shown in Figure 9-6. With six possible outcomes on the slot machine, you have five degrees of freedom. Therefore, if you want to calculate the chi-square that's equivalent to a 0.010362338 level of significance, you could enter the following formula into cell D12:

```
=CHIINV(D10,5)
```

This function returns the value 14.99996888, which is pretty darn close to 15 . . . so I call it 15. Note that I use D10 as the first probability argument because that cell holds the level of significance calculated by the CHIDIST function.

CHITEST: Chi-square test

The chi-square test function lets you assess whether differences between the observed and expected values represent chance, or sampling error. The function uses the syntax

```
=CHITEST(actual_range,expected_range)
```

Again referring to the example of the suspicious slot machine shown in Figure 9-6, you could perform a chi-square test by entering the following formula into cell D14 and then comparing what you observe with what you expect:

```
=CHITEST(B2:B7,C2:C7)
```

The function returns the p-value, or probability, shown in Figure 9-6 in cell D14, indicating that there's only a 2.0256715-percent chance that the differences between the observed and expected outcomes stem from sampling error.

A common feature of a chi-square test is comparison of the p-value — again the value that the CHITEST function returns — to a level of significance. For example, in the case of the suspicious slot machine, you might say, "Because it's not possible to be 100-percent sure, we'll say that we want a 95-percent probability, which corresponds to a 5-percent level of significance." If the p-value is less than the level of significance, you assume that something is fishy. Statisticians, not wanting to sound so earthy, have another phrase for this something-is-fishy conclusion: They call it *rejecting the null hypothesis*.

Regression Analysis

Excel's regression functions let you perform regression analysis. In a nutshell, *regression analysis* involves plotting pairs of independent and dependent variables in an XY chart and then finding a linear or exponential equation that describes the plotted data.

FORECAST: Forecast dependent variables using a best-fit line

The FORECAST function finds the y-value of a point on a best-fit line produced by a set of x- and y-values given the x-value. The function uses the syntax

```
=FORECAST(x,known_ys,known_xs)
```

where x is the independent variable value, known_ys is the worksheet range holding the dependent variables, and known_xs is the worksheet range holding the independent variables.

The FORECAST function uses the known_ys and known_xs values that you supply as arguments to calculate the y=mx+b equation that describes the best-fit straight line for the data. The function then solves that equation using the x argument that you supply to the function.

To use the linear regression functions such as the FORECAST function, remember the equation for a line is y=mx+b. *y* is the dependent variable, *b* is the y-intercept or constant, *m* is the slope, and *x* gives the value of the independent variable.

INTERCEPT: y-axis intercept of a line

The INTERCEPT function finds the point where the best-fit line produced by a set of x- and y-values intersects the y-axis. The function uses the syntax

```
=INTERCEPT(known_ys,known_xs)
```

where known_ys is the worksheet range holding the dependent variables and known_xs is the worksheet range holding the independent variables.

If you've ever plotted pairs of data points on an XY graph, the way the INTERCEPT function works is pretty familiar. The INTERCEPT function uses the known_ys and known_xs values that you supply as arguments to calculate the best-fit straight line for the data — essentially figuring out the y=mx+b equation for the line. The function then returns the *b* value because that's the value of the equation when the independent, or *x*, variable equals zero.

LINEST

The LINEST function finds the *m* and *b* values for a line based on sets of known_ys and known_xs variables. The function uses the syntax

```
=LINEST(known_ys,known_xs,constant,statistics)
```

where known_ys equals the array of y-values that you already know, known_xs supplies the array of x-values that you may already know, constant is a switch set to either TRUE (which means the constant *b* equals 0) or to TRUE (which means the constant *b* is calculated), and statistics is another switch set to either TRUE (which means the function returns a bunch of other regression statistics) or FALSE (which means *enough already*).

SLOPE: Slope of a regression line

The SLOPE function calculates the slope of a regression line using the x- and y-values. The functions uses the syntax

```
=SLOPE(known_ys,known_xs)
```

An upward slope indicates that the independent, or x, variable positively affects the dependent, or y, variable. In other words, an increase in x produces an increase in y. A downward slope indicates that the independent, or x, variable negatively affects the dependent, or y, variable. The steeper the slope, the greater the effect of the independent variable on the dependent variable.

STEYX: Standard Error

The STEYX function finds the standard error of the predicted y-value of each of the x-values in a regression. The function uses the syntax

```
=STEYX(known_ys,known_xs)
```

TREND

The TREND function finds values along a trend line, which the function constructs using the method of least squares. The syntax looks like this:

```
=TREND(known ys,known xs,new xs,constant)
```

LOGEST: Exponential regression

The LOGEST function returns an array that describes an exponential curve that best fits your data. The function uses the syntax

```
=LOGEST(known_ys,known_xs,constant,statistics)
```

where known_ys is the set of y-values, known_xs is the set of x-values, constant is a switch set to either TRUE (which means that *b* is calculated normally) or FALSE (which means that *b* is forced to equal 1), and statistics is a switch that's set to either TRUE (in which case, the LOGEST function returns a bunch of additional regression statistics) or FALSE (which tells the function to skip returning all the extra information.)

In an exponential regression, Excel returns an equation that takes the form $y=ab^x$ that best fits your data set.

GROWTH: Exponential growth

The GROWTH function calculates exponential growth for a series of new x-values based on existing x-values and y-values. The function uses the syntax

```
=GROWTH(known_ys,known_xs,new_xs,constant)
```

where known_ys is the set of y-values, known_xs is the set of x-values, new_xs is the set of x-values for which you want to calculate new y-values, and constant is a switch set to either TRUE (which means that *b* is calculated normally) or FALSE (which means that *b* is forced to equal 1).

Correlation

Excel's Correlation functions let you quantitatively explore the relationships between variables.

CORREL: Correlation coefficient

The CORREL function calculates a correlation coefficient for two data sets. The function uses the syntax

```
=CORREL(array1,array2)
```

where array1 is a worksheet range that holds the first data set and array2 is a worksheet range that holds the second data set. The function returns a value between -1 (which would indicate a perfect, negative linear relation-ship) and +1 (which would indicate a perfect, positive linear relationship).

PEARSON: Pearson correlation coefficient

The PEARSON calculates a correlation coefficient for two data sets by using a different formula than the CORREL function does but one that should return the same result. The function uses the syntax

```
=PEARSON(array1,array2)
```

where `array1` is a worksheet range that holds the first data set and `array2` is a worksheet range that holds the second data set. The function returns a value between -1 (which would indicate a perfect, negative linear relation-ship) and +1 (which would indicate a perfect, positive linear relationship).

RSQ: r-squared value for a Pearson correlation coefficient

The RSQ function calculates the r-squared square of the Pearson correlation coefficient. The function uses the syntax

```
=RSQ(known_ys,known_xs)
```

where `known_ys` is an array or worksheet range holding the first data set and `known_xs` is an array or worksheet range holding the second data set. The r-squared value describes the proportion of the variance in y stemming from the variance in x.

FISHER

The FISHER function converts Pearson's r-squared value to the normally dis-tributed variable z so you can calculate a confidence interval. The function uses the syntax

```
=FISHER(r)
```

FISHERINV

The FISHERINV function, the inverse of the FISHER function, converts z to Pearson's r-squared value. The function uses the syntax

```
=FISHERINV(z)
```

Some Really Esoteric Probability Distributions

Excel supplies several other statistical functions for working with probability distributions. It's very unlikely, it seems to me, that you'll ever work with any of these functions except in an upper-level college statistics course. Thus I go over these tools quickly here. A couple of them, though — the ZTEST and the POISSON functions, in particular — are actually pretty useful.

BETADIST: Cumulative beta probability density

The BETADIST function finds the cumulative beta probability density — something that you might do to look at variation in the percentage of some value in your sample data. The Excel online Help file, for example, talks about using the function to look at the fraction of the day that people spend watching television. And I recently read a fisheries management study that uses beta probability distributions to report on the effects of setting aside a percentage of marine habitat for reserves. The function uses the syntax

```
=BETADIST(x,alpha,beta,A,B)
```

where x is a value between the optional bounds A and B, and alpha and beta are the two positive parameters. If x equals .5, alpha equals 75, beta equals 85, A equals 0, and B equals 1, use following formula:

```
=BETADIST(.5,75,85,0,1)
```

This function returns the value 0.786080098.

If you leave out the optional bounds arguments, Excel assumes that A equals 0 and that B equals 1. The function =BETADIST(.5,75,85), for example, is equivalent to =BETADIST(.5,75,85,0,1).

BETAINV: Inverse cumulative beta probability density

The BETAINV function returns the inverse of the cumulative beta probability density function. That is, you use the BETADIST function if you know x and want to find the probability; and you use the BETAINV function if you know the probability and want to find *x*. The BETAINV function uses the syntax

```
=BETAINV(probability,alpha,beta,A,B)
```

EXPONDIST: *Exponential probability distribution*

The EXPONDIST function calculates an exponential distribution, which can be used to describe the probability that an event takes a specified amount of time. The function uses the syntax

```
=EXPONDIST(x,lambda,cumulative)
```

where `x` is the value you want to evaluate, `lambda` is the inverse of the mean, and `cumulative` is a switch set to either TRUE (if you want the function to return the probability up to and including the `x` value) or FALSE (if you want the function to return the exact probability of the `x` value).

For example, suppose that at a certain poorly run restaurant, you usually have to wait 10 minutes for your waitperson to bring a glass of water. That's the *average wait time*, in other words. To determine the probability that you'll get your water in 5 minutes or less, you use the formula

```
=EXPONDIST(5,1/10,TRUE)
```

which returns the value 0.393469, indicating you have (roughly) a 39-percent chance of getting something to drink in 5 minutes or less.

To determine the probability that you'll get your water in exactly 5 minutes, you use the formula

```
=EXPONDIST(5,1/10,FALSE)
```

which returns the value 0.060653, indicating there's roughly a 6-percent chance that you'll get something to drink in exactly 5 minutes.

GAMMADIST: *Gamma distribution probability*

The GAMMADIST function finds the gamma distribution probability of the random variable `x`. The function uses the syntax

```
=GAMMADIST(x,alpha,beta,cumulative)
```

where x equals the random variable, alpha and beta describe the constant rate, and cumulative is a switch set to TRUE if you want a cumulative probability and FALSE if you want an exact probability.

If x equals 20, alpha equals 5, beta equals 2, and cumulative is set to TRUE, you use the formula

```
=GAMMADIST(20,5,2,TRUE)
```

which returns the value 0.97075, indicating the probability equals roughly 97 percent.

If x equals 20, alpha equals 5, beta equals 2, and cumulative is set to FALSE, you use the formula

```
=GAMMADIST(20,5,2,FALSE)
```

which returns the value 0.00946, indicating the probability is less than 1 percent.

GAMMAINV: X for a given gamma distribution probability

The GAMMAINV function finds the *x* value associated with a given gamma distribution probability. The function uses the syntax

```
=GAMMAINV(probability,alpha,beta)
```

where probability equals the probability for the *x* value you want to find and alpha and beta are the parameters to the distribution.

GAMMALN: Natural logarithm of a gamma distribution

The GAMMALN function finds the natural logarithm of the gamma function. The GAMMALN function uses the syntax

```
=GAMMALN(x)
```

LOGNORMDIST: Probability of lognormal distribution

The LOGNORMDIST function calculates the probability associated with a lognormal distribution. The function uses the syntax

```
=LOGNORMDIST(x,mean,standard_dev)
```

where x is the value for which you want to find the probability, mean is the arithmetic mean, and standard_dev, of course, equals the standard deviation.

LOGINV: Value associated with lognormal distribution probability

The LOGINV function calculates the value associated with a lognormal distribution probability. The function uses the syntax

```
=LOGINV(probability,mean,standard_dev)
```

where probability is the probability of a lognormal distribution, mean is the arithmetic mean, and standard_dev is the standard deviation.

POISSON: Poisson distribution probabilities

The POISSON function calculates probabilities for Poisson distributions. The function uses the syntax

```
=POISSON(x,mean,cumulative)
```

where x is the number of events, mean is the arithmetic mean, and cumulative is a switch. If set to TRUE, this switch tells Excel to calculate the Poisson probability of a variable being less than or equal to x; if set to FALSE, it tells Excel to calculate the Poisson probability of a variable being exactly equal to x.

To illustrate how the Poisson function works, suppose you want to look at some probabilities associated with cars arriving as a drive-through car wash. (This type of analysis of events occurring over a specified time interval is a common application of Poisson distributions.) If on average, 20 cars drive up an hour, you can calculate the probability that exactly 15 cars will drive up using the formula

```
=POISSON(15,20,FALSE)
```

This function returns the value 0.051648854, indicating that there's roughly a 5-percent chance that exactly 15 cars will drive up in an hour.

To calculate the probability that 15 cars or fewer will drive up in an hour, you'd use the following formula:

```
=POISSON(15,20,TRUE)
```

This function returns the value 0.156513135, indicating that there's roughly a 16-percent chance that 15 or fewer cars will drive up in an hour.

WEIBULL: Weibull distribution

The WEIBULL function returns either the cumulative distribution or the probability mass for a Weibull distribution. The function uses the syntax

```
=WEIBULL(x,alpha,beta,cumulative)
```

where x is the value for which you want to calculate the distribution; alpha and beta are, respectively, the alpha and beta parameters to the Weibull equation, and cumulative is a switch. That switch, if set to TRUE, tells the function to return the cumulative distribution function; if set to FALSE, it tells the function to return the probability mass function.

Visit the Web page

```
http://www.windpower.dk/tour/wres/weibull/index.htm
```

to see Weibull distributions for wind speed information.

ZTEST: Probability of a z-test

The ZTEST function calculates the probability that a value comes from the same population as a sample.

The function uses the syntax

```
=ZTEST(array,x,sigma)
```

where `array` is the worksheet range holding your sample, `x` is the value you want to test, and (optionally) `sigma` is the standard deviation of the population. If you omit `sigma`, Excel uses the sample standard deviation.

For example, to find the probability that the value 75 comes from the population as the sample stored in the worksheet range A1:A10, use the following formula:

```
=ZTEST(A1:A10,75)
```

Chapter 10

Descriptive Statistics

• •

In This Chapter

▶ Using the Descriptive Statistics tool

▶ Creating a histogram

▶ Ranking by percentile

▶ Calculating moving averages

▶ Using the Exponential Smoothing tool

▶ Sampling a population

• •

*I*n this chapter, I describe and discuss the simple descriptive statistical data analysis tools that Excel supplies through the Data Analysis add-in. I also describe some of the really simple-to-use and easy-to-understand inferential statistical tools provided by the Data Analysis add-in — including the tools for calculating moving and exponential averages as well as the tools for generating random numbers and sampling.

Descriptive statistics simply summarize large (sometimes overwhelming) data sets with a few, key calculated values. For example, when you say something like, "Well, the biggest value in that data set is 345," that's a descriptive statistic.

The simple-yet-powerful Data Analysis tools can save you a lot of time. With a single command, for example, you can often produce a bunch of descriptive statistical measures such as mean, mode, standard deviation, and so on. What's more, the other cool tools that you can use for preparing histograms, percentile rankings, and moving average schedules, can really come in handy.

Perhaps the best thing about these tools, however, is that even if you've had only a little exposure to basic statistics, none of them are particularly difficult to use. All the hard work and all the dirty work gets done by Excel. All you have to do is describe where the input data is.

Note: In Excel 2002, the Data Analysis add-in is usually already installed (automatically). In Excel 2000, however, you must usually install the Data Analysis add-in before you can use it. To install the Data Analysis add-in (in either Excel 2002 or Excel 2000), choose the Tools⇨Add-Ins command. Next, select the Analysis ToolPak check box and then click OK. When Excel prompts you for the Excel CD, insert that into your CD or DVD drive and wait for Excel to do its magic.

Using the Descriptive Statistics Tool

Perhaps the most common Data Analysis tool that you'll use is the one for calculating descriptive statistics. To see how this works, take a look at the worksheet shown in Figure 10-1. It summarizes sales data for a book publisher. In column A, the worksheet shows the suggested retail price (SRP). In column B, the worksheet shows the units sold of each book through one popular bookselling outlet. You might choose to use the Descriptive Statistics tool to summarize this data set.

To calculate descriptive statistics for the data set shown in Figure 10-1, follow these steps:

1. **Choose the Tools⇨Data Analysis command to tell Excel that you want to calculate descriptive statistics.**

    Excel displays the Data Analysis dialog box, as shown in Figure 10-2.

2. **From Data Analysis dialog box, highlight the Descriptive Statistics entry in the Analysis Tools list and then click OK.**

    Excel displays the Descriptive Statistics dialog box, as shown in Figure 10-3.

3. **In the Input section of the Descriptive Statistics dialog box, identify the data that you want to describe.**

    • **To identify the data that you want to describe statistically:** Click the Input Range text box and then enter the worksheet range reference for the data. In the case of the worksheet shown in Figure 10-1, the input range is \$A\$1:\$C\$38. Note that Excel wants the range address to use absolute references — hence, the dollar signs.

    To make it easier to see or select the worksheet range, click the worksheet button at the right end of the Input Range text box. When Excel hides the Descriptive Statistics dialog box, select the range that you want by dragging the mouse. Then click the worksheet button again to redisplay the Descriptive Statistics dialog box.

    • **To identify whether the data is arranged in columns or rows:** Select either the Columns or the Rows radio button.

    • **To indicate whether the first row holds labels that describe the data:** Select the Labels in First Row check box. In the case of the worksheet shown in Figure 10-1, the data is arranged in columns, and the first row does hold labels, so you select the Columns radio button *and* the Labels in First Row check box.

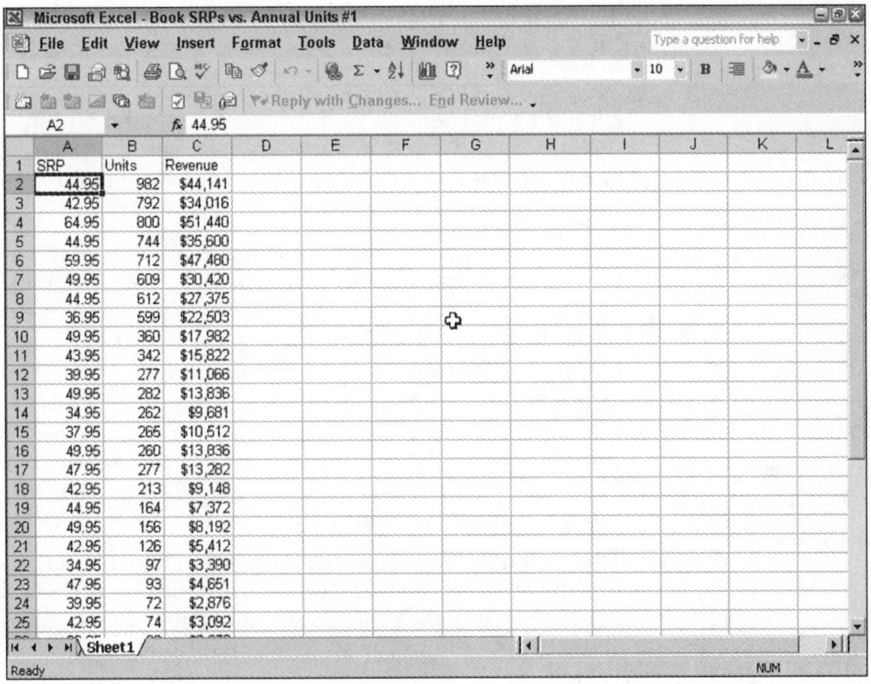

	Microsoft Excel - Book SRPs vs. Annual Units #1												
	File	Edit	View	Insert	Format	Tools	Data	Window	Help		Type a question for help		

A2 ▼ ƒx 44.95

	A	B	C	D	E	F	G	H	I	J	K	L
1	SRP	Units	Revenue									
2	44.95	982	$44,141									
3	42.95	792	$34,016									
4	64.95	800	$51,440									
5	44.95	744	$35,600									
6	59.95	712	$47,480									
7	49.95	609	$30,420									
8	44.95	612	$27,375									
9	36.95	599	$22,503									
10	49.95	360	$17,982									
11	43.95	342	$15,822									
12	39.95	277	$11,066									
13	49.95	282	$13,836									
14	34.95	262	$9,681									
15	37.95	265	$10,512									
16	49.95	260	$13,836									
17	47.95	277	$13,282									
18	42.95	213	$9,148									
19	44.95	164	$7,372									
20	49.95	156	$8,192									
21	42.95	126	$5,412									
22	34.95	97	$3,390									
23	47.95	93	$4,651									
24	39.95	72	$2,876									
25	42.95	74	$3,092									

Sheet1

Ready — NUM

Figure 10-1: A sample data set.

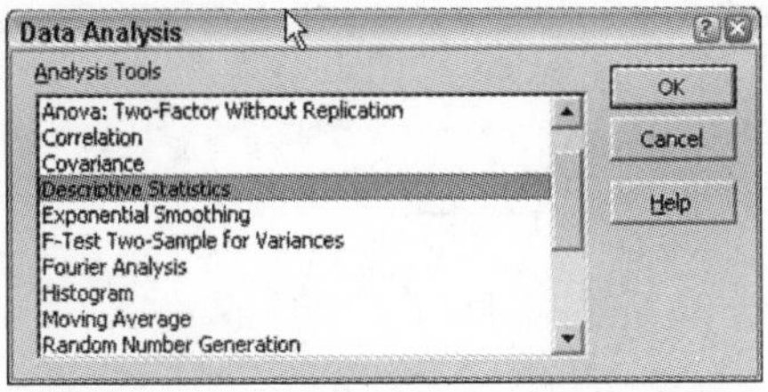

Data Analysis

Analysis Tools

Anova: Two-Factor Without Replication
Correlation
Covariance
Descriptive Statistics
Exponential Smoothing
F-Test Two-Sample for Variances
Fourier Analysis
Histogram
Moving Average
Random Number Generation

OK
Cancel
Help

Figure 10-2: The Data Analysis dialog box.

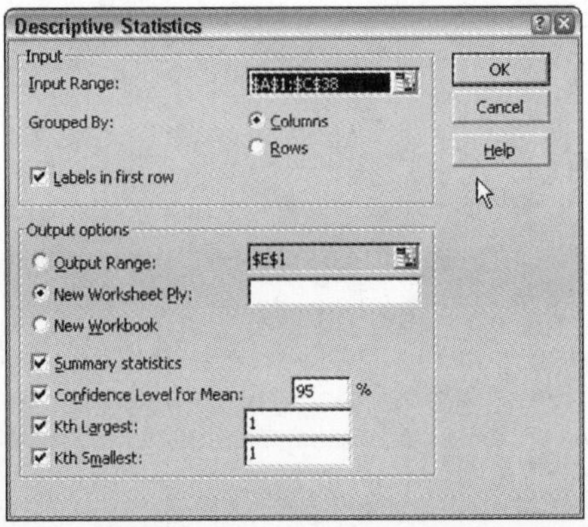

Descriptive Statistics

Input
Input Range: $A$1:$C$38
Grouped By: ⦿ Columns ◯ Rows
☑ Labels in first row

Output options
◯ Output Range: $E$1
⦿ New Worksheet Ply:
◯ New Workbook
☑ Summary statistics
☑ Confidence Level for Mean: 95 %
☑ Kth Largest: 1
☑ Kth Smallest: 1

OK
Cancel
Help

Figure 10-3: The Descriptive Statistics dialog box.

4. **From the Output Options area of the Descriptive Statistics dialog box, describe where and how Excel should produce the statistics.**

   - **To indicate where the descriptive statistics that Excel calculates should be placed:** Choose from the three radio buttons here — Output Range, New Worksheet Ply, and New Workbook. Typically, you place the statistics onto a new worksheet in the existing workbook. To do this, simply select the New Workbook Ply radio button.
   - **To identify what statistical measures you want calculated:** Use the Output Options check boxes. Select the Summary Statistics check box to tell Excel to calculate statistical measures such as mean, mode, and standard deviation. Select the Confidence Level for Mean check box to specify that you want a confidence level calculated for the sample mean. ***Note:*** If you do calculate a confidence level for the sample mean, you need to enter the confidence level percentage into the text box provided. Use the Kth Largest and Kth Smallest check boxes to indicate you want to find the largest or smallest value in the data set.

   After you describe where the data is and how the statistics should be calculated, click OK. Figure 10-4 shows a new worksheet with the descriptive statistics calculated, added into a new sheet, Sheet 2. Table 10-1 describes the statistics that Excel calculates.

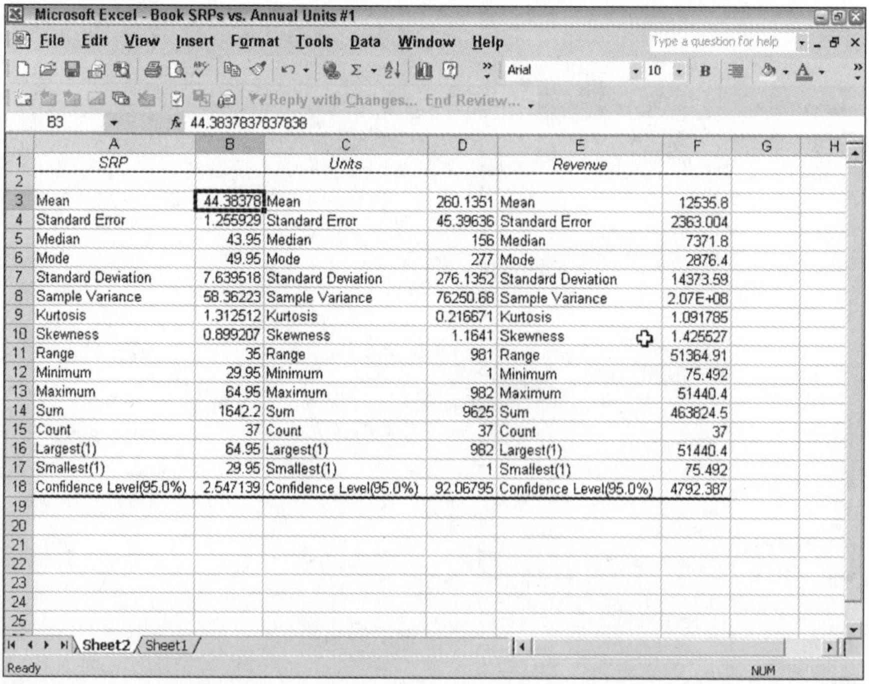

	A	B	C	D	E	F
1	SRP		Units		Revenue	
2						
3	Mean	44.38378	Mean	260.1351	Mean	12535.8
4	Standard Error	1.255929	Standard Error	45.39636	Standard Error	2363.004
5	Median	43.95	Median	156	Median	7371.8
6	Mode	49.95	Mode	277	Mode	2876.4
7	Standard Deviation	7.639518	Standard Deviation	276.1352	Standard Deviation	14373.59
8	Sample Variance	58.36223	Sample Variance	76250.68	Sample Variance	2.07E+08
9	Kurtosis	1.312512	Kurtosis	0.216671	Kurtosis	1.091785
10	Skewness	0.899207	Skewness	1.1641	Skewness	1.425527
11	Range	35	Range	981	Range	51364.91
12	Minimum	29.95	Minimum	1	Minimum	75.492
13	Maximum	64.95	Maximum	982	Maximum	51440.4
14	Sum	1642.2	Sum	9625	Sum	463824.5
15	Count	37	Count	37	Count	37
16	Largest(1)	64.95	Largest(1)	982	Largest(1)	51440.4
17	Smallest(1)	29.95	Smallest(1)	1	Smallest(1)	75.492
18	Confidence Level(95.0%)	2.547139	Confidence Level(95.0%)	92.06795	Confidence Level(95.0%)	4792.387

Figure 10-4: A new worksheet with the descriptive statistics calculated.

Table 10-1	The Measures That the Descriptive Statistics Tool Calculates
Statistic	*Description*
Mean	Shows the arithmetic mean of the sample data.
Standard Error	Shows the standard error of the data set (a measure of the difference between the predicted value and the actual value).
Median	Shows the middle value in the data set (the value that separates the largest half of the values from the smallest half of the values).
Mode	Shows the most common value in the data set.
Standard Deviation	Shows the sample standard deviation measure for the data set.
Sample Variance	Shows the sample variance for the data set (the squared standard deviation).
Kurtosis	Shows the kurtosis of the distribution.
Skewness	Shows the skewness of the data set's distribution.
Range	Shows the difference between the largest and smallest values in the data set.
Minimum	Shows the smallest value in the data set.
Maximum	Shows the largest value in the data set.
Sum	Adds all the values in the data set together to calculate the sum.
Count	Counts the number of values in a data set.
Largest(X)	Shows the largest X value in the data set.
Smallest(X)	Shows the smallest X value in the data set.
Confidence Level(X) Percentage	Shows the confidence level at a given percentage for the data set values.

Creating a Histogram

Use the Histogram Data Analysis tool to create a frequency distribution and, optionally, a histogram chart. A frequency distribution just shows how values in a data set are distributed across categories. A histogram shows the same information in a cute little column chart. Here's how all this works with an example — everything will become clearer if you're currently confused.

To use the Histogram tool, you first need to identify the bins (categories) that you want to use to create a frequency distribution. The histogram plots out how many times your data falls into each of these categories. Figure 10-5 shows the same worksheet as Figure 10-2, only this time with bins information in the worksheet range E1:E12. The bins information shows Excel exactly what bins (categories) that you want to use to categorize the unit sales data. The bins information shown in the worksheet range E1:E12, for example, create hundred-unit bins: 0-100, 101-200, 201-300, and so on.

To create a frequency distribution and a histogram using the data shown in Figure 10-5, follow these steps:

1. **Choose the Tools⇨Data Analysis command to tell Excel that you want to create a frequency distribution and a histogram.**

   When Excel displays the Data Analysis dialog box (refer to Figure 10-2), select Histogram from the Analysis Tools list and click OK.

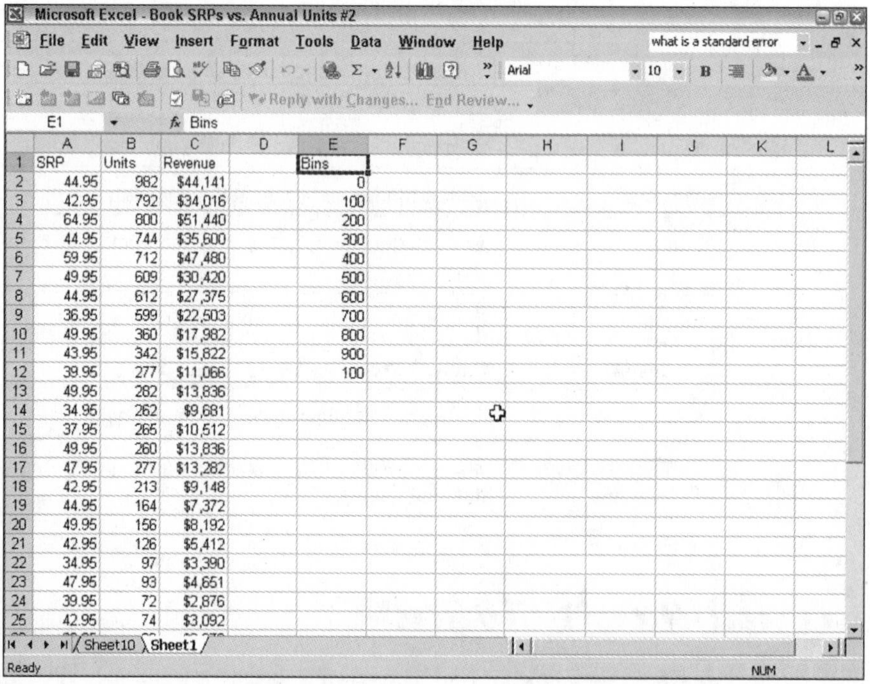

Figure 10-5: Another version of the book sales information worksheet.

2. From the Histogram dialog box that appears, as shown in Figure 10-6, identify the data that you want to analyze.

Use the Input Range text box to identify the data that you want to use to create a frequency distribution and histogram. If you want to create a frequency distribution and histogram of unit sales data, for example, you enter the worksheet range $B$1:$B$38 into the Input Range textbox.

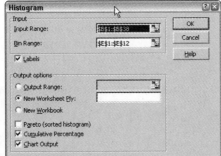

Figure 10-6:
Create a
histogram
here.

To identify the bins that you use for the frequency distribution and histogram, enter the worksheet range that holds the bins into the Bin Range text box. In the case of the example worksheet shown in Figure 10-5, the bin range is $E$1:$E$12.

If your data ranges include labels (as they do in Figure 10-5), select the Labels check box.

3. Tell Excel where to place the frequency distribution and histogram.

Use the Output Options buttons to tell Excel where it should place the frequency distribution and histogram. To place the histogram in the current worksheet, for example, select the Output Range radio button and then enter the range address into its corresponding Output Range text box.

To place the frequency distribution and histogram in a new worksheet, select the New Worksheet Ply radio button. Then, optionally, enter a name for the worksheet into the New Worksheet Ply text box. To place the frequency distribution and histogram information in a new workbook, select the New Workbook radio button.

4. Customize the histogram (optional).

Make choices from the Output Options check boxes to control what sort of histogram Excel creates. For example, select the Pareto (Sorted Histogram) check box, and Excel sorts bins in descending order.

Conversely, if you don't want bins sorted in descending order, leave the Pareto (Sorted Histogram) check box clear.

Selecting the Cumulative Percentage check box tells Excel to plot a line showing cumulative percentages in your histogram.

Finally, select the Chart Output check to have Excel include a histogram chart with the frequency distribution. If you don't select this check box, you don't get the histogram — only the frequency distribution.

5. **Click OK.**

Excel creates the frequency distribution and, presumably, the histogram. Figure 10-7 shows the frequency distribution and histogram for the workbook shown in Figure 10-5.

Note: Excel also provides a Frequency function with which you use can use arrays to create a frequency distribution. For more information about how the Frequency function works, read Chapter 9.

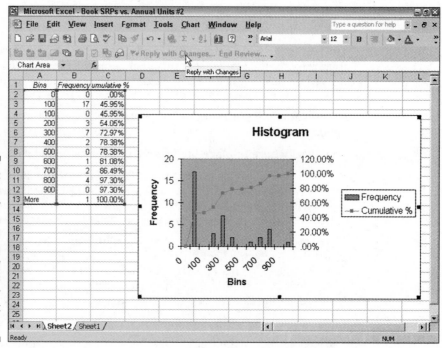

Figure 10-7: Create a frequency distribution and histogram to show how values in your data set spread out.

Ranking by Percentile

The Data Analysis collection of tools includes an option for calculating rank and percentile information for values in your data set. Suppose, for example, that you want to rank the sales revenue information shown in Figure 10-8. To calculate rank and percentile statistics for your data set, take the following steps.

1. **Begin to calculate ranks and percentiles by choose the Tools⇨Data Analysis command.**

2. **When Excel displays the Data Analysis dialog box, select Rank and Percentile from the list and click OK.**

   Excel displays the Rank and Percentile dialog box, as shown in Figure 10-9.

3. **Identify the data set.**

   Enter the worksheet range that holds the data into the Input Range text box of the Ranks and Percentiles dialog box.

   To indicate how you have arranged data, select one of the two Grouped By radio buttons: Columns or Rows. To indicate whether the first cell in the input range is a label, select or deselect (clear) the Labels In First Row check box.

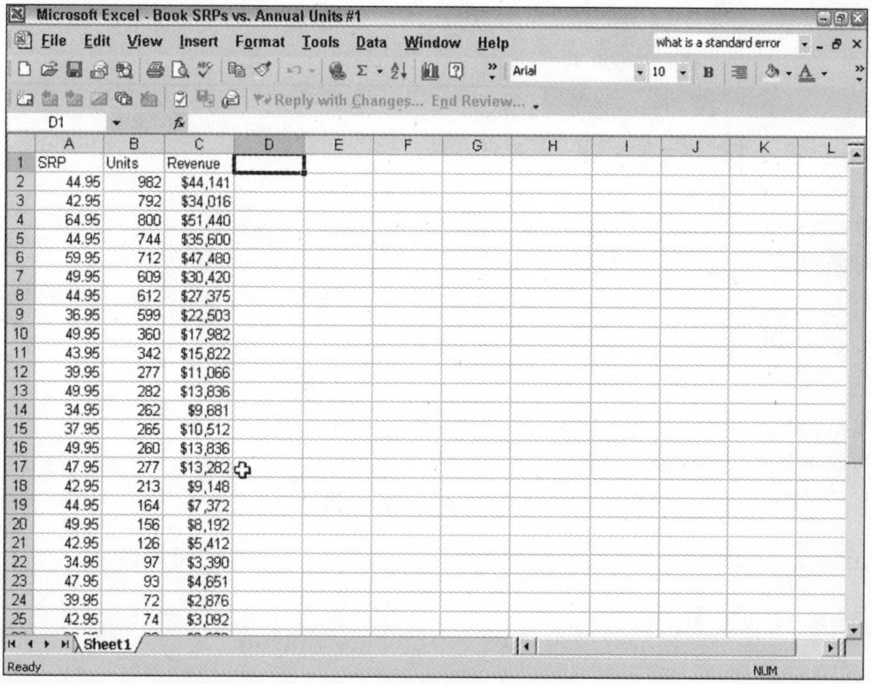

Figure 10-8: The book sales information (yes, again).

	A	B	C
1	SRP	Units	Revenue
2	44.95	982	$44,141
3	42.95	792	$34,016
4	64.95	800	$51,440
5	44.95	744	$35,600
6	59.95	712	$47,480
7	49.95	609	$30,420
8	44.95	612	$27,375
9	36.95	599	$22,503
10	49.95	360	$17,982
11	43.95	342	$15,822
12	39.95	277	$11,066
13	49.95	282	$13,836
14	34.95	262	$9,681
15	37.95	265	$10,512
16	49.95	260	$13,836
17	47.95	277	$13,282
18	42.95	213	$9,148
19	44.95	164	$7,372
20	49.95	156	$8,192
21	42.95	126	$5,412
22	34.95	97	$3,390
23	47.95	93	$4,651
24	39.95	72	$2,876
25	42.95	74	$3,092

4. **Describe how Excel should output the data.**

   Select one of the three Output Options radio buttons to specify where Excel should place the rank and percentile information.

5. **After you select an output option, click OK.**

   Excel creates a ranking like the one shown in Figure 10-10.

Rank and Percentile
Input
Input Range:
$C$1:$C$38
Grouped By:
Columns
Rows
Labels in First Row
Output options
Output Range:
New Worksheet Ply:
New Workbook
OK
Cancel
Help

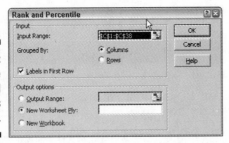

Figure 10-9: Calculate ranks and percentiles here.

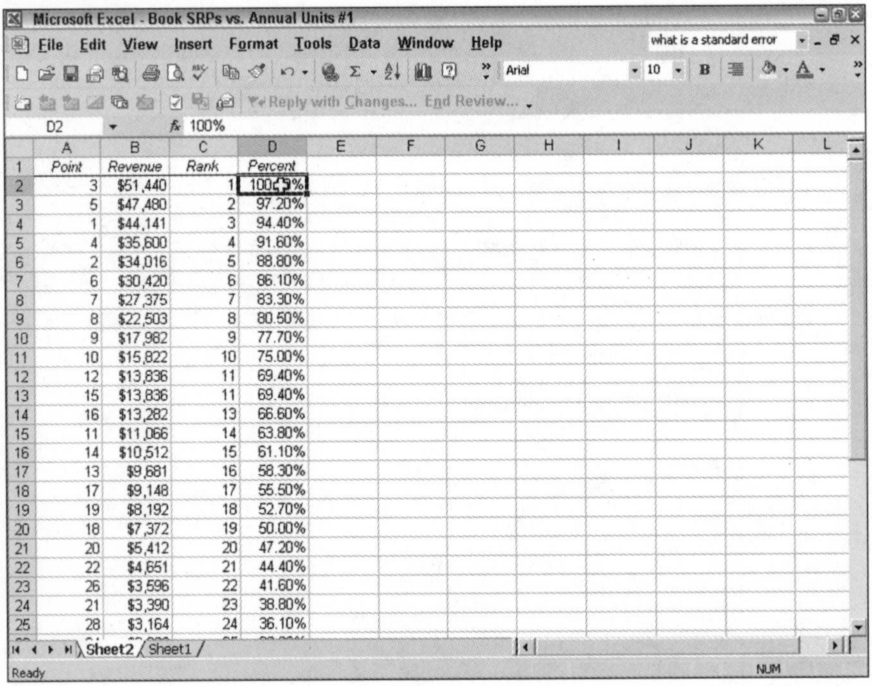

Microsoft Excel - Book SRPs vs. Annual Units #1
File Edit View Insert Format Tools Data Window Help
what is a standard error
Arial
10
Reply with Changes... End Review...
D2
100%
Point Revenue Rank Percent
3 $51,440 1 100.00%
5 $47,480 2 97.20%
1 $44,141 3 94.40%
4 $35,600 4 91.60%
2 $34,016 5 88.80%
6 $30,420 6 86.10%
7 $27,375 7 83.30%
8 $22,503 8 80.50%
9 $17,982 9 77.70%
10 $15,822 10 75.00%
12 $13,836 11 69.40%
15 $13,836 11 69.40%
16 $13,282 13 66.60%
11 $11,066 14 63.80%
14 $10,512 15 61.10%
13 $9,681 16 58.30%
17 $9,148 17 55.50%
19 $8,192 18 52.70%
18 $7,372 19 50.00%
20 $5,412 20 47.20%
22 $4,651 21 44.40%
26 $3,596 22 41.60%
21 $3,390 23 38.80%
28 $3,164 24 36.10%
Sheet2 Sheet1
Ready
NUM

Figure 10-10: A rank and percentile worksheet based on the data from Figure 10-8.

Calculating Moving Averages

The Data Analysis command also provides a tool for calculating moving and exponentially smoothed averages. Suppose, for sake of illustration, that you've collected daily temperature information like that shown in Figure 10-11. You want to calculate the three-day moving average — the average of the last three days — as part of some simple weather forecasting. To calculate moving averages for this data set, take the following steps.

1. **To calculate a moving average, first choose the Tools⇨Data Analysis command.**

2. **When Excel displays the Data Analysis dialog box, select the Moving Average item from the list and then click OK.**

   Excel displays the Moving Average dialog box, as shown in Figure 10-12.

3. **Identify the data that you want to use to calculate the moving average.**

   Click in the Input Range text box of the Moving Average dialog box. Then identify the input range, either by typing a worksheet range address or by using the mouse to select the worksheet range.

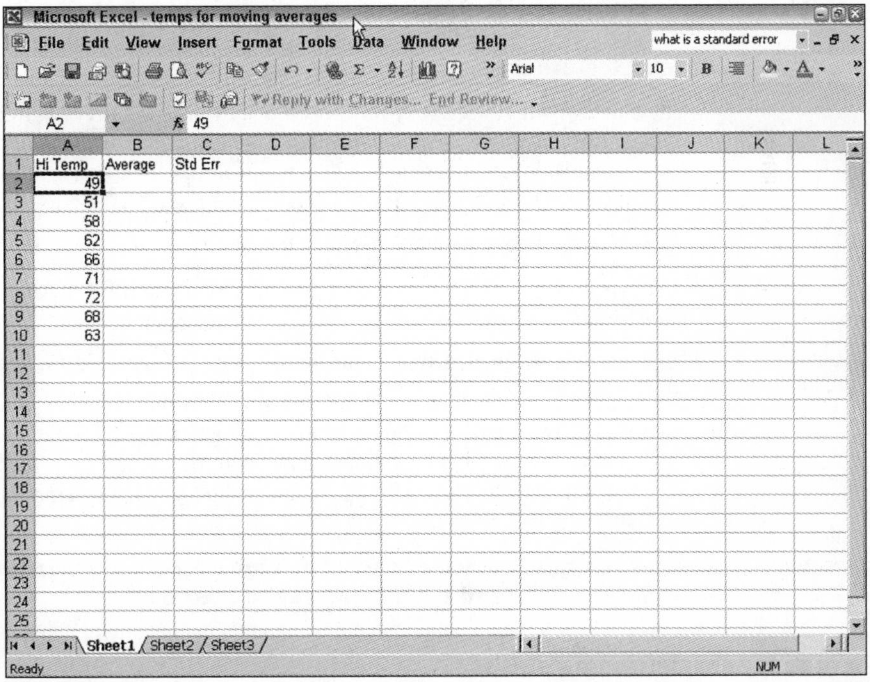

Figure 10-11: A worksheet for calculating a moving average of temperatures.

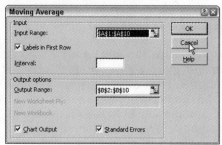

Figure 10-12:
Calculate
moving
averages
here.

Your range reference should use absolute cell addresses. An *absolute cell address* precedes the column letter and row number with $ signs, as in $A$1:$A$10.

If the first cell in your input range includes a text label to identify or describe your data, select the Labels in First Row check box.

4. **In the Interval text box, tell Excel how many values to include in the moving average calculation.**

You can calculate a moving average using any number of values. By default, Excel uses the most recent three values to calculate the moving average. To specify that some other number of values be used to calculate the moving average, enter that value into the Interval text box.

5. **Tell Excel where to place the moving average data.**

Use the Output Range text box to identify the worksheet range into which you want to place the moving average data. In the worksheet example shown in Figure 10-11, for example, I place the moving average data into the worksheet range B2:B10. (See Figure 10-12.)

6. **Specify whether you want a chart (optional).**

If you want a chart that plots the moving average information, select the Chart Output check box.

7. **Indicate whether you want standard error information calculated (optional).**

If you want to calculate standard errors for the data, select the Standard Errors check box. Excel places standard error values next to the moving average values. (In Figure 10-11, the standard error information goes into C2:C10.)

8. **After you finish specifying what moving average information you want calculated and where you want it placed, click OK.**

Excel calculates moving average information, as shown in Figure 10-13.

Note: If Excel doesn't have enough information to calculate a moving average for a standard error, it places the error message #N/A into the cell. In Figure 10-13, you can see several cells that show this error message as a value.

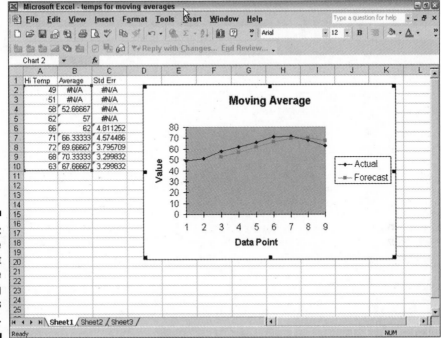

Figure 10-13:
The
worksheet
with the
moving
averages
information.

Exponential Smoothing

The Exponential Smoothing tool also calculates the moving average. However, exponential smoothing weights the values included in the moving average calculations so that more recent values have a bigger effect on the average calculation and old values have a lesser effect. This weighting is accomplished through a smoothing constant.

To illustrate how the Exponential Smoothing tool works, suppose that you're again looking at the average daily temperature information. (I repeat this worksheet in Figure 10-14.)

To calculate weighted moving averages using exponential smoothing, take the following steps:

1. **To calculate an exponentially smoothed moving average, first choose the Tools⇨Data Analysis command.**

2. **When Excel displays the Data Analysis dialog box, select the Exponential Smoothing item from the list and then click OK.**

   Excel displays the Exponential Smoothing dialog box, as shown in Figure 10-15.

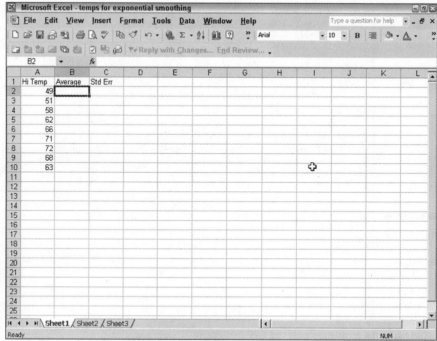

Figure 10-14:
A work-
sheet of
temperature
information.

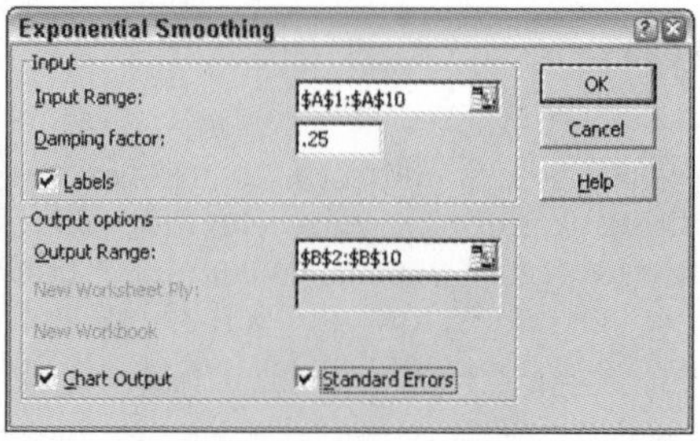

Figure 10-15:
Calculate
exponential
smoothing
here.

3. **Identify the data.**

   To identify the data for which you want to calculate an exponentially smoothed moving average, click in the Input Range text box. Then identify the input range, either by typing a worksheet range address or by using the mouse to select the worksheet range. If your input range includes a text label to identify or describe your data, select the Labels check box.

4. **Provide the smoothing constant.**

   Enter the smoothing constant value in the Damping Factor text box. The Excel Help file suggests that you use a smoothing constant of between .2 and .3. Presumably, however, if you're using this tool, you have your own ideas about what the correct smoothing constant is. (If you're clueless about the smoothing constant, perhaps you shouldn't be using this tool.)

5. **Tell Excel where to place the exponentially smoothed moving average data.**

   Use the Output Range text box to identify the worksheet range into which you want to place the moving average data. In the worksheet example shown in Figure 10-14, for example, you place the moving average data into the worksheet range B2:B10.

6. **Chart the exponentially smoothed data (optional).**

   To chart the exponentially smoothed data, select the Chart Output check box.

7. **Indicate that you want standard error information calculated (optional).**

   To calculate standard errors, select the Standard Errors check box. Excel places standard error values next to the exponentially smoothed moving average values.

8. **After you finish specifying what moving average information you want calculated and where you want it placed, click OK.**

   Excel calculates moving average information, as shown in Figure 10-16.

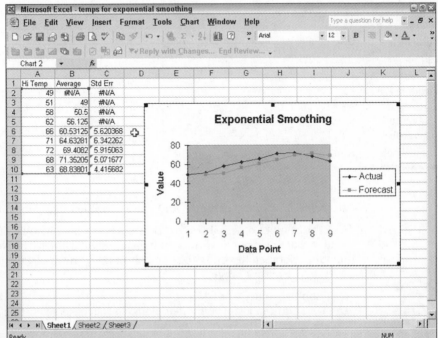

Figure 10-16:
The average daily temperature worksheet with exponentially smoothed values.

Generating Random Numbers

The Data Analysis command also includes a Random Number Generation tool. The Random Number Generation tool is considerably more flexible than the =Rand() function, which is the other tool that you have available within Excel to produce random numbers. The Random Number Generation tool isn't really a tool for descriptive statistics. You would probably typically use the tool to help you randomly sample values from a population, but I describe it here in this chapter, anyway, because it works like the other descriptive statistics tools.

To produce random numbers, take the following steps:

1. **To generate random numbers, first choose Tools⇨Data Analysis.**

   Excel displays the Data Analysis dialog box.

2. **In the Data Analysis dialog box, select the Random Number Generation entry from the list and then click OK.**

   Excel displays the Random Number Generation dialog box, as shown in Figure 10-17.

Random Number Generation		
Number of Variables:		OK
Number of Random Numbers:		Cancel
Distribution:	Discrete	Help
Parameters		
Value and Probability Input Range:		
Random Seed:		
Output options		
Output Range:		
New Worksheet Ply:		
New Workbook		

Figure 10-17: Generate random numbers here.

3. **Describe how many columns and rows of values that you want.**

   Use the Number of Variables text box to specify how many columns of values that you want in your output range. Similarly, use the Number of Random Numbers text box to specify how many rows of values that you want in the output range.

   You don't absolutely need to enter values into these two text boxes, by the way. You can also leave them blank. In this case, Excel fills all the columns and all the rows in the output range.

4. **Select the distribution method.**

   Select one of the distribution methods from the Distribution drop-down list box. The Distribution list box provides several distribution methods: Uniform, Normal, Bernoulli, Binomial, Poisson, Patterned, and Discreet. Typically, if you want a pattern of distribution other than Uniform, you'll know which one of these distribution methods are appropriate. For example, if you want to pull random numbers from a data set that's normally distributed, you might select the Normal distribution method.

5. **Provide any parameters needed for the distribution method (optional).**

   If you select a distribution method that requires parameters, or input values, use the Parameters text box (Value and Probability Input Range) to identify the worksheet range that holds the parameters needed for the distribution method.

6. **Select a starting point for the random number generation (optional).**

   You have the option of entering a value that Excel will use to start its generation of random numbers. The benefit of using a Random Seed value, as Excel calls it, is that you can later produce the same set of random numbers by planting the same "seed."

7. **Identify the output range.**

   Use the Output Options radio buttons to select the location that you want for random numbers.

8. **After you describe how you want Excel to generate random numbers and where those numbers should be placed, click OK.**

   Excel generates the random numbers.

Sampling Data

One other data analysis tool — the Sampling tool — deserves to be discussed someplace. I describe it here, even if it doesn't fits perfectly.

Truth be told, both the Random Number Generation tool (see the preceding section) and the Sampling tool are probably what you would use while preparing to perform inferential statistical analysis of the sort that I describe in Chapter 11. But because these tools work like (and look like) the other descriptive statistics tools, I describe them here.

With the Sampling tool that's part of the Data Analysis command, you can randomly select items from a data set or select every *n*th item from a data set. For example, suppose that as part of an internal audit, you want to randomly select five titles from a list of books. To do so, you could use the Sampling tool. For purposes of our discussion, pretend that you're going to use the list of books and book information shown in Figure 10-18.

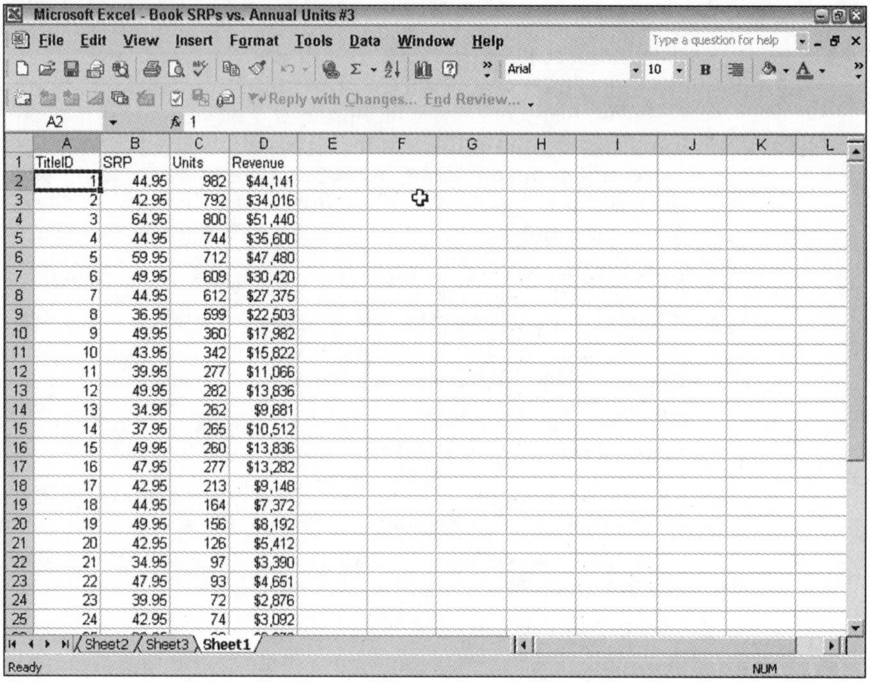

	A	B	C	D
1	TitleID	SRP	Units	Revenue
2	1	44.95	982	$44,141
3	2	42.95	792	$34,016
4	3	64.95	800	$51,440
5	4	44.95	744	$35,600
6	5	59.95	712	$47,480
7	6	49.95	609	$30,420
8	7	44.95	612	$27,375
9	8	36.95	599	$22,503
10	9	49.95	360	$17,982
11	10	43.95	342	$15,822
12	11	39.95	277	$11,066
13	12	49.95	282	$13,836
14	13	34.95	262	$9,681
15	14	37.95	265	$10,512
16	15	49.95	260	$13,836
17	16	47.95	277	$13,282
18	17	42.95	213	$9,148
19	18	44.95	164	$7,372
20	19	49.95	156	$8,192
21	20	42.95	126	$5,412
22	21	34.95	97	$3,390
23	22	47.95	93	$4,651
24	23	39.95	72	$2,876
25	24	42.95	74	$3,092

Figure 10-18: A simple worksheet from which you might select a sample.

To sample items from a worksheet like the ones shown in Figure 10-18, take the following steps:

1. **To tell Excel that you want to sample data from a data set, first choose the Tools⇨Data Analysis command.**
2. **When Excel displays the Data Analysis dialog box, select Sampling from the list and then click OK.**

   Excel displays the Sampling dialog box, as shown in Figure 10-19.

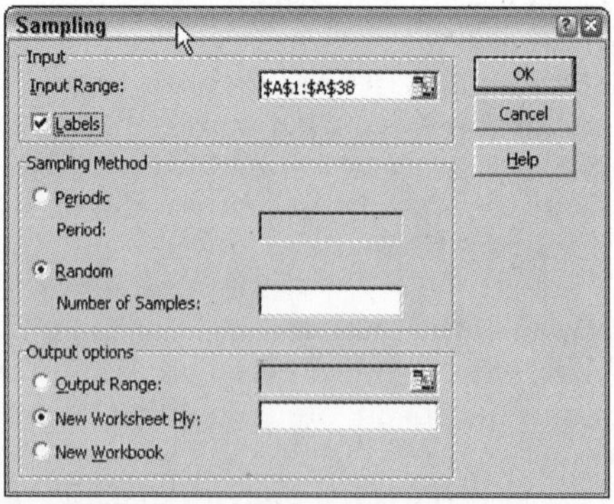

Figure 10-19: Set a data sampling here.

3. Identify the input range.

Use the Input Range textbox to describe the worksheet range that contains enough data to identify the values in the data set. For example, in the case of the data set like the one shown in Figure 10-18, the information in column A — `TitleID` — uniquely identifies items in the data set. Therefore, you can identify (or uniquely locate) items using the input range A1:A38. You can enter this range into the Input Range text box, either by directly typing it or by clicking in the text box and then dragging the mouse pointer from cell A1 to cell A38.

If the first cell in the input range holds the text label that describes the data — this is the case in Figure 10-18 — select the Labels check box.

4. Choose a sampling method.

Excel provides two sampling methods for retrieving or identifying items in your data set:

- **Periodic:** A periodic sampling method grabs every nth item from the data set. For example, if you choose every fifth item, that's periodic sampling. To select or indicate that you want to use periodic sampling, select the Periodic radio button. Then enter the period into its corresponding Period text box.

- **Random:** To randomly choose items from the data set, select the Random radio button and then enter the number of items that you want in the Number of Samples text box.

5. Choose an output area.

Choose from the three radio buttons in the Output Options area to select where the sampling result should appear. To put sampling results into an output range in the current worksheet, select the Output Range radio button and then enter the output range into the text box provided. To store the sampling information in a new worksheet or on a new workbook, select either the New Worksheet Ply or the New Workbook radio button.

Note that Excel grabs item information from the input range. For example, Figure 10-20 shows the information that Excel places on a new worksheet if you use periodic sampling and grab every sixth item. Figure 10-21 shows how Excel identifies the sample if you randomly select five items. Note that the values shown in both Figures 10-20 and 10-21 are the title ID numbers from the input range.

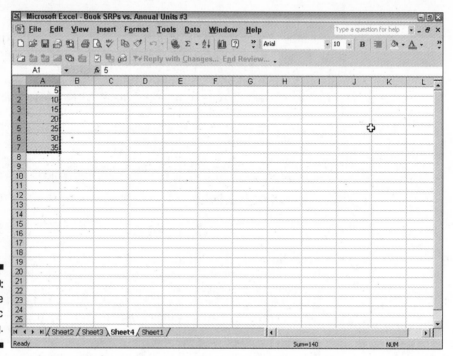

Figure 10-20:
An example
of periodic
sampling.

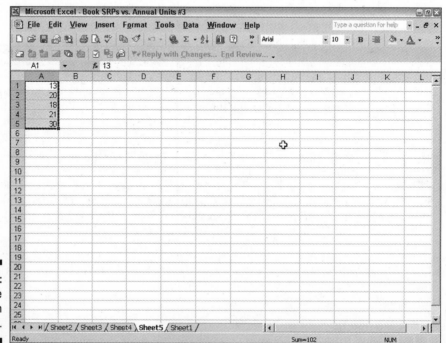

Figure 10-21:
An example
of random
sampling.

Chapter 11

Inferential Statistics

● ●

In This Chapter

▶ Discovering the Data Analysis t-test tools

▶ Performing a z-test

▶ Creating a scatter plot

▶ Using the Regression tool that comes with Data Analysis

▶ Using the Correlation tool that comes with Data Analysis

▶ Implementing the ANOVA data analysis tools

▶ Comparing variances from populations with the f-test Data Analysis tool

▶ Using the Fourier Data Analysis tool

● ●

*I*n this chapter, I talk about the more sophisticated tools provided by the Excel Data Analysis add-in, such as t-test, z-test, scatter plot, regression, correlation, ANOVA, f-test, and Fourier. With these other tools, you can perform inferential statistics, which you use to first look at a set of sample observations drawn from a population and then draw conclusions — or make inferences — about population's characteristics. (To read about the simpler descriptive statistical data analysis tools that Excel supplies through the Data Analysis add-in, skip back to Chapter 10.)

Obviously, you need pretty developed statistical skills in order to use these tools — a good basic statistics course in college or graduate school, and then probably one follow-up course. But with some reasonable knowledge of statistics and a bit of patience, you can use some of these tools to good advantage.

Note: In Excel 2002, the Data Analysis add-in is usually automatically installed. In Excel 2000, you must install the Data Analysis add-in before you can use it. To install the Data Analysis add-in (in either Excel 2002 or Excel 2000), choose the Tools➪Add-Ins command. Next, check the Analysis ToolPak box and click OK. When Excel prompts you for the Excel CD, insert that into your CD or DVD drive and wait for Excel to do its magic.

The sample workbooks used in the examples in this chapter can be downloaded from the book's companion Web site at `www.dummies.com/extras`.

Using the t-test Data Analysis Tool

The Excel Data Analysis add-in provides three tools for working with t-values and t-tests, which can be useful when you want to make inferences about very small data sets:

- ✔ t-Test: Two-Sample Assuming Equal Variances
- ✔ t-Test: Two-Sample Assuming Unequal Variances
- ✔ t-Test: Paired Two Sample for Means

Briefly, here's how these three tools work. For sake of illustration, assume that you're working with the values shown in Figure 11-1. The worksheet range A1:A21 contains the first set of values. The worksheet range B1:B21 contains the second set of values.

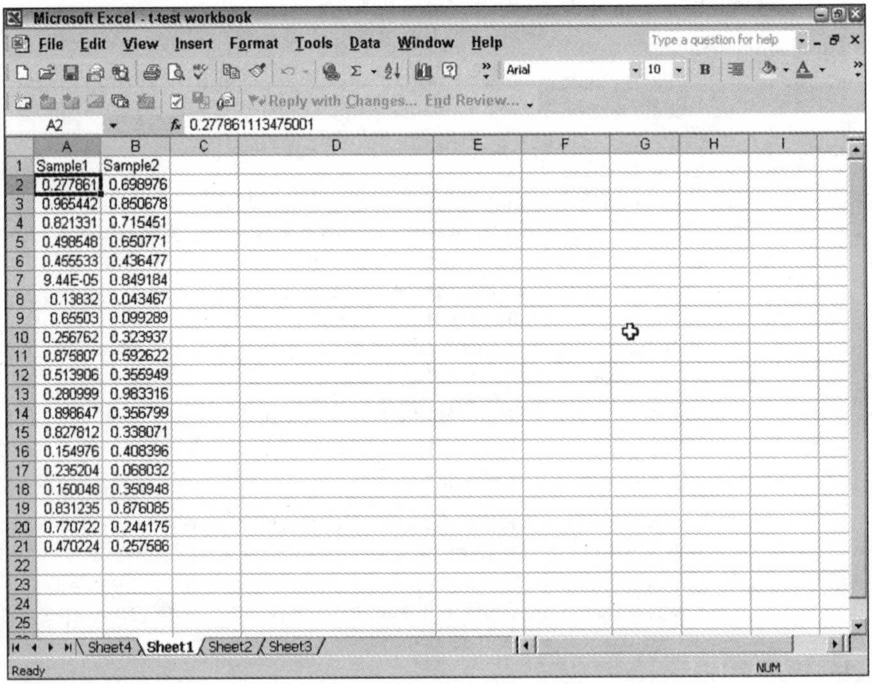

Figure 11-1: Some fake data you can use to perform t-test calculations.

To perform a t-test calculation, follow these steps:

1. **Choose Tools⇨Data Analysis.**

2. **When Excel displays the Data Analysis dialog box, as shown in Figure 11-2, select the appropriate t-test tool from its Analysis Tools list.**

   • **t-Test: Paired Two-Sample For Means:** Choose this tool when you want to perform a paired two-sample t-test.

   • **t-Test: Two-Sample Assuming Equal Variances:** Choose this tool when you want to perform a two-sample test and you have reason to assume the means of both samples equal each other.

   • **t-Test: Two-Sample Assuming Unequal Variances:** Choose this tool when you want to perform a two-sample test but you assume that the two-samples variances are unequal.

3. **After you select the correct t-test tool, click OK.**

   Excel then displays the appropriate t-test dialog box. Figure 11-3 shows the t-Test: Paired Two Sample For Means dialog box.

   The other t-test dialog boxes look very similar.

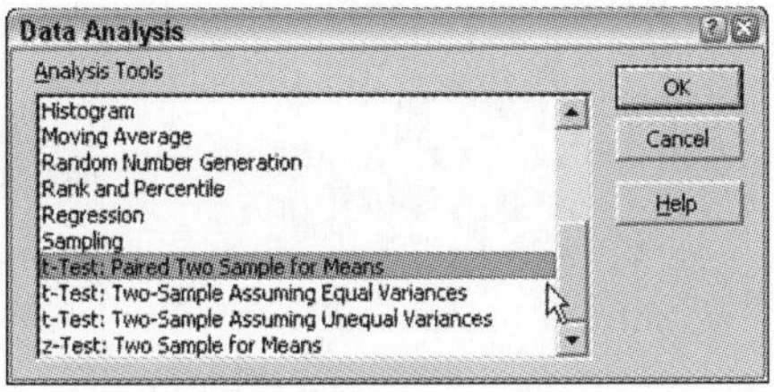

Figure 11-2:
Select your
data
analysis
tool here.

Data Analysis

Analysis Tools

Histogram
Moving Average
Random Number Generation
Rank and Percentile
Regression
Sampling
t-Test: Paired Two Sample for Means
t-Test: Two-Sample Assuming Equal Variances
t-Test: Two-Sample Assuming Unequal Variances
z-Test: Two Sample for Means

OK
Cancel
Help

4. **In the Variable 1 Range and Variable 2 Range input text boxes, identify the sample values by telling Excel in what worksheet ranges you've stored the two samples.**

   You can enter a range address into these text boxes. Or you can click in the text box and then use the mouse to select a range by clicking and dragging. If the first cell in the variable range holds a label and you include the label in your range selection, of course, select the Labels check box.

5. **Use the Hypothesized Mean Difference text box to indicate whether you hypothesize that the means are equal.**

   If you think the means of the samples are equal, enter **0** (zero) into this text box. If you hypothesize that the means are not equal, enter the mean difference.

6. In the Alpha text box, state the confidence level for your t-test calculation.

The confidence level is between 0 and 1. By default, the confidence level is equal to 0.05, which is equivalent to a 5-percent confidence level.

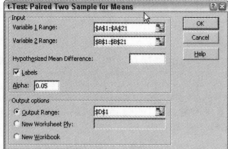

Figure 11-3:
The t-Test:
Paired Two-
Sample For
Means
dialog box.

7. In the Output Options section, indicate where the t-test tool results should be stored.

Here, select one of the radio buttons and enter information in the text boxes to specify where Excel should place the results of the t-test analysis. For example, to place the t-test results into a range in the existing worksheet, select the Output Range radio button and then identify the range address in the Output Range text box. If you want to place the t-test results someplace else, select one of the other option radio buttons.

8. Click OK.

Excel calculates the t-test results. Figure 11-4 shows the t-test results for a Paired Two Sample for Means test. The t-test results show the mean for each of the data sets, the variance, the number of observations, the Pearson correlation value, the hypothesized mean difference, the degrees of freedom (abbreviated as *DF*), the t-value or (t-stat) and the probability values for one-tail and two-tail tests.

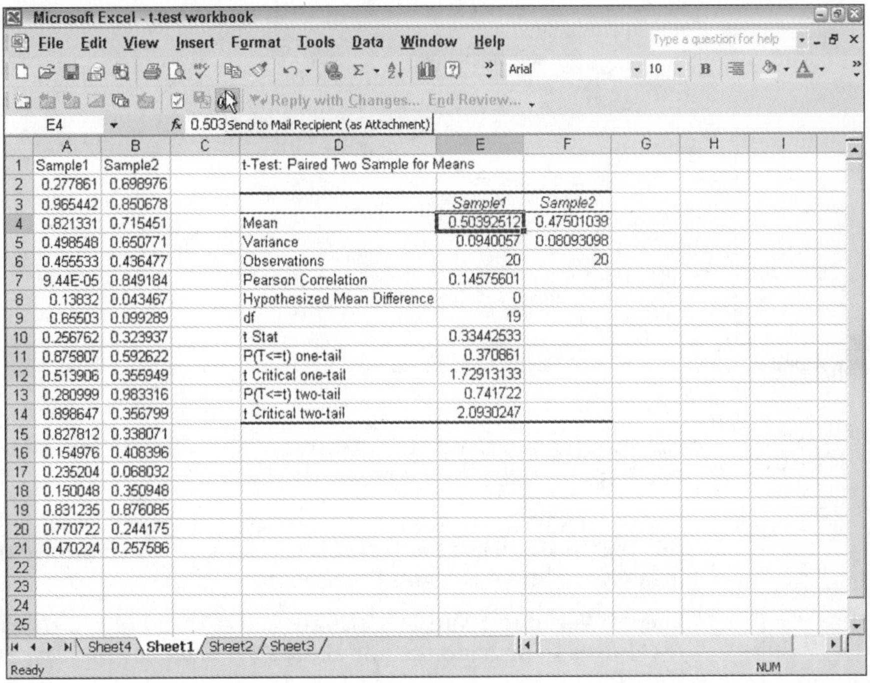

	A	B	C	D	E	F
1	Sample1	Sample2		t-Test: Paired Two Sample for Means		
2	0.277861	0.698976				
3	0.965442	0.850678			Sample1	Sample2
4	0.821331	0.715451		Mean	0.50392512	0.47501039
5	0.498548	0.650771		Variance	0.0940057	0.08093098
6	0.455533	0.436477		Observations	20	20
7	9.44E-05	0.849184		Pearson Correlation	0.14575601	
8	0.13832	0.043467		Hypothesized Mean Difference	0	
9	0.65503	0.099289		df	19	
10	0.256762	0.323937		t Stat	0.33442533	
11	0.875807	0.592622		P(T<=t) one-tail	0.370861	
12	0.513906	0.355949		t Critical one-tail	1.72913133	
13	0.280999	0.983316		P(T<=t) two-tail	0.741722	
14	0.898647	0.356799		t Critical two-tail	2.0930247	
15	0.827812	0.338071				
16	0.154976	0.408396				
17	0.235204	0.068032				
18	0.150048	0.350948				
19	0.831235	0.876085				
20	0.770722	0.244175				
21	0.470224	0.257586				

Figure 11-4: The results of a t-test.

Performing z-test Calculations

If you know the variance or standard deviation of the underlying population, you can calculate z-test values by using the Data Analysis add-in. You might typically work with z-test values to calculate confidence levels and confidence intervals for normally distributed data. To do this, take these steps:

1. **To select the z-test tool, choose Tools⇨Data Analysis.**
2. **When Excel displays the Data Analysis dialog box (refer to Figure 11-2), select the z-Test: Two Sample for Means tool and then click OK.**

   Excel then displays the z-Test: Two Sample for Means dialog box, as shown in Figure 11-5.
3. **In the Variable 1 Range and Variable 2 Range text boxes, identify the sample values by telling Excel in what worksheet ranges you've stored the two samples.**

   You can enter a range address into the text boxes here, or you can click in the text box and then use the mouse to select a range by clicking and dragging. If the first cell in the variable range holds a label and you include the label in your range selection, select the Labels check box.

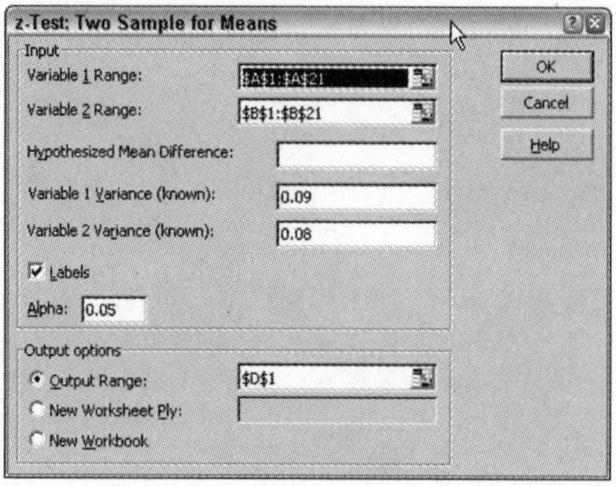

Figure 11-5:
Perform a
z-test from
here.

4. **Use the Hypothesized Mean Difference text box to indicate whether you hypothesize that the means are equal.**

   If you think that the means of the samples are equal, enter **0** (zero) into this text box or leave the text box empty. If you hypothesize that the means are not equal, enter the difference.

5. **Use the Variable 1 Variance (Known) and Variable 2 Variance (Known) text boxes to provide the population variance for the first and second samples.**

6. **In the Alpha text box, state the confidence level for your z-test calculation.**

   The confidence level is between 0 and 1. By default, the confidence level equals 0.05 (equivalent to a 5-percent confidence level).

7. **In the Output Options section, indicate where the z-test tool results should be stored.**

   To place the z-test results into a range in the existing worksheet, select the Output Range radio button and then identify the range address in the Output Range text box. If you want to place the z-test results someplace else, use one of the other option radio buttons.

8. **Click OK.**

   Excel calculates the z-test results. Figure 11-6 shows the z-test results for a Two Sample for Means test. The z-test results show the mean for each of the data sets, the variance, the number of observations, the hypothesized mean difference, the z-value, or and the probability values for one-tail and two-tail tests.

```
Microsoft Excel - z-test workbook
 File  Edit  View  Insert  Format  Tools  Data  Window  Help          Type a question for help  _ 8 x

        E4              fx  0.503925118839197
```

	A	B	C	D	E	F	G	H	I
1	Sample1	Sample2		z-Test: Two Sample for Means					
2	0.277861	0.698976							
3	0.965442	0.850678			Sample1	Sample2			
4	0.821331	0.715451		Mean	0.50392512	0.47501039			
5	0.498548	0.650771		Known Variance	0.09	0.08			
6	0.455533	0.436477		Observations	20	20			
7	9.44E-05	0.849184		Hypothesized Mean Difference	0				
8	0.13832	0.043467		z	0.31362431				
9	0.65503	0.099289		P(Z<=z) one-tail	0.37690326				
10	0.256762	0.323937		z Critical one-tail	1.64485348				
11	0.875807	0.592622		P(Z<=z) two-tail	0.75380653				
12	0.513906	0.355949		z Critical two-tail	1.95996279				
13	0.280999	0.983316							
14	0.898647	0.356799							
15	0.827812	0.338071							
16	0.154976	0.408396							
17	0.235204	0.068032							
18	0.150048	0.350948							
19	0.831235	0.876085							
20	0.770722	0.244175							
21	0.470224	0.257586							
22									
23									
24									
25									

```
H  4  ►  H \ Sheet4 / Sheet1 / Sheet2 / Sheet3 /
Ready                                                    NUM
```

Figure 11-6:
The z-test calculation results.

Creating a Scatter Plot

One of the most interesting and useful forms of data analysis is regression analysis. In *regression analysis*, you explore the relationship between two sets of values, looking for association. For example, you can use regression analysis to determine whether advertising expenditures are associated with sales, whether cigarette smoking is associated with heart disease, or whether exercise is associated with longevity.

Often your first step in any regression analysis is to create a *scatter plot*, which lets you visually explore association between two sets of values. In Excel, you do this by using an XY (Scatter) chart. For example, suppose that you want to look at or analyze the values shown in the worksheet displayed in Figure 11-7. The worksheet range A1:A11 shows numbers of ads. The worksheet range B1:B11 shows the resulting sales. You may have collected this data to explore the effect of ads on sales — or the lack of an effect.

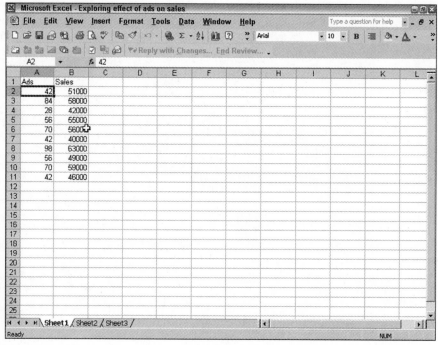

Figure 11-7:
A worksheet with data you might analyze by using regression.

To create a scatter chart of this information, take the following steps:

1. **Select the worksheet range A1:B11.**

2. **Start the Chart Wizard by clicking the Chart Wizard tool on the Excel toolbar.**

   This toolbar button has a picture of a bar chart on it. Or you can choose Insert⇨Chart.

   Either way, Excel displays the first step of four Chart Wizard dialog boxes, as shown in Figure 11-8.

3. **On the Standard Types tab, select the XY (Scatter) chart type from the Chart Type list box.**

4. **Select the Chart sub-type that doesn't include any lines, and then click Next.**

   Excel displays the second Chart Wizard dialog box, as shown in Figure 11-9.

5. **Confirm the chart data on the Data Range tab.**

   Confirm that the worksheet range shown in the Data Range text box does in fact identify the correct data.

Verify that Excel has correctly interpreted the arrangement of your data by looking at the Series In radio buttons (Rows and Columns, either of which you select to tell Excel to arrange data series).

If you aren't happy with the chart as it appears in the Data Range tab, click the Back button to make any necessary changes in the first screen, and then repeat Step 5.

6. Click Next.

Excel displays the third step of the Chart Wizard, as shown in Figure 11-10.

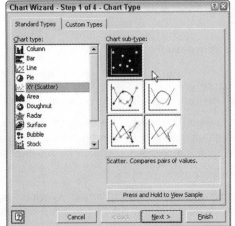

Figure 11-8:
The first
Chart
Wizard
dialog box.

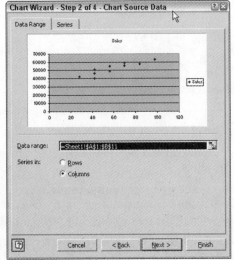

Figure 11-9:
The second
Chart
Wizard
dialog box.

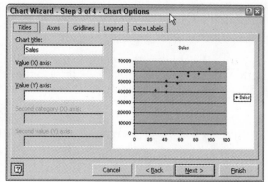

Figure 11-10:
The third
Chart
Wizard
dialog box.

7. Annotate the chart, if appropriate.

Add those little flourishes to your chart that will make it more attractive and readable. For example, you can use the Titles tab to annotate the chart with a title and with descriptions of the axes used in the chart.

In Chapter 7, I discuss in detail the mechanics of customizing a chart using the Chart Options dialog box. Refer there if you have questions about how to work with the Titles, Axes, Gridlines, Legend, or Data Labels tabs.

8. After you select your chart options, click Next.

Excel displays the fourth step of the Chart Wizard, as shown in Figure 11-11.

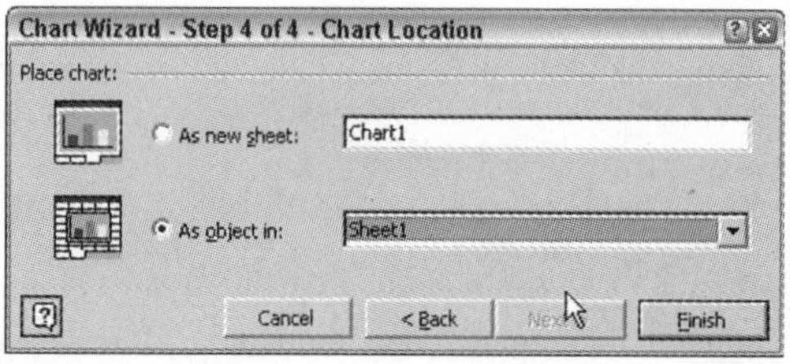

Figure 11-11:
The fourth
Chart
Wizard
dialog box.

9. Choose a location for the chart from the Place Chart section.

Select the As New Sheet radio button to add the chart to a new sheet in the workbook — a chart sheet.

Or you can select the As Object In radio button to place the chart as an object floating over an existing worksheet. You can choose the existing worksheet from the drop-down list box next to this radio button.

10. After you identify where you want to place the chart, click the Finish button.

Excel adds the chart to your workbook in the specified location. Figure 11-12 shows an example of a scatter plot.

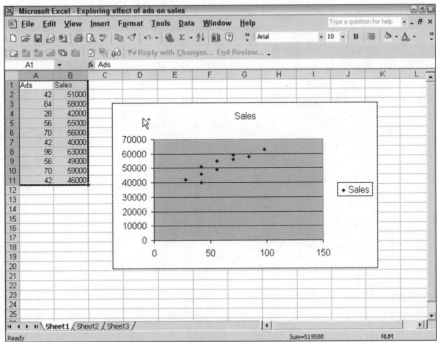

Figure 11-12:
An
embedded
scatter plot.

11. Add a trendline by choosing Chart⇨Add Trendline.

In order for the Chart menu to be displayed, you must have either first selected an embedded chart object or displayed a chart sheet.

Excel displays the Add Trendline dialog box, as shown in Figure 11-13. Select the type of trendline or regression calculation that you want by clicking one of the type buttons on the Type tab. For example, to perform simple linear regression, click the Linear button.

12. Add the Regression Equation to the scatter plot.

To show the equation for the trendline that the scatter plot uses, click the Options tab of the Add Trendline dialog box. (See Figure 11-14.)

Then select both the Display Equation on Chart and the Display R-Squared Value on Chart check boxes. This tells Excel to add the simple regression analysis information necessary for a trendline to your chart.

Use the radio buttons and text boxes on the Options tab to control how the regression analysis trendline is calculated. For example, you can use the Set Intercept = check box and text box to force the trendline to intercept the X axis at a particular point, such as zero. You can also use the Forecast Forward and Backward text boxes to specify that a trendline should be extended backward or forward beyond the existing data or before the existing data.

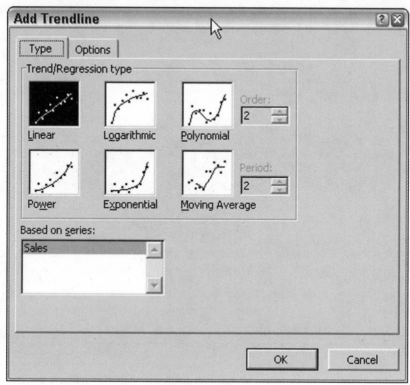

Figure 11-13:
Add a
trendline
here.

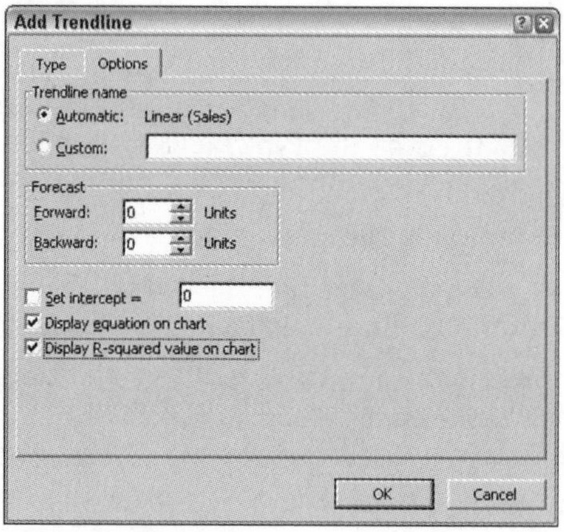

Figure 11-14:
The Options
tab of the
Add
Trendline
dialog box.

13. Click OK.

Excel shows the embedded Scatter Plot chart with the line equation
and the R-squared value displayed, as shown in Figure 11-15. (In Figure 11-15, I moved the trendline information to the top corner of the
chart by dragging.)

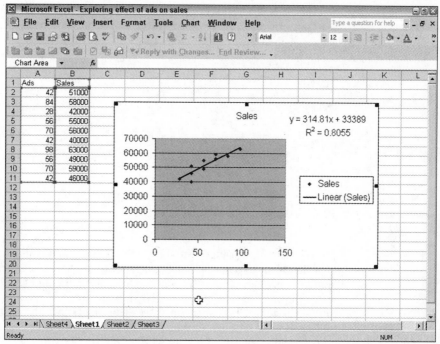

Figure 11-15:
The Scatter
Plot chart
with the
regression
data.

Using the Regression Data Analysis Tool

You can move beyond the visual regression analysis that the scatter plot technique provides. (Read the previous section for more on this technique.) You can use the Regression tool provided by the Data Analysis add-in. For example, say that you did use the scatter plotting technique, as I describe earlier, to begin looking at a simple data set. And, after that initial examination, suppose that you want to look more closely at the data by using full blown, take-no-prisoners, regression. To perform regression analysis by using the Data Analysis add-in:

1. **Tell Excel that you want to join the big leagues by choosing the Tools⇨Data Analysis command.**

2. **When Excel displays the Data Analysis dialog box, select the Regression tool from the Analysis Tools list and then click OK.**

   Excel displays the Regression dialog box, as shown in Figure 11-16.

3. **Identify your Y and X values.**

   Use the Input Y Range text box to identify the worksheet range holding your dependent variables. Then use the Input X Range text box to identify the worksheet range reference holding your independent variables.

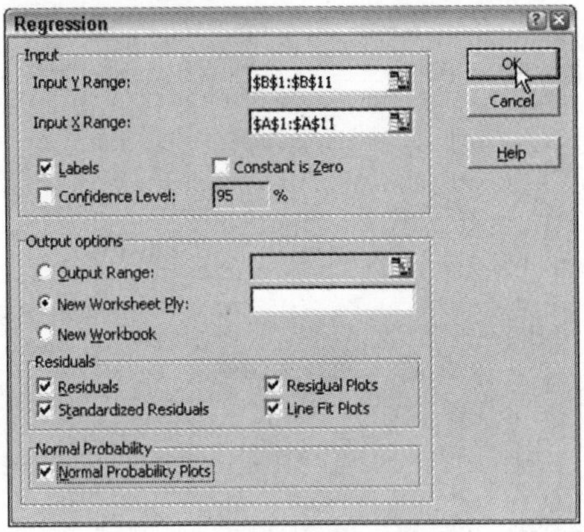

Figure 11-16:
The
Regression
dialog box.

Each of these input ranges must be a single column of values. For example, if you want to use the Regression tool to explore the effect of advertisements on sales (this is the same information shown earlier in the scatter plot discussion in Figure 11-15), you enter $A$1:$A$11 into the Input X Range text box and you enter $B$1:$B$11 into the Input Y Range text box. If your input ranges include a label, as is the case of the worksheet shown in Figure 11-15, select the Labels check box.

4. Set the constant to zero (optional).

If the regression line should start at zero — in other words, if the dependent value should equal zero when the independent value equals zero — select the Constant Is Zero check box.

5. Calculate a confidence level in your regression analysis (optional).

To do this, select the Confidence Level check box and then (in the Confidence Level text box) enter the confidence level you want to use.

6. Select a location for the regression analysis results.

Use the Output Options radio buttons and text boxes to specify where Excel should place the results of the regression analysis. To place the regression results into a range in the existing worksheet, for example, select the Output Range radio button and then identify the range address in the Output Range text box. To place the regression results someplace else, select one of the other option radio buttons.

7. Identify what data you want returned.

Select from the Residuals check boxes to specify what residuals results you want returned as part of the regression analysis.

Similarly, select the Normal Probability Plots check box to add residuals and normal probability information to the regression analysis results.

8. **Click OK.**

Excel shows a portion of the regression analysis results for the worksheet shown in Figure 11-15, as depicted in Figure 11-17.

There is a range that supplies some basic regression statistics, including the R-square value, the standard error, and the number of observations. Below that information, the Regression tool supplies *analysis of variance* (or ANOVA) data, including information about the degrees of freedom, sum-of-squares value, mean square value, the f-value, and the significance of F. Beneath the ANOVA information, the Regression tool supplies information about the regression line calculated from the data, including the coefficient, standard error, t-stat, and probability values for the intercept — as well as the same information for the independent variable, which is the number of ads in the example I discuss here.

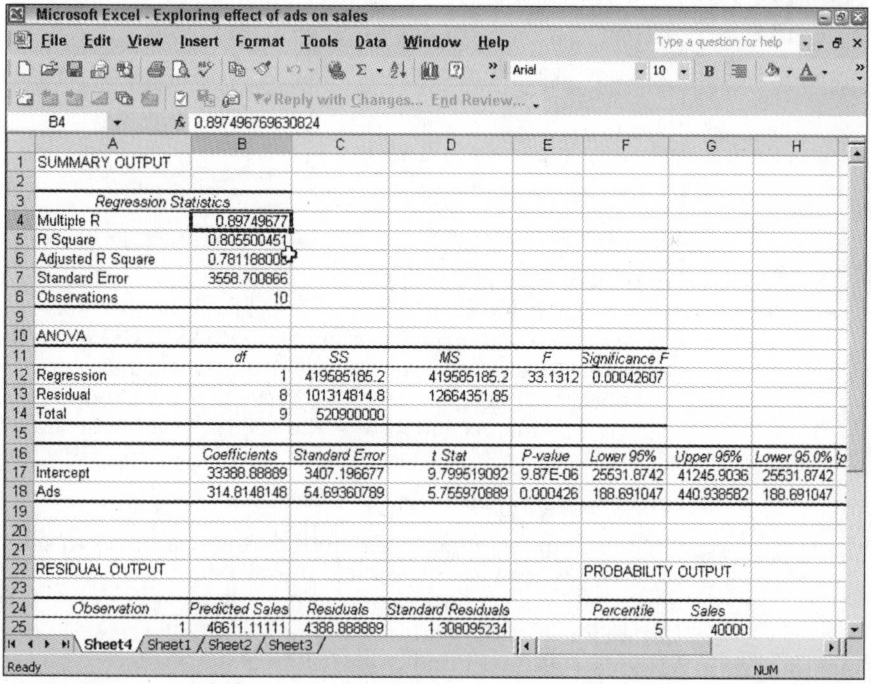

Figure 11-17:
The regression analysis results.

Using the Correlation Analysis Tool

The Correlation analysis tool (which is also available through the Data Analysis command) quantifies the relationship between two sets of data. You might use this tool to explore such things as the effect of advertising on sales, for example. To use the Correlation analysis tool, follow these steps:

1. **Choose Tools⇨Data Analysis.**

2. **When Excel displays the Data Analysis dialog box, select the Correlation tool from the Analysis Tools list and then click OK.**

   Excel displays the Correlation dialog box, as shown in Figure 11-18.

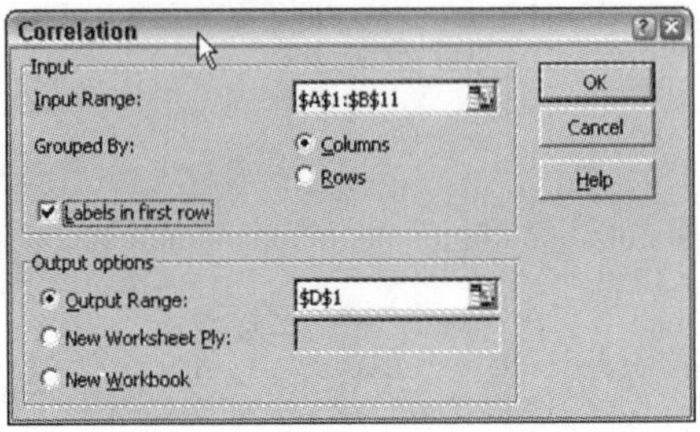

Figure 11-18:
The Correlation dialog box.

3. **Identify the range of X and Y values that you want to analyze.**

   For example, if you want to look at the correlation between ads and sales — this is the same data that appears in the worksheet shown in Figure 11-15 — enter the worksheet range **$A$1:$B$11** into the Input Range text box. If the input range includes labels in the first row, select the Labels in First Row check box. Verify that the Grouped By radio buttons — Columns and Rows — correctly show how you've organized your data.

4. **Select an output location.**

   Use the Output Options radio buttons and text boxes to specify where Excel should place the results of the correlation analysis. To place the correlation results into a range in the existing worksheet, select the Output Range radio button and then identify the range address in the Output Range text box. If you want to place the correlation results some-place else, select one of the other option radio buttons.

5. **Click OK.**

   Excel calculates the correlation coefficient for the data that you identi-fied and places it in the specified location. Figure 11-19 shows the corre-lation results for the ads and sales data. The key value is shown in cell E3. The value 0.897497 suggests that 89 percent of sales can be explained through ads.

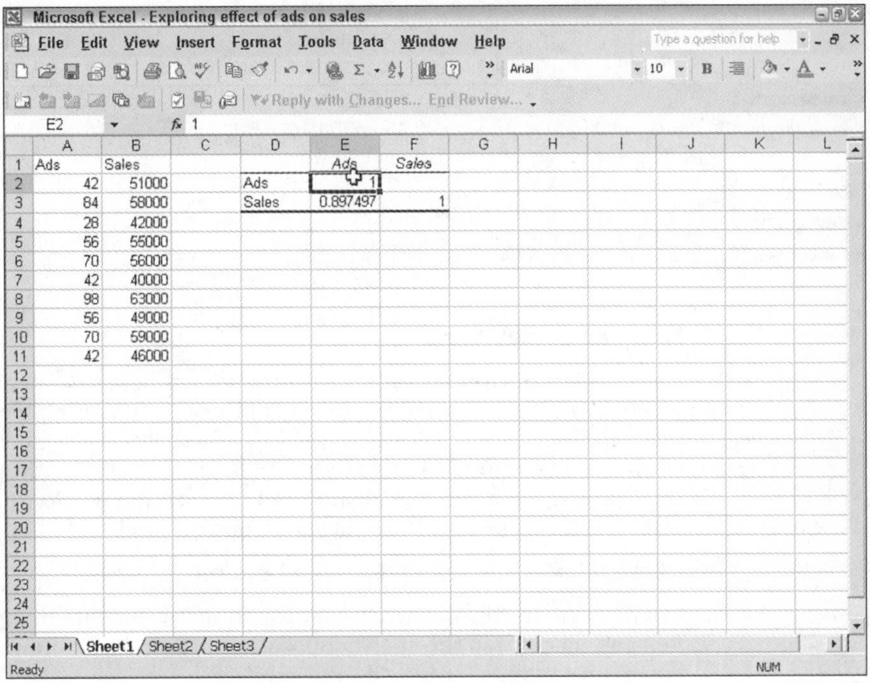

Figure 11-19:
The
worksheet
showing the
correlation
results for
the ads
and sales
information.

Using the Covariance Analysis Tool

The Covariance tool, also available through the Data Analysis add-in, quantifies the relationship between two sets of values. The Covariance tool calculates the average of the product of deviations of values from the data set means.

To use this tool, follow these steps:

1. **Choose the Tools⇨Data Analysis command.**

2. **When Excel displays the Data Analysis dialog box, select the Covariance tool from the Analysis Tools list and then click OK.**

   Excel displays the Covariance dialog box, as shown in Figure 11-20.

3. **Identify the range of X and Y values that you want to analyze.**

   To look at the correlation between ads and sales data from the worksheet shown in Figure 11-15, for example, enter the worksheet range $A$1:$B$11 into the Input Range text box.

   Select the Labels in First Row check box if the input range includes labels in the first row.

   Verify that the Grouped By radio buttons — Columns and Rows — correctly show how you've organized your data.

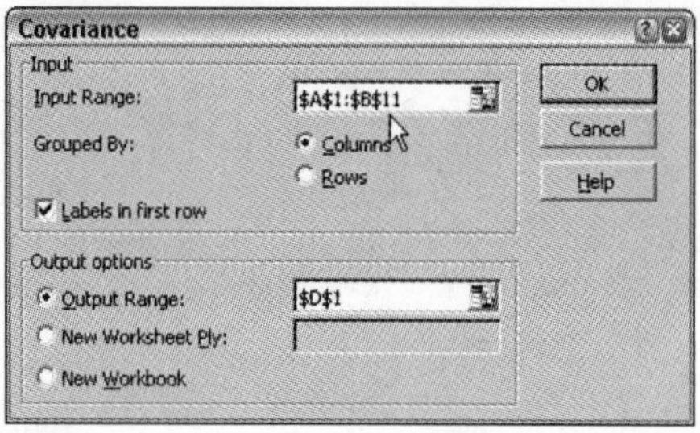

Figure 11-20:
The
Covariance
dialog box.

4. **Select an output location.**

   Use the Output Options radio buttons and text boxes to specify where Excel should place the results of the covariance analysis. To place the results into a range in the existing worksheet, select the Output Range radio button and then identify the range address in the Output Range text box. If you want to place the results someplace else, select one of the other Output Options radio buttons.

5. **Click OK after you select the output options.**

   Excel calculates the covariance information for the data that you identified and places it in the specified location. Figure 11-21 shows the covariance results for the ads and sales data.

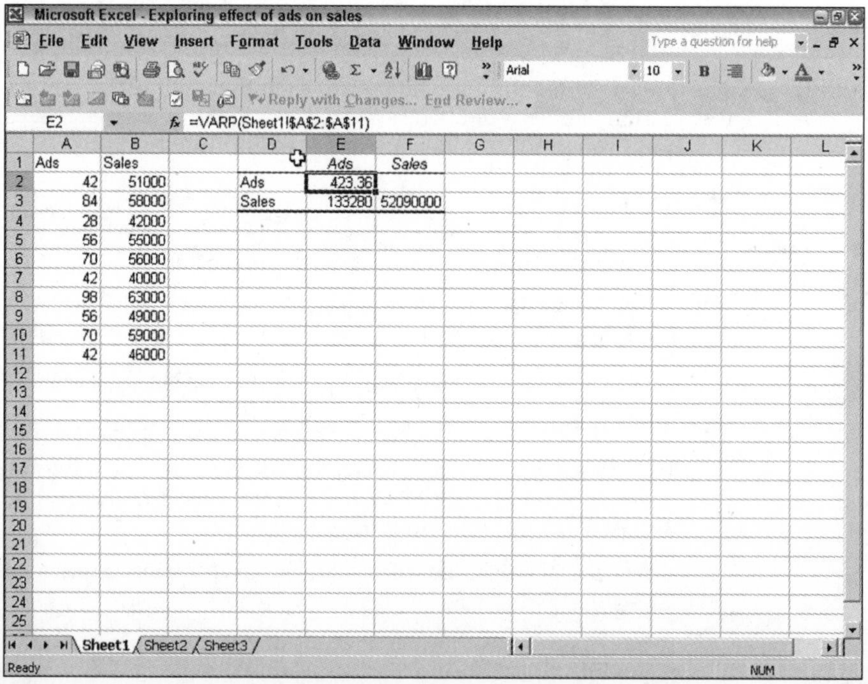

Figure 11-21:
The
worksheet
showing the
covariance
results for
the ads
and sales
information.

Using the ANOVA Data Analysis Tools

The Excel Data Analysis add-in also provides three ANOVA (analysis of variance) tools: ANOVA: Single Factor, ANOVA: Two-Factor With Replication, and ANOVA: Two-Factor Without Replication. With the ANOVA analysis tools, you can compare sets of data by looking at the variance of values in each set.

As an example of how the ANOVA analysis tools work, suppose that you want to use the ANOVA: Single Factor tool. To do so, take these steps:

1. **Choose Tools⇨Data Analysis.**

2. **When Excel displays the Data Analysis Dialog box, choose the appropriate ANOVA analysis tool and then click OK.**

   Excel displays the appropriate ANOVA dialog box. (In this particular example, I chose the Anova: Single Factor tool, as shown in Figure 11-22.)

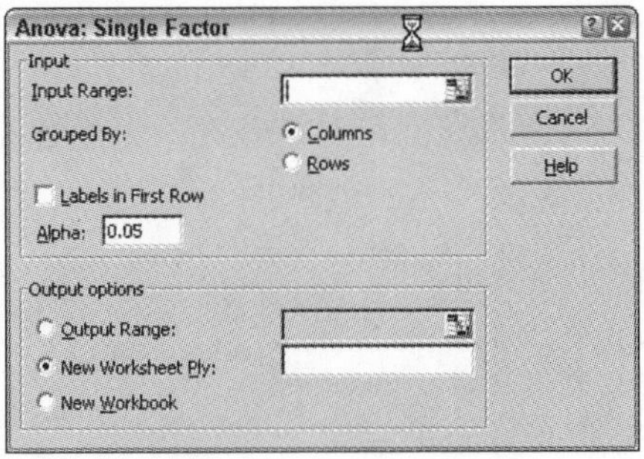

Figure 11-22:
The Anova
Single
Factor
dialog box.

3. **Describe the data to be analyzed.**

   Use the Input Range text box to identify the worksheet range that holds the data you want to analyze. Select from the Grouped By radio buttons — Columns and Rows — to identify the organization of your data. If the first row in your input range includes labels, select the Labels In First Row check box. Set your confidence level in the Alpha text box.

4. **Describe the location for the ANOVA results.**

   Use the Output Options buttons and boxes to specify where Excel should place the results of the ANOVA analysis. If you want to place the ANOVA results into a range in the existing worksheet, for example, select the Output Range radio button and then identify the range address in the Output Range text box. To place the ANOVA results someplace else, select one of the other Output Options radio buttons.

5. **Click OK.**

   Excel returns the ANOVA calculation results.

Creating an f-test Analysis

The Excel Data Analysis add-in also provides a tool for calculating two-sample f-test calculations. f-test analysis enables you to compare variances from two populations. To use the f-Test Analysis tool, choose Tool⇨Data Analysis, select f-Test Two-Sample For Variances from the Data Analysis dialog box that appears, and click OK. When Excel displays the F-Test Two-Sample for Variances dialog box, as shown in Figure 11-23, identify the data the tools should use for the f-test analysis by using the Variable Range text boxes. Then specify where you want the f-test analysis results placed using the Output Options radio buttons and text boxes. Click OK and Excel produces your f-test results.

f-test analysis tests to see whether two population variances equal each other. Essentially, the analysis compares the ratio of two variances. The assumption is that if variances are equal, then the ratio of the variances should equal 1.

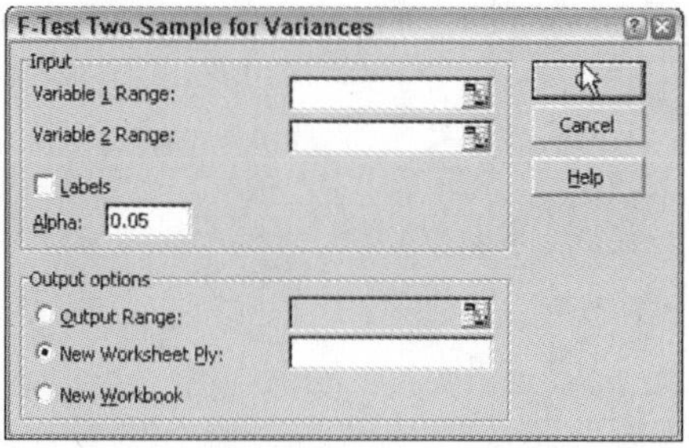

Figure 11-23:
The F-Test
Two-Sample
for
Variances
dialog box.

F-Test Two-Sample for Variances		
Input		
Variable 1 Range:	[ ]	OK
Variable 2 Range:	[ ]	Cancel
□ Labels		Help
Alpha: [0.05]		
Output options		
○ Output Range:	[ ]	
● New Worksheet Ply:	[ ]	
○ New Workbook		

Using Fourier Analysis

The Data Analysis add-in also includes a tool for performing Fourier analysis. To do this, choose Tool⇨Data Analysis, select Fourier Analysis from the Data Analysis dialog box that appears, and click OK. When Excel displays the Fourier Analysis dialog box, as shown in Figure 11-24, identify the data that Excel should use for the analysis by using the Input Range text box. Then specify where you want the analysis results placed by selecting from the Output Options radio buttons. Click OK; Excel performs your Fourier analysis and places the results at the specified location.

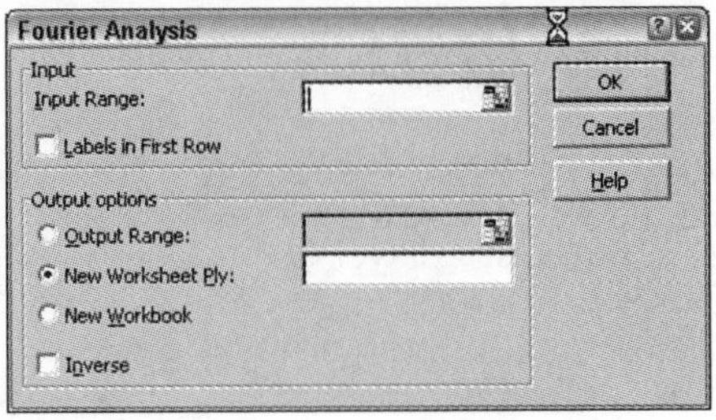

Fourier Analysis
Input
Input Range:
Labels in First Row
OK
Cancel
Help
Output options
Output Range:
New Worksheet Ply:
New Workbook
Inverse

Figure 11-24: The Fourier Analysis dialog box.

Chapter 12

Optimization Modeling with Solver

*I*n the preceding chapters of this book, I discuss how to use Excel tools to analyze data stored in an Excel workbook. However, you can also perform another sort of data analysis. You can perform data analysis that looks not at labels and values stored in cells but rather at formulas that describe business problems. In fact, Excel includes just such a tool for working on these kinds of problems: the Solver.

When you use optimization modeling and the Excel Solver, you aren't problem solving or analyzing based on raw data. Your problem solving and analyzing are based on formulaic descriptions of a situation. Nevertheless, although the abstraction takes some getting used to, analyzing situations or problems based on formulaic descriptions of objective functions and constraints can be a powerful tool. And powerful tools can lead to powerful new insights.

In this chapter, I describe the sorts of data analysis problems that Solver helps you figure out. And I show you a simple example of how the Solver works in action. Although Solver seems terribly complicated, it's actually an easier tool to use than you might think, so stick with me here.

Understanding Optimization Modeling

Suppose that you're a one-person business. This example is sort of artificial, but I need to take some liberties in order to make optimization modeling and what the Solver does easy to understand.

Optimizing your imaginary profits

In your business, you make money two ways: You write books and you give seminars. Imagine that when you write a book, you make $15,000 for roughly six weeks of work. If you work out the math on that — dividing $15,000 by 240 hours — you see that you make roughly $62.50 an hour by writing a book.

Also assume that you make $20,000 for giving a one-day seminar on some subject on which you're an expert. You make about $830.00 an hour for giving the seminar. I calculate this number by dividing the $20,000 that you make by the 24 hours that presenting the seminar requires you to invest.

In many situations, you may be able to figure out how many books you want to write and how many seminars you want to give simply by looking at the profit that you make in each activity. If you make roughly $62 an hour writing a book and you make roughly $830 an hour giving a seminar, the obvious answer to the question, "How many books should I write and how many seminars should I give?" is do as many seminars as possible and as few books as possible. You make more money giving seminars, so you should do that more.

Recognizing constraints

In many situations, however, you can't just look at the profit per activity or the cost per activity. You typically need to consider other constraints in your decision making. For example, suppose that you give seminars on the same subject that you write books about. In this case, it may be that in order to be in the seminar business, you need to write at least one book a year. And so that constraint of writing one book a year needs to be considered while you think about what makes most sense about how you maximize your profits.

Commonly, other constraints will often apply to a problem like this. For example — and I know this because one of my past jobs was publishing books — book publishers may require that you give a certain number of seminars a year in order to promote your books. So it may also be that in order to write books, you need to be giving at least four seminars a year. This requirement to give at least four book-promoting seminars a year becomes another constraint.

Consider other constraints, too, when you look at things such as financial resources available and the capacity of the tools that you use to provide your products or services. For example, perhaps you have only $20,000 of working capital to invest in things like writing books or in giving seminars. And if a book requires $500 to be tied up in working capital but a seminar requires $2,500 to be tied up in working capital, you're limited in the number of books that you can write and seminars that you can give by your $20,000 of working capital balance.

Another common type of constraint is a capacity constraint. For example, although there are 2,080 hours in a working year, assume that you only want to work 1,880 hours in a year. This would mean, quite conventionally, that you want to have ten holidays a year and three weeks of vacation a year. In this case, if a book requires 240 hours and a seminar requires 24 hours, that working-hours limit constrains the number of books and seminars that you can give, too.

This situation is exactly the kind of problem that Solver helps you figure out. What Solver does is find the optimum value of what's called your _objective function_. In this case, the objective function is the profit function of the business. But Solver, in working through the numbers, explicitly recognizes the constraints that you describe.

Setting Up a Solver Worksheet

Figure 12-1 shows an Excel workbook set up to solve an optimization modeling problem for the one-person business that I describe earlier in this chapter. Here I describe the pieces and parts of this workbook. If you've carefully read earlier discussion in the chapter about what optimization modeling is, you should have no trouble seeing what's going on here.

The Solver workbook is available at the For Dummies Web site at the URL address www.dummies.com/extras. You may want to retrieve this workbook before you begin noodling around with the optimization modeling problem that I describe here. Having a workbook set up for you makes things easier, especially if you're working with the Solver for the first time.

If you choose to construct the Solver workbook example yourself (a fine idea), you want to tell Excel to display actual formulas rather than formula results in the workbook. This is what the workbook shown in Figure 12-1 does, by the way. To do this, choose the Tools⇨Options command, click the View tab, and then select the Formulas check box. By selecting the Formulas check box, you tell Excel to display the formula rather than the formula result. Note that the worksheet range B5:B11 in Figure 12-l shows formulas, not formula results.

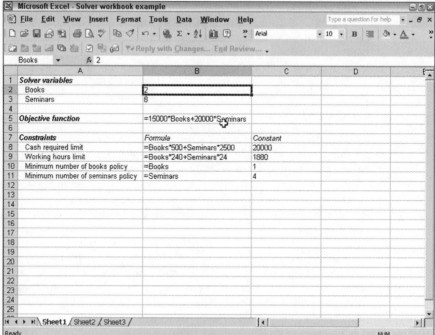

Figure 12-1:
A sample workbook set up to solve an optimization modeling problem for a one-person business.

Setting up a Solver workbook requires three steps:

1. Identify the Solver variables.

The first thing that you want to do is to identify the variables in your optimization modeling problem. In the case of trying to figure out the number of books to write and seminars to give to make the most money in your one-person business, the two Solver variables are *books* and *seminars*.

- **Identify the objective function:** In Figure 12-1, I enter the labels shown in range A1:A3 and then the starting variable values shown in range B2:B3. This part of the worksheet isn't anything magical. All it does is to identify which variables go into the objective function. The *objective function* is the formula that you want to maximize or minimize. The values stored in the worksheet range B2:B3 are my starting guesses about what the optimal variable values should be. In Figure 12-1, for example, I'm just guessing that the optimal number of books to write is two and that the optimal number of seminars to give is eight. You won't know what the optimal number of books and seminars actually is until you work out the problem.

- **Name the variable value cells:** Although you don't have to name the cells that hold the variable values — in this case, cells B2 and

B3 — naming those cells makes your objective function formula and your constraint formulas much easier to understand. So I recommend that you name the cells.

If you set up a workbook like the one shown in Figure 12-1, you can name the variable value cells by selecting the worksheet range A2:B3 and then choosing the Insert⇨Name⇨Create command. When Excel displays the Create Names dialog box, as shown in Figure 12-2, select the Left Column check box and click OK. This tells Excel to use the labels in the left column: This would be the range A2:A3 — to name the range B2:B3. In other words, by following these steps, you name cell B2 *Books* and you name cell B3 *Seminars*.

Figure 12-2:
The Create
Names
dialog box.

2. **Describe the objective function.**

The objective function, shown in cell B5 in Figure 12-1, gives the formula that you want to optimize. In the case of a profit formula, you want to maximize a function because you want to maximize profits, of course.

I should note and you should remember that not all objective functions should be maximized. Some objective functions should be minimized. For example, if you create an objective function that describes the cost of some advertising program or the risk of some investment program, you may logically choose to minimize your costs or minimize your risks.

To describe the objective function, you create a formula that describes the value that you want to optimize. In the case of a profit function for the one-person business as I detail in the earlier section "Recognizing constraints," you make $15,000 for every book that you write and $20,000 for every seminar that you give. You can describe this in a formula by entering the formula **=15000*Books+20000*Seminars**. In other words, the profits of your one-person business can be calculated by multiplying the number of books that you write times $15,000 and the number of seminars that you give times $20,000. This is what shows in cell B5.

3. **Identify any objective function constraints.**

In the worksheet range A8:C11, I describe and identify the constraints on the objective function. As I note earlier, four constraints can limit the profits that you can make in your business:

- **Cash required limit:** The first constraint shown in Figure 12-1 (cell A8) quantifies the cash required constraint. In this example, each book requires $500 cash, and each seminar requires $2,500 cash. If you have $20,000 cash to invest (I assume to temporarily invest) in books and seminars, you're limited in the number of books that you can write and the number of seminars that you can give by the cash, up-front investment that you need to make in these activities. The formula in cell B8, =Books*500+Seminars*2500, describes the cash required by your business. The value shown in cell C8, 20000, identifies the actual constraint.

- **Working hours limit:** The working hours limit constraint is quantified by having the formula =Books*240+Seminars*24 in cell B9 and the value 1880 in cell C9. Use these two pieces of information, the formula and the constant value, to describe a working hours limit. In a nutshell, this constraint says that the number of hours that you spent on books and seminars needs to be less than 1880.

- **Minimum number of books policy:** The constraint that you must write at least one book a year is set up in cells B10 and C10. The formula =Books goes into cell B10. The minimum number of books, 1, goes into cell C10.

- **Minimum number of seminars policy:** The constraint that you must give at least four seminars a year is set up in cells B11 and C11. The formula =Seminars goes into cell B11. The minimum number of seminars constant value, 4, goes into cell C11.

After you give the constraint formulas and provide the constants to which the formula results will be compared, you're ready to solve your optimization modeling problem. With the workbook set up (refer to Figure 12-1), solving the function is actually very easy.

Setting up the workbook and defining the problem of objective function and constraint formulas is the hard part.

Solving an Optimization Modeling Problem

After you have your workbook set up, you solve the optimization modeling problem by identifying where you've stored the solver variables, the objective function formula, the constraint formulas, and the constant values to which constraint formulas need to be compared. This is actually very straightforward. Here are the steps that you follow:

1. **Tell Excel to start the Solver by choosing Tools⇨Solver.**

   Excel displays the Solver Parameters dialog box, as shown in Figure 12-3.

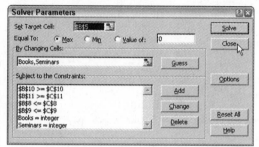

Figure 12-3:
The Solver
Parameters
dialog box.

If the Tools menu doesn't supply the Solver command, you need to install the Solver Add-In. To do this, choose Tools⇨Add-Ins. When Excel displays the Add-Ins dialog box, select the Solver Add-In check box and then click OK. Excel will probably prompt you to find and insert the Excel or Office CD. After you provide the installation CD, Excel or Office grabs the Solver Add-In and installs it. From this point on, you can use the Solver without trouble.

2. **In the Set Target Cell text box of the Solver Parameters dialog box, identify the cell location of the objective function formula.**

   In the case of the example workbook shown in Figure 12-1, the objective function formula is stored in cell B5. If you were solving an optimization modeling problem using the workbook from Figure 12-1, therefore, you enter $B5 into the Set Target Cell text box.

3. **Describe what optimization means.**

As I note earlier, not every objective function should be maximized in order to be optimized. In the case of a profit function, because you want to maximize profits — which is the case here — you want to make the objective function formula result as big as possible. But other objective functions may need to be minimized or even set to some specific value.

Select one of the Equal To radio buttons available in the Solver Parameters dialog box to define what optimization means. For example, in the case of a profit function that you want to maximize, you select the Max radio button. If instead you're working with a cost function and you want to save costs, you select the Min radio button. In the special case in which optimizing the objective function means getting the function to return a specific value, you can even select the Value Of radio button and then make an entry in the Value Of text box to specify exactly what the objective function formula should return.

4. **In the By Changing Cells text box of the Solver Parameters dialog box, identify the Solver variables.**

   You need to identify the variables that can be adjusted in order to optimize the objective function. In the case of a one-person business in which you're noodling around with the number of books that you should write and the number of seminars that you should give, the Solver variables are *books* and *seminars*.

   To identify the Solver variables, you can either enter the cell addresses into the By Changing cells text box or the cell names. In Figure 12-3, I enter **Books,** a comma, and then **Seminars** into the By Changing Cells text box. Note that these labels refer to cells B2 and B3. I could have also entered $B$2, $B$3 into the By Changing Cells text box.

5. **Click the Add button in the Solver Parameters dialog box to describe the location of the constraint formulas and the constant values to which the constraint formulas should be compared.**

   Excel displays the Add Constraint dialog box, as shown in Figure 12-4. From the Add Constraint dialog box, you identify the constraint formula and the constant value for each of your constraints. For example, to identify the cash requirements constraint, you need to enter $B$8 into the Cell Reference text box. You choose the less-than or equal-to logical operator from the drop-down list box (between the Cell Reference and the Constraint text boxes). Then, you enter $C$8 into the Constraint text box. In Figure 12-4, you can see how you indicate that the cash requirements constraint formula is described in cells B8 and C8.

Figure 12-4:
The Add
Constraint
dialog box.

Note that the logical operator is very important. Excel needs to know how to compare the constraint formula with the constant value.

After you describe the constraint formula, click the Add button. To add another constraint, you click the Add button and follow the same steps. You need to identify each of the constraints.

6. **Identify any integer constraints (optional).**

   Sometimes you have implicit integer constraints. In other words, the Solver variable value may need to be set to an integer value. In the example of the one-person business, in order to get paid for a book, you need to write an entire book. The same thing might be true for a seminar, too.

To identify integer constraints, you follow the same steps as you do to identify a regular constraint except that you don't actually need to store integer constraint information in your workbook. What you can do is click the Add button on the Solver Parameters dialog box. In the Add Constraint dialog box that appears, enter the Solver variable name into the Cell Reference box and select int from the drop-down list box, as shown in Figure 12-5.

Figure 12-5:
Set up an
integer
constraint
here.

7. **Define any binary constraints (optional).**

   In the same manner that you define integer constraints, you can also describe any binary constraints. A *binary constraint* is one in which the solver variable must equal either 0 or 1.

   To set up a binary constraint, click the Add button in the Solver Parameters dialog box. When Excel displays the Add Constraint dialog box, enter the Solver variable name into the Cell Reference box. Select Bin from the drop-down list box and then click OK.

8. **Solve the optimization modeling problem.**

   After you identify the objective function, identify the Solver variables, and describe the location of the constraint formulas, you're ready to solve the problem. To do this, simply click the Solve button.

   Assuming that Excel can solve your optimization problem, it displays the Solver Results dialog box, as shown in Figure 12-6. The Solver Results dialog box provides two radio buttons. To have Solver retain the optimal solution, select the Keep Solver Solution radio button and then click OK. In the case of the one-person book and seminar business, for example, the optimal number of books to write a year is seven and the optimal number of seminars to give is six (shown in cells B2 and B3 in the sample workbook shown earlier in Figure 12-1).

Figure 12-6:
Get Solver
results here.

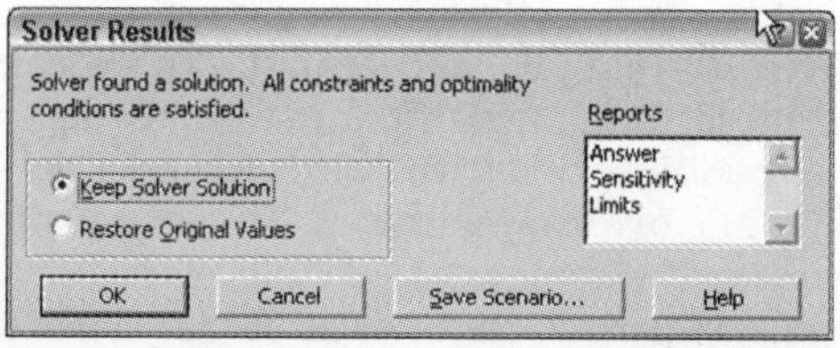

The Solver Parameters dialog box also includes two, presumably self-descriptive command buttons: Change and Delete. To remove a constraint from the optimization model, select the constraint from the Subject to the Constraints list box and then click the Delete button. If you want to change a constraint, select the constraint and then click the Change button. When Excel displays the Change Constraint dialog box, which resembles the Add Constraint dialog box, use the Cell Reference text box, the operator drop-down list box, and the Constant text box to make your change.

Reviewing the Solver Reports

Refer to the Solver Results dialog box in Figure 12-6 to see the Reports list box. The Reports list box identifies three solver reports you can select: Answer, Sensitivity, and Limits. You may be able to use these to collect more information about your Solver problem.

The Answer Report

Figure 12-7 shows an Answer Report for the one-person business optimization modeling problem. I should tell you that I needed to remove the integer constraints to show all the Solver reports, so some of these values don't jibe perfectly with the Solver results shown in Figure 12-6. Don't worry about that but instead look at the information provided by the Answer Report.

The main piece of information provided by the Answer Report is the value of the optimized objective function. This information appears in cell E8 in Figure 12-7. In the case of the one-person book writing and seminar business, for example, the final value, which is the value of the optimized objective function, equals 238945.58. This tells you that the best mix of book writing and seminar giving produces roughly $238,946 of profit.

The Answer Report also shows the original value of the objective function. If you set your original Solver variable values to your first guess or your current configuration, you could compare the original value and the final value to see by what amount Solver improves your objective function value. In this case, such a comparison could show you by what amount Solver helped you increase your profits, which is pretty cool.

The Adjustable Cells area of the Answer Report compares the original value and final values of the solver variables. In the case of the one-person book writing and seminar giving business, this area of the worksheet compares the original value for the number of books written (two) with the final value for the number of books written (a little over seven books). The Adjustable Cells area also shows the original value of the number of seminars given (eight) and the final value of the number of seminars given (roughly six and a half seminars).

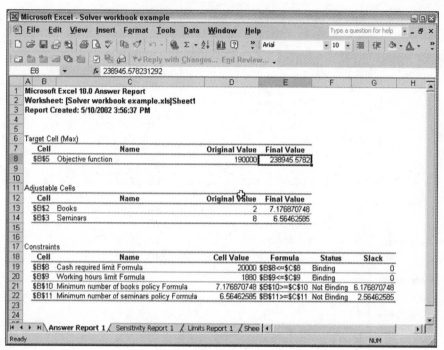

Figure 12-7:
The Answer
Report.

The Constraints area of the Answer Report is really interesting. The Constraints area shows you what constraint limits the objective function. You might, in the simple case of the one-person business, be able to guess what the limiting factors were intuitively. But in many real-life optimization modeling problems, guessing about what constraint is binding or limiting is more difficult.

In the case of the simple one-person business problem, the Constraints area shows that the first two constraints, cash requirements and working hours, are the ones that limit, or bind, the optimization modeling problem. You can easily see this by looking at the Slack column (shown in cells G18:G22). Slack equals zero for both the cash requirements function and the working hours limit. This means that the objective function value uses up all the cash and all the working hours to produce the final value of roughly $238,946. The other two constraints concerning the minimum number of books written and the minimum number of seminars given aren't limiting because they show slack.

The Sensitivity Report

Figure 12-8 shows the Sensitivity Report. A Sensitivity Report shows reduced gradient values and Lagrange multipliers, which sounds like a whole lot of gobbledygook. But actually these values aren't that hard to understand and can be quite useful.

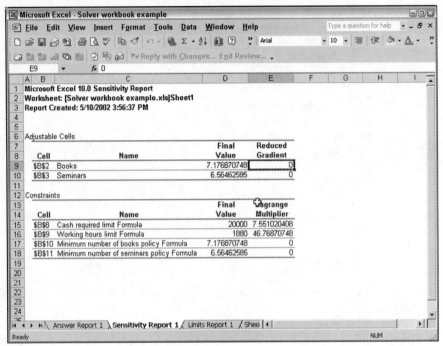

Figure 12-8:
A Sensitivity
Report.

A *reduced gradient value* quantifies the change in the objective function if the variable value increases by one. The *Lagrange multiplier* quantifies how the objective function changes if a constant constraint value increases by one.

In the Sensitivity Report shown in Figure 12-8, the reduced gradient values equal zero. This zero indicates that the variable value can't be increased. For example, the reduced gradient value of zero for books indicates that you can't write more books because of the limiting effect of the constraints. The same thing is true for the reduced gradient value of zero for the seminars variable.

The Lagrange multiplier values sometimes show as zero, too. When the Lagrange multiplier value shows as zero, that means that constraint isn't limiting. For example, in Figure 12-8, the Lagrange multiplier for both the minimum number of books policy formula and the minimum number of seminars policy formula show as zero. As you may recall from the earlier discussion of the Solver results, neither of these two constraints is binding. The Lagrange multiplier value of 7.55102040816327 in cell E15 shows the amount by which the objective function would increase if the cash requirements constant value increased by one dollar. The Lagrange multiplier value of 46.7687074829932 in cell E16 shows the amount by which the objective function value would increase if you had one additional hour in which to work.

The Limits Report

The Limits Report, an example of which is shown in Figure 12-9, shows the objective function optimized value, the Solver variable values that reduce the optimized objective function value, and the upper and lower limits possible for the Solver variables. The upper and lower limits show the range of Solver variable values that still produce an optimal function. In many cases, there is predictably no range of possible Solver variable values.

If you take a close look at Figure 12-9, for example, you see that the lower limit for the number of seminars (shown in cell F14) and the upper limit for the number of seminars (shown in cell I14) both equal 6.56462585. In other words, no range of seminar variable values will produce the optimized objective function result $238,946. The lowest value that number of seminars can be set to is roughly 6.56, and the highest value that the number of seminars can be set to is 6.56. In some cases, however, there would be a range of acceptable, optimal values that the Solver variable could be set to.

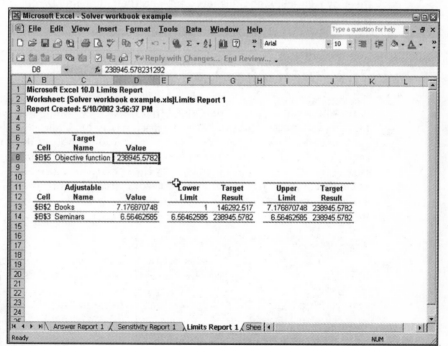

Figure 12-9:
The Limits
Report.

Note that the lower limit and the upper limit for the number of books written does show a range of values. The lower limit shown in cell F13 equals 1. The upper limit shown in cell I13 equals roughly 7.18. I don't think this is correct, however. The target result value shown in cell G13 equals $146,292.517. This is obviously not the optimal objective function result. So you can't really set the number of books to any variable from 1 to 7.18 and still get the optimal function result of roughly $238,946.

Some other notes about Solver reports

You can run the Solver multiple times and get new sets of Answer, Sensitivity, and Limits reports each time that you do. The first set of Solver reports that you get is numbered with a *1* on each sheet tab. The second set, cleverly, is numbered with a *2*.

If you want to delete or remove Solver report information, just delete the worksheet on which Excel stores the Solver report. You can delete a report sheet by right-clicking the sheet's tab and then choosing Delete from the shortcut menu that appears.

Working with the Solver Options

Observant readers may have noticed that the Solver Parameters dialog box includes an Options button. Click this button, and Excel displays the Solver Options dialog box, as shown in Figure 12-10. You may never need to use this dialog box. But if you want to fine-tune the way that Solver works, you can use the buttons and boxes provided by the Solver Options dialog box to control and customize the way that Solver works. Here I briefly describe how these options work.

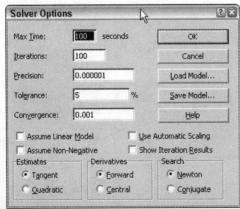

Figure 12-10:
The Solver
Options
dialog box.

Setting a Limit on Solver

Use the Max Time and Iterations text boxes to limit the amount of work that Solver does to solve an optimization modeling problem. Now, the simple example that I discuss here doesn't take much time to solve. But real-life problems are often much more complicated. A real-life problem may have many more Solver variables to deal with. The constraints may be more numerous and more complicated. And you may complicate optimization by doing things such as working with lots of integer or binary constraints.

When you do work with large, complex, real-life problems, the time that Solver takes to optimize may become very lengthy. In these cases, you can set a maximum time limit that Solver takes by using the Max Time text box. You can also set a maximum number of iterations that Solver makes by using the Iterations text box. Both the Max Time and Iterations text boxes accept a value as large as 32,767. 32,767 seconds roughly equals 9 hours of calculation.

You can stop the Solver's calculations by pressing the Esc key.

Deciding how nit-picky to be

Use the Precision and Tolerance text boxes to decide how much nit-picking you want to do about Solver's calculation results.

The Precision text box tells Solver how precise it should be when looking for the optimal value of the objective function. By default, Excel assumes that a precision setting of 0.000001 is okay. Excel interprets that setting to mean that if a constraint formula value is within 0.000001 of the constraint constant, everything is hunky-dory. Excel can consider the constraint met.

You can set the precision box to any value between 0 and 1. To loosen up on your precision, use a larger value. To tighten up on your precision, use a smaller precision value.

In the Tolerance text box, you specify how precise Solver should be in making sure that integer constraints are met. By default, Solver assumes that if an integer constraint is within 5 percent of the integer value, that's okay. If you want to make sure that integer constraints are met more precisely, you can enter a smaller value into the Tolerance text box.

The Tolerance setting only comes into play when you're working with an integer constraint. If you have an optimization modeling problem that doesn't have any integer constraints, the Tolerance text box has no effect.

Predictably, the more precision and less tolerance that you want, the longer and harder that Excel needs to work.

Saying when

Have you ever been to a restaurant where your server wanders around at some point in the meal with a huge peppermill asking whether you want black pepper on your salad? If you have, you know that part of the ritual is that at some point, you tell the server when he or she has ground enough pepper for your green salad.

The Convergence text box provided in the Solver Options dialog box works in roughly the same way. You use the Convergence box to tell Excel *when* it should stop looking for a better solution. The Convergence text box accepts any value between 0 and 1. When the change in the objective function formula result is less then the value shown in the convergence text box, Excel figures that things are getting close enough, so additional iterations aren't necessary.

I should mention that the value that you enter into the Convergence text box only applies to non-linear optimization-modeling problems. (For more on this, read the following section.) Oh, another thing that I should mention: With larger convergence values, Excel reaches a reasonable solution more quickly and with less work. And with smaller or very precise convergence values, Excel works harder and takes more time.

When you assume . . .

The Solver Options dialog box includes two check boxes with which you tell Solver what to assume about your modeling: Assume Linear Model and Assume Non-Negative.

Select the Assume Linear Model check box when you're working on a linear programming problem. This just means that the relationships in your optimization modeling program are linear. Simple optimization functions and constraints like those that I demonstrate and describe earlier in this chapter are linear. In general, non-linear optimization modeling uses much more complicated objective function formulas and constraint formulas (presumably formulas that include things like exponents).

Select the Assume Non-Negative check box if your Solver variables must equal or be greater than zero. This is something that you need to do because in some cases, an optimal objective function result can be created by using negative Solver variable values. But obviously, in many situations, negative Solver variable values wouldn't make sense. For example, in the simple example of the one-person book writing and seminar giving business, you can't write a negative number of books or give a negative number of seminars.

Using automatic scaling

You can select the Use Automatic Scaling check box when you're working with variables that greatly differ in magnitude. For example, if you're working with interest rates and multimillion dollar account balances, you might want to use the automatic scaling option to tell Excel, "Hey dude, the Solver variable values greatly differ in magnitude, so you ought to automatically scale these babies."

Showing iteration results

If you don't have anything better to do, select the Show Iteration Results check box. When you do this, Excel stops after it calculates each objective function using a new set of Solver variable values and shows you the intermediate calculation results. Most people won't and shouldn't care about seeing intermediate calculation results. But heck, I suppose that in some cases, you might want to see how Solver is working toward the objective function optimal result.

Tangent versus quadratic estimates

Choose either Estimates radio buttons — Tangent or Quadratic — to specify how Excel should come up with its first trial solution to the objective function. If Excel should extrapolate linearly from the tangent vector, you select the Tangent radio button. If Excel should extrapolate quadratically because you're using non-linear formulas, you select the Quadratic radio button. If you don't have a clue and find the two terms *tangent* and *quadratic* befuddling and anxiety producing, don't pay any attention to them.

Forward versus central derivatives

Select from the two Derivatives radio buttons — Forward or Central — to tell Excel how to estimate partial derivatives when it's working with the objective function and constraint formulas. In most cases, everything works just fine if Excel uses forward derivatives. But, in some cases, forward derivatives don't work. And in this situation, you may be able to specify that Excel use central derivatives.

Using central derivatives requires much more work of Excel, but some highly constrained problems can more easily and more practically be solved using central derivatives.

Newton versus conjugate algorithms

Select either of the two Search radio buttons — Newton or Conjugate — to tell Excel what or which algorithm it should use to solve your optimization modeling problem. By default, Excel assumes that, "Hey, dude it's cool," if you use the Newton algorithm. However, the Newton algorithm only practically works if your computer has a lot of memory. If your computer doesn't have a lot of memory, you can use the Conjugate algorithm. The Conjugate algorithm takes more time, but it requires less memory. Typically, by the way, using the Conjugate algorithm is only necessary on very large and very complicated optimization modeling problems.

Saving and reusing model information

The Solver Options dialog box provides two buttons, Save Model and Load Model, with which you save optimization modeling problem information. If you click the Save Model button, for example, Excel displays the Save Model dialog box, as shown in Figure 12-11. To save the current optimization modeling information, you enter a worksheet range address in the Select Model Area text box that Excel can use to save the model information.

To later reuse that model information, you click the Load Model command button and then specify the worksheet range that you used to originally store model information.

Figure 12-11:
The Save
Model
dialog box.

Understanding the Solver Error Messages

For simple problems, Solver usually quickly finds the optimal Solver variable values for the objective function. However, in some cases — in fact, maybe quite frequently in the real world — Solver has trouble finding the Solver variable values that optimize the objective function. In these cases, however, Solver typically displays a message or an error message that describes or discusses the trouble that it's having with your problem. Quickly, before I wrap this chapter up, I briefly identify and comment on the messages and error messages that Solver may display as it finishes or gives up on the work that it's doing.

Solver has converged to the current solution

The `Solver has converged to the current solution` message tells you that Excel has found a solution but isn't particularly confident in the solution. In essence, this message alerts you to the possibility that there may be a better solution to your optimization modeling problem. To look for a better solution, adjust the Convergence setting in the Solver Options dialog box so that Excel works at a higher level of precision. I describe how you do this in the earlier section, "Saying when."

Solver cannot improve the current solution

The `Solver cannot improve the current solution` message tells you that, well, Excel has calculated a rough, pretty darn accurate solution, but, again, you may be able to find a better solution. To tell Excel that it should look for a better solution, you need to increase the precision setting that Solver is using. This means, of course, that Excel will take more time. But that extra time may result in it finding a better solution. To adjust the precision, you again use the Solver Options dialog box. Read the earlier section, "Deciding how nit-picky to be."

Stop chosen when maximum time limit was reached

The `Stop chosen when maximum time limit was reached` message tells you that Excel ran out of time. You can retry solving the optimization modeling problem with a larger Max Time setting. (Read more about this in the earlier section, "Setting a Limit on Solver.") Note, however, that if you do see the `Stop chosen when to maximum time limit was reached` message, you should save the work that Excel has already performed as part of the optimization-modeling problem solving. Save the work that Excel has already done by clicking the Keep Solver Results button when Excel displays this message. Excel will be closer to the final solution the next time that it starts looking for the optimal solution.

Stop chosen when maximum iteration limit was reached

The `Stop chosen when maximum iteration limit was reached` message tells you that Excel ran out of iterations before it found the optimal solution. You can get around this problem by setting a larger iterations value in the Solver Options dialog box. Read the earlier section, "Showing iteration results."

Set target cell values do not converge

The Set target cell values do not converge message tells you that the objective function doesn't have an optimal value. In other words, the objective function keeps getting bigger (or keeps getting smaller) even though the constraint formulas are satisfied. In other words: Excel finds that it keeps getting a better objective function value with every iteration, but it doesn't appear any closer to a final objective function value.

If you encounter this error, you've probably not correctly defined and described your optimization-modeling problem. Your objective function may not make a lot of sense or may not be congruent with your constraint formulas. Or it may be that one or more of your constraint formulas — or probably several of them — don't really make sense.

Solver could not find a feasible solution

The Solver could not find a feasible solution message tells you that your optimization-modeling problem doesn't have an answer. As a practical matter, when you see this message, it means that your set of constraints excludes any possible answer.

For example, returning one last time to the one-person business, suppose that it takes 3,000 hours to write a book and that there are only 2,000 hours for work available in a year. If you said that you wanted to write at least one book a year, there's no solution to the objective function. A book requires up to 3,000 hours of work, but you only have 2,000 hours in which to complete a 3,000-hour project. That's impossible, obviously. No optimal value for the objective function exists.

Conditions for assume linear model are not satisfied

The Conditions for assume linear model are not satisfied message indicates that although you selected the Assume Linear Model check box (in the Solver Options dialog box), Excel has now figured out that your model isn't actually linear. And it's mad as heck. So it shows you this message to indicate that it can't solve the problem if it has to assume that your objective function and constraint formulas are linear. (For more on Assume Linear Model, read the earlier section, "When you assume . . .")

If you do see this message, however, your first response shouldn't necessarily be to clear the Assume Linear Model check box. Rather, first display the Solver Options dialog box and then select the Use Automatic Scaling check box. If you get the same message again after making this change, you need to clear the Assume Linear Model check box. Hopefully, you'll then be able to solve your problem.

Solver encountered an error value in a target or constraint cell

The `Solver encountered an error value in a target or constraint cell` message means that one of your formula results in an error value or that you goofed in describing or defining some constraint. To work around this problem, you need to fix the bogus formula or the goofy constraint.

There is not enough memory available to solve the problem

The `There is not enough memory available to solve the problem` message is self-descriptive. If you see this message, Solver doesn't have enough memory to solve the optimization modeling problem that you're working on. Your only recourse is to attempt to free up memory, perhaps by closing any other open programs and any unneeded documents or workbooks. If that doesn't work, you may also want to add more memory to your computer, especially if you're going to commonly do optimization modeling problems. Memory is cheap.

Part IV
The Part of Tens

In this part . . .

The chapters in this part list useful tidbits, tips, and factoids on using Excel to analyze data. Here I give you the quick lowdown on the basics of statistics, as well as lists of tips for presenting list results and for visually analyzing and presenting your data.

Chapter 13

Almost Ten Things You Ought to Know about Statistics

*I*n as much that in a number of chapters in this book, I discuss how to use Excel for statistical analysis, I thought it might make sense to cover some of the basics.

Don't worry. I'm not going to launch into some college-level lecture about things like chi-square or covariance calculations. You'll see no Greek symbols in this chapter.

If you've never been exposed to statistics in school or it's been a decade or two since you were, use this chapter to help you use (comfortably) some of the statistical tools that Excel provides.

Descriptive Statistics Are Straightforward

The first thing that you ought to know is that some statistical analysis and some statistical measures are pretty darn straightforward. Descriptive statistics, which include things such as the pivot table cross-tabulations (that I present in Chapters 3 and 4), as well as some of the statistical functions, make sense even to somebody who's not all that quantitative.

For example, if you sum a set of values, you get a sum. Pretty easy, right? And if you find the biggest value or the smallest value in a set of numbers, that's pretty straightforward, too.

I mention this point about descriptive statistics because a lot of times people freak out when they hear the word *statistics*. That's too bad because many of the most useful statistical tools available to you are simple, easy-to-understand descriptive statistics.

Averages Aren't So Simple Sometimes

Here's a weird thing that you may remember if you ever took a statistics class. When someone uses the term *average*, what he usually refers to is the most common average measurement, which is a *mean*. But you ought to know that several other commonly accepted average measurements exist, including mode, median, and some special mean measurements such as the geometric mean and harmonic mean.

I want to quickly cover some of these . . . not because you need to know all this stuff, but because understanding that the term *average* is imprecise makes some of the discussions in this book and much of Excel's statistical functionality more comprehensible.

To make this discussion more concrete, assume that you're looking at a small set of values: 1, 2, 3, 4, and 5. As you may know or be able to intuitively guess, the mean in this small set of values is 3. You can calculate the mean by adding together all the numbers in the set (1+2+3+4+5) and then dividing this sum (15) by the total number of values in the set (5).

Two other common average measurements are mode and median. I start with the discussion of the median measurement first because it's easy to understand using the data set that I introduce in the preceding paragraph. The *median value* is the value that separates the largest values from the smallest values. In the data set 1, 2, 3, 4, and 5, the median is 3. The value 3 separates the largest values (4 and 5) from the smallest values (1 and 2). In other words, the median shows the middle point in the data. Half of the data set values are larger than the median value, and half of the data set values are smaller than the median value.

When you have an even number of values in your data set, you calculate the median by averaging the two middle values. For example, the data set 1, 2, 3, and 4 has no middle value. Add the two middle values — 2 and 3 — and then divide by 2. This calculation produces a median value of 2.5. With the median value of 2.5, half of the values in the data set are above the median value, and half of the values in the data set are below the median value.

The mode measurement is a third common average. The *mode* is the most common value in the data set. To show you an example of this, I need to introduce a new data set. With the data set 1, 2, 3, 5, and 5, the mode is 5 because the value *5* occurs two times in the set. Every other value occurs only once.

As I mention earlier, other common statistical measures of the average exist. The mean measurement that I refer to earlier in this discussion is actually an arithmetic mean because the values in the data set get added together arithmetically as part of the calculation. You can, however, combine the values in other ways. Financial analysts and scientists sometimes use a geometric mean, for example. There is also something called a harmonic mean.

You don't need to understand all these other different average measurements, but you should remember that the term *average* is pretty imprecise. And what people usually imply when they refer to an average is the *mean*.

Standard Deviations Describe Dispersion

Have you ever heard the term *standard deviation*? You probably have. Any statistical report usually includes some vague or scary reference to either standard deviation or its close relative, the variance. Although the formula for standard deviation is terrifying to look at — at least if you're not comfortable with the Greek alphabet — intuitively, the formula and the logic are pretty easy to understand.

A *standard deviation* describes how values in a data set vary around the mean. Another way to say this same thing is that a standard deviation describes how far away from the mean the average value is. In fact, you can almost think of a standard deviation as being equal to the average distance from the mean. This isn't quite right, but it's darn close.

Suppose you're working with a data set, and its mean equals 20. If the data set standard deviation is 5, you can sort of think about the average data set value as being 5 units away from the mean of 20. In other words, for values less than the mean of 20, the average is sort of 15. And for values that are larger than the mean, the average value is kind of 25.

The standard deviation isn't really the same thing as the average deviation, but it's pretty darn close in some cases. And thinking about the standard deviation as akin to the average deviation — or average difference from the mean — is a good way to tune into the logic.

The neat thing about all this is that with statistical measures like a mean and like a standard deviation, you often gain real insights into the characteristics of the data that you're looking at. Another thing is that with these two bits of data, you can often draw inferences about data by looking at samples.

I should tell you one other thing about the standard deviation. The statistical terms *variance* and *standard deviation* are related. A *standard deviation* equals the square root of a variance. Another way to say this same thing is that a *variance* equals the square of a standard deviation.

It turns out that when you calculate things such as variances and standard deviations, you actually arrive at the variance value first. In other words, you calculate the variance before you calculate the standard deviation. For this reason, you'll often hear people talk about variances rather than standard deviations. Really, however, standard deviations and variances are the same thing. In one case, you're working with a square root. In another case you are working with a square.

It's six of one, half a dozen of the other . . . sort of.

An Observation Is an Observation

Observation is one of the terms that you'll encounter if you read anything about statistics in this book or in the Excel online Help. An observation is just an observation. That sounds circular, but bear with me. Suppose that you're constructing a data set that shows daily high temperatures in your neighborhood. When you go out and observe that the temperature some fine July afternoon is 87° F, that measurement (87°) is your first observation. If you go out and observe that the high temperature the next day is 88° F, that measurement is your second observation.

Another way to define the term observation is like this: Whenever you actually assign a value to one of your random variables, you create an observation. For example, if you're building a data set of daily high temperatures in your neighborhood, every time that you go out and assign a new temperature value (87° one day, 88° the next day, and so on), you're creating an observation.

A Sample Is a Subset of Values

A *sample* is a collection of observations from a population. For example, if you create a data set that records the daily high temperature in your neighborhood, your little collection of observations is a sample.

In comparison, a sample is not a population. A *population* includes all the possible observations. In the case of collecting your neighborhood's high temperatures, the population includes all the daily high temperatures — since the beginning of the neighborhood's existence.

Inferential Statistics Are Cool but Complicated

As I note earlier in this chapter, some statistics are pretty simple. Finding the biggest value in a set of numbers is a *statistical measurement*. But it's really pretty simple. Those simple descriptive statistical measures are called, cleverly, *descriptive statistics*.

Another more complicated but equally useful branch of statistics is *inferential statistics*. Inferential statistics are based on this very useful, intuitively obvious idea. If you look at a sample of values from a population and the sample is representative and large enough, you can draw conclusions about the population based on characteristics of the sample.

For example, for every presidential election in the United States, the major television networks (usually contrary to their earlier promises) predict the winner after only a relatively small number of votes have been calculated or counted. How do they do this? Well, they sample the population. Specifically, they stand outside polling places and ask exiting voters how they voted. If you ask a large sample of voters whether they voted for the one guy or the other guy, you can make an inference about how all the voters voted. And then you can predict who has won the election.

Inferential statistics, although very powerful, possess two qualities that I need to mention:

> ✔ **Accuracy issues:** When you make a statistical inference, you can never be 100 percent sure that your inference is correct. The possibility always exists that your sample isn't representative or that your sample doesn't return enough precision to estimate the population value.

This is partly what happened with the 2000 presidential election in the United States. Initially, some of the major news networks predicted that Al Gore had won based on exit polls. Then based on other exit polls, they predicted that George W. Bush had won. Then, perhaps finally realizing that maybe their statistics weren't good enough given the closeness of the race . . . or perhaps just based on their own embarrassment about bobbling the ball . . . they stopped predicting the race. In retrospect, it's not surprising that they had trouble with calling the race because the number of votes for the two candidates was extremely, extremely close.

✔ **Steep learning curve:** Inferential statistics quickly gets pretty complicated. When you work with inferential statistics, you immediately start encountering terms such as probability distribution functions, all sorts of crazy (in some cases) parameters, and lots of Greek symbols.

As a practical matter, if you haven't at least taken a statistics class — and probably more than one statistics class — you'll find it very hard to move into inferential statistics in a big way. You probably can, with a single statistics class and perhaps the information in this book, work with inferential statistics based on normal distributions and uniform distributions. However, working with inferential statistics and applying those inferential statistics to other probability distributions becomes very tricky. At least, that's my observation.

Probability Distribution Functions Aren't Always Confusing

One of the statistical terms that you'll encounter a little bit in this book — and a whole bunch if you dig into the Excel Help file — is *probability distribution function*. This phrase sounds pretty tricky; in some cases, granted, maybe it is. But you can actually understand intuitively what a probability distribution function is with a couple of useful examples.

One common distribution that you hear about in statistics classes, for example, is a T distribution. A *T distribution* is essentially a normal distribution except with heavier, fatter tails. There are also distributions that are skewed (have the hump tilted) one way or the other. Each of these probability distributions, however, has a probability distribution function that describes the probability distribution chart.

Here are two probability distribution functions that you probably already understand: uniform distribution and normal distribution.

Uniform distribution

One common probability distribution function is a uniform distribution. In a *uniform distribution*, every event has the same probability of occurrence. As a simple example, suppose that you roll a six-sided die. Assuming that the die is fair, you have an equal chance of rolling any of the values: 1, 2, 3, 4, 5, or 6. If you roll the die 60,000 times, what you would expect to see (given the large number of observations) is that you'll probably roll a 1 about 10,000 times. Similarly, you'll probably also roll a 2, 3, 4, 5, or 6 about 10,000 times each. Oh sure, you can count on some variance between what you expect (10,000 occurrences of each side of the six-sided die) and what you actually experience. But your actual observations would pretty well map to your expectations.

The unique thing about this distribution is that everything is pretty darn level. You could say that the probability or the chance of rolling any one of the six sides of the die is even, or *uniform*. This is how uniform distribution gets its name. Every event has the same probability of occurrence. Figure 13-1 shows a uniform distribution function.

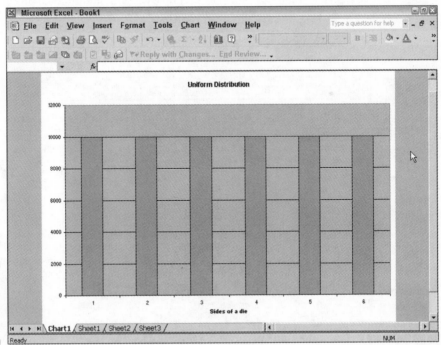

Figure 13-1:
A uniform distribution function.

Normal distribution

Another common type of probability distribution function is the *normal distribution*, also known as a *bell curve* or a *Gaussian distribution*.

A normal distribution occurs in many situations naturally. For example, intelligence quotients (IQs) are distributed normally. If you take a large set of people, test their IQs, and then plot those IQs on a chart, you get a normal distribution. One characteristic of a normal distribution is that most of the values in the population are centered around the mean. Another characteristic of a normal distribution is that the mean, the mode, and the median all equal each other.

Do you kind of see now where this probability distribution function business is going? A probability distribution function just describes a chart that, in essence, plots probabilities. Figure 13-2 shows a normal distribution function.

A probability distribution function is just a function, or equation, that describes the line of the distribution. As you might guess, not every probability distribution looks like a normal distribution or a uniform distribution.

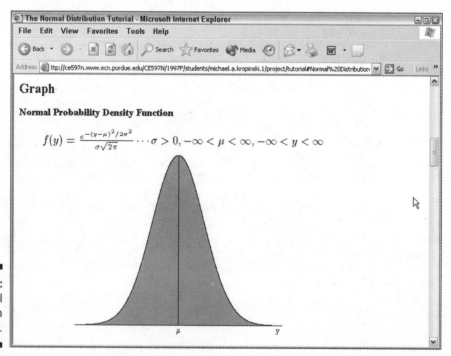

The Normal Distribution Tutorial - Microsoft Internet Explorer

File   Edit   View   Favorites   Tools   Help

Back   •   •   Search   Favorites   Media

Address   ttp://ce597n.www.ecn.purdue.edu/CE597N/1997F/students/michael.a.kropinski.1/project/tutorial#Normal%20Distribution   Go   Links »

Graph

Normal Probability Density Function

$$f(y) = \frac{e^{-(y-\mu)^2/2\sigma^2}}{\sigma\sqrt{2\pi}} \cdots \sigma > 0, \ -\infty < \mu < \infty, \ -\infty < y < \infty$$

μ y

Figure 13-2:
A normal distribution function.

Parameters Aren't So Complicated

After you grasp the concept that a *probability distribution function* is essentially an equation or formula that describes the line in a probability distribution chart, it's pretty easy to understand that a *parameter* is an input to the probability distribution function. In other words, the formula or function or equation that describes a probability distribution curve needs inputs. In statistics, those inputs are called *parameters*.

Refer to Figure 13-2 to see its probability function. Most of those crazy Greek symbols refer to parameters.

Some probability distribution functions only need a single simple parameter. For example, in order to work with a uniform distribution, all you really need is the number of values in the data set. A six-sided die, for example, has only six possibilities. Because you know that only six possibilities exist, you can pretty easily calculate that there's a 1-in-6 chance that any possibility will occur.

A normal distribution uses two parameters: the mean and the standard deviation.

Other probability distribution functions use other parameters.

Skewness and Kurtosis Describe a Probability Distribution's Shape

A couple of other useful statistical terms to know are skewness and kurtosis. *Skewness* quantifies the lack of symmetry in a probability distribution. In a perfectly symmetrical distribution, like the normal distribution (refer to Figure 13-2), the skewness equals zero. If a probability distribution leans to the right or the left, however, the skewness equals some value other than zero. And the value quantifies the lack of symmetry.

Kurtosis quantifies the heaviness of the tails in a distribution. In a normal distribution, kurtosis equals zero. In other words, zero is the measurement for a tail that looks like a tail in a normal distribution. The *tail* is the thing that reaches out to the left or right. However, if a tail in a distribution is heavier than a normal distribution, the kurtosis is a positive number. If the tails in a distribution are skinnier than in a normal distribution, the kurtosis is a negative number.

Chapter 14

Almost Ten Tips for Presenting List Results and Analyzing Data

*T*hroughout the pages of this book, here and there I scatter tips on analyzing data with Excel. In this chapter, however, I want to take a step back from the details of data analysis and offer a handful of general tips. Mostly, these tips summarize and generalize the things that I discuss in the preceding chapters of this book.

Work Hard to Import Data

The first point that I want to make is that working to import good, rich data into Excel workbooks really is worthwhile. I know that sometimes importing data can be problematic. Headaches and heartbreaks can happen when trying to grab data from other management information systems and when trying to work with a database administrator to get the right data into a format that provides for useful data analysis with Excel.

But in spite of the hassles of obtaining the data, you will find — I promise — that importing good data into Excel is well worth the effort. Traditionally, people make decisions by using very standard information sources . . . like the accounting system, or some third-party report, or newsletter, or publication. And those traditional sources produce traditional insights, which is great. But when you can work with a richer, deeper data set of raw information, you often glean insights that simply don't appear in the traditional sources.

Design Information Systems to Produce Rich Data

More than 20 years ago now, as a young systems consultant with Arthur Andersen (yes, *that* Arthur Andersen), I designed accounting systems and financial information systems for large companies. In those days, we concentrated on creating systems that produced the reports that managers and decision makers wanted and that produced forms (such as invoices and checks and purchase orders) that businesses required to operate.

Those items are still obviously key things to think about while you design and install and manage information systems, such as an accounting system. But I think that you also need to recognize that there will probably be unplanned, unorthodox, unusual but still very valuable ways in which the data that is collected by these management information systems can be analyzed. And so, if you work with or design or participate in implementing information systems, I think that you should realize that raw data from the system can and should be passed to data analysis tools like Excel.

A simple example of this will show you what I mean. It applies even to the smallest businesses. The QuickBooks accounting system, which I discuss a little bit in earlier chapters in this book, is an extremely popular accounting tool for small businesses. Hundreds of thousands of small businesses use QuickBooks for their accounting, for example. And the one thing that I would say about QuickBooks users in general is that they often want to use the QuickBooks system simply for accounting. They want to use it as a tool for producing things like checks and invoices and for creating reports that report on profits or estimate cash flow information.

And that's good. If you're a business owner or manager, you definitely do want that information. But even with a simple system like QuickBooks, businesses should collect richer sets of data . . . very detailed information about the products or services a firm sells, for example. By doing this, even if you don't want to report on this information within QuickBooks, you create a very rich data set that you can later analyze for good effect with Excel.

Having rich detailed records of the products or services that a firm sells enables that firm to see trends in sales by product or service. Additionally, it allows a firm to create cross-tabulations that show how certain customers choose and use certain products and services.

The bottom line, I submit, is that organizations need to design information systems so that they also collect good rich raw data. Later on, this rich raw data can easily be exported to Excel where simple data analysis — such as the types that I describe in the earlier chapters of this book — can lead to rich insights into a firm's operation, its opportunities, and possible threats.

Don't Forget about Third-Party Sources

One quick point: Recognize that many third-party sources of data exist. For example, vendors and customers may have very interesting data available in a format accessible to Excel that you can use to analyze their market or your industry.

Earlier in the book, for example, I mention that the slowdown in computer book sales and in computer book publishing first became apparent to me based on an Excel workbook supplied by one of the major book distributors in North America. Without this third-party data source, I would have continued to find myself bewildered about what was happening in the industry in which I work.

A quick final comment about third-party data sources is this: the Web Query tool available in Excel (and as I describe in Chapter 3) makes extracting information from tables stored on Web pages very easy.

Just Add It

You might think that powerful data analysis requires powerful data analysis techniques. Chi-squares. Inferential statistics. Regression analysis.

But I don't think so. Some of the most powerful data analysis that you can do involves simply adding up numbers. If you add numbers and get sums that other people don't even know about — and if those sums are important or show trends — you can gain important insights and collect valuable information through the simplest data analysis techniques.

Again, in echoing earlier tips in this chapter, the key thing is collecting really good information in the first place, and then having that information stored in a container, such as an Excel workbook, so that you can arithmetically manipulate and analyze the data.

Always Explore Descriptive Statistics

The descriptive statistical tools that Excel provides — including measurements such as a sum, an average, a median, a standard deviation, and so forth — are really powerful tools. Don't feel as if these tools are beyond your skill set, even if this book is your first introduction to these tools.

Descriptive statistics simply describe the data you've got in some Excel worksheet. They're not magical, and you don't need any special statistical training to use them or to share them with the people to whom you present your data analysis results.

Note, too, that some of the simplest descriptive statistical measures are often the most useful. For example, knowing the smallest value in a data set or the largest value can be very useful. Knowing the mean, median, or mode in a data set is also very interesting and useful. And even seemingly complicated sophisticated measures such as a standard deviation (which just measures dispersion about the mean) are really quite useful tools. You don't need to understand anything more than this book describes to use or share this information.

Watch for Trends

Peter Drucker, perhaps the best-known and most insightful observer of modern management practices, notes in several of his recent books that one of the most significant things data analysis can do is spot a change in trends. I want to echo this here, pointing out that trends are almost the most significant thing you can see. If your industry's combined revenues grow, that's significant. If they haven't been growing or if they start shrinking, that's probably even more significant.

In your own data analysis, be sure to construct your worksheets and collect your data in a way that helps you identify trends and ideally, identify changes in trends.

Slicing and Dicing: Cross-Tabulation

The PivotTable command, which I describe in Chapter 4, is a wonderful tool. Cross-tabulations are extremely useful ways to slice and dice data. And as I note in Chapter 4, the neat thing about the PivotTable tool is that you can easily re-cross-tabulate and then re-cross-tabulate again.

I go into a lot of detail in Chapter 4 about why cross-tabulation is so cool, so I won't repeat myself here. But I do think that if you have good rich data sources and you're not regularly cross-tabulating your data, you're probably missing absolute treasures of information. There's gold in them thar hills.

Chart It, Baby

In Chapter 15, I provide a list of tips that you may find useful to graphically or visually analyze data. In a nutshell, though, I think that an important component of good data analysis is visually presenting and visually examining your data.

By looking at a line chart of some important statistic or by creating a column chart of some set of data, you often see things that aren't apparent in a tabular presentation of the same information.

Charting is often a wonderful way to discover things that you won't otherwise see.

Be Aware of Inferential Statistics

To varying degrees in Chapters 9, 10, and 11, I introduce and discuss some of the inferential statistics tools that Excel provides. Inferential statistics enable you to collect a sample and then make inferences about the population from which the sample is drawn based on the characteristics of the sample.

In the right hands, inferential statistics are extremely powerful and useful tools. With good skills in inferential statistics, you can analyze all sorts of things to gain all sorts of insights into data that mere common folk never get. However, quite frankly, if your only exposure to inferential statistical techniques is this book, you probably don't possess enough raw statistical knowledge to fairly perform inferential statistical analysis.

Chapter 15

Ten Tips for Visually Analyzing and Presenting Data

*T*his isn't one of those essays about how a picture is worth a thousand words. In this chapter, I just want to provide some concrete suggestions about how you can more successfully use charts as data analysis tools and how you can use charts to more effectively communicate the results of the data analysis that you do.

Using the Right Chart Type

What many people don't realize is that there are only five data comparisons that you can make in Excel charts. And if you want to be picky, there are only four practical data comparisons that Excel charts let you make. Table 15-1 summarizes the five data comparisons.

Table 15-1	The Five Possible Data Comparisons in a Chart	
Comparison	*Description*	*Example*
Part-to-whole	Compares individual values with the sum of those values.	Comparing the sales generated by individual products with the total sales enjoyed by a firm.
Whole-to-whole	Compares individual data values and sets of data values (or what Excel calls *data series*) to each other.	Comparing sales revenues of different firms in your industry.
Time-series	Shows how values change over time.	A chart showing sales revenues over the last 5 years or profits over the last 12 months.
Correlation	Looks at different data series in an attempt to explore correlation, or association, between the data series.	Comparing information about the numbers of school-age children with sales of toys.
Geographic	Looks at data values using a geographic map.	Examining sales by country using a map of the world.

If you decide or can figure out which data comparison you want to make, choosing the right chart type is very easy:

- **Pie, doughnut, or area:** If you want to make a *part-to-whole* data comparison, you choose a pie chart (if you're working with a single data series) or you choose a doughnut chart or area chart (if you're working with more than one data series).

- **Bar, cylinder, cone, or pyramid:** If you want to make a *whole-to-whole* data comparison, you probably want to use a chart that uses horizontal data markers. Bar charts use horizontal data markers, for example, and so do cylinder, cone, and pyramid charts. (You can also use a doughnut chart or radar chart to make whole-to-whole data comparisons.)

- **Line or column:** To make a *time-series* data comparison, you want to use a chart type that has a horizontal category axis. By convention, western societies (Europe, North America, and South America) use a horizontal axis moving from left to right to denote the passage of time. Because of this culturally programmed convention, you want to show time-series data comparisons by using a horizontal category axis. This means you probably want to use either a line chart or column chart.

- **Scatter or bubble:** If you want to make a *correlation* data comparison in Excel, you have only two choices. If you have two data series for which you're exploring correlation, you want to use an XY (Scatter) chart. If you have three data series, you can use either an XY (Scatter) chart or a bubble chart.

✔ **Surface:** If you want to make a *geographic* data comparison, you're very limited in what you can do in Excel. You may be able to make a geographic data comparison by using a surface chart. But, more likely, you need to use another data mapping tool such as MapPoint from Microsoft.

The data comparison that you want to make largely determines what chart type that you need to use. You want to use a chart type that supports the data comparison that you want to make.

Using Your Chart Message as the Chart Title

Chart titles are commonly used to identify the organization that you're presenting information to or perhaps to identify the key data series that you're applying in a chart. A better and more effective way to use the chart title, however, is to use a chart title as a brief summary of the message that you want your chart to communicate. For example, if you create a chart that shows that sales and profits are increasing, maybe your chart title should look like the one shown in Figure 15-1.

Using your chart message as the chart title immediately communicates to your audience what you're trying to show in the chart. Using the chart message as the chart title also helps people looking at your chart to focus on the information that you want them to understand.

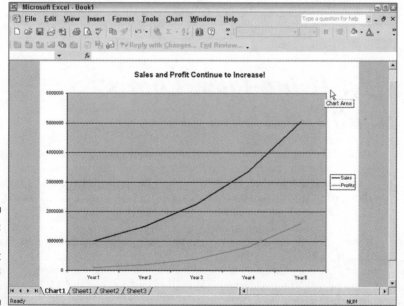

Figure 15-1:
Use a chart's chart message as its title.

Beware of Pie Charts

You really want to avoid pie charts. Oh, I know, pie charts are great tools to teach elementary school children about charts and plotting data. And you see them commonly in newspapers and magazines. But the reality is that pie charts are very inferior tools for visually understanding data and for visually communicating quantitative information.

Almost always, information that appears in a pie chart would be better displayed in a simple table.

Pie charts possess several debilitating weaknesses.

✔ **You're limited to working with a very small set of numbers.**

This makes sense, right? You can't slice the pie into very small pieces or into very many pieces without your chart becoming illegible.

✔ **Pie charts aren't visually precise.**

Readers or viewers are asked to visually compare the slices of pie, but that's so imprecise as to be almost useless. This same information can really be shown much better by just providing a simple list or table of plotted values.

✔ **With pie charts, you're limited to a single data series.**

For example, you may plot a pie chart that shows sales of different products that your firm sells. But almost always, people will find it more interesting to also know profits by product line. Or maybe they also want to know sales per sales person or geographic area. You see the problem. By limiting yourself to a single data series, pie charts very much limit the information that you can show visually.

Consider Using Pivot Charts for Small Data Sets

Although using pivot tables is often the best way to cross-tabulate data and to present cross-tabulated data, do remember that for small data sets, pivot charts can also work very well. The key thing to remember is that a pivot chart, practically speaking, only enables you to plot a few rows of data. Often your cross-tabulations will show many rows of data.

However, if you do create a cross-tabulation that shows only a few rows of data, try a pivot chart. Figure 15-2 shows a cross-tabulation in a pivot *table* form; Figure 15-3 shows a cross-tabulation in a pivot *chart* form. I wager that for many people, the graphical presentation shown in Figure 15-3 shows the trends in the underlying data more quickly, more conveniently, and more effectively.

Sum of Sales $	Month									
State	January	February	March	April	May	June	July	August	Septembe	Grand Total
California	1,591	2,808	15,872	2,156	1,199	1,517	4,420	3,056	3,218	35,837
Oregon	3,249	2,317	13,054	2,158	2,657	4,117	4,486	3,110	1,328	36,476
Washington		2,938	14,115	2,198	3,352	3,212	2,115	2,286	2,516	32,733
Grand Total	4,839	8,063	43,040	6,512	7,208	8,846	11,021	8,453	7,063	105,046

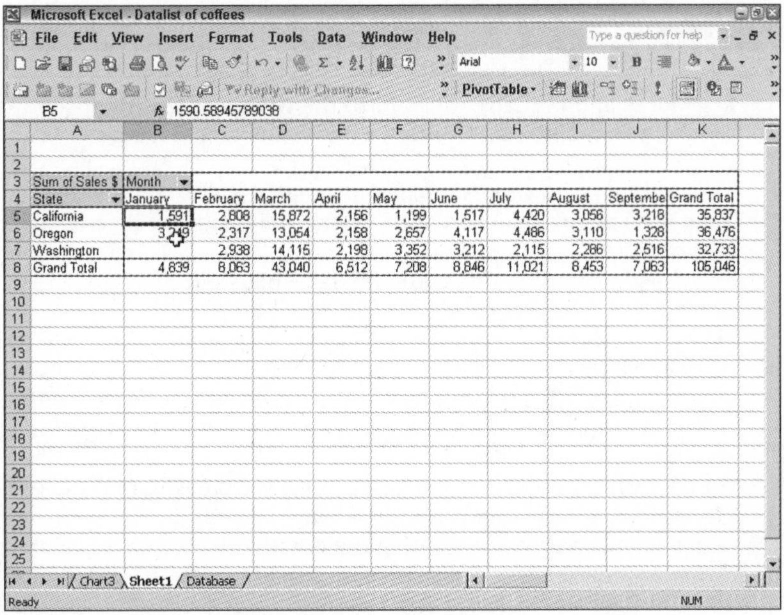

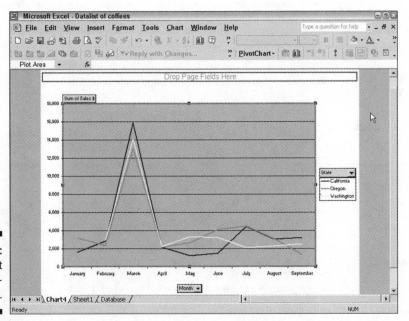

Figure 15-2: A pivot table cross-tabulation.

Figure 15-3: A pivot chart cross-tabulation.

Avoiding 3-D Charts

In general, and perhaps contrary to the wishes of the Microsoft marketing people, you really want to avoid three-dimensional charts.

The problem with three-dimensional charts isn't that they don't look pretty: They do. The problem is that the extra dimension, or illusion, of depth reduces the visual precision of the chart. With a 3-D chart, you can't as easily or precisely measure or assess the data that's plotted.

Figure 15-4 shows a simple column chart. Figure 15-5 shows the same information in a three-dimensional column chart. If you look closely at these two charts, you can see that it's much more difficult to precisely compare the two data series and to really see what underlying data values are being plotted.

Now, I'll admit that some people — those people who really like three-dimensional charts — say that you can deal with the imprecision of a three-dimensional chart by annotating the chart with data values and data labels. Figure 15-6 shows the way a three-dimensional column chart might look if you add this information. I don't think that's a good solution because charts often too easily become cluttered with extraneous and confusing information. Adding all sorts of annotation to a chart to compensate for the fundamental weakness in the chart type doesn't make a lot of sense to me.

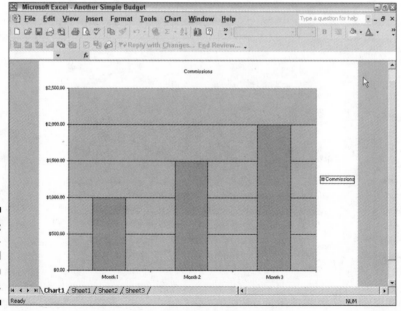

Figure 15-4:
A two-dimensional column chart.

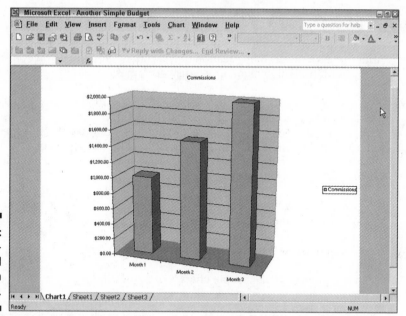

Figure 15-5:
A three-
dimensional
column
chart.

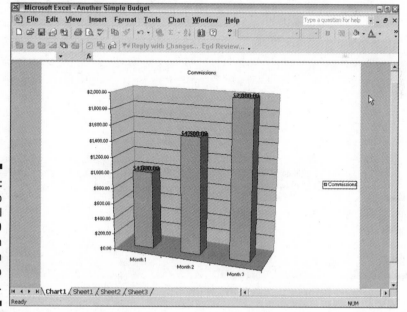

Figure 15-6:
Adding too
much detail
to 3-D
charts can
make them
hard to
read.

Never Use 3-D Pie Charts

Hey, here's a quick, one-question quiz: What do you get if you combine a pie chart and three-dimensionality? Answer: A mess!

Pie charts are really weak tools for visualizing, analyzing and visually communicating information. Adding a third dimension to a chart really reduces the precision and usefulness of a chart. When you combine the weakness of a pie chart with the inaccuracy and imprecision of three-dimensionality, you get something that really isn't very good. And, in fact, what you often get is a chart that is very misleading.

Figure 15-7 shows the cardinal sin of graphically presenting information in a chart. The pie chart in Figure 15-7 uses three-dimensionality to exaggerate the size of the slice of the pie in the foreground. This trick is one that you'll see often used by newspapers and magazines to exaggerate a story's theme.

You never want to make a pie chart 3-D.

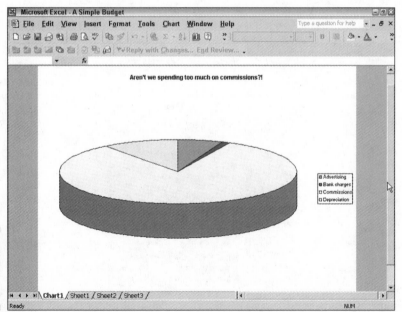

Figure 15-7: Pie charts can be misleading.

Be Aware of the Phantom Data Markers

One other dishonesty that you sometimes see in charts — okay, maybe sometimes it's not dishonesty but just sloppiness — is phantom data markers.

A *phantom data marker* is some extra visual element on a chart that exaggerates or misleads the chart viewer. Figure 15-8 shows a silly little column chart that I created to plot apple production in Washington state. Notice that the chart legend, which appears off to the right of the plot area, looks like another data marker. It's essentially a phantom data marker. And what this phantom data marker does is exaggerate the trend in apple production.

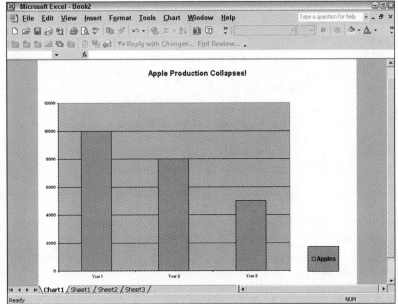

Figure 15-8:
Phantom data markers can exaggerate data.

Use Logarithmic Scaling

I don't remember much about logarithms, although I think I studied them in both high school and in college. Therefore, I can understand if you hear the word *logarithms* and find yourself feeling a little queasy. Nevertheless, logarithms and logarithmic scaling are tools that you want to use in your charts because they enable you to do something very powerful.

With logarithmic scaling of your value axis, you can compare the relative change (not the absolute change) in data series values. For example, say that you want to compare the sales of a large company that's growing solidly but slowly — 10 percent annually — with the sales of a smaller firm that's growing very quickly — 50 percent annually. Because a typical line chart compares absolute data values, if you plot the sales for these two firms in the same line chart, you completely miss out on the fact that the one firm is growing much more quickly than the other firm. Figure 15-9 shows a traditional simple line chart. This line chart doesn't use logarithmic scaling of the value axis.

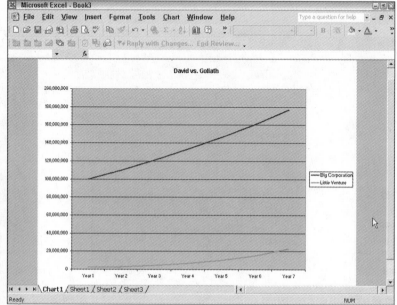

Now, take a look at the line chart shown in Figure 15-10. This is the same information in the same chart type and subtype, but I changed the scaling of the value axis to use logarithmic scaling. With the logarithmic scaling, the growth rates are shown rather than the absolute values. And when you plot the growth rates, the much quicker growth rate of the small company becomes clear. In fact, you can actually extrapolate the growth rate of the two companies and guess how long it will take for the small company to catch up with the big company. (Just extend the lines.)

To tell Excel that you want to use logarithmic scaling of the value access, follow these steps:

1. **Choose the Format Axis command by right-clicking the value (Y) axis and then choosing the Format Axis command from the shortcut menu that appears.**

2. **From the Format Axis dialog box that appears, click the Scale tab.**

3. **To tell Excel to use logarithmic scaling of the value (Y) axis, simply select the Logarithmic Scale check box and then click OK.**

   Excel re-scales the value axis of your chart to use logarithmic scaling.

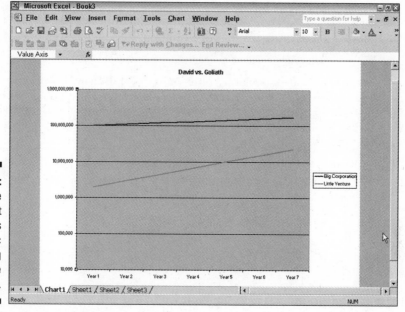

Figure 15-10:
A simple
line chart
that uses
logarithmic
scaling
of the
value axis.

Don't Forget to Experiment

All the tips in this chapter are, in some ways, sort of restrictive. They suggest that you do this or don't do that. These suggestions — which are tips that I've collected from writers and data analysts over the years — are really good guidelines to use. But you ought to experiment with your visual presentations of data. Sometimes by looking at data in some funky, wacky, visual way, you gain insights that you would otherwise miss.

There's no harm in, just for the fun of it, looking at some data set with a pie chart. (Even if you don't want to let anyone know you're doing this!) Just fool around with a data set to see what something looks like in an XY (Scatter) chart.

In other words, just get crazy once in a while.

Get Tufte

I want to leave you with one last thought about visually analyzing and visually presenting information. I recommend that you get and read one of Edward R. Tufte's books. Tufte has written seven books, and these three are favorites of mine: *The Visual Display of Quantitative Information*, 2nd Edition, *Visual Explanations: Images and Quantities, Evidence and Narrative*, and *Envisioning Information*.

These books aren't cheap; they cost between $40 and $50. But if you regularly use charts and graphs to analyze information or if you regularly present such information to others in your organization, reading one or more of these books will greatly benefit you.

By the way, Tufte's books are often hard to get. However, you can buy them from major online bookstores. You can also order Tufte's books directly from his Web site: www.edwardtufte.com. If you're befuddled about which of Tufte's books to order first, I recommend *The Visual Display of Quantitative Information*.

Part V

Appendix

In this part . . .

*I*n this part is a glossary that you can refer to whenever you need to shed light on the meanings of some less-than-apparent statistics terms. Ever been baffled by binomial distributions? Puzzled by p-values? Wonder no more. . . .

Appendix

Glossary of Data Analysis and Excel Terms

• •

3-D pie charts: Perhaps the very worst way to share the results of your data analysis — and often inexcusable.

Absolute reference: A cell address used in a formula that Excel doesn't adjust if you copy the formula to some new location. To create an absolute cell reference, you precede the column letter and row number with dollar signs ($).

Access: The name of a database program developed and sold by Microsoft. Use Access to build and work with large sophisticated relational databases; you can easily export information from Access databases to Excel. Just choose the Access File⇨Export command.

Arithmetic operators: The standard operators that you use in Excel formulas. To add numbers, use the addition (+) operator. To subtract numbers, use the subtraction (-) operator. To multiply numbers, use the multiplication (*) operator. To divide numbers, use the division (/) operator. You can also perform exponential operations by using the exponential operator (^). *See Operator precedence.*

Ascending order: A sorting option that alphabetizes labels and arranges values in smallest-value-to-biggest-value order. *See also Chronological order; Descending order.*

ASCII text file: A type of text file that in essence is just straight text and nothing else. *See also Delimited text file; Importing.*

AutoFilter: An Excel command that helps you produce a new list that's a subset of your original list. For example, in the case of a grocery list, you could use AutoFilter to create a subset list that shows only those items that you'll purchase at a particular store, in specified quantities, or that exceed a certain price.

Average: Typically, the arithmetic mean for a set of values. Excel supplies several average functions. *See also Median; Mode.*

Binomial distributions: Used to calculate probabilities in situations where you have a limited number of independent trials, or tests, which can either succeed or fail. Success or failure of any one trial is independent of other trials.

Boolean expressions: Also known as *logical expressions*. Describe a comparison that you want to make. For example, to compare fields with the value 1000000, you use a Boolean expression. To construct a Boolean expression, you use a comparison operator and then a value used in the comparison.

Calculated field: Used to insert a new row or column into a pivot table and then fill the new row or column with a formula.

Calculated item: An amount shown in a pivot table that you create by calculating a formula. Frankly, adding a calculated item usually doesn't make any sense. But, hey, strange things happen all the time, right?

Cells: In Excel, the intersections of rows and columns. A cell location is described using the column letter and row number. For example, the cell in the upper-left corner of the workbook is labeled *A1*.

Chart data labels: Annotate data markers with pivot table information or list information.

Chart legend: Identifies the data series that you plot in your chart.

Chart titles: Text that you use to label the parts of a chart.

Chart type: Includes column, bar, line, pie, XY, surface, and so on. In Excel, you can create 14 different types of charts.

Chi-square: Used to compare observed values with expected values, returning the level of significance, or probability (also called a *p value*). That p value lets you assess whether differences between the observed and expected values represent chance.

Chronological order: A sorting option that arranges labels or values in chronological order such as Monday, Tuesday, Wednesday, and so on. ***See also*** *Ascending order; Descending order.*

Comparison operator: A mathematical operator used in a Boolean expression. For example, the > comparison operator makes *greater than* comparisons. The = operator makes *equal to* comparisons. The <= operator makes *less than or equal to* comparisons. Cool, huh?

Counting: Used for useful statistical functions for counting cells within a worksheet or list. Excel provides four: COUNT, COUNTA, COUNTBLANK, and COUNTIF. Excel also provides two useful functions for counting permutations and combinations: PERMUT and COMBIN.

Cross-tabulation: An analysis technique that summarizes data in two or more ways. For example, if you run a business and summarize sales information both by customer and product, that's a cross-tabulation because you tabulate the information in two ways. *See also Pivot table*.

Custom calculations: Used to add many semi-standard calculations to a pivot table. By using Custom Calculations, for example, you can calculate the difference between two pivot table cells, percentages, and percentage differences. *See also Pivot table*.

Data Analysis: An Excel add-in with which you perform statistical analysis.

Data category: Organizes the values in a data series. That sounds complicated; however, in many charts, identifying the data category is easy. In any chart (including a pivot chart) that shows how some value changes over time, the data category is time. *See also Data series*.

Data list: Another name for an Excel list.

Data series: Oh geez, this is another one of those situations where somebody's taken a ten-cent idea and labeled the idea with a five-dollar word. Charts show data series. And a chart legend names the data series that a chart shows. For example, if you want to plot sales of coffee products, those coffee products are your data series. *See also Data category*.

Data validation: An Excel command with which you describe what information can be entered into a cell. The command also enables you to supply messages that give data input information and error messages to help someone correct data entry errors.

Database functions: A special set of functions especially for simple statistical analysis of information that you store in Excel lists.

Delimited text file: A type of text file. Delimited text files use special characters, called *delimiters*, to separate fields of information in the report. For example, such files commonly use the Tab character to delimit. *See also ASCII text file*; *Importing*.

Descending order: A sorting order that arranges labels in reverse alphabetical order and values in largest-value-to-smallest-value order. *See also Ascending order*; *Chronological order*.

Descriptive statistics: Describe the values in a set. For example, if you sum a set of values, that sum is a descriptive statistic. If you find the biggest value or the smallest value in a set of numbers, that's also a descriptive statistic.

Exponential smoothing: Calculates the moving average but weights the values included in the moving average calculations so that more recent values have a bigger effect. ***See also*** *Moving average.*

Exporting: In the context of databases, moving information to another application. If you tell your accounting system to export a list of vendors that Excel can later read, for example, you're exporting. Many business applications, by the way, do easily export data to Excel. ***See also*** *Importing.*

F distributions: Compare the ratio in variances of samples drawn from different populations and draw a conclusion about whether the variances in the underlying populations resemble each other.

Field: In a database, stores the same sort of information. In a database that stores people's names and addresses, for example, you'll probably find a street address field. In Excel, by the way, each column shows a particular sort of information and therefore represents a field.

Field settings: Determine what Excel does with a field when it's cross-tabulated in the pivot table. ***See also*** *Cross-tabulation*; *Pivot table.*

Formulas: Calculation instructions entered into worksheet cells. Essentially, this business about formulas going into workbook cells is the heart of Excel. Even if an Excel workbook did nothing else, it would still be an extremely valuable tool. In fact, the first spreadsheet programs did little more than calculate cell formulas. ***See also*** *Text labels*; *Values.*

Function: A pre-built formula that you can use to more simply calculate some amount, such as an average or standard deviation.

Function arguments: Needed in most functions; also called *inputs.* All database functions need arguments. You include these arguments inside parenthesis marks. If a function needs more than one argument, you separate arguments by using commas. ***See also*** *Database functions.*

Header row: A top row of field names in your list range selection that names the fields.

Histogram: A chart that shows a frequency distribution.

Importing: In the context of databases, grabbing information from some other application. Excel rather easily imports information from popular databases (such as Microsoft Access), other spreadsheets (such as Lotus 1-2-3), and from text files. ***See also*** *Exporting.*

Inferential statistics: Based on a very useful, intuitively obvious idea that if you look at a sample of values from a population and if the sample is representative and large enough, you can draw conclusions about the population based on characteristics of the sample.

Kurtosis: A measure of the tails in a distribution of values. *See also Skewness.*

List: Well, a list. This definition sounds circular, I guess. But if you make a list (sorry) of the things that you want to buy at the grocery store, that's a list. Excel lists, by the way, usually store more information than just names of items. Usually, Excel lists also store values. In the case of a grocery list, the Excel version of a list might include prices and quantities of the items that you're shopping for.

Logarithmic scale: Used in a chart to view rates of change in your plotted data rather than absolute changes.

Median: The middle value in a set of values. Half of the values fall below the median, and half of the values fall above the median. *See also Average; Mode.*

Microsoft Access: *See Access.*

Microsoft Query: *See Query.*

Mode: The most common value in a set. *See also Average; Median.*

Moving average: An average that's calculated by using only a specified set of values, such as an average based on just the last three values. *See also Exponential smoothing.*

Normal distribution: The infamous bell curve. Also known as a *Gaussian distribution.*

Objective function: The formula that you want to optimize when performing optimization modeling. In the case of a profit formula, for example, you want to maximize a function. But some objective functions should be minimized. For example, if you create an objective function that describes the cost of some advertising program or the risk of some investment program, you may logically choose to minimize your costs or risks. *See also Optimization modeling.*

Observation: Suppose that you're constructing a data set that shows daily high temperatures in your neighborhood. When you go out and *observe* that the temperature some fine July afternoon is 87°, that measurement is your observation.

Operator precedence: Standard rules that determine the order of arithmetic operations in a formula. For example, exponential operations are performed first. Multiplication and division operations are performed second. Addition and subtraction operations are performed third. To override these standard rules, use parenthesis marks. *See also Formulas.*

Optimization modeling: A problem-solving technique in which you look for the optimum value of an objective function while explicitly recognizing constraints. *See also Objective function.*

Parameter: An input to a probability distribution function.

Phantom data marker: Some extra visual element on a chart that exaggerates the chart message or misleads the chart viewer. Usually phantom data markers are extra embellishments that someone has added (hopefully not you!) that sort of resemble the chart's real data markers — especially to the eyes of casual chart viewers.

Pivot chart: A cross-tabulation that appears in a chart. *See also Cross-tabulation.*

Pivoting and **Re-pivoting:** The thing that gives the pivot table its name. You can continue cross-tabulating the data in the pivot table. You can pivot, and re-pivot, and re-pivot again. . . .

Pivot table: Perhaps the most powerful analytical tool that Excel provides. Use the PivotTable command to cross-tabulate data stored in Excel lists. *See also Cross-tabulation.*

Primary key: In sorting, the field first used to sort records. *See also Secondary key; Sorting;* and if you're really interested, *Tertiary key.*

Probability distribution: A chart that plots probabilities. *See also Normal distribution; Uniform distribution.*

Probability distribution function: A function, or equation, that describes the line of the probability distribution. *See also Probability distribution.*

p-value: The level of significance, or probability.

Query: A program that comes with Excel. Use Query to extract information from a database and then place the query results into an Excel workbook.

QuickBooks: The world's most popular small business accounting program — and one of the many business applications that easily, happily, and without complaint exports information to Excel. In QuickBooks, for example, you simply click a button cleverly labeled *Excel.*

Range: In terms of Excel data analysis, refers to two different items. A range can be a reference to a rectangle of cells in a worksheet, or a range can show the difference between the largest and smallest values in the data set.

Record: A collection of related fields. In Excel, each record goes into a separate row.

Refreshing pivot data: Updates the information shown in a pivot table or pivot chart for changes in the underlying data. You can click the Refresh data tool provided by the PivotTable toolbar button to refresh.

Regression analysis: Involves plotting pairs of independent and dependent variables in an XY chart and then finding a linear or exponential equation that best describes the plotted data.

Relational database: Essentially, a collection of tables or lists. *See also Table*; *List.*

Relative reference: A cell reference used in a formula that Excel adjusts if you copy the formula to a new cell location. *See also Absolute reference.*

Scatter plot: An XY chart that visually compares pairs of values. A scatter plot is often a good first step when you want to perform regression analysis. *See also Regression analysis.*

Secondary key: In sorting, the second field used to sort records. The secondary key only comes into play when the primary keys of records have the same value. *See also Primary key*; *Sorting.*

Solve order: The order in which calculated item formulas should be solved. *See also Calculated item.*

Solver: An Excel add-in with which you perform optimization modeling. *See also Optimization modeling.*

Solver variables: The variables in an optimization modeling problem. *See Optimization modeling.*

Sort: To arrange list records in some particular order, such as alphabetically by last name. Excel includes easy-to-use tools for doing this, by the way.

Skewness: A measure of the symmetry of a distribution of values. *See also Kurtosis.*

Standard deviation: Describes dispersion about the data set's mean. You can kind of think of a standard deviation as an average deviation from the mean. *See also Average*; *Variance.*

Table: In relational databases, where information is stored. Tables are essentially spreadsheets, or lists, that store database information. In fact, an Excel data list is a table.

Tertiary key: In sorting, the third field used to sort records. The tertiary key only comes into play when the primary and secondary keys of records have the same value. *See also* *Primary key*; *Secondary key*; *Sorting*.

Text file: A file that's all text. Many programs export text files, by the way, because other programs (including Excel) often easily import text files.

Text functions: Used to manipulate text strings in ways that enable you to easily rearrange and manipulate the data that you import into an Excel workbook. Typically, these babies are extremely useful tools for scrubbing or cleaning the data that you want to later analyze.

Text labels: Includes letters and numbers that you enter into worksheet cells but that you don't want to use in calculations. For example, your name, some budget expense description, and a telephone number are all examples of text labels. None of these pieces of information get used in calculations.

Time-series chart: Shows how values change over time. A chart that shows sales revenues over the last 5 years or profits over the last 12 months, for example, is a time-series chart.

Tufte, Edward: The author of a series of wonderful books about visually analyzing and visually presenting information. I recommend that you get and read at least one of Tufte's books.

t-value: Sort of like a poor-man's z-value. When you're working with small samples — less than 30 or 40 items — you can use what's called a student t-value to calculate probabilities rather than the usual z-value, which is what you work with in the case of normal distributions. Not coincidentally, Excel provides three t-distribution functions. *See also* *z-value*.

Uniform distribution: The same probability of occurrence in every event. One common probability distribution function is a uniform distribution.

Value: Some bit of data that you enter into a workbook cell and may want to later use in a calculation. For example, the actual amount that you budget for some expense would always be a number or value. *See also* *Formulas*; *Text labels*; *Workbook*.

Variance: Describes dispersion about the data set's mean. The variance is the square of the standard deviation. Conversely, the standard deviation is the square root of the variance. *See also* *Average*; *Standard deviation*.

Web query: Grabbing data from a table that's stored in a Web page. Excel provides a very slick tool for doing this, by the way.

Workbook: An Excel spreadsheet document or file. A spreadsheet comprises numbered rows and lettered columns. *See also Cells.*

x-values: The independent values in a regression analysis.

y-values: The dependent values in a regression analysis.

z-value: In statistics, describes the distance between a value and the mean in terms of standard deviations. How often does one get to include a legitimate *Z* entry in a glossary! Not often, but here I do. *See also Average; Standard deviation.*

Index

• *B* •

• *Q* •

• U •

• V •

Notes

Notes